Berlin, 9. 11. 16.

against the world

for Kemi

Great that you came to our small reading at ACUD

J. B.

THE GERMAN LIST

JAN BRANDT
against the world

TRANSLATED BY KATY DERBYSHIRE

[handwritten inscription] Willie

Enjoy all 882 pages!

Seagull
BOOKS

LONDON NEW YORK CALCUTTA

A number of passages in this book have a special layout, particular typography or a paler font. This is deliberate and not a production flaw.

Citations

pp. 81–2: Elisabeth Borchers, 'Geschichte vom Buch' in *Das große Lalula und andere Gedichte und Geschichten von morgens bis abends für Kinder* (Munich: Ellermann Verlag, 1971).

p. 83: Bertolt Brecht, 'Der Rauch' in *Werke. Große kommentierte Berliner und Frankfurter Ausgabe, Volume 12: Poems 2* (Frankfurt am Main: Suhrkamp Verlag, 1988).

p. 83: James Krüss, 'Das Feuer' in *Der wohltemperierte Leierkasten* (Munich: cbj Verlag in der Verlagsgruppe Random House GmbH, 1989).

pp. 286–7: Ulrich Schiller, 'Man hört, was man hört–Selbstmordsignale von der Platte, das absurde Gerichtsdrama in Reno' in *Die Zeit* 33 (1990).

GOETHE
INSTITUT

This publication was supported by a grant
from the Goethe-Institut India

Seagull Books, 2016

Originally published in German as Jan Brandt, *Gegen die Welt*
© 2011 by DuMont Buchverlag, Cologne (Germany)

First published in English translation by Seagull Books, 2016
English translation © Katy Derbyshire, 2016

ISBN · 978 0 8574 2 337 5

British Library Cataloguing-in-Publication Data
A catalogue record for this book is available from the British Library

Typeset by Seagull Books, Calcutta, India
Printed and bound by Maple Press, York, Pennsylvania, USA

I would like to thank the Berlin Cultural Administration Department, Künstlerdorf Schöppingen, the Lower Saxon Ministry of Science and Culture, Künstlerhaus Worpswede, Ledig House and Yaddo artists' retreat in New York and the archive employees of NDR broadcasting, the Weser-Kurier newspaper, Leer town council and RTL Television for supporting my work on this book.

Special thanks go to all those who shared their knowledge and experiences with me.

For D.

Gerhard Schröder

Federal Chancellery

Schloßplatz 1

10178 Berlin

9 August 1999

Dear Mr Schröder,

I have seen you on television. I have recorded all your speeches
since the election and played the tapes back in slowmo, in some
cases frame by frame. I have watched you very closely and
could not identify anything unusual. You don't have the look.
You're clean. And I am too. But there aren't many men like us
left, real men. And that's why we have to join forces. I'm writing
to you because I need your help, and to warn you. Strange
things have happened in Jericho, which there is no space in this
letter to explain. And lots more strange things will happen if
you don't do anything to stop them. Only you have the authority
to do so. The people there are changing, not on the outside but
on the inside, and not over several years but from one second
to the next. They're changing their nature, losing their charac-
ter, being replaced by identical copies. I don't know if they're
clones, or what happens to the originals if they are. I don't know
when the transformation began either, in which century, or how
far it has come by now. But I am certain that everything is concentrated on Jericho, that something will take place there on
19.9.1999, which will be irreversible if you don't take the necessary steps. The necessary steps are: sealing off the entire region,
screening inhabitants through audiovisual tests, quarantine for
infected persons until it is clear how and whether the transformation can be reversed. If that doesn't succeed, I see no other
option but to isolate them permanently. The substitution of the

There haven't been any reports of doppel-gangers.

whole human race is imminent. But be careful when you go to East Frisia to gain an impression for yourself. Don't look people in the eye; never look at them directly, no matter what they say to you. They'll tell you all manner of stories, crude stuff just to get your attention, but all those imaginary stories are nothing but diversion tactics, however credible they may seem. Trust no one, not even yourself. Forget Berlin. Your new office can wait. Concentrate entirely on your mission of saving the world, at least what's left of it. It's best if you wear sunglasses, mirrored ones, but don't use over-the-counter sunglasses, they're just fakes to give you a false sense of security. In fact, the rays only penetrate faster and more effectively to the brain through them, to switch off your mental immune system. What you need is specially coated pilot's sunglasses. I can get you some if you haven't got any or don't know where you can get my certified ones. They reflect the creatures' gaze. And another thing: they'll greet you. Everyone there says hello to everyone else. They greet strangers as well. Never reply to the greeting 'Moin' with 'Moin'—that's the gateway to hell, the key to your soul. I don't know exactly how it works, but this 'Moin' makes all the defence mechanisms we've built up over the course of our evolution collapse. And keep an eye on the navy radio masts in Saterland. They're not aerials for making contact to submarines in the Atlantic, although that's exactly what your defence ministry will tell you. The signals don't go downwards into the sea; they go upwards into the sky. Find some excuse to switch the things off, at least as long as you're in Jericho, otherwise every word, every movement and every thought you have on East Frisian ground will be recorded and transmitted into space. I know you want my name and address. But I can't reveal my identity, even at the risk of you thinking this is nonsense. I'm being tailed. Not by the Federal Intelligence Service. They're on my side. By the Plutonians. All I can tell you about myself is that

[handwritten left margin] The voices in your head are diversion tactics too.

[handwritten interline] They are Plutonians.

[handwritten interline] More precise studies to come.

[handwritten left margin] Your defence minister's champing has the look.

[handwritten bottom] → At least partly.

[handwritten right margin] Unless you manage, like me, to prevent your own thoughts from thinking. I've only managed through years of toughest training, though. Some call it enlightenment — I call it self-control.

9

I'm a respected scientist. I've solved major puzzles. I've made discoveries. And soon I'll see the white light. During my broad research, I've come across hints in the Bible and other sources, *I've enclosed a copy of* which allow the conclusion that all this conforms to the facts. Please inform your colleagues in Washington, Paris and Moscow. *the evidence.* And make sure that NASA, ESA and Roskosmos stay out of *The under-linings and* it—they're totally infiltrated by Plutonians. I've written to Bill *highlights* Clinton, Jacques Chirac and Boris Yeltsin already, but of course *are mine.* a message from you would lend a lot more weight to the issue. Only a joint approach against the occupiers can be a success now. Only if we all stick together, if all the remaining people on Planet Earth join together via ectoplasmic circuits, can we prevent the total invasion that is to begin in Jericho on 19.9.1999.

Whatever you do, don't look at the sun next Wednesday, not even with sunglasses. That would be the end of you.

PART ONE

Science Fiction

Schatzschneider

The summer was hot and dry. The hottest, driest summer since 1947. They said so in the newspaper, they said so on the radio and on TV, but no one, not even the oldest people, could remember a summer like this one. It hadn't rained for weeks, aside from one or two short sharp showers. The hay languished in the fields, pressed into balls. The air was filled with dust. Bernhard Kuper, whom everyone who knew him better called only Hard, had set up a fan next to the counter and stuck a sheet of orange plastic in the shop window so the boxes and tins and tubes on display didn't bleach in the sun. The customers, especially the tourists, complained of the heat outside, praised the cool inside, wiped their faces with the backs of their hands and bought sun lotion before they continued on their journeys, at low tide to the lake, at high tide to the sea.

Hard stood behind the till from morning to evening, then he wrote and paid bills and developed films in the darkroom. He rarely had a chance for a long conversation. If he did, it was usually about the weather or how much the area had changed since the customer's last visit, how pretty everything was now and how he could think himself lucky to live in a place where other people went on holiday. At times like that he shrugged, put the receipt in the bag with the tubes and said, 'Goodbye then,' or 'Have a good trip.' He accepted prosperity like something perfectly normal, perhaps because it seemed like something long overdue, like something they'd earned after all the years of hardship. They'd finally entered an era of light and he, dazzled by its promises, wanted to have his part in it before this heaven on earth grew dark again.

Up until then he hadn't thought about it, at least not consciously, but it must be true if they kept saying it. All the roads were asphalted and lined by pavements. The lime trees along the village road had gone, and in their place now grew ornamental maples, propped up by wooden poles, held by ropes, with branches that would never extend above the first floor of the houses. The town hall had got a new roof, the dairy a bottling plant. The old fire station and the hose tower had been replaced by a modern appliance building with a communications room, uniform store, washroom and parking spaces for a rescue vehicle, fire engines and turntable ladders. On the B70, Hayo Hayenga had converted the village pub into Club 69 and brought girls from all over Europe to East Frisia. Didi Schulz, the blacksmith, had opened a shop for toys and gifts next to his workshop. Vehndel Fashions had stopped stocking shoes and was now specializing entirely in textiles. And many of the long-established farmers had given up agriculture, set up holiday flats in the old farmhouses and sold their grazing land to the council. It was only the cement works that didn't yet have planning permission, because the site where they were to be built—two fields walled in by hedge banks on the other side of the railway tracks—was a conservation area.

The drugstore's extension had just been finished at the end of May, right before the beginning of high season. Hard had commissioned the building contractor Johann Rosing to extend the shop, the sales area and the stockroom, and add another floor on top of the garage, a second, larger living room for special occasions with large windows, panorama windows, and a terrace lined with terracotta tiles. Hard ate his dinner with Birgit and Daniel there now instead of in the kitchen, talking about the day's takings and outgoings, Werder Bremen and HSV football clubs, school.

Daniel got his first school report on a Wednesday in June: *Daniel can read texts containing new words with occasional help. Daniel can write short sentences and words from those practised in dictation. Daniel can solve most logic exercises independently, can state and note less-than/greater-than relationships between numbers and is capable of addition and subtraction up to twenty without aids. Daniel enriches lessons with relevant contributions. He plays the recorder.*

His parents were proud of him. His father rewarded him with a new bike, a BMX 2000, steel precision-tube cross-frame, reinforced front-wheel hub, freewheel coaster brake. He rode it around the village for hours, always the same route, along Village Road, past the church, through the new estate, Composers' Corner, and back. He pedalled hard. He rode and rode, always in a circle, until he got tired and fell over or came across an obstacle. Once, he crashed into a pile of rubbish sacks by the side of the road. He flew over the garden fence onto a lawn. The front wheel was bent; his father had to fix it.

He spent the entire length of the holidays outside. He and his mother went to Baltrum for a week. She bought him a wooden sailboat. It didn't have any torpedoes on board or any guns. On the second day he let it float too far out and the wind blew it away. The next morning—his mother had left the door to the corridor open while she was in the bathroom—he tugged open the transom window in their hotel room. The draught was so strong

17

that he couldn't keep a grip on the handle. It slammed shut again with a bang, two panes of glass leaping out and shattering on the pavement outside the entrance. When his mother saw the damage he'd done, the fear in his eyes of being punished for his clumsy mistake, she stroked his head and said, 'Shards bring good luck.'

Later, they had breakfast on the veranda, went walking in the dunes and sat together in a wicker beach chair with a roof over their heads, looking out over the water as it came and went. Her hair was long and dark, her skin shiny. She wore a swimsuit with a flowery pattern, her belly rounded beneath it. He built a rampart out of sand around her, wanting to protect her, protect himself; he didn't know what from.

In the evening they went to a restaurant, ate fish, potatoes, salad. His mother told him about *Dallas*, the only thing she missed here, TV, and she talked about earlier holidays with her sisters in Berchtesgaden, in Mittenwald, in Lindau on Lake Constance; then—it was late by then, past nine—she said she'd met his father here on the island. She'd been on a work outing from the office while he'd come over here from the mainland to spend the weekend on the beach with a few mates from the barracks. She'd still been working for Knipper back then, and he was with the army in Aurich. She'd noticed him as soon as she'd arrived in the hotel lobby, in his white coat, his personal uniform, but she hadn't spoken to him until a party in the Fresena Hotel. She'd asked him to dance—Hard, of all people, the *Klutentramper*. Her poor toes.

At night she read him bedtime stories. *The Sea-Wolf*, *Huckleberry Finn*, *The Deerslayer*. His favourite part was where Wolf Larsen crushes the potato in one hand, where Huck and Jim clamber into the house floating on the Mississippi, where Judith snatches the cap off Tom Hutter's head.

On the last day, he wrote his father a postcard. She told him the words to write: that the weather was wonderful and they were fine and he was looking forward to coming home again.

His handwriting is neat and legible.

In the mornings the heat woke him. He lay on the sheet, his covers tossed aside, bathed in sweat. He sat up, leant his head woozily against the wall. After ten or fifteen minutes he got up, splashed cold water on his face in the bathroom, had breakfast and helped his father with his work. He took the empty boxes handed to him and piled them up in the cellar; in the shop, he wiped down the shelves and stocked them up with products; then he swept the car park outside the house.

He completes his tasks in the allotted time.

In the afternoons he watered the lawn, the hedges and the bushes. Afterwards he stood in the middle of the spray. The water rolled off him in drips like from a freshly waxed car. To really cool off, he cycled to the bathing lake. He swam and dived underwater and lay down with the others in the shade of the trees. He still got sunburn, sunstroke.

At the end of July, Daniel and a few friends built a den in a space under the freight shed. Rosing had bought all the land around the village square from the railway after Jericho station closed down. He had demolished the station building—apart from the old coal cellar which was rented to Jost Petersen and his pool hall—and built bungalows next to it, containing offices and workshops. He used the old freight shed for storage. There were platforms on either side of it, one for trucks, one for trains. But the trains sped past now without stopping, on to the jetty at Norddeich or to the harbour at Emden or in the other direction to Neuschanz and the Ruhr region. The building was mainly wood; only the stilts it rested on were made of stone, and the boys crawled between them. It wasn't high enough to stand upright but there was enough space to sit and lie down in there, and that was all they wanted. They got together and dragged in a mattress, abandoned bedside tables and household goods. They sawed sheets of chipboard to size and leant them against the braces. They covered the sandy ground with a rug, stuck pictures to the stilts. To protect them from wind and weather, they encased the whole structure with corrugated cardboard and stuffed tea towels and cleaning cloths in the gaps and slits. From outside, it looked like a giant hornets' nest, and seeing as one of them brought a cassette recorder along it sounded like one too. Once they were finished, they bought ice lollies at the kiosk and sat up on the platform, watching the trains heading to the jetty or on their way back, disappearing in the glimmering haze of the evening's light.

His parents gave him permission to spend a night in the den; there were older boys there too, Ubbo Busboom, Paul Tinnemeyer and Jens Hanken. They gave them sleeping bags and flashlights. When the batteries ran out they lay side by side and talked. They jumped with shock every few minutes. Cats screamed like children, mice scurried past, spiders crawled over their heads. Someone crept around the outside of the building, called something, knocked on the wood. They went home to their parents before dawn even came.

On the first day of school after the long holidays, a new boy was standing next to the class teacher, Mrs Wolters. He was short and fat, as wide as he was tall, a mouth on two legs. He had blue eyes, sticky-out ears and freckles. His head was shaved as if he'd had nits and they hadn't known any way to deal with them other than cutting off his hair. He held a satchel in one hand, which pulled his body down with its weight, and in the other, as if to balance it out, a chocolate biscuit with a bite taken out of it. He pursed his lips and looked down, following the crumbs, at the belly curving out above his short trousers. Mrs Wolters said his name was Volker, Volker Mengs, his father was a teacher at the intermediate school, his mother at the grammar school, he had a younger sister and they'd all just moved here from Hanover. Then she let him sit down.

At prayer time he didn't close his eyes, he didn't put his hands together, didn't move his lips. He didn't even pretend to join in. He didn't take a shower after sport, not with the others and not on his own. All he did was rub down his chest with his sweaty T-shirt. At break time he stood slightly aside, took out a box of sandwiches and ate in silence. His pencils were arranged by colour and his exercise books were wrapped in protective covers. Before he started a new page he put a sheet of blotting paper on the old one, smoothed one hand over it and waited until the ink had soaked in. There were plenty of reasons to beat him up, just no opportunity—his parents brought him in the morning and picked him up when school ended at lunchtime.

After a few days Hard invited the Mengs family over for dinner. He'd thought it all out carefully. First they'd have a good time and then, once they were in the right mood, he'd show them the shop and demonstrate a couple of products, he'd give the wife samples and take the husband along fishing at the weekend, to meet the lads at the pub; via their sons, he'd create a dependency beyond that personal contact—the whole basis of his business. Give and take. That was all there was to it. It all came down to the right ratio.

21

They sat around the table on the terrace, the adults at one end and the children at the other. It was just after seven but still so hot that they were wiping off the sweat. Wasps buzzed around them, dive-bombing the sausages and the mustard, swarming around the fries, the ketchup, the beer and the juice, crawling over the pasta and potato salads, the marinated vegetable kebabs. Birgit flapped her hands and stretched cling film over the pots and bowls. Every few minutes someone leapt up with a yelp, ran a few steps and sat down again, in the hope of having shaken off their pursuers.

The fathers put more charcoal on the barbecue, poked the embers, kept the fresh meat coming. Volker had hardly polished off three sausages and a mutton cutlet before he went up for seconds. On his way back he held his plate like a waiter, balancing it on his fingertips. He knocked over a glass as he sat down. Apple juice spilled over the waxed tablecloth. He slurped it up from the edge while his sister, Verena, slapped at the wet patch.

Hard watched them in horror and then said, '*Herrijeket*! Why don't you say something, that's out of order.'

'We think, I mean, we're of the opinion,' Mr Mengs cleared his throat, 'that children should be allowed to make up their own minds, that they'll come up against their own boundaries in time, that life itself will punish them and *that* punishment is worse than any other.'

'And you use that method to keep your class under control?'

Mr Mengs shook his head. 'You can't—'

'I can't imagine you do,' said Hard. 'Not with the best will in the world.'

'You can't mix private and professional matters. Your own children and other people's children are two different things. Of course there are other rules at school to at home.'

'You can't separate one thing from another like that.'

'Well, we don't tell our children what to do and what not to do, what to eat or wear, how to live. They'll have to find that out for themselves.'

'Where's it all supposed to end?'

'I don't know. Nobody knows. We'll have to wait and see. That's the point, taking a new approach, not repeating our parents' mistakes. Our only motto is: Anything goes apart from drugs.'

'It's the other way round for us,' said Hard. 'Nothing goes apart from drugs.' It was supposed to be a joke, one of his druggist jokes, but nobody laughed. Birgit looked at the ground, Mr and Mrs Mengs exchanged confused glances and the children took no notice. Hard tweaked at his shirt, pointing at the patch sewn on above his chest, *kuper's drugstore*. It was no use. So he laughed himself, reached into the crate, opened a new bottle and poured himself a beer, decanting it so fast it foamed.

To get the conversation going again, he said, 'Can you make a Mexican sentence using the words deduct, defence, defeat and detail?'

'In Spanish?' said Mr Mengs.

'No no, just a normal sentence.'

Mr Mengs rested his head on his hand and rubbed his chin, Mrs Mengs bit her lips and frowned while Birgit, having heard this one before, went to get a wet cloth from the kitchen to wipe down the table. Hard leant back and downed his beer in one, emitting a throaty, hissing sound before he put the glass down. He'd set them a riddle they couldn't solve.

One or other of them kept murmuring, 'Deduct the detail?' or 'Defend to defeat?'—as if they were likely to find an answer by thinking longer and longer about it. Then, after two or three minutes, Hard said: 'De duck over de fence, first de feet and then de tail.'

23

And Mr Mengs said, 'That's not a proper sentence.'

Now Birgit tried to pick up the conversation before Hard climbed on the table and started singing, which happened often enough when he was drunk and thought the best way to fill in a pause was to put on a show of his talent, his tenor. She sighed and said, 'You can call me Birgit, by the way.'

'Petra.'

'Arne.'

Birgit shook hands with them as if they'd only just met, and then said, 'I'm starting to feel like I'm melting, evaporating on the inside.'

'Isn't it terrible?' said Petra Mengs with a smile, grateful for the change of subject. 'I've never experienced anything like it.'

'Not around here,' Arne Mengs specified. 'Although, last year we went to Greece and that—'

'Enough to drive you bonkers,' said Birgit.

And Hard said, 'Only one remedy,' and raised his glass.

They clinked glasses, looking each other in the eye as protocol demanded, and drank. For a few seconds, as long as it took them to swallow, there was silence. Hard had prepared himself. He didn't want to give Mengs any opportunity to get pally and start chatting about his holidays, ouzo and olives and dilapidated temples. He'd invested too much time and money over the past few weeks. He'd read the newspapers and magazines even more closely than usual, compared the final tables, the teams' positions, the facts and figures, and as in previous years he'd placed his bets at the pub, predicted all the results, all the goals and chosen winners and losers. Cocky on past success, he'd wanted to bet on more, on changes of managers, injuries, red and yellow cards, but the others hadn't gone for it. Wiemers, Rosing, Leemhuis, Neemann, Kramer and the other *Bangbüxen*. They really were

24

scaredy-cats. Freese and he would have made them run extra laps for that in the army, or crawl through the mud at low tide—with thirty kilos' baggage on their backs. But he wasn't in the army any more. Only now, here with Mengs, could he raise his winnings, and he had to if he wanted to pay back the loan for the extension and the new car.

'Are you a 96er?'

'What?'

'Are you a 96er.'

Arne Mengs gave him an uncomprehending look.

'Football.'

'Oh, right. Yes, of course, coming from Hanover.'

'You'll never make it back to the first league.'

'We'll see.'

'You should never've let Schatzschneider go. A hundred and forty goals in a hundred and seventy-nine games. No one's ever scored that many in the second league. And now we've got him.'

'Oh, I don't know. He's past his best now. You should have taken Völler instead. Twenty-three goals! In his first season!'

'Wasn't much use to Werder in the end though.'

'Top scorer in the league!'

'Before that it was Hrubesch. And he had twenty-seven!'

'You should never have let him go.'

'No, he was past it. Quit when you're the head.' Hard leant over to Arne Mengs, put a hand on his arm and said, 'We're never going to go down a league.'

'We'll see.'

'*Nix.* We're going to be at the top, there'll be no match for us for years to come. We'll leave the others far behind us. This,'—he stretched his right arm up—'this is us, then there's nothing for ages, I'm talking points now, and then,'—he stretched his left arm downwards—'the mid-table starts from second place, with Werder, Bayern, FC Köln. The gap between us'll be so big,'—both his arms were now as far apart as possible—'so big they'll give up even in February, in March, at the beginning of the second leg, they'll lose all their pathetic hopes for the title. They'll accept their fate, they'll have no other option. They know full well what they're capable of. They'll never get out from down there, what with the players they've bought in. None of them are any use. Schatz makes the big difference! Not Allofs or Rummenigge or Völler! Völler! In thirty years he'll be forgotten, that sausage of a man on legs, but Schatz, Schatzschneider, he'll be a legend by then. A legend! Like Walter! Like Seeler! Like Müller!'

'I wouldn't bet on it.'

'I would,' said Hard. His eyes sparkled. It was right there, his objective, at arm's reach. 'How about it? A hundred?'

He held out his hand to seal the deal. And Arne Mengs shook it. But that wasn't enough. A handshake wasn't nearly enough. To make it valid, a handshake had to be followed by a drink. So he told Daniel to go and fetch the cognac from the lounge. 'The goodsuff,' he said, his tongue already slightly numbed by the alcohol, 'the Hennessy V.S.O.P., you know, Very Sozzled Old Pater.' He laughed again.

By the time Daniel appeared on the terrace with the half-empty bottle, his mother had already taken two glasses out of the kitchen cupboard. She poured two cognacs for the men and topped up the lemonades and the glasses of water so that everyone could drink to their shared future, a toast to the golden age. Daniel reached across the table with his glass. As he touched his father's glass it cracked at the brim, continuing downwards and looking like a tiny flash of lightning frozen in mid-air. His father leapt up

southwards to its source. But he'd never have got there. They'd have asked him beforehand where he was going and he wouldn't have known what to answer, and even if he had known they wouldn't have believed him and they'd have brought him back again. That was what happened when he tried to walk home from his great-aunts' birthday parties. Along the way, somewhere on the B70 or in the *hammrich* fields, someone or other had always stopped alongside him, wound the window down, said he was *de lüttje Kuper*, wasn't he, and asked what he was doing all alone out there. Once he hadn't even been leaving a birthday celebration but walking to one. And still they picked him up halfway. The village was everywhere. That was the realization he was slowly coming to. He'd have to walk a very long way, cycle a very long way, to ever escape it. And then what? Then what? His imagination didn't stretch that far. A car stopped outside the den. A door opened. Someone got out.

Hard called his son's name twice and listened to the words, and then he said, 'You can come out now. I won't do anything. Volker isn't dead, if that's what you're thinking. He just passed out for a while. Do you hear me? He's got concussion. But he's feeling better already. He's in hospital. And he wants to see you.'

There were three patients in the room. Fathers and mothers stood around each bed, talking quietly to their children. Volker was in the bed by the window, his head bandaged up. Above him, on the other side of the room, a TV was suspended from the ceiling. The sound was off. Daniel hadn't wanted to come at first. His parents had talked him into it—it'd been an accident, all he had to do was apologize, give him a present, something important to him, and then everything would be fine and they'd say no more about it.

Hard nudged Daniel closer to the bed. Daniel handed Volker the parcel. Volker sat up, tore the paper off and unwrapped the Cheetah, a 1:35-scale tank with moveable vinyl chains and dual pivoting autocannon. He turned it to and fro, rolled it back and forth over the bedcover, aimed the guns at Daniel, his father and his mother and imitated the thrusting sound of machine guns firing. His double chin trembled, his eyes shone. Suddenly he grasped at his head, his face twisted, and gave a short moan, as if the gift wasn't enough to quell the pain Daniel had inflicted on him.

Daniel heard his mother whispering behind him: 'Haven't you forgotten something? Don't you remember the promise you made? You were going to say something.'

He said it: that he was sorry, that he couldn't explain it either but he certainly didn't do it on purpose. He heard the words coming out of his mouth and echoing inside him.

His mother patted him on the shoulder.

His behaviour is excellent.

He felt like he was remote-controlled.

The incident bound them together. They avoided each other at school but when they were alone in the afternoons they played together as if they were friends. As long as no trains were coming they jumped over the wooden railway sleepers and balanced along the rails. They flew kites on the dyke and threw polystyrene planes into the wind. They made models together in Daniel's room, of fighter bombers, combat helicopters, nuclear submarines. Yet parts of their worlds still remained separate. Daniel never took Volker along to the den underneath the freight shed, and Volker never took Daniel home with him.

By the beginning of September it seemed as if the eight-week drought were coming to an end. The farmers stopped watering their fields with slurry tankers and the sprinklers in the gardens were turned off. Everyone believed in the forecasts that there'd soon be rain and it would get colder and then no warmer again. Dark clouds gathered over the land, trapping the heat beneath them. The air grew more humid and more muggy but the storm didn't come.

It was Saturday afternoon. Behind the house, Daniel's father had driven the new car out of the garage—a green Opel Rekord E2 2.0 S, 1982 model, 74 kW, 100 PS—and soaped up the bonnet on the drive. He'd turned up the radio and was listening to the fifth day of the Bundesliga season. His mother was sitting up on the terrace, under the shade of the awning. She stroked her belly with one hand, flicking through a magazine with the other. Daniel was squatting on the outside staircase, tins and brushes spread out beside him. He was painting a Phantom in a camouflage scheme.

Sometimes his father yelled 'Yes,' or 'No!' or 'Schatzschneider,' depending on what the reporter had said on the radio. He squeezed the sponge every time. White foam dripped onto the ground. A pigeon cooed in the willow. The leaves on the trees moved quietly in the wind. When Daniel looked up and reached for a different tin of paint his mother smiled at him. She waved over at him and he waved back before he turned back to his model. Everything was marked out. The nose was supposed to be black, with a pattern of basalt grey and olive green on the wings and the body. That was what was shown on the packaging, that was what it said in the instructions. Daniel took over the wavy pattern and transferred it to the plastic exterior. Didi Schulz, the blacksmith, had said you should paint the parts while they were still attached to the tree, on the sprue, but that seemed wrong to Daniel, as if they wanted to trick him, as if they didn't trust him to do it on his own without any help.

31

His father shouted again—'Schatzschneider!'—clenched his fist and danced around the car. His mother laughed.

Schatzschneider. He wondered what the name was supposed to mean. Literally, it meant treasure-cutter. But was it someone who cut a treasure into pieces like a cake, so that it was enough to go around, or cut it apart like a ship at the scrapyard because it was old and leaky and no use to anyone any more? His father was over the moon. He was so happy he kissed his mother, Daniel, the car, the sponge.

His mother said, 'If you were always this frisky we'd have six or seven by now.'

'Two's more than enough, Biggi,' said Hard, using a chamois leather to wipe off the mark his lips had left on the windscreen.

'What if I have twins? Then you'll have three in one go.' Daniel couldn't even imagine there'd soon be four of them, that something or someone would soon put an end to their balance.

Five minutes later, Volker came pedalling round the corner. There was a plaster stuck to his forehead as if the wound wasn't quite healed, as if he wanted to remind Daniel of what he'd done for as long as possible. He got off his bike, folded out the kickstand and stood it up in front of him. He was wearing nothing but a pair of red towelling underpants. The fabric constricted his body in the middle like drawstrings, skin bulging out above and below. It was as white as flour, or as milk, depending on what spot you looked at. Some areas, especially on his arms and legs, were dull and grained with dust, others were oily and shiny as if he'd just greased them. The bulges of his neck shimmered in the sunlight.

Daniel dropped the plane in shock. One wing tank and the nose wheel broke off. He'd actually been meaning to show him the den that day. It was time to let him in on it. But now, in that outfit, he couldn't be seen with him there. He couldn't be seen with him anywhere.

Volker said hello to Daniel's father and mother. They both paused for a moment, his father putting his sponge aside, his mother her magazine.

'Aren't you cold?' asked his mother. 'You're welcome to borrow one of Daniel's T-shirts if you're cold.'

'No need for that.'

'Or a pair of trousers.'

'I'm fine.'

'Daniel's got a pair of tracksuit bottoms that are too big around the top and too short at the bottom. I'm sure they'd fit you.'

'I don't need anything.'

'You two should go down to the lake,' said Daniel's father, hands on hips, looking at the sky. 'As long as the weather's still good. Looks like rain.'

'You say that every day,' said his mother and returned to her magazine.

'It's getting more and more likely every day, that's why.'

'Maybe later,' said Daniel. 'I have to show him something first, up in my room.'

'Nix. It's much too hot up there,' said his father.

'I've opened the window. Anyway, it won't take long, I just want to show him something, a model I can't bring down, because, because there's too many parts.'

'What model?' asked Volker.

'You'll see,' said Daniel. And he collected up the broken pieces, put the paint tins and brushes back in the box and went up the stairs to the second floor ahead of him. His room was a mess. A cuddly ET his father had won at the fair's shooting range blocked their way in. The carpet was covered in toys. Daniel shoved the figures and cars and houses aside with one foot and stepped into the middle of the room. He stood between the window and the door, the draught blowing a strand of hair across his face. It was sweltering hot nonetheless. Hotter than outside. Hotter than anywhere else.

'What do you want to show me?' Volker asked.

'Nothing.'

'What, nothing?'

'It was just an excuse.'

'An excuse for what?'

'I can't be bothered to go to the lake. Or the sea. Or keep on playing by the tracks. Or flying kites on the dyke.'

'What do you want to do then?'

Daniel shrugged.

'We could go to your den. To the freight shed.'

'No way.'

'Why not?'

'I told the others, I swore I'd ask them first if I brought someone else along. And there'll be no one there right now, anyway.'

'Then no one will notice you brought me along.'

'Still.'

'What shall we do then?'

'Hide and seek.'

'Here? In the house?'

'It's too easy outside. There's too many hiding places there. But inside you have to find a really good place to not get found. You start, and I'll count to ten.'

'Why do I have to hide and not you?'

'Because I live here.'

'That's not fair. You know every corner of the house.'

Daniel made him an offer. 'If I haven't found you after ten minutes I'll take you with me to the den. If I do find you, you have to show me your room.'

Volker consented. They synchronized watches. It was ten past five. Daniel went and stood in a corner of his room. He closed his eyes and started counting. At one, Volker was out of the door. At two, Daniel heard him panting. At three, his footsteps in the hall. At four, he heard him opening another door. At five, he closed it behind him. At six, nothing. At seven, nothing. At eight, a crash. At nine, he hesitated to go on counting. At ten, Volker was back in his room and telling him to come with him, he had something to show *him* now and it wasn't an excuse for not finding a hiding place.

They crossed the hall to the attic, a room on the same floor with un-insulated exterior walls, used by the whole family as a box room. Volker pointed at the trap window in the sloping ceiling, which the wind had slammed against the tiles as he opened it, and shattered. He said he was sorry, he'd meant to climb out and hide on the flat roof above the extension.

Daniel climbed onto the chair underneath it, looked out of the hatch and saw: the perfect hiding place, not visible from the house or from the street. If you climbed from there onto the crown of the roof you'd have a view of the whole of the village. You'd see Composers' Corner in the north, the flooded sand pits, the rubbish dump and the county town, in the west the railway tracks, the signal tower, the dairy and butchery and the hammrich fields behind them, the Beach Hotel, the custard factory over on the dyke, in the south Petersen's pool hall, the freight shed, Rosing's workshops, the Raiffeisen farmers' cooperative shop, the industrial estate on the other side of the B70 and in the east the centre of the village: Village Road, the post office, Schröder Shoes, Didi Schulz's blacksmith's shop and ironmongery, the Friesenhuus and the Friesen Pharmacy, Doctor Ahlers' and Doctor Hilliger's surgeries, Dettmers' Hairdressing, Wessels' Bakery, Krause Fishmongers, Onken's law chambers, the Flower Barn, Vehndel Fashions and on the corner, where Village Road crossed Town Hall Road, the bank, Kramer's Furniture Paradise on Station Road, the building society, Benzen's Paints, Hanken Solar, Tinnemeyer Upholstery, Plenter Electrical, Busboom Autos, Oltmanns' Cycles, Kromminga Driving School, Stumpe Drinks and Fokken's Snack Bar at the top of Church Road, the church tower with the weathercock, the Reformed Church up on the mound, the cemetery, the monument to fallen soldiers, the morgue, the parsonage and the village hall, Wall Street with the primary school and the kindergarten, the town hall, the fire and police station, Poets' Corner, Superneemann—the supermarket—the schools campus and even the navy radio masts, thirty kilometres away. Twice a year, when the ships put out from the shipyard down on the river, you could see their tall superstructures rising above the trees, over the land across the dykes, as if they were floating on grass. Through binoculars, you could make out the sports centre and the football matches in the Eino Oltmanns Stadium, watch the horse shows at the riding arena. You could see everything and you yourself would be invisible. If you did get caught though there'd be no escape, you'd be stuck like a mouse in a trap.

There was a flash in the distance, followed seconds later by a long roll of thunder. Daniel's father was standing down below on the terrace.

Hard said, 'Stay right where you are, young man.'

From one moment to the next, the sky darkened and a storm rose, hailstones swept across them, drumming on the roof and plummeting onto Volker and Daniel like bullets. Daniel's mother gathered her things together, wound in the awning and drove the car into the garage.

On his way upstairs, Hard went to the built-in wardrobe in the master bedroom and took out a coat hanger, a heavy wooden hanger for winter coats. Volker said it was all his fault. He was trembling, his bulges surging like waves along his body. Hard sent him home. Volker went down the stairs. Daniel crept into the furthest corner of the attic. Hard closed the door behind them, turned the key in the lock and beat a round of good luck into his son.

Science Fiction

1

On the late summer day when Daniel walked into their trap, it suddenly started snowing in the morning. They'd predicted a change in the weather on the radio and TV the night before, but no one had reckoned with it being quite so extreme. It was mid-September. The temperature had fallen overnight from over fifteen degrees to zero, and the first snow fell outside the windows, just a few flakes, white shadows that floated down from the sky and disappeared again the moment they touched the ground, as if they'd never been there.

Hard had pruned back the poplar trees lining the garden in the spring, and now Birgit could look out from the kitchen over the railway lines to the old signal-box, to the dairy. The chimney was smoking and the milk trucks were driving into the yard to make their deliveries. The gates at the level crossing closed—a train rushed by, making the cups on the table tremble—and opened again, cars drove across the railway lines in both directions, and she watched them until they turned off somewhere or their outlines blurred into the horizon in the distance.

The fridge behind her hummed, the dishwasher whooshed quietly, and every time the upper spray arm brushed against one of the plates, the crockery gave a rattle. Other than that there was absolute silence. No screaming any more, no arguing, no high-pitched laughter. The children were out of the worst phase, as she'd said recently whenever she talked to her sisters or old school friends, all far away on the telephone. Daniel left the house at half past seven and cycled to school, no matter what the weather. The twins had to be at kindergarten at eight, and now they preferred to take the short walk with other, slightly older children from the neighbourhood than holding her hands, one on either side. Birgit was glad and proud of having finally got them settled in at kindergarten, but as soon as she shut the door behind them she was scared of having to settle herself back in.

In the first few weeks she hadn't known what to do with herself. All the jobs she'd previously passed on to the home help, a neighbour—vacuuming, dusting, tidying, shopping—she got done in the hours before lunch. She even managed to cook something different every day, and she was surprised she had got down to things with such energy and enthusiasm, plugging the gap that opened up in front of her after breakfast with housework.

Daniel cycled across the junction, past Vehndel Fashions, Superneemann and the sports ground, until he reached the track called the Broadway, which was no broader than the other tracks in the area and wasn't exactly a track any more either, having been tarmacked years ago, before he was even born. There were only a few stony tracks left branching off it here and there, used by the farmers to get to their fields. It would make more sense, Daniel thought, to call it the Longway. He thought that every time he cycled past the *Broadway* sign after turning off Goethe Road. It really was so long that you couldn't see the end from the beginning, even though it ran as straight as an arrow until it crossed Groninger Road and then merged into School Road.

He pedalled harder to ward off the cold and watched his breath coming out of his mouth like smoke and flying away behind him. The grass and hedges all around him were covered in glittering frost and the spiders' webs, otherwise barely visible, stood out clearly against the blades and leaves, every thread white and brilliant. It seemed to him like a sudden return to the Minus World, and he wondered whether the temperature would fall even more, to minus nine hundred and sixty-one degrees, and what it felt like to be an Iceman, a creature with no memory.

The maize stood head-high on either side, green and yellow and already turning brown at its tips, huge fields, some of them up to thirty hectares, which he and Volker had penetrated like a forest the previous summer. Out of rage and high spirits, they had beaten swathes into the field with sticks and laid out labyrinths, where they'd got lost and walked round and round in circles, too proud to follow the seed rows even hours later.

The first time, they'd taken half a dozen cobs, peeled off the leaves and threads, spread butter on the corn, wrapped it in aluminium foil and laid it in a fire they'd lit on a field by the kolk lake. But they'd both only taken one bite. When Daniel told his father about it he'd laughed and told him he'd been out filching crops after the war, at night, always on the run from the farmers, and that even the field corn grown as fodder was edible if you picked it before the middle of August.

Once Daniel and Volker had almost got caught. The farmer who owned the land, a man by the name of van Deest, had posted guards on all sides while they were in there, hunters with rifles who combed the field on his command. They'd only got away unnoticed because there were deer hiding in there too, which had broken out and diverted the men's attention.

Some of the fields had already been harvested and now the snow gathered in the furrows left behind in the damp earth by the tractors. Outside some of the farms he cycled past were towering piles of maize, the ones that weren't covered over and weighed down with old tyres looking like sand dunes. Now, white and uneven, they reminded him more of Christmas stollen cake dusted with far too much icing sugar.

The field outside the school campus was still untouched though. Daniel chained his bike to one of the fence posts and removed the satchel of books and pulp magazines from his luggage rack. Their first class was English, in a room right next to the main entrance. The bike stand was on the other side of the campus and he didn't want to run into Iron, waiting there for him and other Year Five kids, nor to walk all the way across the yard past the gym and the staffroom in the cold.

From downstairs, she heard Hard opening the door and pushing the bike stand outside the shop. She knew he'd be going into the garage to fetch his bike and hers and position them outside the shop so that it looked as if they had customers. Every time she heard him she remembered the time, not long after she'd moved in with him, when she'd stood at the open garage door one morning, shopping bags on the ground, hands on hips, shocked and incredulous that their bikes had been stolen overnight. And she remembered she'd been even more shocked and incredulous when she'd walked round the house to the shop doorway and seen the bikes standing there, both locked up and laden with bags.

Pale in the face but determined to demand the key and take him to task, Hard, *de Sturkopp*—that stubborn bugger—she'd gone inside. She was annoyed at him making plans and putting them into action without talking to her about them. After the wedding she'd told him she was willing to give up her job for him, and he'd assured her he'd let her in on everything to do with the shop. But he hadn't kept his side of the bargain.

'What's this all about?' she'd asked, pointing outside, still upset by the double whammy.

He'd shrugged and said, as if to justify himself, 'It's psychology, Biggi.'

'Give me the key!'

'Doubters find it easier to come in when they assume someone else is in the shop.'

'The key!'

'No one goes in an empty cafe or restaurant when there's one next door with someone sitting inside waiting to be served.'

'That's not psychology, it's nonsense. There isn't any other drugstore in Jericho than yours.'

'Ours.'

'What?'

'This,' he'd said, throwing out his arms, 'is our drugstore.'

'No, it's yours. And now give me the damn key, will you!'

And when she remembered that she thought of *Dallas*, one of the very first episodes when Bobby went into his brother's business, and J.R. refused to let him look at the red files and gave him the feeling that although he might be on the team, he was still an inferior, less powerful member, and that, she feared, was what she'd always be if she gave in to Hard's coaxing to come in on the shop with him.

Sometimes she wished she'd just carried on cycling on one of her bike tours, back before they had the children, kept on and on, taken the ferry across the river back to her parents and started a different life there. Instead, she had cycled aimlessly between the bare East Frisian hammrich fields to the dyke, sat on a bench for hours and hours and stared at the water, the silt. She'd made out the contours of a passenger ship in the distance, and she'd imagined reclining on deck, sun and wind on her face, a book in her hand, travelling around the world into an uncertain future. She still sometimes imagined that, that there was some way, yet at the same time she sensed that everything was just as certain or uncertain in that other life as in this one. Back then, though, she'd simply felt immature and she'd returned home again, not wanting to grant Hard the triumph of having to look for her and then finding her.

Once he'd even borrowed bikes from Oltmanns', dozens of ladies' bicycles that Oltmanns', Oltmanns' Cycles, rented out to tourists during high season. But that day they'd stood in untidy rows outside the shop, every which way as if hastily parked, to reinforce the effect of an ad published that morning in the *Friesenzeitung* newspaper: *Attention all housewives: Spring is on its way! Multipurpose cloths, floor cloths, mops, scrubbers, cleaning fluid, dustpans and brushes and vacuum bags*—special offers from 79 pfennigs!

The first customers had been rather surprised to enter an empty shop through this cordon of bikes, craning their necks past him to the office, the photo studio, the darkroom, holding their breath, listening and then reaching after all for the crates with the special offers set up by the counter. A few of them had asked Hard where the others were, but they had no reply to his question of 'Which others?' and they paid up quickly out of embarrassment. Luckily, the shop was soon so crowded that no one else spotted the disparity between the bikes and the women greedily clutching at packages and purses.

'Psychology,' Hard had told her again that night, as he stowed the cash box under the bed and switched off the light without turning around to her again. 'It's all psychology.'

If there's one thing he knows nothing about, she thought, it's psychology. And it seemed like proof when people started seeing through his bike trick at some point but he continued to believe in its appeal, even as it became less and less effective.

2

Daniel was a zero at English, and he wished at least three times every lesson that he could aim an arkonidic psycho-raygun at Mrs Zuhl to give her posthypnotic commands. *Pick your nose. Pull up your skirt. Give Daniel an A.* Mrs Zuhl was short and fat and had thin, white hair, fluff as fine as feathers—even from behind you could see her scalp and the moles on it—but nobody knew whether most of it had fallen out because of some sickness or because of her age. Having traipsed round all the doctors and pre-scription chemists in the area, she had come into the drugstore. Hard had given her something, a household remedy, *Procapillaris*, a purely plant-based ointment, as he never grew tired of empha-sizing, which would restore her natural volume. After years of strict dieting, the stuff had indeed restored her natural volume—just not in the place where she applied it.

Now Mrs Zuhl was just about to take retirement. Her family had been refugees from East Prussia; she had lost her father in the war and one of her two sisters on the way across Poland, passing through Rostock, Hamburg and Bremen to end up here in the very west of Germany. In a moment of wanton abandon she had mar-ried the senior clerk Hans-Werner Hansen, even though he'd already been married once, and had filed for divorce two years later when she discovered he'd had another woman on the side, his subsequent third wife. She had experienced his fourth and fifth wives, each younger than the last, and seen all the wives, and eventually Hansen himself, die one after another through accidents and illness, and of old age. And she suffered from the fact that she was the only one to have survived and that people still looked askance at her for first letting herself in for him and then backing off.

Aside from that episode, she had stayed on her own. Instead of getting involved with anyone else, she had devoted herself entirely to the task of teaching children and providing them with a small amount of what she liked to call 'skills for life'. She had seen them come and go, grow, blossom and wilt, and yet every year she'd had to start over from scratch with the same hope of making children into better, cleverer people. But she had never heard a word of thanks, with a few minor exceptions; not to the extent to which she had expected.

For the future, for the evening of her life, she had already bought herself a two-bedroom apartment close to her other, surviving sister in Garbsen near Hanover and a new car, and she drove over there whenever she could, three hours there, three hours back, to recuperate from the countryside and its inhabitants. Times had changed. The new world had little in common with the one in which she had grown up. All the other teachers were younger than her and the school had exchanged most of the ideals she had once started out with—cleanliness, discipline, order—for others—long hair, baggy clothes and intense but in her opinion unproductive discussions. At the last staff meeting, she had fought not to have to start over at the very beginning again, with the youngest. She was too old for that, she had said, and wouldn't be there for long enough to take care of the pupils as their class teacher, so it didn't make any sense to take over a Year Five class and then give them up again a year later. But there were just not enough teachers and too many children, and her refusal had made no impression on the school governors.

Daniel's class was one of the mobile classes that had to go to a different room for every subject. Sometimes they spent several hours in windowless spaces used for storing material for woodwork or art lessons. And then there were days when they sat at tiled desks with electrical switches built into them in the science lab to interpret poems or discuss whether Jesus was God's son or Joseph's.

In the beginning they'd been promised a classroom but now, six weeks in, nobody mentioned the idea any more and they had a suspicion it would stay that way until the end of the school year, perhaps even the end of middle school, and they'd have to get used to not having a place to call their own. The class tried to maintain their seating order despite the differing conditions, but they didn't manage it and the teachers kept getting their names muddled up.

Mrs Zuhl held a spontaneous vocabulary test at the start of every class, 'to warm up,' as she put it. She'd drawn up a special class register for the purpose, containing the names of the children and after them the figure one or zero—one for true, zero for false. This binary code provided information on their successes and failures and went towards their grade at the end of the semester. Each time, she said a word from one of the chapters they had worked through in class so far, and called up a different child so that nobody could feel safe. And each time she addressed a child in this way it sounded as if she were giving a dog an order to sit or shake hands.

'Volker,' said Mrs Zuhl, looking at Daniel. 'Rocket!'

Neither of them answered. One of them felt he hadn't been meant, the other felt he hadn't been looked at, and so they sat mutely grinning next to each other until Mrs Zuhl repeated her command to translate the word *rocket* into German.

But instead of saying *'Rakete'* Daniel said, 'I'm not Volker,' because he didn't want to give him an unfair advantage. Volker hadn't given him an unfair advantage either when Mrs Zuhl had accidentally called him Daniel.

Mrs Zuhl looked at the seating plan she'd drawn up during the first lesson. Names had been crossed out and replaced with other names; arrows pointed from one square to another and back again. That sheet of paper proved what she had sensed all summer long—that forty years of English and Maths were enough, more than enough.

'Who are you then?'

'Daniel.'

'Daniel,' she said as though talking to herself, and opened up a red exercise book. A smile flitted across her lips as if she were remembering something she thought she'd forgotten, and she ran a hand over her head. 'Kuper?'

She'd never asked that before. There was no other Daniel in the class, no reason to ask him his surname.

Now she put one and one together. Every sign of strain fell away from her. Suddenly she sensed that she would manage this year, her last year. 'Daniel Kuper?'

'Yes, Miss.' He positioned his finger under the table. *Pick your nose*!

'Kuper's Drugstore?'

'Yes, Miss.' *Pull up your skirt*!

'Bernhard's—Hard's son?'

'Yes, Miss.' *Give Daniel an A*!

'Daniel the zero!'

Last time around, Volker hadn't known what *radiator* meant in German and nor had Daniel, and he still didn't and he hoped she'd give him the same word she'd originally intended for Volker.

'All right then,' she said, taking a red ballpoint pen out of her pencil case and releasing the tip, ready to document her pupil's ignorance. 'Daniel, radiator!'

Warm steam billowed up at her as she opened the dishwasher. She automatically closed her eyes, breathed in deeply through her nose and out again through her mouth. For a moment, she felt fresh and invigorated. The smell and the warmth awakened vague memories in her, of saunas and hot springs, of summer holidays, mountain lakes, lonely hikes—and, once the first gust had passed her by, of dry cleaners, poisons and car exhaust fumes, and she pulled a face and waited for the steam above and below her to dissolve into nothing. As she waited, she wondered whether it was always that way, whether every good thing had an inherent bad side to it, something that couldn't be controlled and broke out of you, no matter how much you wished you could keep it in check. The only thing, the best thing she'd achieved so far, she thought, was her children. Of course they had their dark sides, everybody did, and she was often enough annoyed about her own, her stubbornness, her pride, her tendency to avoid conflict. The children weren't perfect, God knew, and sometimes it seemed to her as if their upbringing wouldn't change much about their flaws, but her feeling for them was stronger and more unconditional than anything she'd ever felt for any person, especially for Hard, her husband. All these thoughts took root within her and withered again before they had a chance to unfurl, in less than a few seconds. For there was nothing she feared more than that—that they might unfurl.

And so she put the plates and cutlery away in the kitchen cupboards and filled up the dishwasher with more plates and cutlery. She put the milk and the jam, the packets of sliced meats and cheese back in the fridge. Then she wiped down the waxed tablecloth, lifted up the teapot and blew out the candle in the tea warmer. Smoke rose from the holes, threads striving towards the ceiling, floating vertically through the air, forming swirls, disappearing. Birgit watched the shapes dreamily, wondering what might have caused the change in the weather, until she registered something moving, down on the pavement. The snow was falling thicker now, and in the flurry she saw Hard standing by the curb behind the house, his broad shoulders luminous in his white coat. He seemed to be talking to someone she couldn't see. Sometimes he looked in one direction, sometimes in another; he pointed at something, nodded, gesticulated, gave some kind of explanations, about the weather, the business, the state of the nation. His lips were moving; perhaps he was chewing something, or perhaps they were trembling with the cold. He reached a hand out as if he wanted a passing car to take him along or wanted to catch one of the snowflakes and inspect its consistency; he shook his head and rubbed it apart like sand between his fingers. That's exactly the way old Mr Knipper used to stand before her, she thought, when he demanded the letters he'd dictated to her, to check back over them.

She'd met him on a stroll through the pedestrian zone in town, only that June. Ten years she'd worked as his secretary, and she'd rarely run into him since she handed in her notice ten years ago. His hair had gone white but hadn't thinned out, and he was still tall. The twins leapt around him as if he were an inanimate object. Julia, her mouth still covered in ice cream, hid behind his back, and Andreas tried to catch his sister between Mr Knipper's legs. He kept grabbing at her, and every time he touched Julia she screamed and jumped aside. Birgit was ashamed of her children but didn't dare tell them off in front of her former boss. He didn't seem bothered by the screaming and the grabbing, or at least he smiled all along, and sometimes he patted Julia's head, her blonde curls, as if she were the dog jumping up at him and begging for his attention, and not Birgit. Daniel was standing a few metres away outside the window of a toyshop, absolutely mesmerized by the almost fifty-centimetre model of the Challenger space shuttle, which had exploded on television that January. He didn't hear his mother asking the man whether he could use her for anything.

'But Miss Bleeker,' he had always called her by her maiden name, 'you know we've got someone else now.'

'I just mean, if she gets pregnant and you need someone to cover for her. I've got time again now and you don't have to show me the ropes, I can still remember everything.'

'Oh yes, I'm sure you can. You'll definitely be the first to hear from me,' he said, scratching his head with one finger. 'I'll be in touch when the time comes.'

But he never had been in touch.

Simone had planted her right elbow on the desk to support her left arm. Her slim fingers clicked in mid-air, making a noise that sounded like a high, clear snap, like the crack of a whip. Mrs Zuhl had nodded at her once to indicate that she'd soon pick her, but that had been a minute ago. Nothing had happened since then, no one had said anything, and Mrs Zuhl's question of what a *budgie* was lay suspended above them all in the room like a burden, descending gradually and unstoppably towards them. Then the bell rang and Simone collapsed onto her desk with a sigh. She hadn't been called on all lesson, even though she'd known everything, everything Daniel hadn't known, a budgie was a *Wellensittich* in German. Unit 1, Acquisition 7: *Look at the bird. It's a budgie. It's Mrs Clark's pet.* They'd talked about it four weeks ago now, and it seemed to her a huge waste of time to keep going over and over what the others didn't know, instead of role-playing the scene with Peter and Betty in the toyshop as planned.

'She's bound to pick you next time,' Volker said to her, sandwich in hand, as they left the classroom together.

'I wouldn't bet on it,' said Daniel.

'I would.'

'How much?'

'Sportsman's bet.'

Volker held out his sandwich-free hand and Daniel shook it. 'I think she's got it in for me,' he said.

'She'll leave you alone if you stop making mistakes,' said Simone, still disappointed at not being picked.

'You mean like she left you alone?' asked Volker and shoved the last bite into his mouth.

'She's never been into me.'

'Exactly,' said Daniel. 'You're a girl, you don't know what it's like when someone's into you.'

'Not yet,' said Volker.

'What d'you mean by that?' asked Simone.

'Oh, nothing.' Simone was taller than Volker, taller than Daniel, and thinner, much thinner, 'a real beanpole,' as her mother always joked, not knowing the reason for it, and she pushed Volker away with both hands and all her strength, but he didn't budge from the spot, only swaying slightly as if she'd pushed a punching bag in PE.

'Or do you know and you just don't want to tell us?'

'Tell you what?'

'That you've got a boyfriend.'

'Rubbish.'

'Simone's got a boyfriend, Simone's got a boyfriend.' Volker stamped off triumphantly upstairs, to the first floor. His voice and his footsteps bounced off the walls, clear and muffled at the same time, and Simone leapt after him to prevent him spreading the rumour he'd invented. They left Daniel alone and didn't see Iron and his friends coming round the corner, walking in front of him and getting slower and slower, so that Daniel bumped into them and trod on their heels and they had an excuse to humiliate him.

Daniel didn't see them either, or at least he didn't recognize them at the first moment, only registering them as shadows because he was looking at the floor, until he ran into them and trod on Iron's heels.

'Well, what have we here?' Iron turned around, hands planted on his hips. 'Little Kuper.'

'Sorry.'

Iron leant down to him, cupped his ear and asked, 'What?'

'Sorry.'

'That's not good enough,' said Iron and straightened up again. 'That's not nearly good enough.' He was a Year Nine at the intermediate school, wore John Lennon glasses, white trainers and black leather jackets with patches sewn onto them, dedicated to bands that were never in the charts, and he always had several devoted boys gathered around him ready to carry out his orders, often before he even gave them. He was tall and broadly built, too tall and too broadly built for his age. It seemed as if he'd shot up a metre in height over a matter of weeks, and not all the parts of his body had kept up with the growth spurt. His real name was Michael, Michael Rosing, but none of the younger kids knew what he was really called. 'You know that's not good enough.'

'Yes,' said Daniel, 'I know.' If he had a gravity neutralizer he could make Iron float up to the ceiling now. And he imagined him wriggling up there next to the fluorescent lamps and falling down and hitting the staircase and breaking his neck and his blood splashing across the linoleum and running down the steps all the way to the school hall and through the hall and out of the school onto the bus parking spaces, across School Road over into the maize field, a huge tide of blood that flooded the land and drowned animals and people. The only problem was that he didn't have a gravity neutralizer and he wouldn't be getting one any time soon.

'Which means?' asked Iron.

'Which means I have to lick your shoes.'

'Exactly,' said Iron to the sound of the second bell, and held out the tip of one of his shoes. The others laughed, one of them grabbed Daniel and wanted to push him to the ground, but Iron held him back. 'He'll do it himself.'

'Why, actually?' asked Daniel. He was playing for time.

'Why what?'

'I trod on the back of your shoes and not the front, but now I have to lick the front of your shoes and not the back.'

'That's the rule.'

'What rule?'

'The rule!'

'Iron, he's getting fresh,' said the boy who'd wanted to push him down before, and he grabbed Daniel again in case he got away before they were done with him.

'Yeah, looks like it,' said Iron. 'You're only making things worse for yourself. The shoes won't be enough now. Where are your two shadows, anyway, Woofer and Tweeter?' He clicked his fingers. 'What's her name again? Silke? Sibylle?'

'You mean Simone?'

'Simone, right.'

'Upstairs,' said Daniel tonelessly. 'They went ahead.'

'Bad luck for them. If they saw what we're going to do with you they could learn a thing or two, for later, for their own torture.

It's always better when you know what's coming to you. What a shame—we've thought up a few really special things for you.'

'What things?' Daniel was building up hope that it was all a bluff and Iron wouldn't know what to say if he asked him.

'Frank here,' he looked at the boy behind Daniel, 'happens to have the key to the chemistry room. There's all sorts of interesting stuff in there. Ethanol, for example. But I bet you've never swallowed it in that concentration, or in our dosage. If at all.'

'He doesn't even know what ethanol is yet,' Frank said over Daniel's head.

'Doesn't matter,' said Iron. 'All the better if he doesn't. And apart from that,' he turned back to Daniel, 'we want to see how conductive your body is, especially under water. And if you're still fit after that, which is unlikely, we'll read you a sample of the finest Vogon poetry.' Iron nodded at Frank, and he shoved Daniel fifty centimetres ahead with one hand, not taking the other off him for a second. Daniel stumbled and another push would have sent him to his knees in front of Iron, but at that moment Mr Kamps came around the corner and asked Daniel what he was doing there. 'You ought to have been upstairs ages ago.' Frank let go of Daniel and pretended to be patting dust or dandruff off his shoulders.

'We were just chatting,' said Iron.

'I see,' said Mr Kamps, who couldn't imagine anyone having a serious chat about anything with Michael Rosing. 'About what?'

'About gravity,' said Daniel, halfway to the stairs already.

And because Iron took that as a comment about his weight, he called after him that Daniel had something coming to him, a miracle, and that he should look forward to the next break time to get a taste of it, because that was when he'd explain to him how the whole gravity and traction thing worked and what it felt like not to get away from the place where he'd nail him down by his knees.

3

On several occasions, Hard had offered to let her work in the drug-store, half-days, on an hourly basis, like back in the in-between time when Daniel was at kindergarten and the twins weren't yet born. He'd even mentioned the possibility of not renewing Mrs Bluhm's contract which expired in December, but she'd turned down all his offers and instead, on the spur of the moment and without telling him, applied to Klaus Neemann and Günter Vehndel. They'd both placed ads in the *Frisian News*, one for a secretary and the other for a bookkeeper, and she was confident she could do either. She'd sent them formal applications by post, containing her CV, samples of her work and references. She'd never been invited to an interview and she'd never received a rejection letter either, and now, two weeks later, she found it awkward to go and say hello to the men she'd written to, because she didn't know why they'd ignored her and it was too late to ask them.

Birgit was born and bred in the county town but she'd known Klaus and Günter a long time, since long before she'd moved to Jericho, since her time at Knipper's. All the local businessmen knew one another, either through business contacts, as competitors or friends, or personally through school, the church, sports clubs. And she'd got to know Klaus and Günter better once she'd got to know Hard better. She'd used their surnames and the formal form of address in her application letters, to show them she wasn't being quite serious—but serious enough for her to hope they'd take her.

Klaus and Günter had been friends of Hard's for years. They sang together in the male-voice choir, played skat—they jokingly referred to themselves as 'the necessary three' because the card game required three players—and stood by the railings on the sports pitch on Saturdays to watch the Germania Jericho boys playing football. Once a week, usually on Saturdays, occasionally on Fridays, they spent the evening at the bar of the Beach Hotel, drinking beer and schnapps and talking politics, football, business— the same subjects they always talked about, just not usually in as much detail and enthusiasm, because now they didn't have to worry about the time and they could have a lie-in the next morning.

Their children went to kindergarten and school together and Birgit was so familiar with their wives, Marlies and Sabine, that she couldn't tell any more whether they were friends or not. They met up regularly for tea or coffee, played Mau Mau while the men were playing skat—they jokingly called themselves 'the necessary three of the necessary three'—went on walks or to the cinema, exchanged stories but not secrets.

Over the years their circle had become closer and closer without them ever noticing. And by now they seemed to be linked together by invisible wires. Not a day passed when Hard and she didn't talk about one or other of them, because one of them had met one or other of them in the village.

And still she'd avoided them all over the past few days, as far as that was possible. When someone came to visit she'd feigned headaches and retired to the master bedroom. She hadn't celebrated her birthday on the 13th of September, with the excuse of having a party some time later. She'd ordered ice cream and cake, fish, meat and peas from the frozen food catalogue and done the rest of her shopping in the neighbouring villages and the county town.

She'd made a list; the piece of paper was on the counter top. Kohlrabi, whipping cream, butter, milk, cheese, salami, bier-schinken, sunflower oil, lettuce, white cabbage, red cabbage, green beans, sauerkraut, parsley, chives, eggs, apples, bananas, oranges, carrots, potatoes, spaghetti, ketchup, mayonnaise, vanilla pudding for Julia, jelly—red or green—for Andreas, chocolate pudding for Daniel, coffee, tea, mustard, flour, Nutella, cocoa, orange juice, apple juice, cola, water, beer, practically everything she'd bought a week ago had run out, and she had to go out to pick up supplies for the family. She went through the list again, comparing her notes with the content of the cupboards, took the car key off the hook, her scarf and gloves out of the drawer, two plastic bags out of the cleaning closet, her jacket from the coat stand, heard the telephone ringing, the in-house line, the green light on the phone lit up, and she crept downstairs, treading on the very edges of the steps. She didn't want to speak to Hard, not at that time of day. She was scared he might stop her from going out with some kind of task and muddle up her morning. He liked giving her tasks, phone calls to customers and reps, errands to run in the village—thin snares meant to loop around her ankles like jewellery and draw her into the business.

Once downstairs, she slowed her pace until she came to a standstill. The office door linking the stairwell to the shop was ajar. She trod on tiptoes, careful not to make the slightest noise. She couldn't see Hard but she could hear him, hear his breath, waiting for her to pick up the phone at last upstairs. She leant forward, enclosed the door handle but then paused after all, knowing he'd notice her closing the front door behind her. It hadn't closed properly for months. You had to slam it to get the lock to snap into place.

Birgit had pointed it out to Hard several times, and he'd promised to take care of it. And now she was annoyed that she'd relied on him and not done something herself and called someone to deal with the problem. She let go of the handle and wondered what she ought to say if he suddenly yanked open the office door and found her there. But then she heard him slamming the phone down, and then the phone ringing almost at the same moment, and he bellowed, irritated by waiting: 'Kuper, Jericho,' and added, more calmly and quietly: 'Oh, it's you. No, everything's fine. It's all going according to plan.'

Kuper, Jericho. That was how he introduced himself every time on the phone. And every time she heard it she shook her head, because there was more than one Kuper in the village and more than one Jericho in Germany and he had the cheek to think himself unique in every respect. And as Hard went on speaking, as he said, 'She's gone out already,' and, 'She'll soon notice,' Birgit left the house without closing the door behind her.

The garage door was pushed up and the car wasn't locked. Nothing had ever been stolen but she was still surprised that Hard, who usually had an eye on everything, had been so careless in this case. She sat down, moved the seat forward and ran a hand across the steering wheel as if to greet the car. They'd had the Opel for three years now and it hadn't given them any trouble so far. They'd driven it to the Black Forest and the Baltic coast, been on outings to the Lüneburg Heath and to Holland, visited wholesalers and trade fairs in Bremen and Münsterland and got home safely every time. Hard took the car to regular inspections, and on Saturdays he washed it with a patience and dedication he never paid to her. There was no reason to buy a new car yet, but Hard had already begun looking out for a new model, got quotes and told her: 'You have to get rid of the old one as long as it's still in good nick.'

And now, when she put the key in the lock and turned it, she thought for herself it was time for a change. The engine wouldn't start. She tried it again and again, but there was no more than a whimper to be got out of it. Even though she knew it wouldn't help, seeing as she didn't have a clue about these things, she opened the bonnet and looked at the battery, the oil level, the spark plugs. Then she went in to Hard in the shop and said, 'The car won't start.'

'What?'

'The car won't start.'

'Nix.'

'It won't.' He went outside with her, sat on the driver's seat, pressed at the clutch and the brake and turned the key in the lock again—nothing but a whimper. He still didn't give up. He got out, pushed her aside, leant over the engine, looked at the battery, the oil level, the spark plugs and came to the same conclusion as she had before—that something must be broken.

'I'll call Busboom and get him to have a look at it. It's probably a loose contact or the battery; I can't think of any other explanation.' He looked past her at the sky, as if he'd find the explanation for everything up there. 'Snow in September. I've never seen anything like it before.'

'Me neither,' she said, following his gaze. 'Do you think something else has happened?'

'Where?'

'Over in Russia.'

'Nix,' he said. 'We'd know all about it by now.'

'But we didn't find out about Chernobyl until days later.'

'I don't trust those Russians either. But now we're much better prepared for that kind of thing. We've got measurement stations and satellites everywhere now. There's probably a perfectly natural cause.' And without a pause for breath he changed the subject again. 'Do you need the car urgently, I mean, right now?'

'I wanted to go shopping.'

'You can take your bike.' He nodded at the bike stand.

'I won't get far on that.'

'It'll get you to Superneemann.'

'But I can't bring everything back, in the basket and bags.'

He shrugged his shoulders, as if to say, 'That's your problem.' Then he said, 'I just tried to get hold of you but you must have come downstairs already. I wanted to ask you to pick up my suit from Vehndel's. I can't go out right now, I'm waiting for a delivery, otherwise I'd do it myself.'

'Does it have to be today?'

'We've got our performance at Johann's at eight, and we're supposed to all come in uniform, and—'

'Johann?'

'Rosing, the building contractor. It's his birthday today, just turned fifty, and, well, anyway, he's invited us along.'

'Us?' She moved one hand to point between Hard and herself.

'No, not us two. Us men. We're singing there. First us, then the trombone band. But you know that, you must know, I told you about it at the weekend.'

'Oh, right,' said Birgit vaguely and looked at her watch, 'but I don't know whether I can manage all that now.'

'*Da mook di man kien Kummer um.*' There were some things, sentences that had become turns of phrase, which Hard said in Low German. 'Don't you worry about that. You go shopping and I'll take care of the kids. It wouldn't be the first time I've cooked a meal.'

The last time he'd offered to cook he'd meant to make pancakes. He'd thought of everything and done everything right, mixed flour with milk and mineral water, added eggs and sugar, poured the batter into the hot frying pan. The only thing he'd forgotten was the fat for frying them in. So now she smiled at him and said, 'If you say so,' went over to her bike, snapped the lock open and cycled off, still smiling, towards new surprises.

The second class of the day was WES, World and Environmental Studies. Working with Globes and Atlases. Elevations and Contour Lines. Mr Kamps unrolled a map and asked Daniel to point out mountains and valleys, using a rod. The Brocken, the Rhine Valley, the Feldberg, the Rothaar Mountains, Königssee Lake, the Alps. Twice, Daniel pointed too high, and Mr Kamps corrected him by pressing his arm a few centimetres downwards. The continental plates drifted faster than his pupils made progress.

Then Mr Kamps asked what the abbreviation ZLE meant. Daniel shrugged, unprepared. Instead of doing his homework he'd flicked back through the WES textbook, unable to believe they'd already left the chapter 'Foray into Space' behind them, as if there were nothing more important than the third planet in the solar system. The whole thing seemed to him like an aborted mission to Mars—they could have crossed the final frontier but they'd made an emergency landing on the moon due to a damaged engine and returned to earth in the next lesson to be on the safe side. Two hundred and forty pages for Urban and Rural Environments, Poles and Equators, Teutons and Romans, two for The Universe. After that lesson he'd told Mr Kamps about the Arkon System, about Naat, about the stellar maelstrom and about the Ploohn-Nabyl Galaxy, five hundred and one million light years away from the Milky Way, but Mr Kamps hadn't shown the slightest interest.

'So, what does ZLE stand for? Does anyone know?' Turning to the class, Mr Kamps realized that the others had been taking no notice of him and Daniel, and were staring out of the windows instead. For a moment he too was fixated; rain or snow or heavy storms had a meditative effect on him—he could watch them for minutes without thinking of anything other than what he was looking at, only to tear himself suddenly out of his trance-like state as if someone had tapped him on the shoulder. 'It's the greenhouse effect.'

'Wouldn't that make it warmer?' asked Simone.

'Not necessarily,' said Mr Kamps. 'The polar ice caps are melting. The Gulf Stream is weakening. The seasons are shifting. It's winter in summer, autumn in spring and vice versa.' He wanted to say more, explain tomorrow's world to them: desertification, broken dykes, flooded fields, extreme heat, a new Ice Age. He pulled down one end of the blackboard and pushed up the other, on which the words *sea level* and *cross-section* and *topographical map* were circled in red, to illustrate what he meant in chalk. The pupils stared longingly outside, wishing they could run out and embrace the snow, but they had to wait until break time and they were afraid it might have melted by then.

Mr Kamps sketched out the end of humankind in a few strokes. The Atlantic was crossed out, the northern hemisphere shaded white, the atmosphere pierced by solar arrows. And when he noticed it wasn't helping and the class were still looking outside as if the cold snap were a first sign of heaven rather than hell on earth, he let down the blinds and took out his secret weapon: before-and-after pictures, photos and drawings, of the Bavarian Forest, the Antarctic, the coast of Bangladesh, enlarged and copied onto transparent sheets. He placed them one after another on the overhead projector and projected them onto the wall behind him. He waited for the horror in the darkness, the silence, and he was annoyed not to see their faces because of the reflected light hitting him from the side. 'This is what will happen, and it'll happen first of all here and to you,' he finished, not switching off the projector; he wanted to let the picture of cows' carcasses stuck in mud take effect on them for a while longer. 'So what is ZLE then?' He heard Simone clicking her fingers and picked her.

'Zero-level elevation.'

'Right. Zero-level elevation, based on the mean sea level, the reference point for elevations above it. At what elevation are we on here?—Yes, Simone?'

'At zero level.'

'At zero level,' Mr Kamps repeated, his voice sliding down an octave in relief at having reached the lesson's objective. 'We're at sea level. And we'll go under if nothing changes.' When the bell rang he raised the blinds again and watched the class dashing out of the room, their heads lowered, glad to play in the snow finally and leave the idea of being zero level behind them for twenty minutes.

Klaus Neemann didn't come from East Frisia. He was born in Lüneburg but he'd grown up near Bremen, in Osterholz-Scharmbeck, and then come to the village, a newcomer with big plans. He'd taken over the general store on Station Road years ago. Mr and Mrs Hinrichs didn't have children and hadn't found anyone to leave the shop to. So they'd placed an ad in the *Frisian News* and Neemann had made them a good offer, a better offer than all the others, and promised to run the little shop the same way as they had.

He'd kept to his promise for several years, until he had enough money saved and got a loan from the bank to buy the field next to the sports pitch and build a supermarket on it, the first in the village, the first in a twenty-kilometre radius. But that hadn't been enough for him. He wanted to start a chain and compete with the corporations, wanted to show everyone that he wasn't afraid, that anyone could stand up to their authority.

He had soon bought up all the food shops in the surrounding villages, closed them down and set up four more supermarkets across the county under the name of Superneemann, all identical to the first one. The widows with no driving licences—and there were plenty of them—were angry at having to walk further to get their shopping at first, but then he'd arranged a taxi service to placate them. They were picked up from home and taken back there, and their bags were even carried to the front door. The families were enthusiastic from the very beginning, though. At last they could get everything under one roof without having to drive from one place to the next and find parking spaces. And Neemann had made arrangements with a few specialist retailers, the most powerful of them, so that he didn't get in their way. Superneemann didn't sell furniture, textiles or cosmetics, only groceries: fruit and vegetables, confectionary and spirits, fish and meat.

Nothing was ever past its sell-by date or bad. There was never any reason to complain, and yet people still stubbornly clung to their belief that a supermarket, especially a chain, couldn't deliver fresh produce. So many of them had bought milk and cheese direct from the dairy, up until the end of April, and driven to the county town on market day or to the farms advertising their products on hand-painted signs along the through roads.

Birgit loved driving to the county town on Wednesdays and then back along the country lanes, listening to the radio while fields and trees passed her by, and talking to people at the stalls or in the shops, people who didn't come into the drugstore day in, day out and didn't know who she was and what she did. She'd stuck to her routine when the market was closed temporarily because of the nuclear radiation, and she was annoyed that she had to change her plans today and forge a path on her bike through the snow, which was now covering the ground and had almost entirely concealed the distinction between the road and the pavement. A smooth, even surface: nothing ahead of her, nothing beside her, only a thin trail behind her that would soon be impossible to follow.

She lowered her head and pedalled. Out of the corner of her eye, she saw cars swerving and stopping in the middle of the road, people coming out of their houses on either side and grabbing at the snow with their bare hands, small children starting a snowball fight by the bike stands outside the supermarket and piling up lumps into shapes. It was like a celebration, except she wasn't in the mood for festivities, and at first she was glad when the sliding doors closed behind her and a song came out of the speakers above her, a song she knew, which made her feel at home.

She got herself a shopping trolley and took out her long list so that she wouldn't have to go back to the fruit stall when she realized at the till that she'd forgotten the apples from New Zealand, Argentina or Chile. She walked along the aisles past the rows of shelves, knowing exactly where everything was, having everything planned out, and yet it seemed to her as if she were reaching randomly into the crates and loading up the trolley, only to get out again as quickly as possible. She kept looking around, afraid she'd meet Klaus Neemann, and at the same time she wondered whether it might not be better simply to march into his office and raise the subject herself and then use her courage to go and see Vehndel as well.

'*Moin*, Mrs Kuper.'

The woman on the meat counter, Mrs Spieker, leant over the glass and handed her a rolled-up slice of mortadella sausage, as if she were a child who could be lured in that way.

'Haven't seen you for a while.'

Birgit took the slice, even asked for another, as if to get her strength up for her plan, and said, not reacting to the reproach: 'Three hundred grams of that, three hundred grams of salami and a pound of bierschinken, please.'

'Sliced?'

Birgit nodded. Mrs Spieker took the long rolls of sausage meat out of the glass counter and pushed them one after another into one of the machines glinting in the neon light on a platform against the wall. She lay sheets of plastic between the slices so they'd be easier to separate later on. She weighed the three types, wrapped them separately, tapped the prices into the till and asked, not looking up: 'Anything else?'

'That's it.'

'*Dan-ke.*' Mrs Spieker said all her thank-yous with a melody that went from the very bottom to the very top, from the lowest depths to the highest heights.

There's nowhere people thank you for not ordering anything except the meat or the cheese counter, thought Birgit, and although she was used to these conversations ending that way—so conciliatory, grateful for nothing—she was still surprised every time. For a moment she had the feeling everything was fine and her little mistakes, the job applications behind Hard's back, wouldn't have any major consequences.

As she took the plastic bag proffered by Mrs Spieker and turned back to her trolley, she saw Klaus Neemann standing by the frozen food chests. He was wearing a plaid jacket with too much padding in the shoulders, his belly flopped over his belt, his trousers were taut over his thighs—everything about him looked pumped up. He smiled and raised both hands, as if he'd been looking for her everywhere and finally found her.

For ten seconds they faced each other in silence, unsure how to greet each other or what to do. Then he hugged her, exuberantly and rather too lengthily for a greeting, to her mind, patting her on the back of the neck with one hand and stroking down her back with the other.

Snowballs came flying through the milky air from all directions. It was hard to make out the frontlines in the schoolyard. There were lots of groups covered from head to toe in snow and thus barely distinguishable: some throwing snowballs at each other, others acting in concert, and yet others who hadn't decided on a common strategy.

Daniel and Volker had started off throwing snow at each other in a corner near the entrance to the main building, concentrating entirely on not leaving out any parts of their bodies. Once they were white all over they had then joined in with the other boys to launch an attack on the girls. Now they were attacking another class their age, who also had to defend themselves against the Year Sixes on the other side of them. It wouldn't be much longer before the fifth-years melted together, just as the other years had melted together, because age was the most visible boundary in all the chaos; its natural authority took effect from the top class to the lowest, with nobody questioning it in any way.

In-between, Daniel kept an eye out for Iron and his friends but he couldn't spot them anywhere. He had to keep ducking, hit from all directions as soon as he stopped for breath. He randomly fired all his ammunition into the crowd, bent down and shaped new snowballs out of the white stuff. As he went to straighten up he felt a pain, stabbing and stronger than any blow. For a moment he hadn't paid attention and had dropped his guard, and during that time he'd fallen victim to the cold. His eyes were crystallized and reflected the light of deep-frozen suns. The temperature had fallen almost to minus nine hundred and sixty-one degrees

Celsius. He was under the spell of the psycho-frost, his consciousness was petrified and he thought the same sentence over and over—that he had to exterminate the Icemen before they exterminated him.

The teachers on playground duty dashed to and fro, holding onto one boy when they had the feeling he'd gone too far and letting him go again when they noticed that another boy, only metres away, had gone even further. They were just breaking up two Year Sevens when they heard baying for blood and saw the crowd of onlookers like a circular wall around Iron and Daniel.

4

He said there was something he'd like to talk to her about, she knew what it was, she could leave her trolley where it was, and he went ahead to the office. He was the only real bass in the male voice choir and his voice boomed around the room at concerts, so low it gave her goose pimples. She had goose pimples now too, and she ran her hands over the sleeves of her jacket and looked around, as if afraid someone had noticed.

Then she followed him along a corridor with other corridors turning off it on either side, until they came to a halt outside a door with his name on it. The room was low and dark, although daylight came in through two large windows opposite each other. But the windows were covered up by thick curtains and the walls were lined with oak panels up to the ceiling.

When he closed the door behind her and all the noises from the supermarket died away—the music from the speakers, the clinking of the cash desks, the customers' conversations—she was reminded of a bunker, as if he had to protect himself from something or someone and used the office as a refuge, an impression intensified by the closed cabinets all around the room and a folded-out bed in the corner.

'Sorry about this,' he said, smoothing the bedclothes, a simple sheet and a pillow which, until a moment ago, had still showed the place where his head had rested. He gestured for her to sit, allotting her a seat in front of the desk. She remembered being in there once before, years ago, with Hard, when they'd met Klaus outside the supermarket and he'd invited them into his office for a drink. But there hadn't been a bed in the corner then and there'd been family portraits on the walls, photos of Marlies and the children.

Everything smelt stuffy and damp. For a moment she thought she couldn't breathe; she swallowed and cleared her throat, and he went to one of the cabinets and folded down a flap to reveal a bar with an ice compartment, from which he took out a bottle and two small glasses nestled one on top of the other.

'Schnapps?'

She shook her head and looked at her watch. It was only half past nine but he filled both glasses to the brim as if he hadn't noticed her gesture. Then he handed one to her and she accepted it like a gift that she knew she already possessed. She didn't touch her glass to his and nor did she drink it in one go with her head thrown back; instead, she put it down on the desk in front of her.

He stepped up close to her again. Now he was standing directly behind her and speaking quietly, his voice lowered to a whisper but still as deep and pervading as if he were massaging her shoulders with words. 'We're from different stars,' he said. She felt a tingle shooting through her skin from top to bottom, felt herself blushing and breaking out in a sweat under her arms. 'You and I don't belong here.'

She stared straight ahead and thought she could do with a drink now after all, something strong to get her through this. She'd already reached her hand out for the glass, was already leaning forward when she saw her application folder opened on the desk.

After break they had double PE, floor exercises, handstands, head-stands, forward roll, backward roll. Cartwheels and back flips. Iron had been sent home with a note to his father, although Daniel would have preferred it if he'd been sent home himself with a note to his father excusing him from PE, at least for one lesson, for one day.

He hated sweating, but what he hated even more was show-ering with the others afterwards. In that respect, he'd become more like Volker than he'd have liked, three years ago. Both of them tried to move as little as possible and preferred to sit slightly sweaty next to each other in German or Maths than reveal their naked bodies to the others, even for seconds. They had different reasons, though.

Daniel was the last one to be called up when teams were picked. Even Volker was a better prospect, because he could use his body in football or handball without having to show any agility. It was enough for him to stand in the line of defence or the middle of a wall, stretching out a shoulder, a knee or his belly to trip up an opponent or bounce off the ball.

Daniel, however, was slim, slow and clumsy. He didn't under-stand the rules, was always in the wrong place at the wrong time and he didn't have his arms and legs sufficiently under control for the balls to take the direction they ought to, if it was down to him and the rest of the team.

He was denied the experience of being part of a movement, despite all differences, and he looked on in amazement at what happened in the gym to the children who sat as far apart as pos-sible in the classrooms. The rules were different in sport; new groups came together, girls and boys who usually couldn't stand each other passed balls between them as if they never did anything else all day long. For an hour and a half they were the best of friends, but as soon as the bell rang these temporary communities scattered again as if they'd never existed. Only Daniel was always an outsider. Whichever team he was on lost. And everyone was relieved when individual sports were on the lesson plan, like that day. The ambitious kids could prove themselves to the teacher, Mr Schulz, the blacksmith's oldest son, and the ones with no hope of getting a good mark didn't have any disappointment or shame to fear other than their own.

Volker bent over, lowered his head as if about to dive into water, splayed his left leg and tried to push himself off with the right leg; Mr Schulz supported him. Volker did push himself off, but without momentum, without energy, and instead of straightening his body he collapsed onto the mat with a sigh and a dull thud. A few kids laughed, quietly behind their hands as if they were scared things might go the same way for them, even though they had more control than he did and a different build, less pudgy.

Simone stepped up to the mat. She stretched, her hands together above her head, and flexed her back like after getting up in the morning. Everyone could see her bones and her veins. *A real beanpole.* Mr Schulz had called her a 'glass girl' a few weeks ago, during gymnastics on the apparatus. He'd meant to help her up to the rings like he helped all the others, and the words had slipped out of him. *Glass girl.* Since then she hadn't let him touch her any more, and he didn't touch her either, kept a distance of two or three metres between them. She didn't need help; she could do without him to put her body in the position demanded of her. Her joints and muscles gave way, released themselves from their lock, slowly and smoothly: press off, roll over, stand up—a single motion.

Daniel had practised the movements at home, first against the wall, then on his bed, and once he was surer of himself on an oriental rug rolled out in the hallway. And still, now that it was his turn, his arms raised, one leg bent, the other straight, he wished he had an Arkonide suit. He could use the light-wave deflector to make himself invisible; no one would see him trembling in mid-air and falling. Or, better than that, much better in fact, he could use the built-in gravity neutralizer to stand on his hands or his head for as long as he liked. In his tracksuit trousers and matching jacket he felt a little bit like a knight, like a soldier, a man whom nothing could harm because he hid his scars and wounds beneath his armour, his uniform.

Someone shoved him from behind and whispered, 'Go on then, you spazz.' Daniel swayed and tipped forward. For a moment, it looked as if he'd fall flat on his face. He felt Mr Schulz's fingers closing around his ribcage from both sides and releasing him again, felt himself rising at the back and gaining hold with his hands. He saw the others standing the right way up and the wrong way round on the ground, on the ceiling. Blood rushed to his head, but he stood his ground until he pulled in his head, rolled himself over and then up again, his arms raised, ready to launch into another handstand.

The handlebars were weighed down with heavy bags and the bas-ket full of fruit and vegetables, beer bottles and packets of juice was jammed onto the luggage rack. Birgit pushed her bike through the snow towards Vehndel Fashions, still rather dazed by her encounter with Klaus Neemann. The way he'd touched her, as though checking the consistency of a piece of meat. The way he'd spoken to her, quietly but firmly, as if he were reprimanding a child who'd done a very silly thing and didn't dare to admit it. *We re from different stars. We don t belong here.* What was that sup-posed to mean anyway? That they were soulmates, stranded in the provinces but destined for higher things? That he loved her and wanted to run away with her? But that wasn't what he'd said.

And they hadn't talked about the future. She went over the events of the past two hours and found not a hint, nothing that suggested what he'd actually wanted from her. And she was annoyed that she'd agreed to go to his office with him in the first place.

As she battled against the snow, against her anger at Klaus, at herself, she thought of her family. She wondered what they were doing now, where they were. She envisioned Hard in his army boots, in his winter coat, trudging to the kindergarten with his ridiculous fur hat on his head and picking up the little ones, pictured Daniel at school, sitting in the classroom between Volker and Simone, his body present but his mind elsewhere, ahead or behind, too slow or too fast, too loud or too quiet, never in synch with the world.

Birgit had always felt a link to him, despite the distance that had come about through the twins' birth. He had liked to be close to her and she to him, although he now dodged kisses on the lips and didn't snuggle up to her while watching TV on the sofa like he used to. But it felt like a rejection that he'd begun locking the door when he took a shower in the morning, over the past six weeks since he'd been back at school. He locked himself in and her out. He hid his body from her because he was ashamed of what was happening to it. She'd guessed this stage would come but she'd expected it later, not at the age of ten, and she was overwhelmed by how much it hurt to lose contact.

The roofs of the houses and the front lawns were perfectly white and the men shovelling snow from the driveways and pavements were so thickly padded that they were hardly recognizable under their jackets and hats. Some of them said hello to her, calling her name, although she was thickly padded too, and she returned their greetings by nodding at them, because she didn't know who they were and couldn't raise her hands without letting go of the bike and losing her balance.

She crossed the road, walked across the crossroads to Vehndel Fashions but stopped on the traffic island, uncertain whether to keep going, filled with fear that she'd have as little bravery for the next encounter as for the last. Klaus Neemann. It was only now that she realized she might have misunderstood him, that *We're from different stars* didn't mean, as she'd assumed, the same as *We're from a different star.*

She wasn't quite on the ball. She couldn't help thinking of Mr Schulz all the time, Philipp. She was new at the school. She'd just finished her teacher-training placement in Hameln and had moved here for the job (worse pay but far away). She had left her boyfriend (thirty-seven, deputy head, divorced, more of an affair, like all her previous relationships) and her friends, who'd actually been his friends. She didn't know anyone in the area, and Philipp, who taught sport as well but not sport, German and religion like she did, had taken her for drives and shown her every-thing. A couple of evenings ago they'd gone out together, to the state theatre in Oldenburg (*The Caucasian Chalk Circle*)—her idea—and then afterwards to a pub—his idea. She had drunk and he'd driven. He'd offered her the informal *Du* and accidentally touched her hand twice, once when he put his glass down and once when he held the car door open for her; nothing else had happened. But now, after the fact, she had the feeling that he'd been coming on to her as he spent hours telling her about his life, although or even because he was married and his wife was expecting a child—which she'd only found out just now in the staff room. 'He had to dash off. His wife called. From the hospital. I think the big day's come,' Mrs Zuhl had said when she'd asked after him, and now she found it difficult to concentrate on the lesson and listen to the boy.

'Making a book takes a lot of people and a lot of time. First it's the author's turn. He's the person who writes the story. Anyone who's written a story is an author. Children can write stories too, or poems.' Daniel felt his way from one word to the next as he read. He didn't understand what they meant in context, didn't understand what the text was about, and he made no effort to do so. He neither emphasized certain syllables nor lowered his voice at the end of the sentences. He wanted Miss Nanninga to release him and call on someone else. There was no subject that bored him as much as German. He wasn't interested in grammar, couldn't remember the parts of speech or the comma rules, and he was convinced that she and the other teachers were playing him for a fool, as if they didn't think him capable of reading something real and talking about the content rather than the form. For weeks on end, he'd been looking forward to this day. But now that they'd finally started the new textbook, *Texts for Secondary Level*, it wasn't much different than before. 'It's important to have an idea if you want to write a story. Having an idea means you know what story you want to tell, about a house or a man on the moon.' After crash-landing thirty kilometres beyond the pole, on the far hemisphere, Perry Rhodan discovers the Arkonides' spaceship, a spherical construction on short, pillar-like legs, surrounded by a flickering green light. He saves the life of the alien Crest, and together they end the Cold War on earth before they set off for further adventures. Daniel had resolved to read one episode every day. There were some cycles he'd never got into and others he'd skipped entirely, but now he'd got back in again. He had volume 1307 in his bag, and in the next break when they didn't have to change classrooms for once, he'd start reading *Foray into the Dark Sky*. And then volume 1308, *The Miracle of the Milky Way*. He wanted to stick with it and at the same time he knew it was pointless because he'd one day lose interest, just like he'd always lost interest in everything else.

'Daniel?' Miss Nanninga was looking at him; everyone was looking at him. 'Please keep reading—properly this time.' The book was from 1973 and she'd used the text a few times at her first school, AEG, Albert Einstein Grammar in Hameln. She knew it by heart; she knew almost all the texts in the book by heart and she thought the children ought to know a few texts by heart as well, not necessarily 'The Story of the Book', but the poems that came later, 'The Fire', 'Smoke'.

Daniel ran his finger down the page, looking for the place where he thought he'd left off, and began to read: 'You have to think carefully about what to write.'

'Further down,' whispered Simone, and showed him. 'If you want to write—'

'If you want to write: The clouds are green, then you write: The clouds are green. Even if someone says there's no such thing as green clouds. Or if you want to write: I'm not happy, then you write it. The story could also—'

'I don't understand that,' said Volker, without putting his hand up. 'There should be a full stop.'

'Where?' asked Miss Nanninga.

'Here, after happy. The way it is, with a comma, it means then you write it is part of the sentence you want to write. And that doesn't make sense, because you don't want to write then you write it.'

None of it makes sense, thought Daniel. If he had an indoctrinator he could give himself hypno-training, multiply his brain's performance potential and make lessons superfluous. He wouldn't have any physical sensations any more, wouldn't remember anything and his brain would calculate at the speed of light, subconsciously. He wouldn't have to think any more when someone set him a problem, no matter how difficult it was. He wouldn't have to work anything out, check anything in a book, everything would be registered and stored and available at any time.

'It's like in that game where you're forced to say something you don't want to say,' said Volker.

'What game?' asked Miss Nanninga.

Daniel leant back and thought about nothing. Then he opened the book to the poetry texts and memorized the lines at a single glance:

Do you hear the blaze blistering,
Clashing, crackling, crashing, whispering,
Do you hear the fire soaring,
Seething, sizzling, raging and roaring?

A little house under trees by a lake.
Smoke rises from the roof.
Without it
How desolate they'd be
The house, the trees and the lake.

They flowed through positronic amplifiers, through feeders to the nerves in his head and were saved in his memory centre. Vogon poetry, he thought, can't be worse than this.

'Say, who do you love?' At the word 'love' a few kids had blushed and started to laugh, and Volker had blushed too but he didn't laugh when he repeated the question 'Say, who do you love?'

Miss Nanninga looked at him, not knowing how to react. She thought it was a trap. Many traps had been laid for her during her teacher training, and she'd walked straight into them every time, out of a lack of experience. But this one was different; she was already in this one, no matter what she answered. If she said a name, the kids would laugh even more and tell everyone in the whole school, and if she said 'nobody' or 'none of your business,' they'd think what she thought: that despite her age she was an old maid, incapable of getting involved with anybody.

Vehndel Fashions was one of the oldest shops in the village. In the black-and-white photos Hard had enlarged and hung up in the village hall foyer, you could see that the words *Colonial Goods* had been painted above the entrance until the fifties, and that the house that now faced directly onto the street had previously been surrounded by a grassy field. Heinrich Vehndel had taken over the company from his father after the war, had the grass cemented over to make a car park and reduced the product range with every decade, every conversion, every extension to the building. He no longer sold spices or animal feed, tools or toys, no more crockery, tobacco or household goods either, only women's and men's fashions in all shapes and sizes. Both his sons, Gerd and Günter, had done their apprenticeships under him, but only one of them had wanted to take over the business. Gerd had found a job with a gentlemen's outfitter in the county town—he wanted to know at the beginning of the month how much he'd have earned by the end of it. And so Günter, the second-born, had superseded his father as managing director six years ago and taken over the house with his family. Doreen, the late arrival as their father called her, was only thirteen, too young to be considered a successor. The parents had built a new house on the edge of the village, in Poets' Corner, one storey for the parents and one for their daughter, and were enjoying their retirement, but sometimes Günter's mother Hildegard helped out when there were too many customers, and sometimes his wife Sabine did.

Since the beginning of the seventies there'd been a hot mangling service and a tailor's shop next door, and this combination, the textile triptych as Birgit called it, worked better than all other combinations before it. People came from all over, even from the county town. There were days when the car park was full and cars double-parked or blocked the pavement or the road. Especially during the sales and in the run-up to Christmas, you could see women and men through the display windows, leaning over tables and chests and tugging at the fabrics from either side, which encouraged others to do likewise. Birgit wondered whether that was where the nickname *Plünnenrieter* came from—rag-ripper—which was imposed on Vehndel time and again like a curse, as if what he sold was good quality but had some kind of flaw to it. In fact he sold branded goods that were on sale in the county town as well. If they had any flaw it was that they came from the countryside and, as Birgit's sisters said disdainfully when they came to visit, stank of stables.

Steam was coming out of the laundry windows, and as she leant her bike against the wall beneath the sign saying *Mangling Service for Closet-Ready Laundry*, she couldn't help remembering that she'd always puzzled over the words *mangling service* and *closet-ready* as a child. *Mangling service* sounded to her like something nobody would want, like making a mess of the laundry—ripping holes in it, dyeing it the wrong colour—and *closet-ready* as if they'd tried their utmost but just hadn't managed to get the sheets, tablecloths and aprons clean and patched well enough to use them again and put them on show.

Günter Vehndel's problem was that he didn't have a spotless reputation and he couldn't do anything about it. And perhaps that was the reason for the fluctuations Sabine had told her about. There were phases, she said, in spring and autumn, in February and October, when not much went on; ten or fifteen customers a day at most and a thousand marks in the till, because the weather wasn't the way they'd expected it to be—it was either too hot or too cold for the time of year. And if nothing changed for weeks they'd be stuck with the collections and they'd have to sell them too cheaply later in the season.

Günter couldn't cope with these phases. Over and over again, he'd count the takings in the evenings, as if the money would multiply through being counted. He trusted his bookkeeper as little as he did the saleswomen. He regularly accused all his employees, including his mother and his wife, of helping themselves to things. And at the same time he was ashamed of himself for voicing such suspicions. Sometimes he did spot checks to be on the safe side. He'd do inventories of certain departments alone at night, walking around the shop with a clipboard and ballpoint pen, noting down what was there and what wasn't, and he'd fly off the handle if a pair of trousers was missing, even if it turned out the next day that a customer had simply put them back in the wrong place.

He refused to see a doctor or talk to a psychiatrist, because he knew the reason for his ailment. He was convinced he'd inherited it from his father and grandfather, and he felt he had to find his own way out. As long as he made a profit he was fine; he invested, took on staff, had the shop renovated, did everything to keep up the success. But as soon as signs of a downturn emerged he was incapable of combating the crisis. Then he was absolutely certain there would never be better days, that it was all downhill from then on, just as it had all gone downhill for his grandfather at the end of the twenties, and he'd decline into a state from which no news, no matter how good it was, could rescue him.

She knew all that from Sabine and from Hard. If the shop was empty Günter would stay away, skip choir practice, cards evenings and football matches, lie in bed all day with the shutters down and increase the financial losses through his absence. Many of the customers, men and women, only came because of him. He knew how to advise them without making them feel they'd been cheated. She'd experienced it first-hand; she'd go to Vehndel's determined to buy only underwear for the children, and come home again with a new dress, a new skirt and a new blouse. The sudden onset of winter must be a disaster for him, she thought.

He wasn't prepared for it, nobody was, but nobody was as upset by changes like that as he was.

As she walked into the shop she immediately heard his voice, hoarse as if he'd been talking or shouting for hours: 'No scarves left.' He was standing by the counter, talking to an old man who had his back to her and was obviously hard of hearing. 'Really, Manfred, take my word for it, I've looked everywhere, the stock-room's empty, we're not getting winter things in for at least another month.'

'Monday?'

'No, in a month!'

'In among what?'

He shouted, 'No, on Monday!' his cheeks red with the effort, and he didn't notice he'd said the wrong thing.

'Right, see you on Monday then.' Now she recognized him. It was Manfred Kramer from Kramer's Furniture Paradise. He pressed the turned-up collar of his coat to his neck and walked out past her with a mumbled greeting.

'We've run out of winter clothes, Mrs—' Günter said to her as if to a stranger. 'I'm sure you heard.'

'I haven't come for winter clothes,' said Birgit.

5

She'd been longing for the last lesson since the first class of the day. He'd be sitting in front of her again, and once again she'd demolish him, bit by bit, word by word, number by number, as a substitute for his father. It wasn't Daniel's fault that Bernhard Kuper was a loser, and it was unfair and cruel to torment his son, but it was for his own good. Mr Schulz was the only other teacher on the staff who shared her opinion, although he hadn't fallen for Bernhard Kuper's tricks like she had. Mr Schulz merely thought a bit of drilling didn't do any harm in general and was good for those who got left behind without it. In the staffroom at the last break-time he'd told her, as if to prove his theory, what Daniel was capable of when he made an effort and prepared for class at home. 'It was incredible. He stood there for seconds, motionless in mid-air. Usually he can't even stand up straight on his feet.'

'Just what I say—everything's possible.'

'Yes, we mustn't give up hope.'

'We're not a grammar school, after all. We have to make the best of the material we've got and work with it. I've never had an alpha or a beta here yet, and I probably never will now, but you see, we can even get something out of these gammas and deltas and epsilons.'

'Right,' he said—he didn't know what she was talking about—'luckily, it's not all a question of genes. Although I do sometimes think it is, when I see the kids, where they come from, what families. Some of them are hopeless cases. Real broken families. No chance from the word go. Some of them can't even speak proper German.'

'We can still make ones out of zeros.'

'But we can't iron out the parents' mistakes.'

'Maybe not iron them out, but—'

'Mr Schulz?' The school secretary had opened the office door a crack and called into the staffroom, 'There's a call for you.'

Now Mrs Zuhl was walking along the corridor, the maths textbook tucked under her arm. She could hear their voices in the distance already, their screams and shouts. It had always paid off in the end when she'd been particularly tough on someone. Several times a year, she received letters or calls from former pupils, children from weak families who were now at university in faraway cities and thanked her for not going easy on them.

The noise died down as she opened the door and those who'd been running around or standing by the windows, still entranced by the snow, sat down in their places. At first she'd thought Daniel had gone home. She thought him perfectly capable of feigning some kind of illness, some fever, headache, stomach-ache, nausea. But then she saw him. He was in the back row, slumped in his seat, his eyes fixed on the floor or a book, hidden behind the others' backs as if he genuinely believed that would help him escape his fate. She pulled in her chair, took her red pen out of the case, opened the maths textbook and the class register and ran a hand over her head.

They were alone, and apart from a fluorescent tube light flashing occasionally with a ping, the shop was absolutely silent. She listened to tell whether there was someone in one of the changing booths after all or next door in the office, in the tailor's shop, the laundry, the staffroom, but there was nothing, not the purring of the sewing machines that otherwise filled the room, muffled by the walls and fabrics, not the hissing and fizzing of the rotary irons or the sales assistants' overly friendly voices.

'I sent them all home,' said Günter, slumping onto one of the seats placed next to every mirror in case a man in the ladies' department or a woman in the gents' department had to sit down, tired from looking on and commenting. 'All of them.'

'Aren't Sabine and Hilde here?'

'Upstairs.' He took a brief look up at the ceiling, then lowered his head again. 'Why should they bother? There's no point. No one's going to come in. And if they do, then only for a pair of gloves, vests, long johns, but they're all sold out, every single thing, and they won't be coming in for ages, not before the beginning of October at any rate.' He waved his hands about, leapt up, walked a few paces along the corridor, past scantily dressed dummies and circular racks of swimsuits, and called out, 'Look at it!' He spread out his arms. 'Look at it! It's all for nothing!'

'Nonsense. The snow will have melted by tomorrow.'

'Even if it does, the summer's not coming back again.' He came back towards her and tapped his index finger against his forehead. 'It's over, up here in people's heads. Doesn't matter how hot it gets. It's over up here. And that's the main thing. They won't want to have any T-shirts now, no more shorts, and I might as well write off the entire autumn collection as well. Up here,' and he tapped his forehead again, 'up here they're all much further along. The only thing they can think of now is keeping nice and warm. And if they can't get what they need from me, they'll go to town.

They're bound to get it there. And even if they don't get it there—seeing as they're there now they'll just take something else, something they could have got just as well, just as cheap, from me, or cheaper. But now they've gone all that way, so they have to make up for the petrol.'

'Nonsense.'

'Of course it's nonsense, but that's how people think, Birgit, you know that. It's all psychology, it's no different with your shop.'

'You can't compare the two,' said Birgit, stubborn. She noticed she'd been drawn into the wake of his bad mood, and she was resisting getting carried along by it.

'You think I don't know what Hard does with the bikes? The ones he parks outside the window even though no one's in the shop? Everyone knows! And everyone laughs at it! We're lying to ourselves, Birgit, we think we can make it, with some kind of trick, but we can't.' He sat back down and pushed a second seat in her direction so she could join him. 'All this,' he said, looking around the room, 'all this will soon be gone, the clothes will be sold at a reduction, twenty, fifty per cent, or given away if we still can't get rid of them, and the shop will be vacant for a long time because no one will want to set up anything new here. All the shops will be vacant.'

The fluorescent light above them had gone off and the place they were sitting was dark, darker than the rest of the shop at least. She had the feeling they were sitting in the shadows, shaded by some large thing that was invisible because of its size. Outside the windows, the snow was falling more slowly now and less thickly, and she hoped it would soon stop and thaw and she'd be able to cycle back, as soon as the roads and pavements were clear.

'Sometimes I think about giving all this up before it's too late, and starting over somewhere else.'

'What would you do, at your age?'

'I don't know. You have to start starting first of all, and the rest takes care of itself.'

'Nonsense,' Birgit said again, instantly annoyed with herself for saying nothing but 'nonsense'. A few weeks ago when she'd written the applications, even a few hours ago when she'd set out from home, she'd thought the same way as Günter. But now she didn't think that way any more. Not because there was no point—no one could predict how things would turn out—but because she no longer believed in having a future without a past. At some point, she was convinced, the things you'd done caught up with you; at some point you'd pay the penalty for your misdemeanours, no matter how small. And perhaps that was her penalty—working for Hard. The penalty for having dreamed of a different life, a life without him, and for still dreaming of it.

'I'll have to let them go.'

'Let what go?'

'All the staff. Apart from my mother and Sabine, of course.' She wanted to say that he could hardly lay off Hilde and Sabine, seeing as he didn't pay them for working in the shop, but he cut her off by putting a hand on hers. 'I'm sorry I didn't get back to you, Birgit. I know you applied for the job here, and at that time I really could have used someone, although I think you're overqualified, what with your references, with your experience, as a secretary for Knipper, *de Kluntjeknieper*, no matter what a sugar-pincher he is. My mother worked there before you, in the typing pool, as a shorthand typist.'

'I know,' said Birgit.

'What you don't know is that she heard nothing but good things about you from her workmates, only the best. That alone's distinction enough. That alone would be good enough to give you a job right away, here, in my shop, anywhere. But then I wanted to wait till autumn, and now, well, see for yourself . . .' He stretched out his arm, which roamed around the room. Then he slumped in his seat, enfeebled like after a long fight.

Birgit drew her hand away, stood up and said, 'Yes, I see. I just wanted to test my market value, and now I know.'

'Don't get me wrong, I—'

'I'm not,' she said quickly. She didn't want to let him see how much his words had hurt her. *Overqualified. With your references. With your experience.* 'I'm not here about the job, I didn't mean that seriously anyway. I'm here for Hard's suit. You've got that performance this evening.'

'Oh, of course,' said Günter. 'The suit's finished,' and he stood up to go and get it.

The bell rang and everyone stood up with a jerk as if on command, packed away their belongings, put on their jackets and pushed the chairs under the desks. It was the signal they'd been awaiting for hours. The kids who took the bus stormed out of the classrooms, wanting to sit at the back or the front of the vehicle, depending on whether they were older or younger, whether they dealt out or received. Every noon there was a battle to get to the very front of the queue at the bus stop, so as to secure the best seats and occupy the optimum positions. Those who came late had to stand, and those who stood and didn't want to sit down next to one of the big kids, even though the seat was free, signalled that they were afraid and prepared to receive insults and blows.

Daniel had often stood, too often, and now he took his time because there was no one for him to fear. In good weather he cycled to and from school with Volker or Simone, although they weren't direct neighbours. They usually met up somewhere along Broadway on the way and parted ways at the same point at noon. Today he was alone, however. Simone's parents had given her a lift to school and would pick her up as well, and Volker had left with his father.

Mrs Zuhl returned his book to him, *Foray into the Dark Sky*, and asked him if he'd like a lift home. But Daniel shook his head emphatically and walked out into the corridor. He strolled along the hallways and listened to the others' voices fading away on the staircase. In the school hall, he stopped in front of one of the Biology Club's display cases and looked at the specimens: beetles and butterflies impaled on pins, stuffed owls and weasels, animals petrified in their motions, their gaze broken, their armour, their fur dry and hard, as if frozen. By the time he left the building all the buses had gone. Their tyres had left deep furrows in the snow. The bike shelter and the car park were empty. Smoke rose from the chimneys of the surrounding houses. There was no one to be seen. Behind him, the caretaker locked the entrance and let down the ground-floor shutters. A car approached on the road at walking pace, a black Volvo 240 estate, 1986 model, 116 PS, 85 kW. It stood out dark against the all-encompassing white and eventually came to a halt right in front of him. The registration plate, the only one in the area with a single-letter district abbreviation, and from far away as well, was coated in snow and dirt at its sides, the figures H-AL 9000 almost impossible to make out. Mrs Zuhl leant over the passenger seat and wound down the window. Beneath the sparse white hair, her scalp shone as if freshly polished.

'Are you sure you don't want a lift?'

'Yes,' said Daniel.

'Get in! The roads are slippery. It's my duty to give you a lift.'

'No,' Daniel said, speaking louder and with more emphasis.

'All right then,' said Mrs Zuhl, more to herself than to him. 'I asked. No one can say I didn't ask.' And she drove off without winding the window up. He heard isolated words over the engine, 'incorrigible', 'Kuper', 'epsilon minus' and 'double zero', and then nothing but an even hum, which gradually dissipated in the distance. After a few hundred metres the red rear lights vanished in the noon haze.

Daniel followed the tracks in the snow, trying to tread in footsteps without leaving any of his own, and he thought he could feel the silence. A pigeon cooed somewhere in the trees, leaves rustled quietly in the wind. He crossed the road with his head down. Then he looked up and saw the second lock on his bike and the sign with an arrow pointing at the maize field.

6

Sometimes Daniel took his time, stopped and sat down in a field to think, read one of the paperbacks and science-fiction novels he always carried around with him, daydreamt. That was nothing unusual. But he never got home later than half an hour after school finished, and when he still wasn't there by two Birgit began to worry. She woke Hard, who had taken a lie-down for an hour after lunch. Lunch break was between quarter past one and quarter past two, and all the children had to be quiet so their father could sleep. He didn't sleep though, only dozing on the sofa in the lounge, shielding his face with one hand, his legs bent, his head facing the wall, breathing evenly in and out. When Birgit spoke to him he took his hand off his forehead and asked, 'What is it?'

'He's still not back.'

'He'll turn up, Biggi, you know what he's like.'

'But he's never stayed away this long.'

'He's probably playing in the snow somewhere with Volker.'

'Volker's at home. I just called them. Maybe something's happened to him. Maybe he's fallen off his bike and can't get up. Or—' she put her hand to her mouth and then took it away again, 'what if he's been abducted?'

'Abducted? Daniel?'

'Yes, like on *Dallas* last night.'

'*Dallas!*' Hard sat up, ran a hand over his face and stroked his hair back.

'It's possible. And the car has to go and break down today,' said Birgit.

'It's probably the battery,' said Hard and got up. 'Because of the cold. It probably de-charged itself over night.'

'What shall we do? We can't walk all the way to school, it'd take far too long, and someone has to look after the little ones.'

'I'll take care of it. You just stay here.'

Hard put on his white coat, took his army boots, his fur hat and his parka out of the wardrobe and went downstairs. The snow had let off but the roads and houses and trees were still white. He stamped a few metres along the driveway, stood outside the shop with his hands in his pockets and wondered if he ought to put on the winter tyres and re-attach the battery he'd unhooked that morning. Then he saw him. Hard's eyes were watering with the cold and he could barely make out the half-naked body in the distance, but there was no doubt: Daniel was walking along Village Road, right towards him.

He couldn't remember anything. Only the lock, the sign on his bike, and that he'd gone into the maize field and come across a clearing. Then the cold element had shock-frozen him and made him into a child of the minus world—his body frosted over, his eyes as hard as diamonds, the present petrified. He heard his brother and sister asking, 'Is he in there?' and 'Is he dead?' and his mother saying, 'Yes,' and 'No,' and stopping them from coming into his room. His father spoke to him quietly. 'What happened to you? I could have come and collected you. All you had to do was call.' He stroked his face and said, louder than before, 'What have you got yourself into this time? Where are your clothes, where's your bike?' With the words and the touch, warmth returned, and for a moment the pain wiped out Daniel's consciousness, only the invisible cocoon wrapped around him preventing him from re-adapting to the laws of continuum or perishing from the after-effects of the thaw rampage. Then he vomited into the bin placed between his bed and his desk, and leant back. He was trembling. Hard stroked his skin with both hands, the bruises on his upper arms, legs and back. He cleaned the wound on the back of Daniel's head, wrapped him in a blanket and put a thermometer under his arm, but he didn't have a temperature.

Doctor Ahlers came—Birgit had called him—and examined Daniel. He lived on Village Road too, in an old farmhouse a few doors down. At the front, where the living quarters had been, he'd set up his practice, and he'd converted the stables at the back of the house, putting in a first floor and dozens of walls. He smelt of 4711-brand cologne and wore a white coat like Hard, and when you saw them standing alongside each other like they were now you might think they were colleagues, two doctors paying a visit.

Hard always felt inferior in his presence. They'd never talked about their professions, about how they saw themselves, but whenever they spoke about medications, creams or treatment methods, he thought he sensed a haughty undertone in Doctor Ahlers' voice, something that gave him the feeling he'd only made it as far as a druggist.

'Has he got a temperature?'

Hard shook his head. 'Nix. Thirty-six point five.' Doctor Ahlers listened to Daniel's chest and heart, took his pulse and took his temperature again, unable to believe someone whose forehead was so hot and sweaty didn't have a fever. He disinfected the wound, put a compress on it and bandaged Daniel's head. Then he stood up and directed Hard outside with a glance at the door.

'Right, right. He'll have to go to hospital. He might have concussion or internal injuries, I can't judge that here, and apart from that,' he halted as he tried to take off his stethoscope and didn't manage at first, 'we'll have to call the police.'

'The police—is that necessary? What if he's just playing a trick on us!' Hard looked out of the window. It had stopped snowing, the clouds had parted and the sun was breaking through on the horizon, several bright rays as if from spotlights. If the neighbours saw a patrol car parked outside they'd be curious and might come to the wrong conclusions, and wrong conclusions were bad for business.

'A trick?' Doctor Ahlers put his stethoscope back in his bag.

'It has been known. Once, a few years ago—'

'This wasn't a trick. Whatever may have happened, Hard, he can't have inflicted those injuries on himself. And I do hope, you know, that you haven't got anything to do with it.'

'What's that supposed to mean? You don't think—'

'I don't think anything. I just see what I see.'

Daniel told the policemen—Joachim Schepers and Kurt Rhauderwiek—what had happened. Haltingly and apparently incoherently, words came out of his mouth, 'Iron, lock, sign, bike, field, clearing, maize,' and he repeated some of them as if randomly, like the needle of a record player repeats sounds and verses, while he rocked his torso back and forth to the rhythm of a music only he heard. They asked more questions, when and how and whether he'd been alone, but there was no more to be got out of him, and they drove off to the school and the maize field to check what he'd told them.

His bike was still exactly where he'd left it, and the swathe that someone—or something—had beaten into the maize really did lead to a clearing, a circular space sixteen metres in diameter. The plants were laid flat anti-clockwise but the stalks hadn't been snapped. The stems around the edge were unharmed, a thin coating of snow still resting on their tops. There were no footprints on the ground or in the snow, at least not directly around the place, and there was no sign of Daniel's clothes or his satchel.

It wasn't long before the news had made the rounds of the village community. A few people gathered at the edge of the field but no one dared to go in. The area was cordoned off. Policemen stood guard and two of the floodlights usually used to illuminate one side of the sports ground next door were turned around a hundred and eighty degrees and lit up the maize at night, so that no one could get in unnoticed and obliterate evidence or lay red herrings.

The next morning the snow had melted and the first reporters arrived, to inform the world that a UFO had landed in the north of Germany and a boy had been injured. One of them broke through the cordon—he lifted up the red and white striped plastic tape—climbed onto one of the floodlight posts and took photos, and when the picture was published in the *Frisian News* the next day, on the front page even above the headline that East Germany was reining in the *Flood of Asylum-Seekers to West Berlin*, everyone saw the corn circle in the middle of the field, a whorl as if from a tornado.

A TV crew got into the hospital and filmed the nurses, the doctors, Daniel's parents and Daniel. He was in the neurology ward, in a single room with his head bandaged and a drip in his arm. He told the reporter what he knew. The doctor standing next to him explained that he had retrograde amnesia, probably due to the blow to his head or the cold or both, and couldn't remember either what had immediately preceded the incident or the incident itself. Everyone hoped Daniel's memory would soon be back in working order. But when the journalists realized they couldn't get any more out of him than what he'd already said to them—*Iron, lock, sign, bike, field, clearing, maize*—they lost interest and turned their attention to the experts who promised an explanation for the phenomenon.

A meteorologist on national radio said, 'In all probability it was a whirlwind that crossed the land from the sea unnoticed at night or in the early morning before touching ground in the maize field. That also explains the sudden temperature drop. The tornado dragged down cold air from the middle level of the troposphere, which led to major snowfall in a perimeter of five kilometres—an unusual phenomenon, without doubt, but a natural one.'

On a local radio station, another meteorologist developed another theory based on the existing data: 'During the night a severe cold front crossed the northwest of Germany, coming from Iceland. The air above parts of East Frisia was extremely humid. And these air masses were attracted particularly strongly by the storm. Inside the cold front there were isolated cases of major snowfall and hailstones the size of pigeon eggs. We received reports of smashed windscreens, dented car paint and destroyed greenhouses from all over the region. In a very small area, such as above the field, the hail densified and reached the size of missiles. I don't want to come to any premature conclusions. We have to evaluate all the data first. All I want to say is that this is what might have happened. Supercells in particular have a strong updraught, which leads to a growth in hailstone size, and then we can't rule out that certain places can be destroyed very precisely, as if a rocket had been fired at a certain target, except with the difference that there's no crater because the warhead breaks down into millions of parts centimetres before it hits the ground.'

On the chat show *Dall-As*, a young, scantily clad woman brought Karl Dall ten small glasses and a bottle of the local corn schnapps, Doornkaat. He filled the glasses, arranged them in a circle—'a corn circle!'—and encouraged his guests, Uwe Fritzmann (the zookeeper in charge of the pandas in West Berlin), the cabaret artist Robert Kreis and the singers Tina York and Bernhard Brink, to raise their glasses with him. 'Uwe, it's not made of bamboo! This is triple-distilled corn schnapps! It'll turn you on! You should give it to Bao Bao! That'll make him take more interest in the ladies. A real Baodisiac!'—'Come on, Robert, your surname means circle!'—'Tina, "They Can't Ban Drinking" was one of your biggest hits.'—'Bernhard, come on, don't leave me to drink it all, you'd usually polish this amount off for breakfast!'

No one took him up on the offer. Instead, Bernhard Brink tried to give Dall a taste of his own medicine: 'If you're not nice to me I'll remind you of the film *Sunshine Reggae on Ibiza*. I saw it the other day on RTL plus.'

'You'll watch any old crap, eh?' Karl Dall rolled his one functioning eye, clearly the master of the situation after years of being rude to his guests.

'That wasn't exactly the high point of your career.'

'You got me there.'

And on the *NDR Talkshow* one of the three presenters, Wolf Schneider, talked to the ufologist Markus Schallenberg. All the other studio guests, Hollywood actress Sigourney Weaver, singer Juliane Werding and nineteen-thirties starlet Marika Rökk, had already been interviewed, and Schallenberg had spent the entire time biting his fingernails while they talked about movies, drugs and ageing. Despite the last-minute invitation, he'd been announced at the beginning as the highlight and he didn't know whether they'd make jokes at his expense, as on previous TV shows.

'I'm afraid Sigourney Weaver's already left,' Schneider said, finally turning to him. 'Otherwise I could ask her the same question I'm asking you now: What are we to make of this corn circle that was discovered yesterday in East Frisia? Was it the aliens we saw in the film clip earlier?'

'Oh no, this isn't a film set on a distant planet. This,' said Schallenberg as he removed his hand from in front of his face, 'this is real, you can get in your car and go and see it,' he waved an outstretched arm at one of the studio lights, 'anyone can.'

'But don't you find it amazing that it's happened right now, just before *Aliens* hits our cinemas? Couldn't it be—and Juliane Werding will be familiar with this kind of thing, coming from the PR industry—couldn't it be a clever advertising campaign?'

'That's just a coincidence. It's not a new phenomenon. There have been corn circles in the south of England since the seventies. The only new thing is that these circles are turning up here now too, and not only in wheat, barley and rye fields, but in maize as well. Maize! Imagine! Do you have any idea how strong maize is, how resistant?' Schneider shook his head, and Schallenberg leant forward and made a gesture with his thumb and forefinger as if trying to grab hold of something invisible. 'The stems are far more stable than other types of grains. It's much harder to lie them down without breaking them. That seems to me the strongest proof that—'

'How did they do it?'

'I don't know, but they must have great capabilities, strong and gentle skills. If you bear in mind the precision with which the circle is laid out, as if with a compass and not damaging the edges.'

'But there's this pathway,' Schneider held a photo up to the camera, an aerial shot, and pointed at the place he meant, 'the swathe that leads into it from the road, into the circle. Isn't that an indication that it was humans who made it?'

'No. Although it really could be some kind of tunnel with the purpose of calling attention to the circle. An entrance to lead us to the interior. But I think it's much more likely that the swathe is part of the circle—like the stick in a lolly.'

'A lolly?'

'Yes, I'd interpret is as a sign of a cautious approach to our culture. A symbol of childhood. They want to show us that we're not alone, that—'

'Who?'

'The circle-makers. This circle—'

'You mean aliens?'

Schallenberg nodded. 'Plutonians.'

'Of course. You've written a book about them, not long ago.' Schneider leant forward, picked up a book from the table, held it up to the camera and read out the title. *'The Plutonians—the Forgotten People.*

'This circle on a stick, this lolly, it's their language, it's a code we have to crack to make contact with them.'

'And this lolly, as you put it, what could it mean?'

'I don't know. We don't know enough about them yet as a whole.'

'But I'm sure you have a theory.'

'Yes, I do.'

Schneider looked around at all the guests. 'Would you be so kind as to share your knowledge with us? Not all of us here—and I assume, not all our viewers at home—are familiar with your work.'

'Yes, of course,' said Schallenberg, leaning back. 'I consider it a gift from the skies. A gesture of peace and friendship. The Plutonians aren't a warrior-like people at heart. It's fear of the unknown that forces them to fight. But if we show them we understand them, then they'll spare us.'

'So they do present a threat?'

'No, no.' Schallenberg raised both hands to ward off the very suspicion. 'Or at the most a very abstract threat. All we have to do is look inside ourselves and discover the Plutonians in us. With this symbol, they want to reinstate a link that was broken many years ago, long before our time. They understand communication as a game and they want to see what we're capable of. What level of intelligence we've reached by now. Whether we recognize the rule behind it for ourselves, and take corresponding action.'

'Couldn't it be bait?'

'Bait?'

'A kind of key with which adults open children's hearts—to stick to your image of the lolly. A reward for good behaviour, hard work, obedience, or, looking further ahead, perhaps it's meant for a different, crueller purpose, a temptation, a round, bright, sweet promise with a bitter aftertaste.'

'I don't quite understand what you're getting at. The thing with the lolly, it's . . . well . . . it's only a hypothesis to begin with, which we have to check out. I'll have to inspect it in detail when I get there.'

'Oh, you haven't even been there yet? I thought you . . . In the green room you said . . . '

'I said I'd been there in my imagination, and I have, during my meditative expedition.'

'Your meditative expedition?'

'A journey into the self. I do it twice a week, sometimes more often when the situation calls for it. How can you make contact to others if you've lost touch with yourself?'

'I don't know. I—'

'It demands a great deal of strength, in here,' Schallenberg pointed at his chest, 'to reach the destination. My soul is a labyrinth from which there's no escape.'

'You mean a maze where you get lost because you've chosen the wrong path?'

'No, I mean a labyrinth. There's only one path and one destination, but there's no going back because it's a downward path, to immeasurable depths, a re-ascent would be too strenuous. That's why I never go too far ahead. I'm sure it's no different for you.'

'Oh yes, it is,' said Schneider and spread his arms wide. 'My soul is an ocean, huge and open.'

'That's not a contradiction. The ocean has the deepest trenches. Every man is an abyss.'

'It makes you dizzy looking down.'

'Only the Plutonians, our forebears, can save us.'

'And what about the boy?' asked Schneider, to get back down to the subject at hand and back down to earth. 'What did they do with him?'

'They took him and examined him, I assume, and then put him back again.'

'Have you spoken to him yet, asked him about it?'

'No, why should I? What would be the point? They wiped his brain and implanted new information.'

On the day the show was aired, residents contacted the *Sunday Pages*, a regional newspaper funded by advertising and distributed for free in Swaarmodig, and reported supernatural phenomena.

A woman who didn't want to give her name said she'd been suffering from insomnia for years, and that night she'd got up and gone to the window because she'd thought a truck was speeding towards her house, even though it wasn't even on a road, and when she'd looked closer the light had seemed more like a white glow in the sky, like a fully lit train carriage turning in circles. Another woman said she hadn't seen any planes that day because of the dense clouds, but she'd heard two bangs in quick succession, like an explosion, like back in 1943 when Hamburg caught fire and she lost everything, her house, her family, everything. A man claimed to have taken photos of the object, but once the editors had developed the film the best pictures showed only the maize field and above it a slice of sky, dull and white and with not the slightest hint of a foreign body.

At some time that day, the inevitable happened; what always happened when East Frisia flickered across the TV screens in two semi-detached halves of one house in Bad Vilbel—Birgit's sisters called. First Gerhild, who was so agitated she could hardly speak and soon passed the phone on to her oldest son Simon.

'Did you see the mother ship?'

'The mother ship?'

'Yes,' said Simon. 'The print in the field is much too small for a large spaceship. It must have been just a shuttle, a transport vehicle for taking soil samples or dropping off troops. There must have been a bigger ship somewhere, maybe behind the clouds. Didn't you see it?'

'No,' said Birgit.

'Maybe that was the reason for the snow, so you couldn't see it, as camouflage. Or they created a forcefield with plasma inductors and immersed themselves in it. Unless—' Simon broke off and fell silent, as if thinking about what to say next.

'Unless what?' asked Birgit.

'Unless the one in the maize field was the mother ship after all—and they're smaller than us. Much smaller. The size of ants.'

'Ants!'

'Or termites.'

'Termites!'

'*Ant Termes Pacificus*.'

'Then they might be among us already!' Birgit spoke to him like to a child in a permanent state of slight excitement, feigning amazement and joy and exaggerating his visions.

'Definitely, yes. They've been among us for a long time now. They've always been among us. And maybe they're even inside us. Maybe they're controlling us without us even noticing. Controlling our thoughts. Even now. It's possible, don't you think so?'

'Yes, Simon, it is. Anything's possible.'

Simon was twenty-five, had been studying biology and theoretical physics in Frankfurt for six years now and still lived at home, and at dark moments Birgit feared the same fate loomed over Daniel—gifted but forever living in strange worlds.

Then the phone rang again, hardly a minute after she'd put it down, and Margret was on the other end. 'At last. I've been trying to get hold of you for an hour. But I just couldn't get through. Constantly engaged. Was that Gerhild just now?'

'Yes.'

'I thought as much. I spoke to her earlier too.'

'Yes, she told me.'

'What you have to go through! Goodness me. I feel so sorry for you.'

'No need for that.'

'Do you need any help? I'd be glad to come if I could, it's just that I can't get away right now. We've just had the garden done, and what with Jochen's heart attack I can't leave him here alone with it now. You know him. As soon as I'm out the front door he launches himself at it, mows the lawn, trims the hedge, starts weeding, the full Monty. It's a good job Gerhild lives so nearby, I'd never manage it all on my own. And he's supposed to be taking things easy! He's off work until the end of the year. He's supposed to start back gradually, the doctor said. He's not allowed to strain himself. At the recovery clinic in Fallingbostel, away from home, it all went fine. But since he's been back home, you know, he's gone right back to all his old habits. Just because he's had open-heart surgery, he thinks he can do everything just like before. He had a quintuple bypass! The operation took more than four hours! I feel fine, he keeps saying. Better than ever. Like I've been reborn. Raised from the dead. You know what he's like, he's never sensible. He's always overestimating himself. He just bites off more than he can chew. No wonder his body's stopped playing along. And at work they're all coming along with their tax returns. Always at the last minute, every year. I'm only there three days a week now, but sometimes I have so much work to do I don't know how I'll ever manage it. If they were at least in some kind of order! But no, they stuff all their receipts in a bag and we're supposed to fiddle it all out again. Is there anything I can do for you from here, shall I send you anything?'

'No, it's fine.'

'Really?'

'Yes. Hard—'

'Is Daniel feeling better?'

'Yes.'

'And what about the little ones?'

'They're—'

'You know you can always come to us, you and the kids. You know there's always room for you here . . . As long as Jochen and I . . . The house is practically empty . . . What with the new loft extension now, for guests . . . You'd all have a room of your own . . . Mind you . . . Well, the twins share a room anyway . . . And Jochen wouldn't mind . . . You know that, don't you?'

'Yes,' said Birgit. 'I know.'

7

The incident commander Uwe Saathoff presented the facts at a press conference. They hadn't found any indications of a UFO landing in the zone in question. Apart from handprints and footprints in the snow, which were in all probability made by the boy, they hadn't found anything at all, but even those couldn't be precisely identified because of the thaw.

When the police removed the cordon from the field it was stormed by journalists, pilgrims and curious members of the public. The farmer who owned it, Arendt van Deest, tried to get rid of them but couldn't. They invaded the maize from all directions, ruining his crop—or what would have been left of it after Chernobyl. He appealed to Mayor Schulz and then to his insurance company, wanting to claim for an act of higher powers as he had back in May, to make up for the loss. And when that didn't work he reported Daniel Kuper to the police for criminal damage.

The circle soon frayed at the edges, its contours barely recognizable. And still more and more people kept coming to the place where they supposed the original circle had been, to meditate or carry out experiments. Some took plant and soil samples, others stood in the middle at night with recorders and microphones, some paced paths of their own making with dowsing rods, and one man spent a whole day walking across the field from different directions with a Geiger counter. They all made unusual discoveries: the tubercles on the stems were enlarged (van Deest had planted a new variety—Aurora—with more solid stalks). A gelatinous mass that couldn't be identified any more closely was found in the earth (a child had buried a tub of berry compote his mother had put in his lunch box, in the hope that trees might grow out of the seeds). In the middle of the circle was a miniature plane with no visible propulsion mechanism, made of an unknown, shiny green metal that was far too heavy for its low density (modelmakers had tested out their latest developments on the field next door over the summer). On the cassettes, a hollow thudding sound could be made out with approximately seventy beats per minute, reminiscent of a heartbeat (it really was a heartbeat; the microphone had been in a shirt pocket). The divining rod made clear upward and downward deflections (water veins). And the radiation was well over the usual standard value, at seven thousand Becquerels per square metre of caesium-137 (there had been strong rainfall over north-western Germany on 4 and 5 May, although not as strong as five days previously in the south-east of the country).

Birgit and Hard took turns at the hospital. At first, Birgit didn't want to leave Daniel's side. They put a bed in his room for her, but Hard persuaded her to drive home every few hours and take care of the twins who were staying with a neighbour while she was away. 'It'll do them good to see you and it'll do you good to get out of this place,' he said as they were drinking coffee in the recreation room. 'Daniel's fine. No brain haemorrhage, the doctor just said. That ought to reassure you, Biggi. Just concussion.'

'Yes,' she said. 'But where from?'

'He'll have got a whack over the head.'

'Who from?' Birgit took a sip of coffee, pulled a face and put the cup down immediately.

'No idea.'

Her lips pursed, she blew at her coffee and looked past Hard out of the window. Then she asked, 'Couldn't it . . . Do you think it was Volker?'

'Volker?'

'Volker Mengs.'

'That fat kid Mengs? You mean as revenge, because Daniel hit him with a hammer that time?'

She nodded. 'He could have killed him.'

'Nix.'

'He might have frozen to death.'

'Maybe he just fell and won't admit it.'

'Oh yes? So why was he naked then? And where are his clothes?' She took a second, smaller sip, but the coffee was still too hot to drink. Hard hadn't even touched his yet.

'He wasn't naked,' he said. 'He had a towel wrapped round him.' And when Birgit looked at him as if she wanted to skin him alive, he added, 'Maybe he was embarrassed about slipping over in the snow, and he took his clothes off and invented the story.'

'What story?'

'You know what he's like, how much imagination he has sometimes, all the stuff he reads and then thinks up for himself.'

'But Doctor Ahlers said the injury came from a blow to the head, he said he couldn't have done it to—'

'Doctor Ahlers! Doctor Ahlers! You and your Doctor Ahlers!' He drank his coffee in one go, wiped his mouth with the back of his hand and stood up to get himself a new one.

All day long, cars parked outside the school. They were moved away for a short while in the mornings and at noon so that the buses could get past to drop off or pick up the pupils. Someone had put up a trestle table by the side of the road and sold T-shirts, key-rings, cigarette lighters, ballpoint pens, postcards, cups—and saucers—printed with the words *This is just a human shell! Next time take me with you! Fuel tank for the first ignition phase! Write home! May the maize be with you! They were here. So were we . . . but too late!* and *Throw me! I can fly!* Men and women wearing long robes and golden amulets set up tents outside the field, on the narrow grass verge between the asphalt and the fence, camping out to wait for the Plutonians' return. When Markus Schallenberg wanted to examine the circle they welcomed him like their leader. They showered him with gifts, lollies made of wood and clay, and bowed down before him, and he left without entering the field.

The schoolchildren who watched the comings and goings from the opposite side of the road were impossible to calm down. All any of them talked about was the aliens; everyone was speculating about what they'd done to Daniel. Some boys were convinced he'd been exchanged for a replica. Others thought individual-reshapers had taken control of him. And a third contingent decided he'd been a shape-shifter all along without knowing, had always taken on one form or another and only now, thanks to the cold shock, knew how to use his powers to the full. The girls dismissed these claims alternately as 'really dumb' or 'totally primitive', yet didn't come up with any better explanation. Lessons were practically impossible. Time and again, the kids would stare out of the windows. Even the teachers couldn't concentrate. They did ask questions but they barely registered the answers and only woke from their daydreams when they noticed the room had gone quiet around them.

Fighter Wing 71 launched four Phantom II bomber planes from Wittmundhafen, and two Tornados took off from Upjever airbase, to cast a glance at the field and the people from zero altitude for a fraction of a second. The Dutch and the Belgians wanted to gain their own impression of the aliens' landing place and crossed the border in the sky. And from their Greenham Common base in England, the Americans flew several reconnaissance flights with their Lockheed SR-71—at such a height that the Blackbird wasn't visible from the ground with the naked eye.

On the roof of the school, several teachers—Mr Pfeiffer, Mr Engberts and Mr Kamps, all members of the Green Party—attached red helium balloons, a metre and a half in diameter. They let them rise to a height of seventy-five metres on nylon strings, to remind the pilots not to undercut the compulsory minimum flight level in the zero-altitude zone. They also wrote protest letters to the Ministry of Defence: *Low-flying aircraft have repeatedly terrorized us with extreme noise pollution. Until you remove the school campus from the army target practice catalogue, we consider ourselves forced to take drastic measures such as this.*

Low-flying aircraft, the Ministry of Defence wrote back, *serve the air force's defence mandate. Practice flights under realistic conditions are irreplaceable for training pilots. Furthermore, the school building is not included in the catalogue, merely the junction of the L1138 and the B589 in Drömeln.*

At the same time, the Aurich public prosecutor instigated investigations against the three teachers who had signed the letter, on suspicion of endangering air traffic, justifying this step by the fact that the balloons had not been approved by the federal aviation authority and had, additionally, been placed too high. The police came and ordered them to remove the balloons immediately or provide them with access to the roof to carry out the order themselves. One of the policemen, Kurt Rhauderwiek, his hand on his holster, threatened to shoot the things down from the playground otherwise. 'We'll shoot them down like they did in the Rhineland.'

But the teachers refused to follow the order and blocked the policemen's way to the staircase. There was a fight with wild, in some cases unintelligible, insults fired off on both sides. And from then on the case was extended to assault and obstructing a police officer in the course of duty.

Several times a day, four Cessnas belonging to a tour operator took off in Nüttermoor and, following a sightseeing flight over the East Frisian islands, flew a circle over the circle, now barely recognizable as such, before they returned to the runway. Police helicopters hovered above the field for minutes at a time, sometimes descending so low that the remaining maize plants were bent to one side and swayed to and fro in the wind from the rotor blades. Some people who saw it said that was the actual cause of the circle, a helicopter, but nobody had seen or heard one on the day when it happened. Apart from that, the opponents of the theory argued, the snow would have been blown away. And all the photos taken on the day and the day after clearly showed that the entire field was covered with a light, even layer of snow.

The sudden attention that fell upon the whole region did not leave the residents unaffected. Each in their own way, they tried to make the best of the situation. Wessels' Bakery started selling popcorn and cornbread with raisins. The five-storey Beach Hotel, rising high above the land, took out half-page ads offering *field-view rooms*. And in the neighbouring village, which extended up to the school from the south in the form of an industrial estate, the newly built Ultravox Disco was promptly renamed—the red neon U had already been mounted above the entrance—the UFO Music Hall.

Ulrich Dettmers, the village hairdresser, offered a new hairstyle in his salon. Instead of concealing bald heads or receding hairlines, as he usually did by leaving men's hair long on one side and then combing it over their heads, he now advised his customers to emphasize their natural tonsures or, if they weren't balding, to let him shave their crowns. He put up pictures of monks between the mirrors, large-format reproductions of old copperplate engravings, he underlined the spiritual dimension of this particular coiffure once he'd asked the customers which cut they wanted, and if they still weren't convinced he added, 'A free spirit needs a free head.' But only a few desperate souls went for it, and Uli Dettmers soon returned to his standard haircut.

On the following Sunday, Pastor Meinders preached in the Reformed Church: 'Do not keep company, if any man that is called a brother be a fornicator, or covetous, or an idolator, or a railer, or a drunkard, or an extortioner—with such an one no not to eat. For what have I to do to judge them also that are without? Do not ye,' he leant low over the edge of the pulpit and pointed at the congregation on the pews, 'judge them that are within? But them that are without God judgeth. Therefore put away from among yourselves that wicked person!' The men and women in the pews cast questioning looks at one another, a whispering arose and ebbed away again as the church choir sang the opening lines of 'O Saviour of the World' from the gallery. No one knew who Pastor Meinders meant by *them that are without* or the *wicked person*. Foreigners? Asylum-seekers? Aliens? The Plutonians they talked about on TV? The antichrist? Daniel Kuper? No one felt directly addressed, and everyone was surprised that he didn't talk about the Revelation as usual, that the heaven in their minds didn't divide and four riders or a horde of black angels didn't descend upon it and cover the land behind their eyes with pestilence, especially now that St John's prophecies seemed to be coming true.

And less than twelve hours later, down in Petersen's underground pool hall, Berger the pool champion, inspired by the sermon, held his cue aloft like a sword and quoted in a trembling voice another passage from Paul's first epistle to the Corinthians, one no less mysterious than the citation Pastor Meinders had chosen: 'For we know in part, and we prophecy in part. But when that which is perfect is come, then that which is in part shall be done away.' Berger, who was otherwise always absolutely certain what would happen—eternal damnation of all men, regardless of their faith and their righteousness—suddenly began prophesying and then, hardly had he finished, potted three balls in one go.

'What's all this?' asked Jost Petersen as he dunked a glass in the brim-full sink. 'Is he having doubts?'

'He's having doubts,' said Heiko Hessenius.

'Then it's all over,' said Gerrit Klopp, dropping his hand of cards—coincidentally, not a very good hand. 'Give us something to drink, quick, before the molten lava of the Last Judgement comes over us and dries out our throats, and the river to wet them again runs dry.'

The drinkers and gamblers who gathered at the tables and the bar every evening ordered schnapps and beer and began arranging the balls and the cards for new games. And even the ex-drinkers and ex-gamblers, who rarely came and had kept up their abstinence over the summer, fell back into their old habits.

'Maybe he's not having doubts,' said Jost Petersen, once he'd dealt with the first onslaught and was taking a break because the beer he'd just poured for himself had foamed over.

'What?' asked Heiko Hessenius.

'Maybe he's not having doubts,' Petersen repeated. 'Maybe he really thinks he's that which is perfect.'

'Him? Berger? You're kidding.'

'Yes, I'm kidding,' said Petersen. 'But I bet he isn't.' He nodded over at Berger, who had just won another game and made his opponent, a truck driver passing through, look like an extra, and

Heiko Hessenius and Gerrit Klopp and the others sitting at and by the bar turned around to him and watched him counting banknotes onto a bundle on the edge of the pool table.

Daniel had no idea of any of this in the hospital. The doctors and nurses didn't mention it to him, and nor did his parents. From outside on the street, muffled voices and sounds made their way into his room: cars hooting, sirens wailing, shouts. Now and then he thought he heard his name amid all the confusion, but he was too weak to get up and take a look whether someone really was calling for him.

The blinds on the windows remained down even during the day. Yet enough light fell through the narrow slits to brighten up the room until the early evening, with no need to switch on the two rows of neon tubes hanging above his head. He spent most of the time lying in bed, staring at the ceiling. He kept drifting off, dreaming of faraway worlds, and when he awoke from that state he'd sit up with a jerk, rock his body back and forth and murmur—scarcely audible, like a prayer—the only words he'd spoken since his admission to hospital. There was one he kept getting stuck on, he couldn't get over it, and he wouldn't stop repeating it out loud until someone put a hand on his forehead, pressed him gently back against the pillow and spoke to him in hushed tones. For those outside him he was silent then, but inside himself he'd still hear his own voice beating through his body, as if it had bounced off the bare walls and returned to him, to sound out his bodily organs for a new, better way out.

Iron, lock, sign, bike, field, clearing, maize, maize, maize, maize,
maize, maize, maize, maize, maize, maize, maize, maize, maize,
maize, maize, maize, maize, maize, maize, maize, maize, maize,
maize, maize, maize, maize, maize, maize, maize, maize, maize,
maize, maize, maize, maize, maize, maize, maize, maize, maize,
maize, maize, maize, maize, maize, maize, maize, maize, maize,
maize, maize, maize, maize, maize, maize, maize, maize, maize,
maize, maize, maize, maize, maize, maize, maize, maize, maize,
maize, maize, maize, maize, maize, maize, maize, maize, maize,
maize, maize, maize, maize, maize, maize, maize, maize, maize,
maize, maize, maize, maize, maize, maize, maize, maize, maize,
maize, maize, maize, maize, maize, maize, maize, maize, maize,
maize, maize, maize, maize, maize, maize, maize, maize, maize,
maize, maize, maize, maize, maize, maize, maize, maize, maize,
maize, maize, maize, maize, maize, maize, maize, maize, maize,
maize, maize, maize, maize, maize, maize, maize, maize, maize,
maize, maize, maize, maize, mars, maize, maize, maize, maize,
maize, maize, maize, maize, maize, maize, maize, maize, maize,
maize, maize, maize, maize, maize, maize, maize, maize, maize,
maize, maize, maize, maize, maize, maize, maize, maize, maize,
maize, maize, maize, maize, maize, maize, maize, maize, maize,
maize, maize, maize, maize, maize, maize, maize, maize, maize,
maize, maize, maize, maize, maize, maize, maize, maize, maize,
maize, maize, maize, maize, maize, maize, maize, maize, maize,
maize, maize, maize, maize, maize, maize, maize, maize, maize,
maize, maize, maize, maize, maize, maize, maize, maize, maize,
maize, maize, maize, maize, maize, maize, maize, maize, maize,
maize, maize, maize, maize, maize, maize, maize, maize, maize,
maize, maize, maize, maize, maize, maize, maize, maize, maize,
maize, maize, maize, maize, maize, maize, maize, maize, maize,
maize, maize, maize, maize, maize, maize, maize, maize, maize,
maize, maize, maize, maize, clearing, field, bike, sign, lock, iron.

'Don't let it worry you. Here's my explanation: if you stand in the middle of a field and turn around three hundred and sixty degrees, all you see in every direction is maize, even underneath you, nothing but maize, and above you, at arm's reach, a white, opaque sky. Your son—Daniel—is simply trying to put into words what he and all of us can't understand,' the doctor told Birgit and Hard with extravagant gestures once they'd left his room for the corridor. 'He's going through it all over again in his daydreams, to try and track down what really happened. It will stop when he feels safe again and finds an explanation that makes sense.'

In fact, Daniel had hardly said anything other than what he kept repeating. He couldn't get a complete sentence out. When he asked for something to drink he simply said, 'Water' or 'Cola'; when he was hungry he said, 'Food'. But the doctor wasn't willing to rule out the possibility that the blow to his head might have affected his language skills, and he consulted a colleague. The two of them prescribed an MRI scan but the images showed no anomalies or lesions.

The psychotherapist Bernd Reichert said Daniel probably had a blockage. Something—or someone—was putting him under pressure and preventing him from communicating. He suggested hypnotizing him. Hard said, 'Great! Hypnotize us! First him, then me.' He wasn't being serious, but Birgit said, 'Absolutely no way.' She was afraid Daniel would never wake up from the trance and she'd lose him entirely.

Instead, she brought him books and magazines from home, toys, cuddly animals, familiar objects, and told him what she'd experienced that morning. At last she had him to herself, and she hoped he'd need her presence and the consolation of her words for longer than three or four days or, as many people thought, a week. Every doctor gave a different prognosis. Now that she was sitting by his bed and holding his little hand, which he had reached out to her from under the sheet, he was her baby again, and the memory of the elated feeling of forming a single unit with him on her lap, at her breast, mother and child, returned with all its might. For months, she had only had to look at him or hold him, and all the tensions between her and Hard were forgotten, everything that had happened before his birth was forgotten. Never before and never since had she felt so strong, so untouchable.

She didn't think of Jesus and Mary when she looked at him. Birgit wasn't particularly religious, although she'd always wanted to be because she noticed that those people, especially women, who had a religious faith, no matter which one, appeared more confident, more confident and more determined, it seemed to her, than she was. And she went to church every few weeks to be closer to God or the divine—whatever that was—closer than at home, at least. There were some aspects to the words Pastor Meinders spoke that she thought were good and right, but she didn't share the rapture that the other members of the congregation went into when they sang hymns or prayed or gathered in the churchyard after the service and touched one another's hands and shoulders. Even on the way home, on Church Road, she was always over-come by an ineffable emptiness and perplexity, which she over-came again as soon as she was standing at the cooker in the kitchen, making lunch.

She put her fingers in Daniel's hand and his fingers closed around them like a shipwrecked man reaching for a rope, and all at once the time before he'd gone to kindergarten and to school, before she'd given him away, seemed to have been the happiest time in her life.

Back then she'd so often sat by his bed and read to him, or if she hadn't had a book at hand that he wanted to hear, she'd told him stories. She'd simply thought something up, characters she couldn't remember later on, when he wanted her to tell him about little Patrick and his dog Duffy again. Sometimes she'd told him her own story, how and where she'd grown up, what her parents had done and said or what she'd done all day long. And now she did that again. She stroked his head or his arm and spoke to him quietly. She hoped it would help him remember what had happened to him, and when it didn't help she asked him if it had anything to do with Volker, if Volker had hit him.

Daniel shook his head. 'Iron,' he said, and then again: 'Iron.'

She didn't understand what he meant, assuming that the object he'd been hit with was made of iron, until Volker and Simone visited him and she told them what he'd told her.

'Iron's an idiot,' said Volker and then, when Birgit raised her eyebrows, added, 'This boy at school.'

'What boy at school?'

'Just a boy.' He shrugged.

'He's in Year Nine,' said Simone.

At school, she learnt nothing new from Mrs Zuhl, Daniel's teacher whom she'd never liked from the very beginning, other than that it was all Hard's fault, that he was a bad influence on his son. From Mr Kamps she learnt that they'd had a fight, Daniel and Michael, Michael Rosing, the son of Rosing the building contractor, and it hadn't been the first time.

'He's a decent lad,' said Hard when Birgit wanted to inform the police, 'he wouldn't do a thing like that,' but Birgit wasn't convinced. Not knowing any other number, she dialled the emergency services on one-one-zero.

Johann Rosing told the police his son had been with him all that day, after he'd been sent home from school 'for some kind of nonsense,' and several guests at his birthday party, friends of his, confirmed his statement.

Once his efforts at gaining compensation for what had happened had failed—the cases had been instantly dismissed—van Deest wanted to get justice another way and either defend his property against the invaders, 'those lowlives,' as he called them, by violent means or at least make a profit out of their presence. He put guards around the field overnight, and the next morning he demanded five marks' entry fee, but no one was willing to pay. They didn't let the men stop them, simply clambering over the wire into the field. He swore he'd sue them, and he wrote down their car registration numbers to lend weight to his threat. He had an idea that wouldn't change anything, that they wouldn't let him stop them because they really did believe in higher powers, but he didn't want to leave anything untried before he turned to his last resort: violence. That same evening, he came driving up from the other direction on a tractor and ploughed the plants under, shielded by policemen. He thought he'd put an end to all the nonsense. And he had.

8

Birgit never knew what to do with herself when she came home from the hospital. As soon as she was there she wanted to go straight back. The twins were still at the neighbour's place and they'd stay there as long as Daniel didn't get any better—he was still under shock. And Hard was busy in the shop, mainly fending off curious people, crazies as he called them, who wanted to see the boy, his boy, and talk to him. A writer came by who wanted to write a book about the 'Kuper Case', and a director spoke to him to negotiate the film rights, but when he referred to Daniel as the 'UFO boy' Hard threw him out. Later, at night, when he told Birgit about it and she asked him who it had been, he couldn't remember the man's name. 'Nobody famous,' he said, 'nobody we know.'

And she said, 'We're getting more of them every day.'

Daniel received post from all over Germany, especially from 'over there' in the East—the East German TV channel DDR 1 had shown *Guests from the Galaxy* that evening, which the letter-writers agreed couldn't have been a coincidence. But letters came from Austria and Switzerland too, from England and Holland and France, even from America and Japan. All of them reported UFO landings, alien abductions and experiments on their bodies. Birgit and Hard didn't know how they'd got their name; it had been abbreviated in the newspaper and not mentioned at all on TV. And still they got forty or fifty letters and cards a day. Birgit didn't understand all of it, but she inferred the content of the others from the few foreign letters she managed to decipher. She read some of them to Daniel when she visited him, and some of them, the ones in German, he read for himself.

A lot of the people who came into the drugstore to see 'the boy' bought something: toothpaste, all-purpose cleaning fluid, small pet bedding or moisturizer, products with price tags on them, anything that said *kuper's drugstore*, as a kind of souvenir. In fact business was going so well that Hard couldn't keep up with his orders and had to drive to the competition in the town or the nearby villages to buy up supplies. He left more and more often and stayed away longer and longer. When he did come into the shop, usually at noon or just before closing time, then it was only for a few minutes to check the stock, pick up new orders and change his white coat. Mrs Bluhm couldn't deal with the crowds on her own so Birgit helped her out on the cash desk in the mornings. She entered the prices, wrote receipts and gave information and interviews. Yes, she was the boy's mother; no, she didn't know what had happened; 'Silica capsules are right at the back with the nutritional supplements'; Daniel was fine, just concussion; 'Nursing pads are sold out, they're on order, they should be in by Monday'; he was still in hospital, they were keeping him in there until the excitement was over; 'Cold wax strips on the shelf on the left, below the nail-care sets'; he'd be discharged at the end of the week, or maybe not until the weekend, they'd have to wait and see. All along, she kept her temper and her friendliness, and at the same time she defended herself against the euphoria welling up inside her, not wanting to admit she was enjoying the fact that he, Hard, needed her.

Lying exhausted on the sofa in the evenings, she caught herself dwelling on certain TV shows—*Wonders, Mysteries, Phenomena* and *Research and Technology*—and reading the articles about Daniel or about what had happened to him, even though she'd vowed not to do so.

One Thursday, Marlies and Sabine came by after work to wish her a belated happy birthday. They brought her flowers and chocolates and a pile of newspapers and magazines, several issues of the *Magazine for the People of Tomorrow* and the *UFO News*, which were about extrasensory perception, psycho-kinesis, prophecy and encounters of the third kind.

She didn't understand a word of it and she was surprised her friends believed in that kind of thing. 'Have you all gone crazy?' asked Birgit as she went ahead of them into the kitchen. But they both said they hadn't even looked at them; two men had come round to talk about these things, and Klaus and Günter had given them the newspapers before choir practice, for her, for Birgit, and that made her even angrier. 'They came to me too, but I wasn't having any of their rubbish,' she held up two of the magazines. 'I threw that nonsense in the bin.'

Marlies said, 'You know what they're like,' and Sabine said, 'Is that new?'

'What?'

'Your dress.'

Birgit looked down at herself—navy blue, the top trimmed with white piping, side zip, artificial-leather belt—and shook her head. 'I haven't worn it for ages.' She put the magazines, which she'd wanted to fling across the room a moment ago, on the table, on the pile with the others.

'Pleated skirt. We stock those too but it's not from our shop.'

'No, it's from Brandt in Ihrhove.'

'You went all the way to Ihrhove specially?'

'I've done that before,' said Marlies. 'They have some really nice things there.'

'No wonder Günter's always complaining, if you two go behind his back. You're his most loyal customers.'

'It wasn't me, it was a present from Hard. For our anniversary.'

'It's pretty,' said Marlies.

'Yes,' said Birgit. 'And it's really light.' As if to prove it, she turned half a pirouette. 'I thought I'd wear it again before it's too late. It's more of a summer dress.'

'How much was it?'

'I don't know, do I, I didn't pay for it.'

'We've got it in the window for sixty-nine ninety. Not the same one, not that colour, not that fabric. What is it, actually? Silk or jersey?' Sabine stroked a hand over Birgit's shoulder, not waiting for an answer, and felt the material between her fingers. 'Or polyester. Feels like polyester if you ask me. Let's have a look.' She fiddled around the collar at the back of Birgit's neck and then, when she couldn't find what she was looking for, bent over, grabbed the bottom of her skirt, searched for the label, found it and called up from below, 'I told you so, here: a hundred per cent polyester.'

'Doesn't it make you sweat?'

'I don't think I could stand it!'

'Me neither.'

'It doesn't make me sweat. I never sweat when I'm wearing it.'

'I bet you don't. I bet you never break out in a sweat.'

'What's that supposed to mean?'

'Nothing.' Marlies and Sabine exchanged glances and started to giggle.

'You're so childish. Can't you ever think of anything else?'

'I bet you do when you're cooking.'

'What?'

'I bet you sweat when you are cooking, I said. Well, I do anyway.'

'Me too.'

'Yesterday, I was making lentil soup, and I was practically dripping with sweat, even though I had the window open and the extractor on. I got changed especially, and then when I ate them I got really hot—'

'Brown or red?'

'—really . . . What?'

'Brown or red?'

'Brown. The red ones cook quicker but they're no good for my digestion.'

'Same here.'

'You know what Hard did the other day?'

'What?'

'He cooked. He wanted to make lentils, lentil soup with smoked pork, but he didn't soak them first.'

'What?'

'The lentils?'

'Dried lentils?'

'Yes.'

'And he didn't soak them overnight?'

'No.'

'He could have used a pressure cooker. That would have been fine.'

'Or tinned lentils.'

'He didn't though. He just put the dried lentils in boiling water and left them in there for twenty minutes.'

'Twenty minutes?'

'That's not nearly long enough.'

'Exactly.'

'I always cook them for at least twice that, otherwise they're too hard.'

'At least.'

'That's what I told him, afterwards. We didn't even eat them. I made sandwiches for everyone, with mortadella and bier-schinken. Good job I'd just been shopping.'

'At our shop?' asked Marlies.

'Yes,' said Birgit. 'At your shop.'

'Why was he even cooking in the first place?' asked Sabine.

Birgit shrugged. 'He probably wanted to prove himself. Or take some work off my hands.'

'Klaus gets like that once a year too. On my birthday he wanted to make cauliflower cheese, but he used far too much flour and it was all lumpy, and then we went out to eat.'

'Where did you go?'

'To Fokken's.'

'Fokken's? You don't mean the snack bar?'

'Yes, I do. The kids wanted French fries. And Klaus had already had a drink and I didn't want to let him drive, so we went to Fokken's.'

'We get sausages for everyone there now and then, they're pretty good.'

'No, they're too spicy for me.'

'Me too.'

'The only thing Hard can do in the kitchen is make tea.'

'Same as Günter.'

'But Hard doesn't use an egg timer.'

'I could do with a nice cup of tea now,' said Marlies, 'or a coffee,' and Birgit said, 'Me too.'

While Birgit put the kettle on and Sabine put cups on the kitchen table, Marlies looked for cream in the fridge. 'Right at the top, by the margarine,' said Birgit. 'Go ahead and open a new one. I think the old one's gone off.'

'By the way,' Marlies said into the fridge. 'Have I told you we're getting an au pair girl?'

'Really?' asked Sabine. 'Where from?'

'Yes,' said Marlies. 'Klaus sorted it out, she's from France, Paris, via an agency.'

'It must cost a fortune.'

'Two hundred and fifty a month.'

'Pretty steep,' said Sabine, and Birgit said, 'Pretty good.'

'But she has to work five hours a day for that, six days a week.'

'Does she speak German?' asked Sabine.

'Her German's very good, she's already written to us.'

'She could have just copied it.'

'No, I don't think so. There were a couple of mistakes in the letter. You could tell she's not from here. Mind you, her mother's German, she wrote, or her grandmother. I can't remember now, I'll have to check.'

'I don't understand how you can invite a complete stranger into your home, a foreigner. What with all the stories you hear. The Ahlers had one, didn't they, that dark-haired girl who always brought the washing to us at the laundry because she was too lazy to do it herself. Where was she from again? Greece?'

'That's got nothing to do with us,' said Marlies.

'Italy,' said Birgit.

'And then she just disappeared one day, upped and left.'

'That's a whole different story.'

'No, she was from Spain. Madrid, I think.'

'And then later they noticed she'd taken all their jewellery.'

'Oh yes!'

'You can't compare the two.'

'Or was it Barcelona? Didn't she come from somewhere on the coast as well? I think I remember her saying something like that.'

'And the silver cutlery, all gone.'

'They caught her though. In Neuschanz, she didn't even make it over the border.'

'Yes but the Ahlers never saw their belongings again. Those lovely pearl necklaces, real cultured pearls, I always thought it was a bit over the top, the way Eiske put them on display, with all her goods on show,' she unbuttoned her blouse a little way and pulled the fabric apart with both hands, stood on tiptoe and paraded to the door and back until Marlies and Birgit started laughing, 'but they were still lovely, white and shiny, not at all matte.'

'I thought they were too big.'

'They were a bit chunky, that's true.'

'That was just a one-off case,' said Marlies. 'They were just unlucky.'

'You hear that sort of thing all the time.'

'Didn't he have an affair with her?'

'Who?'

'Gerald, I mean Doctor Ahlers,' said Birgit. 'Someone told me there was something going on between the two of them. That's why she ran away and took the jewellery, to get her revenge.'

'On Doctor Ahlers, you mean?'

'Maybe it was her who started it. And then the whole thing got too much for her.'

'Probably. Gerald would never start something with a house-keeper.'

'No, I don't think so either.'

'Maybe you're right.'

'Certainly.'

'Especially not with someone like her. The way she acted. And the clothes she'd wear. Either a kaftan or jeans. Either too baggy or too tight. As long as she got plenty of attention.'

'Some people like that kind of thing.'

'Not me though.'

'Me neither.'

Outside, a train thundered past the window. The floor trembled and the glasses in the cupboard clinked against each other.

'Why now, though?' asked Birgit when the kitchen was quiet again.

'What?' asked Sabine.

'I mean,' Birgit turned to Marlies, 'why are you getting an au pair girl now, now that the kids are all at school and you've just started back at work?'

Marlies looked at the floor, then at her stomach, and then up again and from one to the other. She raised her eyebrows and pursed her lips, and then she said, 'Well.'

'No,' said Sabine, and Birgit said it as well: 'No.'

'You're kidding!'

Birgit hugged Marlies. 'At your age!'

'I can't believe you're putting yourself through it again,' said Sabine, once she'd let go of Marlies. 'I wouldn't want to do it again. Three's enough for me.'

'Me too,' said Birgit.

'You even had two at once. Are the twins back home again, by the way?'

'Yes, they're asleep.' Birgit pointed at the ceiling, and Marlies and Sabine looked up. 'They were wiped out.'

'I can imagine.'

'It must be a bit much for them.'

'Oh no, they're much too little. They don't understand any of it. We told them Daniel's sick. I took them along to the hospital today but they spent the whole time running around.'

'Let's hope you don't have twins as well.'

Marlies shook her head. 'I had a scan. I don't want to get a surprise like you did.'

'How far gone are you?'

'Four months.'

'You're not showing yet.'

'I am a bit.' She sat up straight and stuck out her belly.

'Only a little bit.'

'Let's drink to it!'

'Not me,' said Marlies.

'But I will,' said Sabine, and Birgit said, 'Me too,' and she fetched a bottle of schnapps and two glasses from the lounge.

Later, at a quiet moment—Sabine had gone to the bathroom, the conversation was interrupted—she asked Marlies whether she and Klaus had any problems because of the pregnancy, whether he was having difficulties with becoming a father again, but Marlies said she didn't understand what she meant, and Birgit didn't want to explain. Sabine came back and told them about Günter, not that anyone had asked, about how even-tempered he'd been recently, so calm and confident since that unexpected winter's day had arrived, all of a sudden a different man, as if transformed. 'Turnover's not quite as expected, a bit worse than last year even, but that doesn't seem to bother him at all.'

'That's nice for him,' said Birgit. 'Did you know he and I had a talk that day?'

'Yes,' said Sabine. 'He told me. I think it did him good to talk to someone else for a change, about his problems, I mean, his depression.'

'It didn't do me good,' said Birgit.

'I can imagine,' said Sabine, and Marlies said: 'Me too,' but Birgit didn't mean it the way they'd understood her. Looking back, that morning at Neemann's and at Vehndel's seemed unreal. There was something unreal about the whole day, not just because of the snow or what had happened to Daniel. They talked for a while longer, mostly about the weather and the autumn, and while Marlies and Sabine got on to the autumn holidays the week after next, about what they wanted to do with their children, Birgit scanned their faces and their way of speaking for a hint as to whether they knew about her applications or not. Marlies kept running a finger along one eyebrow, curling her lips, and Sabine cast her a few sidelong glances, and every time she did so she yawned with her mouth closed, and Birgit couldn't shake the feeling that both of them were trying to supress laughter. Then Marlies said in a distorted voice, a robot version of Birgit's voice, 'Dear Mr Neemann, I would hereby like to apply to your advertisement for a secretarial post.' And Sabine said in the same tone, 'Although I have not trained as a bookkeeper, I do secretly adjust my husband's accounts—to his advantage. That could be to your advantage too.' And they both started laughing, burst out in peals of laughter, and Birgit laughed along with them, relieved that they saw her applications as a game, a joke, a foolish trick among adults, nothing that had to be taken seriously.

After they'd left, Birgit went to check on the twins. They were asleep in their beds in their room. Out of habit, she went into Daniel's room too, and it was only when she was halfway into the room, in that dark, phosphorescent universe, that she remembered he was in hospital. She felt dizzy; she'd drunk too much schnapps. Planets and spaceships orbited around her, and above her on the ceiling, stars glowed toxic green. In the kitchen, she made herself a pot of herbal tea and looked at her watch as the water boiled. Hard was still with the male voice choir at the Beach Hotel, although practice must have been over for hours. She lay down on the sofa and stroked the scar on her belly, the place where her navel had been. For the first time since the twins had been born, she was glad she couldn't get pregnant any more.

Then she flicked through the newspapers and magazines Marlies and Sabine had brought along, listlessly and yet still half-expecting some kind of explanation for what had happened to Daniel. She barely read more than the first paragraphs of the reports. She asked herself what it all had to do with her son—he wasn't usually named at all—and what these people, these self-appointed scientists, wanted from him. The story had broken loose from him, and Birgit hoped it wouldn't come back to him, or to her.

9

Three days later, some kids found Daniel's satchel two kilometres away from the maize field: a sports bag, a T-shirt, a pair of tracksuit bottoms, a pair of trainers, a sandwich box, a pencil case, four textbooks, four exercise books and two issues of the science fiction series *Perry Rhodan*. The clothes damp, the bread mouldy, the pages of the books rippled.

When Mrs Zuhl heard that—a neighbour told her about it—she remembered the slim paperback she'd confiscated from him, *Foray into the Dark Sky*. Perhaps, she thought, he assumed the aliens would come and take him away if he made them a suitable landing place. Snow in September. That's the signal, the herald of their advent. That's how it's been passed down, that's what it says in the paperbacks, and he alone knows what to do now. He rams a wooden stake, decorated with hieroglyphics, into the earth, fastens a steel wire to its blunt end and walks eight metres eastwards until the wire has unwound. Like using compasses, he draws a circle in the maize so that they'll recognize it as soon as they pierce through the clouds. There is nothing to see yet. But the time of their landing has not yet come: thirteen thirteen. He undresses, despite the cold. He even rubs his body with snow from head to toe, to stand before them as pure and natural as possible.

Then he waits for their arrival, for a ray to lift him upwards, a convoy ship to take him in, creatures with four eyes—one for each direction—which materialize in from of him and accompany him on his journey to their people. He won't have to understand the sounds they make, and they won't need to translate his language into theirs; they'll communicate solely through the power of their thoughts. He looks up again and again, into nothingness, rubbing his arms and legs together to stave off the cold. At some point he can no longer stand and he does a handstand to take the pressure off his half-frozen feet. He stands there as straight as a number one, his neck and knees locked in place, his feet drawn in. Standing upside down is the only skill he's mastered, the only thing that makes him happy. An epsilon-minus, who accidentally ended up on the rocket-scientist shelf as an embryo. Unusually, though, he can't seem to keep his balance there in the clearing. He sways, he wriggles, he tries to get a hold with his hands on the plants and the snow. Perhaps it's too cold, perhaps the ground is too uneven, or perhaps he's simply reckless, convinced he's overcome gravity in his cold ecstasy. Whatever the case, he falls over and hits his head on the stake in the flat-pressed maize alongside him. For a moment he loses consciousness. He loses contact to the world, he thinks he's floating, flying, he feels himself being lifted up by a power that exceeds all that is human, and he only comes back when his limbs begin to tremble. At first he thinks they've taken him to a space that looks identical to the space from which they took him. A simulation. He can tell straight away. The snow is far too dry and powdery to be real snow. The light is too bright, the air too clear. But he accepts the demonstration of their skills as what it is—a welcome gift. They want him to feel at home. And he is at home. He's where he always wanted to be. In the dark sky. In the middle kingdom. At the centre of the universe. Then he thinks he hasn't moved one millimetre away from Earth. The circle in the maize is his circle—his work. He reaches for the stake and picks it up, wanting to test out its texture, its weight, to be on the safe side, and as he does so he gets a splinter in his finger. Sitting up, he realizes what a stupid thing he's done, how silly it is, and he realizes he'll be in trouble if people find out who's behind it. So he gets rid of the things. He flings the stake over the fence, as high and as far as he can, and he stuffs his clothes in a skip behind the school. He takes the towel out of his sports kit and wraps it around his hips, ashamed of his genitals and not daring to walk around completely naked. He dumps his satchel on the way back and covers it with leaves and twigs. He walks across the fields, climbs over fences, jumps over ditches, taking the shortest route home. On his way he gives himself bruises by running into trees and walls, to put the blame on others and make himself look like a victim. It's not a conscious thing. He acts intuitively. He can't help being the way he is. It's in his nature, the nature of the Kupers. They're not responsible for the effects, the side-effects of their actions.

Then the telephone rang, a former pupil calling, and she abandoned her thoughts.

Another three days later, van Deest was harvesting a field and came across a wooden stake with a wire attached to it, the same length as the circle's radius. He took it to the school to show it to all of them. He marched across the playground in his rubber boots, past the staff-room windows, encircled by kids, and he held the stake up high with two hands, like a flagpole without a flag. When Mrs Zuhl saw him, when she heard him shouting, 'It's the proof, it's the proof, I done said all along the boy did it himself,' until he went hoarse and his voice gave out, her theory seemed much more likely. She went to the secretary's office and placed a call to the *Frisian News* and told the new editor-in-chief, Martin Masurczak, what had really happened that day in the maize; the true story.

I Am a Master of Loneliness

I am travelling on the orders of the Privy Council. The initiates forgot the deeper motives for my journey at the very moment they dispatched me to fulfil their will. No one knows where I am flying to and why. I deleted the files that might have informed anyone before I set out. No one knows my route; even I have lost sight of it. Officially, I am on an exploratory mission. According to the coordinates, there ought to be nothing at the place where I am now, nothing but the dark emptiness of outer space.

I was sent to the ice planet Tubal IV as a courier, to meet a metamorphess by the name of Variola and receive a message from her. Twelve days and twelve nights I spent at the base. I wandered the corridors and hangars. In the Parabar, with the mutated spider women, in the middle of the trading centre, I waited for a sign. But there was none, other than those hirsute, many-legged, dancing twins who fished butterflies out of their nets with their tongues and hypnotized me with their rhythmic movements. I thought I discovered a pattern in their steps, in the twitching of their muscles, a code I had to crack, which would brand itself onto my visual nerves unless I turned away. In my nest, lying in the dust, I found no rest. No one had told me where and when I would meet Variola or how I might recognize her.

One evening, a severe snowstorm raged outside. On intuition, I set out for a colony in Section Twenty-Three, an eastern sub-section near the Tubal caverns. There, between fire pits and steaming caul-drons, I was approached by a female worker, or a being in the form of a female worker, with hundreds of phosphorescent shishir cat's eyes. I asked her whether she was Variola. She said some-thing in her language that may have been a negation or a greeting, covered my lips with hers and offered me, back at the base, a cup of anft in the Parabar. I distrusted her affection, turned down her offer, ordered my own anft and insisted on paying my own tab. We sat down at a table a little isolated from the others. Not because I am shy of public attention but because she insisted. She said something else I couldn't understand. Then she leant forward and grabbed two of my twelve claws, as if to measure her strength against mine. It was no great effort to press her onto the tabletop and hold her there until she abandoned her resistance and sub-mitted to me.

To be quite certain she had no other intention than losing in front of an audience and thereby proving her humility to me, I whipped out my gornik, its butt in a firm grip, ready to bathe in her yellow blood. All along, she stared at me with her cat's eyes and repeated the same words over and over: *Specta me. Animum diligenter attende ad ea, quae tibi nunc dicam. Te absconde in spelunca obscura. Occlude sensus tuos. Propugnaculo te praepara in animo. San-guinem inflamma. Radios per corpus mitte. Vigila omne tempus. Incumbe mentem in res futuras. Delinea finem. Vade viam tuam, etsi aspera sit. Resiste illecebris. Ne moratus sis. Oculos ne retro verteris. Ne dubitaveris de verbis. Chandos adversarius potens est multas facies habens. Ne alicui confisus sis, ne tibi quidem ipsi. Nuntius in te est. Eum expedi.* When our claws released I had a rupture in my chitin, fine and smooth as if from a cut. I wanted to launch myself upon her, numb her with my venom gland, cut out her heart with my sting and share it among the bar's patrons as a feast. Yet when I looked up she had vanished. I don't know whether she was Variola or someone else, but that night I slept as deep and long as an Alvoranian anteater.

I stayed three more days at the base in the hope of her revealing herself to me. I flew to Section Twenty-Three again and called her name into the darkness, but there was no answer. Then I set out again.

I don't know my mission. I don't know what message I am supposed to transmit. Variola said nothing that made sense to me. I didn't memorize the sound of her words, so I couldn't repeat them in the presence of an interpreter. They didn't select me for my memory, but because I can hold my tongue and know no fear. Even if I knew something I wouldn't reveal it. The threat of torture instils no terror in me. I feel no pain and no sorrow. Glarum, the truth-finder that sifts our enemies' brains and records their thoughts, has no effect on me, as a number of tests have proved. My mental training is almost complete but I am not yet a Siddim Master. Despite that, the highest level, which accomplishes total obliteration, has not destroyed me but put me into a pleasantly even mood. For the first time, I feel at one with Gibbesh. I have told no one of it and will tell no one of it, until I hold her guu in my hands. Then, however, everyone will find out at the same time, and they will be grateful to me for telling them. My inner peace will be transferred to them and make them better, more unconditional soldiers.

There is no point in following me. And yet someone is following me. I have spent hours shaking off the ship that has latched onto mine. The sensors show nothing. The screen is black. But that doesn't mean there isn't something out there that might be a danger to me: a power that forces me to abandon my conviction and adapt to its own. Many have the ability to camouflage themselves or manipulate their enemies' perception. I must not exclude the possibility that they have long since taken control of my thoughts and are merely waiting for the right moment to initiate my self-abandonment.

At moments like this, floating and looking down at a strange world, it seems as if I haven't yet been born, as if I were merely a distant shadow of the future. It is certainly possible that I have flown through a wormhole during my escape. Some open up suddenly in front of you and are so small that you can't evade them. In Kardeus, I heard of monks who breathed one in or swallowed one. Since then, the past has spoken through them. That is the highest level of enlightenment.

All I know is that I have lost my course and entered the atmosphere of an unknown planet in the constellation of the Great Gog. My ship is badly harmed. But even if I did manage to repair the damage, the fuel will not be enough to return to Kedron. Even though I have a mission to fulfil and the probability is high that I am carrying a message within me that I don't understand, no one will miss me.

My mother lives in the Old Quarter, deep beneath the earth. I have not seen her for years. She protects her spawn; I am merely one of many. My father burned in the war, after he had slit four thousand Laomers to pieces with his mandibles, already aflame. My brothers were considered missing in action until their corpses were found on Thos. They wore their innards over their shoulders like sashes and had kicked out with all their legs at their opponents even as they died. They had to cut their claws out of rumps and heads to bury them. I have no female companion, or not a steady one who might cry for me. They will declare me dead immediately, a leader, fallen honourably in battle with enemy powers, and send someone else, someone equal to me, to complete the mission. He will take my place and suffer the same fate. Or, if he's lucky, a worse fate that forces him to prove his true greatness. Only the battlefield makes heroes out of soldiers. My sole consolation is that I won't have to envy him for it.

I have sent out a distress signal, which only the initiated can understand. It is an old atter udder recipe. The preparation method reveals my location. But if they do decipher the data they won't come to get me. They'll give me up. Where nothing is, nothing can be. My message is a farewell note. They won't read it until after my death and they'll decide it's far too late to save me.

Wherever I may be now, it is just as inhospitable as Tubal IV. They say you take the image you have of one world into another, to make it easier to adapt to the new conditions. You look for the familiar in the new, until the new becomes familiar. Severe snowfall makes it impossible to see anything with my own eyes. If I were to look outside now I would recognize nothing to use as orientation. Everything is white. At first glance, that appears more helpful than if everything were black. At least it's light. Yet I am not capable of determining the position of the sun by the shadows cast by the equipment. The snow might also be a new strategy to veil our arrival. We've been experimenting with weather phenomena in this field for some time. I can't rule out that I might be part of another promising test run, which, like the others before it, ends in disaster. They didn't inform me. Some spaceships that were equipped with manipulators melted in mid-air, others caused floods. Since then, the tests have been carried out underground, in tiny laboratories with consoles smaller than the tips of my claws.

The instruments before me register values exceeding all proportion. All of them are glowing as brightly as possible. Even though I'm shielding my eyes their constant glimmer bedazzles me like a dozen suns. I have to rely entirely on my instincts. At the moment I'm floating half a malec above the surface. But I'm sinking all the time. Something is pulling me down. I've had plenty of opportunities to simulate emergencies. I've been through all the phases during my five-year flight: pain, desperation, indifference. But now that the end is within claw's reach, I yearn for it. Having recourse only to your own thoughts, no matter how great they may be, leads you back to the beginning of your thinking over and over again, the longer the journey takes.

I consider landing in a chasm before I crash or come to land in a place with no cover. On my approach I saw mountains and valleys and domes, shining golden like the roofs of the Holy City. I flew over streets and houses, over pyramids and temples, peaked and strong and reaching high into the sky, deceptively similar to the temples of my home. It may well be that we have already settled this planet and there are occasional Kedron colonies here and there already. Or it might just be a projection to put me off my guard. The first rule you learn at the imperial academy is to distrust everything, including and above all the first rule. Every image could be a copy and every word a quote.

If I were to land on one of the poles I could hide the ship for centuries. In every other place on this goddamned planet, I have to hope to float down from the sky unnoticed. In densely populated areas, the inhabitants, if they were below me, even here in this all-encompassing white, would see me as a light, as the reflection of an even brighter light which they have no idea exists. But the less they know, the greater the risk of being glorified. Every discovery gives birth to a new legend and every legend brings new disciples. They might take me for a meteor and make pilgrimages to the collision point to dig up every millimetre of ground in search of a lump of charred rock. They raise dead stars to the status of gods and worship their relics. How often have I seen Alvoranians and Laomers amazed at the prospect of their own insignificance, their limbs entwined and pointing at constellations whose existence arises solely from the restrictions of their own intellects. They make a connection that doesn't exist, and they think they can make deductions about the future from it. Nothingness has always been a firm part of their faith, and there is little hope that anything will change in that regard. All attempts to tell them the full truth have failed. They're not yet mature enough. And it is hard to bear when you find out your life is based on a mistake. That must be how companions feel who think they form a happy community, until one of them finds out the other has been cheating on them from the very beginning. First they don't want to believe it, then they accept it because their anger finds a valve in hate and a separation makes a new order possible. But how can you separate from yourself? Reality is a borderline experience, one that drives even the strongest minds to insanity.

Whoever is down there would recognize me instantly. Not as one of them, unless they really are Kedrons, but as an outsider, as someone who has come to take their queen, divide her into two equal halves with a single blow in a duel and decapitate her eggs. The news of my arrival and her death could not be kept secret. Barely had her ptomaine diffused in the corridors, I would have to fight against an entire people. I'd have to fight hundreds of battles and I'd be alone against a world. That would change little about the mission with which I'm inscribed. I, Kraan, son of Kron, am a master of loneliness.

Perhaps they've been waiting for someone like me. I could be their saviour. I would relieve them of the burden of forever having to concentrate on themselves. The fantasy that my presence releases in them would explode their imaginations and mobilize unsuspected powers within them. They would grow through my greatness. My strength would challenge theirs. Their evolution would skip several stages at once and yet never achieve the level of my intelligence and our collective abilities.

They prepared me to be persecuted. They prepared all soldiers for it. Those who conquer the gods always attract the mortals' hate. Two ships took off along with mine, swinging in to match my course shortly after we left Tubal IV's orbit. One smashed against an asteroid, one stuck to my tail despite many direct hits, like a rabid dwar. No one can forget thousands of years of war. The universe is our enemy. All peoples despise us, and we despise them. Between them and us is a wall of blood. All I have to do is reach out my antennae and their tips are instantly red or green, depending on which direction I choose. The attachments we make are of a purely strategic nature. They serve the sole purpose of protecting the empire and our ancestors' honour and securing the continued existence of our species.

The engines have failed and the protective shields have retracted. I'm losing more and more altitude. Making impact is unavoidable. Clouds seem to be circling around me but below me is an opening that reveals a field. My ship's rear is still coated in snow. Yet soon they will see me.

I touch down with a crash. I open the hatch and descend the ramp. For a while, I stand there, in the middle of a clearing, enveloped in clouds of the hot, bloodthirsty breath streaming out of my tracheae. Before me stands a human, clothed only in a loincloth, and stares down at me and my spaceship. I hadn't realized humans were so large. Upright, I only reach up to his toes. They looked much smaller in the pictures they showed us. But there were no sizes or scales given. All that mattered was their outer appearance, their weak points, the mouth, nose, ears, eyes, open wounds. Easy prey.

I whip out my gornik. I will fight, if need be against the whole world. I will hold out until the very end. If I sacrifice my mandibles I will use my claws as clubs and my forehead as an axe to split my victims' skulls. Only when all my limbs are severed, my mouth and eyes are sealed, will I admit defeat. Even then I would express my chagrin through the rising and falling of my chest. They can stab ten of my kidneys, and still the others will do their duty. They can eat my brain, tear out my stomach and feed it to their animals, and my eight-chambered heart will beat all the more wildly. My death must be agonizing. That is my destiny.

Dirk Schmidt

Federal Intelligence Service

Heilmannstraße 30

82049 Pullach near Munich

17 September 1999

Dear Mr Schmidt,

We have only met once, or at least that's the only meeting you
can remember. I've been watching you, and you haven't spotted
me. So you were right to assume I would be extremely well suited
for a position in your organization. I am a master of playing
not only with words and numbers but also with masks. On 23
July, you were sitting in Kiepenkerl, Table 1, right next to the
entrance. Excellent choice, an excellent overview of the whole
restaurant and a wonderful view of the Spiekerhof out of the
window. You can see who's there, who comes and goes and who
prefers to wait outside, for whatever reason. You ordered a bottle of Condrieu, 1997 vintage, venison stew with mushrooms
and vanilla fool with rum and flaked chocolate for dessert, and
you spent four hours talking to a woman who was far too young
and far too blonde. The two of you then took a taxi to your second home on Goldstraße 23. On 2 August, on your return by
train from Munich, you took a room in the Krautkrämer Hotel,
Room 23, directly adjacent to that of Halil Pandza, a Turkish
underwear rep of Bosnian extraction who is suspected of contacts to the Balkan mafia and Islamists. He was supposed to
meet a man in the city—you didn't know who—and take receipt
of an envelope—you didn't know where. You tailed him all day.
You followed him into every fashion store in the pedestrian
zone. You strolled twice around the city centre with him on
the promenade. You ate together, at separate tables, at Schloß
Wilkinghege, mussels for him, lobster for you, and afterwards

[handwritten annotations:] I won't write now where and when that was — You'll have to find it out yourself. My disguise is so perfect that I sometimes think I've already been through the transformation. But when I look in the mirror I can't spot any symptoms to indicate it.

153

you sat in the Schloß Theatre, Row 12, Seat 14, *The General*.
Later, you had the privilege of watching him down one vodka
after another at the hotel bar. You tried to keep up with him,
with his pace, with his stamina, but in the end you had to admit
defeat. His skill at leading you astray was a hundred times superior to your skill at keeping your attention up. He checked out
at 6.14 a.m., you at 8.37, still drunk. [*You paid with your own credit card.*] I don't envy you your life;
the reports you write testify to the boredom and sorrow you feel
at having to note down every detail of these equally boring and
sorrowful existences. If you were honest to yourself you'd admit
that you've long since stopped enjoying watching others, especially when you're being watched, as you're now realizing, not
only by those you watch yourself. The romantic idea with which
you began your career, fed on books and films, has given way to
dreary everyday life. You spend more time at the office than in
fast cars, your foreign postings are limited to two per year, [and] [→ *in places where you'd never go on holiday*]
instead of climbing the ranks at HQ, planning operations or run-
ning your own department, you've spent the past twelve years
as a field representative in Münster with the code name 'Boned
Ham'. And yet you dream of one day finishing the screenplay
you're working on, *The Snake*, so you can make your name as a
writer. But you're not Ian Fleming or Robert Ludlum. Knowledge of procedures, experience, talent, style, discipline—all
that's not enough, and you know it. You have to experience
more to tell an exciting story. [*212. 185. 191. 128, IBM Thinkpad 600, Windows NT 4.0.*] It's not important how I got all
this information and insight. [*You forgot the SP and ignored the DLLs and paid no attention to who was standing behind you*] As you can see, I have no interest
in working for you. But I do have an exciting story for you. And [*at the Cebit trade fair. Microsoft, Hack the Evil Empire!*]
you could experience something that's worth writing down. In
other words: I want to offer you a job. However, you'd have to
take a number of precautions and forget everything you think
you know. What use is your insight into human nature if it's
based on false assumptions, if the humans you concentrate on
so intently that you've become alienated from yourself aren't

humans at all? What if they're all wearing masks and you can't trust anyone, not even your superior officer? If the commands you receive violate the principles to which you're obliged? If you yourself, without even realizing, walk through a mirror and suddenly find yourself on the other side? Too abstract? Aliens have been landing on earth for centuries. Some of them—I call them diplomats—live to a biblical age. Others have shorter life-spans. They die with the bodies they occupy. You can spot both kinds by the way they look, a flicker in their eyes. I think they reverse our polarity with that look and a word that they use. Not deliberately, not out of malice. That's what they're pro-grammed for. They're simbionts. As they're dependent on us, I assume they must have dispersed all around the world. But only isolated individuals so far. That's why we have to build net-works, before they build their networks. There's a Big Festival planned in Jericho for Sunday. That's their name for it, not mine. What it means is a comprehensive attack. Slaughter fes-tival would be a better name, although no blood will flow. I've found a way to stop them. I don't want to say any more about it here. I could have sent you huge amounts of documents, but I assume there's no need for me to convince you any more. I'll explain everything else when you're here. As I gathered from the Outlook calendar on your computer, you're currently at HQ in Pullach. By the time this letter reaches you, I will have taken the essential step. I don't know if I'll have regained enough strength by then to fend off the Plutonians alone. It may be possible that the transfer from one dimension to another might weaken me so much that I'll need hours or days to ready myself for an attack. In that case, I'll need your help. Keep my parents, who aren't my parents, and the police off my back. I've informed the chancellor and the presidents of several other states. I'm not really counting on their support, but I didn't want to let anything go untried. The more authorities find out about the

→ My girlfriend will be here too, if she gets through to me and passes the final test. Unlike you, however, she has never doubted in our world. But makes it more difficult to activate her.

155

invasion, the greater the chance to evade it. Of course, that also increases the risk of the Plutonians pre-empting us. I haven't let Tony Blair in on it, by the way. He doesn't have the look, but he has the mouth, if you get what I mean. And now the rules: Destroy this letter. Don't think about what you've read. Cancel everything. Come to Jericho right away. Don't talk to anyone on the way here. Put on your mirrored sunglasses, the ones you wore in the park on the 20th of June. They're mine. Follow these clues: a composer from Berlin, the van is parked outside, the model is the key, count backwards, 16 23 18 9 3 1 24 21. 17 3 1 10 14 14 17 3 15 24 2 1 10 1 10 21 21 18 25.

I know you have a department meeting

wilful duty tomorrow afternoon, and 800 kilometres is a long way.

I hope you didn't look into the sun on 11 August, either with or without sunglasses, otherwise you've either one of them now (my bad luck) or blind (your bad luck).

156

PART TWO

Heavy Metal

The Sea of Glass

He was late again, even though he'd left the house earlier than usual. He'd even taken the short cut past the parsonage across the churchyard to get to the old church hall on time, and still something—as always—had held him up. He could never say exactly what it was that made him late; it was something different every time. The way seemed longer and longer and he'd have to come up with a good excuse, a better one than last Thursday and all the Thursdays before that.

The *warft* mound on which the Reformed Church was built was surrounded by great oaks. Their branches were bare as bones and loomed, dark from all the rain of the past few days, into the gradually brightening afternoon sky. Leaves swept across the paving stones, got caught up in the withered flowers, in the grass, in the wire fence, trembling soundlessly in the wind. Aside from the chatter of a magpie perched on a cast-iron cross, all was silent. Daniel walked past the monument for the fallen soldiers, past the graves of farmers and foremen, employees and unemployed, and then over the hill, past the vaults erected by the area's largest entrepreneurial families—the Kramers, the Vehndels, the Rosings—until just before the bell tower, where he came to his own stone.

He clamped his bag more firmly under his arm, intending to walk straight on. He was almost halfway past the stone when he turned around, as if to reassure himself that the inscription hadn't vanished overnight. It hadn't. It was still there and it would always be there, as long as someone paid for the stone's upkeep: *Here lies Daniel Kuper. RIP.* Only the dates, *1898–1974,* didn't tally with his own.

In the eyes of his parents, neighbours and relatives, there was no doubt that his grandfather was resting in peace, as his grandmother had insisted on being buried a few metres away from him and had been given her own stone, which said *I have overcome the world.* Those who'd known her said she couldn't bear the thought of lying next to her husband in death like she'd lain next to him in life, side by side, him on the left, her on the right, breathing in his schnapps fumes every night. And as all the others lay to the left of him, the whole Kuper family and their *gespüüs,* and there was only enough space for her and all her descendants to his right, she'd had no other option but to leave a gap between him and her, to be filled in one day by their children and grandchildren—like the gap between the two mattresses on Daniel's parents' double bed, except that this gap would stay for ever, through all eternity.

Daniel had no memory of his grandmother. She had died of heart failure not before he was born, like his grandfathers and his other grandmother, but soon afterwards. Nevertheless, she had a firm spot in his consciousness, unlike all the others. She'd left to the family not only black and white photos, in which nobody could identify anyone any more, but also religious and medical literature, magazines like *The German Christian* and *The German Druggist,* and books: Goethe's and Schiller's collected works in individual editions, a reference book of flowers, *A Guide to Good Behaviour, The Young Lady's Beauty Book, My Struggle, My Son* and *My Path to God.* She'd been a doctor and had made his mother swear on her deathbed that Daniel would one day follow in her footsteps and would never take on his father's or grand-father's profession.

Almost everything Daniel knew about his grandmother, he knew from his mother. Once he was older she'd told him about her last hours, her legacy. He'd been playing in the attic and found a wooden box with his name on it, and he'd asked his mother what it was. Instead of saying he was too young for it, as usual when he found something, she had spread out the books and magazines in front of him and explained that it all belonged to him, although he wouldn't understand it yet, and that his grandma had lain in bed after a fall and whispered feebly the words that had been bottled up inside her all her life: 'Druggists are bad pharmacists, and pharmacists are bad doctors. The ones who fail their final medical exams become pharmacists, and those who fail their first medical exams become druggists. There's no lower you can go. The boy mustn't start at the bottom if he wants to achieve anything. He has to get in at the very top. Otherwise he'll get stuck, like my husband and your husband too, and us with them.' And once his mother had assured her she'd tell that to Daniel as soon as he was old enough, and give him the books and the money for university, his grandmother had fallen asleep and never woken up again.

From time to time, Daniel crept up to the attic and took out the books and magazines and flicked through them. He spent a long time looking at the anatomical atlases with their schematic drawings and the *Pschyrembel* clinical dictionary with its pictures of malformed and scrufulous bodies, filled with excitement and disgust. He took *My Struggle* for a novel about knights because of the golden sword on its blue binding, but he never got further than the first few pages. He picked up the others, with their brittle paper jackets and half-decomposed pages full of dust and shame, cast a brief glance at their titles—*Sexual Developmental Disorders* or *Thou*

Shalt Lead a Chaste and Decent Life—and put them back. The bible, with the words *The Holy Scripture* written in golden letters on its black binding, was the only book he took down to his room. At first he thought the Holy Scripture was a code, secret symbols only comprehensible to the initiated. Then his father explained that it was printed in Gothic type, and he taught him how to distinguish the *s* from the *f*, the *k* from the *t*, the *x* from the *r* and the *y* from the *h*, and Daniel vowed to read it, like he'd read *Treasure Island*, *Robinson Crusoe*, *Gulliver's Travels* and *Perry Rhodan* in the weeks before—from morning to night in school holidays and on the weekends, during the school term from lunch until dinner and then on and on after that, until his eyes fell shut, like on a high, addicted to never-ending new words and sentences and actually suffering withdrawal symptoms as soon as he'd reached the end of a book and wasn't yet ready to start the next one, afraid it might be less adventurous. But he gave up after only a few chapters. The register of names and ages from Noah to Abraham was too much for him so he skipped a few pages, started again, read about Sodom and Gomorrah, about Lot's daughters, about Abraham and Isaac, about Joseph and his brothers, and then he came to the first section that was underlined in red:

> And Onan knew that the seed should not be his; and it came to pass, when he went in unto his brother's wife, that he spilled it on the ground, lest that he should give seed to his brother. And the thing which he did displeased the LORD: wherefore he slew him also.

He didn't understand what it meant, so he asked his mother. But she didn't want to explain it and told him to ask his father; he knew all about it, she said. And when he went to his father he got almost the same answer, except that this time he was supposed to ask his mother.

'But she sent me to you.'

'How do I know what your grandma underlined,' said his father, not interrupting his shelf-stacking in the storeroom. 'Your mother's the one who was always huddled with her talking about things.'

'But—' Daniel began, holding out the book as if to prove the opposite.

'Nix,' his father butted in. 'Give it a rest with that stuff. You'll find out soon enough.'

He did find out, but not until years later—a few months ago— did he realize what it meant and why his grandmother had written a treatise by the name of 'On the Prospects of Operative Therapy in Certain Cases of Masturbation among Young Males'. His father said one thing about it and his mother another, but both stories had one thing in common—his grandmother had published the essay, originally planned as a dissertation, of her own accord after her supervising professor had rejected the subject as not scientific enough and religiously loaded, and she'd distributed it among students at the University of Kiel, which earned her the nickname 'Castrata', until she did gain her doctorate with a dissertation *On Haematometra and Pyometra at Climacteric and Preclimacteric Age*, set up a gynaecology practice, met her husband and gave up everything she'd achieved to live with him and start a family. And so the core of her theory, that those who didn't abide by the Ten Commandments fell sick and wasted away mentally and physically, had passed down the years and one generation to Daniel Kuper junior. After two sleepless nights of doubt and renunciation, he had rejected it.

When he looked at his watch he noticed they must have started already and there was no point in hurrying now, but he still hurried, ran down the hill, yanked open the gate and dashed across the road to the old church hall, in the insane hope of thereby turning the clock back and catching up by a few minutes.

The desks were arranged in five rows of pairs facing the pastor's lectern. All the seats were taken, except for one chair at the very front. He usually sat at the back because he was the last to arrive and the first to leave and he didn't want to disturb anyone when he sat down or got up. And he bridled as he closed the door behind him, hesitated to walk further into the room and past the others, who were first looking round at him and then back to the front so as not to miss Pastor Meinders' reaction. But the pastor remained calm and showed no outward sign that he was going to make an example of Daniel that day. He stood there—in his black suit and black shirt, leaning forward slightly, his eyes small and red behind his glasses, inflamed from hours and hours of lying in wait—and merely nodded, as if giving Daniel his permission to discard his jacket and bag and sit down in front of him, not punishing him for his lack of punctuality, his misbehaviour.

The old church hall had once been a kindergarten. Daniel had spent two years here before they'd all moved into the new building on Wall Street. The two sinks where they'd cleaned their paintbrushes were still next to the entrance; the picture rails on the walls were now used for hanging up coats. The parquet floor, weathered by a thousand tiny hands and feet, was coming loose in places, and as he walked he felt pieces of wood giving way beneath him and knocking together, lifted by his soles. Before the church had moved in, the building had been empty for a short while, only a few months but still long enough to give Ubbo Busboom, Paul Tinnemeyer, Jens Hanken and other older boys the idea of smashing the latticed windows with stones. By the time he and Volker had finally joined in, there was hardly anything left for them, only four or five panes, but while they were breaking them Daniel's father had driven past, as if he'd been drawn from kilometres away by the sound of smashing glass.

'I—' Daniel began, wanting to apologize for being late. He had thought it all out. He intended to say he'd been helping his

166

father in the shop after school and had lost track of time. He hadn't used that excuse for a while and it had always worked. But Pastor Meinders raised a hand, gestured at the desk in front of him and nodded again, this time looking at Volker, and at his sign Volker began to read from the Bible. 'In the beginning was the Word, and the Word was with God, and the Word was God. The same was in the beginning with God. All things were made by him; and without him was not any thing made that was made. In him was life; and the life was the light of men. And the light shineth in darkness; and the darkness comprehended it not.'

'So how do the four gospels differ from one another?' asked Pastor Meinders. He waited for the children to put their hands up but no one put their hand up apart from Simone. No one ever put their hand up apart from Simone.

'Simone.'

'Matthew begins with Jesus' family tree. Mark starts straight in with the baptism. Luke tells the story of the Baptist. And the Gospel of John has this prologue, which—'

'According to.'

'What?'

'According to,' said Pastor Meinders with a tired sigh, like someone who knows he won't improve people but can't stop trying. 'It's called *the Gospel according to John*, not of.'

'Oh, yes.'

'Why is that?'

'Because it's not by him, it's a record of Jesus' words, and some parts that we can't exactly—'

'No, I mean, why are there several versions of the gospel?'

'Because they weren't all written at the same time and there are different addressees and manifestations of the revelation,' said Simone.

'They could have just put it all together in one text. Why didn't they do that?'

'Because—' Simone began, but Pastor Meinders raised his hand again and looked over the heads of the front row. There was a crackling sound coming from somewhere. Some of the children ducked down behind those sitting in front of them, others flicked through their books or looked out of the window, through the flawless glass of the new panes, to the graveyard, until the pastor said 'Volker' and a sigh of relief passed around the room. Volker slipped the packet of liquorice he'd just torn open back into his pocket and said, 'So it's more realistic.'

'What's that supposed to mean? Are you trying to say it's made up?'

'Perhaps not made up, but they didn't know everything exactly themselves back then. There were some things they just picked up from others and only wrote down later on.'

'That doesn't mean it couldn't be made up,' said Daniel, and Pastor Meinders gave him an angry stare. 'I mean, when we tell a story about someone who's dead, someone we might not even have known personally, not everything is true either. Everyone would tell the story differently, in different words, and sometimes they do contradict each other, Matthew, Mark, Luke and John, I mean.'

'I see, you think so, do you?' said Pastor Meinders.

'Yes,' said Daniel, 'I do.'

'You turn up here, quarter of an hour late, I don't even want to know why because you'd only have to break the ninth commandment, and you have the temerity to maintain it's all made up!'

'Not all of it,' said Daniel. 'Some of it. And maybe not even with ill intent. We have to think of it like Chinese Whispers—the more often the message is passed on, the more it gets distorted.'

'I see,' said Pastor Meinders. 'We have to, do we?'

'Yes,' said Daniel. 'We have to. Or at least that's how I imagine it. I mean, they'd all been waiting centuries for the saviour, they hoped so much that he'd appear, and then when he got there maybe someone exaggerated a bit or didn't look too closely, and someone else got the wrong end of the stick, and that's why there's all these differences. I mean, it is a bit funny that Jesus heals two blind men in Matthew and only one in Mark.'

'That's not the point,' said Simone.

'What is the point then?' asked Pastor Meinders.

'It's about the truth,' said Simone. 'A higher truth.'

'No,' said Daniel. 'It's about faith.' Pastor Meinders nodded. A vague hope flashed through him that Daniel was now on the right path, not all was lost after all, he was just a soul gone astray who needed his guidance, like so many others, to return to the path of illumination, but then Daniel said: 'It's about ignoring all the contradictions and not resolving them.'

'Oh, man,' said Onno. Onno Kolthoff. Daniel had just started in the same class as him at school in the county town, Wilhelmine Siefkes Grammar School. An only child, parents divorced. 'It doesn't matter at all if it was two blind men or five or ten.' He lowered his head, his hair fell back over his face, and he picked up his two pencils again and resumed drumming the erasers on their ends against his thighs, inaudible to Pastor Meinders.

'Right,' said Volker, 'the main thing is that Jesus could heal blind people in the first place.'

'But if one guy writes it was one,' said Daniel, 'and the other one writes two, don't we have to doubt the rest of it too? I mean, if they're not even quite sure themselves what's true and what isn't—that makes the whole story totally implausible.'

'Doesn't it make the story more plausible, in fact, because there are two variations on offer?' asked Pastor Meinders, leaning forward and breathing a gust of putrefaction into Daniel's face. 'Would it have been better to hush up the contradictions and harmonize the four gospels?'

'No, definitely not,' said Daniel, pulling a face as if he was swallowing something rotten, 'but what I mean is that these four are trying to convince us that it all happened exactly like they say, more or less, and that's not possible, if you accept the contradictions. It can't have been like this one day and like that the next, depending on who's telling the story. I mean, either there are eyewitness reports or there aren't.'

'I'm beginning to doubt you're in the right place here,' said Pastor Meinders. 'We agreed at the beginning that we'd discuss the Bible and its interpretation, and I said I was willing to permit critical opinions, but what you're always doing is questioning the Word of God as a whole. And that's why I ask myself, and I've been asking myself for a while now, whether you want to be confirmed at all, whether you're at all ready to be accepted into the community. Or are you only doing it, like almost everyone here,' his hand gestured around the room, 'for the money?'

'No,' said Daniel.

'Then let yourself be drawn into it.'

'Into *what*?'

'Into faith. Release yourself from what you know, and let yourself be drawn into what's beyond the bounds of your imagination.'

'OK.'

'Just saying OK and agreeing with me isn't enough. You have to agree with HIM,' he pointed a finger at the ceiling and everyone followed the finger's direction with their eyes, 'and it has to come from yourself, from deep inside you. Don't think it'll just happen, like it or not. It won't work without your input, without effort and discipline. Take Volker's example. He's not baptized, hasn't been raised a Christian, and yet he's still here because he decided on it. Or Onno, whose own father has abandoned him and who now, although he might not yet admit it, is seeking a new, spiritual father, one who will never abandon him, no matter what happens.' Everyone but Pastor Meinders knew that Onno was only here because he needed money for records, records which, played correctly, contained messages from the devil. He'd told his mother you had to know evil to combat it, and confirmation classes were his way of releasing himself from Satan's temptations. 'And that's the most important prerequisite,' said Meinders, his eyes fixed on Daniel, 'no matter which path your parents took with the baptism after your birth, you're old enough now to make your own decisions. You have to know whether you want it or not. But if you do want it, you have to really want it. And that's why I'm asking you: Do you want it?'

'Yes.'

'Do you really want it?'

'Yes.'

'Do you commit yourself with your body and soul?'

'Yes.'

'Good,' said Pastor Meinders. He stepped back from the lectern, removed his glasses, wiped the sweat out of his wrinkles and the bags beneath his eyes, put his glasses back on, looked at the clock above the door and compared it to his watch. 'We'll take a short break now. Five minutes.' He'd never had to fight for anyone's consent in the old days, and now he struggled for every one of them. The devil and his angels had grown overpowering; they had scattered their enticements across the world and found fertile ground in the young souls. There, in the twilight of their hearts, doubt germinated, ready to take shape and unfurl. There was little to be seen of it yet but a few shoots pushing through here and there, which could be cut back with the right words, however. No one is without sin. Not even me. And he called out into the chair-scraping and standing-up and putting-on of jackets: 'I hope you've read the text I handed out last time, the *Heidelberg Catechism*.' It sounded like a threat, and when Daniel turned around to him again he saw Pastor Meinders taking a pack of Mother Superior's Melissa Spirit and a silver flask out of his pocket and unscrewing the lid. Daniel wondered how old he was and how many groups he'd confirmed before theirs, and he guessed there must have been many, because an earlier version of him featured in his parents' confirmation photos, standing upright alongside the boys and girls in his cassock and preaching bands, two heads taller than them, a giant with thick hair and a clear gaze, filled with zeal, pride and assurance.

Outside, some of the girls were sitting with their knees drawn up on the steps or the bike stand, Simone Reents, Tanja Mettjes and Susanne Haak, their arms folded across their chests. The boys were walking in a circle around the church and dragging at their cigarettes when they felt they weren't being watched.

There was nothing else to do. The slide, see-saw and swing that used to be next to the church hall had been taken down and put up again three streets away outside the new kindergarten, otherwise some of them, driven by boredom, might have succumbed to their attractions.

The sun was low in the sky, its rays barely reaching over the gables of the surrounding houses, and the roofs and trees cast long shadows. Daniel shivered, turned up his jacket collar, buttoned it up to his chin and put his hands in his trouser pockets. The weathercock on the church tower was now pointing north-east, so the wind must have changed in the past half hour. Not long to go and it would be winter.

He saw Volker and Onno disappear behind the church, and followed them. Standing in front of the tall building, he noticed the freshly grouted cracks, not for the first time, and the granite blocks that formed the base, the dark parts standing out against the pale bricks. There were sandstone inlets in the bell tower, which had been used as arrow slits during the wars between the East Frisian chieftains, and where windows and doors had once been their arches and cornices still protruded from the brickwork. But suddenly the church, with its extensions and conversions, seemed like the Bible; they'd made it and changed it, extended and narrowed it, added and taken away, depending on the needs of the time, until it had taken on its current shape.

He kept walking and arrived at the bricked-up northern portal which came up to his shoulders. For a long time he'd assumed it was built so low because people used to be shorter, but then Pastor Meinders had explained to them that it had been on the instructions of the Normans, who had come across the sea on ships in the ninth century and occupied the land in only a few years, not experiencing any major resistance. The low doorway was supposed to force the Christians, he said, to bow to the north as they left the church and pay respect to their new lords. Pastor Meinders had ignored Daniel's objection that the church had only been built three centuries later, and had quoted Jeremiah instead of responding. 'Behold, a people shall come from the north, and a great nation shall be raised up from the coasts of the earth.'

Volker was leaning against the wall lighting a new cigarette, and Onno spat on the gravel once he'd taken a drag from his own.

'All right?' asked Daniel.

Onno nodded.

'Pretty close cut,' said Volker. 'Lung yearnings increase exponentially with length of boredom.' He handed Daniel the packet and the lighter. 'Sometimes I wonder why I'm putting myself through all this in the first place. The lessons are getting longer and longer and the breaks are getting shorter. There's hardly any time left for living.' He inhaled deeply, expelled the smoke through his nose and looked at the ground. 'Oh well, it doesn't matter anyway.'

'What doesn't matter?' asked Daniel.

'Everything. Are you through yet?'

'Through what?'

'The Bible.'

'Halfway.'

'Well, then you know by now,' said Onno, stroking a strand of hair out of his face. 'Volker told me about it just now. His epiphany.' He rolled his eyes.

'What epiphany?'

'That we don't have a chance,' said Volker. 'No matter how hard we try, no matter what we do.'

'Why not?'

'He says because we're first-born sons,' Onno said and spat on the gravel again.

'God favoured Abel and not Cain,' said Volker. 'He said to the pregnant Rebecca: The elder shall serve the younger. And so it came to pass. Esau served Jacob. Out of the twelve sons of Jacob, then, the ten oldest were bad, they murdered, robbed and defiled their father's bed, and only the two youngest were good and selfless and were blessed. And God disliked Judah's oldest son, and he killed him. And Onan, the second-born—'

'I know,' said Daniel, 'he kills him too.'

'Yes, and it went on and on like that. When the Pharaoh wouldn't let the Israelites leave Egypt, God sent plagues across the land. He made the water rot in the rivers and destroyed the harvest with hail. He deluged houses and fields with frogs and gnats and flies and locusts. He infected people and animals with plagues and boils and draped the world in darkness for three days.'

Onno looked at Daniel and circled his flat hand around in front of his face several times, making sure Volker couldn't see it. Then he spat on the ground again.

'The tenth and worst plague, however, was upon the first-born. He killed them all at the same time. And if you think that only affected the Egyptians and not the Israelites—that's where you're wrong. Their first-born belonged to him alone and they had to pay a ransom if they didn't want to sacrifice them to him. They shall not appear before him empty-handed, it says. And us? Has a ransom been paid for me? For you? Or for Onno here?' He put one hand on Onno's shoulder. 'God's against us.'

'No one has to pay for me,' said Onno and took a step back out of Volker's reach. 'There's definitely no more kids coming after me. I'm an only child. Only children are spared.'

'Not at all,' said Volker. 'You're damned, damned to be lonely. It's—' A low-flying combat aircraft thundered over them. Volker kept talking but no one could understand what he said. He couldn't hear himself either and at some point he simply stopped.

'If it was true,' said Daniel once it was quiet again, 'then Rosing and Iron ought to be long dead.'

'What d'you mean by that?' asked Onno.

But before he could answer, Volker said, 'Cursed be the man before the LORD, that riseth up and buildeth this city Jericho: with the loss of his first-born shall he lay the foundation thereof, and with the loss of his youngest son shall he set up the gates of it!'

'Oh, that,' said Onno.

'Exactly,' said Daniel. Everyone in the village knew the quotation but hardly anyone ever said it out loud. In the Bible he'd inherited from his grandmother there was a bookmark at the place where it dealt with the conquering of Jericho, with a picture of an angel, a guardian angel. 'Rosing is a building contractor, he tarred the streets here and paved the pavements and built practically every new house—apart from ours, I hope—and he and Iron are in the best of health.'

'He's paid penance already,' said Volker. 'His wife—'

'You should know,' said Onno.

'What's that supposed to mean?' Daniel asked.

'He's paid penance already,' Volker said again.

'Nothing.' Onno shrugged. 'I'm just saying. 'Cause of the UFO.'

'That was years ago.'

'He's paid penance already,' Volker said for the third time, louder and faster this time. 'His wife had an accident, and his daughter,' now *he* moved his open hand around in front of his face, 'Wiebke, she's not quite right in the head. The prophecy only hasn't come quite true because it's from Joshua and not from God.'

Daniel said: 'I think you're getting tangled up in something that has nothing to do with you or me or Onno or anyone else.' He suddenly thought he knew why they'd been spending so little time together since they'd been at different schools—because they'd grown apart without noticing. He no longer agreed with what Volker said, and now, with Onno present, it seemed absolutely inconceivable that he ever had. 'And apart from that, it's different in the New Testament, and that's what's most important for us, if at all, and Jesus is the first-born in that part.'

'Yes, exactly,' said Volker. 'And what did he do?'

'What do you mean?'

'He told his apostles the parable of the prodigal son. Again, it's the younger son who's favoured. He moves away and squanders his inheritance, and when he comes back poverty-stricken and dirty the father gives him the finest robe, puts a ring on his finger and slaughters the fatted calf for him. The fatted calf!'

'They're all just stories,' said Daniel, lighting up a cigarette at last. But he'd barely taken his first drag when one of the three bells above them began to ring. 'The zombie bell!' said Daniel.

'Yep,' said Onno. 'Time to go.'

The three bells had been melted down and replaced by new ones twice over, and Pastor Meinders had given them a list of their inscriptions at the very beginning of their confirmation classes, telling them to memorize them. The smallest bell, which rang at every hour or announced children's deaths, had been inscribed before the First World War *In honour of the remembrance of all deceased and missing seamen* and before the Second *Be thou faithful unto death, and I will give thee a crown of life.* Since the 1st of October 1951—they had to learn all the dates too—it had borne the verse *Thy dead men shall live, together with my dead body shall they arise*, and that was what Daniel thought of whenever he heard the sound of the bell, and every time he thought of it he shuddered, even though he didn't believe in anything any more, neither in zombies nor in what it said in the Bible.

Once they'd trodden on their cigarette butts and stepped out into the graveyard, they saw that the others had already vanished into the village hall.

'We're in trouble now,' said Volker, not turning around to the other two.

And Daniel said: 'More than in trouble.'

'Have you learnt the text?' Onno asked.

Daniel shook his head.

'May God have mercy on you, then.'

'That won't happen,' said Volker as he opened the door for them. 'Not according to everything I've read.'

There was a tense silence in the room. Nobody was saying anything; nobody was flicking through the books on the desks. Pastor Meinders had been waiting for them. He looked at them from his lectern, watching their every move as they came towards him, took off their jackets and sat down at their desks, and this silence prepared him for the outbreak that was to put an end to it all.

'From where do you know your misery?' he asked Daniel.

But before he could respond, all the others answered in unison: 'From the Law of God!'

'What does the Law of God require of us?'

'You shall love the Lord your God with all your heart, with all your soul, and with all your mind. This is the first and great commandment. And the second is like it: You shall love your neighbour as yourself. On these two commandments hang all the Law and the Prophets.'

Some couldn't keep up or lost track in the middle, and they waited for an opportunity to join in again. Until one arose, they tried to adapt to the others' rhythm or underpin it with a loud hum like on Sundays with the Lord's Prayer after the sermon at church. The words hailed down around Daniel like bullets. He turned around and around, as if that might help him dodge them, but all of them hit their mark because Pastor Meinders showed them which way to take with his strict stare.

'Can you keep all this perfectly?'

'No,' they all said, 'for I am prone by nature to hate God and my neighbour.'

'You haven't prepared, Daniel Kuper,' Pastor Meinders said at last, in a voice with which Daniel was familiar. Relieved, he breathed out and slumped forward, unable to prevent it. He smiled; it had all been a joke.

Pastor Meinders smiled too and wrote something on a piece of paper. Then he looked up. 'Will God allow such disobedience and apostasy to go unpunished?'

'No,' said the others, 'He is terribly displeased with our inborn as well as our actual sins, and will punish them in just judgement in time and eternity, as He has declared: Cursed is everyone who does not continue in all things which are written in the book of the Law, to do them.'

He put the sheet of paper in an envelope and handed it to Daniel. 'Give this to your father, please.' Daniel was reaching out his hand for it when Pastor Meinders withdrew the envelope. 'No,' he said. 'I can do it myself. I see him every day.'

'What is it?'

'You'll see soon enough.'

'You're not going to confirm me, are you?'

'I don't plan to, no.'

'But I gave you my word.'

'Your word! You're always late, you never take part in the lessons, you—'

'That's not true.'

'All right, you do take part, but your contributions always undermine the class. And you never prepare for lessons. If you really wanted to be confirmed, you ought to behave like it. Whatever you promise, you break at the same moment. If you say, for instance, I'll never squint my eyes again, you squint your eyes while you're saying it. And before, when you agreed with me three times, there was a twitch at the corner of your mouth every single time, there, there it is again, like someone who doesn't take himself seriously. There's nothing to rely on with you. You assert goodwill but you never show it.'

Daniel couldn't help thinking of his grandmother again, of the underlinings and notes she'd made, but he didn't have the guts to raise the subject because then he'd have to mention the other thing, the one he didn't dare talk about. 'It's just,' he began, thinking about what to say. Then he said: 'I can't manage it, it's too much.'

'What's too much?'

'The homework.'

'Nonsense, it's nothing at all. God—'

'God is dead,' someone said from the back. It was Onno, and Pastor Meinders leant forward to see who had said it. Some of the kids laughed, having seen the words countless times alongside the swastikas, sketches of genitalia and phone numbers on the walls of school toilets and considering it a great slogan, although they didn't know its true originator or understand its full meaning.

'Oh no,' said Pastor Meinders, 'God isn't dead. He's alive.' His face had turned red all of a sudden; he was breathing heavily and he ran the back of his hand over his lips. 'He's more alive than ever, don't you see that? All you have to do is open up a newspaper or turn on the television. Right now he's destroying a realm of darkness and delusion, tearing down its wall, razing its fortress, he's driving the people onto the streets and leading them to the light. And all that with no violence whatsoever. Never has God's rule shown itself more powerful and milder than in these past weeks.'

'That's got nothing to do with God,' said Daniel.

'Oh, really?' said Pastor Meinders, straightening up again. He was exhausted. They were finishing him off. The stake was already deep in their flesh, deeper than he'd thought. He dabbed the sweat from his forehead with a handkerchief. 'How do you think they stood it for so long over there in the first place, for forty years? And how did it all start, and where? Don't underestimate God's power—it's hope and life, it's all we have, all that's left to us, and that means everything else is nothing.'

'But Daniel's right,' said Simone. Everyone except Pastor Meinders turned around to her. Et tu, Simone? 'We've got so much homework at the moment, and we come here once a week and Sundays there's church and—'

'I have mercy on whom I will have mercy, and I will have compassion on whom I will have compassion,' Pastor Meinders spoke very quietly, barely audible for the others, as if saying a prayer to himself, his eyes closed and his hands folded in a whisper and a murmur as if to calm himself. But it was too late; Satan's messenger was here, and he could not be got rid of using words alone.

'I've been wondering for a while now what the difference is between school and *konfitje*,' said Daniel.

Pastor Meinders paused, opened his eyes and called out: 'The difference? The difference is that you have to go to school, but you don't have to come to confirmation classes. You can leave whenever you want.'

'All right, if you say so,' said Daniel, and he gathered up his belongings, took his bag and his jacket and stood up.

'Where are you going?' asked Pastor Meinders.

'Home. You said this is voluntary, so—'

'Sit down. Sit down this minute.' He was shouting now, and his voice broke as he spoke. 'And stay sitting down until the end of the lesson. There'll be consequences. I won't let you get away with this, not this.' His lips trembled, he was dizzy, and he felt the yearning rising within him to reach for the flask in his pocket. He had already stretched out his hand for it when he remembered the doctor's advice, Doctor Ahlers' words—to take a deep breath in and out if it happens again, and look for something to focus his eyes on. He found something on the piece of paper in front of him and said: 'Now let's come to the *Salvation of Man.*'

It was growing dark outside already and he instructed Volker to switch the light on. Then he asked more questions but the answers, now recited by individuals at his prompting, didn't reach him any more. Later, when the others had long since left and he and Daniel had been sitting facing each other in silence for a while, he made notes in a book in the shape and design of a class register, but much smaller, only half the size, which fitted into any pocket. He didn't know himself exactly what he was doing. He simply hoped the sentences he wrote would give him strength to counter evil, as soon as it assumed its true form. Once again he recollected the course of the lesson, before saying, not looking up or putting the pen aside, 'Aren't you even ashamed of yourself?'

And Daniel said, 'Shame is my constant companion.'

Again he drew the pen across the page, as if he were noting down the statement word for word so as to use it against him as evidence of his guilt at the next opportunity.

'Have you got no sense of decency?'

Daniel remained silent, not wanting to read or hear again what he'd once said. But Pastor Meinders wrote minutes of his silence as well. He took even more detailed minutes of it than of his speech. The silence seemed to be an irrefutable admission, but one that was more difficult to capture as it took up more space in the book than the words Daniel had said. Pastor Meinders turned the page, started over on the top left of the next sheet and wrote and wrote until that page was full too, and only when Daniel rose from his seat and leant forward to see what he was writing did he stop writing mid-sentence and slam the book shut.

'I'm starting to realize that you not only have something against faith, against the Bible, the church and the community, but also and especially against me.'

Daniel shook his head. 'That's not true.'

Pastor Meinders opened the book again. He didn't write anything, though, but merely pointed the pen at the windows behind which it had now grown so dark that they were both reflected in the glass and the tip of the pen was aimed at Meinders' double. 'First you smash the windows here, then,' he nodded at the ceiling, 'the nonsense with the aliens, with which you made fools of us all for weeks, and now this.' He slapped the page so hard that it made a bang, as if Daniel had polluted the paper with his words and not the air that he breathed. 'How can I interpret it as anything but a personal attack?'

'I only wanted to demonstrate that—'

'Oh yes, demonstrate, your generation are good at that!'

'No, I mean, I wanted to show that *konfitje* is voluntary. I got up because I have the right to get up and leave whenever I want, you said so yourself.'

'You do have the right, yes indeed. Nobody's forcing you to stay, least of all me.'

'Fine,' said Daniel, 'then I'll leave now.' He got up, wedged his bag underneath his arm and walked to the door, determined to leave and never come back. But he'd hardly got there, his hand already reaching out for the handle, when he heard the loose wood panels of the parquet floor knocking against each other. He wanted to turn around but at that moment Meinders clipped him round the ear.

'God won't let you leave as easily as that,' he roared, holding Daniel by the collar with his left hand, slapping him again with his right. 'Not until you've paid penance and asked Him for forgiveness.'

Daniel dropped his bag and it fell soundlessly to the floor. He tried to pull away and he managed it, even making it outside, but then he tripped on the step and fell flat on his face. Pastor Meinders bent over him and pressed him to the ground. Daniel struggled and wriggled, but every movement merely dug him deeper into the earth. Pastor Meinders held him down with his knees. The seven angels had come to give him succour, and they handed him the vials of wrath so that he might pour them out. And he poured them out as he had never poured anything out, with vigour to the very last drop. He laughed, his face pale with fear and horror at his own deed: 'Cursed shalt thou be in the city, and cursed shalt thou be in the field. Cursed shall be thy basket and thy store. Cursed shall be the fruit of thy body, and the fruit of thy land, the increase of thy kine and the flocks of thy sheep. Cursed shalt thou be when thou comest in, and cursed shalt thou be when thou goest out. The Lord shall send upon thee cursing, vexation, and rebuke, in all that thou settest thine hand unto for to do, until thou be destroyed, and until thou perish quickly; because of the wickedness of thy doings. The Lord shall make the pestilence cleave unto thee. The Lord shall smite thee with a consumption, and with a fever, and with an inflammation, and with an extreme burning, and with the sword, and with blasting, and with mildew. And thy heaven that is over thy head shall be brass, and the earth that is under thee shall be iron. The Lord shall make the rain of thy land powder and dust: from heaven shall it come down upon thee. The Lord shall cause thee to be smitten before thine enemies: thou shalt go out one way against them, and flee seven ways before them: and shalt be removed into all the kingdoms of the earth. And thy carcase shall be meat unto all fowls of the air, and unto the beasts of the earth, and no man shall fray them away. The Lord will smite thee with the botch of Egypt, and with the emerods, and with the scab, and with the itch, whereof thou canst not be healed. The Lord shall smite thee with madness, and blindness, and astonishment of heart: And thou shalt grope at noonday, as the blind gropeth in darkness, and thou shalt not prosper in thy ways: and thou shalt be only oppressed and spoiled evermore, and no man shall save thee. Thou shalt betroth a wife, and another man shall lie with her: thou shalt build an house, and thou shalt not dwell therein: thou shalt plant a vineyard, and shalt not gather the grapes thereof. Moreover, all these curses shall come upon thee, and shall pursue thee, and overtake thee, till thou be destroyed; because thou hearkenedst not unto the voice of the Lord thy God, to keep his commandments and his statutes which he commanded thee.'

It was only when he collapsed in exhaustion over Daniel that Pastor Meinders saw it wasn't seven angels standing beneath the lamp, but seven boys and girls. They had been waiting for Daniel and now they scattered to proclaim the tale to all the village.

The very next day—Daniel had only suffered a few scrapes and bruises, to which no one, not even he, paid any heed—Pastor Meinders had departed for Israel. It must have seemed like running away to them all, but he'd booked the holiday months previously, and now he used it to find peace again, *his inner balance*, as he wrote to Daniel once he'd apologized to him, *peace in his soul*, and he did find it there, albeit differently than expected. First he worked in a kibbutz, then he wandered the Negev Desert for forty days and nights. Over Christmas—the vicar held the Christmas service—there was a rumour he was dead, or at least missing, or at any rate his wife Marie had lost contact with him. At the end of January, however, he came back as if he'd never been away. As though nothing had happened, he took up his old position in the village, leading the services, communions and confirmation groups. The voice in his head had gone mute.

Daniel hadn't wanted to go back to begin with. His father and mother coaxed him, saying the other parents had been concerned about sending their children to him. But Pastor Meinders had put paid to all their fears that there might be another outbreak by immediately approaching them with outstretched arms, reformed and sober, to make reconciliation. He asked for forgiveness, as they in turn had asked him for forgiveness all the years before, although they weren't Catholics. And they forgave him.

Daniel was confirmed on a Sunday at the beginning of April. It was warm, almost summery. The sun was shining and the boys started sweating in their new suits early in the morning as they walked through the wide churchyard gate, accompanied by their parents, towards the Reformed Church. Dandelions blossomed on the graves and the leaves on the trees were fully formed.

The sacristan held the door open for the confirmands, and Daniel instantly thought he was walking into a village meeting. The vestry was tightly packed with people, all with their backs to him, looking over the heads of those in front of them as if at a faraway goal. There was no getting through, and it was only when one nudged another and they all shifted apart that it emerged that there were several passageways through which they proceeded inside. The oak pews on the left and right were fully occupied; up in the gallery people were standing on either side of the organ stops, some half-leaning over the balustrade, pushed from behind. He spotted his parents and the twins on the pastor's family pew. His father took no notice of him, talking animatedly to Mrs Meinders who was sitting next to him, her head almost resting on his shoulder, probably to hear him better in all the noise. The twins laughed when they saw Daniel and pointed their little fingers at him. His mother waved at him. He didn't wave back, though; the thought that they might be related to Meinders, no matter how distantly, paralyzed him almost entirely for a moment, his arms dangling, his polished shoes shuffling along the floor. He wished he had overcome the world already, like his grandmother.

The only thing still propelling him forward was the hope that it was a coincidence and there hadn't been any other seats available in the church.

The candles in the crown of lights above him were burning, although the whitewashed walls and the high windows made it so bright that their flames were barely visible in the milky light and he had to shade his eyes to see them. The organ was playing and the confirmands paced two by two over the large sandstone slabs of the central aisle towards the font.

Pastor Meinders came and all conversations died out. He ascended the pulpit and greeted the congregation, they sang a hymn, Simone and Volker took turns reading Psalm 27, Pastor Meinders recited the opening prayer, and at the deacon's bidding Daniel read from the first Book of Kings, Chapter 19, Verses 2 to 8, an extract from the story of the divided kingdom. 'Then Jezebel sent a messenger unto Elijah, saying, So let the gods do to me, and more also, if I make not thy life as the life of one of them by to morrow about this time. And when he saw that, he arose, and went for his life, and came to Beersheba, which belongeth to Judah, and left his servant there. But he himself went a day's journey into the wilderness, and came and sat down under a juniper tree: and he requested for himself that he might die; and said, It is enough; now, O Lord, take away my life; for I am not better than my fathers. And as he lay and slept under a juniper tree, behold, then an angel touched him, and said unto him, Arise and eat. And he looked, and, behold, there was a cake baken on the coals, and a cruse of water at his head. And he did eat and drink, and laid him down again. And the angel of the Lord came again the second time, and touched him, and said, Arise and eat; because the journey is too great for thee. And he arose, and did eat and drink, and went in the strength of that meat forty days and forty nights unto Horeb the mount of God.'

The longer Daniel read, the heavier and more stifling the air seemed to him, inhaled and exhaled by a thousand lungs. Suddenly he was overcome by a fatigue that pressed him to the floor; he only picked up isolated words of the sermon, 'bread' and 'blood' and 'betrayal', and he didn't even have to move to receive the blessing, as he was already kneeling before Pastor Meinders like the others alongside him. He closed his eyes and relinquished himself to the hand that had driven the curses into him six months earlier.

'Do you want to be a member of the congregation that confesses the faith?' asked Pastor Meinders.

And Daniel answered as if in a trance: 'Yes, yes I will, yes.'

As a permanent symbol of this affiliation, the deacon put a nylon thread holding a droplet of glass around his neck and handed him a certificate with the appropriate aphorism: *And before the throne there was a sea of glass like unto crystal : and in the midst of the throne, and round about the throne, were four beasts full of eyes before and behind.* For longer than all the others, Daniel stood motionless before the font with his head lowered and his hands folded, as if he wanted to savour the feeling of submission to the full.

Heavy Metal

1

Peter Peters had never done anything to them. He had never done anything to anyone. They'd chosen him because he'd put up the least resistance. Weeks ago, they'd begun testing him out in the schoolyard. They had insulted him, laughed at him and tested his reactions. And now they were lying in wait for him.

They hadn't reckoned with him that autumn afternoon. They'd been sitting by one of the flooded sandpits which had been dug out decades ago, long before their time, for sand for the railway embankment. They had pelted ducks and anglers incessantly with acorns and stones, and smoked cigarettes until dark clouds gathered in the sky above them and the wind they brought with them chased through the half-bare trees and they got up and ran off so as to get home as quickly as possible. They didn't know that he'd take that route, or even that he was out that day, but when his shadow appeared before them in the haze of rain, they decided to take the opportunity to baptize him.

Peter Peters, whom they called Penis because of his name and his high forehead, had come towards them alongside the embankment on the Hoogstraat that connected Jericho and Drömeln. They spotted him from a distance, his drooping shoulders, his dragging gait, his figure always leaning forward slightly, and to prevent him looking up and disappearing before they got to him, they hid at intervals in the bushes on either side of the path until he was exactly between them.

Peter Peters was pushing his bike along the gravel because it had a flat front tyre. A few kilometres previously, he'd cycled through broken glass and been caught out by the rain in the hammrich fields. He often went on cycling tours; he loved the hollow sound of the tyres beneath him, the wind driving him on or holding him back, and the silence out in the fields, at the dyke, empty of people. He could cycle for hours without getting tired. When he went out on a tour, which happened several times a week, his brown leather bag held not only classification guides and notebooks, insect jars and a net, but also a thermos flask of coffee and sandwiches, as if he were going on an excursion and would stay away for longer than an afternoon, as if he were meeting someone for a picnic. But he never did meet anyone. He simply sat there, somewhere by the edge of the road, on the banks of a river, by a lake, on the beach by the sea, looked at the guides and wrote something in the notebooks—a line, an observation, a thought. He wanted to be a naturalist, a zoologist or a botanist. While others changed their career wishes every few weeks and adapted them to new needs, his always stayed the same. Sometimes he would get up, catch insects, put them in the jars and wait for them to stop moving. Then he'd give them a good shake and laugh as soon as they came back to life, eat the sandwiches he'd brought along with satisfaction—like after a long, hard day—and drink his coffee which was strong and hot. But not strong enough to stop him falling asleep and waking up again in the rain and walking into his tormentors.

By now he was soaked to the skin, just like them. And as he came closer they heard that he was sobbing—not like someone who's crying, not out of grief, but like somebody who's fallen through the ice and got out of the water, cold, wet and shocked. One of the boys, Stefan Reichert, was the first to come out of his hiding place and block Peter Peters' path. 'Hey, Penis, you *arm Bloot*,' he said, hands on hips. 'All alone out here, you poor thing? So far away from Mummy?'

Peter Peters didn't hesitate for a second. He let go of his bike, which fell with a clang and a crash to the ground along with his bag and an iron rod used to strengthen the luggage rack, and wanted to run away in the opposite direction. He did run a couple of metres, but when the other two boys, Onno Kolthoff and Rainer Pfeiffer, blocked his way he veered off and jumped into the trees—right into Daniel Kuper's arms.

For an instant they stood facing each other in silence, their hands interlocked, two wrestlers after the starting whistle, still careful, tentative, assessing the other's strengths and weaknesses through glances and touches, pale with amazement and horror. The rain pattered onto the leaves above them. A freight train loaded with new cars rushed past them, frightening a few animals that had sought protection in the trees and bushes around them. All Daniel had to do was step aside, and Peter Peters would have run past him, climbed the embankment and got away. He'd have had enough of a head start to reach one of the farms or the B70, to flag down a car and get a lift. But Daniel didn't step aside. Neither of them betrayed the slightest emotion, and the only thing Peter Peters said in the end, before the others grabbed him, was 'You too.'

Daniel and Stefan each wedged one of his legs under their armpits and Onno and Rainer took care of his arms. Peter Peters yelled and wriggled and they were occupied for a full half-hour with holding onto him, turning him on his stomach and not letting him go again, because he resisted every touch and kept slipping through their fingers, as wet as they were. Then all of a sudden his strength seemed to run out. They still felt the pressure in their hands, the desperate attempts to escape their grip, but there was no more determination, as if he sensed that every false move he made now would double the pain that awaited him.

When they got to the fence Rainer, the oldest and strongest in the group, grabbed both their victim's hands so that Onno could draw the bolt aside. Stefan pulled off Peter Peters' left boot to get a better grip on him, and Daniel did the same with the right one. They dragged him across the grass until the path along the embankment was only visible as a blur and then not at all. Their clothes stuck to their bodies, the ground was uneven and muddy and they made slow progress. At one point they all fell flat on their faces, but before Peter Peters could make a break for it they'd grabbed him again. Twice he called for help, but the rain was so loud that every sound was drowned out by the drumming of the water.

In the middle of the field, beneath a buzzing high-voltage power line, they took a break by pressing Peter Peters against the grass with their feet before they switched hands and picked him up again.

'We should have thrown his bike in a ditch,' said Stefan, 'or in the bushes.'

And Rainer said: 'No one'll come past in this weather anyway.'

'Penis came past.'

'Good job he did,' said Onno, 'or he'd have missed a treat,' and nodded sideways towards the drainage ditch as a sign to continue.

'Thirsty, Penis?' Stefan asked.

'No, I—'

'You must be thirsty, you've been out so long. You have to drink something, something other than rain, with more of a taste, more nutritional.'

'Leave me alone. Let me go. I won't—'

'You won't what? Tell on us?' asked Stefan. 'Why would you? Nothing's happened, has it?'

'No,' said Rainer, 'not yet,' and added, turning to face Onno: 'Do you know what he's talking about?'

'No, do you?'

'No,' said Daniel.

'Let me go.'

'Not until you've drunk something,' Stefan decided. 'Not before that.'

And so they dragged him on.

Out here, not five hundred metres from the river, the fields were larger than directly by the village and not divided by hedge banks but by broad ditches into which the rain and slurry flowed via underground drainage pipes.

They weren't intending to throw Peter Peters in one of these ditches or dunk him in the river until he ran out of breath. All they wanted was to give him a going-over, for his appearance and his name. That was what they called a baptism, among themselves.

Cows grazed on the lower fields and some of them had stepped out of the fog up to the fences, into the clear light, and were looking over at them in curiosity.

'Look at them,' said Stefan, pointing at them. But they held Peter Peters in such a way that he couldn't lift his head high enough to make out more than the cows' front feet behind the tall grass on the bank. 'Take a good look at them,' Stefan repeated. 'You'll soon be one of them.' And he grabbed him by the armpits from behind and shoved him towards the drinking trough, an automatic drinker where the cows pressed their muzzles against a long yellow cast-iron tongue to pump water out of the ditch into a green bowl. But the stuff Peter Peters pumped up with his forehead was brown, a thick, murky liquid.

Daniel sat on the boy's legs, Onno bent his arms back behind his back and Stefan kept pushing his crossed hands against the back of his head, ten or fifteen times, as if he were trying to bring a drowned man back to life and not the other way around, making a live man drown.

Then Rainer said: 'That's enough. That'll do now.'

And that was it.

They let Peter Peters go and ran, howling and treading on one anothers' heels from behind, across the field, along the Hoogstraat back to the village, not turning round to look at him. They never talked about what had happened.

When Peter Peters got home later, covered in dirt and with blood on his face, he said he'd fallen off his bike and lost consciousness for a moment, perhaps longer. His parents, fearing the worst, took him straight to the doctor. Their other son, Peter's older brother, had been trampled by a breeding bull the previous year as he took it out to pasture, then stood up as if nothing had happened and died the next night. They didn't call the doctor in advance, just got in the car and drove off. So they only found out from a note on the door that their GP was on holiday and anyone who needed treatment should go to Jericho, to Doctor Ahlers, whom they'd never been to before.

The waiting room was full and they had to wait a long time, and the other patients looked at them all along, out of the corners of their eyes, not saying anything. Their clay-smeared, manure-splashed boots had left marks on the linoleum, wet brown footprints leading from the entrance past the reception desk to them, and their farmers' clothing, rough and covered in stains, would dirty the upholstery just as much as the floor, only more strongly, more deeply, less easy to remove. The Peters were locals; they lived in Drömeln, on a small farm on the B70 that had been in the family for generations. But they didn't have much land or livestock, so they had no influence. The father wasn't on the board of the cooperative bank or the dairy; he didn't even live entirely on agriculture, earning half his income as a metalworker at the shipyard. And the mother had a job on the side too, as a cleaning lady in wealthier farmers' houses. The moment their name was called and the door closed behind them, voices were raised in the waiting room.

Peter Peters told Doctor Ahlers what he'd told his father and mother. Doctor Ahlers listened attentively and made notes, then he disinfected the abrasion on the boy's head, shone a flashlight in his eyes, took his pulse and blood pressure and prescribed an anti-epileptic drug.

Propping each other up, the Peters family left the surgery, crossed the road and collected the prescription in the Friesen Pharmacy.

Wilfried Ennen, the pharmacist, told his wife about it that evening, and she told her friend the next morning at Dettmers' Hairdressing. From then on people saw Peter Peters as someone who'd fallen once and would fall again.

After that afternoon, during that night, Daniel lay awake for a long time. The rain hit the dormer window with all its might. And the walls groaned at every gust of wind, as if they wouldn't withstand the next one. Every time a train went past the house and the bed trembled to the rattle of the wheels, he thought of Peter Peters, of what he'd said to him in the bushes. And every time, a shudder ran down his spine.

2

They'd known one another ever since they could remember, since they were children. Stefan, Onno, Rainer and Daniel. Perhaps they'd played together in a garden sand pit or in their bedrooms or under their parents' supervision, but the memory of those days was as if erased. They didn't know when and where they'd first met, none of them could say, and whenever they talked about it everyone came up with a different occasion and an earlier one—

It is early morning, the fog is low on the fields, and when I look out at the land from the driver's cab, only the railway embankment ahead of me and everything white to the horizon, I feel like Jesus, borne by clouds to the heavenly kingdom. I've never flown but this is how I imagine it, floating high above the earth and looking down at something you've left behind you, at least for a while. It reminds me of my first times working on steam engines, of that quaking feeling of setting the whole world in motion with one hand movement, when we, the fireman and I, drew a comet's tail top and bottom behind us, and all those who heard us turned their heads and thought we'd take off the next instant and pull them along with us, despite the weight pressing us against the rails and

a birthday, a carnival procession, a day at the lake, at the seaside, at the swimming pool.

They'd gone to primary school together, in two different classes, had played football together and later tennis against each other. Onno and Daniel had been confirmed on the same day, and Stefan and Rainer had shared an early interest in machines and exchanged their knowledge, but they'd never really been friends until they were put in the same class at grammar school. For a while, two years, they'd shared the fate of coming from the same village and going to school in the county town, and that had made them allies despite all their differences.

In their very first summer, a few weeks before the assault on Peter Peters, they had met up one afternoon at one of the flooded sandpits alongside the railway embankment without any of them arranging anything beforehand. They took this silent agreement as a stroke of destiny, as a sign that they belonged together—especially as none of them had a fishing rod with them, unlike the other boys squatting between the bushes and trees on the banks

---

often enough forcing us to a halt. I thought that myself, as a child, when my father lifted me up and showed me the trains that passed by our house and made the walls tremble. He wanted to take away my fear of the nightmares that plagued me by night, wanted to show me there weren't any demons sweeping through my room in the dark, but all he did was make the demons take the form of trains, until I was old enough, with his help again, to tell real and imagined horrors apart.

Today I'm hauling tank wagons filled with liquid gas from Emden to Rheine. Someone else will take the freight from there to Cologne while I switch platforms and trains and return to the coast with new cargo. I've just left the town, I'm making good

to either side, baiting hooks with worms, with maggots, casting out lines and waiting until it got dark or they'd caught enough to view the day as a success. The four of them just sat there leaning against a tree stump, not knowing where else to sit if they didn't want to stay at home. The ponds were easy to reach along the train tracks but still far enough away not to be found immediately if anyone happened to look for them. They sat alongside each other almost motionless for hours, smoking, staring at the surface of the water speckled green with duckweed, throwing in stones from the railway track to annoy the anglers, and talking about school, music and horror films they'd seen or pretended to have seen.

Sometimes older boys joined them—Ubbo Busboom, Paul Tinnemeyer, Jens Hanken—when they didn't have any cigarettes and came to scrounge some from them. And they let them join in their conversations because they hoped to learn something from them in return, something they didn't know yet that might get them on in life, new things about girls. Everything they found out that way seemed both compelling and contemptible at once. They

time and I lean back, my hands behind my head. I hardly slept last night, another one of those sleepless nights. And now fatigue threatens to overpower me. I yawn and rub my eyes. Not looking, I take the thermos flask out of my work bag and wedge it between my legs. I unscrew the lid and pour out a stream of coffee. I drink it like wine, inhaling the scent, savouring the flavour before I take a sip. And it tastes like wine, sweet Amarena cherries, black truffles, dark chocolate, warm and soft and woody in the finish. I instantly feel the warmth starting to take effect. It shoots through my body like an electric shock and I feel awake. I stand up and put my face out of the window. The oncoming air hits me. I screw up my eyes and turn my head first in one direction, then in the

assured one another, their faces red with shame, that they'd never do any of those things, but they never got tired of talking about them and incorporating girls' names picked up from the TV or magazines into their negative fantasies.

'I wouldn't kiss Clarissa,' said Daniel. Nobody knew a girl called Clarissa. 'At least not with tongues.'

'No way,' said Stefan.

'Not Gabriele either.' The name Gabriele always made them all laugh; nobody knew why.

'Nope,' said Onno. 'Gabriele least of all.'

'She stinks,' said Rainer. 'And she does it with anybody too.'

'That's where you're wrong, young man,' said Daniel. 'You're confusing her with Bettina.' Bettina was hilarious, because they pronounced the name *Bett*-Tina and any mention of a bed was hilarious.

Over the weeks the girls developed a life of their own. Clarissa had first blonde, then black hair, but from day one she had large

other, looking at the multicoloured tanks behind me, seven hundred and twenty cubic metres of propane and butane, and I can't help thinking what I always think when I'm hauling tanks— bombs on wheels.

Dazed by that image, I lean back in my seat and look at the main air pressure gauge, the brake-cylinder pressure gauge, the speedometer. But I barely register the measurements because I'm imagining the stuff behind me blowing up in the middle of a residential area, perhaps even in Jericho, a wheel of fire rolling over the place and the people in a single instant and suffocating all life, a glowing breath faster than the wind, human torches staggering out of the flames before they stop, their arms raised in search of

breasts that she pressed together to make a crack in the middle into which everyone who met her stared as if down a canyon, with dizzy fascination. One day she met a farmer and got pregnant by him. She had to marry him even though she didn't love him, and she left him again when she found out he didn't only milk the cows in the stable but stimulated them from behind with his breath to make them give more milk.

Gabriele, short and fat, had a clubfoot and God had blessed her in the same department as Clarissa. Unlike her, however, Gabriele granted both breasts maximum freedom, so that when she moved, especially with the way she had of dragging one leg, they flopped around her hips like two bulging shopping bags. Due to her corpulence and her heavy, limping gait, she sweated so strongly that a puddle pooled beneath her wherever she stopped for a few minutes' rest. Her sweat ascended across the entire village and had an identical effect on men and flies—they felt magically drawn to her.

protection, and freeze in position, burnt into lumps. The fog is thinning. The sun is shining. The engine is humming. I drum my fingers on the handwheel, lost in thought.

I like driving freight trains. There's no one for me to take into consideration. I don't have to wait until the passengers have embarked and the man in the red cap raises his signalling disk. I simply speed through. The barriers are closed, or ought to be closed. The colleagues in the signal boxes and stations wave at me and I wave back. I've got orders and I carry them out. I collect my cargo and take it to its destination.

Something familiar or new appears before me at every second, and in the next second it's past me again. On clear days, you can

Bettina, though, was tall and slim, had green eyes, thick, curly hair that reached down to her waist and glowed coppery red as soon as the sun shone on it, her skin delicate and white as ivory and covered in freckles, a real beauty—with a single flaw: she had no arms. She had lost them in an accident. Stefan said it had been a riding accident. But Onno and Rainer disagreed because no one lost their arms that way, unless they fell off the stallion directly into a shredder. Instead, they claimed they'd seen with their own eyes that a tank had driven over her on the main road, failing to provide an explanation for why a tank might stray into the village in the middle of peacetime, which was why Daniel claimed she had done it herself, with a bread knife, to make herself even more interesting. At any rate, Bettina didn't have arms so she couldn't wash herself, and she insisted—even at an advanced age when her beauty had faded entirely and she lay in bed, weakened by all the admiration—on boys taking care of this task for her, boys like them, Stefan, Onno, Rainer and Daniel, and soaping her up and rinsing her down from top to bottom—especially the bottom.

see the whole route stretched out before you—four lines coming together on the horizon. At the height of summer there's often a shimmer above the rails. In the far distance I can still see cars and people dashing across the tracks, dark spots dancing in the air like gnats before a light. And then I'm there. And they tremble in front of me before I disappear from their lives again and they from mine. Now, at the end of April, the air is heavy with blossoms; pollen floats dense as snow across the land. Cows graze in the meadows. Farmers till their fields. The heavy smell of slurry rushes in at me and out again through the other window. Women clean the windows of their houses in risky positions. Children play in gardens. The paths on either side of the tracks are full of cyclists

There were other girls too, Sophie, Melissa, Hannelore, and other stories that tended to overlap. Dozens of life stories condensed down to a few years. None of them managed to tell them all apart, and at some point they lost interest again. They turned to new subjects that seemed more entertaining, more important, more pressing. But the girls' names still existed and became a kind of secret language that they used to exclude other people who didn't understand their true meaning. Sometimes even they didn't understand what one of them wanted to tell the others in the presence of outsiders, but whenever any of them mentioned Clarissa, Gabriele or Bettina without giving any kind of explanation of whom they might mean, it wasn't long before they were alone together and could speak plainly.

In the wet, cold summer after that they had camped by the lake for ten days and caught pneumonia which got them a week's stay in hospital. They had barely been discharged when they climbed over the fence of the municipal open-air pool, peed in the water, kicked hedgehogs across the lawn like footballs and took

and hikers, dogs hurtling from one tree to the next and rolling in the dirt, cats ducked down in the grass, shorn sheep on the dykes and lambs, dozens of lambs, still full of sap, escaped the Easter slaughter.

Petkum, Oldersum, Tergast. Long before I reach Jericho, the place flashes up inside of me. The flooded sandpits, dark between the trees, the industrial estate with its white warehouses, the custard factory, the Beach Hotel over on the dyke, the dairy, the new signal box and the old station, the freight sheds, Rosing's workshops, the old farmhouses no longer used for farming in the middle of the

out films from the video shop next door, which they were several years too young to watch and which cost significantly more in lending fees than their pocket money. Sometimes, when they didn't know what to do, they roamed around the village at night, extinguished streetlamps with a kick, set fire to chewing-gum machines and drove dogs in kennels into a white rage by sticking branches through the bars and poking the tips at their flanks. Together, they had skipped school for the first time, smoked joints and drunk *kruiden*—too much of the herbal liqueur, as it turned out in the course of the evening at Onno's place. And once, on a hot summer day—later they said it was the day after they got drunk—they'd met the Kelly Family in the hammrich fields. The red and green double-decker bus in which the musical family travelled around Europe was parked by a field in the middle of Clay Road. Visible for miles, it stood out from the flat landscape and hordes of people gathered from all directions to admire it and stroke it like a brightly coloured beached whale. It was standing at an odd angle; from a distance it looked like it had slipped into

village, my house, my garden, my son, on the swing, pushed by a strange man, the new estate, the lake, the Reformed Church with its bell tower, high up on the warft mound, towering above it all like a castle.

I never used to go there often, but for twelve years now I've sat in the front row on occasional Sundays. I fold my hands and listen to the sermon, but I don't join in with the hymns. I can't keep in tune and I'm not going to learn it at my age. There's the mixed choir in the gallery for the singing. They practice twice a week for their big appearance. And every time those men and women—simple people, people like me—stand up and raise their voices, I get goose pimples.

a ditch, but when they got closer and pushed their way through the tightly packed crowd they saw that one of the front tyres had burst and four men were busy mounting a new one. As they did so, Dan Kelly and his children, some of whom were younger than Dan Kuper and his friends, walked out onto the road and played music in the flickering heat—with a natural sense of dedication that Daniel, Stefan, Onno and Rainer had never experienced before. At the first moment they had frozen still in amazement, even though it wasn't what they called music.

They'd had more experiences. The time when a bottle of bromine fell over in the chemistry lab and the building was evacuated. When Stephanie Beckmann, a girl from their class, won against the presenter Thomas Gottschalk when the *You Bet!* TV show came to Emden. When their physics teacher took a camera out of his briefcase at the station and took photos of trains. When some of the cupboards in the classrooms collapsed with a crash as soon as a teacher opened their doors, because someone—there were people who suspected Stefan, Rainer und Onno—had

Every now and then Hans descends the pulpit to me, and we talk about the topic he's chosen or wants to choose. In summer he leans over the wooden fence, and if he notices me sitting in the garden or on the patio he climbs over to me or rings my doorbell and I let him in. Until a few months ago, he always brought along the first draft of his sermon and a bottle of wine, one like an apology for the other.

He's been coming empty-handed for a few weeks now.

Sometimes I make us something to eat, fried eggs with fried potatoes, some kind of fish I've caught and put in the freezer, and we drink a Chardonnay or a Riesling with it, and sometimes, if I'm too lazy to cook or we've both had dinner already, I fetch a

removed the screws in the side walls. And the time when Peter Peters had a fit, had to leave school and died.

Then Daniel had left. He had Es in Maths and Latin and he didn't want to repeat the school year, and so the original reason for their closeness was gone all of a sudden. Still, they promised to keep in contact—too much had happened in the meantime. They had spent two years together, two years with Herlyn and Weers, two decisive years, as they agreed unanimously after the last day of school, which they couldn't give up just like that. The last day was a month ago now, though, and they hadn't seen one another for the past four weeks, almost the entire summer holidays. Daniel had spent a long weekend in Bad Vilbel with his mother and the twins, Stefan and Onno had been in Italy and Denmark and only got back a few days ago, and Rainer had been working at the custard factory and still was, in fact, to earn enough money for a Vespa because his parents and grandparents refused to buy him one, saying he'd have to finance his death out of his own pocket.

tin of peanuts out of the cupboard, and we eat them greedily before we pack our kit and go fishing.

On the way to one of the lakes, we talk about sport or the railways, about fish and bait or something that's happened in the village. But at some point he's guaranteed to ask my advice, on which parable is best suited for illustrating the temptations of evil, our daily misconduct, our doubts and our lusts. Or he'll want to know how the congregation found his sermon in church on Sunday. I can only speak for myself, and I tell him what I think of it and whether I liked it or not.

Often he speaks too fervently for my taste, too solemnly. Those who've turned their backs on him, and those who face him

They'd reached the age at which they only used surnames when they talked about adults. The respectful form of address, the *Herr* they'd once used as a matter of course when they talked about the pastor, doctors and teachers, had vanished from their stories. And the women who held the same positions were only distinguishable from the men by the fact that they put a feminine definite article in front of their names. There were times when they'd address each other by their surnames too. If anyone had asked when and why it had happened, none of them would have known what to answer. They didn't think about it, they just did it.

'Sure, Kuper, come on over. I'm at home. If you really want to lose another game.'

'Did you see what a show Meinders put on again today!'

'Epilepsy? That was the diagnosis? Ahlers must be crazy. Ian Curtis had epilepsy, not Peter Peters.'

'Remember *die Zuhl*? She was an odd one.'

'She was more than odd.'

down, say he's a fanatic. They admire him and despise him for the same reasons. And both types fear his persistence. He believes in what he does, and he's convinced of the effect of his words. He feels responsible for the whole community, even for those who've left the flock, and he regards it as a personal failure if one of the congregation only appears in church three times, for their baptism, confirmation and wedding, before they're laid out next door in the new church hall now used as the morgue. There were times last autumn when I got the feeling he was gradually realizing he'd chosen the worst conceivable place for his mission, in Jericho. Especially after the episode with young Kuper, Hard's son. They say Hans beat him, the day before he left for Israel. I don't know if it's true or not; we've never talked about it.

'Odd to the power of ten, I'd say.'

They didn't want to show themselves up by being polite or respectful to one another. Any semblance of cowardice had to be avoided, and they were determined to put up a front against adults—as long as they were among themselves, at least. Seen from the outside, that was exactly what it was—an act of diminishing, a kind of quiet rebellion. It was as though they wanted to bring the people who controlled their lives down to their own level. It was only when they faced them directly and looked up at them, when they addressed them personally, that they still said *Entschuldigung* and *Bitte* and *Danke* and *Herr* and *Frau*.

Herlyn had been their class teacher for two years. He was always punctual, always wore a suit and always demanded more than the pupils were capable of. He taught Latin and German, and his first act in office had been to break up the structures and move apart those who knew each other from their previous schools and had

Shortly after that, some time in December when I was buying bait at Kuper's, Hard told me how angry his son got him sometimes. And then I realized I've never experienced that, I realized Tobias always does what I ask of him, in my imagination. He's at that age himself now, and I can only hope he doesn't put up with everything and he'll put up a fight when it comes down to it.

I wouldn't want him to chose the pastor as his adversary, though. Hans Meinders has just got back on his feet and he might not be able to take another knockback at his age. Fewer and fewer people come to his services every Sunday. The old are dying and only a handful of the newly confirmed stay true to him. He doesn't give up, though. The break he took in the winter seems to

banded together at the grammar school, around two tables pushed together. Before their first class, Daniel had been sitting in the back row next to Stefan, and next to Stefan were Rainer and Onno, and next to them sat two girls, Tanja Mettjes and Susanne Haak, also from Jericho.

Even when the classes were divided up, as they'd been waiting in the schoolyard until their names were called, Daniel had missed Volker and Simone. Volker had been recommended for grammar school but decided against it and his parents hadn't pressured him, and Simone had gone to a different grammar school, a Catholic one with a better reputation, in her parents' opinion, a lyceum in a different town. The only person he didn't miss was Iron. Iron had left school at sixteen and done a year's basic vocational training and was now apprenticed to his father, the building contractor Johann Rosing. They hadn't run into each other for a long time and Daniel hoped they never would again. But it was hard to keep out of someone's way in a village like Jericho. From the back row Daniel could see almost everyone, and when he looked around and saw the heads

have given him new strength. He seems more determined than ever, but he doesn't lean over the pulpit and shout any more if someone stands up before the final organ music or doesn't put anything in the collection. It's as if he were trying out a new, milder tactic so as to reach his goal after all, just before he takes retirement.

He spent weeks walking in the desert, in Israel. When no one heard from him, lots of people here wrote him off. Even Marie, his wife, who flew out there to look for him, soon gave up hope of finding him alive. The wildest rumours were flying around the village. Some thought he'd had an accident, broken his leg, hit his head, something like that, and died of thirst; others believed it

and backs of his classmates from all over the district, he looked forward to a shared future, to things new and uncertain.

Then Herlyn had come in. He had greeted them and introduced himself. He had put his briefcase on the lectern, snapped open its two locks and taken out a grey tin box, as long and wide as a shoebox but not as tall, like a coffin for roadkill. Daniel and Stefan looked at each other, everyone in the class exchanged glances and a few girls giggled.

Stefan asked, 'What's that?' so quietly that only Daniel could hear.

And Daniel said at the same volume, 'No idea. His pencil case?'

Everyone whispered their interpretations between the desks: 'Chalk holder.'—'Glasses case.'—'Cigar box.' Words were hissed around the room for several minutes.

Herlyn had been standing motionless at the window all along, his back to them, until he turned to face them with his arms

---

was kidnapping or suicide. But I knew he'd come back. He's not the type to put himself in danger or end his own life.

I'm gliding high above the Rorichum Tief river. Fields as far as the eye can see. Neermoor, gravel pits on either side, shimmering turquoise like oxidized copper. Sautel Tief, Uthusen, Neuschwoog, Altschwoog, Klostermühle. Under the B70, Eisinghausen, Bollinghausen, Heisfelde. At Leer Station the number of tracks goes up to fifty-six, before it falls again only metres along. Just after Connemann, the oil mill, towards the Leda Bridge, the line only has one track. The signal's on stop. There are often men waiting by the line here in Leer but they don't want a lift; they take photos of trains. They're mainly interested in the old engines,

folded, ready to hold a speech like every year on the first day of school, the same one every time. 'Don't think you're something special just because you've made it this far, because someone recommended you for grammar school at some point. You're nothing. You have to prove what you can do—you have to prove it to me,' he pointed first at his chest and then at them, 'and to yourselves. I won't give any of you preferential treatment. I don't know your parents, I don't know who they are or what they do or how much money they have, but I'm going to get to know them, you can count on that. I haven't looked at your old school reports and I'm not going to. I don't care whether you had an A or a D for history or WES or whatever your old school called it, and I don't want to know which texts you read in German and which not. Everything you're used to from home no longer applies. And now,' he picked up the box and took off the lid, 'each of you will write your name on a piece of paper and put it in here and pass the box to the person next to you, once around the classroom.'

the ones that have actually been phased out but then do get used every now and then. They're in search of lost time and they want to complete their collection, but today I can't see a soul with a camera on either side of the embankment. The air shimmers above the tracks. Jackdaws are perched on the bridge, cawing and waiting like in that film with the birds. But these ones here will rise up and fly away as soon as the tracks begin to buzz behind them. I light a new cigarette and look at the clock—twenty to eight. A passenger train comes towards me, the seven four three seven. I know that without looking at the timetable. I know it off by heart. I could say at any time where and when which train arrives and departs; I could even list the production series used

Everyone did as they were told. Daniel scribbled down his full name, barely legibly, and folded the sheet of paper in half several times over, put it in the box and handed it on to Stefan. No one could take their eyes off the box migrating along the rows of desks and no one had any idea that they were signing their names beneath Herlyn's power with this game.

Susanne had just put her paper in and taken the overflowing box back to the front, when Herlyn ordered them all to pack their things and line up against the wall facing the windows. Then he shuffled the sheets of paper and took them out of the box, one after another. He didn't unfold them though, merely placing them on the desks as they were. And when he was finished, he said, 'You,' and beckoned Susanne, because she'd been the last one. Now she was to be the first; she was to unfold the pieces of paper and read out the new seating plan. And so it came that from then on Daniel sat next to Peter Peters, and Stefan, Rainer and Onno were spread out around the room. Herlyn thought he'd broken

on all the lines, their engine power and year of manufacture. I'm full of it, full of knowledge that's no use to me in real life. It's like a game of trumps, except there's no one to play with me, no one I could beat.

The bridge was blown up in the war and then rebuilt straight afterwards. It originally had two tracks but for some reason only one of them was put back in operation. Next to the track a narrow path runs across the river, with just enough space for pedestrians or cyclists. Once, at sunset a few weeks ago, I experienced what it's like to stand there when a train comes thundering past you, not two metres away. And at that moment I remembered how it all began, how promising everything was, the first time I climbed

down old allegiances. What he didn't know was that they only came all the more to life in the breaks, on the way to and from school, in their free time.

Weers was different to Herlyn, milder and less concerned about his appearance. He had thinning hair combed to one side and a beard which always harboured a few crumbs. He wore wool sweaters in winter and T-shirts in summer, but no matter what it was, it always seemed to be one size too small, as though it was very important to him to show off his proportions instead of covering them up like his colleagues and other men of his age. He wasn't ashamed of his belly, of his passion for home-baked biscuits, and he wanted the students to establish a relaxed attitude to their bodies at a time when they wished for nothing more than to step out of their skin and exchange it for a different one, a more childish or more adult one.

Weers—whose name is pronounced *verse*—taught Mathematics and Music. His parents had always seen him as a wunderkind because he had perfect pitch and began composing sonatas and

up into a driver's cab and felt that huge power, the power of the sky and the earth, the fire and the water, forces of nature united in a machine, effortlessly setting a thousand tons in motion and hauling them for kilometres. I remember the first fireman patting me on the back with his hefty hands, so hard that I bumped into the automatic lubricant pump, and pressing his shovel into my hand; me taking far too many coals at once, dropping half of them on the way to the firehole door and finally, after days of sweat and welts, finding my own rhythm.

I still wear the same uniform: black trousers, black shirt, black cap—the stoker's uniform, even though I haven't been a stoker for a long time now and I don't have to wear a uniform any more. To

KILL MISTER

Edzardstrasse 3

Wednesday, 19. July 1989

Begins 8 p.m.

School Hall

WILHELMINE SIEFKES GRAMMAR SCHOOL

suites at the age of nine. And for a while, during his degree at the music school in Hanover, he'd been a saxophonist in a jazz band that toured Western Europe. He still played the saxophone but not in front of audiences, only at home for his wife and himself. The two of them didn't have children but sometimes when Weers told off a boy in class for saying something rude or annoying one of the girls, he'd make a pun on his own name. 'If I had a son like you, with your behaviour, I'd call him Per.' Every few months someone asked him why he didn't write music any more and whether he didn't want to play in a concert hall or a jazz bar now and then. He knew his limitations, he knew he'd never be capable of more than interpretation and imitation and he wasn't what some people saw in him, a genius or a virtuoso. His pupils only saw Weers in him, their Maths and Music teacher. Once he'd heard them mimicking him, on the staircase on his way to the classroom, mimicking his slow way of speaking and the way he hummed or whistled songs to fill the pauses between words.

begin with, in my early days as an engine driver, I did it out of solidarity; I didn't want to put myself above them. I knew I wouldn't get anywhere without them. I needed them, to oil everything properly, to keep the firebox glowing all the time, and they knew the line as well as I did. They had to know when a left-hand curve came and they had to look out for a signal I couldn't see from my side. We were linked together like wheels on an axis. We were one man before the machine. Every motion was attuned to the other's. And later, when everything was switched over to diesel and there were overhead lines in our region too and no steam engines or stokers were needed any more, the clothes had become a habit. I thought that by merely changing my outfit in the mornings and

Despite all that, he had a certain standing with his pupils that they didn't accord to other teachers, because he taught something that had to do with their lives outside of school—music—and because he seemed to have mastered all instruments equally. For some of them, those from good families whose parents could afford it, like Stefan, Onno and Rainer, he gave private lessons in the afternoon. In his living room was a black, highly polished grand piano with *Grotrian-Steinweg* in golden lettering—'the grotty Steinway' as Weers always said when someone he liked played the wrong keys—a violin, a cello, an accordion, several alto and tenor saxophones and (something no one would have though possible) an electric bass, an electric guitar and a drum kit. He didn't insist on anyone playing or learning a classical instrument, but at the end of the school year he held an orchestra performance in the school hall with each class, and nobody got around at least beating a triangle or a tambourine.

There was only one way to avoid the humiliation of making a public show of failure or lack of ambition with one of these

evenings I'd be able to put on and take off my work and not take it home with me.

They don't quite fit any more. The trousers are taut, the shirt is unbuttoned halfway, and that's although they're both new, not even a year old. The three women I've slept with in the past twelve years didn't care. They never said a word about my figure, or not in front of me, not as long as we were on tour together. But sometimes when I give a colleague a lift, he'll make the odd comment. Suck your belly in, Walter, your fat's pressing on the safety switch. The safety switch is the dead man's handle, which I have to let go of and then press again every thirty seconds, or the train will stop. It's my monitoring system to make sure I'm still alive. If I don't

instruments in your hand—taking the bull by the horns, and that bull in this case was starting a band, Kill Mister, and performing as the opening act for the orchestra. It had been Onno's idea and Weers had picked up on it with great enthusiasm, although like everyone else he did ask what the name was supposed to mean. 'Kill Mister? There's something missing! What Mister do you want to kill? Mr Mister? Mr Blue Sky? Lemmy?' And like everyone else, he never got an answer.

For six months, Daniel, Rainer and Stefan regularly met at Onno's place, because he had a drum kit, and rehearsed three songs: two cover versions, Slayer's 'Criminally Insane' and Metallica's 'To Live Is to Die', and their own ambiguous composition 'Hang Your Dead Up High'. It suited Daniel, who hadn't mastered any musical instruments apart from the recorder and couldn't play either guitar or bass, that the lyrics of all three songs were very short and very hard to understand by the way he yelled them into the microphone, more screeching than singing. And as he refrained from announcing the songs at their gig, the provocation everyone

react after thirty seconds because I'm collapsed somewhere, fully conscious but incapable of moving, a blue light flashes for two and a half seconds, and if I don't do anything then, a horn sounds for another two and a half seconds, and if I still don't react the emergency brake kicks in. It's all happened before.

At last the train comes across the bridge. I see its outlines getting larger and larger. The tracks hum, the jackdaws startle out of their torpor and rise, cawing, but otherwise there's absolute silence and I'm surprised once again by how quiet everything's got. No panting and booming any more, no raging and roaring; all that's had expected from them never came about. Once silence had descended on the school hall, a handful of parents and teachers even clapped six or seven times out of politeness, and someone or other demanded an encore—which prompted Onno to split up the band after only one gig and rule out a comeback for all times.

Although that meant they had no actual reason to meet up, they continued to get together by the old pits or at one of their houses, apart from Daniel's, and they spent entire afternoons together in their bedrooms, ostensibly doing homework they couldn't manage alone. In fact they listened to music, smoked cigarettes at the open window and spent hours playing simple computer games, until they got blisters on their hands from the joysticks or one of the appliances broke down.

left is the whooshing, and that's only when the cars rush directly past you.

I raise my hand in a greeting and Ernst Taute, the other driver, greets back. The signal flaps up, I start moving slowly, and it's only once I'm well past the bridge, by the rubbish dump, that I reach my old speed. Jericho is less than a kilometre away now and my thoughts are focused on nothing else. If an axle breaks now and the tanks spring a leak during the crash, if all that stuff behind me escapes and catches light, through someone lighting a cigarette for instance, there'll be a lovely fire, one that people won't forget too quickly, and I'll be in the middle of it.

I am the beginning and the end.

3

In the previous years, there had always been short bursts of rain in July and August, showers with thunder and lightning, typical summer storms that usually only lasted a few minutes, rarely longer than two or three hours even if they were particularly severe. Then the clouds had moved inland or floated out to sea and disappeared. But that year there was a drought, drier and longer than the heat wave seven years earlier. The temperature

The industrial estate is coming up ahead of me, the sandpits, the first houses of Composers' Corner. I turn my head to the left to look at our garden, and at the moment when I think I see someone standing in it, the blue light goes on. I press the safety switch and then the whistle, but I've gone past now.

Every time I come into the village I sound the signal. Not to greet them but to keep them awake, the way they keep me awake, night after night, day after day, Nella and he.

Nella doesn't turn her nose up at the money I put in her account every month. And she doesn't send back the presents I give Tobias for his birthday, for Easter and Christmas. But she doesn't want

rose to thirty-eight degrees, fields and meadows withered, streams dried up, ozone alarms were triggered in some towns, and in the woods and moors south of Jericho no one was allowed to smoke or leave the official paths.

Yet the day when Daniel set out to visit his friends was one of uninterrupted rain, sometimes heavier, sometimes lighter, from morning to night. The wind blew the raindrops ahead of it, whipping them against the windows of houses and cars as if God had told his angels to wash the earth clean of all sins at last and flush the people, his creation gone wrong, off its surface, no matter whether they bore a seal on their foreheads or not.

Daniel had been working in the shop in the morning. He hadn't signed up in time for the Christian summer camps his contemporaries went to when they didn't want to go on holiday with their parents, and he hadn't found a summer job. He hadn't made any serious effort to do so, though, because his father had offered him

me to get too close to our son. She's never said it or written it explicitly, but I think I can tell by the way she used to turn me away on my nightly visits to our front door. Her eyes lowered, her arms folded across her chest, drawing an invisible line in the gravel with the tip of her foot, a line I presumed I'd better not cross if I didn't want to risk getting arrested in front of my son, by his new father. And all that in white dresses and wraparound skirts that look like curtains, with tassels and fringes and golden hems. I think she's scared that the sorrow and the anger I carry within me might rub off on him, that he might become just like me—bitter.

Sometimes I think I ought to insist on my right to see Tobias. It would be easy to get my way through the courts, nothing more

fifteen marks an hour for helping to stock the storeroom or keep the shop clean so that Birgit could concentrate on the twins, and that was more than Rainer got at the custard factory. But the offer only held as long as Daniel didn't start smoking. His parents hadn't yet noticed that their son smoked until his eyes watered whenever he got together with his friends. He brushed his teeth afterwards, or sucked on a Fisherman's Friend if he didn't make it to the bathroom before he came across them, thinking he could cover up one smell with another, stronger one.

In the summer, during high season, tourists stopped off in the village on their way to the sea, and Hard made sure he always had plenty of bathing mats and sun cream, sticking plasters and film cartridges in stock. Trucks stopped outside the house every day to deliver cartons, and every day Daniel went to the post office, which was just opposite, and collected parcels, some of them so big and heavy that he pulled them along behind him on a string like a cart without wheels.

than a formality. We didn't make a marriage contract and I didn't care about anything during the divorce. I never looked at the papers, I don't even know if I've still got them, but I know for sure there was no mention of me not having visiting rights. I did break a few things in my anger back then, glasses and plates and a couple of chairs. And I kicked a hole in the bedroom door and stuck a knife in the kitchen table. But I never laid a finger on either of them, and Nella never said I did. But then I think, what would be the point, what would come out of it, for him and for me? It might make him happy to meet his real father from time to time, as an alternative to Kurt, the copy that lives in our old house and pretends to have been there all along. But it might be the opposite; it might confuse him

Once Daniel had unpacked and shelved the contents, he took the empty boxes down to the storage basement. Hard kept them there for a few weeks in case anyone made a complaint or a product didn't sell and he had to send the goods back. But at some point the time came when the room was full. The boxes were stacked up to the ceiling and pressed against the door from inside, so that Hard had to press his whole torso up against it to get in, and even then he could only pull out the nearest box, a small, battered one he hadn't even been looking for. Then he gave his son the assignment of abandoning everything else and immediately ripping up and disposing of 'those bloody boxes down there,' as he said, every single one of them.

Daniel got down to work as if it were his greatest pleasure in life. He launched himself upon the pile with all his might, to begin with at least, for the first half hour, treading on the lids and stamping on the corners, then tearing open the sides and piling the pieces of corrugated cardboard on a trolley and tying them together with a thin strip of hemp string. Twice a month, they

and hurt him. And I might feel even sadder and angrier at every one of those meetings arranged under adverse conditions, because even the thought of Tobias makes me realize what I've lost and can't get back, no matter how much I wish for it. Hans helped me to see that. I probably wouldn't have realized it on my own, or not straight away. Not long after I moved out, he said, you're getting further and further away from the point where your family life stopped existing, the more you try and get back to it; what's done is done. Back then, I expected his words to heal me and I trusted in them like a tried and tested medicine.

Whenever I think back to that conversation in his office, the first of many, it reminds me of Lathen Hill near the Tinnen Pines,

took the bundles to the rubbish depot and Hard gave part of the money he got for them to Daniel. Daniel hadn't yet quite decided what to buy first with it plus what he'd got for his confirmation. He was saving up for a CD player and larger speakers and a more powerful computer, and he liked the idea of fitting out his bedroom with everything at once and catching up with Stefan, Onno and Rainer.

Once he'd got through half the boxes he stood, hands on hips, facing a mountain of cardboard. Sweat ran from his forehead to his eyebrows, and his mouth felt dry although the cellar was cold and damp. He looked around for a bottle of water which he thought he'd brought down with him, but he couldn't find it anywhere and he couldn't be bothered to look for it. So he decided to go upstairs to the kitchen for something to drink and a quick break, or in fact the more attractive option of a long break, lasting until the next day or longer, until the end of the holidays, even if that meant he couldn't afford what he wanted to buy.

a slight elevation, the only one for miles around. It's not a problem for today's engines. But in the steam engine days we used to crawl up it. And if we didn't have enough steam because the piston rings had a leak and the pipes started singing, we had to give it all we had to keep moving. By the time we got to the top, we'd usually run out of water. And that meant we wouldn't make it to Rheine. I'd stick my head out of the window at the next signal box and mime knocking back a drink, to show the signalman we needed water. What else could I do? Stop and let them know? Shout? Above all the noise of the engine? And we didn't have walkie-talkies back then. We had to keep going until the standpipe in Lingen or let the fire go out.

He had just got to the top of the stairs when he heard voices and stopped in his tracks.

'Ten days, not even ten days, and the whole world collapses,' said a man. Coming around the corner, he recognized him as Uncle Günter, Günter Vehndel, Vehndel Fashions, a friend of his father's. 'We didn't have anything over there,' Günter gestured towards a poster for herbal cosmetic products next to the office door, 'in that B&B on Texel that Klaus recommended, no radio, no TV, no newspapers. It was the first time we didn't get the paper sent on to us. And now I feel like a complete idiot—everyone knows, except me.'

'That's nothing new, Günter,' said Hard, resting his elbows on the counter and picking at his fingers.

'And on top of that,' Günter pushed a book, *The Name of the Rose*, the Bertelsmann Book Club edition, closer to Hard, 'I still didn't get round to reading this, even though we had nothing else there, and I won't now either.'

The boiler explodes without water, and it always blows out backwards because it's fixed at the front. There's no room to dodge and if all the rods come with it they take you along with them. It never happened to me. But I've heard stories, horror stories, from colleagues who say it happened just like that. That's what they always say once they get started—just like that and no different. Lots of those men have more imagination than common sense; they've never even driven a steam engine themselves. If they had a bit of brains, an inkling, the slightest experience, they'd keep their mouths shut and get on with their work and leave me in peace with their fairy tales.

Every time I went up Lathen Hill I was scared of getting stuck. Especially with the ore trains, fifty wagons in a row, four

'It's worth it, though. Especially the ending. The tribunal.' It was the only novel Hard had read for years, and that was only after he'd seen the film on TV but missed the beginning and the book had been sent by the book club because they'd forgotten to order a different one, as they did every quarter.

'We shouldn't have gone away in the first place.'

'Come on, don't exaggerate. It would still have happened down there if you'd have stayed at home.'

'Right, but I'd have seen it coming. I'd have been prepared.'

'I saw it coming.' As if to prove it, Hard tapped at his patch, the words sewn onto his chest, *kuper's drugstore*.

'Yes,' said Günter. 'You did.'

'Shame we didn't have a bet going on it. I could have made a packet.' Hard continued picking at his fingers.

'Have I ever taken you up on one of your stupid bets?'

'No.'

---

thousand tons. And on moonless nights, when you could hardly see the rails with the forty-watt headlights, I often imagined the elevation never ended, there was no peak and no incline on the other side. I felt the weight of the world pressing us down on the rails, I felt us getting slower and slower, and I longed for every thrust that took us forward. At the same time I doubted with every thrust that we'd reach Lingen, that we'd ever get anywhere again, because the gaps between the thrusts got longer and longer, all the levers and handles trembled with tension and we heard the pipes singing.

'I'm not going to let you rip me off! I know your methods. I,' now he tapped at his own chest but there was no patch on it, no words sewn on, 'I can see right through you, I can. You can't fool me. Not me.' Then he took a step back from the counter as if dodging a blow. 'I know you better than you know yourself.'

'Oh, do you now?' said Hard, looking up from his fingers.

'Yes, I do.'

'If you can see through everything so well, Günter, why don't you just join in next time? What have you got to lose?'

'Everything. I've always got everything to lose. We all do. We're businessmen, Hard, retailers. We have to put our property on the line, our souls. At any time. Now too, especially now that it comes down to it.'

'And it was so clear, so predictable. They shouldn't have believed him from the beginning, him and his assurances of peace. You just can't trust the brothers down there.' Hard shook his head. 'Arabs and Jews. No matter what they say, in the end their temper gets the better of them.'

When Hans doubts, then in the details. An image that doesn't seem appropriate, a formulation he's not sure describes what he wants to express. I don't know why he always comes to me with his doubts. The simplest explanation is that we live next door to each other. I'm not an expert. I've never been one for books, apart from my own ones, my notebooks. And there are plenty in Jericho who know their Bible better than I do and are more suitable to judge the right choice of words, teachers and lawyers. I think he's just looking for someone to talk to, someone he can try things out on. Because he rarely does what I advise him. He takes notes, writes it all down word for word. Even when we're out fishing he'll sometimes take out his book in the middle of the night, a

'You can't trust anyone,' said Günter. 'Least of all your allies. Next thing you know, they turn around and stab you in the back. From one day to the next.'

'Down there maybe, but not here, not where we are.'

'Oh, yes. Here too. Where we are too. Best friends can become your worst enemies in a matter of minutes, and no one can say afterwards what actually caused it. Without batting an eyelid, they'll go over to the enemy if they see some benefit in it. Just look at Italy or the Czechs.' They always talked about the Second World War as if they'd been involved in it personally and might still manage to bring about a decisive change as long as they spoke about it this way, in the present tense. They'd both done national service, Günter in the navy and Hard in the army, but they'd never been in any real battles, only ever taken part in manoeuvres, on the North Sea or the Lüneburg Heath. They'd never come close to death, and perhaps that was why they'd declared their fathers' war their own, although they didn't even know it from family

---

black notebook like my one, and I'll shine my flashlight for him until the batteries run out. But when I look up to him on Sundays and listen to his sermon, I can't tell any difference from the version he read to me two days previously at the kitchen table or by one of the lakes.

Hans comes from Emden. He was born and bred there and we know a few people in common. I know some people who went to school with him and have worked on the railway for a long time, longer than me. When I mention them he pretends he only vaguely remembers them. He nods and say, oh yes, yes, and tells me to say hello from him, and then he gets right back to Isaiah, Daniel or one of the other prophets, a little too quickly, it seems

stories. 'Let me tell you something, and I'd even put a bet on it. There's going to be a war. As sure as eggs is eggs.'

'It already is a war,' said Hard, unimpressed, and waited for Günter to withdraw his outstretched hand before he went on. 'No one can invade a country and topple the government unpunished, no matter how corrupt it is.'

'Especially not when there's oil involved.'

'It's pure provocation. The Yanks mustn't put up with it.'

'Not just the Yanks,' said Günter. 'We're just as wrapped up in it. That's the price for our independence: we'll have to go over there in the end, whether we want to or not.'

'Us?' Hard stood up straight, as if to steel himself against an invisible threat. He smoothed his white coat and pointed first at Günter, then at himself, then back at Günter.

'Maybe not you and me. But the current soldiers, the air force, the navy. And if it lasts a long time, longer than the first Gulf War, our children too.'

---

to me. I know things about him that he'd never tell me himself, how rebellious he used to be, how quick-tempered and lecherous, but perhaps it's all just stupid talk and the person you were at ten or fifteen isn't the same as the one you are forty years later, and there's no point in playing one off against the other.

Jericho is behind me now. I'll pass it again on the way back, and then, I promise myself, I'll sound the signal again and pay more attention to who's in the garden, and I hope it'll be Tobias, my Tobias. I hope he'll be home from school and standing by the fence waiting for me, like other boys his age stand by the fence

'Daniel? You think so?' He looked over at his son, who had meanwhile stepped into the aisle in front of the cash desk, as if doubting he'd be capable of driving a tank or operating a weapon and killing a person.

'Every one of them,' said Günter, having noticed Daniel as well now. 'And if it goes on that way, if push comes to shove, we'll all have to join up. All of us, Hard. You too.'

'Nix,' said Hard. He knew how easily Günter got carried away, everyone knew that, and he didn't want to provide him with even more arguments to fuel his bleak visions. 'Saddam's a Satan all right, but Kuwait's a long way away.'

'I read today that he's the most dangerous man in the world.'

'I can think of someone who'd give him a run for his money.' Hard looked out of the raindrop-studded window; something was occupying his attention. Günter followed his eyes and a second later the door opened, the bell rang and Klaus Neemann, Superneemann, entered the shop.

and wait for trains to pass by. I haven't run into him much recently and I've only spoken to him a couple of times. The last time was a few months ago. But I can imagine what he looks like now. I went to his baptism and his first day at school. I sat at the very back of the church, and the school hall, right by the door, and no one noticed me because they were all looking towards the front, at him. So no one could tell Nella I was there, and perhaps Tobias won't believe me if I tell him later, if he accuses me of abandoning him and Nella and never being there for him. Sometimes I'd watch him from my car when he came rushing out of kindergarten into the waiting arms of his mother or his father; not mine. At football matches, I stood a little way away from the other spectators at the edge of the pitch and cheered when he shot a goal or prevented

'Ah!' said Günter and raised both hands as if he wanted to embrace him but had decided against it at the last moment. 'We were just talking about you.'

'This awful weather,' said Klaus, taking no notice. 'Incredible.' He shook himself like a dog.

'It wasn't him I was thinking of, actually.' Hard's eyes flitted between Klaus and Günter.

'At least the Bundesliga's started over again,' said Klaus, who had no idea what Hard and Günter were talking about and no interest in finding out. 'Mind you, it was no fun to watch. Did you see HSV versus Kaiserslautern on Saturday? Boy oh boy, what a match. Enough to drive you crazy! Two penalty shootouts, two counters and that was it. Unbeatable for years—don't make me laugh. The fall of the Wall hasn't done us any good, apart from a few empty promises and false expectations. They spent four million marks in the East. Four million! Imagine it. And what did it get us? Nothing.' And as if to prove his theory, he slammed down a newspaper, corrugated from the rain, on the counter.

one. He won a reading competition when he was eight. And once, when he was ten, I bumped into him at Neemann's, Superneemann, by a shelf of video games. He was looking at the pictures on the packaging when I pushed my trolley past him on the way to the freezers. I didn't recognize him at first: a boy with dirty hands and black hair. His T-shirt sweaty, his trousers patched. A boy like any other boy. But then he turned around and ran off, right into my shopping trolley. I helped him up and said, nothing happened, nothing happened, nothing happened, over and over, nothing, nothing, nothing, like a crazy person, my mantra, my stupid mantra. And instead of thanking me or looking at me, he got up and ran away.

'A bet's a bet.'

'I know.'

'What you don't know is,' said Hard, in an attempt to regain command of the conversation, 'why they call camels "ships of the desert".'

Klaus and Günter exchanged glances.

'Something to do with rocking,' said Klaus.

And Günter, who couldn't come up with anything better, said, 'Because they rock around the clock.'

'Nope,' said Hard. 'Because they're full of Arab seamen,' and as neither of the others laughed he started laughing himself.

Daniel took advantage of the opportunity to slip past them into the office, which was nothing but a walk-through space on the way to the staircase, a room with a desk, three filing cabinets, a chair and two doors. On the walls were photos of houses and people, photos of the shop at various stages, before and after the

---

Just before Papenburg I notice my head drooping onto my chest, just for a second. I jerk it up again and close my eyes. I feel the burning behind my eyelids, a stabbing like from a thousand needles meeting at one point, and I think I can dull it by rubbing my eyes and drinking another sip of coffee, the last one.

The further I go into Emsland, the colder and darker it gets. I'm in the middle of the forest, just after Dörpen, pine trees alongside me, densely planted. I'm cold and I rub my hands roughly up and down my arms, a cigarette clamped between my lips. The track goes straight on for kilometres here. The only way I can tell I'm moving is by the rise and fall of the overhead wire and the treetops above me. But that could be a projection too. Perhaps I'm

conversions and extensions, and photos of his father, grandfather and great-grandfather, three generations of druggists side by side, their eyes and expectations bearing down on him like a curse. In dark, dull voices, the men in the shop returned to their favourite subjects. Daniel could make out occasional words through the first door, but the office was cleansing like a decontamination chamber. Once he'd closed the second door behind him all was quiet. Only in his mind did Daniel continue to follow the conversation, and on his way upstairs he was astounded at their persistence in talking about things they could never change.

At lunchtime, Daniel sat freshly showered and changed at the kitchen table with his parents and siblings. His mother had said a prayer, thanked God for his blessings and asked him for better weather, but the sun still hadn't put in an appearance. For four years now, since the incident with the snow, she'd been going to church almost every Sunday, and she encouraged the children to follow her example. She prayed and fasted and occasionally read

just imagining driving. Like when you're sitting on a train in a station and you look over at the wagons just pulling in on the next track, as if they were the ones not moving. Perhaps I'm not heading southwards at a hundred kilometres an hour, perhaps the earth is moving northwards at the same speed and I'm using all this energy just so I don't get pulled along with it.

If there weren't any trees in the way, I could see the Transrapid on the left, gliding to and fro at four hundred kilometres per hour without ever reaching a destination. Sometimes the white stilts of the elevated track flash into sight between the trunks. There's no better expression of the nature of travelling than this test facility. If someone hadn't previously had the idea of using a horizontal

the Bible, but no matter what she did, her wishes went unheard. The clouds were suspended so low and dense above the land that there was little visible beneath the dark sky. No treetops, no pylons, not even the chimney of the dairy opposite, nothing higher than the train tracks, shiny black welts she looked down upon from the kitchen.

The twins had mushed the potatoes and carrots together but eaten next to nothing. As usual, they had left the table and run off to their room before everyone else had finished eating, and their father's scolding had dissolved into thin air before it even reached their ears. Birgit forked the leftovers into the bin.

'Let's hope they don't turn out like you,' said Hard, still agitated and on the lookout for a new victim.

'Like what?' asked Daniel.

'As lazy as you are.'

'At least he doesn't have to repeat the year,' said Birgit.

eight as a symbol of infinity, it would have veritably forced itself to mind when viewing the track from above. Two loops connected by a line, which turn into two circles touching at one point. I've tried it out a thousand times: The more often you draw them with a pen on paper, the closer they get to each other.

Since they set up the testing facility, I've thought a lot about the benefits of maglev technology. Even though we don't see Lathen Hill by the Tinnen Pines as a problem any more and trains rarely get stuck on the tracks, even though we've improved engine power, speed and capacity from year to year, the Transrapid is still ahead in all areas. It's long since achieved that personal ideal. It's kept in levitation through constant repulsion and attraction.

'That'd have been even worse. Grammar school's out of your league. I said so from the very beginning. And I was right. But don't you go thinking you'll have it easier at intermediate school. No pain, no gain.'

Daniel had barely taken his last mouthful before he got up and put his plate in the dishwasher.

'Have you finished in the cellar?' Hard asked.

'Ages ago.' Daniel took a step towards the door.

'Where are you going?' asked Birgit.

'Out.'

'In this weather? You'll catch your death.'

'Chance would be a fine thing.'

'Don't talk nonsense,' said Birgit. 'There's no thunder, thank goodness.' She wiped her hands on a tea towel and looked out of the window. 'And thank goodness we don't have tornados here like in America. There was one on *Dallas* last week, at J.R.'s wedding.'

There's no rolling noise and no structure-borne noise, and wear and tear is minimal.

I went along on one once, only a few months ago. On a works outing, of all things. And that was when I first felt what it's like to be part of the future. Since then I've wished I could steer one of them myself, raised up above all resistance, out of reach for people, travelling thousands of kilometres and still not getting anywhere.

I've always dreamt of taking Tobias along with me one day. Him just climbing into the cab with me and asking me about the switches and controls. Him asking me to sound the signal, like men sometimes ask me to when they're standing at level crossings—

'*Dallas*,' said Hard. 'When's that going to be over?'

'Never, I hope.'

'It's not real life, Biggi.'

'Oh, isn't it?'

'No. This is real life. The Kuper family. Kuper's Drugstore. All our everyday craziness. They should make a film of that.'

'Someone wanted to. You wouldn't let them.'

'With good reason. I don't like it when strangers come round calling my first-born, my son and heir, UFO boy. Hey, UFO boy,' said Hard to Daniel, 'when will you be back?' and he glanced past him at the clock.

'Don't know yet,' said Daniel, in the doorway.

'Don't let them beam you up and undress you again. I could use your help in the storeroom later. I'm expecting a delivery of sun cream.'

'What, now? In the middle of August? You should cancel it,'

one arm around their son's shoulders, the other raised, their hand clenched in a fist, they pull an invisible string. Him accompanying me on my journeys and keeping me company. I don't want him to be a railwayman himself; I wouldn't recommend that to anyone, least of all him, not after all I've experienced. All I want is for him to know what I do, so he understands me better. If Nella's told him who I am and given him my presents, he must have at least an idea of what driving trains means. But she probably hasn't. He probably plays with wooden trains and wooden cars and plasticine men with no guns. But I think I wouldn't even take him along if I were still with Nella; I'd be far too scared that someone would step onto the rails at the very moment he was behind

said Birgit and looked out of the window. 'We won't sell it this summer anyway, not with this weather.'

'Too late now.' Hard turned to his wife, and Daniel used that moment to take another step into the corridor and disappear from their view.

'We've still got enough on the shelves,' he heard his mother. 'There's plenty. And even if it wasn't enough you can always go to town and pick up some more.'

'Nix. The cancellation deadline's passed. I have to take it now, whether I want it or not. Look on the positive side, Biggi. It won't go bad just because we store it a few months, it'll keep till next year, and when the season starts we'll be all ready.'

'Yes, but it goes on the books this year.'

'It all evens out at the end.'

'What end?'

'Our end.'

the handwheel. On the other hand—I've thought about this often recently—it might be the best thing that could happen to me and him. Everything would be clear with one blow. I wouldn't have to try and explain things to him in great detail, things he wouldn't understand anyway at his age, and there'd instantly be such a strong tie between us, the kind that never comes about between father and son under normal circumstances.

Although my father worked for the railways until his dying day and I used to drive past his signal box every day for a while, the two of us had hardly anything to do with each other apart from

'And when's that supposed to be?'

'In the distant future.'

'I hope the bank sees it the same way. What with all the out-goings recently.'

'They always have up till now.'

'Because they know you.'

'No, because they know things always go uphill after they've gone downhill, that's how business works, and the world—and women, too.' Hard had stood up and put his right hand on Birgit's back.

'What's that supposed to mean?'

'In cycles.'

'Stop it,' said Birgit, as quietly as she could. 'It's too late for that as well, now.' She hoped Daniel wouldn't hear, and then she said more loudly, her voice almost breaking as she spoke, 'Until there's a crash.' And she tried to free herself from Hard's grip but

work. He worked his shifts and I worked mine, and when we sat together at breakfast or dinner we'd talk about our day, about what was coming up or what we had behind us.

We usually sat in the kitchen. I could hear my younger brothers and sister playing with the model railway in the other room. When I looked up from my wooden plate decorated with railway motifs I'd see photos of engines and carriages my father had taken as they passed our house, and when we sat down after-wards in the lounge to read the paper or turn on the TV, my eyes might well alight on the shelves holding the timetable books of the past twenty-five years, in chronological order and as neat as if they'd never been used. I can't remember a single real conversation

didn't manage; he was clutching her firmly now and huffed his breath at her hair.

'Why would there be a crash?' asked Hard, almost as loudly.

'If someone behaves out of line.'

'Who?'

'You, for example.'

'Me?'

'Yes, you. You and the likes of you.'

'What do you mean by that?'

'Nothing.'

'Come on.' He ran his tongue along her neck.

'No.'

'What's this?' He'd reached her earlobe.

'What? My perfume? 4711 cologne.'

'No, this here.'

---

between us about anything other than the railways. Even when he punished us as children, for our strong will, our disobedience, he brought the railway into it. He'd drag us out to the track, hold us tight from behind, standing on a set of points, so that we couldn't miss the approaching train and we'd think we were going to get run over up to the very last moment. I hated him for that at the time, but now I can't hold it against him. The cancer that wiped out my mother wiped him out too. It was too much for him, on his own with four children. It all had a knock-on effect, of course. My brothers went to the railway and my sister married a railwayman. And sometimes I think it would have been better if I'd left the railway instead of my family. But the railway was there first

'You know what it is.'

'Yes,' said Hard. 'But I want you to say it.'

'My earring . . .'

'*My* earring?'

'Your anniversary . . . What are you doing? . . . Don't . . . don't do that . . . it tickles.'

'Does it?'

'Really!'

'And this?'

'That too.'

As his parents went on talking, whispering, muffled by skin and hair, Daniel put on a yellow raincoat and yellow rubber boots and set out, as if on rails. First he'd try Stefan on Lortzing Road. He always tried Stefan first. He hoped he was at home, tinkering with some appliance or other in the basement, his workshop, as usual. Before the holidays they had regularly arranged to meet up

and it'll still be there after me. That's an obligation that goes far beyond any oath people swear, to God or to themselves.

Tobias will be starting confirmation classes in August. Yesterday Hans took me aside after the service and told me in confidence that Nella had signed our son up and that he didn't want to turn anyone away who came to him out of their own free will, neither me nor him. And he said he was certain faith would bring us together again, all of us, not as a family but as friends. But that's where he's wrong, he's absolutely wrong. And I told him so as well.

there after school in the afternoons and evenings. In the end Daniel had spent so much time there that he'd stopped announcing his visits and simply showed up in time for tea and stayed until dinner, or midnight. The Reicherts had taken him in as if he were part of the family, and there were days when Daniel had wished he didn't have to go back to the house with the drugstore where his parents and the twins lived. He had wished he could be part of a family with more to connect them than the same surname.

Cars drove past him, slowly, at walking pace, with their rear fog lights on, headlights on full beam and windscreen wipers twitching to and fro in a frenzy, and every other second he saw men and women leaning so far forward in their seats, out of fear of causing an accident, that their faces almost touched the front window.

Daniel was looking forward to the time after the rain, to the scent that would rise from the streets, trees and houses. But that time hadn't come quite yet. The raindrops were still hitting the road,

---

Nella is a believer, but not in the sense Hans would like. She lives in a complete other world, not in this life and not in the hereafter, but somewhere between them. Back when I still lived there, our old house was bursting at the seams with her books about summoning spirits, autogenic training and self-healing, and it probably still is now. She never throws anything away, especially not if it was once sacred to her—apart from me of course. She believed in telepathy and aliens and her reincarnation as a man. Whenever she sensed I doubted her spiritual explanations, she'd say, we humans are like all living beings, body and spirit with no beginning or end, including grasshoppers, ants, mosquitoes and horseflies. Her standard phrase. And I'd say in reply, I might as

the roofs and him with unabated force. On the other side of the road a woman was struggling with her umbrella. Over and over, she tried to turn it into the wind, but no matter what direction she faced, the quills bent upwards over and over, until she gave up and folded the thing up as it was, semi-destroyed, and fled inside the Flower Barn, where others had also sought protection, as Daniel could see by the shop window fogged by their breath. He pulled his hood tighter at both ends and braced himself against the gusts whipping along in waves. Suddenly, a man stepped out of a doorway and blocked his way. He was wearing a hat pulled down deep over his face and a coat, both absolutely soaked.

'Kuper!' yelled the man, slamming his walking stick against the ground. 'When will you develop those photos at last?'

'What photos?' Daniel asked at the same volume.

'Don't ask me what photos! You always ask that when you haven't developed them yet. You won't get away with it this time.' The man tapped his stick against Daniel's chest.

well go fishing then. My standard phrase. Back then I still fished for pikes, which landed on my plate later on, iridescent and tasty but not a challenge at all.

Nella was always eccentric, always had wonderful, crazy ideas, even in our schooldays. Incredibly realistic animal noises in lessons. Phone calls to strangers in the middle of the night. Putting out cigarettes with her tongue. Smoking through her nose. Raising her elbow at right angles as she drank. Sliding down banisters. Climbing trees. Breaking into vacant houses. Spending a whole day at the cinema. Chasing cows across fields. Swapping price tags at Superneemann. Always getting the last word. Taking every joke to the brink. Painting red traffic lights green. Sticking slogans

He must be getting him muddled up with someone else. And Daniel knew who that was. 'I'm Daniel.'

'I don't mean the ones of your son,' the man shouted, 'although he's hardly got a clean slate either. I mean the ones of mine, that bomb-planter, that terrorist. The Jews and the Bolshevists are our ruin. I said it back then and I'll say it again now. Not that anyone listens to me.'

'Tomorrow,' shouted Daniel. He had no idea what the man was talking about.

'Monday? Not until next Monday?' He raised his stick in a threatening manner. 'Woe betide you if they're not ready!'

Daniel nodded. The man raised his hat—now Daniel recognized old Kramer from Kramer's Furniture Paradise—and went on his way. And Daniel went on his way as well. White funnels splashed up in front of him, instantly bursting and replaced by new ones only millimetres away from the old. On the pavement and in the potholes in the road, brown puddles formed with

on election posters: More! Much more! Even more! Hilarious, for onlookers.

But what can you expect from a person called Nella Allen. Her real name is Annalena Allen, but no one who knows her calls her that, not even her parents. As a child, her younger sister Lisamarie couldn't pronounce her name. And she called her Nella, for the sake of simplicity. Others picked up on the short version, probably grateful they didn't have to decide on the first or second part of her name, Anna or Lena. And that was how it stayed. Nella. The forename an ananym of the surname. We looked that up in our good years, in the exciting times. I'd never have thought Latin words could ever get my adrenalin flowing like

yellow streaks, flowing into the gutter, growing into small streams and disappearing down one of the drains.

Four weeks. His memory of the things they'd experienced together was beginning to fade, and as they faded the images blossomed in inverse proportion, grew bigger and brighter, much bigger and brighter than they'd ever been. Every meeting seemed to Daniel like an adventure, in hindsight, every word they'd exchanged worthy of being preserved and endlessly repeated.

The summer holidays were an interim period. Something new would begin for him after they ended, while for the others life went on as they were used to it. Daniel still thought he could be part of it because the classrooms of Wilhelmine Siefkes Grammar School, the teachers and the pupils, were so familiar to him. And to make sure they were part of his future, he decided to tell them all about it as soon as it happened.

---

that. All one of us had to do was take the orange Duden dictionary of foreign words down from the shelf and put it on the table, and there was no stopping us. My name's Anna Nym, she'd say, fumbling with her flies, whereby Nym stood for *nympha*, nymph, nymphomania—we looked that up too. And I'd say, half in a trance, Nice to meet you, Miss Nym, my name's Amos Soma. And then we'd tear each other's clothes off. At some point even something in the same shade of orange was enough, a rubbish truck, a lamp, a boiled sweet, anything in that decade so rich in orange, or a word we didn't yet know, kayak, civic, radar, mentioned in passing at a party, and we'd head straight home and have long, hot, wild sex sessions.

When he got to the *warft* hill below the church and the memorial, Simone came towards him. He saw her from a long way off, despite the rain, and waved at her. She raised her head, a red headband holding her hair back, and waved back as she ran. Every step she took on the asphalt made splashes; fountains scattered from the road to the pavement when she stepped in a pothole, slapping onto the stones, ebbing away into the water-soaked flower beds. She came to a stop before him, panting. Her hands on her thighs, she rested for a moment and then stood upright, looked at her watch, pressed one of the buttons to stop the time, and said, 'Daniel, great to see you. How are you? What are you doing?'

'I'm out in the rain.'

'Me too.'

Her black, loose-cut T-shirt and leggings were plastered to her skin and he couldn't take his eyes off her. Her ribs and nipples protruded alongside the print, an encircled A, and drilled their way into his brain from either side. Simone Reents. He couldn't

---

She's still called that: Nella Allen. She never changed her name. Perhaps that's why she had something like a fool's freedom, for a long time. No one took what she did the wrong way. No one found her behaviour strange. Quite the opposite, in fact. Everyone loved that about her and would have been disappointed if she'd given it up all of a sudden. Myself included. But when Lisamarie, whom I'd secretly christened Lima, moved to Düsseldorf and started work for Fuji and married a Japanese man and invited us along on a trip to his homeland, something snapped inside her. I couldn't go; too high and too far. Flying's not my thing. So she flew alone with them. Three weeks of rice wine and incense sticks, straw mats and sliding doors, much too brightly coloured carp and

remember when he'd last seen her, and he had to admit that whenever it was she'd changed since then, much to her advantage—and to his.

'Yes,' said Daniel, 'but you're going faster than me.'

'That's not difficult.' Raindrops bounced off her lips, ran down her chin and her neck, mingled with other drops, drops of sweat, and vanished in the hollow between her breasts. 'Just doing my endurance training.'

'How far do you jog?'

'No idea,' she said, 'an hour a day, and two on the weekends. I run further every day.'

'That must be twenty kilometres.'

'Maybe. It's all about keeping up your endurance.'

'And why?'

'What, why? Why not?'

far too small trees, men and women in flip-flops and flowing robes, whom you can't even tell apart by the pitch of their voices, and all those temples and pools high up in the mountains, made her lose her mind entirely. Ever since then she hasn't eaten meat, not even fish, no animal products at all. And she swore off alcohol and cigarettes as well.

She meditates in the morning, before sunrise, singing and chanting for an hour at a time, and she built a lotus blossom-scented shrine to her new God, Nichiren. But she still keeps up Christian traditions. In her opinion, Tobias ought to know the Bible before he can decide against it. We never talked about it, of course not, but I know how she thinks about it. She accused me

246

'No, I mean, are you in training for something? The national youth championships? The Ossiloop?'

'No, just for myself. To keep fit and not get fat,'

'You can't get fat.'

'Oh, yes I can! It can go really quickly with girls.' As if to prove it, she pulled her T-shirt up at her hip and let it flap back against her skin and the hip-bone standing out beneath it.

'Boys too—look at Volker.'

'He's always been like that.'

'But he doesn't do anything about it.'

'And what are *you* doing?'

'Nothing. Going to visit friends.'

'Friends?'

'Yes, school friends. Stefan Reichert, Onno Kolthoff, Rainer Pfeiffer.'

often enough of allowing myself an opinion on things I know nothing about. I have to admit she's right about the church. I didn't know how good it could do to be around people who are sure of their cause. I don't share all their views, and the strength and unshakeableness of their faith will always be closed to me, but still some of it rubs off on me when I sit next to them on a pew or talk to Hans by the lake in the evening, as the last glow of daylight extinguishes above our heads and the fish begin to bite.

For a while, perhaps five or ten minutes, I drive parallel to the Dortmund-Ems Canal, a long, dead-straight stretch of track.

'Oh, them. The freaks. Are you one of them, then?'

'I suppose so.'

'Well then,' she pressed a button on her watch again, 'have fun.' And off she went, disappearing into the rain, sucked up by moisture.

The nerds. One day they were supposed to play their favourite records in Music, and Onno put on Napalm Death. As he walked to the teacher's desk at the front of the music room and took the record out of its cover he smiled beneath the hair falling over his face. He'd been waiting a long time for this moment, for this chance to show everyone what true music was in his view—chaos, hate, resistance, an expression of the refusal to fit into the dominant system and accept the rules, a form of protest impossible to close your mind to, the thorn in the flesh of the conformists. Weers listened to the A-side thoughtfully. His eyes slightly reddened, his

Every time you come out of the forests and moors of Emsland it's a relief to see a patch of water between the trees, even though the canal's not a real river and the Geeste Reservoir, just before Lingen, isn't the sea. I stand up and look out of the window. The white smoke of the cooling tower, still kilometres away, rises vertically to the sky. I draw my arms back a couple of times, stretch out my torso and roll my head in circles. I put my work bag down on the safety switch, dash to the other cab at the back, and I'm back before the alarm goes off at the front. All the models in the V-61 family are the same at the back and the front. You can drive forwards and backwards without having to turn the engine around. They're like a head with two faces, both absolutely identical.

chin propped on his hands, staring alternately at the ceiling and outside at the playground, he sat there just as during the previous presentations, just as always, completely unmoved. He didn't even seem to notice the girls holding their ears and demanding he turned the screeching off, by screeching at him over the screeching. Then, as the needle slipped into the run-out groove after the one-second song 'You Suffer' and swivelled back to its starting position, he rose from his chair, stepped up to the blackboard and asked, 'So . . . well . . . what do we have here?' emphasizing the last word as if he'd just made a great discovery and were really astounded at what they'd just listened to.

Susanne, one of the girls who had just been demanding the screeching be turned off, put her hand up and said, 'Heavy Metal,' frowning as if the very words caused her grievous pain.

Weers turned around, picked up a piece of chalk and wrote *Heavy Metal* on the board, beneath the words *Classical*, *Rock*, *Pop* and *Blues*—the styles of music they'd covered previously. Onno,

---

The sun reflects off the water's surface. The light flickers in to me, gleaming so bright that I fold down the shade. Exhausted by my race against time and myself, I look out at the water until the trees rob me of the view of the canal again and I arrive in Lingen. Past the boarded-up water tower and the half-collapsed railway repair works, buildings as red as fire, glowing in the morning light like newly baked bricks. At some point they too disappear, and it may be that I'll be the last person to remember what they were once built for, on the day they're demolished. Except nobody will be interested any more, and perhaps it would be better to demolish everything that's lost its function immediately; better than hoping the old days will come back again, because they won't. And that's

still standing next to the record player as if he expected to be allowed to play the first twelve tracks from *Scum* a second time, shook his head.

Rainer put his hand up and said that it wasn't actually Heavy Metal, to be precise, it was Death Metal.

Stefan picked up Rainer's opener. 'To be precise,' he said without putting his hand up, 'it's Trash Metal.'

Weers wrote these words on the board as well, indicating them as sub-genres of Heavy Metal by placing hooked arrows in front of them.

Onno shook his head again. 'To be precise,' he said in the same tone as Rainer and Stefan before him, 'it's neither Death Metal nor T*h*rash Metal, but Grindcore.'

Weers wanted to write that on the board too but paused after *Gr* because he wasn't quite sure how to spell *Grindcore*, with a *t* or a *d*, turning to the class and asking once again: 'So . . . well . . . what do we have here?'

not something Hans told me, for a change. It's from me, though it's not all that original. But it's something I have to keep reminding myself of, because some scattered cells in my brain are always trying to persuade me it's not like that, that life doesn't just move in one direction, forwards, inevitably heading for death.

The old decommissioned nuclear power station comes along on the right and on the left, on the level of Hanekenfähr, the new one with its huge cooling tower. It went into operation just after Chernobyl, despite major protests. Nella took part in the demonstrations. And I assume Tobias accompanied her on her crusade, in a yellow mackintosh and yellow boots, waving a peace flag like the other children they drafted in for the cause, whose photos were

Tanja put her hand up and said at Weers' nod: 'An argument.'

'Right,' said Weers, 'an argument . . . but that's not what I mean . . . it's more than that . . . something that can come about through an argument . . . though sometimes it develops over a longer period of time . . . so that you don't notice a difference at first . . . a change . . . a variation, from which a new . . . higher order eventually originates.' He spent a full minute looking around the class, into dim, vacant faces, and added, 'I mean the structure . . . the principle of this process . . . the extension . . . or differentiation,' without getting an answer from anybody. Then, after further minutes of oppressive silence, he turned around again and wrote the word he meant on the blackboard. 'We call it . . . di-ver-si-fi-ca-tion.' And everyone except Onno copied it down.

Another time, months later, they were supposed to read poems aloud and interpret them. *Sturm und Drang*, German Classicism, Goethe and Schiller. Even when Herlyn announced it, many of them, especially the boys, groaned out loud as if the very words and names corroded their eardrums.

---

on the front page of the newspaper the next day. It's actually much safer, perhaps the safest power station in the world. A plane would have to crash directly into it to cause a meltdown; a low-flying combat plane, one of the Tornados or Phantom II bomber planes that circle above us every day like hungry vultures; or a Soviet MIG-23 with an engine failure, speeding out of control across half of Europe until it crashes, a thousand kilometres further west, onto the dome-shaped pressurized water reactor, and not onto a boy, like last summer somewhere in Belgium.

That or a convoy of liquid gas tanks exploding right next to it.

I cross the River Ems, which runs together with the canal at this spot for a few hundred metres before they divide again, and

'Poetry!' Onno had whispered from the back, 'two-hundred-year-old rhymes, two hundred years dead.'

And Stefan had asked, 'Do we have to? Can't we do something else?'

But he hadn't had an answer to Herlyn's counter-question of 'What then?'

That was on a hot day in September, in Daniel's second year at grammar school. And for the first time he felt like he was in the right place, with the right people in the right place. He was in the front row on the third floor of a nineteenth-century brick building, in front of him the teachers, by his side and behind him the other kids. He didn't understand everything they said and he didn't think he had to understand it all to get by. He was convinced he'd fulfil his parents' expectations of him. He really thought he could do it if he made an effort, and he resolved to spend less time in front of the TV and the computer and more time on his schoolwork, because everything was the way he thought school ought to be. It

after that the land opens up, small villages, children in garden sand pits, women hanging out the washing, farmers tilling freshly furrowed fields. Preparations for a future they have yet to experience, provided the catastrophe they stand in the shadow of doesn't happen.

Up to Tobias' birth I made every decision in the belief that I could take it back at any time. I can drop out of my training course and start up again. Change jobs over and over until I'm sure I've found the right one. And others before me have proved that man can tear asunder what God has joined together. So I didn't consider my

was an unfamiliar feeling, and it filled him to the brim; he was at one with himself and the world. Everyone thought what he thought, and someone or other spoke the thoughts before he did. It wasn't embarrassing to know something other people didn't know or to get good marks, and no one had to be ashamed of not knowing something as long as they had a prospect of changing the situation before the next test.

A few girls straightened their backs and shoulders. Tanja and Susanne smiled at each other over people's heads, as if the day for which they'd been preparing for weeks had finally come. Stephanie Beckmann, the best in the class, closed her exercise and text books as if she had no need to look at them to know what the lines she was about to read or hear were supposed to mean. Breasts stood out under her T-shirt, more pronounced than the other girls' of her age, even more pronounced than Simone's, and at that moment everyone looked at her and the only one she turned around to was Daniel Kuper, because his desk bordered directly on hers. But Stephanie had made it unmistakeably clear

marriage to Nella a big deal. Neither of us did, actually. But Nella loves ceremonies and rituals, every kind of show, and she doesn't miss any opportunity. Hans says he noticed straight away by the way we said 'I do,' without any expression. He likes to brag about knowing which couples he marries won't stay together until the end. He even makes bets with newly wed couples after the ceremony, and there are some stupid enough to take him up on it. He didn't make a bet with me, or actually he tried; he doesn't leave anything untried to put his flock to the test. But of course his sense hit the spot. If I hadn't seen any possibility to get out of it at some point, I'd never have let myself in for it. I didn't realize until much later that you can only build up a deep relationship with someone

to him and all other boys in their year that she was out of bounds for them by flirting with older boys at break-time and by being picked up after school by a man in a dark blue BMW 325i, 1986 model, 170 PS, 160 kW, who was old enough to be her father and perhaps—nobody quite knew—really was her father.

Every time Daniel looked at Stephanie like this, as if hypnotized, he thought of Simone. Not because they looked alike; they didn't look alike, not in the slightest; but because they had the same aura, the same confidence. Learning came easily to them, and so did passing on what they'd learnt. They always concentrated in class and had all the answers. And although they weren't always the right answers, they didn't let that put them off making more mistakes. They both came across as if nothing bad had ever happened to them. He had never seen them sad, never doubting or anxious. In their presence, he felt strong, stronger than usual, invulnerable. And that was more attractive than anything else, not only for him.

if you put things on a permanent footing. It's no coincidence that soldiers stay in close contact after a war. If you look death in the eye together with someone, you can never part with them for all your life.

Outside Salzbergen Station is the last steam engine to be taken out of service. On tracks but with no access to a platform. With a roof over it and a fresh lick of paint. Preserved for all eternity. Somewhere in my head, the points always get switched around here. It happens with the precision of a light signal. Every time I pass the spot I can't help thinking of the day when my life went

Herlyn's metal box went around the classroom again. Every double-desk was allocated first a Schiller poem, then one by Goethe. One student was to read it out and the other had to interpret it. 'Over every mountaintop lies peace,' read Peter Peters once he had disentangled the multiply folded piece of paper with some effort. He didn't emphasize any syllable and he ignored the rhyming structure, the metre, the melody. 'In every treetop you feel scarcely a wind. The little birds fall silent in the woods. Wait, soon there'll be peace for you too.'

When Daniel heard the last two words he froze. A realization came to the surface within him and stuck in his throat. For seconds, he thought he would suffocate. His breath came shallow and fast and he felt sweat breaking out on his forehead. He looked at Peter Peters but he seemed either not to remember what he'd said to him in the bushes, or to be giving no sign that he was referring to it. Without altering the look on his face, Peter Peters put the piece of paper back in the box and passed it on to the next row. Daniel told himself it was just a stupid coincidence; there was

off the rails. If there is a hell, then it's a place where everything repeats itself, a place with no history, with no beginning and no end.

It didn't happen on the day Tobias was born but the day before, the 26th of October 1977. The last 44 engine had just been taken out of service as we drove out of Emden. Crowds of people were still lined up along the track with handkerchiefs, flags and cameras. Children were sitting on their fathers' shoulders to get a better view. And all they got to see was us in our ocean-blue 216 with two dozen wagons behind us. Perhaps they'd got the time wrong and come too late. Or perhaps they simply hadn't wanted to believe it really was the end. They'd already announced it once,

nothing behind it. And yet he still believed from then on that that was what Peter Peters had wanted to say to him: 'You too. Soon there'll be peace for you too.'

A few months after that, towards the end of his time at grammar school, they had to translate Cicero's dialogue *Laelius de amicitia* in Latin. Herlyn had raised the difficulty level because he suspected Stephanie Beckmann had a copy of the answers book. She got top marks in every exam. On one occasion he'd made a mistake while typing up a test. Instead of *decollare*—to behead—he had written *delocare*—to relocate. Yet she still translated the word correctly, that is, put it into German in the original meaning given in the answers book. And in fact, as he found out at the parents' evening, her mother's brother was a Latin teacher at another grammar school in another town. So now he was no longer using the book *Cursus Novus I* as the basis for their exams, but took paragraphs from Roman sources at the stage they had reached: Tacitus' *Germania*, Caesar's *De bello Gallico* and of course Cicero's *Laelius de amicitia*.

in fact, just before the oil crisis. And then they'd put the steam trains back into service after all.

As we moved past them slowly, Hermann Gerdes and I shook our heads. We raised our shoulders and stretched out our arms as if we wanted to rock a child to sleep, to show them they could go home now. But when we looked back at them we saw they hadn't let that put them off staying where they were and waiting. Unmoved, they stood there waving at us, thousands of them, dressed up and decorated as if for a celebration and not, as would have been more appropriate, for a funeral.

We had a cargo of cars, Beetles in all shades, new Beetles fresh from the VW production lines, which we were to take to Rheine.

The metal box under his arm, he entered the classroom, closed the door behind him and said, '*Salvete, puellae puerique*,' whereupon the entire class, standing, recited in unison, '*Salve, magister*.' Only then were they allowed to sit down. Nowhere else did they maintain this outdated ritual, not even in German, the other subject Herlyn taught. But as it was the same teacher who taught them vocabulary and grammar in both cases, they felt they were both dead languages.

Every time Herlyn greeted them like this, Daniel thought of the time Onno had told them that Herlyn, out of contempt, as an allusion to their age, the development stage they were at, never actually said *puellae* and *puerique*, but *pudores*—shame—and *purisque*—pus—but Stefan said the vocative form was *pura* so he ought to say *puraque* or the feminine form *puresque*. And as soon as Herlyn's footsteps rang out in the corridor, Stefan said into the noise of them standing up, '*Audite!*' Since then, Daniel always listened very closely and he was sure the others who knew Onno's

There, we would change over to the train in the other direction and return empty or, if anything unexpected happened, if a train was delayed and we couldn't keep to our timetable, we'd travel off duty, as passengers.

Actually, I could have operated the 216 on my own by that point. But during that changeover period, only a few months, none of us was allowed to drive more than eighty kilometres in one go. They feared someone might lose concentration and an accident might happen. So there were two of us in the cab that day. Hermann Gerdes had more experience than I did. He'd been working for the railways back when my father was still a points operator, and now he was just coming up to retirement age

theory did the same. Sometimes it sounded like *puresque* and sometimes like *puerique*.

Herlyn told Peter Peters to hand out the exercise books they wrote the tests in, and when Daniel took his, a thirty-page document of his failure, the proof of his laziness, he sensed that he'd make too many mistakes again that day to make his grade up to a D. An unwritten book, plain white but for the thin grey lines, might have brought about the change he had predicted to Herlyn in a one-to-one conversation six weeks previously. But on seeing his past inability, he began to lose courage.

From the first page on, the right-hand margin was full of red comments such as—*Wa, F, | F eum, | C* !!? or *past!, ablative!, terrible!, meaning?* ('*The call of the mountain?*'), and the left column consisted of texts riddled with blanks, made up of the words he thought he'd recognized. *Odysseus, ⸺ of the Greeks was of great wisdom and ⸺.—And he would never have ⸺ from the terrible cruelty ⸺ to benefit the gods with his killed son.—If Tantalus*

himself. He was looking forward to it, to being retired; he thought he couldn't keep up with the technical progress and it was better to get out now than later, when he'd sense he'd missed the right moment. He wanted to make way for younger men, for engine drivers like me. That was why he let me take over the first part of the journey although he'd been the first on the roster.

It's your turn now, he'd said, now you can show me all you've learnt in your training.

And I'd said yes, yes Hermann, maybe I can teach you a thing or two.

I'd be surprised. But I'm happy to give it a go. You never know what theory's good for.

had not been summoned from Olympus, ————————
———————————. Beneath that were numbers marking the degree of his failure, *-18, -21½, -37½,* although some texts were only seven sentences long; descriptions of his grades: *just sufficient (D), inadequate (E), unfortunately a fail (F)* and sad, analytical, constructive comments: *A bitter disappointment!—Too many construction errors. It s obvious you haven't paid enough attention to word endings. —You will now revise (a) vocabulary and (b) declina-tions (a/o/ e/u/i and the consonants) until you know them better than your forename. You have no command of the pronouns either!* It was only the vocative and the imperative he had down pat, thanks to Stefan and thanks to Herlyn, almost perfectly.

Once everyone had opened their books, Herlyn passed around his tin box. They each had to take out a sheet of paper. On each sheet of paper was a different sentence, so that no one could copy from anyone else. Daniel took out his sheet, laid it on the table with the blank side up and passed on the box to Stephanie. Then

So we looked out of the windows and shook our heads until only a handful of onlookers lined the tracks, and then, after Petkum, none at all. The land stretched out ahead of us, broad as the sky. The fields were still green and full of cows. Gulls hovered in the air above us. The tracks shimmered black in the evening light. Hermann cleaned his glasses by breathing on the lenses a couple of times and then wiping the moisture off with his shirt. Then he cleared his throat and asked whether it wasn't due soon.

Any day now.

What's her name again?

He'd forgotten we were expecting a boy. I'd told him weeks ago. I'd told everyone. A boy. A railwayman. A man like me.

Herlyn said, '*Circumvertite!*' And everyone turned over their sheets of paper. His first sentence was: *Namque hoc praestat amicitia propinquitati, quod ex propinquitate benevolentia tolli potest, ex amicitia non potest; sublata enim benevolentia amicitiae nomen tollitur, propinquitatis manet.* Although he'd revised little more for this test than for the last one, he was still confident he'd manage it this time, because many of the words were repeated and he knew all but two of them. Unfortunately, though, he was lacking the key verbs, which meant that the sentence he wrote, like the previous and the next, made no sense: *For in this point friendship is better than kinship, because affection can —— from kinship, but not from friendship; for when affection ——, the name friendship ——, that of kinship remains.*

Tobias.

Funny name for a girl.

When he'd finished cleaning his glasses he took a pack of cigarettes out of his breast pocket and offered me one. I hesitated; I'd just given up smoking. But he knew I'd already given in once. Come on, he said, holding the box out to me, just for today. I took one, he gave me a light, and we smoked our cigarettes in silence until Neermoor.

Doesn't your son have kids too? I asked once I'd thrown the cigarette end out of the window.

Two, he said. A son and a daughter.

4

The tracks of the western line, leading from the sea, from the pier to the south towards Rheine, divided the village into two halves. On one side were Petersen's Pool Hall, the freight shed, Rosing's workshops and the Raiffeisen cooperative store, Village Road and Station Road with their old farmhouses, shops and tradesmen's workshops, the Reformed Church, the monument, the graveyard, the abandoned building site for the mortuary, the old and new

---

How old?

The boy's ten and the girl's at college. She wants to do something else, I reckon. I can't blame her. He paused, as if expecting me to contradict him, and threw his cigarette butt out of the window too, but then he said, as if to himself, she knows best, she's old enough now.

Yes, I said, she's old enough. And then I got to the point I'd been meaning to ask about, about baby equipment. I asked everyone back then; Nella and I couldn't afford everything we thought we needed.

They must still have some, he said, somewhere in the cellar. What do you need?

church halls, the village hall, the fire station and the police station, Poets' Corner with its old people's homes and flats and behind that, on open ground by the sports field, Superneemann, the supermarket.

On the other side, towards the dyke, where once cows had grazed and potatoes had grown, was now the new estate, populated by doctors, teachers and architects, by locals like the Reicherts and the Kolthoffs and newcomers like the Pfeiffers and the Mengs, but suddenly, since the fall of the Wall, also by refugees and ethnic German immigrants, families with names like Szkiolka, Michalak or Zywczgk, Composers' Corner with its rubber bollards, speed bumps and raised curbs, its parking bays, flowerbeds, trees in tubs, playgrounds, cul-de-sacs and turning circles: Verdi Road, Wagner Road, Brahms Road, Mozart Road, Offenbach Road, Beethoven Road, Händel Road, Haydn Road, Bach Road, Lortzing Road, Schubert Road, Schumann Road, Johann Strauß Road I and Johann Strauß Road II—father and son—the street entrance, the only way in by car, flanked by blue-and-white traffic signs.

Anything really, I said. Mostly clothes, and a car seat.

Wait a minute, I'd better write it down or I'll have forgotten it by tomorrow. He took a pen and paper out of his leather bag, made a note with his back bent over, the piece of paper pressed against his thigh, and when he straightened up and looked ahead again, he said, there's someone on the tracks. He said it quite calmly, like you might say to a woman, a new conquest, I was born in that house, and there's the lake where I used to go fishing. And it wasn't until that moment that I saw him too, even though I'd been looking ahead all along. A person, right on the tracks. I sounded the whistle, once, twice, three times, and then we were a hundred metres further on. I heard Hermann saying, there's no

In the summer, when the sun shone until evening, the rattle of dozens of lawnmowers echoed off the houses on Saturday afternoons and the scent of freshly cut grass dispersed above the roofs. Boys played football in the road and girls hopscotch, men polished the chrome of their cars in their driveways or stood on ladders, clipping hedges of Japanese cypress or thuja that separated their property from the neighbours', and women unpegged bed sheets and towels from rotary clotheslines in front gardens, until the church bells rang in the end of the working day here too. Then barbecues were lit in the lee of the houses and bottles were uncorked, and some untiring souls pulled on running shoes, heart-rate monitors and headbands to combat their consciences and raced around the streets again, before darkness descended over the land and the people and put paid to all the resolutions made at the beginning of the week.

When it rained, however, like that day, there was not a soul to be seen. In the front gardens, plastic chairs and tables were leant against the walls so that water didn't pool on the surfaces. Tarpaulins

point, and at the same time I pulled full on the brake, because I'd noticed for myself that the person standing there hadn't ended up on the track by coincidence. A man in a long, dark coat. A young man, no older than I was back then. He spread his arms and leant his head back, as if he wanted to embrace us. And he did embrace us.

We coasted three or four hundred metres over him before we came to a standstill. I called the control centre over the radio. Hermann got out to take a look from close up. You stay here, he said, it's not for you. He walked once around the engine and then walked back along the wagons. I looked out of the window, saw him bending down, stretching out a hand for something and

were thrown over the sandpits. Over at Rosing's workshop a German flag, the remnant of the euphoria over the football World Cup, hung limply from a pole and would stay there until the day of German reunification—whenever that might be.

Daniel pulled his hood down lower to stop the rain running into his eyes. Aside from that, he was afraid Volker might recognize him as he trudged past the Mengs' house on Mozart Road, and engage him in a conversation on how he'd been right about God making the first-born die, and the second-born too if the first sacrifice wasn't enough. They had lost contact since their confirmation and Daniel would pick it up again soon enough, in only two weeks when they went to the same school again.

His trousers were stuck to his knees and from below, from his boots, he felt cold and wet creeping up, but no matter how often he looked down at himself or stopped walking and put his hand inside and felt his socks, the rubber was watertight. The curtains in some windows were twitched briefly aside as he walked past

---

drawing it back again. When he came back he said, wasn't your fault, nothing you could do. He wiped his hands on his handkerchief, although they weren't dirty.

Yes, I said, I know.

But that powerlessness was no consolation, not for either of us. During my training they'd told us it would happen and how to behave when it did, and I'd kept to the instructions. I'd done everything right and yet still killed a man. I knew Hermann Gerdes had a few on his conscience. One of the first times we met, he greeted me with the words, Just hit one again, near Uthusen; thought it was an animal at first, but it wasn't. That was the way we'd talk about it. And even as we waited for the police and the

them, garage doors purred automatically up and down, doors slammed, engines wailed, tyres screeched on the wet road surface, but all the sounds were muffled as if they couldn't develop fully in the wet air. Only the rushing and the rattling of the fast trains, the freight trains that raced past the village every half hour, shattered the rain-heavy stillness on both sides. Sometimes the train drivers gave a signal, a high, penetrating whistle, to shoo animals off the tracks or, if they came from nearby like Walter Baalmann, to greet their relatives and friends in passing.

There were six level crossings on the entire stretch of track. There were two directly by the dairy and the freight station, which linked Station Road and Village Road with Dyke Road, eight barriers with bars, railway-crossing signs and flashing lights, controlled by a signal tower within eye's view. Two were a couple of hundred metres further north and south, each with two simple barriers without bars, just before or after the estate, leading into the hammrich fields or the village depending on the direction.

---

ambulance and the state prosecutor, we didn't talk about it any differently. We made our statements for the record and we were in a taxi back to Emden before the track was opened up again.

I called in sick and Tobias came the next day. In the delivery room, I had the overwhelming feeling of having taken one life and given it to another, though it hadn't happened at the same time. And when I looked at Tobias, the baby who threw his head back and waved his arms, I saw the man in the long coat. I saw death in his eyes. At first, I hadn't wanted to tell Nella about the accident, and then I did, the day after Tobias was born.

That's why you got home so early.

Yes, I said, that's why.

Their barriers only opened on request, via two intercoms mounted by the edge of the road, two yellow plastic boxes with grey buttons in the middle, which were seldom pressed because drivers rarely used the road—it wasn't a shortcut—and pedestrians simply ducked under the poles, some to get across quicker and others so as not to cause any bother to the level-crossing attendant. And in the hammrich fields, at the place where the line to Neuschanz branched off, the Holland line, there were two more level crossings with no barriers. Three years previously, Doctor Ahlers had had a car accident at the first one, on Clay Road. He'd been on his way to a patient. Magda van Deest had called him and said her husband had keeled over during milking and wouldn't respond to her, and he'd driven straight off at dawn because he was on weekend callout duty and thought it was an emergency. He'd treated old van Deest for cardiac irregularity not long before, so it was an emergency. It really was a matter of life and death—but, as he discovered after the crash with the 2030 express train from Oldenburg to Rotterdam, also of *his* life and *his* death.

She leant forward to hug me, but she was holding Tobias and she collapsed back against the pillows.

After a while I said, at least it had its good side—otherwise I couldn't have brought you here.

How can you say that, she asked indignantly, sitting up in bed. Then someone else would have done it. Someone would have been there for me. My father, my sister, Kurt.

Kurt? Kurt Rhauderwiek?

Yes. With sirens and flashing lights.

I said I'd promised to be there, and I kept my promises.

Yes, she said, you do, you did, but he could have come at any time, even two weeks from now, and she stroked Tobias' back as

The car, a red Porsche 911 Turbo, 1981 model, 260 PS, 190 kW, was impaled on the buffers and dragged along with the train for several hundred metres until the engine finally came to a standstill. The train driver got out and inspected the damage; pieces of metal, broken glass and the front wheels were scattered along the embankment and the car was a solid lump, dented from all directions. He spoke to Doctor Ahlers, who was dripping with blood and hemmed in by metal and plastic, struggling for air and incapable of answering the man's questions even with a nod. A surgeon on his way to a conference in Leyden gave him first aid. And Magda van Deest, who had seen the collision from the farm, called two ambulances, one for Doctor Ahlers and one for her husband. While old van Deest died in the kitchen—it really was a heart attack— Doctor Ahlers survived the accident with no lasting damage; except that his hair turned white that day and stayed white from then on.

he lay on her chest, his head pressed to hers. Nobody knew it would go so quickly. And then she asked me whether I didn't want to hold him. I reached out my hand for him and drew it back again. I couldn't touch him. I knew if I touched him I'd vomit there and then, all over her, and him, and myself. So I said, I don't feel well, and I jerked the door open and before I closed it behind me I heard Nella laughing and saying, You don't feel well, that's just like you, I'm the one who shouldn't feel well, after what I've been through.

Downstairs in the foyer, I bought a coffee from a vending machine. I paced the corridors, not drinking a sip. I went outside into the grounds and threw the full cup into a bin. It had cooled down. The cold air burned in my lungs. But that fire brought no

There was nothing to betray the house from the outside. A large garden with flowerbeds and a fishpond, bordered by neatly trimmed hedges, their leaves pale and half-parched, and a simple brick building with a double garage like almost all the houses in the new estate in which Stefan lived with his parents—both doctors, general practitioners and psychotherapists—and his younger sisters. Nor did the hallway into which one of the sisters led Daniel give any clue to the chaos that awaited him in the basement. A mirror on the wall, a coatrack covered in rain jackets, a chest of drawers, a green push-button telephone, a door and a sign: *No entry*. But as soon as anyone had gained entry—they only had to use the door handle—then descended a narrow wooden staircase to the cellar and reached the first landing, the vapours of melted solder and plastic attuned them to the end of the world.

Next to the utility room and a larder storing wine and preserves was Stefan's workshop, a low-ceilinged, fully panelled room stuffed with screens and apparatus, televisions, video recorders, record players, radios and keyboards, joysticks, walkie-talkies and

clarity, merely clouding my senses. I went back inside just before it got dark. Tobias was still lying on top of her. His body rose and fell to the rhythm of her breathing.

Come here, she said, waving me closer with her free hand. He's asleep. He's a calm spirit, free from all toxins.

On my way home I thought, who is he, kept thinking, who is he? That raw creature with black fuzz on his head and blue, glassy eyes bore no similarities to her or to me. Nor did I recognize the woman I'd once loved and married any more. We must have grown apart long ago, without me even noticing, perhaps even before Japan. It must have happened after we finished school and took different directions but stayed together, because we thought

measuring devices, adapters, lighting consoles, batteries, acoustic couplers, telephones, microphones, headphones, aerials, keypads and folding clocks, an electric guitar, an amplifier, a mixing desk. On one side was a home-made work bench which occupied almost the entire wall, on another, below the basement windows, tables of various heights and sizes, shelves piled up with CDs and magazines, in the middle three armchairs covered in books and papers—circuit diagrams, construction and instruction manuals— and right next to the door was a bar with stools and a beer pump, a reminder that the basement had once been used as a den. Spherical speakers hung from the ceiling in each corner; they rarely emitted music but often distant white noise, buzzing and crackling, indefinable high-pitched tones that condensed, if anyone listened long enough, into words and sentences, secret messages only meant for the listener. Everywhere were opened-up metal casings out of which spilled cables and copper wires, emerald-green-and-golden circuit boards, looking, with their soldered surface elements, with their processors, capacitors and resistors,

we could get through the contradictions arising from our different interests and wishes. In one of our rare man-to-man conversations, my father once told me people change every seven years, and the great challenge in life was adapting to the current conditions. Back then when I was fifteen or sixteen, I hadn't wanted to know. But now, whenever I look at old photos I think the first part of his theory might not be all that wrong. At least, I can't possibly understand now how I could ever have worn flares, brightly patterned shirts with wide collars and long, bushy sideburns.

It seemed that after twelve years together, Nella and I had entered a phase of our relationship in which there was no space left for each other. Barely a day passed when we didn't criticize

like miniscule models of depopulated industrial towns, grey boxes with buttons, flashing diodes or flickering monitors on which numbers and jagged lines displayed frequencies—the vital parameters of an ailing technical organism.

Everything seemed to vibrate and be just about to implode at all times. Some devices did implode, letting off a hiss like when water splashes onto a hot frying pan or a bang that caused another bang upstairs in the hallway, in the fuse box, and downstairs immediate darkness and silence. Most things did not announce their death, however. The light that signalized they were working simply went out, and the sounds they emitted fell silent without crashing the entire system.

No one could say what Stefan was working on at any given moment or what purpose his experiments served. He couldn't say himself, and when he tried to explain he got lost in specialist terms. It was a never-ending series of experiments which aimed to prove nothing except that everything that existed separately

each other. Sometimes, after hour-long arguments with dozens of foreign words, we ended up in bed and succumbed to the illusion of being right back at the beginning, not at the end. Then she'd got pregnant. I'd never wanted children and neither had she. But she'd forgotten to take the pill out of anger and lust, and I was incapable of reminding her, for the same reasons. And with this new mutual goal in sight, we'd stopped fighting and stopped having sex, and stopped succumbing to any illusions, except perhaps for that of soon being parents and caring for our child. We'd reached a kind of biologically determined ceasefire. On the surface, peace reigned supreme, but on the inside the fighting continued by other means, or at least mine did. I asked myself how I could get rid of

could be interconnected, radio stations to computers, musical instruments to screens, cameras to speakers, people to machines, people to people.

Across flokati rugs worn thin in the middle, which had lined the floor upstairs in the living room until they were exchanged for wall-to-wall carpet, ran cables in many colours and thicknesses, providing the appliances with power. The entire floor was covered in these colourful strands. One false step could trigger a chain reaction, pull appliances from tables or rip them out of the walls. So the first thing Stefan said whenever anyone came in was, 'Watch where you step.'

'I know,' said Daniel. 'There's no need to tell me that.'

Stefan was standing at the workbench, his back to the door. He had a soldering iron in one hand and was bending over a circuit board.

Daniel took off his boots, hung his raincoat on a hook on the wall and stepped into the room.

---

her and prevent the little monster from hatching, the kicking, invisible inevitability that would chain me to her for all eternity. I hoped those thoughts would fade or disappear with time, at Tobias' birth at the latest. But they didn't. My hate for her had been transferred to him.

A few days later the three of us drove home to Jericho from the hospital, and when we turned into our road I saw a removal box outside our front door. I let Nella out on the driveway. She picked up the basket containing Tobias from the back seat and walked to the house, our new house. It had only been finished a few weeks previously. Some rooms still had wires dangling from the ceilings, furniture positioned randomly, and not all the boxes

'You can put that stuff there on the table, next to the biscuit tin.'

'What stuff?'

'That stuff,' said Stefan, waving the soldering iron at the papers that had almost completely buried one of the armchairs. Daniel made an attempt at picking them all up at once by inserting both hands between the fabric and the lower strata on either side. Semi-raised, he asked, 'Which table?'

'Any one. Just put them down on top. But in the right order. It's all sorted.'

'What are you doing?' Daniel asked once he'd sat down.

'Hey,' said Stefan and paused again, not looking at him this time either.

'What?'

'We agreed you wouldn't ask me that any more.'

'Did we?'

had been unpacked. Only Tobias' room was fully decorated. I parked the car in the garage and pulled the door closed behind me. It was only when I reached for the handle that I noticed I was trembling. Nella was leaning over the box, a note in her hand.

That's nice, she said. It's from Hermann, baby clothes.

I never drove with Hermann Gerdes again. Not because of the accident, but because he finished working before I went back. After that we ran into each other a few times, at the Christmas party in the Friesenhuus and at people's birthdays. We never talked about the accident. But colleagues told me he couldn't forget that suicide, his last one, just as little as I could. Up until he died only six months later, by which time I'd moved out, he

'Yes, we did.'

'I don't remember that.'

'Have a good hard think then.'

'Maybe you're getting me muddled up with someone else.'

'Maybe,' said Stefan, 'maybe not,' and he got back to work.

Daniel picked up a Conrad Electronics catalogue from the floor and began flicking through it. The pictures of components and page-long product lists were strangely familiar. What Stefan did—whatever it was—seemed to Daniel the natural next step on from model-making; no longer encasing nothingness but filling it, moving things, bringing them to life. And he wondered when he had lost track, when he'd lost interest in technology, in anything at all, and why.

'Right,' said Stefan. 'It ought to work now.' He put aside the soldering iron and inserted the circuit board into a box. 'Can you just press that switch there?'

blamed himself for having given me the first turn at the controls. He thought none of it would have happened if he'd been driving, none of the stuff with Nella and me; everything would have been different. I wish I'd told him that fate doesn't depend on our decisions or on leaving the house a second earlier or later, but I didn't get a chance because he got cancer, lung cancer, and he died five days after the diagnosis.

Shortly after his funeral, I was allowed to drive on my own for the first time, the whole journey from Emden to Bremen or Rheine and back. Someone put up a cross at the place where it had happened, and someone else took it away again before I could see what was written on it. I didn't need to see it though. I knew

'Which one?'

'The one by the socket there.'

Daniel leant over the right armrest. 'On your left.'

'The white socket or the black one?'

'The white one.'

Daniel pressed the switch on the white extension socket but nothing happened.

'The black one then.'

Daniel pressed the switch on the back socket and there was a bang upstairs in the hallway. At the same moment the lights went out downstairs and all the sounds died.

'What did you do?'

'What you told me to do.'

'But not when the white switch is on too.'

'How am I supposed to know that?'

---

the man's name from the newspaper. Reinhard Renken. 10 May 1952–26 October 1977. Beneath that, the names of his relatives and the address for letters of condolence.

On days when I didn't know what to do with my anger and drove around for hours in the car, I stopped outside the Renkens' house and stared over at it. A large house, bigger than ours, Nella's and mine, and much bigger than the house I live in now. I'd park on the other side of the road, listen to music, smoke and drink nine or ten bottles of beer, until I was tired enough to sleep. Sometimes I was so tired that I fell asleep right there and woke up in the morning, not long before my shift started, with stiff limbs and a malty, metallic taste in my mouth.

'You know how sensitive everything is down here.' Daniel heard Stefan trying to clamber past him over the cables, heard him saying 'Damn!' and something crashing to the floor directly in front of him, heard Stefan, now very close to him again, saying first 'What was that?' and then another 'Damn!' and then the door opening and slamming behind him. Then all was quiet, but for the sound of the rain that came in to him through the basement windows opened at the top. Then the neon tubes above him flickered on and the machines around him began to hum and flash again.

'What are you doing here anyway?' asked Stefan before the door closed behind him. It was only now that Daniel saw how tanned Stefan was. He must have spent days lying in the sun, possibly too long. On his nose and forehead, along his hairline, his skin was peeling and scattered onto his T-shirt whenever Stefan brushed against it, like dandruff, white as snow.

'I thought we could play computer.' Daniel stepped up to one of the tables, which held a TV, a keypad, a disk drive with toggle

---

When I reported for duty once after one of those nights, a passenger train to Rheine, Hans was standing on the platform in Emden. I hadn't seen him for months. I didn't know him then as well as I do now.

Can I give you a lift to anywhere?

Wherever you like, he said.

There's only one direction, I said, only ever one direction, and I let him get in at the front with me, although that's not allowed.

Along the way I told him what had happened, and he said, We must needs die, and are as water spilt on the ground, which cannot be gathered up again.

closure, a console and several joysticks. Next to it, on a wooden structure, hundreds of cassettes, diskettes and modules were piled high. 'Something simple we haven't played for ages. Wonderboy or Space Invaders.'

'You're the expert on Space Invaders.'

'What's that supposed to mean?'

'Oh, nothing,' said Stefan. 'The problem is, it won't work.'

'What won't work?'

'There's something wrong with the connection ports, I think, or maybe it's something else. I haven't worked it out yet.'

'Let's have a look.'

'There's no point, I've tried everything. There's nothing we can do, especially not now,' Stefan looked over at Daniel, 'now that the fuse has just blown again. Maybe it's just time I got something new. All this stuff,' he gestured around the room with one outstretched arm, 'is no use any more.' As if to prove it, he picked

What? I said, absent-minded, concentrating on the controls. I hadn't expected him to give me a sermon.

It will change your life. More of his wise words, but I'd realized that for myself. And when he got off the train in Jericho—the station was still there then—he said, I can't do what you expect from me. I couldn't do it even if I was the Pope, because I don't think a few Hail Marys and a few Our Fathers will help. I can only see one way—you have to go to his people, you have to talk to them, and then God will forgive you.

I didn't expect forgiveness, neither from God nor from people, but I followed his advice and went to see the Renkens that same day, to talk about their son, about his last few seconds. I rang the

up one of the joysticks and added, almost in the same breath, 'We can go round to Onno's.'

And that's what they did.

bell and a short woman opened the door. She burst into tears when I introduced myself. She swayed on her feet, clutching at the banister. Her knees kept collapsing. Her husband had to help her stand. The two of us took her into the living room and sat her down on the sofa. The man offered me a beer. He brought one for himself as well. He put a glass of water on the table for his wife. We didn't clink glasses, but drank silently in short, fast gulps. Golden lemons, blood oranges, passion fruits, slightly wrinkled, effervescent and fizzing, but with a bitter aftertaste. There was a clock on the wall. The even ticking had a calming effect on me, as if my heartbeat was adapting itself to the rhythm. My eyes roamed around the room, a wall unit, a tea trolley, a TV, orchids

5

Onno Kolthoff lived not far from Stefan, a few hundred metres down Verdi Road in a similar house, a new building that his father had designed for the family shortly before he'd met another woman at his architect's office and moved out. Now Onno lived there alone with his mother, he up above the garage, she next door. He had one room that housed the drum kit—a black TAMA Artstar II double-bass drum set, four crash cymbals, four hanging

on the windowsill. When I looked back at the old man I saw that they'd calmed down too. I told them about that day at work. About the last steam engine, the people everywhere, about the sun piercing the clouds, about the land stretching out ahead of me, back then in the autumn, about the mood, like saying farewell. At the word farewell, the woman began to cry again; the man was fighting back tears as well. He blew his nose on a handkerchief embroidered with the initials RR. After a while, he got up and fetched new beers for us from the kitchen. Although his wife's glass was empty when he came back, he didn't get up to fill it for her. Then they told me about Reinhard, their son, about his life, about how they didn't know why he'd done it.

toms, two floor toms, one hi-hat—a wall of shelves full of records, a fridge and an old three-piece suite, and a bedroom that was at least as large and could be accessed via an outside staircase from the driveway. He could come and go whenever he liked without his mother even noticing.

They all envied Onno the space, the independence and the double attention bestowed on him. They often came round spontaneously on Friday or Saturday evenings, sat around the table drinking beer they brought along from the petrol station on the B70—the only place in Jericho where they could buy alcohol without having to show any ID—smoking and listening to music for hours until they were tired enough to go home again. Onno nodded whenever anyone said how great his rooms were, how big, how far away from everything, turning the music up to prove his exceptional circumstances, and he was never angry with anyone who came round at night because he couldn't stand it at home any more.

He didn't leave a letter, the woman said in a brittle voice. And he didn't talk about it to anybody. Not his brothers, not even Vera.

We don't know that, the man said.

He didn't talk to us anyway, about his problems.

What problems, said the man. Didn't he have it good here? Didn't he have everything? Didn't we give him everything he wanted? And did he ever say a word of thanks? Did you ever hear him say thank you?

He never said much at all, said the woman, turned to me. Reinhard was a very quiet boy.

They told me he'd done his national service after he took his A-levels and then got an apprenticeship, as an industrial clerk at

The label on the bell next to his front door didn't say *Kolthoff*, it said *Metallica*. Every time Daniel pressed the white button next to it he couldn't help remembering the Jehovah's Witnesses who had traipsed around the village in pairs the past May to convince the Jerichoans of the true faith, and had rung at Onno's door too. It had happened during the preparations for Kill Mister's first and last gig. They'd been taking a break and Onno had ordered four pizzas from Fokken's Grill. And when there was a ring at the doorbell after over an hour, they'd all run to the door like starving children waiting for their parents to come home, only to find two women clutching the *Watchtower* and addressing Rainer, the tallest and eldest of them, with: 'Herr Meta-lit-sha?'—'Have you ever thought about God?'

When Onno opened the door to them this time he went straight back into his room without a word and collapsed into one of the armchairs.

Daniel said, 'Helloah, great that you're at homoah.' That was another one of their secret languages, like the girls' names—

the shipyard, the Nordseewerke. And they told me he had a girlfriend, Vera Bohlsen, and they'd been expecting a baby.

Do you have children?

I nodded. The woman nodded too and pointed at a photo on the wall behind me, and she got up to take it down and show me. A portrait of a young woman with blonde hair and a man of about the same age, his arms around her swollen belly from behind. She was smiling; he wasn't. I got up after two hours. At the door, we embraced like old friends who wouldn't be seeing each other for a long time.

I resisted the impulse to visit Vera. I looked up her address, drove there and waited outside her house, the motor running. She

speaking the way James Hetfield sang, with a deep, pressed-out *oah* at the end of every sentence.

'What's up with your haioah?' asked Stefan.

'It's getting longoah and longoah,' said Daniel.

'And greasioah!'

'You might want to give it a washoah!'

'With shampooah!'

'Or you'll get in trouble with your mothoah!'

But unlike usually, when a single word was enough to get them talking like that for hours on end, Onno didn't join in this time. He didn't even raise an eyebrow, simply staring at them or rather through them, at the wall behind them, with cold, glazed eyes.

Daniel and Stefan sat down on the sofa across from him. The whole drum kit, which occupied almost half the room, was covered in a layer of fine dust. There were crinkly copies of *Rock*

---

lived not far away from the Renkens. I imagined us consoling each other. But I knew I was no consolation. And I drove on, along the country roads to the sea. The wind was so strong that I had to lean against the car door to get it open. I buttoned up my jacket and stuffed my hands in my pockets. Walking backwards, my collar turned up, I climbed the ramp to the top of the dyke. The waves slapped against the land below. In the darkness, I could see lights on the other side of the Dollart bay, Emden, the lights of the city. I drove along the coast until dawn, with no destination. When I'd almost run out of fuel I stopped at a petrol station. I bought a map in the shop. I knew where I was but I wanted to know where else I could be. The attendant, a huge man who seemed to have breathed in too many petrol fumes in his life,

Hard and *Metal Hammer* lying around everywhere. Opened up somewhere in the middle and turned upside down, they covered the radiators, standing lamps and speaker cubes. The ashtray on the table was full to the brim with cigarette butts. Next to it was a tin of Fisherman's Friends, a Zippo lighter, a packet of cigarette papers and a thin, crumpled pouch of Schwarzer Krauser extra-strong tobacco, which seemed to contain hardly enough to roll a cigarette. The shaft of a bread knife poked out of a honey jar as round and high as a paint pot. And a dozen crusts of bread in all shapes and sizes protruded from a paper bag. Both windows were opened at the top and the half-drawn curtains danced lightly in the wind. The clouds had parted and for seconds a few rays of sunshine fell almost vertically into the room.

Stefan explained that Daniel had come round to see him and broken everything, and he had brought him round here so he could continue his work of destruction. He laughed, even slapped his thigh and said, 'Funn-ny,' but no one joined in with his laughter.

---

looked over at my car with a blank gaze, then at the map in front of him, then at me. Have you lost the way?

I shook my head, paid and drove on, until I reached a place where no one would disturb me. A factory site, an old brickworks, long since abandoned. I'd heard stories about the place. The windows were shattered. The gates were missing. Grass grew up between the stones. The chimney, half collapsed, rose above the land, visible for miles. I spread out the map on the front of the car, pressing the edges to the metal with both hands. There were hundreds of possible turnings to take, new, different routes, which could take me to the end of the world. But I got back in the car and drove home.

Daniel looked at him and said with far less emphasis, 'Very funn-ny.' Onno still didn't say anything. Instead he took a swig from a bottle of water standing on the floor next to him, next to an empty biscuit tin. Something wasn't right. Daniel had the feeling he was being dazzled, but it wasn't the light coming from outside.

It was the room itself.

It was brighter than usual.

It was brighter because something was missing.

Then he saw it.

The records were gone.

All of them.

He hadn't been able to see it before, when he came in, but now he saw it: the shelves that filled the entire wall in the alcove behind them were empty. 'Where are all your records?'

'Gone.'

'What—gone?'

The next day, I went to a bar by the harbour with a few work-mates. It was only lunchtime but I'd put my engine on the siding for the day, the others too had finished all their assignments. We ordered beer and schnapps, or rather, I ordered beer and schnapps; I don't know how much. I must have fallen asleep and when I woke up it was dark outside and dazzlingly light inside. The landlord shook me and slapped me in the face. All the others had left.

I stumbled outside, the night hitting me like a blow from a hammer. I staggered to my car, the only one in the car park, wound down the window and turned on the engine. The road markings intersected each other in my head. I had to keep one eye closed to stay on the right side of the road.

Now Stefan turned around to the shelves as well. Onno owned hundreds of records, some inherited from his parents—the Beatles, Pink Floyd and the Electric Light Orchestra—but most of them he'd bought himself. Even as a child, he'd saved up and spent all his money on singles and albums. Initially unsure what was good or bad, guided by what was played over and over on TV or the radio, he had picked what he knew out of the record boxes and then, at Weers' recommendation, discovered Edgar Varèse, Gene Krupa, Keith Moon, Mitch Mitchell, Klaus Dinger, John Bonham and Ian Paice. Ian Paice! Deep Purple, 'Paint It Black' on *Scandinavian Nights*, live in Stockholm 1970, Connoisseur Collection DP VSOP LP 125, Record One, Side Two, six minutes of only drums. And from then on he'd continued on his own and taken every opportunity to go to Negativeland, a small record shop in the county town, to listen to and buy everything new, new to him. Doom. Fear Of God. Naked City.

'My mother's locked them away.'

The light was still on in the hall and the door to Tobias' room was ajar. I lay down in bed next to Nella, and when she went out for a walk with Tobias the next afternoon I packed my belongings, the most important things—fishing rods, clothes, papers. I wrote her a note, saying I was the cause and effect of all evil and wouldn't create any more karma from now on, at least not around her, saying we needed some distance and I had to find my way back to myself, to restore my inner equilibrium; things she'd accused me of or advised me to do only days previously; and I put the note on the kitchen table. Throughout the drive, I was ashamed of my inability to say it to her face, to tell her that our son's screams were a dead man's screams, echoing in my head and

'What? She must be crazy.'

'Why on earth?' asked Stefan.

'Because of the messages.'

'What messages?'

'How do I know? She read this article that said there are hidden messages on records which you can only hear if you play them backwards.'

'Back-masking. That's nothing new. I'm thinking *Revolution No. 9, Strawberry Fields Forever, Stairway to—*'

'It's not new, but these two guys in America killed themselves because of them.'

'*Heaven* . . . Because of what?'

'Because of the messages.'

'What messages?'

'How do I know? Read the article for yourself.'

---

robbing me of my sleep, and that her new God and her prayers and her robes, her whole patchwork religion was driving me round the bend, had been for years now, ever since she went to Japan with her sister. I'm still ashamed of that. But it's too late for apologies now. The train's left the station.

I got myself a room in Emden, right by the station; I only had to cross the road to get to work. I stayed there for two months. Once, I called Nella. When she heard my voice she put the phone down. I tried it again later that evening. And a couple more times over the next few days. But no matter when I called, as soon as I said my name, as soon as she realized it was me, she'd hang up or not even answer and let the phone ring, and at some point, a week

He went over to his desk, plucked a newspaper clipping from *Die Zeit* off the pin-board and handed it to Daniel. Four paragraphs were highlighted in yellow.

In 1985, two young men committed suicide. One died instantly, the other three years later. The parents are now suing for damages, claiming that hidden signals and commands underneath the music of the Heavy Metal band Judas Priest on CBS Records drove James Vance and Ray Belknap to suicide.

They began their Christmas celebrations on 23 December 1985—in Ray's bedroom, with beer, marijuana and the Judas Priest record *Stained Class*, which at one point refers to the world as not worthy of living in. 'Let's see what comes afterwards,' James is alleged to have said. They had gone to the church playground with a sawn-off shotgun, and after Ray had been the first to put it in his mouth and shoot and was instantly dead, James failed to kill himself with his own shot.

---

later, the line was dead and an artificial-sounding woman's voice said, This number is no longer in service. I rented a furnished flat in the town centre, with a view of the *delft*, the lightship and the town hall. But I didn't stay there for long either. I thought I could undo everything I'd done and start over from the beginning if I moved back to Jericho, not with her or my parents, but into a small old house next to the rectory, which had just become vacant.

I don't know what Nella found harder to forgive—me leaving or me coming back.

Under hypnosis, he gave his version of the events on that 23 December. He stated that he could quote Judas Priest lyrics like the Bible and that he considered Heavy Metal music encouraged killing, rape and robbery. And Ray, before he raised the gun to his head, allegedly called out 'You too, you too.'

Howard Shevrin, a psychoanalyst at the University of Michigan, did not hesitate to confirm the danger of subliminal messages. He said the brain absorbed and internalized them (!) as the individual's own thoughts. Under the specific circumstances—of the behaviourally disturbed young people, therefore predestined for suicide—the subliminal message 'you too' had been imperative, Shevrin detailed in court. It had 'pushed Ray and James over the edge,' he claimed.

At first glance, Daniel had really read *you too* and not *do it*, and he had to start again and point to the place with his finger to

My hands are trembling. I look up and the train is in the activation area of a level crossing. The alarm howls in my ears and I break out in a panic. I don't understand what's happened. It takes me a moment to think clearly and press the safety switch. I pick up the radio handset, call the control centre and tell them I'm just outside of Rheine and will be arriving slightly late and everything's fine, forgot to press the safety button, I don't know, just got up for a moment because I had cramp in my leg and didn't get back in time. I release the brake valve, turn the hand wheel to the right, and gradually get moving again.

I swipe both hands across my face. I wish I had a bucket of cold water or a bed I could sleep in. I wish I could sleep at all

make sure it really did say *do it* and not *you too*. 'Do it,' he said to himself and to the others too. 'Do it.'

'Yeah,' said Onno. 'Do it.'

And although his fear hadn't been confirmed, the shock had still paralysed him. He was suddenly back in the bushes. Yes because now we're here we might as well yes yes sure I get it I get what he's saying he doesn't have to say it three times over I heard everything he said I'm not deaf but I still don't understand why we have to hide we can walk towards him he can't run away anyway with a flat tyre or why else is he pushing his bike in this weather we ought to get it over with quickly drag him across the field to the thing that drinking trough there it's ridiculous it's another one of Rainer's stupid ideas baptism why does he always have to go over the top why simple when you can make it complicated there's no point it's much too far away and then we have to go through with it even though no one can be bothered any more we can't just leave him lying there that's no good cause what

again, just a couple of hours, a night, a day. The doctor, Doctor Ahlers, said it's not unusual in your line of work, the varying hours, all the sitting down—you don't need sleeping tablets, you need to make up for it, more sport, more physical exercise, push your body to its limits, give up smoking. And I did that. I ran along the dyke every day. I braced myself against the wind or let it buffet me along. At low tide I ran through the mudflats; I ran as far out as I could and then, the tide around me, ran back again. I swam at the swimming pool; I don't know how many lengths. I even bought myself a bike, me and a bicycle, a racing bike with curved handlebars. I lost weight, ten kilos in ten weeks, and for a while I was fitter than ever before. My trousers and shirts were

does that look like half measures once you've started something you have to finish better we get it over with right here right now mind you it doesn't matter now I'm all wet now anyway from top to toe up to my ankles in mud why did I have to wear my Chucks today typical well at least you can wash them but they never look as good as before Onno's black ones are totally faded who knows how often he's put them in the washing machine Mum's going to flip her lid when she sees them cost a fortune they're in the window at Schröder's Shoes for ninety-five marks Auntie Margret and Auntie Gerhild from Bad Vilbel gave you them for your birthday Bad Vilbel I can't stand the place to hell with Bad Vilbel and to hell with my birthday and to hell with Auntie Margret and Auntie Gerhild with your semi-detatched houses and your front gardens right next door to each other your neatly mown lawns and shiny clean cars on Saturday afternoons your tweed and taffeta clothes your permanent waves and permanent husbands your Peter Alexander and Hildegard Knef records the landscape prints above the settee your porcelain dogs pewter cups crystal glasses

suddenly too loose and I had to buy new ones, a size smaller. I told myself I felt better and slept better, but whenever I woke up and looked at the clock I'd notice that only a few minutes had passed. So I gave it up again, not right away, not from one day to the next, but I didn't run as far, I swam fewer lengths, and the bike gathered dust in the garage.

I pass fields and meadows, going under the B70 for the seventh time and finally arriving in Rheine, almost punctual down to the minute despite the incident. When I drop the train off at the depot I feel relieved. And at the same time I keep watching the wagons with a sense of longing, as if it pained me to have once again left unused all the possibilities for blowing up the world.

everywhere and you're not allowed to touch anything it might break keep nice and clean top and bottom you haven't even said thanks they'll never give you a present again especially if you treat it so carelessly but that's typical of you first you want them and three weeks later you don't even look at them any more that's the way with all your things as long as you get your own way we have to work so hard for it we've worked so hard for you it adds up to hundreds of thousands but that doesn't interest you that doesn't interest anyone no one sees it it's all taken for granted as long as everyone's nice and full up all morning I stand here in the kitchen for you lot peeling potatoes and making dessert yummy dessert strawberries puke with strawberries yuck strawberries and then your dad starts in as well I get fish from Krause's specially fresh fish the best salmon they have the most expensive the finest fillets fried golden brown all you have to do is sit down at the laid table go ahead take a seat not that you'd lift a finger in your valuable holidays without asking for something in return as if he could cook as if he ever and in next to no time you lot have gobbled up

---

At the engines office where I collect my new assignment, I have to answer two questions. Does it happen often, that cramp in my leg, and am I capable of driving back? I say yes twice, and then they advise me to go to the works doctor in Emden and get him to sign me off sick. I think about it for a second; the thought of having nothing to do for two weeks is tempting. If it was warmer I could go camping by the Leukermeer. I could try out my new carbon rod and new bait, boilies from Holland, and try and break my personal record, thirty-five pounds. Carp bite well in April but the nights are still cold and long, and my old gas heater for the tent is broken and the new one hasn't come yet, and I'd only end up sitting at home in front of the TV.

the meal like any old grub at a greasy spoon the same old thing every day and no one helps me I have to do everything myself maybe if I just put them in water just soak them rinse them scrub them but the stains won't go away for sure the stuff's just running in through the eyelets and the seams sure it was bound to squelch when I walk I should have thought of that right away but he won't hear it anyway the rain's much too loud and he's got other things on his mind he only ever thinks of his insects maybe if I didn't keep slipping up like crazy here I'll be in the ditch in a minute it's all on a slope here maybe I should dig myself in all I have to do is lift them up and I'll sink in deeper and get stuck but then maybe I won't get out quick enough to grab him as soon as the whistle comes maybe I should just bugger off through the opening there they wouldn't even notice just up the railway embankment and along the tracks back to the village they wouldn't even get it there's far too many bushes in the way by the time they notice I'll be long gone maybe they wouldn't even miss me they'd deal with Penis on their own without me they don't need my help never have but

Then I go into the canteen, buy a pack of cigarettes from the vending machine, take a tray, bread rolls and meat and fill up my thermos flask without anyone noticing. I sit down at a table by the window, at a distance from the others, scribble down words and numbers on my timesheet and watch my younger colleagues as I flick lazily through my notes. They're so scared to miss something during their break that they run from one table to the next, talking to this or that person about the fall of the Wall, the upcoming football World Cup, decommissioned tracks and decommissioned wives, never more than a few minutes, swapping the latest stories and rumours. They come to me too, of course. They gather round me like someone lying on the floor begging to be counted out. I

if I do that I might as well not show my face around them any more they'd hold it against me for ever they'd say I've got no guts I left them in the lurch and so on and so on I'm a chicken all the usual stuff they'd really get their rocks off on it I would if I was them too what's going on now must be Penis what a funny sobbing sound he's crying before he gets so much as a slap in advance like preventive medicine what trembling breathing sounds like an animal caught in a trap or a person coming in from the cold the thing from the swamp damn where's it coming from anyway not from there and not from over there that sobbing everywhere when I listen in one direction it comes from there when I listen in that direction it comes from over there where's that stupid farm boy got to now has he gone past already or what or did he turn around there's no path branching off he can't have turned off he has to come this way or turn back again unless he walks across the fields but I bet he wouldn't dare he'd never leave his things in the lurch not if his life depended on it not just like that he won't have noticed we're waiting for him here no he's much too dumb for

put my notebook aside, push the flask and the plate away and listen to what they have to say.

Heard you had another unplanned stop, over at Salzbergen.

What was up with you, old boy?

Yeah, Walter, what happened?

Drunk again, were you?

Had too much coffee again?

How do you manage to get so drunk on coffee? Or did you have another visitor?

It wasn't one of your girls, was it?

that and then the others would be after him and I'd have seen that they have to go past me but the sobbing's there I'm not imagining it am I I'm not stupid am I or is it coming from me I'd feel it wouldn't I I'm not sobbing not so strangely like especially how would I with my mouth closed I'd notice that what's the matter they're all there already why didn't anyone let me know didn't I hear the whistle or what the sobbing's not that loud not so loud you wouldn't hear it when Onno puts his fingers in his mouth he can wake the dead who's Stefan talking to there Penis' handlebars and front wheel bent looks pretty far gone I bet the frame's bent someone must have jumped on it and the bag there the books a thermos flask and the jars those nasty old jars with his insects in they're broken at last I always wanted to smash them against the wall in Biology he showed off with them all the time with his snails and spiders and moths what a swot all he wanted was to suck up to Mrs Mengs well I just happen to have a few samples with me sure we believe you thousands wouldn't and then his typical know-it-all face his stupid grin all the time he managed it all

My break's not over yet but I get up, pack my things away and walk over to the track. I've been assigned a 216 again and I wonder why they bothered electrifying the track if they still keep sending out the old diesel engines. This time it's a fast train from Cologne, which has the advantage that I only have to stop seven times until Norddeich and my day's over by lunchtime. Before the conductor's closed the door behind him, I'm moving off.

I thought about asking for a transfer, of course, working in admin. Back then, after the first time, they offered me a good job in a signal tower. But that's not for me. I can't spend all day in front of a

right they always do the teachers are happy as Larry when someone's actually interested in what they're teaching when someone joins in and uses their brain but as soon as you use yours a bit more as soon as you ask the question what's it got to do with you and your life what's the point of all this what purpose does it all serve that we sit around all day long and shovel all this crap into our brains that's going a step too far and you'll soon be on the brink very soon my friend this is not the time and place for that what you're spouting has nothing to do with the construction plans of animals what do I care about the construction plan of snails put salt on them and that's it there are Onno and Rainer too mind you a pretty long way away considering what are they doing back there by the level crossing there where the Kelly Family's bus Danny Boy the pipes the pipes are calling with their funny robes are they crazy or what and what's Stefan saying there he's talking to them or isn't he I can't understand a word can't see his head frseeeeeeeeeeeeeeeeeeeeeefrong oh now of all times a train has to come frseeeeeeeeeeeeeeeeeeeeeeeefrong I bet it's that Baalmann he

screen or a wall full of switches and levers, waiting for a command and then pressing that one button on that one command, like my father. It'd drive me crazy. Nella is convinced I already am, crazy that is, that I'm locked in a struggle with myself and the grief has eaten away at me, but that's not true. She just couldn't take it that I had to go on driving. She didn't understand it. Lots of people didn't, and they never will understand; only my workmates, they do, because they're in exactly the same boat as I am. Going on driving is the only way to forget what happened, and the only way to deal with it. At first I hated the relatives for putting up crosses in the places where it happened. I thought, they want to remind me of what I've done; they want to punish me with those signs

always whistles when he goes past because of his wife or whatever so she knows he'll be home soon and put the food on the table frseeeeeeeeeeeeeeeeeeeeeeefrong what are you saying I can't hey Daniel all alone here so far away from did he really just say Daniel now it's starting to buzz as well a flickering in the rails a screeching I bet it's a freight train with new cars we threw stones at them once from a mast that was such a laugh climbed up each of us a handful of stones and then bambambam right at the windows at night of course full moon otherwise we'd have got caught was pretty hard to keep your balance with one hand and aim with the other in our state and all totally wasted and then everything was trembling as well when those heavy ones especially the ore trains twenty or thirty wagons in a row so loud you can't stand it and we were just as close to the tracks even closer awokwokawok what was that sounded like when Dad beats the carpet in the garden like a dull thud that echoes off the walls and what's that red stuff now is that blood or what where's that come from all of a sudden I haven't hurt myself I haven't bumped into anything or did I did I

of their misery. But now I don't hate them any more. I know they're more responsible for those people's deaths than I am.

The second time, I was on my own. I was coming from Bremen. It was in the middle of summer, the 21st of July 1983, and I had a clear view for miles. I remember I was just thinking how much had changed along that stretch of track, what was still there and what wasn't, because there were sleepers piled up everywhere, wooden sleepers. Tracks had been taken up and new ones laid. They'd renewed the track ballast and laid new sleepers, made of concrete, I was thinking. And then, when I came around the curve

tear my skin on the thorns over there won't come off the bloody stuff won't come off you have to wash it out right away or it'll never come out it's not me is it it's coming from up above from the clouds the sky my God it's raining blood it's really raining blood the day of wrath has come hail and fire mingled with blood it can't be true and now the ground's quaking as well there's thunder and noise and lightning Meinders was right after all that old bastard was right although the earth has been quaking all along that's normal that's the train it'll be gone in a minute then there'll be peace in every treetop you feel the reeds over there aren't moving any more he must have gone past I'd better go over to the others been standing round here like an idiot for too long shit what was that now Peni I mean Peter how did you get here so quickly his eye's missing my God his eye's missing what happened to you how dumb of course I can't think of anything better right now that's what everyone says with accidents a totally sick automatic reaction that's what Dad said back then after the thing in the maize field with Iron but this is a joke in comparison half of

near Stickhausen-Velde, I saw someone standing on the track at the end of the long straight stretch. I sounded the signal three times, then I pulled on the brake. Screeching, the train slid along the rails, getting slower and slower but still not slow enough to come to a stop in time. It was a woman. She was wearing a white dress like a nurse's uniform. Her blonde hair danced in the wind before she disappeared below me.

Michaela Klopp, 21 July 1963–21 July 1983. That's what it said in the paper two days later, and underneath that two names, Erika and Aiko and the address, nothing else, no information about the funeral, no word of regret, no bible passage. I was better prepared this time. I bought a bunch of flowers for the mother at

Penis' face has gone he's got a hole in his head the size of a fist like in that book on the shelf at the Reicherts' place War against War or whatever it's called the skin all torn away and tied up with wire like it's been torn to shreds and just patched up again to meet me thanks a lot Frankenstein's monster that's what he looks like just the same kind of face that makes you want to run a mile his right arm a stump his whole body naked except for some leftover scrap of trousers furrowed like by a rotary tiller now he's swaying to and fro as well stumbling and wobbling around like a spinning top just about to fall over shit why doesn't he fall over the way he looks he ought to collapse any minute now or fall apart what's this what does he want now what's he doing with that stupid rod that's the thing he always lugs around with him he probably takes it to bed with him and all and shoves it up his arse I wouldn't be surprised nothing would surprise me with him it's certainly long enough to stick it through you from bottom to top and as sharp as a sword and that's exactly what he's holding it like just like an executioner's sword like in that armoury in Emden where we went

the station, nothing big, nothing brash, ready packed in cellophane with a ribbon round it; for the father I took along a bottle of schnapps. We could probably both do with a drink, I thought. And apart from that I didn't want them to fob me off with one or two beers and then be high and dry for hours. But when the woman opened the door to me, just a chink, she was already so tanked up that her breath took mine away. When I introduced myself she adjusted her glasses, which occupied half her face, and asked, what d'you want? Once I'd explained everything she went inside without a further word. I followed her along a narrow hallway crowded with junk. In the living room, she flopped down onto a grease-spotted leather sofa. Next to her I saw a boy, maybe

with school in the museum in the town hall and I bet he's going to whack me in the head with it like an overripe thanks a lot saw that one coming saw it all coming just keep on keep on bashbashbash like at confirmation like at bloody confirmation when I knelt there in church with my eyes closed and my hands folded in front of Meinders like a total idiot like Meinders and said yes three times I said yes yes I will yes. All that flashed through him in one second.

'She cut it out specially for me,' said Onno.

'Who?' asked Stefan.

'My mother. So I know all about it.'

'But it's nonsense,' said Daniel, shaking his head to get rid of the images the article had conjured up from the depths of his soul.

'She came in my room while I was in Denmark, saw that I've got the same record,' he tapped the article with one finger, 'the one it's all about, *Stained Class*—'

'Great album,' said Stefan and then, turning to Daniel and pointing at the clipping, 'give it here.'

---

twelve or thirteen. The TV was on at full volume; they were both watching the Smurfs. The blinds were down and the lights on, illuminating the swathes of smoke drifting past them.

I told her how sorry I was about her daughter, although it wasn't true. Then I held out the flowers to her for a few seconds, and when she didn't react I simply put them down on the table in front of her, between empty beer bottles and full ashtrays. Don't be, she said, her voice so hoarse I thought it'd be gone any minute and she wouldn't be able to say a word. But then it rose in one fell swoop, as if she'd discovered some last vestige of energy somewhere inside her after all. I'm not sorry about her, it was her own fault, she didn't get it from me and—she pointed at the ceiling—

'It's pretty conventional if you ask me, it might have been ground-breaking in the seventies, hard rock, but now all it has is documentary—'

'Judas Priest isn't hard rock! Maybe the early stuff, *Rocka Rolla*, *Sad Wings of Destiny*, but with *Sin After Sin* at the latest they were totally metal, they were pretty much at the forefront back then. I'm thinking *Dissident Aggressor*.'

'Anyway, she saw that I've got it, and then she probably looked more closely at the others as well and decided I'm at serious risk of suicide. So—'

'It does say *death* all over them,' said Daniel, handing the clipping to Stefan.

'—to protect me from myself she locked them all away.'

'What, where are they now?'

'How do I know? Somewhere in the cellar, probably in the furnace room. I've looked everywhere but I couldn't find anything, and the furnace room's locked.'

---

not from him neither. She lit a cigarette, and then she told me the condensed version of a life she saw as wasted. Dropped out of school, dropped out of her apprenticeship, and one man after another. She started throwing herself at men when she was only fourteen. She looked at the boy as she said that, but he spent the whole time staring at the screen. He was Smurf-blue with its reflected light, shovelling peanut flips out of the packet with both hands. She couldn't ever be alone, she always had to have someone around her, especially after Roland died. At the word Roland, she pointed at the ceiling again. He wasn't her father but he cared for her like a father, more than that, he was always there for her while I was looking after the little'un here. She patted the boy's

'Bad news,' said Daniel.

'Very bad news,' said Stefan, 'very bad climate down there, very bad climate. I'm thinking subtropical.'

'Yeah, Stefan,' said Onno. 'Thanks a lot for the tip.'

'They'll never survive it, the temperature variations, I mean. They'll get warped. Much too humid and much too warm.'

'Shut it, will you?'

'Have you got anything to smoke?' asked Stefan. He banged his fist against his chest several times. 'I could use one.' No one ever said 'I've got lung yearnings' like Volker. Once Daniel had said it, 'lung yearnings,' and everyone had looked at him as if he wasn't right in the head, as if he had a speech defect that could only be got rid of with a lot of practice, if at all.

'No,' said Onno, squeezing the tobacco pouch on the table as if to prove his point. A couple of strands wafted out and sank onto the marble table-top like brown snow.

knee and he drew his leg away. But once Roland died she was all alone, and it was all too much for me and all, I had to go back to work myself, at the custard factory, all he left us was debts, and then the two kids, but I rolled up my sleeves and got on with it, no point sitting around at home all day long, and she rolled up her sleeves as well, up to here. She pointed at the inside of her elbow. I don't know how many times she tried to quit, three times at least, but all that rehab's no use if you don't want to give up, if you haven't got the message up here—she tapped her forehead—that you're just killing yourself.

I lit a cigarette, unscrewed the schnapps lid and drank a swig out of the bottle. White blossoms, billowing hay, smoke and turf

'Nothing at all?'

'No. You?'

'Only cigarettes,' said Stefan. He slipped down in his seat and extracted a box from his trouser pocket, dented at the corners. Then he took out a cigarette for himself, passed the pack on to Onno and Daniel and gave them both a light.

'And when,' Daniel cleared his throat to weaken the desire to cough, 'I mean, and when are you going to get them back?' Tears pricked his eyes and he turned his head so the others couldn't see.

Onno crossed his legs and extended his chin, expelling smoke upwards. 'It looks like never.'

'You won't be able to play them anyway in that state,' said Stefan and knocked the ash off his cigarette with a tap of his fingertip.

'She must be crazy,' Daniel repeated. 'She can't do that.'

Onno shrugged.

---

and fern, and hot as pepper. I noticed she wanted some too, because she looked over at me with greedy eyes when I put the bottle to my lips, but I didn't give her any and she went on talking, and the longer she talked the hoarser she got again, and at some point, when her voice really did fail, she got up and got herself a bottle of schnapps out of a cupboard.

After she sat down again she said, Well, let's see what we've got here. She held her glass out to me, dull from her greasy fingers, and raised it for a toast, but this time I didn't react. She'd barely necked the glass before she started in again. I always told her, keep your hands off that stuff, you'll go and catch something, I told her a hundred times.

'What's much worse, if you ask me,' said Stefan, holding up the newspaper clipping, 'is that she's indirectly insulting you, all of us actually.'

'How?' asked Onno.

'Look,' said Stefan and read out the passage, 'the behaviourally disturbed young people, therefore predestined for suicide. I'm thinking subliminal message!'

'You mean—' said Onno, looking at the clipping again.

'Exactly. That's what she's trying to tell us—that we're behaviourally disturbed. And predestined for suicide.'

'She's the one who's predestined for suicide,' said Onno. 'She's been totally off the rails since Achim moved out.'

'She's transferring her fears to you. Maybe she should go and see my old man, he could prescribe something for her.'

'Like what?'

'All kinds of stuff. She just has to tell him what she wants and he'll write her a prescription.'

I can't remember how long I sat there listening to her. At some point I got up and asked where the bathroom was, and she said, the toilet's right over there by the front door, but instead of going to the toilet I went outside into the front garden and pissed on the flower bed, a long, strong jet. On the way home I decided never to do that again, never to talk to those people again.

Everything repeats itself, only in reverse order. Farmers drive their tractors across the fields, laundry bulges in the wind, and the sand pits have the same attraction and fascination for the children even two hours later. The new nuclear power station appears on the

'It'd have to be pretty strong stuff. She's been lying in bed downstairs all day like in a coma.' He put out his cigarette.

'She can come round this evening. That's no problem. People are always picking up prescriptions outside practice hours, even at night sometimes. Or she can make an appointment with him, for a session. He offers that as well,' he pointed at the article. 'Conversational therapy.'

'She'd never do that. She'd rather run over to church every day and pray it away.'

'Maybe you can drop a subtle hint by giving her a Therapy? single.'

'Therapy?' asked Daniel.

'Yeah,' said Stefan. 'A new band from England or Ireland.'

'Northern Ireland,' said Onno.

'Whatever.'

'I heard them on the radio the other day, on Bremen Four.'

---

left, and on the right, after Hanekenfähr, the old one with its huge cooling tower from which no steam has risen for years now, and never will again. I cross the Dortmund-Ems Canal, which flows together with the river here for a few hundred metres before they divide again, and just after that I'm alongside the red ruins of a vanished world. On the platform, the waiting people clot together in front of the opened doors. The passengers on the train push their way out and the ones on the platform push in. It's always a pleasure to watch that moment when the two groups' movements cancel each other out, but it's nothing compared to the high when you pass through a station at top speed without having to stop. Every person is a delay, a hurdle to be overcome. The man in the

'Can you get Bremen Four?'

'Yeah, sure.'

'On that thing there?' He gestured at the stereo.

'Yeah.'

'Put it on then.'

'Not now.'

'Put it on!'

'No.'

'So you can't get it, I thought so.'

'I don't have to prove anything to you.'

'No?'

'No.'

'Then you can turn the radio on, can't you?' said Stefan, wedging his cigarette into the notch in the ashtray even though it had burnt down to the filter, and bracing his hands against his knees as if to get up. 'Or shall I? I know the frequency by heart.'

---

red hat raises his signalling disc. The doors close. I turn the hand wheel to the right, wait till the gears are full, and then I pull off.

I don't have the best relationship with my brothers and sister. After our father died we went on meeting up regularly but then, when the children came, their children, the gaps in between got longer and longer. And when I left my wife and my boy, when I ducked out of my responsibilities, as they put it, we had no contact for years. Responsibility! What do they know about responsibility? Who was their father? Who spent all those years looking after them and protecting them from the worst? But I can't blame them for condemning me. They can't help it. They don't realize how easy they had it. They don't know there were stones in their

'Go ahead,' said Onno with a wave at the stereo.

Stefan stood up, went over to the stereo and pressed Power on all the decks, but nothing happened.

'What's the matter? No power?' He pulled the cabinet away from the wall slightly and leant over the amplifier.

'She took the power cables as well,' said Onno and took another gulp out of his water bottle.

Stefan pushed the cabinet back against the wall and sat down again. He shook his head with a disdainful grin. 'Now that's totally brain-dead. She could have just left the records then.'

'You don't say.'

'You really are an *arm Bloot*.'

'Thanks,' said Onno. 'Thanks for reminding me of how shit it all is.'

'Why don't you move in with your old man?' asked Stefan.

'They may not have had the same opinion on many points, too many probably, but they're agreed on one.'

---

path that I cleared for them, and for myself. They're simply not the first-born. In their shoes, I might have done the same. For a while we didn't even say *Moin* on the street, and that's saying something because people say *Moin* to everyone here, even tourists. Now I just don't see them very often, more by chance if it does happen.

I don't have many friends any more either, not since Nella and I split up, and with the few I still have—two or three who work on the railways or at the public order office, like Theo Houtjes—I talk about other things than our wives or ex-wives or God and deep subjects. We usually go fishing together. And when you sit next to each other for hours by one of the flooded sand pits, drinking beer,

'Which one?' asked Daniel.

'My one,' said Onno. 'That it wouldn't be good for me to live with him and his new girlfriend.'

'Why not?' asked Daniel.

''Cause she doesn't like me and I don't like her. And their house is much too small. And my mother would freak out if I did it.'

There was silence for a while.

At last Daniel finished smoking as well. He pressed the cigarette out and reached for the Fisherman's Friends tin on the table, but before he got there Onno said, 'Forget it, it's empty.'

Daniel shook the tin—there was no more to be heard than a slight rustle—and put it down again. 'Remember Weers?' he said. He wanted to perk up their mood, remind them of the old days, hoping that would release the tension that must have overcome them over the past few weeks. He didn't know what was up, why the two of them were so short-tempered. Things were always

absolutely concentrated on the slight vibrations of the rod bell, it frees up your mind, or makes it freer than anything else I've experienced anyway. At those times I think of nothing. Nothing is, nothing was, nothing comes back to me apart from the hook.

I do go to church services, and I close my eyes and fold my hands and repeat the words, but my heart's not in it. I value the community, spending time with Hans; as I said, I draw strength out of all these things, and yet there's nothing that goes any further. I don't feel what I ought to feel. There's no illumination inside me, no ecstasy, not what I hoped for. And that's why I pray to the stars and the trees and the fish in the water. The lake is my church. That's where I find my peace. That's where I have

breaking down in Stefan's basement and there'd always been problems with Onno's mother, much worse than this one.

Once she'd launched into Onno for a really petty reason.

At breakfast he'd said, 'The tea's cold.'

And she'd picked up the cup and chucked the tea in his face and said, 'It's hot enough for you.'

And another time, just after she and her husband split up, she had run away in the middle of the night and Onno had thought she'd do herself harm if he didn't stop her. She'd already threatened to take tablets or throw herself under a train, and he had to call the police and drive around with the officers, Kurt Rhauderwiek and Joachim Schepers, until they found her. She was standing by a cigarette machine at the end of the village, at the junction to the B70. Dazzled by the headlamps, she shielded her eyes with one hand while she fumbled in her pocket for coins with the other and, walking slowly towards the car, claimed all the other vending machines were out of order. 'They keep on swallowing up my

the feeling I'm entirely myself. No one asks anything of me, and I don't ask anything of anyone else, only that the fish bite.

I'm never alone, even if Hans or the others don't come along. The kids make their noise far away on the opposite bank, lighting fires, throwing things in the water, presumably stones they gather up from the railway embankment, and they roar and shout until their boredom bores even them and they leave or fall asleep. In the darkness, I see the other anglers' cigarettes lighting up and glowing to an end. I hear their belches echoing over the lake, the scrunching sound when they crush their beer cans. And by the exclamations they make when they reel in their lines, I can tell how good or bad their catch was.

money . . . Eight marks I've lost today . . . Eight marks! . . . That's
. . . two packets! . . . Those damn machines!' she called into the
open police-car window, struggling from one sentence to the next,
not noticing her son on the back seat.

'Is everything all right?' asked Rhauderwiek. 'Have you been
drinking?'

'No,' she said. 'I'm . . . tired.'

'Well, it's the middle of the night.'

'Yes . . . night.' She looked around as if she'd only just realized. 'Middle of the night . . . Those damn machines! . . . That's
what you should be dealing with . . . Not with me . . . I'll be fine
. . . Always been fine . . . Never alone . . . God is with me . . . He
shows me the way . . . '

'The Lord is my shepherd, I shall not want,' said Rhauderwiek.

'Right . . . exactly right . . . '

'Except for cigarettes.'

To begin with, Hans refused to believe how liberating it is to
spend a night by the lake. During one of our first conversations I
said to him, if there's a God then he's out there, and I pointed out
of his study window. But it took me years to persuade him to try
it out for himself. And right after that first night he asked when I
was going next and could he come with me again. Back then I
thought he just wanted to drink undisturbed, but now that he's
sworn off the alcohol, our shared demon, I don't think that any
more.

On that first night, we sat next to each other in silence. We
held our rods in the water all along, twice changing position but
not catching anything. And when something did bite around

'Have you got any?'

'No,' said Schepers. 'Only tobacco. No filters.'

'Even better.'

He leant over his colleague and handed her a pouch, and she took out the cigarette papers and rolled two cigarettes, one for herself and one for him. 'Can I buy this off you?' she held up the pouch.

'No, you can't. You can keep it though. Do you need more papers? There aren't many left in there.'

'I've got enough papers . . . more than enough . . . I just didn't have any tobacco left . . . at home . . .'

But he'd already ducked down. 'I've got some here somewhere,' he said, his head half-submerged in the glove compartment. 'Here.'

'Thanks very much,' she said once she'd taken her first puff.

'No need.'

---

dawn, a small bream, and he fetched it out, I asked him, how can you do that, catch fish?

And while he fiddled the hook out of the gills and threw the mutely thrashing fish back in the water, he asked me, how can you do that, drive a train?

Clouds have moved in front of the sun and the glinting of the Geeste reservoir that dazzled me only hours ago has disappeared. There's a languor above the water now like in autumn. The buds on the birch trees have lost their intensity even before they unfurl, the willows are less green, the sky less blue. The colour has

'Heaven must have sent you.'

'No,' said Rhauderwiek and gestured behind him at the back seat. 'It was your son.'

Onno had told the whole story to his best friends, Stefan, Rainer and Daniel, hoping they wouldn't tell anyone else, even though he hadn't expressly told them to keep everything about his mother and him to themselves. But they had done so far. None of them spoke to their parents about what they'd been through together or knew about one another, and sometimes Daniel thought that was the very essence of their friendship—that it only existed in the moments when they were together and there was no space for the past or the future. But now he had the feeling something had changed since they'd last been together, something decisive, something that had nothing to do with the failed experiment earlier or the lack of music now but with him leaving, the fact that they didn't go to school together any more and never would again.

leeched out of everything, the colour of spring. Looking at the land, you know that summer has irretrievably passed and the air will grow ever cooler and milkier. And yet I still cling to that stretch of grey water before I re-immerse myself in the forest after Meppen. I drink another swig of coffee to get my strength up.

I've been fishing there too, just out of curiosity. The reservoir was only dug out a couple of years ago, as cooling water for the nuclear power station, and there's not much in there yet apart from a few ruffes and sticklebacks. And unlike as I thought in the car on the way there, they're neither unusually large nor do they have three eyes or fangs or any other spectacular mutations that might justify hours of waiting. Even though the conditions in that

'What do you mean?' asked Onno.

'Napalm Death.'

'That's ages ago,' said Onno.

And Stefan added, 'No one gives a shit about that any more.'

'Maybe you don't,' said Daniel. 'I'm thinking: *Trash* Metal.'

'Are we so old we've started talking about the past now, or what?'

'You're the one who always brings it up.'

'Brings up what?'

'The past.'

'Just leave it,' said Onno. 'It doesn't matter.'

'No,' said Stefan and struggled halfway to his feet from the sofa. 'First I want to know what he means by that.'

'Nothing,' said Daniel. 'Forget it.'

'All right then, if you say so,' said Stefan, leaning back.

---

stone tub might well be ideal for mutations. The lake is Europe's largest asphalted surface, the water floating in a gigantic concrete bowl. Worse than the nuclear power station or the artificiality of the whole setting, though, are the swimmers and divers and windsurfers who prevent any natural development before it can happen.

If I lived nearby and could take the car there every night and drink until dawn without worrying about being stopped on the road, I might even think about it, despite the paltry catch. But it doesn't make sense the way things are. And I'd never even dream of moving to Meppen, for whatever reason—too big and too Catholic.

There was another silence. Onno took a last sip from the water bottle and looked at his watch. 'Where's Rainer anyway?'

'Don't know,' said Stefan. 'At home, I guess. He must have finished work by now, at least. He's on the early shift this week.'

'Let's go over there,' said Onno. 'I can't take it here any more.'

'Yeah,' said Stefan. 'It's a bit quiet here. A bit too quiet.'

'Wait,' said Daniel. 'I can hear the silence.'

And Stefan said, 'Silence is Deafening.'

'Is that it?' asked Onno. 'Have you made enough of your comments yet?' Once the two of them had nodded they all went through the bedroom, left the house by the outside staircase and went over to Rainer, who lived two streets along on Bach Road.

Jericho isn't big but it's big enough to go out of people's way if you want to. Seeing as my working rhythm is very different to most people's and I often do my shopping on the way home, in one of the supermarkets along the B70 and hardly ever at Superneemann, I rarely come into contact with people from the village. I can lead a normal life for weeks without deliberately avoiding them. And when we do run into each other, at the post office, at the village hall, in Doctor Ahlers' waiting room, they're always amazed at how long we haven't seen each other, and they ask me where I've been all this time, have I been on holiday or run away, or—with a wink—in the closed ward in Emden.

But I do have phases when I feel drawn to my old family, phases when I think all I have to do is get out of the car and ring

6

The rain had lessened off, only a few isolated drops falling from the sky and splashing onto the wet, steaming roads here and there, and above the sea, far out on the horizon, the darkness was brightening. The sun had disappeared between the clouds again but everyone felt the warmth it emitted. Daniel screwed up his eyes and sucked in the scent of the trees and bushes. Soon the layer that had lain on the land like a dark cloth all day would have evaporated.

---

her doorbell and she'll welcome me in like a prodigal son. I drive around, stop outside my old house, look out of the windscreen at the brightly lit windows and spend a while dazzled by the idea that I might return, the way we're dazzled by the white shadow of long-extinguished galaxies by night. I enjoy sitting in the office all day, inserting corrections into timetables. I've never wanted anything else. I get home in the best of moods at five every afternoon, park the car in the driveway and slip into the living room via the back door. Mother and son are watching TV. We eat together at a richly laden kitchen table, roast goose with red cabbage and dumplings. I read Tobias a bedtime story. Then Nella and I snuggle up on our orange artificial leather sofa, smoking and drinking wine, a full-bodied Spätburgunder, deep, saturated

He walked a little way behind the others; there was no room for three abreast on the pavement and he didn't want to walk in the gutter, despite his boots. He found the thought of being shorter than them degrading. Stefan and Onno were still talking about music. When they'd got their teeth into a subject they couldn't abandon it until something new commanded their full attention.

Daniel trod on the back of Stefan's heels.

Stefan didn't trip up though, but instead drew back his arm as if he'd been expecting the attack and rammed his fist into Daniel's stomach. For a moment he couldn't breathe. Daniel bent double and as he gradually fell to his knees he saw that Stefan and Onno had simply kept on walking, not turning around to him again. It took him a full minute to get his breath back. Then he stood up, his hands pressed to his belly, and walked after his friends.

---

red, almost black. Morello cherries, smoked game, forest floor, broad and viscous on the palate and bursting with minerality. We watch a video, one I've taken out of the video shop, casually, not taking any notice of the actors' gestures and actions. But still, inspired by their choreography we touch and kiss and tear each other's clothes off. She sighs and screams and wraps her legs around mine, and we sway to and fro to the rhythm of our lust, like we did back when we were sixteen, when we first met, long before our love faded out. But we can't remember that. We can't remember anything. Our former lives don't exist any more. No collision, no irritation, no powerlessness and no guilty conscience, no guilt at all, no misunderstandings leading to hours of arguing, no objects flying through the air, passing dangerously close to our

The house, a bungalow, was new, as new as the others in the estate. All the houses here looked as though they'd been built in the space of a week, apart from one row on Wagner Road which was older, from the sixties, when Johann Rosing, the building contractor, had started to build cheap accommodation for builders so they'd sign up with him and not the competition. But then he'd realized he could make more profit if he sold the land to the village council, dozens of hectares of best construction land—it simply had to be designated as such—and he had broken off the project of a workers' estate on the other side of the railway tracks and left the land fallow until the council had come to a decision.

The bungalow on Bach Road was the first building in the new estate to be finished, after the ones on Wagner Road, and the Pfeiffer family had lived there at a time when everything else around them was a building site; the earth dug up and loose, the sky full of noise and sand, concrete mixers rotating loudly, trucks pulling in and driving off. It had been impossible to ignore the hammering, sawing and knocking from morning to night and the

---

heads, no healing conversations or morning prayers, no smashed-in doors or stabbed tables, no accusations or insults, no sleepless nights or gruelling, sad days, no Fuji, no complaining. All that is outside of our universe, in a faraway, unfamiliar world. We're newly born, a new species.

Where I barely felt the elevation earlier, at the Tinnen Pines, I now feel the incline just as little. There's no tickle in my stomach, no tingling like I used to get when we raced down the slight hill at full speed. One hand on the handwheel, the other on the safety switch, I glide along with an absolutely even temper, no preliminary

fine, grainy dust that fogged the glass and made its way inside through all the cracks in the doors and windows.

The house wasn't visible from the road, only the tiles framing the gritted roof, the chimney and the TV aerial. It was slightly set back and surrounded by a two-and-a-half-metre wooden fence covered in ivy. Werner Pfeiffer, Rainer's father, had put up the fence himself back then in a desperate attempt to keep all the dirt away from him and his family and his ideal of life in the countryside, and then left it there, to the neighbours' great annoyance. Some were annoyed by it casting too much shade on the pavement or their gardens, the others by it robbing them of their view. They simply didn't know what went on behind it, whether Pfeiffer used pesticides, he and his wife ran around the garden naked and their boys really were tinkering with motorbikes, as they claimed, or building a bomb to blast the whole estate to pieces whenever they felt like it.

Even before Stefan pressed the bell next to the gate they could hear the clanking and rattling, and Rainer saying to someone, 'Hand me the sprocket, will you?' He was talking to his brother

---

signals in warning position, no boiler problems, no speed control lamps, only interrupted by the people I set down and pick up in Lathen.

For Christmas and Easter every year, Hans gives me a notebook, the same kind as he uses, black with a hard cover and an elastic band around it, running parallel to the spine, to close the book when you're not using it. He's never said anything about it; not that it might help me to keep a diary or write down my thoughts and resolutions. It's probably the kind of present you give because you can't think of anything else, because he knows I wouldn't read his self-published writings on the Apocalypse, the prophets of doom and the return of the Great Dragon, and I'm

Marcel who was two years older. He rode a scooter and was a real mod, with a suit and a target badge—not like Rainer. Even if he had the money to pay for it all he wouldn't want to run around looking like that, so style-conscious, such a pop fan, as Rainer called it when he was with Stefan, Onno and Daniel, his hair cut and combed, wide collars and patent leather shoes. Rainer simply wanted to ride a scooter, an old black scooter, because he'd fallen in love with its shape, the legshield with chrome edging that curved in at the bottom, the large headlamp built into the handlebar and the floor strips that shimmered silver in the sunlight. But he kept that to himself after a failed attempt at explaining his aesthetics to them. When he spoke about it now, about his passion, his aim, he mentioned the high-torque four-gear engine with driving-key transmission and kick starter, the multiple plate wet clutch on the crankshaft, the self-supporting steel bodywork, the hydraulically cushioned suspension struts front and back, the Dell'Orto carburettor, the high compression and the overwhelming feeling of bombing along the coast at eighty kilometres an hour

not interested in much apart from fishing and drinking and train-driving, and I'm better than him at all of them. I often simply have the book open in front of me and don't write anything in it. Usually, I draw little sketches in it, absent-mindedly like on the telephone, or I mark down lines, dozens of tallies, one next to another. I count the trains that come towards me, the streets or the bridges or decommissioned stations I've passed. Mostly, though, I let the pen glide aimlessly across the paper like a pendulum, the seismograph of my soul. I rarely get anything useful out of it because my own tremors can't be distinguished from those of the train. Or I trace the route of the Transrapid with the tip of the pen. Even now as I'm driving past it again, I draw my

for no reason. And that feeling was mainly so overwhelming because he wasn't allowed to drive that fast at his age. Next year, when he had his driving licence and a scooter of his own, testing the boundaries would be less tempting, and in the year after that even less so. But as long as there was a vague prospect of beating his brother's Primavera on his Prima, he kept tinkering away at his Hercules. He had already replaced the old chain, taken out the reduction on the exhaust and planed the cylinder head to raise the compression, but so far he hadn't got above a top speed of fifty kilometres an hour. When the bell rang and Marcel got up to open the door, Rainer had been extending the transmission by exchanging the eleven-tooth sprocket for a twelve-tooth one.

'It's for you,' said Marcel, pointing his thumb on the way back to his Vespa.

Rainer looked up. 'Oh, it's you lot.'

'Yes, us lot. Just us lot,' said Onno. 'Were you expecting someone else?'

circles on the paper. The book's full of them. The black book of infinity.

I'll have to start a new one soon.

I could give it up whenever I like, of course I could, but I've noticed that drawing makes me feel contented. Every one of the lines is nothing, taken on its own. It's only through the oscillation, through the curve that leads back to the starting point and extinguishes it, that something unique comes about, something that lends me a power no one else can claim. No one can tell afterwards where I started drawing and where I stopped. Only me. I alone.

'I wasn't expecting anyone,' said Rainer, his eyes reddened, his hair full of dust, and he stared at the sprocket in his hand as if at an unknown object. Then he laid it aside and put the wrench back in the tin, picked up a rag to wipe his fingers and got to his feet, his joints cracking so loudly that everyone could hear. He had given up hope of going back to work in peace. Since he'd started work at the custard factory he'd had only a few hours' time to do what he actually wanted to do, and usually he was too tired even for that when he got home in the afternoon or evening. It was absolutely exhausting standing by the conveyor belt all day long and checking the packaging moving past him for damage. It exhausted him more than anything else, and he had to keep telling himself why he was doing it and that it was worth it, so as not to go mad or chuck in the job and enjoy the summer holidays like his friends.

'We're here now, Mister Meta-lit-scha,' said Daniel, and that made it perfectly clear that they didn't intend to leave any time soon.

When I used to go cycling to get tired enough to sleep all night long, I'd often come here to the northern part of Emsland and cycle past the old labour camps, burial mounds, moor bodies and shooting ranges. Mined territory wherever you tread; too much history. But the wind isn't as strong and there are mile-long stretches of road blocked for cars; for civilian vehicles, not for tanks. The whole area is a nature reserve and a military training area in one, a conservation zone for animals and at the same time a testing place for weapons and ammunition. There are signs every few metres—Military Zone—bunkers and hangars, and when you leave the roads there are tiny splinters of shell on the ground that slit open your tyres if you're not careful. The likelihood of being

'Yes,' said Marcel, although Daniel hadn't said it to him.

Rainer said 'Yes' as well, not picking up on the remark, and to stop him sounding like he was merely repeating his brother's words, he added, 'I can see that.'

In their oil-smeared blue overalls, it was almost impossible to tell Rainer and Marcel apart. The way they stood there underneath the carport, one behind the other, and rubbed their hands clean on two ragged vests, they looked like twins who had made a pact against their father, the cyclist. At the sound of the bell, Werner Pfeiffer had come out of the large greenhouse that occupied almost all of the garden and then, once he'd seen the visitors weren't there to see him, gone into the house with a semi-dismissive wave.

He didn't know anything about these things. He didn't even have a driving licence. He taught Biology and Chemistry at the intermediate school, and to begin with had tried to prevent his

---

hit by a bullet is relatively low, as long as you stick to the right times. Deep inside the forest is a place where the Krupp company once wiped out a whole village, years ago. It's all gone now, the houses, the roads; they even pulled down the church, one of the tallest for miles around. All that's left is the graveyard, the graveyard of Wahn. The village's name means delirium, of all things. Once, in summer, I'd only meant to take a break and I'd got off my bike, leant it on the graveyard wall and laid down on the grass outside the gate. A horsefly settled on my sweaty arms and legs every few seconds. I'd hardly killed one when the next one came along, and I was starting to think Nella might be right, that the beasts really were without beginning and end and were reborn at

sons from taking an interest in engines, cylinders, capacity and output. He had taken them along to the Bremen Overseas Museum and the Emden Art Museum, they had spent their holidays on islands with no cars or motorbikes, and before Chernobyl they'd taken the train to the mountains and spent weeks hiking through dense forests and across bare fields from one hut to the next, picking mushrooms and drinking goat's milk. But it had been no use. It might even have had the opposite effect and reinforced their desire for speed and noise. At least when he asked Marcel and Rainer why they were busy with their bikes all day long, though, they explained they were working on reducing the fuel consumption. And although he didn't quite take their word for it, he did settle for it, in the hope that they'd one day be in a position to use their technical knowledge for a real good cause.

'Do you want something to drink, boys?' Their mother, barefoot but in jeans and a T-shirt, was now in the garden too—her husband had obviously told her who was at the door—and had come out of the house out of curiosity, or to convince herself of

the moment of their death, when I fell asleep for the first time in weeks, it seemed to me. And when I woke up, covered in stings and absolutely relaxed, possibly intoxicated by all the insect poison, there were tanks roaring around me.

They say there are still unexploded bombs in the fields, leftovers from the war or from manoeuvres, which might explode at the slightest tremor. Another time, when I really did have a flat tyre, I walked a good way across the fields to the next village, my bike over my shoulder. At every step on the blossoming heath I thought I'd trodden on something. The ground felt hard and soft by turns, and I expected either to sink in or fly into the air at any moment as soon as I lifted my leg. I didn't put my life at risk deliberately. I didn't

what he had said. Her hands were sheathed in brown oven gloves up to her elbows.

'Yeah, sure,' said Stefan. 'Thanks, Mrs Pfeiffer.'

And Onno said, 'Always,' so quietly that she couldn't hear. 'And put more than zero proof in there.'

'What's in there?' asked Daniel, as if in reply. He had only been round to Rainer's house two or three times and he was looking over at the greenhouse. The plastic was transparent but it was matte, illuminated from within and covered in splashes of earth from the ground up. Apart from a blurry, cloudlike green there was nothing to be seen from the outside.

'Plants,' said Rainer.

'Yeah, but what kind of plants?'

'Since when have you been interested in botany?' asked Rainer, and then, turning to the others, 'What do you lot want here, anyway?'

want to challenge fate. I only saw the warning signs about buried explosives once I'd got to the path on the other side, and felt like a dud myself.

And since then I've realized why all those desperate people go and stand on the tracks. It's because the tracks form a line, because the decision they've made can't be influenced by anything, not even by me. Fate comes straight at them, and the consequence of their action unfolds immediately, unlike all the other options they may have gone through in their minds—the rope you knotted around the roof beam isn't short enough to hold you above the ground like an inverted exclamation mark, or it breaks when you put all your weight on it; when you jump from the

Stefan repeated his earlier joke. 'Daniel came round to my place and broke everything. And we went round to Onno's so he could continue his work of destruction,' he nodded at Onno with his head to one side, 'and once he'd broken everything there we thought there might be something worth smashing up round here, and we could help him complete his work.' He grinned.

Unlike the last time, he didn't say 'Funn-ny' at the end though, so Daniel didn't say 'Very funn-ny' either, but instead, 'Not true,' as if he suddenly even had to justify himself for what he hadn't done.

'There's nothing here,' said Marcel and looked over at his brother's semi-disassembled moped, a black Hercules Prima 5S, 1989 model, 1.36 PS, 0.9 kW, manual two-gear change. 'Nothing Rainer hasn't already destroyed himself. Sorry to tell you this, but you've come too late.'

'You could still demolish the Vespa over there,' Rainer pointed at the freshly polished Primavera 125, 1967 model, 5.6 PS, 4.1 kW.

church tower you miss the cast-iron grave fences and land on the soft grass, a pile of leaves or next to one of the freshly dug graves in warm, moist earth; someone finds you in the bathtub before you bleed to death; the sleeping tablets do nothing but give you a deep and dreamless sleep; the stones you tied around your legs to stay underwater come loose from their ropes and you float to the top again. After one of these attempts you come to the conclusion that you can't even do that properly. And you begin to look for new, more efficient methods. Even if you walk out onto the motorway at night, the car you've chosen for your delivery might still swerve around you. In the worst case, the driver might die and you'd remain unharmed. You stand there and have to watch

'Sure,' said Marcel. 'If you want to die as young and as fast as Peter Peters, feel free.'

They all stared at him.

'Feel free.' He waved his outstretched arm at the Vespa, as if asking someone into his bedroom, and he took a step aside but nobody moved.

Daniel was struck dumb. What he was thinking of, what they were all thinking of, was dipped in glass, a film played back soundlessly in slow motion and yet crystal clear, every detail perfectly visible. Peter Peters.

He could see the others' brains working behind their eyes, each of them pursuing thoughts that came together at a single point in their midst.

'What's up?' asked Marcel. 'What are you looking like that for? Are you scared? Of course you are! You chickens. Your mouths are bigger than your trousers. You—'

---

someone you don't even know dying, and it's all your fault. None of that can happen on the tracks. Everyone's always complaining about the railways. But you can count on them for this one thing.

One more station and then I'll be there; then I'll see Tobias again, or maybe not. It's a Monday. The Easter holidays have been over since Wednesday. He ought to be still in school at this time, unless the last two lessons are cancelled and he gets out earlier and is on his way home. A sudden shower of drizzle obscures my view and I switch on the windscreen wipers. There are bare branches on the trackbed, pine trees billowing in the wind. The weather can

His mother came out with five glasses of ice cubes and a carafe of freshly squeezed orange juice. She had taken off the brown oven gloves. She put the tray down between them on the drive, on the dry paving stones, said, 'Help yourselves—if you want any more let me know. You know where to find me,' and went back into the house.

Once he'd taken a drink, Rainer said, 'We're not chicken.'

'Oh no? What are you scared of then? I'm alone, there's four of you.'

'Exactly,' said Rainer. 'That's why we'll win.' He'd had an idea. He suddenly knew how he could manage to hold out against Marcel. He might not be able to overtake him, but he could stay abreast for long enough to make his brother feel like he'd lost. 'We should have a race.'

'What?' asked Marcel.

change here from one moment to the next. Forecasts may apply to the rest of Germany, but they're no use for East Frisia. You have to be prepared for anything at any time, here.

In one of the freshly ploughed fields, four deer leap away. I drink a swig of coffee and light a new cigarette. I haven't hit one for seven years now. But not a day has passed when I didn't think it might happen again. I think of it when I'm in the car to Emden and getting on my train, and I think of it when I go home and get into bed. The dead are my constant companions. Those I've sent to the other side, and those I have yet to send there.

Three or four years ago, just outside Oldenburg, something scurried in front of my engine. It was dark outside and the new

'We should have a race. In the hammrich fields. On the Hoogstraat. We can really let the engines rip there.'

'Why? What's the point? We've had ten races and you always lose, because that thing,' Marcel pointed at Rainer's moped, 'is no use and never will be. The engine's crap. When are you going to see sense?'

'I'm going to change the sprocket,' said Rainer, unmoved. He squatted down again, the twelve-tooth sprocket in his hand. 'And then we'll see what happens.'

'That'll only get you up to sixty, tops. That's still not enough.'

'You forgot the ballast.'

'What ballast?'

'The extra load you're going to carry.' Rainer made half a turn, nodded over at Stefan, Onno and Daniel and then looked at his brother.

'No way,' said Marcel. 'Forget it.'

---

headlamps hardly give off more light than the old ones. I couldn't see much, not more than a shadow, and not a second later I heard a bang. A train engine's a blunt instrument, and over time you get to know whether it's a deer or a dog or a person. They all have their own sound. Animals make a bang. They're all skin and bone. A short, sharp bang, like the sound of a shot. People are more muffled, because of their clothing. And I thought I'd run over a deer or maybe a dog. I didn't stop. I didn't pull on the brakes as usual, like the times before. I simply went on, through Wechloy, through the town centre, between the windows of the houses with the people behind them, people occupied with something quite different, with themselves.

'Come on, don't be like that. We've done it before.'

'Yeah, but we were drunk. We were totally rat-arsed.'

'All the better that we're sober now.'

'We nearly died. We didn't even make it a hundred metres. We just got out of the car park and then we were flat on our faces. In the middle of the B70.'

'All I remember is lying on the grass,' said Rainer, suddenly staring up at the glass roof of the carport as if inspired. 'After the final, after Brehme's penalty . . . It was raining, like now . . . and we were lying on the grass . . . our arms and legs outstretched . . . We were looking at the sky . . . We eliminated the clouds with our eyes and saw the stars, all at once . . . And then the sun went up . . . and we tore off our wet clothes . . . and one of the girls, Marianne, had something to smoke with her . . . fantastic stuff . . . pure blossoms . . . and she let us all try it . . . It tasted like gold . . . It felt like gold . . . It was gold . . . Our bronchia were dusted with gold . . . We decorated our lungs with the most valuable gold

---

I slowed down until I pulled into Oldenburg Station, convinced my senses and experience hadn't been playing tricks on me. The rolling stock inspector who would take charge of the train was already on the platform, a flashlight at the ready. I told him about the collision and asked him to inspect the undercarriage, which he would have done anyway because the train was due to be sent for cleaning. And then he did find hairs, brown hairs, hard and smooth and smeared with blood, which could just as well have come from a person, and a scrap of cloth, checked like from a shirt. I went to the train dispatcher and called the police and had the track closed. An hour later we got the news over the radio that they'd found a deer between Bad Zwischenahn and Bloh.

. . . And with every breath we took we grew lighter . . . We were floating . . . We were light as a feather . . . And we floated home . . . Marianne and me.'

'Don't talk crap,' said Marcel. 'You don't even know how to inhale.'

'You don't have to inhale to get high.'

'You weren't high. You were drunk, that's all. Drunk as a skunk. We all were. But unlike the rest of us, you weren't even responding after the crash. Nothing. No reaction. You didn't blink. No pulse. Absolutely nothing. Clinically dead. We took you straight to hospital from the UFO. You had a broken nose and your T-shirt was covered in blood. And they had to pump your stomach or you'd have suffocated on your puke. The truth is, you can't take your drink. The girls filled you up for a joke. Marcel's little brother. Little Rainer. They made bets on how many brandy and Cokes you'd need before you passed out.'

'No,' said Rainer. 'It really happened.'

How the scrap of shirt got there, I don't know. Perhaps someone got caught on a screw during maintenance work, or it was on the tracks and the draft blew it up there. All the time I sat with the dispatcher in his office and we numbed ourselves with cigarettes and stories full of death and violence, two men who'd been up far too long, I held it in my hand. I turned it over and over as if waiting for the rest of the jigsaw puzzle, the right place to insert it. But there was no jigsaw, just this one piece. I put it in my pocket and carried it around with me like a talisman, although I didn't believe it would prevent me from becoming a murderer again. But perhaps Nella and I are more similar than I'd like to admit, and in truth her religion is my salvation.

'In your dreams maybe.'

'Who's Marianne?' asked Daniel.

Everyone stared at him as if he'd said something incredibly stupid.

Then Rainer said, 'Are we going to have a race or not?'

'One kilometre.'

'I get a hundred and fifty metres' head start.' Rainer held out his hand to Marcel and Marcel shook it to seal the bargain.

I lost the scrap of cloth, probably in the wash or when I took out my keys somewhere to unlock the car; who knows. It's two or three years ago now. And I only noticed it was gone when I saw a similar shirt in the window at Vehndel's and reached into my pocket to compare one pattern with the other. I didn't feel any effect, if there was one. The thoughts and faces were there all along, in the same sharp focus, clear and cold, like now, like always when I'm stone cold sober and haven't had enough sleep.

There are men I know, older colleagues, who go to psychiatrists or psychotherapists and try to get taken off the job before retirement age. I even know some who've managed it with only a couple of sessions, a few deep conversations. But it's got more

7

The train tracks across the Hoogstraat, the second level crossing with no barriers, marked the finishing line. The Hoogstraat ran parallel to the tracks for several kilometres until the tracks took a bend just before Jericho and crossed the road. Whoever crossed the rails first was the winner. It was Daniel's job to wait next to the railway-crossing sign with his arms outstretched, until the others finished their preparations a kilometre away, and then give

difficult to get out that way now. You have to go all the way now and get yourself committed to a mental hospital to cash in on at least part of your pension. That's not for me. I'm forty. I can't spend the next forty years weeding the garden or washing the car and tidying the house. Apart from fishing, I don't have any hobbies, and if I did that all day it wouldn't be a hobby any more. I haven't got a family to look after, although it's not too late to start a new one. I haven't ruled that out for the future. I don't know if I'm already over the hill. But I'm well on the way. I don't feel the elevation any more, neither at Tinnen Pines nor any other. No resistance whatsoever. There's no spanner in the works and no stone to be cleared from the path, for me or for anyone else. Everything's running like a well-oiled machine. I'm gliding along

them a sign, the starting signal, by clapping his hands above his head. He pulled back the sleeve of his rain jacket and looked at his digital watch. Quarter past five.

Rainer came back to him one last time to provide him with final instructions. 'To give us a bit more edge, wait until you hear the train,' he said with his engine running. Daniel couldn't hear properly and he had to repeat it, this time more loudly.

'Which train?'

'The one from Holland.'

'What?'

'What's your problem? Calm down. Stay cool. Nothing's going to happen to you. And we won't get to the tracks at the same time anyway. We'll be there before it. Or after it. Either way, we'll have our eyes on it and we can brake if we have to. Just give the signal when you hear it, OK?'

'You know what happened to Ahlers.'

soundlessly. I'm floating. I'm at one with the engine. The world can stay the way it is. Nothing has to explode or come tumbling from the sky, not for the moment. The seven trumpets aren't heralding the end of Jericho and no one is marching around the village in a torch-lit procession. I know I'll be able to sleep again at some point, perhaps not as long and deep as I used to before it all happened, but certainly for more than three hours in a row. I'll buy myself a new notebook and one for Hans too. I'll take my best rod and combine bait or invent my own recipe and soon I'll catch a carp bigger and heavier than anything I've ever fetched out of the lakes and pits before. I'll talk to Nella, perfectly normally, full of reverence, respect and genuine interest for her life, without letting her words or clothes influence me, and I'll

'That was different. You can't compare the two. That was on Clay Road. Ahlers was coming from the other direction. From there,' he pointed at a couple of trees, 'from the village. When he came out of the bend he drove alongside the tracks. The train was in his blind spot. And the engine of his Porsche was so loud he couldn't hear anything. He didn't know there was anything coming. We do. We're prepared for it. And anyway, what do you care? Nothing's going to happen to you. Just give the sign when you hear it, right?' Then he drove back to the others and they all took up their positions.

Through the rain, which had grown stronger again, he had a hazy view of Stefan and Onno climbing onto Marcel's Vespa, the engine running, making an initial attempt to keep their balance and drive off together, then stopping and trying again a few metres on by jumping on while the scooter was moving. He saw that fail too and then, a bit further now, he couldn't quite make out how this time, he saw that they'd found a way not to fall over. Rainer had watched it all too, a hundred and fifty metres away from

meet Tobias and be a friend to him, or at least try. I can't turn the clock back. I can't replace the years we've both lost; nobody can. But I can venture a new beginning. I'll spread my arms and he'll come running into them, I'll embrace my old family and they'll embrace me. I can see the ending coming. I feel it rising inside me, spreading out in my lungs and cleansing me from within, like when I take a steam bath when I have a cold or rub Pinimenthol on my chest or under my nose. I feel light and free and I'm ready to get involved with someone again. The mists are clearing. I've got everything under control. I've got myself under control, my history, my story. I'm awake, wide awake. I'm breathing. I'm alive. Nothing can stop me now.

them, and then he turned to face Daniel, his hands on the handlebars, playing with the accelerator. He revved the engine several times.

Daniel looked at his watch again. It was like a reflex. He knew it didn't matter how many minutes they took for the race, only who came first. He wondered why Rainer had brought the train into it, as if that was his way of dealing with the Peter Peters thing, and whether he wanted to feel the same flicker of excitement Peter Peters must have felt, alone on the tracks in the face of death.

He pulled back his hood and listened. But apart from the engines and the rain dripping onto his jacket and the tarpaulin over the silage pile behind him, he couldn't hear anything. He looked along the Hoogstraat and took in some of the tension ruling Marcel and Rainer, freezing them in the same position— both feet on the ground, both hands on the handlebars.

Then he heard it. The buzzing. The high, rising tone. The train was sending out heralds to announce its arrival.

So that everyone where it arrived—wherever that was—paid it the necessary respect.

So that everyone welcomed it.

Or fled.

Daniel took an involuntary step forward, away from the tracks. He stepped into the middle of the road and ran his eyes once along the horizon, and although the railway embankment inclined to the west, towards the river up to the top of the dyke, he couldn't see any sign of the train. Only the bridge. And the trees lining the route. But suddenly it was there. One after another, the birds rose from the trees and fluttered away. Somewhere back there, it was whipping through the rain. More than a hundred kilometres an hour and several hundred tons behind it. Nothing would stop it from one moment to the next.

Daniel spread his arms, closed his eyes and counted to three. Then he clapped his hands together above his head.

Marcel was still behind, perhaps by a hundred metres, but with every metre the gap between the two motorbikes grew smaller, and the train alongside them was catching up too. Its contours flashed between the trees and bushes. Soon they'd be parallel and, as the tracks bent towards them, they'd meet at a point directly behind Daniel.

Now he heard the train's engine too, not its stamping but its humming and gliding. The ground was vibrating but the waves emanating from the wheels and conveying to the tracks were even and came at short intervals, small, fast, violent thrusts. The brackish water in the ditches on either side of the tracks splashed against the sides hollowed out by muskrats, the fields quaked, the tops of shrubs swayed to and fro, until even the road, shaken by this invisible force, began to tremble. And then there was the rushing sound, swelling, like a gust of wind sweeping through the leaves from far away, and that crackling full of promise on the rails and up in the overhead wires, as if someone had lit a forest of sparklers for their race.

The others could hear it too now. The air was full of it. Rainer looked to the right and then leant low over his handlebars, lower than before, lower than ever. Stefan or Onno, one of the two, pointed at the train, at which Marcel turned his head in his direction, apparently surprised by the development. If he didn't draw level with his brother he'd crash into the train. Unless he slowed down—or got rid of the ballast fidgeting on the seat behind him.

Daniel heard the train whistle, three short bright blasts, and he waved his arms. He wanted them to stop, to abandon their pride and hate, but they just speeded up even more to get all they could out of their engines, out of themselves.

Then they shot past him and past the finishing line, alongside each other. Daniel couldn't tell which front wheel came before the other. Rainer and Marcel stood up above their handlebars and their bikes made a jerk as they reached the crown of the dyke. For a second, the tyres were suspended in mid-air, floating above the road, the tracks, and then setting down on the tarmac again. Daniel could just see Stefan and Onno, their faces contorted in panic, clutching hold of Marcel so they didn't fall off, before the train cut off his view. And when the last goods wagon was past him he saw that they'd simply gone on driving after the level crossing instead of stopping as they'd agreed. On the long Hoogstraat, which extended far into the hammrich fields in a dead straight line, they grew smaller and smaller until at some point they vanished. Daniel stood motionless for a while longer, looking after them to the place where their friendship had begun, to the flooded pits; to the field where they'd taught Peter Peters a lesson for life; and to Clay Road, where years before the Kelly Family's brightly painted bus had broken down. They were the only band he'd ever seen live and they could never split up, in his mind, even if they announced their breakup and didn't play any more gigs or release any more records, they would always stay the Kelly Family for him and themselves, whatever happened, until the end of time.

Then he walked home. He took the shortest route, along the tracks to where the Holland line met the Western line, in eyeshot of the signal tower. From there, he cut through the bushes. A trail, semi-overgrown by plants and rubbish, led alongside the tracks to the village. He reached out a hand and tapped against the branches and leaves. He kicked a stone along in front of him, and when that stone leapt away from him and wasn't instantly visible he took another. Then he kicked at something he thought was a stone, but it wasn't a stone, it was the tip of something else, metallic, something he knew because it spent night after night and sometimes the days, like today, slitting open his head from the inside.

8

After the drinking trough thing they had never laid hand on Peter Peters again. They hadn't even insulted him, but others had and that had pushed him over the edge. The nickname they'd given him in the beginning had stuck in their minds, even though they didn't use it in his presence any more. Yet still the word was said in class, at break-time, on the bus, not referring to him. And every time someone said 'penis' in his presence, there was someone else who'd slap Peter Peters around the head and say, 'We were just talking about you.'

At some point Peter Peters had decided to cycle to school, no matter what the weather. He defied the wind and rain and at break he always kept his distance, usually standing near an entrance so he could slip into the building at any moment. There, though, the teachers would waylay him and make him copy down the school rules, two densely printed pages, as a punishment for violating their instruction to spend the time between lessons out of doors, as a punishment for his cowardice. Daniel sat next to him in almost all subjects, but they didn't speak to each other any more than necessary. Peter Peters never asked a question and he only answered when the teacher or a fellow pupil spoke to him directly, apart from in Biology, where he put his hand up to volunteer information and carry out his own experiments. He knew how to test for protein in foodstuffs (by heating them), what anthozoa are (coral, for example) and under what circumstances plant guttation takes place (after humid nights), and all without preparing for lessons.

No one could say what set it off, but one day before the Easter break he went crazy.

Peter Peters had taken the iron rod he used to reinforce his luggage rack into the classroom, a sawn-off, forty-centimetre, cold-galvanized bolt hinge which he swung through the air like a club. And the way he held it, sideways away from his body, making swipes, coming closer and closer until it swished in everyone's ears, left no doubt that the heads he reached with it were nothing more to him than balls to be impaled on his stake. But like at the shooting range at the village fair, where an endless row of white rabbits rattled past the iron sights, the heads were moving targets. And he was moving too. He had to be. More moveable than them. He had guessed that this test would be hard, harder than all previous tests, and he had spent long hours preparing in the hamm-rich fields. He had stood on the dyke, the rod in both hands, and fought against shadows, their shadows and his.

Now he ran towards Daniel, towards Rainer, Onno and Stefan, and chased them around the desks. Nothing he said was comprehensible; he didn't understand it himself. He whirled around, turning in a circle like a hammer thrower to increase the force of his blows, but he hit no one because he wasn't fast enough, because he didn't aim precisely enough, because the desks and chairs were in the way and because Herlyn came in and put a stop to it all.

'What's going on here?' he asked as he put his briefcase on the lectern. 'What are you doing, Peter? Have you lost your mind?'

'I've had it up to here,' said Peter Peters. 'I've had enough. I'm going to get them now.'

'Who are you going to get?' asked Herlyn.

'Them,' shouted Peter Peters, pointing the rod at the class huddled in a corner of the room.

'What have they done to you?' Herlyn opened his briefcase, took out an exercise book and a pen and closed it again, as if intending to begin the lesson like any other morning. Peter Peters had the feeling the question was mocking him, but he didn't know how to answer. Both options, 'everything' or 'nothing' seemed equally stupid and he didn't dare, not here in front of all the others, to tell what had actually happened, what had built up inside him over months, over years. The worst thing though was that the anger that a moment ago had filled him and driven him to extremes had now evaporated, and he feared it wouldn't come back to him. He lowered the rod, dizzy, and was almost grateful when Herlyn took him by the hand and led him out of the classroom and along the corridor, talking quietly, up to the third floor, to speak calmly and collectedly to the headmaster in his presence about his expulsion.

Four weeks later, during a Music class—the Easter break was over, the seat next to Daniel remained empty, and he had got used to sitting alone after only three days—they found out what had happened to Peter Peters. No one knew what school he'd ended up at, no one had seen him after he was expelled or heard anything of him, but no one, not even the parents and teachers, had stopped talking about him, about how he'd flipped out and what would have happened if he had hit one of them, one of the other students, with his rod.

At first, Stefan had considered publishing the whole story in the *Blackboard Jungle*, the school newspaper, under the headline *Penis Came to School with Stiff Rod*, and it had cost the other editorial board members in their class, Tanja and Susanne and Daniel, some effort to persuade him against it. Rainer and Onno had done impressions of Peter Peters at break or at parties, waving sticks around them and roaring something incomprehensible, and the girls had run away screaming and laughing.

Weers never came too late. The music room was his staff room and recreation room, which he only left for important meetings or discussions with other teachers. He was usually sitting at the grand piano or next to the record player with the window open when the first pupils filed into the room, beating out the last bars of a suite or slowly fading out a trumpet or saxophone solo, and he completed the pieces in hums and whistles, inaudible for others, or so he thought—Gustav Holst's *Planets*, Miles Davis' *Solar*, John Coltrane's *Satellite*. They were all the more amazed when they found the room empty and absolutely silent after the bell rang for the second time that Monday at the end of April. Some of them stood by their chairs, hoping Weers was sick and the lesson would be cancelled and someone would bring them that very message any minute, so it wasn't worth removing their jackets and sitting down. Others stood because they thought they'd made a mistake with the timetable, and they took out their books to check. In the end they did all take off their jackets and sit down at their desks. They told themselves he was bound to turn up, or a stand-in, Fischer perhaps, the other music teacher, or that someone would at least give them something to keep them occupied for the next forty-five minutes.

After a while Daniel, who sat at the very front here as in all other lessons, spotted Weers' bag next to the record table. He went over and picked it up; it wasn't closed and an apple and a round tin rolled out. He opened the tin and a sweet scent pervaded the room. It was full to the brim with biscuits. He took one and was just about to bite into it when Rainer grabbed him by the arm. 'Hey, they're all counted, he'll notice. He's not stupid.' And Daniel put the lid back on and put the tin and the apple back in the bag.

At some point Susanne stood up to open a window. The air, still heavy with the smell of biscuits, was stuffy and stale, as if no air had been let in for hours. At the window, she saw that there were no teachers in the other classrooms. 'There's none over there either,' she said. 'They've all gone.' Others joined her and saw it too, and from then on no one said a word.

Then Weers came in. His face was pale, his remaining hair standing on end, and there were sweat patches under his arms. He felt for the table as though he couldn't get his balance quick enough, sat down, ran a hand though his beard, over his forehead, breathed deeply in and out again and looked up at the ceiling for a moment. And then he said that something terrible had happened, something awful. 'Your classmate Peter Peters is dead. They found him on the railway embankment this morning.' A few of the girls started crying, the boys looked at the floor or shook their heads mutely, and Stephanie Beckmann asked what was on the tip of everyone's tongue: 'Really?'

'Yes,' said Weers. 'Really.'

Peter Peters had had nothing with him but his old student ID card, nothing to identify him except the number and the name of the school—all that had still been legible on the card—and that was the reason why the police called the grammar school first and then his parents.

When Stefan, Onno, Rainer and Daniel cycled home that day, the route they usually took, along the tracks through the hammrich fields, was blocked; they had to take the B70 to get to the village.

Daniel's mind was still on the race and the way they'd simply left him behind, and he'd taken a diversion past the freight shed and Petersen's Pool Hall; but he was home in time for dinner. For the sake of simplicity, out of laziness and habit, he went into the house via the shop. The bell rang and everyone in the room turned round to him. Two customers, Mrs Meinders and Mrs Ahlers, paused at the shelves and squinted over at him. His father and his friends, Günter and Klaus, were standing around the counter caught up in a new conversation, one so similar to the old one that it might seem there hadn't been any interruption since that morning.

'I saw it though, Doll's not such a doll,' said Klaus with a broad grin. 'He's totally overrated, he overrates himself.'

'Maybe he just hasn't settled in with the team yet,' said Günter. 'Maybe he has to get acclimatized first.'

'Forget it. He'll never get acclimatized. None of those Easteners will. Not in twenty years they won't.'

'It must have been a shock for Coach Schock,' Hard said with a grin as broad as Klaus', but his eyes firmly fixed on Daniel. 'Seeing his protégé, his big hope fail.' He'd been trying to top Klaus' pun and he was pretty sure he'd managed it. But instead of bursting out laughing as he usually did when he'd made a joke nobody laughed at, he pursed his lips again as if at the touch of a button. 'To begin with you don't know what'll become of these great talents. Anything's possible. They might fill you with pride and satisfaction. They might give you a good feeling at the end of your life that you've done everything right. But they might turn out to be absolute losers, or worse, liars and traitors, despite the love you invested in them.'

'And the money,' said Klaus.

'And the money,' said Hard. 'Not to forget the money.'

Daniel tried to get past them as quickly as possible so he wouldn't have to excuse his absence from the basement in front of an audience. He heard his father calling his name several times, his voice getting darker and darker, and he heard Günter saying, 'Let him be,' and Klaus saying, 'He can't get away from you, that's the good thing about children,' and then he was in the office and out through the office.

'Where were you all day?' asked Hard, still agitated and ready for anything by the time they were all sitting at the kitchen table, only minutes later. 'I told you I was expecting a delivery. I had to spend all afternoon unpacking and shelving sun cream, no time for anything else. And God knows I had plenty of better things to do, plenty.' Daniel felt like asking, 'What?' but he sensed his father had only made that comment to give him a reason to ask back, and to give himself a reason to let out his anger on him. He often laid bait like that, and Daniel had learnt not to bite. 'And you haven't finished in the basement yet either!' Hard meant to go on. He had thought it all out but the twins, who were refusing to eat the black bread and liver sausage he'd made them, even though they were old enough by now to spread their own sausage, occupied his full attention for a moment. It was only when he threatened to stop them watching TV, his hand raised as a sign that he meant it, that they gave in and he turned back to Daniel. His nostrils trembled. 'Have you been smoking?'

'No,' said Daniel and put his hand in front of his mouth to shield his breath and test it at the same time.

'Have you been smoking that stuff?'

'What stuff?'

'Don't act all innocent. You know what I mean.' He had stood up and leant halfway over the table to him.

'I don't know.'

'Smells like it,' he said, sitting down and turning to Birgit, as if she knew better. 'Doesn't it?'

'Yes,' said Birgit. 'Smells just like it.'

Hard picked up his knife and fork, sliced off a piece of his black bread with cheese, used it to dab a few crumbs from the wooden plate and put it in his mouth. 'You just keep on like this,' he said once he'd swallowed his mouthful.

More bait. Daniel knew his father wanted to hear 'I will.' He'd often replied 'I will,' and got himself a clip round the ear, but he didn't do him the favour this time.

'I hope you know what smoking means,' said Hard. 'And I assume you want more than a handshake for what you've done over the past two weeks.'

'Stefan and Onno were smoking,' said Daniel, not looking at his father and mother.

'Don't you even start,' Birgit pointed a finger at him. 'It messes up your metabolism. Especially when you're still growing. Or do you want to end up like Volker?' She paused and shaped her hands into a ball. 'All round?'

'You're a real hero,' said Hard, dabbing at his mouth with his napkin. 'Put a bit of pressure on you and you betray your friends to save your own skin. The Spanish Inquisition would have had a field day with you.' Then he shook his head, as if he'd thought of something even more reprehensible. 'So you've been round the compunists' again, have you?' Many of the villagers, especially the locals whose families had lived in Jericho for generations, regarded the residents of Composers' Corner as nothing but hippies and communists. *Compunists*. No one could remember who had come up with the name. Hard bragged that it had been him, and whenever an opportunity arose—and opportunities arose often when he was around—he used it in abundance. Not an evening went by at the bar of the Beach Hotel without someone or other railing against foreigners or compunists and the others feeling prompted to tell their own stories. It made no difference to them whether the residents of Composers' Corner were right- or left-wing, where they came from, who they really voted for and what they smoked, injected or snorted to get high. Some of the men who lived there had been to university, even some of the women, and that was reason enough to keep a good eye on them, in case the revolution was suddenly proclaimed for some reason and both parties had to take up arms, shotguns and small-bore rifles on one side and rakes and shovels or whatever pacifists kept in their sheds on the other.

'Yes,' said Daniel, making an effort not to give in to his urge to correct his father. 'I was.'

'Your mother and I hoped that was all over.'

'It is now.'

'Is it now?' said Hard with a sceptical look.

'Yes,' said Daniel. 'It is.'

That evening Daniel left the house again. The sun had set but it wasn't yet quite dark. On the horizon, high above the dyke, a colourful glow shimmered through the clouds like from distant fireworks. There was still a slight drizzle but the rain wasn't so heavy that he had to put on his boots or pull up his hood. He walked along Village Road, across the railway tracks, past the signal tower and into the hammrich fields. He wanted to go back to the tracks and see if he could find the rod he'd thrown away. He thought if he found it and kept it or buried it in the ground he wouldn't have to keep thinking about Peter Peters. But he didn't find it. Not on that day and not on any other.

No one knew whether it was coincidence or intentional that Peter Peters had been lying on the rails on the Hoogstraat on the first Monday morning after the Easter break. He hadn't given any sign, hadn't behaved strangely, or no more strangely than usual, and hadn't left a suicide note, just a few full packs of Diazepam, and many Jerichoans took that to mean he must have had a fit while crossing the tracks. The only indication against that was that the path he'd taken didn't lead to his new school but to his old one. But that, as Doctor Ahlers later told the police and the state prosecutor, could just as well be to his confusion, the aura, the time before the actual fit.

Rainer Pfeiffer died three years later in a road accident. Not on his souped-up moped and not on the scooter he bought the year after that—with the money he'd earned at the custard factory in the school holidays—but in a car: a silver VW Golf III, 1993 model, 75 PS, 55 kW, his eighteenth-birthday present from his parents.

They had wanted to get him away from 'those hellish bikes,' as they said, and had gone on a family outing to Wolfsburg to collect the car directly from the VW factory. On the way back, Marcel and his mother had driven off first and he and his father had given them a minute's head-start.

Rainer missed the wind and the vibrations of the engine beneath him, the feeling of being at one with the countryside and the machine. At the Hattorf and Flechtorf junction, he wound the window down and stuck his head halfway out until his father shouted at him to stop that nonsense.

The girls he gave lifts from now on would no longer automatically snuggle up to him, and the boys wouldn't boast about their top speeds any more, because that was far less dependent on skill than on the engine itself—and on the courage to test out the boundaries of possibility.

'So,' his father asked, 'do you like it?'

'Yes.'

'It's much better, isn't it?'

'Yes,' said Rainer. 'Much better.'

The only advantages to driving a car, in his view, were listening to music on the journey and using the back seat after parties and discos.

'There they are, look,' said his father, pointing at the road through the windscreen from the passenger's seat.

A dot was visible about a kilometre away, gradually getting larger and larger.

'Yes,' said Rainer and put his foot down. 'We'll catch up any minute.'

'Don't drive too close,' said his father. 'We'll overtake them on the A2.'

And that's what they did.

It didn't happen that day or the next day either. It happened the weekend after that, after a party thrown by Stephanie Beckmann, the only person he knew personally who had ever been on TV. The Beckmanns owned a shipping company, a medium-sized enterprise with twenty ships, mainly gas tankers but also two freight ships with more than eight thousand gross register tons' loading capacity, which transported coal and cellulose from one godforsaken part of the world to another. They were affluent enough to live in a house with five bedrooms and three reception rooms, a villa directly on the Dollart bay, thirty kilometres from Jericho, but they were stupid enough to leave their only daughter, their only child, alone there over New Year.

Rainer couldn't remember who'd invited him, whether it had been Stephanie herself or someone else. Since she'd won against the presenter Thomas Gottschalk on the *You Bet!* show, she'd become a minor celebrity. One thing had come after another, and whenever a car showroom was opened or a ship was launched in the months after the show aired, Stephanie Beckmann was the person who cut the ribbon or smashed the bottle against the bow. More people came to her birthday parties than the previous years, and on this occasion the entire young generation of the county town seemed to be there. Rainer ran into dozens of people he'd never seen before in every room. The tables and sideboards were strewn with half-empty bottles full of cigarette butts, a glass was always smashing somewhere, and Stephanie was running around issuing warnings that nobody heeded. The beds on the top floor were occupied from the beginning, or at least the doors were locked and from behind them came either giggling or moaning, so loud and high pitched that anyone who walked past thought it was put on and groaned back. The bass made the walls vibrate and the guests feel vibrant, the whole house moving to the rhythm of the music—furniture, pictures, vases, model ships lined up on the shelves, cushions, light as a feather and weightless, all danced through the air.

Rainer had only had one beer, afraid he might lose control and not know when to stop once he got started, and then stuck to Coke for the rest of the evening. He had spent most of the time standing around awkwardly, watching Stefan and Onno trying to lose their minds as quickly as possible. They drank and smoked and ate everything they got their hands on, and it wasn't even two hours, just after midnight when the New Year's fireworks went off outside and inside, before they slurred their words and swayed on their feet and fell asleep at the same time, side by side on one of the sofas in one of the reception rooms. He didn't want them to vomit in his car and he thought they'd sober up by morning, get sober enough to tell him to pull over before they puked up.

At one point, at around one, he had danced. He had squeezed his way between the others and shaken his head, not taking his feet off the floor, and raised his right arm, his forefinger and little finger splayed out, the rest clenched in a fist. But all the time he danced he couldn't help watching himself, and every one of his movements had seemed false to him, as if there were some kind of rules he no longer mastered. The moment the song finished he made his way out of the crush and leant against the wall, his arms folded. He hoped nobody had been watching him, and when he looked around the room he saw that everyone else was occupied with themselves or each other—everyone except Stephanie Beckmann.

'Just when you were dancing, you know, I thought about you guys,' she said to him. Her voice was slightly slurred and she was having difficulties finding the right words.

'Who?' shouted Rainer, surprised she was even talking to him, and also because he had hardly understood what she'd said.

'You guys. Kill Mister.'

'Long time ago,' said Rainer.

'Yes,' said Stephanie. 'What did Kill Mister actually mean?'

'What?' shouted Rainer, pulling a face and pointing at his right ear which he turned in her direction. 'It's so loud in here.'

They stepped aside slightly, away from the speakers and towards the door, and Stephanie repeated her question but Rainer shrugged. 'What did you say? I can't understand you.'

'Oh, never mind.' Stephanie took his hand, pulled him out into the hallway and changed the subject. 'There's a new girl in my German class, from the intermediate school, and she used to know Daniel too.'

'Really?'

'Yes.'

'What's her name?'

'Simone.'

'I know her,' said Rainer. 'Everyone knows her in Jericho.'

'Yes, she said that too.'

'You know what,' said Rainer, looking through the open door into one of the reception rooms and at the same time leaning closer to her, 'I've decided to spend less time thinking about the past and more about the future.'

'About what to do when you finish school, get a job, go to university?'

'No,' said Rainer, not even five centimetres away from her mouth. 'About us.'

'Get up,' said Rainer and shook first Stefan, then Onno. Both of them opened their eyes briefly—Onno said his name, 'Rainer, Jesus, Rainer,' and Stefan laughed as if in a delirium—and then fell back into the semi-conscious state he'd forced them out of. He shook them again but achieved no more than the last time.

'They'redead,' said someone next to him, a boy in a T-shirt and lumberjack shirt, fifteen or sixteen at the most and similarly out of it as all the others slid low on the seats around him. 'Might aswellforget'em.'

Rainer took no notice of the boy and began slapping Stefan and Onno around the face by turn. It seemed to have an effect. They both looked at him with astounded, empty gazes, as if staring at a stranger.

'Get up, we're leaving now.'

'Now?' said Stefan. 'Why now?'

Onno held his right arm steady with his left hand and leant over his watch. 'The party's not even over yet.'

'Yes it is,' said Rainer.

'It isn't,' said Onno. 'It's only half past one.'

'You can come with me or not. I don't care either way. I'm leaving now.' In the hallway, he threw their jackets at them and to his surprise, they put them on. Together, holding each other up, they stumbled towards him. Outside, the cold took their breath away for a moment. Stefan gasped for air and Onno pointed up at the night sky. 'Look, the stars.'

'There,' said Stefan. 'That one's moving.'

'No it's not,' said Rainer.

'Oh, yes it is. Look—it's moving, and it's flashing. It's sending us a sign.'

'Yes,' said Onno. 'He's right. It could be a code.'

'It's a plane,' said Rainer, his car keys in his hand. 'Come on. I can't be arsed to stand around here any more like an idiot.'

They got into the car, Rainer and Onno at the front and Stefan at the back. Rainer wiped the windscreen with his elbow and switched on the radiator and the fan, but it took a whole five minutes before he could see anything. Onno turned on the light and rummaged in the glove compartment for a tape, as he'd done on the way there.

'What are you looking for?'

'Guns N' Roses.'

'It's in the tape deck.'

'*Use Your Illusion*?'

'It's in there.'

'Really?'

'You put it in yourself. Before we went in.'

'One or two?'

'How do I know?' said Rainer. 'What difference does it make?'

'A big difference. One is bad, but two is unlistenable.'

'Why do you want to put it on then?'

'Because of "You Could Be Mine". The solo at the beginning. If it was up to me it would go on for ever. Just drums. For ten minutes, twenty, thirty. No guitars. No vocals. No anything. A drum sonata.' Onno ejected the tape and held it under the light. 'Doesn't say anything on it.'

'No,' said Rainer with a sigh. 'Only on the boxes. We've discussed this already.'

'Doesn't make sense to write on the boxes but not the tapes.'

'We've discussed this already, I said.'

And Stefan said from the back, 'I feel sick.'

'Can we go now at last?'

'So how do you know which one is which?'

'I feel sick,' Stefan repeated.

'Then open the door and puke outside,' said Rainer and turned the key.

'Not that sick.'

Rainer put the car into reverse and Onno put the tape in the tape deck. Wheels spinning, they pulled out of the drive and onto the street.

At the first bars of 'Right Next Door to Hell' Onno said, 'Shit, it is Tape One,' pressed Stop and began searching hectically through the sparsely lit glove compartment for Tape Two. He unearthed a couple of tapes without boxes and inserted them into the tape deck one after another until Rainer, at the end of his tether, switched it off. 'Hey, what's that all about?' asked Onno and switched it on again, turning the volume up to full for a second.

'You're driving me crazy.'

'You are crazy. You always have been.'

Rainer wound down the window and pressed the eject button, but before he could take out the tape and throw it out Onno had it in his hand and held it above his head like a trophy, as far away from Rainer as possible.

'Give it to me,' said Rainer, trying to reach for the tape with one hand.

'No.'

'Give me the bloody thing.'

'No. It doesn't belong to you.'

'Oh, doesn't it? Who does it belong to then? You?'

'No. No one.'

'But I bought the tape, and I put the music on it. And it's in my car. So I can chuck it out the window if I want to. And I do want to.'

'You can't throw me out the window either, even though you want to.'

'You're not a tape.' Rainer couldn't believe he'd really said that.

'Music belongs to everybody,' said Onno. 'You're not allowed to destroy it. No matter how bad it is.'

'We'll see about that.' Rainer grabbed Onno by the shoulder, whereupon the tape fell on the dashboard. Now it was almost equidistant from them and they both instinctively reached for it. But as Rainer stretched out his right hand, his left hand, with which he was holding the steering wheel, slipped. The car veered to the left, swerved towards Club 69, and the tape slammed against the panel on Onno's side. Rainer tried to steer in the other direction to dodge the posts on the grass verge between the road and the cycle path, and yanked the steering wheel around. As he did so the tape slid towards him, but only a few centimetres, only back to the middle. Onno had caught it and was holding it like before, pressed against the sun visor above him.

'Give me the bloody thing, will you,' said Rainer, who had regained control of the car. His voice sounded calm and controlled, certain of victory. The wind whipping round his head and ruffling his hair did him good. He felt the pride and hate falling away from him and the cold giving him new strength. Suddenly he knew what had to be done, and he laughed because it hadn't occurred to him sooner, because he hadn't done it much earlier, to himself or someone else. At the same time, in a single motion, he put his foot down on the accelerator and pressed the black button with the symbol of a lit cigarette. He waited until the green circle of light extinguished. The night raced past him. He felt the speed, the trembling of the cylinders.

Then he bored the glowing metal spiral into Onno's forehead.

'Watch out,' shouted Stefan from behind into Onno's shout, and pointed, leaning forward, between the front seats to the windscreen, at the light hissing towards them.

Onno Kolthoff put an end to his life—three years after the car crash—with a single blow. He didn't use a gun, although he had access to weapons as a member of the marksmen's club. He didn't take sleeping pills, didn't slit his wrists, didn't walk under a train. He didn't throw himself off the church tower onto one of the grave fences reinforced with sharp points, which some did to be on the safe side. Onno chose an absolutely new method—he played a gig.

The blinds were half down and let in little light, just enough for him to make out the contours of the drum kit, for him to see what he hit, although he'd have hit the cymbals and toms blindfolded. He drummed listlessly for a while until another, duller knocking made him lose the beat.

'What?' Onno called into the self-imposed twilight.

'You have to eat something,' said his mother once she'd come in, a plate in her hand.

'I've already eaten.'

'This stuff?' She nodded at the table strewn with empty packets and bottles and cigarette butts, and pushed everything aside to make room for the plate. 'That's not proper food.'

'Oh, isn't it?' said Onno. 'And what is proper food?'

'Something healthy. Here—potatoes and green beans, I know you like them so much. I made them specially for you.'

'Potatoes, beans and bacon.'

'No bacon.'

'No bacon!'

'No bacon.'

'Your vegetables aren't going to make me healthy again, no matter how much I eat of them.'

'Meat won't either.'

'Who knows?'

'And you ought to go out for a change,' she said, going over to the windows and reaching for one of the strings for the blinds.

'Don't!'

'It's such lovely weather outside.'

'Don't, I said. Are you deaf?'

His mother put her arms down. 'The sun's shining!'

'So what?'

'You can't always sit around in here!'

'Why not?'

'You could go to the lake.'

'And what would I do there? Go swimming?'

'Stefan called. He's staying with his parents over Easter and he said he'd come round later.'

'How nice for him.'

'If you like, you can come downstairs for lunch. Walter and I are out in the garden.'

'Walter "I've suddenly found Anne-Marie Kolthoff" Baalmann.'

'Stop it! You know very well how upset he was about your friend back then.'

'What friend?'

'Peter Peters.'

'He wasn't our friend.'

'I thought he was.'

'You thought wrong then.'

'Well anyway, you shouldn't make fun of Walter, he's had a hard time of it.'

'Harder than me?'

'Harder than all of us.'

'Walter "I've suddenly found God" Baalmann.'

'That's enough. We'll be in the garden. You can think about it. Maybe it might take your mind off things.'

'Oh yes,' said Onno. 'I'm sure it would.'

'And stop making such a racket,' she said, her hand on the door handle. 'It's Easter Saturday.'

The instant she closed the door behind her, he threw both drumsticks after her. Then he picked up a bottle of beer from the floor and took such a big gulp out of it that it ran out of his mouth on either side. Nothing would take his mind off things. Nothing but that. And that only when he'd drunk enough of it.

He could hardly remember anything that came before the accident. They'd been coming from that New Year's Eve party at Stephanie Beckmann's house, Rainer and he had fought over a tape in the car, and he had told Rainer that no one was allowed to destroy music, no matter how bad it was. Whenever he thought of it he was amazed at his own words, because he himself had never done anything but destroy music, especially the bad kind. Even after they'd discharged him from hospital, all he'd cared about was smashing out at everything at arm's reach, with all the strength he had. But it was that strength that he'd lost. His left arm had never been all that strong, and since the accident he couldn't manage more than a hesitant knocking with his right arm, enough to stroke a brush over a drum but too little to break it. When he sat behind the drum kit he had to use his left hand to lift the right hand onto the snare or one of the toms and jam a stick between forefinger and thumb and make sure the hand didn't slip off the edge in between.

The arm usually dangled by his side. When someone wanted to shake his hand to say hello, he'd stand there motionless apart from a barely perceptible nod of his head. Onno rarely ventured out among other people. Instead, he spent hours and hours behind the drum kit in his room, in the hope of reaching the level he'd been at before the accident, or a new one, a more original and spectacular level due to his altered beating technique. But no matter how hard he tried, how much he worked with the foot pedals to make up for it, he never managed to play anything that expressed his anger over his disability.

The arm adhered to him like a foreign body and when he concentrated on lifting it, as the physiotherapist he went to three times a week demanded, his whole body broke out in a sweat. Nothing else happened. Afterwards he was so exhausted that he fell asleep on the couch in the treatment room while electric impulses massaged his muscles, and didn't wake up until the session was over.

At moments like that he wished he'd lost his arm entirely, like Rick Allen, the drummer of Def Leppard. He could still tap out the beat, well enough to join one of the many Grunge bands setting up all over the place, regardless of the waning enthusiasm for the music, but he was simply too weak for Heavy Metal. There were some people, as Stefan had told him, who called him Cripplehoff, and others who knew him from before, from the time when he'd played with a bare chest and still had full command of both arms, called him The Hoff—a reference to David Hasselhoff and also because he was now lacking what they connected to the first part of his surname, strength, energy, force—whatever it was. And that was how he felt himself, like a cowboy without a Colt. The only advantage to the accident was that he didn't have to do military or social service. They hadn't even taken Stefan after the army medical examination, once they'd finished school, even though he hadn't come out of it with any visible damage, unlike Onno.

Onno put the beer down and stood up. The stool he'd been sitting on fell over and knocked the bottle over as well. A dark stain spread across the carpet, blending in with other, older stains. He took no notice. Instead, he pulled *Master of Puppets* off the shelf, took the record out of the sleeve and put it on the record player. He pushed the starting lever to the left, put the needle down in the middle of 'Welcome Home (Sanitarium)' and turned the volume up to maximum. Then he went over to the windows, opened one after another and pulled up the blinds. He put the speakers on the windowsill. Down in the garden, he saw his mother and Walter Baalmann sitting at the table. They both looked up at him at the same time. His mother shaded her eyes with her hand. She said something that was lost in the flare of guitars, the barrage of drums.

After Kill Mister's split he had played in bands that called themselves Necrosis, Decomposed or Final Death, where every member regarded himself as an artist. The singer always thought he had a divine voice even though the sounds he emitted were more reminiscent of barking or grunting than of words. The bassist was more interested in playing solos than paying attention to the beat or the riffs. And the two guitarists would argue over who played the rhythm and who played the melody. They all felt equally responsible for the song lyrics—'Rotten Flesh', 'Burning in Heaven', 'Satan's Salvation'—regardless of the fact that none of them spoke any more English than what they'd learnt at school.

When it came to their musical skills they overestimated themselves beyond measure, but Onno liked the thought that this kind of Metal, where every band member hogged the limelight with their fast, wild improvisations, came closest to his ideal, that of Metal Jazz. The songs often went totally off course, the instruments came in at the wrong moment, chromatic scales mingled with diatonic ones, the chords didn't go with the keys, and no one took care of the cadence, rhythm or articulation. And yet the racket they made was music in his ears, as if they'd stretched out 'You Suffer' for an hour or, even better, as if they'd played 'You Suffer' three thousand six hundred times in a row and interpreted it differently every single time.

But those days were over now, for him and for the others.

Hardly anyone had come to the last few gigs he'd played before the accident, with Final Death. It was mainly because most of the Metal fans had moved to Hamburg, Berlin or Münster after they finished school and their social service and only came back to East Frisia in the university vacations or on holiday, and the concert organizers were putting more effort into the younger generation, bands who were still at school and, as some bookers thought, not only looked more civilized and played better but also—and more importantly—asked for less money and promised more profits.

In hospital and at the rehab centre, he'd refused to believe what Stefan and Stephanie told him, that Metal was dead, and he'd made plans to prove them wrong as soon as he got home. But when he got there, when he marched across the village with his sticks in his hand, he realized they'd been right, Stefan and Stephanie.

He could hear the silence from a long way off, even from Village Road, as he walked past the stainless steel vats of the disused dairy, which stood out against the sky like fuel tanks for a space shuttle left on the ground. There were shards of glass everywhere. Someone had sprayed swastikas on the walls, not with phosphorescent paint like Daniel five years before but in black and white, and someone else had crossed them out or turned them into squares. The ground-floor windows were nailed up with planks of wood, there was a birch tree growing in the gutter, and on the old dairy building, where it had once said *Jericho Cooperative Dairy* in shiny white letters, there were two letters missing in *Jericho*, the *J* and the *o*, and the remaining letters were weathered and eaten away by rust.

Usually, crashes and hums and booms came up from the cellar, from the band practice rooms, the asphalt vibrated and the few unbroken panes of glass trembled from the force of the bass. But once Onno had opened the door all he heard at first was a jangling like from a tambourine and then, when he reached the bottom step, high, light voices and something that sounded like an acoustic guitar. He felt like a soldier returning home from war, or at least he imagined soldiers returning from war must feel this way—robbed of any illusions about the homeland—and like them, he consigned himself to his fate.

The bands now were called Marble Juice, Violent Green or The Spoonmen and the songs 'Jonathan' or 'Fridge' or 'Ear Pollution'. Their hair was shorter—apart from Onno's—their clothes more colourful and fleecier and their lyrics were comprehensible, which wasn't necessarily a good thing for their composers. Unlike in the old days, when Onno had insisted on sitting next to all the others with his drum kit, it suited him fine to be at the back, barely recognizable behind the cymbals on the rear edge of the stage. He thought all he was good for now was accompanying the other musicians, and he contented himself with the role of the person who set the beat.

He had never wanted to make compromises; he despised gigs where twelve-metre pig-shaped balloons floated above people's heads, blood was splashed over the audience or the instruments were sliced up with flaming chainsaws. Nothing ought to distract from the music. At Marble Juice gigs, the lights were directed at the fans while the stage was in darkness; with Violent Green each guitar was tuned for precisely one song; and The Spoonmen used plastic spoons instead of plectrums, which were constantly breaking, although that didn't prevent either the guitarist or the bassist from clinging to the ritual. Even Onno had once been persuaded to play the drums with wooden spoons, but he'd noticed right away that the result didn't meet his standards. One of them he'd thrown at the singer, whose idea it had been, and the other he'd simply dropped on the floor because he couldn't throw with his right hand. Then he'd got up and gone home and hadn't turned up to rehearsals for three weeks.

When Onno heard his mother saying 'He's up in his room,' he was lying on the sofa, his right arm jammed beneath his head. He was smoking a joint—finest grass, which he'd bought only a few days previously on the other side of the Dutch border in Winschoten—and staring at the ceiling, at the panelling, the grain and texture of the cut wood. In the lines and dark knots, he made out faces and objects, and he saw a message in their arrangement. He was just about to decipher it.

'All right, mate,' said Stefan, tearing him out of his thoughts. 'What's going down?' Since he'd been studying Mathematics, Biology and Computer Science in Münster, Stefan was constantly saying that kind of thing, and he wondered whether he talked to Stephanie like that as well, so pseudo. 'Woah, mate. What kind of a state is this place in? It's worse than our flat-share. I thought Hegel was the king of chaos, but at least you can find a path through his mess, at least there's somewhere to sit.' His hair was shorter and his clothes were baggier and hung lower than a few years ago; he looked like a skater but he wasn't one, or at least Onno had never seen him on a skateboard. 'Are these in any order?'

'What?' asked Onno, not moving his head.

'These magazines here.' Now Onno did turn around. Stefan pointed at a pile of *Metal Hammer* magazines on one of the two armchairs.

'Does anything here look like it's in order?' Onno slid back into his original position.

'The records do.'

'The records are sacred.'

Stefan swept the magazines off the chair, and as they fell to the floor on either side of him he sat down and took a drag on Onno's joint. 'Nice one, mate, where d'you get this from? Better than the crap from the Sputnik Hall. The stuff they sell there tastes like grass, and I mean grass and not grass, if you get my meaning.'

As Stefan went on talking, something about an exam he'd never have passed without grass, Onno closed the windows, turned the speakers back around and the volume down to two, put *Master of Puppets* back in its sleeve and put on *Kill 'Em All*.

He felt like every movement took him hours.

'Is that one of the ones your mother locked away back in the old days?' Stefan asked that every time.

Onno rolled himself a new cigarette, this time not sprinkling anything onto the paper other than tobacco, clicked his Zippo lighter open and closed, inhaled and exhaled again.

'You can tell by listening,' said Stefan, leaning over to the record player. 'And by looking.'

Onno went over to the fridge and took out a new beer bottle. Stefan said, 'I'll have one too,' and pointed first at the empty bottles on the table and then at his chest, but Onno didn't react and dropped down onto the sofa again.

'You should have moved away,' said Stefan once he'd fetched his own beer.

'Where to?' asked Onno. 'Not to Münster.'

'Why not?'

'What would I do there?'

Stefan shrugged. 'Get a degree.'

'How would that work? I never got my school-leaving exams, did I?'

'Technical college.'

'And what would I study at technical college? Care Management or Health Studies or some crap like that so I can heal myself?'

'Still better than what you're doing now.'

'Oh yeah, what am I doing now?'

'Gigs with those idiots.'

'What idiots?'

'The Spoonmen.'

'How do you know about that?'

'Everyone knows. The news has even made its way to Münster.'

'Oh really,' said Onno. 'Has it now?'

'Yes,' said Stefan. 'It has.'

He used a pseudonym on announcements—Ulrich Larsson— his face was unrecognizable in photos because of his long hair combed forward, and if someone wanted to interview the band, which rarely happened, he told the others not to tell the truth at all cost. But still a few of his old fellow metalheads recognized him at festivals, and still they fell to their knees before him when he turned up anywhere off-stage. They raised their hands above their heads and bowed down before him, not in awe because of his past achievements or respect for what he'd been through, but as an ironic gesture. The glowing cigarette lighter Rainer had pressed into his face before the accident had left a circular scar on his forehead, and since then a few people had regarded him as a chosen one, someone who could redeem them all from the decline of Thrash Metal. Except he didn't know how he was supposed to do that, not with his arm.

'Even Hegel knows. He saw you the other week at the Platform. And he never usually goes to gigs. I couldn't believe it when he told me. Guess who I saw yesterday, mate—your old friend Onno Kolthoff.'

Onno regretted playing with The Spoonmen at Platform 22, a youth club right by the station, and he regretted ever visiting Stefan in Münster, ever staying overnight in his shared flat.

'He was just there by chance because of some girl from the student council. I don't know her, maybe it's not true either—he's been hanging out at the Platform loads lately. Steffi's seen him there a couple of times too, but always on his own or with other philosophers. Anyway, he said, I never knew Onno was playing with The Spoonmen, I thought they'd be too dumb for him, Grunge. He said maybe you're doing it on purpose though, to show how bad they really are, if they even play with a hemiplegic. Don't get me wrong. He said you're playing badly on purpose, below your abilities, to pull the rug out from under Grunge, to show everyone who still believes in Grunge that it's no good and won't last long. That's Hegel's opinion, not mine. But in principle, Hegel's absolutely right, of course. Except his conclusion's not right. You don't want to unmask Grunge. It's unmasking itself. You're only doing it so the others don't feel like they're not as good as you. So you all work as a band. Like we used to work as a band in the old days.'

'We never used to work as a band,' said Onno. 'All the bands the two of us ever played in were based on not working.'

The record was over and Onno got up to put on another one.

Once the vocals set in, Stefan asked, 'This isn't Judas Priest is it?'

'Yes,' said Onno from the fridge. In the light of the small bright lamp, the two remaining bottle bottoms shimmered like round emeralds, and he stroked them as if touching treasure. Kneeling before the last beer, he had the feeling he had to make a decision. He didn't know what to do with Stefan. All he knew was that he had to decide. Either he ignored him until he left of his own accord, or he threw him out. But then he asked, turning in his direction: 'Do you want another one?' And at the moment he asked it he couldn't feel either of his hands any more, nor his legs, and yet he didn't collapse but straightened up again. He felt like someone had dropped an anvil on his head and smashed it to a pulp.

Stefan nodded. 'I thought you couldn't stand Judas Priest. I thought they were too soft for you.'

'Not *Painkiller*,' said Onno, putting the bottles on the table and sitting back down. The sensation was gradually returning to his limbs. '*Painkiller* is OK. Especially with the new drummer, Scott Travis.' *Judas Priest*. He suddenly remembered them sitting here with Daniel, in absolute silence. The article his mother had cut out of *Die Zeit* and pinned to the wall had disappeared and the records she'd hidden from him were back on the shelves in alphabetical order. Apart from that, the room still looked exactly as it had six years ago, with the same old living-room furniture, the same drum kit, the same mess.

'We could give it another try.'

'What?'

'Gigging.'

'Who with? Decomposed?'

'No, just the two of us. Guitar and drums. Totally reduced. Not that bombastic rock, none of that opulent crap. Reduced to the essentials—Minimetal. There's another open-air festival in Wacken in August and they're looking for bands, mate. It'd be just the right place for a comeback.'

'A comeback for what?'

'For us.'

'With this?' Onno pushed his right arm up with his left and then dropped it again.

'I could make you a drum kit like the one Rick Allen has. That's no problem, mate. We just have to add a couple of drum pads and connect your second pedal up to the PC. You'd have to do without one of the bass drums of course, but in principle you can program it so it sounds like two, really deep.'

'You mean a disabled drum kit.'

'It's just about strengthening your beat. Think about it—you could play a double-speed snare pattern again! We'd record the beats from your left hand and use the pads, piezoelectric triggers, to activate the sampled sounds. No one would notice the difference.'

'I would.'

'Only because you'd know.'

'You might as well use a drum computer in the first place. What do you need me for then?'

'For the show, mate!' Stefan took the tobacco, arranged papers and a filter, opened the bag Onno had brought over from Holland and skinned up a joint. 'For the show,' he said again and flicked open the lighter. 'Is it from that coffee shop we went to at the Braderienacht fair?'

Onno nodded. 'White Shadow. It's been around for years. You can get it here in Jericho as well but it costs more.'

'Really? And who deals it?'

'Iron Man.'

'Black Sabbath?'

'That too.'

'What else?'

'My continually successful dealer in three areas.'

'Do I know him?'

'Definitely.'

'And who is he?'

'A man of villainy, tricks and strength.'

'You won't reveal your source.'

'He'd kill me. And that's a triumph I refuse to grant you.'

'Certainly better that the stuff from Pfeiffer, anyway.'

'Much better,' said Onno and reached out his hand. 'But more dangerous too.'

'Dangerous?' Stefan handed him the joint and Onno took it.

'You can't take too much of it. It fogs up your brain.'

'I thought it expanded your consciousness.'

'Yours, maybe.'

'I might even be able to stand your avant-garde crap with this.'

'Speaking of which,' said Onno, gave him back the joint, got up from the sofa and pulled *Naked City* off the shelf.

'Shit, I shouldn't have mentioned it.'

'Too late,' said Onno and swapped the records over. But shortly before the end of Side One he pushed the lever to stop.

'Hey, I was just starting to like it.'

'I'll never be able to play as fast as that again,' said Onno. 'Not even with your disabled drum kit.'

'In a couple of years even that won't be necessary,' said Stefan, screwing his eyes up, taking a last drag although the joint was burnt almost all the way down to the tip, and putting it out in the ashtray. 'Jesus, that's good stuff.' He leant back and blew smoke rings. Then he straightened up and looked at the ceiling. 'Woah.'

'What?'

'Kohl.'

'Where?'

'Up there!' Stefan pointed upwards at the wooden ceiling panels. 'Helmut Kohl.'

'Don't talk crap.' Onno jumped up, getting dizzy from the sudden movement, and looked at the spot he'd been staring at all along before Stefan invited himself in.

'Totally, mate. The glasses, the high forehead, the droopy jowls. Kohl. Our eternal chancellor.' He slid off the seat to his knees and folded his hands as if in prayer.

'You've had to much to smoke.'

They both sat down again.

'And you've got Helmut Kohl on your ceiling. Big Pear is watching you!' He paused to skin up another joint. 'Have you got any more?'

'Only what's in the bag.'

'Maybe we could go over again in the next few days. I'm here till the next semester starts. Mate, if I think of the crap from the Sputnik Hall I feel sick already. The stuff they sell there tastes like grass, and I mean grass and not grass, if you get my meaning.'

'Yes,' said Onno. 'You said so earlier.'

'Mate, next time you come to Münster you have to try it. I think it really is just grass, dried grass from some field.'

'What won't be necessary?' asked Onno, to get back to what Stefan had said before, because he couldn't imagine sitting in the car next to a stoned Stefan, watching him smoke a couple of grams of finest marihuana in front of his nose and possibly driving back himself in his Audi A4 automatic, 1995 model, 150 PS, 110 kW, which his father had given him after he got out of the clinic.

'What?'

'My drum kit.'

'Oh right, yeah.' Stefan rolled the paper together and sealed it with his saliva. 'They'll just plant a chip inside you. Then you just have to think of the beats to make sounds. How fast do you think you'll play then, mate? Dave Lombardo's two hundred and forty-eight BPM on "Necrophobic" will be nothing then, you'll be getting more than four beats a second, easy. Think of all the possibilities. Your arm, both your arms, will be totally superfluous, only the power of your thoughts will count. Here,' he tapped his forehead, 'that's where you'll be playing. Beethoven could have gone on to a ripe old age, even though he was deaf. And Shostakovich would probably still be composing one revolutionary symphony after another, never mind his age. You can be blind and deaf and dumb, like Tommy, you can even be completely paralysed, totally stiff as long as your brain's alive, and you're still a musical genius. You'll overcome the limitations your body imposes on you with ease.'

'Maybe in twenty years' time.'

'You don't know anything about it.' Stefan lit the joint and took a drag. 'Technological progress is increasing exponentially. It can happen practically overnight. They already have a device for tinnitus sufferers like me, which is implanted behind your ear and releases medication at the touch of a button to reduce the damn ringing.' He bent his ear forward with one finger and then let it flap back. 'In two or three years a machine like that'll be replaced by a chip, I bet, an adaptive chip, one that automatically develops itself. It might be pretty primitive to start with but the brain's permanently feeding it information, and soon it'll be capable of solving the tasks it's posed on its own. The whole process will become automatic, so that the computing power is one day just as efficient as a purely biological brain. And you know what's the best thing about it, mate?'

Onno hated rhetorical questions, especially from people talking stoned shit, especially from Stefan. He suddenly knew it would have been better to throw him out. But it was too late now. Now he'd have to pick apart his argument or, if he didn't manage that, outdo his knowledge so as not to end up the loser.

'The thing they implant doesn't even have to be a silicon chip. It'd even be better if it wasn't. A silicon chip could compute fairly quickly but only process a small amount of binary information at the same time. What they'd have to implant is a genetic computer, one made of pure DNA. It would be slower but it would have the advantage that it makes its calculations at billions of points at once.'

'Do you know what kind of crap you're talking? No one's going to implant a chip in my brain.'

'Maybe you're right about that.'

'About what?'

'That no one's going to implant a chip in your brain.' Stefan raised his forefinger. 'Maybe they're not *going to*.' He leant forward and lowered his voice. 'Maybe someone already *has* implanted a chip in your brain. And mine too. How are we supposed to know? Maybe our thoughts are already being monitored and remote-controlled.'

'Oh yeah, yours definitely are.'

'No seriously, mate,' said Stefan. 'Wouldn't it be possible that we're part of a huge program, that all of us here,' he waved a hand around the room, 'have been programmed for a specific purpose?'

'And what purpose would that be?'

'Consumption, mate! Consumption!'

'You don't need to programme anyone for that. People do that all on their own.'

'That's the proof!'

'Ridiculous.'

'Don't you think it's remarkable that Zuse developed his first computer at exactly the same time as Keynes published his *General Theory of Employment, Interest and Money*?'

'No,' said Onno. 'I don't think so at all. It's a coincidence.'

'Coincidence is the same as extrinsic necessity. Says Hegel.'

'I don't give a shit what Hegel says.'

'Not *that* Hegel, the other one, the real one.'

'Either you were in a coma too long after the accident or you smoke too much!'

'Look who's talking, mate. Look who's talking. Want some more?' Stefan held the half-finished joint out to him.

Onno shook his head. He didn't want to be mollified. 'Let's assume what you're saying is true, and someone or something has implanted a chip in my brain, then why doesn't this living computer—'

'Genetic processor.'

'Right, whatever. Why doesn't this genetic processor work so that I can play the drums again? That would fit better with your sick hypothesis. Because then I'd go right out and buy a bigger drum kit, play more gigs, make records, print T-shirts, travel round the world and knock up a couple of underage girls backstage. I'd serve the market all-round and keep the whole economy thing running.'

'Because that's not what they want.'

'Who? The capitalists?'

'The ones who programmed the chip.'

'And who are they? The Plutonians?'

'Don't talk crap, mate.'

'You started it,' said Onno. 'So who, then?'

'How do I know? If I knew that I wouldn't be sitting here any more. They'd switch me off before I even thought the thought.'

'The thought police!'

'If that's what you want to call it.'

'OK, OK. So you don't know who it is. But I still don't get why they won't help me, if they've got so many great supernatural skills. I'd move out of here right away. I wouldn't just buy a new drum kit and all mod cons, I'd be so happy I'd get my own place and another car, a much more expensive one, and I don't know what else, and I'd take out a loan for it all that I'd never be able to pay off. They ought to be rubbing their hands with glee about an idiot who'd sell his soul to them so cheap.'

Stefan shook his head. 'Don't take yourself as an example. It's not worth it for them, long-term and for society as a whole. You're forgetting alcohol, and drugs and medication.' He pressed out the joint although he could have taken a few more drags. 'The therapies. They earn much more out of a depressed cripple. You're a negative role model. The whole of society suffers from guys like you.'

'Not necessarily. What if I die young? What if I kill myself?'

'That's no use to you. None at all. Then you'd be a martyr. And that's exactly what they want. Look at Kurt Cobain.' Stefan took a large gulp of beer, too large, put the bottle down and wiped his mouth with the back of his hand. Onno waited for him to finish his sentence, thinking it was a rhetorical imperative, but Stefan simply looked at him with tired, glassy eyes.

'What about Kurt Cobain?' Onno asked in the end.

'Nirvana sell more records now than they ever did. He's not our Jesus. He didn't die for us or for Rock 'n' Roll, he died for himself, to go down in history and establish himself as a trade mark.'

'I'm not Kurt Cobain.'

'That's true,' said Stefan and stifled a belch. 'You're telling the truth there.'

'I haven't achieved anything yet,' Onno said in the same crazy intonation as Stefan. 'I'm not done yet. My mission is not yet completed.'

'Yeah, that's why they're waiting. And then, when the time comes, they'll flick the switch.'

They drank their beers in silence. Then Stefan said, 'Hey, are you going to eat this?' pointing at the plate of potatoes and beans.

'No,' said Onno, who was standing in front of his records looking for something, something he hadn't listened to for a long time, which he hoped would give Stefan a tough time of it.

'There's no bacon in it,' Stefan said with his mouth full. 'And it's cold.'

'You don't have to eat it. No one's forcing you.'

'Too late.' He looked up at the ceiling. 'The Higher Powers ordered me to do it.'

The cover depicted a green monster trampling the devil under its feet. Onno held it so that Stefan couldn't see it and set the record in motion.

'Rad!' said Stefan, throwing his head back as if he still had enough hair to mosh, and raising the hand holding the fork up in the air, his fist clenched. 'Flotsam and Jetsam, *Doomsday for the Deceiver.*'

Onno lifted the pick-up arm off the record and put it back on the support.

'Hey! What are you doing? Put it back on. It's rad.'

'Maybe a few minutes' silence will do us good,' said Onno as he put the record and the cover back on the shelf.

'Silence is deafening,' said Stefan. '*Stille macht taub.*'

'I get it,' said Onno, 'but I'm not going to do you the favour of putting on Napalm Death, even if you say it in French or Russian or Chinese.'

'*Le silence rend sourd.* тишина оглушает. I don't speak Chinese.'

Onno stood by his records as if in a mental jam. He wondered what would go best now, thematically, and he decided on Motörhead's *Ace of Spades*, even though he was afraid it would get another 'rad' out of Stefan.

But Stefan didn't say 'rad' and didn't shake his head or raise his fist either. He simply sat there, put the knife and fork back on the plate and looked at him. 'Mate,' he said, patting his stomach with both hands. 'That was good. No bacon and a bit cold, but good.' He leant forward. 'And now we ought to get to the point.'

'The point being?'

'The Easter Fire. In the square behind the dairy. Steffi's going too.'

By the time they got there the mountain of branches and fir boughs, hay bales and euro-pallets had already been ignited in several places. Flames surged towards the evening sky. Sparks flew. The villagers were standing closely packed around the fire, staring into the red, entranced by the glow. Onno spotted Postman Schmidt from a distance, Miss Nanninga, Mayor Rosing, Simone, Iron Man, several school kids like Tobias Allen and Volker's sisters Verena and Venja, who made him feel like he'd got stuck in Jericho, and his father, Achim Kolthoff, in one hand a beer, in the other Susanne Haak. Onno knew she wanted to be an architect and was a trainee at his office, but he didn't know what the training programme consisted of. As his father whispered something in her ear, she began to laugh and he laughed too, but all at once their expressions darkened. Everyone's expressions darkened. Onno couldn't see what it was. Something coming towards them was capturing their attention, and they were backing off. Then he saw it for himself—a burning rabbit raced towards them and ran, directed by their screams, back into the fire.

'How terrible. The poor bunny.' Stephanie stepped out of the crowd, the zip on her jacket pulled up to her chin, the sleeves folded over her hands, her hair in a plait. She wrapped her arms around Onno, around Stefan, and then pushed him away. 'Are you crazy? You're off your face.' On the way back to the others, she turned around and showed him both her middle fingers: 'Fuck you, go fuck yourself.'

'What's the matter?' asked Onno. 'What have you done?'

'Nix,' said Stefan. 'I haven't done anything. Nothing forbidden. Nothing you wouldn't have done in my place with a healthy arm. And I wouldn't call it a bunny.'

An hour later, they were leaning against one of the wooden stalls that sold mulled wine and sausages, drinking beer out of half-litre cans. In the vanishing light of the setting sun, the contours of the old dairy were darkly visible. The air was heavy with smoke, voices and the scent of burnt resin. Less then ten metres away, a train rushed past them.

'We still need a name,' said Stefan after a long pause. 'For our gig.'

'What gig?'

'The one in Wacken.'

'I haven't even said I'm going to do it.'

'You haven't really got a choice. The whole Spoonmen thing's not going anywhere. You know it and I know it.'

'You don't know nix,' said Onno. But after thinking about it, he had to admit that Stefan was right. It was better to end his career with a huge, unforgettable gig than to drift into oblivion with a hundred smaller and smaller gigs. 'OK, but let's have another smoke first.'

'And a drink wouldn't be bad either,' said Stefan, crushing his can. 'My head feels pretty dry.'

Towards midnight when the wood had burnt down to the thickest branches, they were still discussing what they might call themselves—a stage some bands they'd played in had never got past. They'd already considered names like Axillaris, of Death and Naked Fear, when Onno said suddenly, 'Aaaaaaarrghh!'

'What's up? What happened? Did you catch a spark? Is this thing on fire?' They were sitting on a hay bale and Stefan jumped up, turned around and sat straight back down again, exhausted by the sudden movement.

'Everything's fine,' said Onno.

'So why did you scream?'

'I didn't scream. I said Aaaaaaarrghh!'

'Yes,' said Stefan, 'but why?'

'Because that's what we're going to be called.'

'Aaaaaaarrghh! What kind of crap name is that, mate? That's even dumber than Kill Mister.'

'It's not a name, it's a quote,' said Onno.

'From who?'

'From Venom. It's'—'

'I know. Without Venom we wouldn't be here today.'

'What do you mean?'

'Insemination,' said Stefan.

'What have your or my parents got to do with it? They definitely didn't listen to them, never, especially not when they—'

'That's not what I mean.'

'What then?'

'Osmosis!'

'Osmosis?'

'Yeah, mental osmosis. Biology. The penetration of materials through a semi-porous membrane—'

'I know what osmosis is. Everyone knows that. Mengs made us learn it off by heart, we'll never forget it.'

'That's all right then.'

'Yes,' said Onno. 'It is.' His eyes kept closing of their own accord.

'Anyway,' Stefan said after a while, 'without Venom there'd be no Metallica, and without Metallica no Thrash Metal, and you'd never have got into music, and we'd never have met.'

'We met on the estate, long before any of us was into music.'

'That doesn't make any difference.'

'Yes it does.'

'OK,' said Stefan. 'Then we'll call ourselves Aaaaaaarrghh!' He said 'Aaaaaaarrghh!' again, this time more loudly though, and turned around and yelled into the night, 'Hey, listen up, we're called Aaaaaaarrghh!'

Onno yanked his eyes open one last time. 'Who was that for?' Then they fell closed again and the beer can slipped out of his hand.

'For the record.'

'What record? We're not an official association!'

'We're not. But they are. They record everything,' said Stefan. 'It all gets saved. Everything we say. Everything we think. They're here. Not up there. All around us. Look at these people, mate. Take a good look. They're like remote-controlled. It could be anyone. The postman, the teacher, the mayor. Your parents, my parents. It could be us. Their exterior appearance is humanoid. At first glance they're hard to tell apart from humans. You have to look them right in the eyes, mate. Their blink frequency reveals their true identity. Their camouflage isn't perfect but it's impossible to tell in the dark. And yet I do know they're here. Now. At this moment. I can sense their presence. I hear their voices, their orders. They're calling me. They're saying, stay calm, stay sitting still, we've come to collect you.'

So ended the Silent Saturday, and so began the resurrection of the redeemer.

Stefan Reichert connected himself up to the world on 19 September 1999 and burnt out. He sat almost fully strapped down to an old hairdresser's chair, writhing with cramps. His right arm twitched in mid-air as if he wanted to point at something. Foam came out of his mouth. The blood coagulated in his veins. For a moment time stood still and space disappeared. Then flames surged out of his head—a wreath of fire encircled his face—and there was a crackle before the first sparks fell to the floor in a brief, intense fizzle and extinguished.

The call came early in the morning. Stephanie was still in bed when the phone rang. She picked up and Britta, Stefan's mother, was on the other end. 'You've got to come.' Her voice was trembling. 'Stefan's locked himself in the basement.'

'That's nothing new,' said Stephanie, annoyed at being woken up by it.

'No,' said Britta. 'It's different this time. He's screaming and shouting. He's been screaming all night.'

'What is he shouting?'

'We can't understand all of it but it sounds terrible.'

'Is he shouting numbers?'

'Yes.'

'Rational or irrational?'

'Irrational, I'd say. Totally irrational.'

'Put him on the phone.'

'I can't.'

'Why not?

'He won't talk to us.'

'Then call him and tell him I want to speak to him.'

'We've tried that already. He won't come up, no matter what we say.' She sobbed but she didn't start crying. 'Steffi?'

'Yes?'

'What does it all mean?'

Stephanie looked at the clock—quarter past seven. 'I'll take the next train.'

'Oh, thank goodness. Wonderful. I'll pick you up at the station.'

Stephanie didn't take the next train, nor the one after that. If it had been up to her she wouldn't have taken any train at all, but spent the day in bed, eating crisps and watching TV. She'd got home late and drunk from a party and now her head was buzzing from too much wine and too little sleep. She was annoyed that she had to go back to East Frisia again because of Stefan, even though the reason, however upsetting it might be for his mother, was a positive one. They'd been there together at the beginning of the summer break, not even two months ago. She'd stayed with her parents and he with his, and they'd left after a week, exhausted by the rituals to which they had to submit—breakfast, lunch, dinner and two lots of tea in between, accompanied by comments on their appearance and their way of life.

'Do you have to wear that rubbish, those second-hand clothes? Don't we give you enough allowance? Or are you spending our money on other things?'

'Don't you start taking drugs, young lady. You can see what they've done to that ne'er-do-well.'

'I don't understand how you can do it, make so many sacrifices for him. He's bleeding you dry, down to the last drop.'

'When are you going to finally finish your degree? And what do you want to do with it after that? Mathematician—that's not a proper job.'

'What's the point of those ridiculous sunglasses? We can't look you in the eye properly.'

'At least he's cut his hair.'

That was why she hadn't understood why he'd gone back there two weeks ago, why he couldn't say what he wanted to say to her here and why his parents being there was suddenly so important to him. And she also wondered why he hadn't asked her to come ten days earlier, if she had to come to him in the first place. 9.9.99 would have been a much better date, ideal timing.

She was also annoyed because she couldn't take her own car, now that she needed it, a black Mini Cooper MK VI, 1996 model, 63 PS, 43 kW. Something was wrong with the engine. The ignition was OK but it made a strange noise. And as she'd thought she could go without a car for a while, at least while she was staying in Münster revising for her repeat exam on number theory, she had taken it to be repaired on Friday.

At least she could sleep or read on the train.

She stood under the cold shower for a long time, pressing her arms close to her body and struggling for breath as though at risk of drowning. And while she put on her best dress that she'd recently bought in London and packed her bag, she drank three cups of coffee, hot and black and so strong it gave her palpitations. And still she felt numb. In her new high heels, she lost her footing even in the hallway, and the blazer she'd bought specially for the occasion suddenly seemed too tightly cut, but it was her most special outfit. She put a pair of trainers in her bag, to be on the safe side. Just before she left the flat she called the Reicherts again to tell them her arrival time. The answer machine picked up and she left a message.

On the way to the station she stopped at the bakery on the corner. It was a branch of a large chain. The bread was delivered and the rolls were only baked on the premises, not made there, but the small shop was always crowded. It was right at the beginning of the medieval town centre, and anyone going to the university or the pedestrian zone passed it. Even on days like this, when the library and all the shops were shut, people stood tightly packed in front of the display counter, placing their orders and examining their small change.

Stephanie couldn't remember how often she'd been in there before, alone or with Stefan, but whenever she was waiting to be served she was reminded of one of their professors, Professor Ischebeck. She'd only met him here once, two years ago, but she couldn't shake the thought that it might happen again. She'd been on her way home from jogging after a round of the city, and it had been embarrassing standing next to him in her sweaty sports outfit. At first he hadn't noticed her and she'd hoped it would stay that way, but he'd spoken to her as they left. 'Good morning, Ms Reichert.' He knew neither her forename nor her surname, although she'd attended his seminars on number theory and geometry. All he knew was that she was with Stefan, and that was all that interested him. 'How are you?'

'Fine.'

'How's the work going?'

'Making progress.'

'I hope so. We're all looking forward to it.' He didn't mean her work. None of the professors who asked about it did. For them, Stephanie was nothing but the moon that orbited the earth.

While other students attended lectures on calculus or stochastics in their first and second semesters, Stefan had gone straight to the big subjects: the arithmetic of the Abel differential equation,

389

the cohomology in Grothendieck's topologies, the minimal super-symmetric standard model, the analysis of three-dimensional incompressible Navier-Stokes equations, and Hilbert's as yet unsolved problems concerning whether physics can be axiomized, whether the real part of every nontrivial zero of the Riemann zeta function is ½, and how the Kronecker-Weber theorem can be extended to random number fields.

He read the most important essays and papers on each task, talked to older students who hadn't managed them so that he wouldn't repeat their mistakes, and he asked his lecturers to confirm the significance of the conjectures and problems. Only then did he begin to take notes.

Professor Ischebeck had noticed him when Stefan had shown during a stochastics seminar how Grigori Margulis' work on ergodic theory could be simplified, and he had encouraged him to continue his research—in all directions.

And that's what Stefan had done.

For days.

For weeks.

For months.

It took him a long time to find his subject. He felt he had to have mastered all the subdomains before he could devote himself to one thing. He wanted an overview of the whole before he turned to a fraction. To begin with, it was only ever ideas that didn't work, taken on their own. Whenever he talked to Stephanie about it, which he rarely did and only in the form of hints, he complained about his inability to link the many different ideas together. He hoped he'd manage what he'd once managed again, if only he worked hard enough. The theorems were clear and well ordered in his head, but as soon as he wrote them down it all went out of focus. With every word, his proofs lost precision and elegance.

The longer he sat in the library or on the Bridge—a glass corridor between the main building and the lecture theatres, equipped with desks and chairs—the further he seemed to get from the solution to a problem. Sometimes Stephanie brought him a coffee before her teaching lectures, but when she went to see him again later the cup would still be in the same place and he hadn't drunk a single sip. Stefan got to university before her and went home after her, often falling asleep slumped over his books or his laptop, and he often had the feeling he never woke up, because he accepted everything not related to mathematics or biology or computer studies with almost complete apathy.

She had got used to going out on her own, to Platform 22 at the station or the Luna Bar or to private parties like yesterday. She met other, less interesting men, went on holiday with her friends Charlotte, Antonia or Julia Hamm, and when she got back Stefan didn't seem to notice she'd been gone. She was the only one who noticed her absence—the whole flat was covered in piles of dirty plates and empty pizza boxes, and his books and notes were scattered across all the rooms. She had always felt superior to her fellow students, who lurched from one adventure to the next, and she'd never regretted her decision to move in with Stefan. But the chaos he left behind whenever she turned her back upset her every single time.

Once, she'd turned on her heel and left again, in a rage. Still holding her suitcase, she'd got in her car and driven home—to her parents. And she'd let them persuade her to pour her heart out over three or four glasses of wine. From then on, her father had called Stefan a ne'er-do-well and her mother had always eyed her with an accusing, pitying look, as if commiserating with her daughter for having made the wrong choice in life. She had never openly pressured her to leave Stefan, but she herself had thought about it in the past, especially because she never knew what he was working on, and that was more hurtful than anything else.

Every time she'd had enough of his taciturn brooding she'd take him to task, and every time she'd get the same answer.

'I can't tell you.'

'Why not?'

'Because then I'll lose hold of it.'

'Lose hold of what?'

'Everything. Everything I say takes on a life of its own.'

'I won't tell anyone. I swear.' Stephanie raised her right hand to make an oath. They didn't argue; they almost never argued. These conversations, when she wanted him to reveal more about himself, always drifted into nothingness.

'That's not what I mean.'

'What do you mean then?'

'I'll tell you when I've finished, OK?'

And when he was finished, when they were both finished, back then in summer two years ago, he had handed her several notebooks one morning, hundreds of pages of theorems, formulae and equations. Then he'd fallen asleep on the sofa and hadn't woken up until the next day.

Although she was studying mathematics, she was one of the students taking maths to teach it at primary-school level. The other maths students mocked then as 'schoolmarms' and the professors didn't take them seriously. She did no research and she wasn't interested in doing any. She wanted to work with children, teach them reading, writing and arithmetic and the basics of the Christian faith, which she considered the most important thing in life, the foundation everything else was built upon. She'd been good at school, one of the best, but she found university difficult. She only passed most of her exams with Stefan's help. And she tried to help him in her own way, by enabling him to concentrate entirely on his work. She did the shopping, took care of the household, made the dinner. That was what her mother reproached her for, for betraying the feminist ideals she'd fought for when she was a student in the early seventies. But Stephanie liked cooking and cleaning, she enjoyed trying out new recipes, walking around a clean flat and lying in a freshly made bed. These activities gave her a feeling of having achieved something visible and necessary at the end of the day—a feeling she didn't get from her studies. And it hardly bothered her that Stefan did next to nothing in the household. All she asked of him in that respect was not to make too much of a mess.

She didn't understand enough of mathematics to assess Stefan's proof of the Riemann hypothesis properly, but she knew enough to tell that, if everything in the notebooks was correct, he had done something out of the ordinary. Although the professors who had examined his proof—including Professor Ischebeck—thought they had found a few gaps and inaccuracies in his argumentation and weren't all positively surprised by his unconventional methodology, they did show respect for his achievement and urged him to publish as soon as possible. Stefan had agreed in principle, under the condition that he first wiped out all the errors that were doubtlessly contained in his paper. He said he only wanted to submit something perfect, a proof that held down to the very last detail. In fact, however, he had put the manuscript in the bottom drawer of his desk and devoted himself to what he considered more pressing tasks, molecular genetics and bioelectronics.

Time and again, the professors spoke to him and her about the notebooks, asked when he expected to hand his work in and offered their support in getting it finished. Enquiries came from all over the world—some of the mathematicians who had examined his proof must have made copies and handed them on. Stefan promised he'd soon be ready and he'd send every one of them their own personal copy for re-examination, but at some point a new hypothesis arose, the Reichert hypothesis. And that said that he hadn't come up with the proof on his own and that older, more experienced scholars had been involved. Some even said they'd developed the whole structure of his proof at the same time as he did, but they couldn't prove that; others wrote letters to the dean of the mathematics faculty, intended to show that Stefan had taken theorems and lemmata from them without marking them clearly as citations, and they demanded that the dean immediately expel Stefan, his best student, or they would expose them both for plagiarism—which never happened.

And when Stefan was considered for the Fields Medal, regardless of these accusations, an award to be bestowed for the first time ever in Germany, the press caught wind of him too. Journalists called him at home; they ambushed them when they left the flat or came home from university; some even followed them into the bakery in the hope of gaining their trust, or if not then at least provoking a statement. Although he turned down all interview requests, there were dozens of reports on him in newspapers, on the radio and TV, the genius, the fraud, the Reichert Case. That and the severe reactions, veering between adoration and abhorrence, to lectures he held in Münster and at other European universities, confirmed his belief that it was better to publish nothing at all than nothing complete.

During that time, a man approached her and Stefan in the Maths Institute. He had no camera, no tape recorder, no note pad with him, and he asked no questions either. All he said was, 'With your abilities and your language skills you could make it a long way in the senior service. We have far too few people with clean political records, fluent Russian and a good understanding of algorithms.' He gave him his card, added 'Munich's a very nice city with the best primary schools in Germany. I'm sure your wife would like it there,' and left without casting a single glance at Stephanie. 'Call me any time, and I mean any time.' She wondered whether that was the reason why Stefan had withdrawn entirely, wore mirrored sunglasses whenever he left the house, spent even more time at the lab or the library, got up at night to calculate endless decimal points, specify bases, translate amino acid sequences and read the bible, as if he'd discovered the secret of all humankind.

'What can I do for you?'

Stephanie had finally reached the front of the queue. The man next to her at the counter took his paper bag, stepped back and bumped into her as he turned around. 'Sorry.' It was Professor Ischebeck. 'Oh, good morning, Ms . . . Beckmann? How are you?'

'Fine. How are you?'

'Aren't you resitting one of your exams with me? Numbers theory or geometry?'

'Numbers theory,' she said. 'I'm revising for it now.'

'I hope so too. In your own interest. You haven't got much time left.' With that, he left the bakery and Stephanie placed her order.

When she'd moved to Münster, finally moved away from home, she'd thought she had to try new things for herself, and she'd avoided everyone she knew from school. In the first few weeks she spoke to strangers every day after lectures, men and women. Some of them had common names like Thorsten and Anja or Michael and Julia, and she connected these names with attributes, with their hair colour or their origin, to distinguish them from other Thorstens and Anjas, Michaels and Julias when they came up in conversation. Thorsten Brown, Anja Black, Michael Kassel, Julia Hamm. Some of them had names she'd only ever come across in books, though: Robert, Charlotte, Gregor, Antonia.

Many of them she never saw again because they decided to attend a lecture at a more convenient time or study a different subject, in a different city. But the ones she saw again, she told about her life, from kindergarten to leaving school, everything she could remember. She didn't invent anything. She didn't make up stories, the way some people did to make themselves more interesting or to gauge their listeners' reactions, and she added nothing new to her experiences and impressions. The only thing she did was leave things unsaid that she found unpleasant.

She spent hours sitting in the kitchen, talking to her flatmates. For the first time, she had sole control over her memories. There was no one to contradict her, no one to correct her.

Never before had she revealed so much about herself. Or concealed so much.

After a lecture on Paul Celan she went to the cafeteria with Thorsten Brown. Then they had a beer at a cafe on Prinzipalmarkt. They felt very daring because it was only three o'clock and they'd never done anything like that in the middle of the week, drinking in the afternoon. They bought two new bottles at a kiosk, strolled along the promenade, threw fallen leaves at each other and rented a pedal boat in the shape of a white swan on the Aasee lake. Thorsten told her about his past and she told him about hers. His father was a pastor and his mother had died young of cancer, and one of his brothers had been hit by a car out playing and been severely injured. They talked about books, about their favourite writers. He admitted that he wrote himself—poems. She asked him to quote one and he offered to read some out to her as soon as they got to his place, his shared flat, his room, behind closed doors.

Late that evening—it was dark by then—they went outside again and had a pizza in an Italian restaurant on Rosenplatz. She'd often been on holiday with her parents, to Scandinavia, England and America, but never to Italy. Her father didn't have any ships there or any port he could call on. There were dozens of unusually named pizzas on the menu with the usual toppings, Chiosco, Lungomare, Foglie, Pedalo, Poesia, Cigno, Pastore. Stephanie couldn't make her mind up. Thorsten recommended one with rocket, and she picked that because rocket was something she'd never tried before, and that day she had the feeling she was doing everything for the first time, drinking, eating, kissing, loving.

Anja Black, who had gone to school with Thorsten Brown, told her his father was a scaffolding worker and his mother was still alive and one of his sisters had run over a child, who now lived in a home for the severely disabled, and Antonia said, 'Did he read you his poems too?'

'The Camp Tinnitus,' said Anja Black, her voice devoid of expression.

Antonia closed her eyes and supressed a laugh. 'The drumming of the bones—'

'In my ear—' Stephanie joined in the recitation and looked at Anja to continue Thorsten's death fugue.

From then on they took turns. 'I still hear it now,'

'After all these years.'

'The tiny man,'

'In my ear,'

'Beeping and whistling,'

'Beating the bones,'

'In time,'

'Beats out the death march and won't stop drumming, after all these years.' They recited the last lines together, and then they cheered and clapped each other's hands like sportswomen who have scored a surprising point against an overpowering opponent.

She hadn't noticed Gregor at first. In fact he wasn't the kind of person who could be easily overlooked, tall and slim and fond of brightly coloured clothes—a green sweat jacket, brown cord trousers, various coloured trainers made of rough, matte suede. Black horn-rimmed glasses. Freckles. Blue eyes. Dark, chin-length, home-cut hair. He was standing at a slight angle, as if leaning against a wall, one leg crossed over the other, and he spoke to her.

It was just before ten and she'd just got out of a lecture on mathematical logic. The professor, Professor Diller, had filled up all six blackboards so quickly, pushing them up and down and wiping them clean again, that she felt like he'd run the sponge across her own brain. Only the sentences, 'The following sentence is false. The previous sentence is true,' were still echoing in her mind as she stepped out into the corridor and met Gregor.

'Hello,' he said, and followed up, before she could return his greeting, with a question—would she like to get an ice cream with him? He wanted to ask her before the ice-cream season was over and another ice age began.

'I don't even know you.'

'What isn't now can never be?'

According to her own logic, any man who approached her in a sober and open manner presented no danger. He wouldn't be able to hurt her because he'd ventured the first step into the void, because it was him dangling above a precipice and not her. Lots of men had spoken to her, but most of them weren't themselves when they did so. They had mustered the courage to approach her only under the influence of drugs, and that was nothing that deserved her respect.

'Chocolate chip or nut?'

'Both.'

On the way to the ice-cream parlour, he said, 'Tell me everything you know, where you live and what's your name.'

And that was what she did. Of course, she didn't tell him everything she knew, but she did tell him where she lived and why she'd moved to Münster and what subjects she was studying and what she was interested in: Mathematics and Literature, England and Finland. He spent the whole time watching her attentively and licking his ice cream. Sometimes he asked a question, sometimes he told her to go into more detail, and it wasn't until she was back at university and sitting in the mathematical logic class that she realized she knew little more about him than his first name. With a twinge of panic, she feared she herself was now three steps away from the precipice; she feared he might lie in wait for her, knowing her address. And that was what he did, but not outside her house; outside the lecture theatre where she'd first met him. This time they didn't go out for ice cream but for fish 'n' chips.

'Are you here on Saturday?' she asked him.

He nodded.

'That makes you an exception. Everyone goes home on the weekends.'

'I don't.'

'It's the Send on Saturday.'

'Saturday is suicide.'

'They ought to do something to make them stay, something better that that stupid funfair, a festival or a rave, something big.'

'The idea is good,' he said, 'but the world's not ready yet.'

They went anyway, took a turn on the bumper cars and the ghost train, the big wheel and then back to her place. There, it turned out that everything about him was skewed and large and yet hard to grasp.

When she woke up in the night and climbed down the ladder of her raised wooden bed, still woozy from the alcohol, from the bumping and the circling of the fairground rides and her and his motions, he and his things had disappeared. On her desk was a piece of paper, folded up like a letter. She decided to read it as soon as she got back from the toilet. She thought, that's it, I messed up. In her mind, she went over the evening and the night again, what she'd said and what she'd done. Then she thought for a moment, he's left me his number, he wants to see me again, he liked it.

He hadn't left her his number, and if he'd liked it then not in a way that made him want to see her again. The piece of paper said: *Thank God we two had each other.*

At the beginning of November a band from Hamburg played at Platform 22. Julia Hamm had a spare ticket and offered to take Stephanie along. The name Tocotronic didn't sound familiar and she couldn't even remember it to begin with. She'd only gone along as a favour to Julia. The audience, all in sweat jackets and cord trousers, like members of a sect, stood packed tightly all the way up to the bar. Stephanie got them two beers, and when the music started and they'd finally fought their way to the stage with their bottles, she saw Gregor standing right next to a speaker, chanting along to every line with his hair over his face.

'Thank God we two had each other.'

'The idea is good but the world's not ready yet.'

'Saturday is suicide.'

'What isn't now will never be.'

Lines that stabbed her through the heart, no matter whether they were true or false.

Robert was in her pedagogy seminar on The School of the Future. He didn't look like the kind of student studying to be a teacher— he didn't wear knitted sweaters and flared trousers but white shirts and black suits. He had short hair, trimmed above the ears and at the sides, shaved at the back of his neck. He always arrived too late, took no notes and never joined in the discussions about alternative teaching methods. Stephanie thought him rather stiff but once, as they were leaving the room together after the fourth or fifth class, he said something she'd thought about the seminar herself—'What a load of crap.'

The week after that she had overslept and met him outside the university as he was just locking his bike. 'It's started already,' she said.

And he said, 'All the better, then it'll be over sooner.'

He held the door to the institute open for her and as they climbed the stairs he made the suggestion of skipping the seminar and going to see a film instead, at the cinema called simply Cinema where they screened old French films in the matinée showing, *Contempt, The Mischief Makers, The Samurai.* And Stephanie consented. To get there in time they took a taxi, afterwards they went to a bar, and when they parted ways at midnight he paid her taxi fare home without asking for the money back or insisting on coming with her.

One evening in December, he invited her over for dinner. He shared a small flat in the Kreuzviertel district, where he served up a five-course meal: artichokes in mustard and cream sauce, tomato soup with pumpernickel croutons, wild boar ragout with chestnuts and potatoes, crème brulée and almond tarte. There was red wine to go with it, a Châteauneuf-du-Pape, 1995 vintage. Later, while he was fetching another bottle from the cellar, the woman he shared the flat with popped into the kitchen, gave her a wink and said, 'He's never done this before, cooked for a woman.'

His room was full of books, lined up on simple pine shelves all the way up to the ceiling, large-format photo books and exhibition catalogues, the collected works of Kierkegaard, Nietzsche and Schopenhauer, mythological and art-history encyclopaedias, novels by Kafka, Sartre and Camus, books with titles like *On the Heights of Despair*, *The Trouble with Being Born* and *Seduction*, which made her curious—not about the books themselves but about the man who'd read them.

In the middle of the room was a big, wide bed with white sheets and white covers, surrounded by candles and red roses, like an altar on which he meant to sacrifice something to himself. Once the flames had died down he admitted to her that he wasn't studying Teaching but Art History and Philosophy, and only went to the seminar because the lecturer was his father. He talked about his childhood, about demonstrations, concerts and rural communes, about moving house over and over, holidays and pilgrimages to India, about how much he wished he had brothers and sisters and longed for clear rules. 'Somewhere,' he said, digging around in a box in the dark, 'I must still have a tape of me as a seven-year-old kid.' And while she lay in his arms and listened to him, his childhood voice, she felt like she'd known him for years.

Over breakfast at noon the next day, he asked what plans she had for the day, and whether she'd like to go to Paris with him; he had a car.

'Now?'

'Yes, now.'

In the past ten minutes he had eaten two croissants and drunk half a pot of coffee while she was still facing an empty plate and a full cup, incapable of even contemplating eating or drinking. She wanted to take things slowly this time, not go as fast as with Thorsten and Gregor. 'That sounds tempting. But I always go to the sauna with a friend on Sundays.'

For a while he simply looked at her, his eyes cold and piercing. Then he said, 'Can I come with you?'

She'd never been in a sauna with a man she knew, apart from her father, but she didn't want to look uptight so she said, 'Sure, why not?'

'Is it OK if I bring someone else along too?'

'Sure. I don't mind. And I'm sure Charlotte won't either. It's a mixed sauna anyway.'

Charlotte was also in the seminar on The School of the Future. Stephanie had only been to the sauna with her once before; although they'd planned to go regularly they'd never managed it after that one first Sunday.

She'd have to call her, she'd have to explain why she wanted to go that day, and she feared Charlotte would say no when she found out who'd be coming along. But she didn't. 'If he's like in the seminar it's bound to be great fun.'

'What do you mean?'

'So stiff,' said Charlotte, and they both laughed.

They arranged to meet at five. To begin with, they leant against the wall and looked at the palace grounds across the road, at the dark, bare trees. Charlotte lit a cigarette and Stephanie asked for one too, although she hadn't smoked for years. The first drag made her cough, the second made her eyes water, the third warmed her heart, and she was annoyed with herself for not taking up Robert's offer to take her to Paris.

'I bet he comes late,' said Charlotte once she'd put out her cigarette on the ground, 'he always comes too late.'

'Not last night,' said Stephanie, and they laughed again. But Charlotte was right, Robert really did come too late, and as it was more pleasant to wait in the sauna for him and his companion than out in the cold, they went inside. They stowed their clothes in a locker, took a shower and spread their towels on the top bench. Stephanie was glad they had enough space and the others there were almost all women, pairs of young friends and mothers with their daughters. A man sitting directly by the sauna stove scooped water out of the wooden barrel with the ladle and tipped it over the stones. Stephanie felt her pores opening and the night's sweat running down her back.

Then the door opened and Robert and his father came in.

She only ever saw Stefan at a distance. He would wave at her and she'd wave back. But she heard him saying things to other people, like 'All right mate, what's going down?' 'Hot chicks, mate, top location here,' 'Man, this weed goes straight to your brain,'—things he'd never said in her presence. And she heard other people talking about him, about his skills and talent. About what he said to the professors in the seminars, and about the findings of his biological experiments, as if he were one of them. Sometimes when they were in the queue in Cafeteria II or passed each other on the Bridge, they'd stop and talk. But as soon as anyone else came along she'd say goodbye. Not because she was afraid he'd embarrass her with anecdotes from their past, but because she didn't want her old life to mingle in with her new one. Soon, however, she realized that a city like Münster was too small and much too densely populated with exiled East Frisians of her age group to keep that separation up permanently.

'Hey,' Michael Kassel said to her at a party. 'I hear you were on *You Bet!*'

'Yeah, right,' said Antonia. 'I saw photos of you at Gesa's place.'

'Really? What photos?'

'From the paper. With Thomas Gottschalk. And outside a car showroom place. At the opening. You cutting the ribbon.'

'I've never seen them. But didn't you have that legendary party at your house? I think I've seen photos of that. Pretty wild.' He shook his head. 'Man, I wish I'd been there. Seems to have been a really great party.'

Antonia nodded. 'The party of the century.'

'Did you move out afterwards?'

'No, we didn't,' said Stephanie and went to get a new drink.

She met Stefan two days later at university. At first she made accusations, thinking he'd shown people photos of her, but then he said, 'I can't even remember that night.' And she realized there was more connecting them than their old school—they'd both lost a friend in Rainer. Maybe, she thought, that was why I've been avoiding him, so I don't get reminded of it, and maybe that was a mistake. Maybe we ought to talk about it. Maybe we ought to get together and talk about it.

And that's what they did, not guessing that they'd soon lose another friend because of it.

Stephanie locked up her bike in the new underground bike park, went up the stairs to the station, bought a ticket and a coffee to take away and waited on the platform for the Regional Express to Norddeich. The wind was cutting and cold and kept getting under her dress. She buttoned up her blazer and sought shelter behind one of the vending machines. The temperatures had fallen below fifteen degrees Celsius over the past few days, and she was glad to be holding something warm, even if it was only a cardboard cup of coffee.

Now, in retrospect, running into Ischebeck seemed unreal. As a child she'd been convinced that people appeared if only she thought about them hard enough—be it that she really bumped into them during the day, at school, in the village, at her father's office, or that they called or someone mentioned their name. For a while she'd even believed she could bring the dead back to life merely through the power of her thoughts. And later, at the end of a long evening rich in discussion and hash at his shared flat, Stefan had told her about biologists who thought the world only existed inside our heads, that reality was a construct of the brain, that Hegel, his flatmate, had said, 'That's not a new idea, in philosophical terms. It's called solipsism: I am me, and nothing else exists. And in that case all this here,' he gestured around the kitchen, 'is only a projection, the table, the chair, the oven, and you two are nothing but a dream.'

'Yes,' Stefan said back then, 'but one that's about to cause you so much pain you'll wish you'd never fallen asleep.' Stefan hated it when other people knew more than he did, especially Hegel—one reason why it had been so easy to persuade Stefan to move out of that flat and in with her. And since then it hadn't mattered to her whether the world only existed in her head or not, as long as she could look at it and smell it and touch it and taste it.

Opposite, on the other side of the platform, a train stopped and no one got out. Minutes passed as the conductor checked every single carriage by looking in through the windows. Once he knocked at the glass and the doors opened with a hiss after all. A girl stepped onto the platform, huddled over like an old woman. She had a trekking backpack on her back and bags in both hands. First she went in one direction and then, after noticing her mistake, she walked past her to the staircase. Stephanie couldn't help remembering how she'd arrived here herself, four years ago, with nothing but a map of the city and a couple of addresses. A few students, boys she knew from the UFO, had waxed lyrical in shouted conversations over the loud music, praising the palatial university, the burgher houses and Gothic churches, and advised her to start her degree there because the city was just the right size. Big enough to avoid people. Small enough to run into people again. A place where it was easy to get by, where you could develop at your own pace, where you never lost control.

Back then, on her arrival, she'd been disappointed. On her journey from one flat to the next she had seen neither the palace nor burgher houses, only 1950s buildings with low-ceilinged, over-priced rooms. And later, when she saw the old town centre, the town hall, St Lambert's Church, the cathedral, her initial enthusiasm had given way to even greater disappointment once she'd found out that these buildings too had been bombed in the war and then reconstructed as faithful copies. Every time they passed them, Stefan would say, 'You see, forgeries are accepted. Münster is the centre of illusion.'

She'd never regretted her decision though. And soon there'd be new decisions to make. If she passed the repeat exam she'd only have a few months left of her degree, and she'd already talked to Stefan about moving to Hamburg or Berlin after that. She hoped that would take his mind off things. Some people she'd studied with had set up their own companies there and were earning a lot of money out of the future. They were developing websites, databases or mobile devices, of which no one could say with any certainty what they would be used for one day—apart from making phone calls, writing messages, taking photos, listening to the radio and going on the net.

Stefan had always been scathing about these things; for him they were signs of mental and moral decline, symbols of the end of the world. The New Economy combined everything he hated about capitalism: gluttony, incapability and the praising of a young generation acting out unconventionality. CEO, B2B, IPO, venture capital, content development, e-commerce, synergy effects, Nemax, flat hierarchies. Smoke and mirrors, nothing but smoke and mirrors to conceal the real aims, exploitation and control of the people. She knew his theory, that the history of computer technology was tied to that of capital, that one only existed to help the other to rule the world, and she'd had enough of it. 'Richard Nixon, the biggest capitalist of all times, becomes president—and the Pentagon implements the ARPANET project. Milton Friedman publishes his critique of the welfare state—the most important work since *Capitalism and Freedom*—and IBM puts the PC on the market. Tim Berners-Lee writes the Hypertext Transfer Protocol, the basis of our civilization—and the Berlin Wall comes down. All at once, boundless freedom on all levels, freedom of travel, communication, trade. And that's supposed to be a coincidence? We definitely have entered a new age. Welcome to paradise—in the ninth circle of Hell! Now we think we can do whatever we want, because they want us to think that! Send and intercept messages via every computer, every modem. Play games with millions of other players. Meet people and be totally honest to them. Or totally dishonest. And still not get knocked back. Listen to music. Watch films. Read books. Carry an archive around in your pocket, a gigantic, multimedia diary. Explore the world without leaving the room. Never lose your bearings. Always be available. Have friends everywhere. And know where they are and with whom. It's all nothing more than a permanent simulation of reality.

'I'm not saying it doesn't exist. Or couldn't exist. But what you need to fulfil all these wishes costs you a lot of money and a whole lot of time, maybe your whole life. You think you have to be up to date all the time, you update your software, you exchange your old hardware for new, higher-performance versions and still you're always a tick too slow. On the other hand—if you don't go along with it you get left behind. If you drop out of the system you're out of it all. So you keep on logging in again. You register and you reveal your data, you surf and leave a trail, you use the net, and suddenly, without even noticing, you're drawn in. That's what it'll be like.

'The truth is, we're letting ourselves be enslaved all over again through the Internet, only much more subtly and comprehensively than before. More democracy, more freedom! Don't make me laugh. Who profits from it? You? Me? Society? Or capital, power? And you want to tell me there's no connection, it's all a figment of my imagination? Wake up, Steffi! You start getting nervous when you haven't checked your emails for five days.' There was nothing she could say against these tirades. He smothered every objection she made with names and data, alleged proof.

Stephanie looked at her watch and took a step towards the edge of the platform. No train in sight. She went over to the timetable, thinking she'd made a mistake with the departure time, and as she stood there an announcement came that the Regional Express to Norddeich was delayed by approximately twenty minutes. The flap display above her relayed the information at the same time. Stefan's mother couldn't tell rational and irrational numbers apart; perhaps he'd shouted neither π nor e and was simply despondent after a failed experiment or new proof. She wondered whether there was any point in still going to Jericho under the circumstances. Stefan had probably long since calmed down by now, like he always did, and she was going all the way to him and his parents for nothing. At the same time, she found the idea of strengthening their connection exciting, and she decided to call the house again, hoping he'd come to the phone himself. She drank a last sip of coffee and threw the cup in the bin.

She walked along the platform in search of a phone booth, went down the stairs, found an empty one on the square outside the station and pulled out her Telekom card, but the twelve Deutschmarks of credit was used up and she'd spent all her change at the bakery. Even though she thought mobile phones were ridiculous accessories, she was annoyed she didn't have one now.

Passing the kiosk inside the station, she thought for a moment about changing a note or buying a bottle of water and taking the rest back outside, but she instantly rejected the idea as too complicated, went up the stairs again and stood in the same place from which she'd set off five minutes previously, determined to stay in Münster, in the shelter of the vending machine.

Her feet ached.

The wind had got stronger.

The display board said: *Approx. 30 min. later.*

Exhausted, she sat down in one of the glass-walled waiting areas and swapped her high heels for the trainers. On the wooden bench opposite her, someone was snoring loudly, lying there like a corpse. She was certain it was a man. He had his back to her, a denim jacket, leather trousers, trainers, long straight hair down to the ground; that was all she could see of him. But the way he lay there, his hands beneath his body, his legs drawn in, and his stature—he could be a woman. She got up to look him in the face but his hair covered his entire head, so she sat down again. Rainer,

410

Stefan and Onno used to tell her stories, she remembered now, about people approaching them in the street and asking, 'Boy or girl?' And from then on she had often thought that they looked like girls, like swotty, unkempt girls. Except they had never behaved like girls. None of them had ever been capable of giving in. Perhaps then none of it would have happened. Perhaps Rainer wouldn't have had the car accident, and Onno wouldn't have killed himself, and Stefan would have stayed normal.

A few months ago, coming home from a night out at the cinema with Julia Hamm—*Notting Hill* at the Palace Theatre—she had found Stefan kneeling on the carpet in the living room, surrounded by records. Heavy Metal thudded out of the speakers.

'I'm such an idiot,' he shouted at himself over the music, and she got the impression he'd been shouting it for a good while even before she'd opened the door.

'What's the matter?' she asked, turning the volume knob to the left. 'What's going on?'

'I should have known!'

'What?'

'Onno! He had it all planned out. When I went to see him, when I persuaded him to do another gig, he played it for me. But I was too out of it to notice anything.'

'What did he play for you?'

'His death. How he was going to do it. Here!' He stood up, came over to her and held out a slightly wavy record cover. 'Metallica, *Kill 'Em All*.'

'What about it?'

'What do you see?'

'A hammer. And blood. A pool of blood. And a hand. The shadow of a hand.'

'Hammer and blood! That was the first record we listened to that afternoon. And then it went on. Here!' He went over to the record player and exchanged one record for another. 'Judas Priest, *Painkiller*, Track Seven.' He came back to her, held out the cover and tapped his forefinger at a point on the back of it.

Stephanie read out the title. 'Between the Hammer and the Anvil.'

'Then he put on Naked City.' Stefan took Judas Priest off the record player and put on Naked City. 'Track Twelve.'

'Hammerhead,' Stephanie read.

Stefan stopped the record player and picked up another record from the floor.

'Flotsam and Jetsam, *Doomsday for the Deceiver*, Side One, Track One.'

'Hammerhead.'

'His little joke. It's a song about sex.' He stuck his tongue in his cheek and moved it back and forth, back and forth.

Stephanie pulled a face and gave him back the sleeve, and he threw it over to the others. 'And now, the grand finale.' He swapped the records again, the tone arm moved into its orbit automatically, and Stefan lowered it at a point near the middle. 'Motörhead, *Ace of Spades*, Track Twelve.' He held out the sleeve.

'The Hammer.'

'The Hammer, right. I was so stupid!'

'But you couldn't possibly have known.' She wanted to go to him and embrace him but he dodged her and went over to the chest of drawers, piled high with papers, photocopies and printouts.

'All I had to do was put two and two together: one, seven, twelve, one, twelve.'

'Thirty-three? What does that mean?'

'Not thirty-three. A-G-L-A-L. AGLAL. In this case it's the other way round—every number stands for a letter.'

'AGLAL?'

'AGLA is an acrostic, a cabbalistic acronym. It stands for *Athah Gabor Leolah Adonai*. It means something like You, Oh Lord, are mighty for ever. For Samuel Mathers, the founder of the secret society Golden Dawn, A stood for the beginning and the end, G for the trinity in unity and L for the completion of the Great Work, for the perfected opus magnum. According to the Count of St Germain, AGLA is the name of God, in the shape of one of the two angels who save Lot from destruction. The added L is either a reference to Lot himself or to the Lord. Or it has another meaning that goes even further, one that can't be named.'

She had dozens of questions, but all she said was, 'Who's the Count of St Germain?'

'An adventurer. Secret agent. Composer. Occultist. Alchemist. I call him the Supreme Diplomat. Not much is known about him and most of the reports are contradictory. Some say he was the son of a Transylvanian prince, others that he was a descendant of the English philosopher Francis Bacon, an Italian violinist by the name of Catalani or the illegitimate son of the Portuguese king Peter II. In the eighteenth century, he's said to have advised the war minister at the French court, poached a number of ladies from Casanova in Venice and been governor of the Indian town of Chengalpattu, all at the same time. During the First World War he tried to cross the German border on the Vosges front, disguised as a civilian, and when he was interrogated he prophesied defeat, revolution and inflation and the rule of the Antichrist. Because of his ability to be in several places at once, some people say he was responsible for the lightning spread of the Spanish flu. In 1944 he wanted to kill Hitler at his Berchtesgaden house, this time in the uniform of an ordnance officer, but other than usual he wasn't allowed in to the Führer. He couldn't prevent John F. Kennedy's assassination even though he knew about the plan. Some say that was because he was still touring with the Beatles as the real Paul McCartney, to present their second album *With the Beatles*—hence the title—which came out on the same day, and he wanted to savour his fame, but I think that's unlikely. Kennedy's death suited him fine because he blamed him for the suicide of his lover Norma Jean Baker. And he wanted to watch the president of the United States of America die on camera, for all to see. Then he turned up at a press conference in East Berlin in 1989 and gave a tip to an Italian journalist to ask Günter Schabowski about the new exit regulations. And that's just the fairly well-documented incidents. No one but he knows what else he's done. He speaks six different languages and plays several musical—'

'Stop! That's enough.' She could never stand history, not because of all the dates but because it had always been about key-words, about dull repetition of knowledge. At first she'd found it not enough of a challenge, and then once she'd got left behind it was annoying. And that was how she felt now too. Superficially connected names and numbers flashed through her head and allowed only one conclusion: 'Does that mean he's still alive?'

'According to Voltaire he's a man who never dies and knows everything.'

'Do you know what that sounds like to me?'

'I can imagine.'

'And what's it all got to do with Onno?'

'I don't know yet. But the count's written several books.' Stefan picked up one of the photocopies. 'And in one of them he not only mentions AGLA, he also describes himself as someone who stands above things, here, as an explorer of all of nature who has found out the principle and the earth from the great All. Do you remember Daniel from our class?'

'Daniel Kuper?'

Stefanie nodded. 'He said he'd been abducted by aliens.'

'Yeah, right. Super excuse. Except it didn't work.'

'Maybe it wasn't an excuse at all.'

'Yeah, right. And he wasn't responsible for the swastikas. They suddenly turned up on the walls of their own accord.' Up to that point she hadn't been sure whether what Stefan was saying made sense or not. His proof of the Riemann hypothesis contained many lemmata, intertwining paths that might seem idiotic at first sight but did lead somewhere in the end. And in biology and computer studies too, which she understood even less, he was supposed to have reached astounding findings via similar diversions. But this wasn't about mathematics or biology or any other generally accepted science. *Golden Dawn. The Count of St Germain. Aliens.* Stefan must have lost his mind.

'Here,' Stefan picked up another photocopy from the pile. 'The Count of St Germain reports on a similar incident. Within a fraction of a second the plains below us were out of sight and the Earth had become a faint nebula. Finally he raised me with him to an immeasurable distance. For quite a long time I rolled through space and I saw globes revolve as I travelled at a speed comparable with nothing but itself.'

'Where did you get all that?'

'From the Internet.'

'You went on the Internet? I thought it was the devil's work.' She crossed her fingers as if to ward off a vampire. 'I thought the Internet was evil, an evil drug that gets us hooked and makes us compliant.'

'The Internet's just a means to an end for me. I'm not going to get sucked in. I'm not tempted to follow every single link—I only look at what I really want to see. And anyway I've checked everything. I've read the sources, the original texts, printed paper, books bound in pigskin leather, falling apart. The real problem is somewhere else entirely.'

'Oh really? Where?'

'It's in us. Us ourselves.'

'It all sounds totally crazy to me.'

'It does to me too. But the clues Onno gave me are pretty clear, don't you think?'

'No.'

'Why else do you think he left me his records in his will?'

'So his mother didn't get her hands on them?'

'He knew something, Steffi, maybe he knew too much.'

'You're being crazy. You're just blaming yourself for not realizing earlier and stopping him.'

'You do too. You were there too.'

'But I wasn't up on stage with him.'

'No, but you were in front of the stage.'

'Yes, squeezed in with all the others.' It was the first and only time they spoke about the Aaaaaaarrghh! gig in Wacken.

And now she pictured Onno again. Hurling his sticks into the audience over her head and coming out from behind his drum kit, a hammer in one hand. Thrashing at the drums and cymbals with it before using the tip of it on himself, with all his strength. The middle of his forehead bursting open, the circular scar left there by Rainer's cigarette lighter. Onno falling over and getting up again and bowing down to her, covered in blood, as if the last blow had had no effect on him.

At that moment the train arrived.

A man with five children, five boys, got on at Greven. Three of them squeezed onto the seat next to him, and two sat next to Stephanie—at a distance, pressing against the armrest, their legs dangling above the floor. Every couple of minutes, they leapt up and ran around the compartment but the sliding doors were too heavy for them and the man didn't do them the favour of opening them so they could run wild all over the whole train. 'Stefan! Ansgar! Come and sit back down,' he kept saying, with varying emphasis, and sometimes they obeyed him and sometimes they didn't.

'Sorry,' the man said to her.

'It's all right,' said Stephanie, although it wasn't really all right at all. She'd hoped to revise her number theory or get some sleep on the train, as compensation for not taking the car, and she decided to get off at the next station and move to a quieter carriage. But in Salzbergen a crowd of football fans stormed the compartments and more joined them at every station, so that not only were all the seats taken but even the corridors were populated by drunken singers in their club's colours.

The man pulled the window down, the boys sat on their seats, and Stephanie unbuttoned her blazer, unpacked her croissant and began to eat it, half-concealed in its paper bag. At least this way she found out that the man was the father of Stefan and Ansgar, was separated from their mother—he winked at her—it was Stefan's birthday and they were all on their way to the coast for a hike along the sand flats from Dornum to Baltrum, and had to be back by the evening. 'It's back to school tomorrow,' he said. 'For them and for me.' It turned out that he taught Maths and General Studies, and when he asked her what she did for a living she answered, 'I'm unemployed.'

'Oh, I'm sorry to hear that.'

She didn't want to be rude but she didn't feel like talking either, especially not to someone who'd told her his entire life story in five minutes, possibly even in the hope that she'd join him and the boys on their trip to the coast. As she'd expected, the man returned his attention to the children. She looked out of the window. The sun was shining and the sky was blue and clear. In the distance, above the treetops, she could see the red-and-white navy radio masts.

Stefan, her Stefan, had never celebrated his birthday, not even as a child. There were photos of him holding a number baked by his mother up to the camera, but none showing him with other boys or girls of his age or with relatives or unwrapping presents or blowing out candles—documents of normal people's lives.

He had always accepted her gifts half-heartedly, with half-hearted thanks. On his last birthday, four months ago, she'd wanted to go on a trip with him. The flight and the hotel were already booked; they'd be getting away from Münster at last, away from Germany, and he'd promised her to leave his books and notes and even his laptop at home and spend a few days with her on the Mediterranean. When she woke up that morning his side of the bed was crumpled and empty—like every morning. At first she'd assumed he was in the bathroom or had gone to fetch bread rolls, at the bakery she'd just been to earlier.

As she leant against the counter in the kitchen, drinking coffee and casting a glance at her suitcase standing packed in the hallway, it dawned on her that he'd thought better of it or, worse still, he'd had no intention other than staying on the ground from the very beginning. She thought about flying to Spain on her own, out of defiance. She thought about packing the rest of her things into boxes and looking for a new flat with a new boyfriend, as revenge. She thought about knives, candles, cake and the heavy glass ashtray on the windowsill next to her, out of hate. She thought about him, his words, his skin, his smell, and she went to the university.

He was in the library, in the place where he always sat in the morning before he went to the lab, a single desk flanked by bookshelves at the end of the reading room, far enough away from all the others to work in peace, but still too close to stage an argument in public.

'What's going on?' she shouted at him. 'What are you doing here?'

He turned around to her, his mirrored sunglasses in front of his eyes, a pen in his hand. 'I'm working.'

'We wanted to go away. We ought to be on the way to Düsseldorf by now. Did you forget about it?'

'No. I know—' he raised his hands as if to calm her down.

'You don't know nix.'

'Don't get upset.' He put the pen between the pages of a thick book and shut it. There was nothing on the black cover but a large golden cross.

'Don't get upset? I'll show you how upset I am.' She reached out for the shelf, pulled out a couple of books and threatened to throw them at him. But all she did was hold them in her hand. Stefan stood up and looked Stephanie in the eye for a few seconds, then took the books away from her and put them back on the shelf. Next he put his glasses case in his pocket and led Stephanie out of the library, past all the swots and the desperate cases in search of immortality, just like him. On the way to the exit she resisted him, batting away the hand he was holding her with, holding onto a pillar when he wanted to pull her along, and telling the staff to call the police because she was being abducted.

'By him?' The man on duty was a student library assistant from their course. 'He's not going to abduct anyone. Only himself, maybe.'

And then they were outside, on the Bridge, and she looked at him, her nerves tense and full of anger.

'It's like this,' said Stefan. 'I can't leave. I can't abandon my work now.'

'What work?'

'Can you please be a bit quieter?' He looked around in the corridor but there was no one there apart from them.

That really made her shout. 'Why? So nobody notices you here? You can forget that. Everyone knows you here. And I can tell you what they think of you.'

'I know what they think of me. I don't care.'

'But I do. I do care.' She sank into one of the chairs, exhausted by her feelings, and looked at her watch. She'd given up all hope of making it to the plane on time. 'The Whitsun break starts tomorrow,' she said, not looking up at him. 'At least take off those awful glasses. I've had enough of looking at myself. The sun's not even out.'

'It's nothing to do with the sun.'

'What then?'

He sat down next to her, looked under the table, under her and his chairs, and then sat up straight again.

'What are you doing?'

'Nix. I never have a break. If I take a holiday now, it'll take me weeks to get back into it. And I don't have enough time left for that. I'm—we're—running out of time.'

'Hey, come on. You're twenty-five. And so am I.'

'Einstein formulated the theory of relativity at twenty-five. Von Neumann proved the minimax theorem at twenty-five. And Ramanujan—'

'You proved Riemann's hypothesis.'

'No I didn't. My proof was imprecise.'

'So why is everyone always pushing you to publish it?'

'Because they don't understand it. I'm the only person with a full overview of the problem, my problem. And that's why I'm the only person who sees the weaknesses they can't see.'

'That's just petty stuff. The result is consistent. Or at least it can't be disproved.'

'Publishing a flawed proof is no use to anyone.'

'Flawed proofs get published all the time.'

'Not by me.'

'No, not by you. You never publish anything.'

'That may well change soon.'

'What's that supposed to mean?'

'It's in the early stages so far. But I'm going in the right direction.'

'What's it about this time?'

'Everything.'

'Everything's always about everything for you.'

'I mean the theory of everything.'

'There is no absolute formula.'

'That's what they tried to tell us in our degrees. That's why I stopped going to lectures. They don't want us to find out.'

'Who doesn't?'

'Do you remember our code?'

'The digit sum code?'

The digit sum code was a secret language they'd used at the beginning of their relationship, their personal first and second semesters. The curriculum, their diaries, included seminars such as Sociology of Emotions, Experiments in Practical Biology and Introduction to Stephanie Beckmann. And after one of these seminars, which took place in her or his high wooden beds, he'd told her about the girls' names, about Clarissa, Gabriele and Bett-Tina, and about the suffix oah, which Daniel, Rainer, Onno and he had added to every sentence, and she'd called him 'Sixty-fiveoah'—which stood for S-T-E-F-A-N. From then on they transformed all words into numbers, added them together and communicated via the results, often leading to misunderstandings because one sum could have several different meanings. But at that time the misunderstandings were still of the kind that always took them back to the source of their secret language, no matter what he had meant and she had understood.

Standing in a group at a maths party and getting bored, for instance, Stefan might say 'Forty-eight,' and Stephanie 'Seventy-eight'—totally unrelated to the conversation going on around them, although the conversations were also usually about numbers. Once someone even said, 'Forty-eight is wrong,' and someone else said, 'And so is seventy-eight.' Stefan and Stephanie took no notice of their objections; they'd barely been listening anyway. Instead, they put down their bottles or glasses, put on their jackets and cycled as quickly as they could to his or her place. She had never told him that seventy-eight, along with many other possibilities, meant not only 'let's go' but also 'no way'. But he'd never asked why she didn't just say 'twenty-six,' or 'forty-two,' which would have been simpler, so she assumed he knew—that she wanted to keep all her options open up to the last minute.

They'd used the code on other occasions and for other purposes, on visits to their parents or at exams, as swearwords and terms of endearment. At some point they'd stopped, though; not because someone had seen through it but because the playfulness with which their relationship had begun had given way to a more serious side, a kind of sorrow over the omnipresence of everyday life.

'Forty-two.'

'Yes,' said Stefan. 'Forty-two.'

'What about it? You're not telling me the digit sum code is the theory of everything?'

'Don't be silly.'

'Then what?'

'This isn't about string theory or loop quantum gravity. Or let's say, it's not just about them. Of course the Big Bang plays a role, the beginning of the universe. Have you ever asked yourself what's behind it?'

She looked out of the window, at the square below, hundred of bicycles parked in concrete brackets on either side, at Einstein Road and the trees opposite. 'A place beyond time and space. The big nix.'

'That's not what I mean.'

'What do you mean then?'

'What's behind it. The meaning of life.'

'That's what I said: forty-two. *Hitchhiker s Guide to the Galaxy.* Grab your towel and you're ready to go.' She laughed, thinking he was making a joke, albeit one that had cost her a few hundred marks for a holiday not taken, and a good few illusions.

'No,' said Stefan. 'The question of who we are. And whether we are the people we think we are.' He looked round again. 'I don't even know myself yet how far-reaching my discovery is, but I assure you everything depends on it.'

'What depends on it?'

'Everything. The past and the future.'

'Our past and our future?'

'The whole world's.'

'Oh, if that's all it is.'

'Steffi,' he took hold of her shoulders, 'I'm not kidding. Listen very carefully—if we don't spend the eleventh of August together, for whatever reason, don't look at the sky, no matter what happens, no matter who wants to persuade you to watch the event of the century. No total eclipse, do you understand me?'

She gave him a disappointed nod.

'Hey, there's good news too—we know now. We've cracked DES. In twenty-two hours and fifteen minutes.'

'DES?'

'Data Encryption Standard, one of the world's most secure symmetrical encoding algorithms, the official standard of the US government. It won't be long before we can do it simultaneously. We ought to be prepared when the time comes. We ought to know the basics.'

'Who's we?'

But Stefan didn't respond. 'And another thing—if I ever mention irrational numbers in the near future, π or e, no matter what the context, no matter where, that means it's starting, then we have to be together. And then there's no going back. Neither for you nor for me.'

She raised her eyebrows and smiled. 'Are you making me a proposal, Stefan?'

'No,' he said. 'It's a mission, an official mission.'

And then he kissed her, and so she did regard it as a proposal, as his strange way of telling her he loved her, that he wanted to spend the rest of his life with her, until death did them part—or united them for ever.

'And put these on,' he took another pair of mirrored pilot shades out of his glasses case, 'as a sign of our affinity.'

At the station in the county town, it wasn't Stefan's mother waiting for her, it was his father, Bernd, dressed all in white— white shoes, white trousers, white polo shirt. He hugged her the way people embrace at funerals, full of pain and powerlessness, and took her bag. As they walked through the underground passage linking the middle platform with the main building, he asked her only inconsequential questions, whether the train had been crowded and how her studies were going, and she gave him only inconsequential answers.

'Sorry I'm so late.'

'Doesn't matter. I've only just got here myself.'

But the moment they were inside the car words came gushing out of him. 'There's been a break-in at my practice.'

'No! When?'

'Yesterday or last night. I only just noticed. I wanted to pick something up on the way to the station, and when I got in there all the cupboards were broken open.'

'Is there anything missing?'

'Yes, but not much, nothing valuable. Syringes. Disinfectant. Swabs. Surgical instruments. A bit of medication. I presume it was junkies.'

'Yes,' said Stephanie.

'Or one of our temps. We've been having problems with one young woman recently, but not that kind of thing. She didn't keep to instructions and then Britta gave her a piece of her mind, and she couldn't take it. She was the last to leave on Friday. That's why I haven't called the police yet.'

'But you can't let her get away with it. You have to place a complaint against her.'

'I will. But not until I've talked to her, when I'm sure it was her.'

There was silence for a while. Then he said, 'Why does every-thing always have to come at once?'

'What else?'

'Stefan.'

She'd fallen asleep on the train, despite the noise, and woken up shortly later, and since then she'd been feeling absolutely drained, incapable of thinking clearly. For a moment she'd for-gotten why she was here in the first place, why Stefan had got her to come, what doubts had come over her at the thought, and what certainty that he and she needed exactly that, stability, a new level for their relationship.

'He's not himself. I don't know who he is. But I know one thing—that's not my son. If I wasn't a doctor I'd say he was possessed.'

'He is possessed,' said Stephanie, not looking at him.

'By what? A demon?' He laughed for two seconds.

'By an idea.'

'What idea?'

She shrugged. 'I don't know either. He doesn't talk to me about his work,' she raised both hands and crooked the first and second fingers on each side twice, as she said, 'not until it's finished.'

'I wish I knew what he's planning. Since he got here he's taken away all sorts of junk and brought new stuff. And now he's hard at it in the basement.'

'What junk?'

'Mostly rubbish. Two huge fridges, old halogen lamps, adjustable chairs, hood dryers and all sorts of other stuff from Dettmers', Dettmers' Hairdressing.'

'I don't know the place.'

'Doesn't matter. It's closed down now. Lots of things have gone now in Jericho.'

'Only Stefan's come back again. The Return of Stefan Reichert.'

'When did it all start, Steffi?' He looked at her. There was a flicker in his eyes, short and fast as if his lids weren't moving. 'He got over the accident pretty well back then.'

'That's what I always thought too.' Stefan obviously hadn't told his parents anything, not even dropped hints. And whatever he was planning with her, with them, she didn't want to spoil the surprise of him revealing his news himself. 'But we didn't see each other for a while afterwards.'

'There weren't any anomalies, no complications.'

'Apart from the coma.'

'That might have been a good thing for him. The only odd thing was that he spoke perfect Russian afterwards. Russian! No one ever spoke Russian to him, not even his granddad, and he was a prisoner of war there. I mean, how does something like that happen?'

'Who knows? And he was never very interested in maths before either. He was never really good at it.'

'Maybe it was all just too much for him. Maybe it was too much of a strain on him, on his intelligence. Like a fuse that blows because too many appliances are on at the same time. I can't find any other explanation.'

'Maybe it's to do with Onno though.'

'Maybe.'

'He was really upset about it. I was too.'

'Yes, but he won't admit it. He refuses to see it.'

'It was only after that that he started throwing himself into his work.'

'Mathematics—even the thought of it gets my synapses tied in knots.'

'Not just yours. I think it's the same with him.'

'Is he still taking drugs? Does he still smoke that stuff, White Shadow? I don't want to criticize, Britta and I used to smoke a lot of hash as well, and we've never held it against him, but that stuff,' he shook his head, 'no, it's not good for him.'

'He doesn't even drink any more. He's totally straight edge now. But sometimes he acts like he's drunk.'

'Why didn't you come to me?'

'I thought he'd sort himself out, like he always does.'

'Stefan needs help, Steffi.'

'I'm sure he does.'

'I mean medical help.'

'What he needs is a good psychotherapist.'

'If you're thinking of me, no way. I've tried it already. He even turns down the colleagues I've recommended, experts in the field.'

'What field?'

'Schizophrenia.'

'Don't say that.' The thought of it shocked Stephanie, that Stefan might be seriously crazy, although everything certainly looked that way. 'Do you really think so?'

'Absolutely. The hallucinations, the delusions, the letters, the phone calls, the anger he vents on his mother and me.'

'What letters?'

'Crazy collages made out of newspaper articles, formulae and photos, messy and cryptic, hard to understand. Before-and-after pictures he says prove that we've changed, that we're no longer the same people—but they're harmless compared to the phone calls.'

'What phone calls?'

'He must have called us at least fifty times a day before he arrived, even at night. Usually about three or four in the morning. You must have noticed. He called here every night, and he called the neighbours too. In the end we left the phone off the hook.'

'What did he say?'

'He showered us with abuse. He said, you're not my parents, my parents are dead. You've taken them over. Capgras delusion.'

She stared straight ahead. Suddenly she wasn't sure whether the conditions under which she'd come here still applied. 'So what does he want here, then?'

'He wants to catch us out, I think. Reveal our lies. Tear the masks off our faces. Kill us. Who knows? Britta's scared of him. So am I. He's capable of anything in his state.'

'What state?'

'I've seen it with other patients, less severe cases but still similar. He's in a kind of fundamental opposition. Stefan against the rest of the world. He's even broken off contact with Dani and Kerstin. And his sisters have always meant the world to him. You seem to be the only person he still trusts.'

'It doesn't feel like that to me.'

'We may have to have him committed, if the worst comes to the worst.'

'First he'll have to come out of the basement.'

They turned off the B70 towards Jericho, circled the centre of the village to get there quicker, drove alongside the hammrich fields, where the sound of the concrete factory was audible even through the closed windows, and pulled into Composers' Corner. Once they drove into the estate they passed several rubber bollards, speed bumps and raised brick panels, detoured around a few flower beds built into the middle of the road to slow drivers down, and gave way to vehicles coming in the other direction by means of hand signals, because the lane was too narrow for two cars.

'Didn't even say thanks,' said Bernd when they'd passed the last car. 'Typical. One of those new people, the Russian-Germans.'

Stefan's VW T3, 1990 model, 70 PS, 51 kW, was parked outside the Reicherts' house, an olive-green minivan that gave up the ghost every few hundred kilometres.

As they got out of the car Britta came out of the garden, a pair of trimmers in her hand. On the grass between the flowers were piles of branches and leaves, and there was a wheelbarrow laden with weeds by the fishpond. 'Nature doesn't respect Sundays,' said Britta as if apologizing for not picking Stephanie up, and she took off her gardening gloves, dropped the trimmers on the grass, hugged Stephanie and led her into the house. 'At last. I'm so glad you're here. And look at you! So smart! Wonderful. Just wonderful.' Her eyes were small and moist and twitched with fatigue. Her skin was pale and her hair was mussed as if she'd just got up. 'Maybe *you* can make him see sense.'

'I don't think so,' said Stephanie. 'But I'll try.'

'He's still down there,' said Britta, pointing at the door to the basement, at the *No entry* sign.

'I've turned the electricity off on him a couple of times,' said Bernd. 'That only made it all worse, though. Then he really started flipping out.'

Stephanie knocked at the door, first hesitantly and then, when Stefan didn't react, more firmly, in the end drumming both fists against the wood.

'Have you called the police yet?' Britta asked behind her.

'No, not yet,' said Bernd. 'I wanted to talk to Anita first. I couldn't get hold of her from the practice. And, you know, I don't like the idea of getting the cops involved. I'd rather let sleeping dogs lie.'

'Maybe it's enough if you get them to come here, if we have a talk to them here. You know Rhauderwiek, don't you, you went to school together.'

'Exactly.'

'Who is it?' she heard Stefan asking.

'It's me.'

'Which me?'

'Steffi.'

'Is there someone with you?'

'Your parents.'

'They're not my parents. My parents are dead. Tell them to get out of there. Tell them to go away—no one's allowed to be with you.' She turned around to his parents and began repeating what he'd said, but they'd heard too and went into the living room. Standing in the doorway, Bernd signalled that he'd watch her by pointing two fingers first at his eyes and then at hers.

'Have they gone?'

Stephanie waited for the door to close behind them and then said, 'Yes.'

'All right. I'm coming up now.'

She heard footsteps on the stairs, the key turned in the lock and she took a step back because the door opened outwards.

Stefan only opened it a crack and she had to pull it towards her. She'd expected him to come out to her, but she couldn't see him even when she moved onto the top step. She couldn't see anything; he must have covered the windows downstairs. Suddenly something shone in her face. She screwed up her eyes involuntarily.

'What's that?' she asked. 'What are you doing?'

'Look at me.'

'Turn the light off first. I can't see a thing.'

'That's the point. I want to look at you.'

'But you can see me.'

'I want to look you in the eye.'

She tried to open her eyes but the light was too strong. 'Turn the damn light off.'

'Better?' He must have turned a dimmer switch; when she opened her eyes she could still see the light, a lamp with the luminosity of a flash of lightning but now it wasn't so strong that she couldn't stand it.

'What's this all about? Have you totally lost it?'

'Not me, but maybe you have. If you'd been wearing the glasses I gave you, you could have saved yourself that test. Five. Four. Three. Two. One. OK. Everything's alright. You can come in.' He pressed two switches and the light went out with a flicker and another, less bright one came on. 'But watch where you step.'

'What's happened to your hair?'

'Shaved it off.'

Stephanie ran a hand over his head. 'You're bald.'

'I had to do it. Too much resistance.'

'You're not growing up, are you, Stefan?' she said, walking past him. 'Or are you just adapting to the conditions?'

'What conditions?'

'The biological ones. Your age.'

'I doubt that.'

She'd only been down here once, years ago. Back then his workshop, the Reichert family's former party den, had been a complete mess. A mountain range of CDs and records, books and magazines, the walls papered with notes, a tangle of wires and aerials, flokati rugs covered in ash and cigarette ends and dried lumps of solder. Now she was surprised to find everything clean and tidy. No wooden panelling on the walls, no bar with stools, no rugs. In their place, a bare wood floor with a small number of cables snaking across it, attached to multiple power socket strips, studded foam sheets on the ceiling, door and walls, the windows covered with metallic first aid blankets.

'Have you started making music again?'

'This soundproofing wouldn't be suitable for recording. No high notes, reflections too strong and problems with medium frequencies. It's more the other way around. Nothing's allowed in. A studio of silence.'

The walls swallowed up his every word. If he'd been shouting out irrational numbers, then he must have been standing outside the laundry room or the pantry, on the staircase, up in the hallway. She looked around. Different noises, different voices, were coming out of four spherical speakers suspended from each corner of the ceiling. It was as though he were listening to four radio stations at once.

'Well, it's not exactly silent in here.'

'What do you mean?'

'The voices?'

'What voices?'

'Those ones.' She pointed at one of the speakers. 'What is that? Radio?'

'Police radio.'

Two fridges were humming in one corner of the room. In another, on a long, handmade table on wheels, was a neat row consisting of a roll of tape, a pair of scissors, a hair trimmer and four different attachments, several ampules labelled *Amidate*, a white plastic container, two bottles, one of acetone, one of saline solution, a bucket full of cleaning cloths, three hypodermic needles sealed in plastic, a syringe filled with a colourless fluid, two sets of jumper cables and a pack of disposable gloves. On the workbench were a binocular microscope, books, an amplifier, a printer, something that looked like a miniature washing machine, the top-loading kind, computers and monitors—screens on which figures flashed up and disappeared again.

The middle of the room was occupied by two chrome seats with scuffed leather upholstery, two hairdresser's chairs with extendable footrests. There was a white coat thrown over one of them, and since there was nowhere else to sit, she took a seat on the other one. She put down her bag and took off her blazer. The armrests and footrests had straps attached, belts affixed to them. Above her, at the head end, a salon hood dryer was screwed to the wall, a white model reminiscent of an astronaut's helmet, with a chin bar dangling from it. She leant back and looked up. Where the holes for the hot air had once been were now blue and red electrodes.

'What on earth's this supposed to be? A hairdressing salon in the basement? Like one of those dark restaurants? Blind haircutting? Stefan's cuts—fast and short?'

'Something like that.'

'If that's the only hairstyle you can do I'll stick to mine, thanks.'

He locked the door and pushed a beam across it at hip height, a wide galvanized iron bar, as if bolting a barn door.

She stood up. 'I want to get out of here.' She didn't believe he was capable of anything like his father did, and she wasn't scared of him either, but she wanted to stay in control of the situation.

'It's just for our protection. From them.' He pointed a finger at the ceiling.

'I want to get out right now!'

'Just listen to me first.'

'Open the door!'

He took the bar away and turned the key in the lock. 'Happy now?'

'Yes.'

'You can leave whenever you want.'

She sat down again. 'I'm just a bit tired. The party yesterday was a bit much, and then your mother called at seven to tell me you'd been shouting all night long. Irrational numbers. I imagined it all a little differently, Stefan.'

'Me too.'

'And then the train journey with all the football hooligans really finished me off.'

'You came on the train?'

'How else? Hello? Remember? My car's broken.'

'Shit. Did you meet anyone on the way?'

'Ischebeck.'

'Where?'

'At the baker's.'

'What did he say?'

'We talked about my exam, the re-sit. He even knew my name, imagine that. So it was worth going to his office appointment after all.'

'Did he ask about me? Did he tell you to say hello?'

'No.'

'Because he knows!'

'He knows what?'

'He knows you were coming to me, my God, that you'd come here.'

'Rubbish. How should he know that? I didn't say anything, anyway. And if you—'

'Did you speak to anyone else?'

'—didn't either . . . What? . . . No.'

'At the station? On the train?'

'No. Well actually, only briefly, with a man on the way to the seaside with his sons, but I didn't know him.'

'Did you notice anything unusual about him?'

'What's all this about? Why do you want to know?'

'It's important. Did he look like me?'

'No. Mind you, the tramp might have.'

'What tramp?'

'There was a tramp at the station in Münster. In the waiting shelter on the platform. Like you guys used to look, with long hair.'

'And the man on the train?'

'He didn't look like you. But one of his sons was called Stefan.'

'That's it!'

'That's what?'

'They've guessed something's going on. Damn, I should have known. Steffi, they tried to influence your perception, maybe even take control of your conscious.'

'Who?'

He clenched his fists, paced up and down by the workbench, looked at one of the screens and then turned back to her. 'I'm sorry. I wanted to call you first but I haven't got a phone down here. And I can't use the one upstairs. They don't know what I'm planning because I never thought about it outside the studio. We're safe down here, Steffi, no one can hear or see us here. Their rays can't get through to us. Not for the time being anyway, for a few hours, until they've adjusted their search frequencies.'

'What is it you're planning?'

'You'll see in a moment. I told you about Cabbala, didn't I?'

'Did you?'

'AGLA. The acrostic, the cabbalistic acronym.'

'Oh, that thing.'

'The basic idea of Cabbala is that the microcosm and macrocosm are one—every human is formed in God's image. The whole universe is concealed inside us. We are perfect and complete. By nature. We just don't know how to deal with that perfection. Why is that?'

'No idea,' said Stephanie, but Stefan hadn't expected an answer.

'What holds us back? Our own inherent limits are a problem I've been looking at for some time. Why aren't we capable of computing arithmetic problems, even though we're superior to computers in many different respects? There's no explanation. Neither in mathematics, nor in biology or medicine. Only conjecture.

That's why, starting with Onno's pointer to AGLA, I began reading the Bible, for the first time in my life. From front to back. The whole thing. And all along I had this feeling that something wasn't right, that something was going absolutely wrong. I asked myself, what are all these names and numbers for? These ancestral lineages that end up going nowhere? Many of the people named in those lists never crop up again—they live, thrive, reach the age of a thousand and vanish for ever more. If the bible was a novel an editor would cut it by half. And then I read this book,' he picked one up from the workbench and held it towards her like a cross, '*The Bible Code*, and then it was clear what the problem is—the text itself. Hebrew is written from right to left, and so is Aramaic, Jesus' mother tongue. Do you know what that means? We've always been reading the Bible the wrong way round! In the language of the murderers! Who enslaved and gassed those who read the right way round! The devil's message is in the Latin! For centuries we've been following the false prophets. Not the New Testament is key for us, it's the Old Testament, only in reverse order. And that's why the Book of Revelation is worthless—we have to stick to Isaiah. To Ezekiel. To Daniel. The signs—'

'Daniel Kuper?'

'I'm serious, Steffi. The signs were right there in front of us all along, we just didn't recognize them.' He lowered the book. 'I know you think I'm sick.'

'No, it's—'

'Everyone does. But I'm feeling better than ever before. I didn't believe it myself when I came across it. You know me better than anyone else, you know I'm my own greatest critic—I never say or publish anything without checking it a dozen times. The facts speak for themselves—God is an alien. You can't deny that either. He's the only alien whose existence is acknowledged by millions of people. And the Bible is his word, his message to us—

we just have to learn to read it. Drosnin is right, the Bible really does contain a code, a text within the text, but not one that predicts the future—one that helps us to understand the past, our own origin, the nature of humankind.'

'Who's Drosnin?'

'The author of *The Bible Code*. An American journalist. Wrote it all down here.' He flipped a few pages through his fingers. 'The story of this Bible code, only with reference to the Torah. And that brings us full circle to Cabbala. Some Cabbalists see the Torah as a living organism with movable letters, in which every word has infinite meanings. Every single letter counts. Nothing must be corrected or changed. For them the Torah is God himself. It's inscribed with the great mystery, the formula for creation. And only one person has got through to that mystery so far—Moses. He saw the White Light, the original light of Creation. But when he came down from Mount Sinai and saw the Golden Calf, he decided to take that knowledge to his grave. And that's exactly what he did. Even Newton suspected a secret truth in the Bible. But it was only two hundred and fifty years later that a rabbi from Prague managed to crack the code, although not completely of course, so it was ultimately of no use. What he didn't have was a simple and fast search engine, a computer and a mathematical genius.'

'You!'

'No, Eliyahu Rips at the university in Jerusalem.' Stefan put the book back, went over to the screens and pointed at two words highlighted in red, which Stephanie couldn't make out from her seat. 'I've applied his method of equidistant letter sequences to the Latin version, the vulgate, and looked for patterns in it, sequences, letters at the same distance to each other in the text, horizontally, vertically, diagonally, forward, backwards, in a shape corresponding to Euclid's two-dimensional metric system.'

'Why the vulgate? I thought only the Torah was God's word.'

'The Hebrew gave me the first clue here too. The name of God is Yod, He, Waw, He—JHWH, Yahwe, and in Hebrew every letter has its own numerical value, in this case ten, five, six, five.'

'Twenty-six.'

'Exactly. Twenty-six.'

'Unless you add each separate figure again, so you get eight.'

'That too. Eight for the never-ending. Twenty-six for the alphabet. The Latin alphabet, not the Hebrew one. That was the first key. Then I defined the letter sequences without spaces or punctuation, using the ones Onno showed me with his playlist, one, seven, twelve, one, twelve. AGLAL. That was the second key. And what made me abandon all my doubts was a discovery I made right at the beginning, in Genesis. There's a crossover of letters seven and one, the letter S, in *malleus* and *sucni*, so *incus* — *hammer* and *anvil*. Nowhere else in the bible do these words appear in this combination again, neither in the Old or the New Testament do they come together in such a significant way. And although I don't believe in coincidence I carried out a random test, and lo and behold, the p-value was very low, almost zero. That encouraged me to keep going and search for more conspicuous combinations. I programmed skip sequences at intervals of one, seven, twelve, one, twelve. And in the books of the great prophets I came across coded words in a conjunction that goes just as far beyond the extent that statistics allow for random deviances.' He looked at one of the screens again and pointed a finger at separate letters. 'Here. *Homines, somata, machinae, orbis, Hiericho, hostes,* whereby *somata* is Greek, of course, but here it comes: *Moriantur plutonii!*—*Death to the Plutonians!* And this is at the point where Ezekiel describes the sky opening above him and a fireball floating down to earth.' Stefan took a thick book with dozens of bookmarks between its pages from the workbench and opened it up. 'And I looked, and, behold, a whirlwind came out of the north, a great cloud, and a fire infolding itself, and a brightness was about it, and out of the midst thereof as the colour of amber, out of the midst of the fire. Also out of the midst thereof came the likeness of four living creatures. And this was their appearance; they had the likeness of a man. And in Isaiah, in his announcement of the Last Judgement, if you take every twelfth letter, you find the sentence *nos transformamur totaliter in deum et convertimur in eum*—We are totally transferred into God and converted into him. What is that? A pious hope on the part of Jerome, the translator? A joke? Hidden criticism of the pope? Or a secret message to us, those born later? The message of a mystic or heretic, a chosen one or a renegade? A pointer to the fact that people lose their identity by being replaced by something else, something higher? If that's the case, then only those who subjugate themselves are the righteous. Only they will be saved. That's exactly what the perfectly readable words of the Bible say: Follow the commandments—or go to hell! But that would be the end of humankind, the true apocalypse, a herd of lambs on the way to the slaughter. Unless we meet them at eye level and make ourselves into gods. And how? Here!' He put the Bible aside, pressed a key and pointed at the screen. 'At the point when Daniel reports on how the great prince will appear and the time of need begins and he receives the book of seven seals, the words *nostra salus* and *ortus computator* cross at the first O: our salvation, the calculator of our origin.'

'You see what you want to see,' said Stephanie. 'Every major text contains the whole universe, if you take it apart like that.'

'That may well be, but not every text fits back together in this way, if you use Onno's key. Everything interlocks absolutely harmoniously, like the base pairs of a double helix. Our DNA is the perfect equivalent—a data storage device of gigantic proportions, compressed into a tiny space and, used correctly, capable of solving the most complex of problems in a matter of seconds. Do you understand? The answer is here already, Steffi. It's all about asking the right question.'

'And that would be?'

'Whatever you like. The answer is concealed within you. But you alone won't find it, your processing power's too weak and your life expectation too short. And apart from that your capacity decreases the longer you think about it. Our brains use a quarter of the oxygen we breathe and the glucose we eat, and still a large part of our intellectual potential goes unused. And the small amount we do use gets less and less all the time. We're on standby, if you like. Life's no more than a dream. That's why we're such easy prey for them. They assault us in our sleep and we don't even notice. In fact it'd be pretty simple to hack their system and switch them off—we'd just have to bring our brains up to a hundred per cent.'

'And how's that supposed to work?'

'Every cell in our bodies processes information coded in our DNA. That happens uninterruptedly. Your body acts without you doing anything. That's exactly the point where a genetic processor comes in. Its task is to act on command. And all you have to do to get it working is manipulate the molecules. To put it in simplified terms: we feed the molecules with our questions, and our brain will give us the answers. Without our thinking. You don't have to tell your heart to beat—it just beats. And it's just the same—you won't have to tell your new brain where these aliens are vulnerable, it will find the spot and penetrate it like a spear. Every cell is upvalued by the genetic processor and turned into its own control centre which works autonomously and reacts at the speed of light. And the best thing is—the cells renew themselves. It's an unintentional side effect but it's very advantageous. Nix gets lost. Everything is saved. Death is overcome. That, in brief, is exactly what I've been working on over the past few weeks. With NewMan 2000 here,' he gestured at the device that looked like a miniature washing machine, 'I've optimized my and your DNA and modified our molecules using viruses in such a way that they develop computing operations of their own accord.'

'Where did you get my DNA?'

Stefan ran a hand over his bald head. 'Steffi, we live together. The flat's full of you. You're practically everywhere.'

'And how did you do it? I mean, how did you optimize the DNA?'

He pressed a button and the circular lid of the machine he called NewMan 2000 opened with a hiss. Once the mist had cleared, pairs of test tubes were visible, filled with a transparent fluid. 'By exchanging individual nucleic acids and changing the sequence of the DNA. Of course, the difficult part was getting the right—' Stefan paused, stared at one of the speakers and said: 'Did you hear that?'

'What?'

'Someone just said Lortzing Road.'

'Where?'

'There,' he pointed at the speaker closest to him, 'on the police radio.' And he turned up one of the controls, with the result that the voices in all the corners got louder and louder.

'I can't hear anything.'

'Quite clear. Fifty, Lortzing Road. It's starting. They're on their way. They're coming here.'

'Because there was a break-in, at the practice.'

'No. Because they want to prevent my discovery.' He pushed the lid of NewMan 2000 closed again.

'Rubbish.'

He turned the volume back down, stepped up to Stephanie and knelt down in front of her so that their heads were on the same level. He put a hand on her cheek and stroked back her hair. She hadn't been expecting it any more, but now, she thought, now it's coming. It was all just a joke, a fantastic, crazy show.

'What day is it today, Steffi?'

'Sunday.'

'What date!'

'The 19th of September.'

'So 19.9.1999. Do you know what that means?' Stephanie shook her head. 'A-I-I-A-I-I-I.'

'I don't understand.'

Stefan stood up again. '*Artificial intelligence in action, artificial intelligence in Jericho.* Whereby the second A stands for both *action* and *artificial* and the last I is a J like in the classical Latin alphabet. *Artificial* can mean the same as *alien,* and it can even be both at the same time. That's what's worrying me. If they're artificial it'll be much harder to penetrate their system. It could be the methyl groups don't match up, or—'

'You don't think, if they're as intelligent as you say, they'd be dumb enough to use such a simple code?' She folded her arms, disappointed that he was simply continuing with his theory instead of paying her attention, and she hoped he'd see the mistake he'd made if she disproved it piece by piece.

'That's the whole trick. Just like it used to be our trick. Everyone who tried to get behind what we were saying to each other didn't imagine we'd take the simplest code in the world. That's why no one ever found us out. Like that story about the purloined letter—it's on the table for all to see, and that's just what makes it invisible. Remember? Poe?'

'The fireplace.'

'What?'

'It was over the fireplace, the letter.'

'Never mind. It's just an example. What I mean is—'

'All right. Let's assume you're right about the code. Couldn't it mean a different Jericho, one that's better known?'

'Then why would I be the person to decipher it? That's not logical. They're here, Steffi, here in Jericho, East Frisia.'

'And who are they?'

'By all indications, they're Plutonians after all, which is surprising because Schallenberg's crazy, his books are no good—the evidence he provides is as confusing as his conclusions. I keep wondering how he arrived at the term Plutonians. None of it has anything to do with that lousy little planet on the edge of our solar system, at any rate. No life is possible there. And this much is clear—the Plutonians are more human than we would like. I've tested their DNA. Their camouflage is perfect. The ones up there could really be my parents.'

'They are your parents.'

'No, they're not. They're hosts, living husks, sad figures unaware of their true identity. Their transformation is complete. The Plutonians need an earth-like atmosphere, and they need us.'

'Why?'

'No idea. I'm not quite clear about the nature of this alien power. I don't know whether it has a natural origin or consists of machines and whether, if they are machines, it's remote-controlled or has reproduced itself and thus functions autonomously. And I haven't found out yet how they manage to get inside us unnoticed. It must have something to do with the eyes, the way they look at us. Maybe they fixate us and get into the brain via a ray, through the iris, to switch us off. Or perhaps it works via words, through what we say to them or they to us, like a password they use to crack us.'

'Maybe it's a combination of both?'

'Good idea. The question is, which comes first? The eyes or the word? As soon as the processor's up and running I'll know, then I'll know everything.'

'So this is all just conjecture?'

'I know they're using us.'

'What for?'

'To secure their survival.'

'You know, it all sounds a lot like *Matrix* to me.'

'There is no true or false world. There's only one. This one. And it's false. But the film's right about one thing—everything you perceive is nothing but an electrical signal. We're made up of a hundred per cent bio-electricity. If you like, we're little walking molecular power stations. Except that we've absolutely neglected that energy up to now. All the impulses we transmit or receive contain information, and all these impulses can be converted into computer-compatible data. But we don't have to dial into some matrix—we don't need telephones, entrances and exits. We are the matrix.'

'I'm sure we are.'

'Steffi. It's much simpler than you think. The whole universe is made up of numbers. Every human being is a number. In rough terms, that's the core of Cabbala. On our own, we're powerless. On our own, we can't do anything against the Plutonians. That's why we have to join together. We have to optimize and network our DNA. That's the only way we can avert the total invasion. But I know that will never happen. Not by natural means. Humankind will never all pull together. Even when there's a global threat. There'll always be some people trying to make a profit out of every situation, traitors, collaborators. And aside from that there'd be no point now anyway. We've already been infiltrated. Maybe from the very beginning, or maybe it took place at intervals, centuries apart. With the landing of the four winged beings in the Old Testament. The appearance of the Count of St Germain. With Daniel Kuper's vision in the corn circle on the 17th of September 1986, at 1313 hours, Central European Time. In any case there are too many now who would deliberately refuse a connection. The program would never be complete. So I've constructed all the possible numbers, all the possible values, and entered them in the database. What we need now is a body that reacts, that can process the influx of impulses. That's why I'm going to connect myself up. I'm going to be the new Moses. I'll see the White Light, the knowledge that holds the world together in its innermost. And I'll share that knowledge with you. We'll amalgamate, Steffi. We'll be one. Man and woman. To get the genetic processor running, you see, it takes a second organism. And that will be you.'

'Me?'

'You also happen to be the only number that's missing.'

'That is?'

'Zero.'

'You're crazy.'

'It's like the poles of a battery, cathode and anode, plus and minus. If only one side's connected up nothing works. It's only with both, in the right order, that electrical energy comes about.'

'You're not going to connect me up to anything.' She got up from the hairdressing chair again, picked up her blazer and her bag and walked towards the door. 'I'm leaving.' And she was, she was determined to go, upstairs, home, back to Münster, if she didn't manage to persuade him against his plan—whatever it was. She felt she owed that much to him, and to herself.

'What a pity,' said Stefan. 'I thought you were on my side.'

'I am on your side. I'm just really tired, and I'm finding it really creepy down here. Why don't we go upstairs and have a coffee and talk about everything in peace, in daylight?'

'There's no place more peaceful than this. This,' he spread his arms, 'is the eye of the storm, the centre of reality. And today is the day of days. I have to take it to an end here and now. And I had hoped you'd support me.'

'I will. Later.'

'There is no later. But maybe I was wrong, maybe one body is enough to activate the processor, if I—' He turned to the workbench, looked at one of the screens and tapped a few keys. 'Yes, it might work like that.' Over his shoulder, he asked, 'Can you do me a favour?'

'Sure.' Now that she'd decided to leave and was certain she could, she was willing to fulfil any wish he might have. 'What then?'

'Can you press that switch there?'

'Which one?'

'The one on the socket over there.'

Stephanie looked at the floor. Next to the hairdressing chair she'd been sitting on were two multiple plug sockets, both switched off.

'The white one or the black one?'

'The black one.'

She pressed the switch with her foot but nothing happened. 'The white one, then.'

Stephanie pressed the switch on the white one and there was a bang upstairs in the hall. At the same time the light went out downstairs and all the sounds died.

When she came to, the room was brightly lit again and she was naked and strapped into one of the hairdressing chairs, her head pushed halfway into the dryer. Her forehead felt damp and heavy and her limbs were as if paralysed. She wanted to scream but she didn't manage more than a dull moan. She couldn't get her lips apart. 'Sorry,' said Stefan. 'I had to strap you down.' He was now wearing the white coat and white disposable gloves. 'I couldn't let you go. The tape's just for your own protection. The room's not completely soundproof and I can't risk them coming down if you scream, even if all they hear of it is a whisper. They're standing outside the door up there. The power cut got them worried. It won't be long before they crack the lock and start playing around with the fuses. We have to hurry. This,' he ran a finger over her head, her chest, belly, private parts, 'is nix against you, it has nix to do with you or me. You might be cursing me now. But I only want what's best for you. I'm fighting for a higher cause, we both are. Once we've entered the world of activation you'll see that too. And you'll be grateful to me for opening your eyes. Then it'll all be clear to you at one fell swoop, everything that seems strange now. I can sense your fear, and I can't take it away from you. I'm afraid of this step too. But it's unavoidable. Not taking it would mean abandoning ourselves.' He tied a belt around her lower arm. 'We're pioneers, Steffi. We'll be the first ones, the first living computers, developed out of humans. I've only tested it on rats so far, and they survived, and the speed at which their brains computed makes me certain we'll survive as well, although you won't be the Steffi you once knew any more.' He shaped her fingers into a

449

fist—she couldn't resist—and disinfected the inside of her elbow with an alcopad. 'I'm going to raise you to a new level of existence and put you into a state that other people wouldn't even achieve through years of meditation. You'll be powerful, fast and strong, you won't feel any boundaries, neither physical nor mental. I'm afraid I haven't got time to adjust you properly. We're diving without radar, to some extent, and I can't even teach you to swim. The sudden insight is like a shock. To begin with you'll have a terrible headache. You'll feel numb in your back, your legs, you'll be incapable of moving. But then you'll swim like you've never swum before, at an incredible speed. You'll see the White Light and hurry towards it. You'll be aware of the great distance you cover, thousands of kilometres in a few seconds, but you won't feel it. You won't even feel the pressure surrounding you, trying to compress you. All you'll feel is the force driving you on. And suddenly you're there. And I'm with you. For all time. These,' he pointed at the two chairs, 'are the thrones of our rule. Our realm will never perish. We'll live for eternity.' Then he leant over her to kiss the tape he'd used to seal up her mouth but she turned her head, the only movement she was still capable of, and then she saw him go over to the two fridges and come back with two ampules. One had her name on it, the other his. And then he pulled the wheeled table over, took two tubes out of their wrappers, inserted the needles, broke off the tip of her ampule and drew the liquid into one of the syringes. She tried to get free, to turn her arms and feet towards the door, but the straps were pulled too tight and every motion stabbed at her flesh. 'Save your strength,' he said as the needle went into her. 'You'll need it. In the beginning you're soft and weak, your body has to accustom to the new surroundings, at the beginning you'll be vulnerable and they'll try to make use of that.' He removed the syringe and put it back on the table. Dull thuds came down to them from above. Stephanie looked at the door. 'They'll be too late,' said Stefan and unbuttoned his white coat.

As he kicked off his underpants there was a crash at the door and a piece of the studded foam fell on the floor.

'OK, listen, they can hear us now. I'd hoped to say at least these things before they find us. They're important for the transition, for your own protection.' He took two cleaning cloths out of the bucket, soaked them with saline solution and clamped one of them to her left foot with a jump lead and the other to her right foot. 'Increases the entry area. We need a bit of thrust. We have to overcome the world before we can rise from the dead.' He fished another two cloths out of the bucket, lay down on the other hairdressing chair next to her and clamped two cloths and two jump leads to his own feet—now they were both connected to the socket and crosswise with each other. The door gave way a crack, the plaster flaking off the wall next to it. Stephanie thought she could break her ties by casting herself to and fro in the seat, but what seemed to her like a convulsion was only a tremor. At least she managed to raise her head despite the chin strap and look at Stefan, in a moment of absolute clarity. He calmly tied a belt around his arm, disinfected the place where the needle was to go, broke open his ampule and filled the second syringe with the clear, transparent fluid she had seen before in the test tubes, in NewMan 2000. 'You have to listen very carefully now, because you have to remember what I've said to you when you're in the light. And that will be hard, as hard as when you try and remember a dream after you wake up. I told you about AGLAL, about the second L, and that I wasn't sure what it meant straight away. At first I thought it was a mistake, something superfluous, incidental. But nothing is superfluous or incidental. Every single letter counts. The second L is the end of everything. L is Lucifer, the light-bearer, the devil, Satan, call him what you like. Who if not he was equal to God by birth? And that was his ruin.' He pulled out the needle and threw the syringe on the ground. He rubbed his head with saline solution and put it all the way into the dryer. He fixed the chin strap and began to strap himself in. Only one arm, the right one, remained free. 'And? Can you feel it yet? Can you feel everything getting faster and easier, how clear everything is suddenly, even the most complicated things? How straightforward? We're beating them at their own game. We're going to be like them.' A hand came through the gap in the doorway. Someone called her name. 'This is the third key, the code that will protect you,' said Stefan. 'Repeat it as soon as you open your eyes. Salted__õ◊8¡ ö#˘#„µ÷|•r)ΩnÈ‹ „@Ø˜GóâmVPzD@ÀÄTDÑVP‡↵µ€,≤ËOl∞ øcBNèw_Ω"µ–¡>°ã?í↵]NÇßëÅn,8>∞fÙè*/}€‰ÌOo*m.'

She didn't understand a word.

Then he put his finger on the start button. 'Let's go, baby!'

That was the last thing she saw and heard.

This is what happened to Daniel Kuper.

Birgit Bleeker

c/o Weber

Waldweg 3

61118 Bad Vilbel

1 August 1999

Dear Mrs Bleeker,

I don't know if the address is correct. I got it from your ex-husband and he told me it might not be up to date any more. I used to be a friend of your son, Daniel. We met a couple of times at your house. And you know my parents. If I told you my *[handwritten: → who aren't my parents.]* name you'd know who I am straight away. But that has to stay a secret, as long as I haven't overcome the boundary and I'm not certain the Plutonians can't do anything to me any more. I can imagine what that word makes you think of. I doubted in Markus Schallenberg's theses for a long time too. His interpretation may be controversial, but the word isn't. I don't know where he got it from and I'm not going to ask him. Unlike him, I've found evidence for the Plutonians' existence on earth, which I won't keep from you.* It's the result of years of research. At first, I couldn't get my head round it. But then the separate symbols came together into a message. The letters and numbers next to each other without any link suddenly made sense. *[handwritten margin note: I still do. I consider him a charlatan.]*

I don't know everything yet, there are still more questions than answers, but if I interpret the indications correctly, I should have more answers than questions in a matter of days.

I didn't always treat Daniel decently. I denied him when he needed me by his side. He was never aware of his abilities, his influence. And we never let him sense it, out of pride and prejudice. We thought we were better than him, and didn't realize

[handwritten] * See enclosure.

that it was actually the other way round. He never talked about you much, but I assume he still had the closest relationship to you, at least up to a certain age, even though you'll probably think differently.

I don't want to open up old wounds for you. The pain of losing a son is immeasurable, and there are no words that might give you comfort. I only wanted to inform you that I may well soon be in a position to make contact with him. Not the way you think. Not with the aid of a medium. Unless I'm the medium myself. But if it works, he won't speak through me. I'll talk to him, perfectly normally, face to face. Just not in our world, but in his. I know that sounds pretty crazy, and I can't promise you I'll actually meet him in the place where I'm going. The plan is to stay for only a few seconds, just as long as it takes to activate me. No one has ever dared to take this step before. It's not a near-death experience, although the light some people who've experienced it talk about, the light I anticipate seeing, must be quite similar. I remember the next day when it was all over and half the village was a pile of rubble, and you were standing wrapped in an aluminium rescue blanket by the smoking remains of the goods shed while the police and fire brigade retrieved the dead girl and looked for Daniel's body. You were waiting. But not for them to find him. You were waiting for him to come back, completely unharmed and younger than before, like a phoenix rising from the ashes. You're still waiting for him. I don't have children; I'm a scientist. But I can imagine in a very abstract way that parents feel what happens to their children. And when I do that, and I've done it a lot in the past few years, I come to the following conclusion: Daniel isn't dead, and he didn't run away like some of the newspapers wrote. Just because he's no longer visible to us, it doesn't mean he's invisible. Extra terrestrials! Back then, I believed him as little as you did. I thought it was a cheap excuse so he didn't have to go to school, because he was scared of Mrs Zuhl. Now I'm certain he saw something in that maize field and that that something, those Plutonians, saw him too. Plutonians, as I've since found out, possess the amazing ability to take control of human beings. They infiltrate us in a certain way and make us into servants of their will. We don't experience that as a burden. On the contrary, we're still convinced we possess our inner freedom, perhaps even more than ever. 'Our thoughts,' as they say in the folk song that the men's choir used to sing, 'Our thoughts they are free.' But that doesn't apply to those who've been transformed. For them, freedom is nothing more than an illusion, a beautiful dream that will never come true or is permanently true. I didn't see any signs in Daniel that are characteristic of the metamorphosis: passivity, flickering in the eyes. And I can't explain why he's immune, how he's the only one who managed to resist the Plutonian gaze. I'm following his example. But in my own way. I'm going to disappear and come back at the same moment as a new person. And if I meet him along the way I'll bring him with me. But don't be scared. He still looks just like he did then. Eight days for him are eight years for us. Time moves on for us but he doesn't notice. I'm confident you'll soon see him again. You should be too.

Which of us would recognize paradise in everyday life? Don't you only know what's good when it's gone?

Stay indoors on 11 August. Resist the temptation to look outside. It's not the moon moving in front of the sun, it's a death star, a gigantic Plutonian eyeball, of which you'll only see a shadow because it's outshone from behind. From there, out of the darkness, the Great Gaze will come over us. The first step of the invasion is meant to open our hearts, and the second to lock them up for ever.

PART THREE

White Shadow

In the Rex

In the space of a few months, Daniel Kuper's life had changed entirely. All contact had broken off with his friends from grammar school, Rainer, Onno and Stefan, and at intermediate school, where he sat next to Volker again, a void had opened up inside him, a black hole that drew in his thoughts and swallowed them up. He didn't know how it had happened; all he noticed was that he had lost interest in all sorts of things, model kits and adventure novels, science fiction and Heavy Metal, things that had been his whole life for a long time, and so far nothing comparable had taken their place—except writing for the school magazine.

He had always liked watching films too, feature films, and he still did now; it was just that they suddenly seemed to have lost their magic. Six months ago, he and Volker had cycled to the county town on their own after school every Thursday, on their new racing bikes. First they'd had a banana split at the ice-cream parlour—one portion for him, two for Volker—and then they'd bought tickets for the film club at the cinema across the road, for classics like *The Graduate*, *All the President's Men* or trilogies like *Back to the Future* and *Star Wars*, and they'd had moments of great happiness. But now that the new boys in the class, Paul Tinnemeyer and Jens Hanken, were coming along with them, the past wasn't worth talking about, and Daniel drank beer and schnapps and smoked cigarettes, hoping that would make everything like it was at the beginning, new and exciting.

It wasn't friendship that connected him to Paul and Jens. They had built a den together in the hollow space underneath the goods shed and later smashed the windows of the old church hall, and sometimes they'd met at one of the flooded sand pits, shared cigarettes and stories, stories about girls, but they were a year older than Daniel, they'd always been a year ahead of him and they always would be. Yet now that they'd been in the same class for almost eight months, now that the hopes their teachers and parents had placed in them hadn't been fulfilled, they came together. They didn't have any common interests or views; they didn't even like one another. What united them was the feeling of disappointment they'd experienced, the feeling of being unable to meet their own and other people's expectations, of having failed themselves and the world.

There was no one boy who made himself a leader and the others into executors of his decisions, there weren't any decisions at all, not even ones made together, they weren't a gang—although they might have made that impression on others. They didn't have a plan, except perhaps for the plan of killing time and experiencing something that would fill the void inside them. Although they only met up spontaneously after school, they did have a pecking order, a vague, unspoken one that resulted from the type of disappointment they felt. Paul—the Big Red Giant, as they called him in secret—had never had any ambitions and deliberately got bad grades so he didn't look like a swot. He'd wanted to prove that you could be lazy, inconsiderate and successful at the same time, and Jens, his satellite, had followed him on the path to damnation. Until the last moment both of them had hoped, against better judgement, they would go up to the next school year with three Es on their reports for the first half-year and no improvement in the second. Daniel, in contrast, came from the grammar school, had been catapulted into the stratosphere and crashed back down to earth. And Volker was their sun, the fat, grease-glossed star holding them in his orbit at the correct distance from one another.

Paul was tall, one metre ninety, and out of time. He always combed his hair into a quiff, apart from a single strand that fell over his forehead in a thick coating of gel, and instead of jeans and T-shirts he wore trousers and shirts. His father ran a small upholstery workshop and people said he wouldn't let anyone in the family wear jeans because denim wore down the fabric he stretched over chairs and sofas, destroying all his hard work. When Daniel heard about that, when Volker told him in the first week at intermediate school why Paul looked the way he did, the thought seemed paradoxical to him; an upholsterer made a living out of wear and tear. 'How stupid is that? If everyone wore jeans and slid across their sofas in them, he could make a fortune. Paul ought to set a good example.'

'An example of what?'

'Of destruction.'

'You can tell him that.'

'Maybe I will.'

'I don't think that's a good idea.'

'Why not?'

'Jens.'

'What about Jens?'

Volker tapped one of his front teeth.

'You mean Paul knocked it out?' Jens wasn't missing a whole tooth, just part of one, and above the tooth his lip was blue and swollen, like a bruise—except that this bruise didn't go away, not like the others, the normal kind.

'Long time ago.' Volker shrugged. 'Anyway, I wouldn't say anything to him about his clothes. And certainly not about his old man. He's sensitive about him.'

'Who isn't?' When he said that, Daniel was thinking of himself, of his father and the drugstore, but he could just as well have meant Volker or Jens. Volker didn't exactly enjoy the other kids' respect, being a teacher's son. Jens' father had a tanning studio. And Jens' skin colour implied that he made use of it often enough, which some girls, who didn't have to worry about trouble because they were too pretty or too confident, used as an excuse to take the mickey out of him.

'Hey Jens, did you fall asleep on the beach again?' said Simone, who combined both traits, whenever Jens entered the classroom with a winter suntan as he had recently.

They had met outside the station at seven, bought a bottle of corn schnapps at the kiosk and then roamed the streets, drinking and making trouble. Dark streetlamps, tipped-over bikes and shards of glass on the asphalt marked out their route to the movie centre, where they were showing *Darkman* that spring evening, *The Man with the Mask*, although they suspected they wouldn't be let in, not at their age. Paul claimed to have seen the film several times already and only to have come along again for their sake. Paul also claimed to have seen and stomached *The Evil Dead*, *The Evil Dead II*, *Hellraiser*, *Hellbound: Hellraiser II*, *Night of the Living Dead* and *Day of the Dead*. In class and at break time, he would sometimes lean over to girls and say in an unnaturally high or low voice, 'The trees are alive! It's the trees. They know!'—'It's me, Frank, it's Uncle Frank. The blood on the ground brought me back. But now I need more. Come to Daddy! Come to Daddy! Come to Daddy!' And then he'd reach his hands out to them and touch them everywhere and tell them what he planned to do with their brains. But because none of them knew the films and they weren't available at the video store, and because not even Jens' older brothers had seen them, there was no way to check Paul's detailed descriptions of the violence scenes and horror effects.

It was just before eight and the shops were still open, as on every late-opening Thursday, but the pedestrian zone was already dead. Only a handful of couples were standing in front of the lit-up shop windows, pointing at the items on display. Daniel watched them for a while, both hands buried in the pockets of his parka—a Christmas present from his father—before he turned around to the others, who were emptying their cans behind him, behind the display cases. Volker dropped a full can, then picked it up and tapped his finger on the lid.

'That doesn't do anything,' said Jens.

'You don't know anything about it,' said Volker and carried on tapping at the aluminium. 'It's to do with excess pressure. When you shake it gas is released and—'

'Maybe when *you* do,' Jens interrupted and moved his curled hand up and down in front of his stomach as if rubbing at something invisible.

'Yeah,' said Paul. 'You wouldn't get anything more than gas out, fatty.'

'Idiots,' said Volker. 'You've got no idea of chemistry. When you shake it gas is released, my dad told me, and if you tap on the lid the gas bubbles come away from the edges and rise to the surface, and the carbon dioxide has nothing left to hold on to, to escape.'

'Rubbish,' said Jens.

'Your old man's crazy,' said Paul, and Volker said, 'No, really, look, I'll open this.' He pressed the tab into the can and beer spurted out. 'Damn. That was the first time. Honest. It's just because of these new openings. It always worked when you had to pull the ring.'

Once they'd stopped laughing, Paul asked, 'Got anything with you?'

'Course,' said Jens.

'And what about you?'

'Sure,' said Daniel, 'always,' although he didn't know what Paul was talking about.

'I should hope so too,' said Paul, flicked his cigarette end across the square to the monument and went inside to see who was at the cash desk. Paul had predicted that it might be tricky getting in with the kids, depending on who was on duty, and when he came out again he said, 'No chance.' He'd had a holiday job at the cinema for a while. He had carried the heavy reels and put the films on the projectors and sat in the back row during the screenings. Afterwards he had cleaned the cinemas, collected up empty bottles, swept crisps, salt sticks and popcorn up from the floor, scraped chewing gum off the bottom of the armrests and kept the small change he found under the seats. One day he'd found a fat wallet and quit the job from one day to the next, not giving any reason. But he still knew all the employees, said he was still friends with some of them and knew who would close a blind eye and who wouldn't.

They looked up at the green wooden sign above the entrance, illuminated from below, on which the evening's four films were announced, and agreed on *The Silence of the Lambs*.

'It's supposed to be better than *Darkman* anyway,' said Daniel.

Volker said, 'I bet it's much more subtle than *Zombie 7* too.' He said it perfectly calmly, as if he knew what he was talking about, as if he had no need to worry despite his age.

466

And Paul said, looking at Volker and Daniel, 'I don't normally watch kids' films, but I guess I don't have any other option with you two.'

Daniel knew it wouldn't work for him, that he didn't even look old enough for the so-called kids' films. *The Silence of the Lambs*, like almost all the films they wanted to see, was a Sixteen certificate, and so when he got to the counter after the others, he said, 'One ticket for *Awakenings*, please.' At the same time he was annoyed with himself for not even trying, for giving in immediately.

Three spotlights fixed to the ceiling bathed him in glinting light, like an actor at the theatre. He actually felt reminded of performances in the school hall—he had stepped onto a stage on which everyone except him knew their lines and there was no one to prompt him. Instead, they stared at him as if they could coax words out of him with their eyes, words of forgiveness or anger, anything to destroy the silence and move the action along.

The others were standing by the staircase that went up to the cinemas. Daniel had his arms folded in front of his chest. The woman behind the desk shifted her gaze to and fro between him and the money he'd put on the counter, as if there were some similarity between him and Dürer's *Young Man* on the banknote, as if it were a clumsily faked passport or a cheap attempt at bribery, for the purpose of travelling into her country. Then she exchanged the banknote for two coins and a ticket and yelled at the ticket collector on the other side of the room. 'Nella, keep an eye on young Kuper here,' pointing at Daniel, 'he'll probably try and go over.'

He wondered how she knew him, how she knew his name, whether Paul had said something to her just now or she knew his parents, but he couldn't remember ever seeing her anywhere outside the cinema. The others laughed; he heard them talking about him on their way to the Rex, until they disappeared behind a black curtain. The ticket collector—Nella—who was standing next to the staircase, was wearing a white, semi-transparent dress. The fabric was so thin that her underwear was outlined beneath it. When he looked closer, though, driven by a sudden desire, he thought he made out the pattern of the banister she was leaning on in the wave-like stripes; the shape and colour matched, the foreground and background blended into each other seamlessly. He guessed she was thirty, forty at the most. Her lips were glossy and she smiled at him in pity and stroked his hand when he gave her his ticket. Her skin was rough and chapped, weathered like an old man's. Shocked, he stepped back and almost dropped one of the cans concealed underneath his parka.

Once he'd left the woman behind him he felt lighter, as if he'd passed a test and crossed an invisible boundary. But the further he went, the quieter and darker it got. Sounds were swallowed up by the thick fabrics with which everything around him was upholstered, the glaring light of the foyer was nothing but a distant glow, contours faded with every step, and soon he could no longer distinguish where the walls stopped on either side of him and the ceiling and the floor began, and so he started swaying on the sloping ground and almost lost his equilibrium and reached his hands out pointlessly in the hope of finding a hold somewhere. This was the payback for drinking too much of the schnapps too quickly on the way from the station, because he'd been so nervous. He was dizzy, he started sweating and trembling and only calmed down again when he reached the door at last, after what seemed like hours, above which the word *Urania* was lit weakly from behind and flickered hectically—the smallest of the four cinemas, where *Awakenings* was showing for the last time.

He had only seen two horror films so far, *Swamp Thing* and *A Nightmare on Elm Street*, both by Wes Craven, both at Onno's house, and he'd had nightmares afterwards; not the kind in which someone killed him but the kind in which he slit someone open or strangled or skinned them, his parents, his brother and sister, his friends.

Him stabbing a knife into them, cutting off their breathing with a belt, cutting the flesh off their bones, pouring petrol over them and warming himself by the fire as their bodies burnt. That had shocked him more than anything else, the realization that he was capable of such things, even if it had only happened in his mind and in his sleep and he couldn't put up any resistance to it. That impotence was no consolation. The opposite, in fact—it gave him the feeling there were forces acting inside him that were out of his control and would one day come to the fore. He never dreamt of falling off a roof or off a bridge into a canyon either; it was always the roof or the bridge collapsing and him floating above these works of destruction, like an angel of death who had plunged the world into chaos with a single gesture or word.

Paul organized a horror movie night every few months when his parents were away on business, buying new fabric. He showed videos for a small, select audience in the family living room, amateur films he said weren't available for hire because they were on the index or had never made it to public release.

'And what's in them?' Daniel asked Volker, who had been along once.

'Nothing special. Blurry, shaky pictures and really bad sound quality,' he answered, making an effort to hide his pride at being invited to join this exclusive circle. 'You can hardly even understand what the tortured women and children are screaming.'

Daniel had not been party to an invitation so far. He had never expressed an interest either. Still, he saw their night out together at the cinema as a kind of test of whether he'd prove worthy of the honour or not.

He sat directly by the entrance. There was a bar in every separate cinema, below the projector window, where you could buy drinks, snacks and ice cream while the ads were showing. In the old days, when he'd come here with his parents, the buttons installed every two metres on the back of the seats in front had still worked and you could call up the staff and place your order from your seat. But by now they'd either broken or been switched off, or at least no one had ever come when Volker and he had pressed them and no one came now when someone in front of him or next to him pressed them, and he was glad he'd brought his own beer because the woman who'd taken his ticket earlier was now behind the bar to his rear.

He tapped his fingernails on one of the cans because he believed in Volker's theory about gas and carbon dioxide and feared the beer might come shooting out after all the toing and froing if he didn't tame it with patient tapping. When he pressed the tab in it spurted out anyway, and he had to lean over and slurp up the foam so it didn't go everywhere. Jens was right; Volker's theory was rubbish. Perhaps the tapping did less to calm the beer than to calm the person doing the tapping, and all you had to do was leave the can alone for a while to let the gases dissolve of their own accord, or perhaps neither of them had found the right place yet, the spot that deactivated everything. He waited until the lamps on the side walls had gone out and only the green exit signs were lit up, until the woman had left her post and everyone was looking forward, at the screen, watching the first trailer, and then he got up and went out into the corridor.

A few metres on, he sensed the woman behind him. Her steps were inaudible on the soft carpet, her outline barely visible in the subdued light, and yet he knew she was there, a white shadow following him at a constant distance. He didn't even have to turn around to her, and he didn't turn around when she said, 'Where are you off to, Daniel? There's no point even trying.'

'The toilet. Just the toilet. Be right back.' Daniel hastened his steps as if that would help him escape her and reach his goal faster, even though he had no hope of that now.

She guarded him like a prisoner, stood outside the door until he was finished, accompanied him back to the cinema and whispered in his ear as he sat down, 'Stay where you are, or else—'

'Or else what?' he asked at an exaggerated volume.

'*Namu Myōhō Renge Kyō*,' she said as if to herself, and then, 'Don't try and find out.'

'And what if I do?'

'Very bad karma.'

After the trailers and a second beer, he undertook a second attempt. He looked around; the woman was nowhere in sight. Perhaps she'd sat down somewhere, or perhaps she'd left because she had to go back down for another film and didn't expect him to dare go against her command, her empty threat. Once again, he got up and walked along the corridor to the Rex. A few latecomers dashed past him, making accusations at each other because of the time.

He pushed the curtain aside and closed the door behind him, crept along the wall and up the slope to the back row. He had almost made it, he was standing in front of them, just about to push past Paul and Jens and take the free seat next to Volker, whose sweater was sprinkled with popcorn, when the woman said behind him, 'Nice try.'

Daniel turned around, not knowing what to say, and said, 'I just forgot my ciggies.'

'I see,' said the woman. 'Forgot your ciggies.'

'Yes,' said Daniel, glad his excuse was working.

'I've never seen the guy before, Nella,' said Paul.

And Jens said, 'You're in the way, I can't see,' sliding left and right on his seat and trying to peer around him.

Anthony Hopkins hadn't showed up yet but Jodie Foster was already running through the forest in her sweat-soaked grey FBI sweater, and even Daniel and the woman looked around at her, until Volker said, 'He's causing such a commotion it's spoiling my enjoyment of *The Silence of the Lambs*,'—a few popcorn crumbs fell out of his mouth—'could you, I mean, could you please remove this individual immediately?' Sometimes, Volker talked in this pompous manner when he wanted to be particularly mean to someone, and Daniel remembered that he usually laughed at his stiff sentences, only he wasn't laughing now that they were directed against him. 'Stop all this crap, will you?' he said. 'And give me a ciggie.'

But Paul and Jens exchanged grins, their faces pale and blue, contorted by the light reflecting off the screen, and as if they'd discussed it earlier they both blew smoke in his face.

'I haven't got all day,' said the woman. 'If you don't come right away I'll have you thrown out. I hope you know what that means, being banned from the cinema in a place like this.' Apart from the movie centre, which had originally housed only one cinema, the Delphi, there were no other cinemas left in the county town. In the early sixties they had opened up the Rex next to the Delphi for film premieres, a large cinema with five hundred seats and a sequined curtain. The Apollo had been rented out to a discount supermarket and then demolished to make way for a car park. And the Urania had moved from Weser Street into the movie centre to join the Delphi, Rex and Apollo, because it belonged to the same owner and he wanted to have all his cinemas under one roof. 'The nearest cinema is twenty kilometres away,' said the woman and repeated the distance for added emphasis, hoping to shock Daniel into obedience. 'Twenty kilometres!' Hisses came out of the darkness from all directions. But the woman was savouring her power to the full, apparently not holding her sermon for the first time. 'I'm sure you don't want to risk the privilege of going to the cinema, not at your age when everyone wants to join in the conversation. I know that from my own boy.'

'I only come over here for the ciggies,' said Daniel.

'Came.'

'What?'

'Came over here. It ought to be came over here, not come.'

'If you say so,' said Daniel, and to overplay the unpleasant feeling of having made a mistake and been corrected, he added, 'I saw *Silence of the Lambs* ages ago, I don't want to watch it again, it's not worth it.'

'It's only just started its run,' she said, pointing at the screen. 'This is the premiere.'

'So?' said Daniel, and he opened his eyes wide and looked from one boy to the others and made hectic movements with his hands and lips. He held his index finger and his middle finger in a V in front of his mouth, pouted as if in a kiss, and pushed them back and forth, back and forth. He repeated the gesture several times to no avail. Paul frowned, Jens shrugged, and Volker shook his head.

Then Paul said, 'I'll swap you for a beer.'

'I haven't got any beer,' Daniel said and looked at the woman. 'Honest.'

'I thought you had some with you.'

'You've got the wrong idea,' said Daniel. 'It's not allowed, bringing drinks in.'

'Oh right,' said Paul. 'I didn't know that. When I used to work here I could bring in as much beer as I liked.'

'I'll throw the whole lot of you out in a minute,' said the woman.

'All right then.' Paul started patting his pockets. 'Here.'

Expecting a new cigarette, Daniel stretched out a hand to him, but instead Paul extinguished his old one on his palm. Daniel clenched his fist until the glowing tip went out and then dropped it, not pulling a face. 'A whole one,' he said. 'Not one you've licked.'

Eventually Volker gave in and handed him his box and his lighter, and Daniel lit himself a cigarette. He inhaled briefly, once, twice, and looked down at Paul. And at that moment he thought of Peter Peters, of what Stefan, Onno, Rainer and he had done to him, and of what had happened to him, but Daniel didn't want to end up like him, ripped apart by a train. All of a sudden he knew what he'd do to Paul: chophimuppiecebypiecestartingwith hisfeethishandshiscockandthenallthewaydowntohisrumpjusthave tomakesurehestaysawakeconsciousofwhat'shappeningtohimI'll stuffitallinthemincerandshoveabigpileofmincemeatdownhisjaw forcehimtoswallowandgrabitalloutofhisstomachwithmybarehands andshoveitbackdownhisthroatagainandonandonandonandonfor everandever. For a second, the fantasy soothed his wound. Then he pulled his hand away, not wanting them to see how hard he was trembling. He wouldn't be able to stand there like that for long, cool and untouchable like a hero, and he was almost grateful to the woman when she said the words she'd wanted to say immediately after his crude excuse—'*Awakenings* is a 12 Certificate film. There's no smoking in the Urania.'

He was sitting closer to the front now. The seat next to the entrance where he'd been sitting before was occupied. Five rows behind him, the woman was watching his every move. Once, he'd turned round to her; her eyes were fixed on him, not on the screen, so he'd soon slipped so far down his seat that his head no longer protruded above the backrest, his legs angled, his knees pressed against the edge of the seat in front so as not to slide onto the floor or get trapped in the upholstery. From his toes up, he felt his legs going gradually numb. He took a new can out of the side pocket of his parka, held it in his hand for a while to cool the burn and then emptied it in a few gulps. Then he set about drinking the last one as quickly as possible and forgetting what had happened to him.

The film was a great help for this plan. He thought he must have seen the characters, the scenes and the places a hundred times before. In the role of Dr Malcolm Sayer, Robin Williams looked like Mr Mengs, Volker's father, their Biology and Physics teacher. Brown suit, round metal glasses, beard, his feet turned in slightly as he sat, his entire appearance insecure, a person afraid of people, who therefore prefers the company of ivy and worms. And the neurological department where he worked, with its patients staring straight ahead or talking crazed nonsense, reminded him so strongly of school that he fell asleep a few minutes in and didn't wake up until the lamps above him and at the sides were lit up and everyone else had left; even the woman had disappeared.

There was only a boy sweeping up the rubbish the cinema-goers had left behind. Here and there, he bent down and picked something up from the floor, but most of the time he held the broom firmly in both hands, the muscles in his lower arms tensed to snapping point, a body full of strength and expectation marching across the room in zigzags from top to bottom, and while he came towards Daniel he was whistling the 'Imperial March' from *The Empire Strikes Back*, thinking he was alone, a sound more beautiful and terrifying than anything Daniel had ever heard.

White Shadow

1

The symbols were everywhere. On the walls of vacant houses, the concrete pillars of the bridges, the bus stops along Village Road. Three letters, two slogans, a swastika, *NPD*, *Foreigners Out*, *Germany for the Germans*, in bright white. Daniel saw them one morning on the way to school, and when he went home from school at lunchtime they were still there. He told his parents about them over lunch. He sat there, hunched over, his head resting on both hands, as if dazed or numbed. He watched his brother and sister reaching into the serving dishes, piling potatoes and cauliflower florets in Hollandaise sauce onto their plates, his mother serving veal and putting the jug of brown gravy down in front of him.

'Eat it down,' she said and sat down on her seat opposite him. Every time his mother said 'Eat it down,' he said, 'Up.' Whenever he said 'Up,' his father said, 'What?' Whenever his father said 'What?' he said, 'Nothing.'

Then his mother said grace and they all wished one another a good appetite.

This time it seemed unfitting to point out his mother's mistake. Instead, he said, 'Someone ought to call the police about it!'

'How about you?' said his father. 'They know you already.'

'Exactly.'

'I'm sure they've already seen it for themselves,' said his mother. 'No one could miss smears like that. They're bound to find them.'

'No need,' said Daniel. 'I know who it was.'

'Oh, do you now?' said his father. 'Who was it then?'

'Rosing.'

His father started laughing, his chest above the white coat quaking as if shaken by cramps. His brother and sister laughed as well. They thought Daniel had made a joke. His father's laughs soon turned into coughs because he'd choked on his laughter. The twins went quiet. His mother thumped his father on the back. Once he'd calmed down and drunk a glass of water, he said, 'Oh no, I really can't imagine Rosing spraying words, not with the best will in the world.' He said 'words' rather than 'graffiti', afraid he might not pronounce it correctly, and then his son would point it out and kick off a discussion there was no way of ending.

Daniel said, 'I don't mean Rosing went round the village at night himself. Maybe he sent one of his men. Or Iron. Or, just as likely, even more likely actually, he incited someone to do it with his speeches.'

'Rosing,' said Daniel's father, 'talks a lot when the day is long. No one takes everything he says seriously. Mind you, there must be something in it, otherwise he wouldn't be so popular. I wouldn't be surprised if he got voted in as mayor in October.'

'What about Didi?' asked his mother.

'Didi Schulz? He's out of the running. He just didn't do enough for the retailers. What can you expect from a blacksmith? It's obvious he's only interested in his own kind. Farming. Industry.'

'I'm amazed he's even running for office again at his age. He's over seventy now.'

'It's time we had a breath of fresh air in Jericho. Rosing can't count on my vote though. I'm voting for Wiemers from the FDP. I've always voted liberal and I always will.' Daniel, who hadn't seen his father so worked up for a long time, wanted to say something but couldn't get a word in. 'And when it comes to Rosing, he's not a National Democrat, if that's what you're thinking, he's an independent candidate. He's a decent man. I won't let you say anything against him. He's never had it easy. Never. He had to bring up his children all on his own because his wife died on him early, much too early.' He looked at Daniel's mother and then back at Daniel. 'Did you know he built this house?'

Daniel shook his head.

'He did, though. And not just this one. Practically all the houses here,' he waved a hand around the room. 'If it wasn't for him there'd be no Jericho, no new Jericho. The custard factory, the village hall, the football stadium, all built by him. And with the concrete works out there,' he pointed out of the window, 'out in the hammrich, he's bound to create a few more jobs. Saying it's him defacing the village is slander. And let me tell you one thing, buddy—if you don't want even more trouble, you should keep your opinions to yourself in future.'

Hard was lying on the sofa in the living room, shielding his eyes with his hand and trying to sleep. The twins were making a racket above him. He could hear them running from one end of the landing to the other, to and fro, to and fro, untiringly. Every footstep gave him a stab. He'd hoped they would calm down once they started school, and he'd got his way over Birgit, who wanted to send them to kindergarten for an extra year. But their first day at school hadn't been the short sharp shock he had in mind when he thought back to his own childhood.

In his view, the teachers were too lenient, let the kids get away with too much, and the fact that almost only women taught his youngest two, even for Sports and Mathematics, seemed to be proof to him of how badly children needed male role models to learn their own boundaries. A clip round the ear had never harmed anyone, least of all him. His class teacher back then, Headmaster Itzen, had been a soldier through and through, first in the Wehrmacht, then in the West German army. That was why Hard had signed up himself later on, and not only for military service like all the other boys in his class who passed muster, but to become a sergeant and adopt responsibility. He didn't regard the job of defending the fatherland as a bothersome duty, a necessary hurdle on the way to family life. For him, it was an honour to bear the insignia of power, and he had let everyone feel that who hadn't crawled through the mud with the same devotion as he had years previously.

If you decided on something, his father had always told him, you had to do it wholeheartedly, whether as a civilian or a soldier. And as the lads had decided on the army, he demanded wholehearted effort from them. And they ought to be grateful to serve under him as well—the other training officers in Aurich were even tougher. *Bangbüxen* who chickened out right after the medical examination and came over all conscientious objector ended up behind bars, or they ran off to West Berlin in the old days, which made no difference, as Staff Sergeant Freese always said—one was a prison and the other was too, just bigger and brighter and less strict.

And he'd spent years training recruits to protect that gigantic biotope of layabouts and terrorists, until his father died and he had to take over the business. And now his own son was coming along with these left-wing accusations, calling people Nazis. Music started playing upstairs. They'd have to wait and see who was a Nazi here and who wasn't. On that thought, he got up to take care of peace and quiet in the house—at least until the end of his lunch break.

The next day the symbols were still there, the day after that too. Daniel didn't talk about them to his parents any more, and at school, on the school campus, two two-storey concrete blocks, he sat silently. In Social Studies they were doing the local elections coming up that autumn, and the teacher, Mr Engberts, shared Daniel's indignation over the National Democratic Party and its positions, but when the word 'graffiti' was mentioned and he asked Jens what he thought of it, Daniel already had an idea where it would lead.

Jens said, 'Graffitis are cool.'

Mr Engberts corrected him. 'The word comes from Italian. The plural of *graffito* is *graffiti*, not *graffitis*.' He paused for a moment, looked around the room and said, 'I'd like to hear someone else's opinion.'

Paul, who had an opinion on everything, said, 'Graffitis are a modern form of urban art,' and to provoke Engberts he added, 'Anyone who rejects graffitis is reactionary.'

Simone, the class representative on the student council, put her hand up. She clicked her fingers three times before Mr Engberts called on her. 'It's not about graffiti,' she said, brushing her henna-red hair out of her face, 'it's about the content they transport.' An hour earlier, in History, Colonial History, German Southwest Africa, Herero Uprising, she had recommended not calling black people black any more but coloured people or Afro-Americans.

Which was why Paul now said, 'The best graffiti artists are niggers.'

Simone's face turned red and she called him a racist. Paul and Jens threw paper pellets at her from behind, over the others' heads. Mr Engberts appealed for quiet.

Volker, who sat next to Daniel, asked in a whisper, 'Hey, what time is it? I'm getting lung yearnings.'

Daniel looked at his digital watch. 'Nearly ten.'

Volker groaned as if he'd had a stroke and returned the cigarette packet recently removed from his jacket pocket to its place. He took two half-slices of brown bread spread with liver pate and wrapped in aluminium foil out of a plastic box. A low-flying combat plane thundered over the building. Mr Engberts made a note in the register. Then the bell rang.

At break time, Simone and Daniel sat together in the cafeteria, the former staff room, a long, brightly lit space between the two main buildings. They wanted to write a report for the school magazine. Daniel had one of the bread rolls with raw minced pork and onions displayed on the counter and then they both had a coffee. Simone had brought her own cup along, a white bowl that she clasped in her thin fingers like a heavy dish.

Daniel was glad of every moment the two of them spent together. Sometimes it seemed to him as if they were the only human beings on a planet populated by apes. They shared the fate of having left grammar school, although they'd made the decision for different reasons—Daniel hadn't wanted to repeat the school year, and Simone hadn't wanted to be mediocre, and she had kicked up such a fuss at home that her parents gave in and let her switch to the intermediate school. He had acted out of necessity whereas she had fallen prey to her own ambition to be the best at all times and everywhere—or at least in her immediate surroundings.

Daniel put his cup down. He wanted to say something; he had the headline and the text in his mind already. But Simone said, 'How can you drink out of those plastic cups? I told you old Mrs

Klautzki, or whatever her name is, fishes them out of the bins in the yard. Everyone knows this place is riddled with rats. I'm in favour of recycling in principle, but the thought of drinking out of cups pissed in by rats turns me right off. Totally! And when it comes to those pork rolls you're always stuffing your face with,' she pointed at his mouth, 'I bet they're a day older than they ought to be. We ought to write about that. We're not allowed to report on anything that happens outside of school in the *Chalkeater* anyway. Apart from the dumb work-experience placements coming up in April. As long as no one paints on the gym walls or the pillars in the foyer, you won't get Nazis into the *Chalkeater*. And you know Schulz. How often has he got rid of a story at the last moment because it wasn't directly related to school? Maybe it'd be better to organize a panel discussion in the school hall, with antifascist activists. I've got pretty good contacts to the scene. There's this guy I went out with. Nothing serious though. Not for me, anyway. I never have anything serious.'

Hard had often sent Daniel over to Rosing on errands. Little things he wanted to get over and done with, for which it wasn't worth going all the way himself if he hadn't got hold of anyone on the telephone. The terracotta tiles cracked in the frost and needed replacing every two years, the flat roof leaked after every major rain shower, in a different place every time, and the concrete slabs outside the stockroom subsided into the ground after two or three fourteen-tonne trucks had unloaded there.

There was always something to be done around the house but Hard didn't always consult the experts. He did a lot of things himself and he left a lot of things to his son. He thought Daniel was at an age now when he ought to learn how to paper a wall, use a drill and change a car tyre, so he didn't have to rely on others later. Whenever an opportunity arose he called Daniel, showed him

485

how to do it and supervised his implementation. Hard wasn't a handyman and he'd learnt what he taught Daniel from his own father, Daniel Kuper senior, who hadn't been a handyman either. All the mistakes had thereby been passed on from one generation to the next and, as all the Kupers ignored technical progress, amplified. Often enough, Daniel would hit an electric wire while drilling, plane off too much wood or apply the wrong paint, even though he'd followed Hard's instructions to the letter, and in the end they had to call in an expert after all to repair the damage they'd done. That didn't stop Hard from getting Daniel to do the job first next time round, though.

Sometimes, if something had broken in his room or his racing bike had a flat tyre, Daniel turned to his father. But he'd never come to him with a problem that didn't concern himself.

'The plaster's coming off the wall in the stockroom.'

'So?' said Hard, hunched over his books, the balances of the past few years. 'No one ever goes in there.'

'I do.'

'Then you can trowel it over, can't you?'

'Don't you think we ought to tell Rosing to begin with?'

Hard looked up at him. 'I thought he was a Nazi.'

'He's certainly a building contractor and he knows about these things.'

'What things? Plaster?'

'Mould.'

'Nix,' said Hard. 'There's nothing wrong with that wall. We don't have to call in a professional for a little thing like that.'

'And what if more plaster comes down?'

'You can give it a try.'

And that was what he'd done. He had gone into the stock-room with a hammer and a bucket of water, knocked the plaster off and wiped over the exposed brickwork with a sponge, so that it looked like the whole wall was damp. Then he'd called his father. And now Daniel was walking down Village Road past the post office to Rosing's place.

From Petersen's Pool Hall, the basement of the demolished station, the hollow click of balls against each other came up to him, and on the other side of the road at Kramer's Furniture Paradise two men who had just put a wardrobe in the shop window collapsed onto a sofa, folded their legs and got out their Tupperware boxes and thermos flasks. They waved their sandwiches at him and Daniel waved back.

Rosing's office was housed in a white bungalow. Behind it were the administration building, the warehouses and the workshops. From the outside, it looked like a perfectly normal home, its flat roof tiled with brown shingles, curtains at the windows, windowsills full of geraniums. Except that the words *Rosing Construction* shone above the entrance in orange letters all day long and the doorbell was labelled *JR*. The door was always ajar during business hours, unless the weather was bad. On that day, though, when Daniel set out to save the village from its doom, the sky was cloudy and milky white but it wasn't raining, it wasn't windy, and there was no snow falling either.

The receptionist, Mrs Duken, said the boss was in the main warehouse, and pointed at the wall. The main warehouse was the wooden freight shed bordering the bungalow. Daniel remembered playing underneath that shed as a child, in the hollow space between the beams. He and Paul and Jens and a few other friends had built a den there and fitted it out with bedside tables from the rubbish collection. For a while they'd considered moving into their grotto, but they'd abandoned the idea after spending a night wrapped in sleeping bags, thronged by cats, mice and spiders. Other children after them must have taken away the remains they left behind. When he bent down to look now, all he could see was the mattress he'd lain on back then, shrunken and black, as if burnt or charred.

He climbed the ladder and stepped onto the ramp. The gate was pushed half-open. Hundreds of bales of rolled-up glass wool were stored in the high, dark room, some piled on palettes and packed in cellophane, some loose and standing upright in several rows. The only light spilled in through the gaps in the board walls, chopped into slices, narrow strips saturated with dust.

There was no one to be seen. The secretary must have meant a different warehouse, the new one in the newly designated industrial estate on the other side of the B70, far away, too far to walk. He couldn't think of any other explanation. He listened to see if someone was there after all. He called something and heard his voice echo. Then he decided to seize the opportunity to take his time and look for evidence, spray cans and stencils, leaflets, books and pictures. Sometimes he stuck his hand between the bales. His fingers reached into nothingness every time. He walked up and down the rows. The boards made a groaning sound at every step. At one end, towards the bungalow, there was a door. He tried the handle, tugging at it, but it wouldn't open. Just as he turned around to leave, Wiebke was standing in front of him, in a much-too-short and much-too-colourful dress and with plaits sticking out from her head like bent antennae. Some people said she used them to pick up signals from a faraway galaxy, whispered messages from aliens, secret commands. The fact was that she had problems with reading and writing and had to go to a special school. Daniel didn't care what some people said and what not. All he knew was that she had a whole lot of other problems, and reading and writing encountered conditions at the special school about as favourable as those for human life on Mars.

'Daniel, what you doing here?'

'How do you know my name?'

'Everyone knows.' Wiebke plucked at her dress. 'You come to see me?'

'No, I'm looking for your father. I have to talk to him about something.'

'About what?'

'None of your business.'

'Isn't it?'

'No.'

'Maybe it is.'

'I don't see why.'

'Cause you want to know where he is.'

'Where is he then?'

She shrugged. 'Just left in the van. Five minutes ago.'

It couldn't be true.

'Where's he gone?'

'Don't know. He told me to wait here. And then you came along.'

'Did he go to the building site? To the factory?' Although he didn't have planning permission yet, Rosing had pegged out the land for the cement works and had a pit dug to test the quality of the ground.

She shrugged again.

He wasn't getting anywhere like this. They said nothing for a while, simply standing there in the middle of the freight shed and looking at each other. He noticed she bore no similarity to Iron, or to Rosing either. He had no memory of her dead mother.

'Do you want to play with me?'

Daniel shook his head. 'I haven't got time for that now.'

'You've got time for my father but not for me. I'll show you my hiding place if you play with me. I got a hiding place here in the shed.'

When he turned her down politely in the hope of getting out of it, she promised to let her father know he'd been there. Hopping from one leg to the other, she scurried out of view. He was electrified. If Rosing found out he'd been snooping around there'd be trouble. He called her name. At the same time, he set out in her direction. He walked up and down the rows. Again, the floorboards made a groaning sound at every step, only this time it seemed more major to him, like a quake. He felt the sweat underneath his parka, under his arms. Once he got to the gate he rested his hands on it and called, still out of breath, 'I'm off now.'

At that point she came out and pulled him between the bales into her hiding place—a clearing in the midst of the glass wool. She squatted down in front of him, her legs wide, leaning back so that her dress slipped up above her knees, up to her thighs, and assigned him a place in the opposite corner. He hesitated. The likelihood that she'd tell her father about his visit increased with every minute they spent together.

The moment he sat down she demanded he read to her from one of the books piled up next to him. 'When you've finished,' said Wiebke and opened her legs further, 'I'll show you my sluice, my sluice gates, maybe even my sluice chamber, it depends.'

'On what?'

'On you.'

He picked up a book. *Live and Let Die*. Outside, an engine roared and died down. A car door opened and slammed. A man threatened to bolt the gate. On the platform, she swore not to tell her father he was a spy, as long as he came back.

He didn't have a choice.

Günter Vehndel and Klaus Neemann were already sitting at the very end of the bar, in their usual places, each with a half-litre of beer in front of him and a pile of cards between the glasses. When Hard took a seat on the free stool with the words 'We're all here now' and indicated with a nod to Enno Kröger, the landlord and barkeeper, that he was also ready for a freshly tapped Jever, Doctor Ahlers approached them, his cheeks sunk, his skin pale, his hair as white as the smoke forming a cloud around him. 'And I'd hoped I could join in your game.'

'Not a chance,' said Günter.

And Klaus said, 'Not as long as we live.'

'Life could be over sooner than you think.'

'You should know.'

'Is that a threat, Gerald?'

'Just a fact.' He took a last drag on his cigarette and pressed it out in the ashtray between them. 'Death is my job.'

'I thought it was life,' said Hard.

'Depends how you look at it,' said Doctor Ahlers and took his leave, dragging a cloud of 4711 cologne in his wake.

'Bit of an odd one,' said Klaus once the door had closed behind the country doctor.

'It's a miracle he even survived that train accident back then.' Günter took a gulp of his beer.

'Maybe he didn't.'

'He doesn't look exactly healthy.'

'I never thought he was quite right, even before,' said Hard.

'Isn't he your GP?' asked Klaus.

'He is, but just because he wears a white coat doesn't mean I trust him. I haven't been to see him for years. I help myself. Birgit was there the other day, though. Her whole left side was swollen, covered in bruises, just like that. And do you think he found anything? Nix. Just said it was her nerves. She could hardly see for three days.'

'He always finds something with me,' said Günter.

'I bet he does,' said Hard.

And Klaus said, 'If you're so fed up with him, go somewhere else.'

'How can we? They're our neighbours, they're good customers. Eiske is, anyway. She comes into the shop all the time. And we can use every mark right now—thanks to you.'

'Listen, Hard, how often do I have to say it? I had to change the merchandise range. If I hadn't added grooming products, my customers would have left in droves. The competition never sleeps. I don't know why you're always going on about it—they're all brands you don't even offer. I'm not treading on your toes.'

'And where else would we go?' asked Hard, not responding to what Klaus had said. 'You don't go to the Reicherts, do you?'

The other two shook their heads.

'I'd have been surprised if you'd let the Compunists get their hands on you. Who knows what they'd prescribe.'

'Whatever it is,' said Enno Kröger, who had been listening in and now put Hard's beer down for him, 'there's bound to be more in it than in this stuff here.'

Hard raised his glass. 'To the Necessary Three.'

'To the Necessary Three,' said Klaus and Günter as if from a single mouth.

Then they clinked glasses.

After a week, Daniel decided to do something about it. It was a Thursday, after midnight, and his parents and the twins were all in bed. He had been lying in bed as well, fully dressed. His mother had come into his room one last time to check on him. As soon as all the sounds in the house had died down he put on his parka and crept down the stairs to the basement in his stockinged feet, clutching his shoes. He took a tub of latex paint and a brush out with him; he and his father had recently painted the kitchen. He left the basement via the entrance next to the garage. The streets were dark, the lamps switched off hours ago. Only the *S* on the savings bank and the *A* for Apotheke on the pharmacy lit up the night. He passed by the vacant houses, the concrete pillars of the bridges and the bus stops, covering over the swastikas and letters with white paint. Suddenly it was light. Two spotlights were trained on him like rifles on a man sentenced to death. A police-man stepped up, and a second came towards him out of the dark on the other side and cut off his escape route.

'Aha,' said one of them, whom Daniel recognized, now that he was in the spotlight, as Kurt Rhauderwiek. 'Now we've caught you at last.' And the other one, a very young man, four or five years older than Daniel, said, 'The repentant criminal always returns to the scene of the crime. Because he wants to take back what he did. Won't work, though. Never does. It's to do with time. What's done is done.'

Daniel couldn't think of his name but he recognized the face instantly. Then he remembered everything, the run-in at school, the grip on the back of his neck, the boy trying to force him to lick Iron's shoes, back then, that day of the snow, when he lay naked in the maize field and a shadow descended over him.

Daniel let them arrest him with no resistance. They hand-cuffed him anyway, 'for his own safety,' as they said, to protect him from himself. As they put him in the car he saw Iron on the

493

other side of the road. His motorbike. His leather biker suit. His glasses.

Later, during the interrogation in the county town, in a white, windowless room, he found out that someone had seen him and informed the police. The officer, a plain-clothes man, wanted to know why he'd done it.

Daniel explained it to him.

'That's the first I've heard of it.' He flicked through a file. 'There's nothing here about symbols. And no one's filed a report.' He put his right forefinger on the paper and reached out to the intercom with the other hand. 'Mrs Freese?'

'Yes?'

'Send me in that,' he looked at the sheet of paper in front of him, 'Tebbens, Frank Tebbens.'

'Right away, Mr Saathoff.'

Saathoff let go of the button and looked at Daniel. Then he stood up, walked around the table and leant over him from behind, his hands on the back of the seat.

'I've got a boy your age. Henning. I know what it's like when you're young and you want to try things out and you get up to all sorts of nonsense because you can't anticipate the consequences. I understand that. Henning got up to no good once, he stole when he was five, not much and nothing valuable, a model jet, plastic, Made in China, all one piece, very rough, but still: theft. And even though he was underage I still reported it to the police. I wanted him to feel the consequences, to understand'—there was a knock at the door, and Saathoff called out, 'Come in!'

The young police officer who had arrested Daniel entered the room, his cap jammed beneath his arm. 'You wanted to speak to me?'

Saathoff righted himself and tapped Daniel on the shoulder. 'This lad here says there were things painted around the village. Is that true?'

Frank Tebbens nodded. 'Graffitis. Zigzags and lines.' He traced them out in mid-air.

'What kind of zigzags and lines?'

'Some kind of message.'

'What message?'

'Hard to make out.'

That same night, his parents picked him up in the new car, a gold Audi 100 C4, 1990 model, 101 PS, 74 kW. His father and mother at the front, Daniel at the back. His mother said nothing, fighting back tears.

'Why must you always make us worry like this?' asked his father. 'Couldn't you just have let it be? What good has it done you now?'

Daniel leant his head against the window, cooling his cheek and staring out through the glass. In the east, behind the dyke, the sun was rising. He thought, The birds will start soon.

As they drove through the village he saw what he'd done.

His father saw it too, pointed at the white patches on the walls, at the white shadows on Daniel's soul, and said, 'Your behaviour is bad for business.' He was shouting.

His mother was crying now.

That enraged his father even more. 'They'll come at me tomorrow, at me and the whole family. Kuper. That name used to stand for something. For quality! For service! For cleanliness and purity! And now? You've dragged our family's name into the dirt. As if it wasn't hard enough already to stand up to the chains, spreading out their branches across the countryside like carbuncles on a face. Only six months ago they opened up a branch of Schlecker in Achterup and made the drugstore there go bust. Hamann Drugstore! A traditional company! One like mine! In the family for ninety years! Ruined in nine weeks! And now this!' He pointed out of the window again at one of the white patches.

Daniel thought, I'm whitewashing my father's house.

At the next cards night at the Beach Hotel, Hard said, 'Looks bad for you,' as he noted down numbers in a notepad, Günter's latest defeat. 'Looks like you'll be getting a round in later.'

'Unless,' Klaus said, 'unless his hand gets better.'

'I'm just out of luck today.' Günter pulled the cards over to him and shuffled them several times by picking up a pile and putting them down in a different place, in front or behind, so quickly that no one could follow his movements, not even him.

'Anything's possible with skat,' said Klaus.

'If you've got bad cards there's pretty much nix you can do.'

Günter let Klaus cut the pack, dealt three cards to all of them and put two down in the middle of the table. Then he dealt another round of four, and then another three.

Hard picked up his hand. Ace of hearts, ten of hearts, king of hearts, queen of hearts, nine of hearts, eight of hearts, seven of hearts, ace of spades, ten of spades, seven of spades. 'Well, ladies, you might as well give up right now.'

'You haven't got anything,' said Günter. 'You're just bluffing.'

'He's always bluffing,' said Klaus.

'Cheer up, ladies. There'll be better days ahead. At least we don't have to go to war after all, eh, Günter?' He patted him on the back. 'You're in luck, mate.'

'You mean to the Gulf, because of Saddam?' asked Klaus. 'We wouldn't have had to anyway.'

'Would have been better though,' said Hard. 'What's the army there for anyway? All these manoeuvres won't get us anywhere. We need a proper emergency now and then. It's like if HSV only ever practiced and never played a match.'

'Did you see the thing against Bochum earlier, how Eck got it in the back of the net? Bloomin' Eck. Boy oh boy, if they beat Werder as well next week they might manage it this season after all.'

'I'd be careful if I was you,' said Günter.

'About what?' asked Klaus.

'About statements like that.'

'Why?'

'Because you'll only be disappointed in the end.'

'Look who's talking.'

'You start blubbing right at the beginning,' said Hard. 'Before it even gets going, you're always painting the devil on the wall.'

'You mean,' said Günter, arranging his cards—four jacks, ace of clubs, ten of clubs, queen of clubs, nine of clubs, eight of clubs, seven of clubs—'like your son?'

Klaus said, 'Eighteen.'

And Hard said, 'Yes.'

'Twenty.'

'Yes.'

'Two.'

'Yes.'

'Zero.'

'Yes.'

'Out.'

Günter said, 'Twenty-four,' and Hard went along up to 'Fifty' and then he said, 'Out.' Günter picked up the skat pile in the middle, put down two cards face down and said, 'Grand.'

'With grand you play aces,' said Hard, confident of victory, and slammed his ace of spades on the table, 'or you shut your faces,' but Günter outplayed him with a jack and then played an ace of clubs, which meant Klaus and Hard had to give up.

'Oh, kiss my arse,' said Klaus.

And Hard said, 'What's this: black-red, black-red, black-red—white?'

Günter gathered up the cards, tapped them together on the table and pushed the deck over to Hard to deal the next round. Klaus ordered a new beer for all of them by raising a hand in response to a glance from Kröger. While Hard was noting down his own first defeat—which was to be followed by many more that evening—the other two kept murmuring, 'Black-red, black-red, black-red, white,' not coming any closer to solving the riddle. Hard drank one last gulp and began shuffling the cards, smacking his lips at the taste. He might have lost the game but he didn't want to give them the added satisfaction of winning the conversation.

'The old Reich flag?' asked Günter.

'Coal briquettes,' said Klaus. 'You buy them black, you use them red, they go white.'

'Nope,' said Hard. 'A nigger masturbating.'

Shortly before the Easter holidays Daniel was told that the police wouldn't press charges if he was willing to repair the damage he'd caused of his own accord. His father thrust an old rag and a canister of cellulose thinner into his hands. It wasn't the first time. Once, a few months ago, someone had sprayed *I love you* on the front wall next to the shop window, and he'd had to scrub it off.

Nothing but *I love you*. He didn't know who'd written it and whether they meant him. He'd still had to scrub it off, though. No one had admitted to *I love you* and his eyes and hands had stung afterwards as if he'd held them too close to a fire for too long. Now he put on special gloves made of butyl rubber and walked from wall to wall. The twins followed him, like gnats, like dogs. He sent them away over and over, and over and over they came back.

Little by little, a crowd gathered around him. They watched him getting rid of the patches. Some of them cheered him on. Others gave him advice on the best scrubbing technique. He took no notice, soaked the rag in cellulose thinner and scrubbed across the paint evenly from top to bottom. His father brought new rags. It took Daniel hours to deal with each patch. He didn't manage it all in one day.

The next morning—the school holidays had started—the crowd of onlookers was larger than the day before. His old and new classmates had come along as well to take part in the spectacle. Rainer and Marcel cruised close behind him on their Vespas. Stefan followed them on his bike. Paul and Jens stood to one side, their arms folded across their chests, spitting on the ground every few minutes. Simone wanted to help him but her parents stopped her. Volker smoked and ate the liverwurst sandwiches he'd brought along, one after every cigarette. That was how it went from morning to evening. To Daniel, it felt like a procession.

On the third and last day almost everyone came together, almost the entire village. His father, his mother, their neighbours and acquaintances. The teachers Werner Pfeiffer, Jürgen Engberts, Dieter Kamps and Arne and Petra Mengs with their daughters Verena and Venja, Klaus Neemann and Günter Vehndel with their families, Heiner Oltmanns, Marco Klüver, Tobias Allen and Guido Groenewold, still wearing their dirty football shirts, Old Kramer with his employees, Schröder the cobbler, Onken the lawyer and Mrs Bluhm, Achim Kolthoff, the Hankens and the Tinnemeyers, Jost Petersen, Gerrit Klopp, Heiko Hessenius and Berger, his cue still in one hand, Kromminga the driving instructor, the Reicherts and the Hilligers, Krause the fishmonger and Postman Schmidt, Eino and Klaas Oltmanns the bicycle seller, the former cooperative dairy chairman Anton Leemhuis, bank director Hoyer, wearing a suit and tie even on his day off, Freerk-Ulf Dänekas from the savings bank, Uli Dettmers, his hair out of place from the wind, Captain Fechner, Susanne Haak and Tanja Mettjes with their parents and siblings, Stumpe from the drinks shop and Harm Fokken from the snack bar, Enno and Gerda Kröger from the Beach Hotel, Meta and Alwin Graalmann, Pastor Meinders and his wife, who came from church because it was Sunday, Schulz, the blacksmith and mayor, his son, the headmaster, a head taller, the farmers Appeldorn, Wübbena, Brechtezende, Harders and Watermann, Anne-Marie Kolthoff and Walter Baalmann, Hayo Hayenga from Club 69 with his girls, Abbo and Ubbo Busboom, Doctor Ahlers with his wife and children, Wilfried Ennen the pharmacist, Volker and Simone, and right at the front Mrs Nanninga, their new class teacher, Wiebke, Iron and Rosing and the three policemen, Kurt Rhauderwiek, Joachim Schepers and Frank Tebbens, with a young reporter from the *Frisian News* who introduced himself as Tammo Tammen and said he wanted to get an idea of the situation on the ground. They stepped out of the crowd together, as if they'd all been friends for years. Rosing had his coat and shirt unbuttoned. Daniel thought, Chest hair like a monkey.

Rosing said, as if to apologize for his presence: 'I just want to know if what they're saying is true. You see, I heard you painted over something else with the white paint, some kind of symbols. If that's the case, we ought to be able to see what's hidden under the white.'

Daniel got down to work, soaked the rag in cellulose thinner and scrubbed across the paint from top to bottom. White shadows that dissolved into nothingness in the light.

2

It was in mid-March, when Daniel began his work experience placement at the *Frisian News*, that the fog descended. It came with the rain, and to begin with many people thought it would go away with it as well, the way the morning mist went away as soon as the sun was high enough in the sky. But it didn't. It stayed suspended above the fields. Sometimes it was thicker, sometimes thinner, sometimes it barely reached above the stalks, sometimes two-storey farmhouses disappeared in it. For weeks, the grass from the village to the dyke was covered in a thin white layer like by the smoke from a peat fire which broke out in the moor south of Jericho every few years. The farmers had driven the cows out of the sheds to the meadows after the hard winter, and often there was no more to see of them than their heads, and the few bare trees protruded from the fog like signposts, their arrows pointing in all directions.

Hard took Daniel into town. He had polished the car to a shine only two days ago, and as they left the driveway now the sun was shining too, so brightly that they were dazzled by the reflection from the radiator hood. But they'd barely left Jericho behind them when they saw the clouds coming towards them from the sea, a wall of grey reaching from the earth up into the sky and swathing all the land in darkness. Hard could hardly believe his eyes; he'd never seen anything as large, and then he switched on the lights and held the steering wheel with both hands to stand up to the storm winds threatening to blow the car off the road. Bare branches flew over them, wilted leaves, a plastic bag. And then the first raindrops fell too, unusually large and hard, seeming to him like bullets from a spaceship. 'Good job you've got your seatbelt fastened,' said Hard as he switched on the windscreen wipers, 'then nothing can happen to you. This time they'll have to work a bit harder to take you with them.' It was supposed to be a joke, although he wasn't in the mood for jokes. He was afraid for the car's bodywork if the rain turned to hail. Once, seven years ago, hailstones the size of fists had made dents in the radiator hood, the fenders and the roof of his Opel Rekord, and in his attempt to repair the damage from inside with a rubber hammer he had ended up making them into lumps, so now he looked around for somewhere undercover, a carport, an open barn. But they were too far outside the village, nothing but fields and hedges on either side. With relief, he realized that the wind and rain weren't turning into weapons and the wax he'd applied was doing its work, and he hoped there'd one day be a similar thing for people, some kind of tablets to waterproof Daniel's confused soul and protect it from the forces of nature inside him.

On the B70, once they'd reached the refuse dump, he said, 'You should be glad you got out of it so unscathed. Onken said nix is allowed to happen now, though. You're still subject to juvenile law. It's all up to you, he said, it's up to you whether you want to mess up your future or not.' He looked over at his son.

Daniel rubbed the sleep out of his eyes. He'd been too excited to sleep much that night. He'd been looking forward to this day for weeks. Now he felt like he was underwater, like Dustin Hoffman in *The Graduate*—the words barely got through to him.

'Are you listening? Did you even understand what I've been saying?'

Rain slashed against the windscreen, was wiped away, a hare ran across the road ahead of them, slashed, vanished into the bushes, was wiped away, appeared again behind them, slashed, cowered in the grass, was wiped away. 'I said, did you understand?' his father repeated, louder than before.

Daniel nodded. He couldn't help remembering the day when they'd ambushed Peter Peters in the hammrich fields, and the day when he'd walked through the village to visit Stefan, Onno and Rainer. It had been raining cats and dogs both times, but not as much as it was now.

Hard went on talking. He'd thought everything out and he spoke of responsibility, decency, duties to society. 'You can't afford to behave like that at the newspaper. Anyone who makes speculations into facts is a bad journalist and has consequences to face, much more drastic consequences than scrubbing off scribbles. Don't you go thinking they'll let you write anything for them. You can forget that right away.' He tapped at the folder on Daniel's lap, the notepad with suggestions for stories. 'But they still have the accounts department, distribution, computer equipment and all the other stuff. What with that report today, that photo of you, I had trouble convincing Martin, the editor-in-chief, Masurczak, remember his name, on the phone earlier of you, of your honesty. We went to school together, Masurczak and me. I used to call him Mamasurczak because his father never came home from the war. But you'd better keep the Mamasurczak thing to yourself. Otherwise your career'll be over before it even gets started. You can't afford to make mistakes. They abbreviated Kuper and your face isn't recognizable, but of course everyone round here knows who they mean by Daniel K. and what you did. You've got a reputation.' He shook his head. 'Not really acceptable for a newspaper.

That's why I had to vouch for you personally. The only alternative would have been doing your work experience with me. In Kuper's Drugstore! In your father's business!' He broke off his speech and gripped at his chest, at the patch sewn onto his white coat, the writing *kuper's drugstore*. Then he said, 'There's nix more embarrassing than being apprenticed to your father, even if it's only for three weeks. No one knows that better than me. But I'll bet you didn't want to do work experience at a drugstore. And even if you did want it, I wouldn't have let you. I can't imagine you as a druggist, you see, not with the best will in the world. You'd be no good as a druggist. You don't have the necessary sensibility, the right temperament, the understanding of people. A druggist has to put himself in the customers' shoes, doesn't matter if they're housewives or bank clerks or farmers' wives, fat or thin, blonde or brunette, small or large pores. You have to have the right creams and perfumes in stock and the correct sanitary towels and tampons, nail and hair scissors, natural- and plastic-bristle brushes, massage belts, exfoliating sponges, pregnancy oils, absorbent pads, milk pumps, breastfeeding cushions, the whole range. You have to spot what a woman wants the moment she walks in the door. You have to read it in her eyes, in her figure, in her whole appearance, even before she opens her mouth. You have to divine her wishes and penetrate to her innermost core at a single glance. And I don't think you're capable of that. You can't expect that of any boy of your age, though. I mean, it takes years of experience with the opposite sex. I don't mind you making mistakes. Everyone makes mistakes. Mistakes are part of life. But I can't afford for you to make them in my shop. Because it'd fall straight back on me. If you interpret those first key seconds wrong, you've already lost. You can never make up for it, no matter how much you offer them afterwards or spray on their skin. Women have a feeling for whether a man understands them or not. They have a *sexth* sense.' Hard laughed, looked over at his son to see if he was joining in,

and when Daniel didn't laugh he looked ahead again. 'My customers are almost entirely female. There's no point in kidding
myself about that. And I don't kid myself! No women, no business. If I didn't sell film and cameras and angling supplies, not
one man would ever set foot in my shop, not for white spirits or
insecticides, to say nothing of aftershave and condoms.'

Daniel stared straight ahead. His father's words slashed
against his head. 'And no one gets photos developed either any
more. Apart from Old Kramer of course,' were wiped away, 'only
passport photos at most!' slashed, 'Once every ten years!' were
wiped away, 'Every ten years!' slashed, 'I mean, imagine it! How's
anyone supposed to make a living out of it? I can't make a living
out of it, or not for much longer anyway.'

His father talked and talked. He kept gripping at his chest as
he spoke. Daniel hoped they'd be there soon. But they were
making slow progress because of the weather and the animals
crossing the road at that time of year. As soon as the temperatures
rose above freezing and the rubbish heap thawed, rats, hares,
hedgehogs, stray cats and dogs, attracted by the scents and
vapours, came out of their holes, out of their hiding places, ran
across the fields, slipped beneath fences and waited at the edge of
the road in the bushes for the right moment.

'Can't you drive a bit faster?' asked Daniel. 'It's a hundred
kilometres an hour here.'

'That doesn't mean you have to drive a hundred.'

'You're not even doing fifty.'

'Have you looked outside?'

'Yeah, but we're late.'

'And whose fault is that?'

'Mine.'

'Exactly. And what does coming late make?'

'A bad impression.'

'Exactly right.'

'And who,' Daniel asked, repeating one of his father's sayings, 'does that fall back on?'

Hard accelerated involuntarily, put his hand on the gearstick and switched to fourth and then fifth gear. The rain slashed harder and harder against the windscreen. The wipers flapped to and fro at the highest speed, the fan was rotating at full power, and still there was barely anything to be seen outside apart from the white lines of the lane markings and the reflection of the headlights. Hard leant over the steering wheel to get a better view and suddenly, from one second to the next, the rain stopped and started again, and he saw the hare transfixed by the light, and he heard the high, dull thud as if from a shot.

In the car park outside the newspaper building—the rain had turned into drizzle—he inspected the damage. He circled the car twice over. He stopped in front of the radiator, ran his hand along the bumper, leant over to the tyres and found nothing.

'Something happened?' a man asked out of an orange and brown striped van, a Mercedes MB 100, 1990 model, 72 PS, 53 kW, with the words *Johann Rosing* on one side in large white letters.

'Everything's fine,' said Hard, sticking out a thumb. Then he patted Daniel on the shoulder; he wanted to say something else, something important, something fatherly, and he said, 'See you later,' and got back in the car.

The glass doors slid aside and Daniel walked into the entrance hall. There were cables dangling from the ceiling, several of the grainy white panels above him had been pushed open, the floor was covered in newspaper sheets and there was a smell of fresh paint. A woman was sitting behind a counter that took up almost the entire room. She was filing her nails. On one wall opposite her, two men in blue dungarees were busy mounting new electrical sockets, while two others, standing on a ladder above them, were filling in drill holes. The doors on either side of the hall were open. Daniel could see men and women sitting around tables, their hands behind their heads or folded as if in prayer or gesticulating wildly. A tangle of voices buzzed around him, seeming to come from every direction, as if words flew through the air here, at their source, until they were captured on paper and sent out to the world. He looked at his digital watch: ten past ten. The time for writing had not yet come. He shivered.

'What's up with you?' called the woman from the reception desk. 'You coming in or out?'

The builders stopped working and looked at him. It was only then he noticed the automatic doors constantly opening and closing behind him, because he was still standing too close to them.

He took a step towards the desk.

The doors closed.

The builders went back to work.

The woman put her nail file down.

'I've come for, er, I've come for my work experience.'

The woman picked up the telephone and said into it that the boy had arrived now. A white-haired, white-bearded man came down the stairs and introduced himself, his right hand outstretched, as Mr Sievers, his work-experience supervisor. While he was showing Daniel around and explaining where the different departments were, he said, 'Daniel Kuper, boy oh boy. I've heard a lot about you this morning.'

'Heard what?'

'You're a bit of a celebrity now,' said Mr Sievers. '*Jericho cleaned up again. Boy cleans walls, mayoral candidate Rosing congratulates.* Oh yeah, he's good at that. But he was the one that started it, with his slogans, all that less Europe, more East Frisia. Mrs Wiemers told me all about it, boy oh boy.' He patted Daniel on the back. 'Who dares to stand up to a powerful man like Rosing? Rosing the man of vision, the construction king, the advertising customer! There'll be no help from them up there.' He pointed at the neon strip lights. 'They're in his pocket—they eat out of his hand. Rosing's a shining light for them. But I won't let him and his promises blind me. Not me! Can you smell that? Smell that stink! I can't stand it! I've been a card-carrying Social Democrat for thirty years,' he counted off on his fingers, 'in the trade union for ten and on the works council for three. I know the contracts, the working conditions, all the tricks, guys like him. I could tell you stories, dozens of stories, you wouldn't believe your ears. Better not, though, you'd only lose faith in whatever you believe in. And if you don't believe in anything, all the better. These fumes are making me all woozy, boy oh boy. Is this supposed to be paint?' He ran his hand along a freshly painted wall but not hard enough that anything came off on his fingers. 'It's poison, that is, pure poison. Just keep it up! Make it all new! Lovely and shiny! A brand new building! A whole new look! Don't make me laugh. Oh yes, they're good at that, painting over scandal. Rosing's going to knock us all off. But that doesn't interest the lords and masters upstairs. All they care about is filling the pages, best of all with adverts.' He dabbed the sweat off his forehead with a handkerchief. For a moment he gave Daniel a confused look, as if he couldn't believe he was talking to a young boy about the depths to which local journalism would sink. Then he put the handkerchief away and took a paper box out of the inside pocket of his suit. He pushed out the plastic packing, popped a couple of pills onto his hand and threw them in his mouth. 'I shouldn't have started on the subject,' he said once he'd swallowed them, but as they went on down a flight of stairs he still couldn't stop talking about it.

At the bottom of the stairs, in the middle of a long corridor full of junk, Mr Sievers opened a fireproof door bearing the legend *Office for Beginners*. 'Right, here we are.'

The office looked like a storage closet. The shelves were piled high with yellowed newspapers, dusty expired typewriters and shabby books, address directories, encyclopedias and dictionaries, deposited any which way. In the middle of the room were two chairs and a television cabinet. Mr Sievers pressed the buttons on the remote control until the screen went blue. He dimmed the light and promised to collect Daniel when he'd watched the film, a documentary about the newspaper's history. The video recorder switched off automatically after ninety minutes. Daniel sat in the semi-darkness for a while longer, staring at the flickering screen, and then got up and went to the door. He looked left and right along the corridor—no sign of Mr Sievers. There was no sign of anyone. At the reception desk, he found out Mr Sievers had gone home. 'He wasn't feeling well,' said the woman behind the counter, rolling her eyes. 'He had another one of his turns.'

'What kind of turns?'

She waved a hand. 'Nothing serious, don't you worry. It's not unusual for him. They say it happens twice a year. And he usually takes two or three weeks off every time. So you might not see him here again. You can do your work experience without a supervisor, though. Without a supervisor is better, actually. Then you learn to work independently quicker.'

They put Daniel in Accounts. The office also smelt of fresh paint, there was masking tape still hanging from the window frame, and the floor in front of it was covered in old newspaper. Two women, Mrs Geuken and Mrs Wiemers as he gathered from the sign outside the door, both in their late fifties, were sitting at two desks pushed together. They turned around to him simultaneously when he knocked and introduced himself.

'He looks just like Bernhard,' said one of them, turning around to the other. 'Don't you think so, Theda?'

'The splitting image,' said Theda. 'Except younger, much younger. Not as worn out.'

'Maybe it is him. Maybe he just wants to give us a demonstration of how young all his anti-wrinkle creams really make you look. Come over here, Bernhard, come and sit with me.'

'Nix,' said Theda and pulled up a chair. 'Hard's all mine. I want to be the first to find out the secret of eternal youth.'

Daniel sat down next to her and she introduced him to accounting. She explained the filing system and asked him to punch holes in the receipts piled up in the pigeon holes on the shelves behind them, and put them into ring-binders. He made messy pile after pile of papers in front of him, punched two holes in one side of the sheets and snapped the binders open and closed. There was no sign of the hectic atmosphere of the entrance hall here in this room; the slatted fronts of the cabinets radiated an air of absolute calm, they could conceal everything and anything, profit and loss, assets and liabilities, the secrets of a company. You just had to know how to read the numbers. But he didn't know. And he didn't want to know either. But still, he toed the line, for the women's sake and because he hoped he'd be moved on to the editorial office after all if he proved himself. After a while—Daniel was absolutely absorbed in his task—the other woman said, 'If only it was true.'

'What?' asked Theda, not looking up.

'If we could stay young.'

'Oh, Irmi, don't start that again. We all get older. That's life.'

511

'Yes,' said Mrs Geuken. 'I know that, but it'd still be nice if we could live on in our children.'

'Part of us does, though.'

'Yes,' said Mrs Geuken. 'But not always the best part.'

At lunchtime Daniel sat on his own in the cafeteria, up on the fifth floor, directly beneath the roof. The large windows gave a good view far across the land, all the way to the horizon, but now that the fog was covering the hammrich and only a few trees and houses, high-voltage pylons and navy radio masts rose above it, there wasn't much to see other than a billowing white surface. Daniel spent a long time looking at the panorama. He got up every few minutes and exchanged one tray for another, a starter for a main course, the main course for a dessert, and returned to his table. The coffee tasted better than the coffee at school and the minced pork roll did too. He didn't go back to his desk until three. The old newspapers on the floor and the masking tape on the window had disappeared. But shortly before the end of the day, a man with white stains on blue dungarees from Benzen Painting and Decorating came in and checked. 'All nice and dry,' he said, 'at least in here,' and he began putting the flowerpots back on the windowsill.

At four o'clock one of the women, Theda Wiemers, offered to drive Daniel home, and she called up his father to inform him that she'd be taking care of his son during his work experience, if he didn't mind.

Daniel wrote his daily report that evening: *Filling in a remittance order. Comparing invoices. Filing manuscripts.* Two days later he was moved on to Advertisements. *Sorting advertisements. Measuring sizes. Completing database.* The day after that he moved on to Distribution. *Addressing envelopes and sending pay cheques to delivery employees. Receiving and documenting complaints.* All these things took him three or four hours, and it was a while before he noticed that he ended up sitting around doing nothing if he finished them too quickly. Then they'd send him back to Advertisements or Accounts, depending on where they could make use of him.

Wilfried Ennen, the pharmacist, was sitting at the piano, bashing out a tune with one hand while the other men gathered around him in a semi-circle and inserted sweets into their mouths. Some of them were missing; they had cancelled over the telephone, mentioned headaches, coughs and hoarse throats, wanting to disguise the fact that their wives and children wouldn't let them go. He was subject to the same power, the power of the family, but he was the choir director so he had to turn up to rehearsals, no matter how he was feeling, no matter what state his marriage was in.

He played the first few bars of 'Winter Won't Last Much Longer', a children's song he had recently arranged for four vocal parts and now played to warm the men up, to loosen their tongues. Every choir practice needed a kind of prelude, nothing happened of its own accord, and sometimes he felt he started over at zero every Thursday. He thought of the embroidered motto, *Singing means understanding*, on the wall of his music room above his desk, a present from his wife on the occasion of the German Choral Association's annual festival in Hamburg in 1983, and of the fact that the motto didn't apply to the Jericho Male Voice Choir, or to people in general. If singing really did lead to greater understanding, to improved ability to grasp and remember, they wouldn't have to keep repeating everything all the time.

He greeted every man with a nod and waved his free hand at the chairs he had set up for them here in the large hall of the Beach Hotel. The first tenor section at the front left, behind them the second, next to them the first bass section and the second at the front right, the foundation of the movement, seven strong men, but none of them as good as Klaus Neemann. He might not be the best businessman—four of the supermarkets he'd opened up all around the county had just closed down again—but he certainly earned his nickname of Superneemann in the choir. Apart from that he was always on time, unlike some of the others, although Wilfried Ennen felt that was only to be expected of a chairman. He had to be more than a basic member of the association and set a good example, even if no one followed him. And so Klaus was sitting in front of him drinking a beer, and he wished he had a beer of his own on top of the piano so he could toast him. He never drank before rehearsals and never very much afterwards, not because he was scared of losing control, but because he didn't want to get too pally with the others. His was an honorary position, and he regarded it as an honour and feared he'd lose the men's respect if he ever gave them a chance to ridicule him. He had good reason. Old Kramer, who had founded the choir after the war, was so hard of hearing that he regularly missed his cue when they sang a circular canon and got nudged from all around, not that that stopped him from simply carrying on singing. And Günter Vehndel came up to him after every performance to ask how he'd done. 'How was I, Willy? I had this really bad scratching in my throat. That's what I get for smoking. Your vocal chords are like your brain cells, right, once they're gone they're gone, is that right? You ought to know, you're a pill-maker.' He always thought he'd been singing out of tune, and he was often enough right about that, but if a choir director were to judge everyone by their wrong notes there wouldn't be more than a handful of men here, the youngest, and many of them were already around fifty, Johann Rosing, Klaus Neemann, Anton Leemhuis and Bernhard Kuper—an excellent soloist who didn't need sheet music or a conductor and could thrill the audience merely with the power of his voice and his performance. He didn't even need a choir behind him; give him two or three beers and he'd climb on a table at birthday parties or weddings and steal the show from the hosts. As usual he was the last to arrive, and as usual he was wearing a white coat as if he'd just dashed over from the drugstore. Wilfried Ennen knew why he did that, everyone knew—he wanted to show them he was on the same level as the choir director and knew just as much about medications as a doctor or a pharmacist. 'We can get started at last, then.'

'I had a customer,' said Hard, hung his coat up and took his seat in the front row.

'A female one, no doubt,' said Klaus.

Wilfried Ennen ignored the laughter and counted in, 'Two, three, four—and!'

And they all sat up straight on their chairs and sang at the tops of their voices, 'Winter won't last much longer, soon the sun will shine, then spring will come upon us with all its songs so fine. The larks sing in the hedges, the cuckoos in the wood: cuckoo, cuckoo, the sunshine does us good!'

'Yes, thank you, and now the tenors.'

'Do we have to sing this?' asked Hard.

'You don't have to do anything,' said Wilfried Ennen. He knew how much the men hated singing songs like this one, where they imitated animal calls, but there were worse ones in their repertoire that asked nothing more of them than repeating childish words, 'Bella Bimba', 'Diridonda' and all the other *hey nonny-nonnies* and *la la las*.

'So why are we singing it?'

'Because it's spring.'

'You call that spring?' Hard pointed out of the window at the moonlit fog.

'That'll soon pass. Right, from the beginning.' He played the first few bars on the piano again, and the voices raised before him on his command. He mustn't allow fundamental discussions, there wasn't time for that, and apart from that they expected him to make decisions, even though he'd upset singers that way in the past. Once, a few years ago, he had chosen 'Kalinka' for the men to sing and Old Kramer, who had fought in Russia, had left the choir, but not without encouraging the retailers in his retinue to leave along with him, and he had only come back on condition that they didn't have to sing any more 'Russki songs', as he put it. Now there were even fewer members than back then, and it was all too possible that Günter Vehndel and Klaus Neemann wouldn't come back either if Bernhard Kuper followed Kramer's example, and then he could scratch one vocal part entirely and cancel the Easter concerts in the church, and that would be the end to all of it. 'Yes, thank you. That'll do for now, we'll practice again another time when everyone's here.'

'When will that be?' asked Hard.

'Next week.'

'The dead won't rise from their graves.'

'Who knows? Jesus did. And it's Easter in ten days,' said Wilfried Ennen as he handed out sheet music. 'Meinders asked me to perform "Holy is the Lord" on Good Friday, and I've—'

'Isn't that Catholic?' Hard interrupted. 'I mean, isn't that part of the Holy Mass?'

'—complied with . . . What? Yes,' said Wilfried Ennen. 'Yes, it is.'

'But we're not Catholics. And neither is Meinders.'

'No, the Lord knows he isn't.'

'So why are we singing it then?'

'Because it's Easter,' said Wilfried Ennen, who'd had enough of justifying every song, 'and he asked me for it, for whatever reason.' And then he hit the keys and called upon the voices, and the men lowered their heads. 'Don't look at the music before we've even sung a note—and!'

And then they sang, pious and swaying: 'Holy, holy, holy, holy is the Lord, Holy, holy, holy, holy only He. He who never began, He who always was, always is and forever more, always will be Lord. Lasting, lasting, lasting, lasting is his Word, Wisely, wisely, wisely, wisely heed his deeds.'—'Yes, thank you,' said Wilfried Ennen, 'it's not quite right yet. We'll have to have a quick run through it separately. The melody's clear, Franz Schubert,' he played the opening on the piano again, 'first tenors—and!' After four verses he called on the second tenors, then the first and the second bass sections. 'We won't sing loud where it says *fortissimo*. We're starting very quietly, as quietly as we can, and then *mezzo-forte*. It's best if we all stand up—and!' And they did, apart from him, and they sang the Sanctus together.

He was using both hands for the piano now and watching them over the edge of it. The way they were standing there, in their sweaters and shirts, in their everyday clothing, they had no shine to them, just two dozen men who had come together to sing. But as soon as they put on their suits and fastened their ties and stood in the gallery at the church with the coat of arms on their chests, they'd make a powerful impression. Then their wives would look up to them again and discover something about them that they thought they'd lost. And perhaps, Wilfried Ennen thought now, that was what the motto in his music room meant: Singing means understanding that there is more to them, more than they think, that together they can rise above their everyday lives.

517

On Friday, Daniel went to a party. Jens' father had inherited his parents' farmhouse in Drömeln years ago, refurbished it on his own and put in two holiday apartments at the front. The Hankens rented out the barn for family celebrations. When there were no bookings—and there were never any bookings out of season—they let the 'children', as they still called their grown-up sons to friends and relatives, hold parties there. So the children partied every weekend, drank alcohol, smoked, danced and made out with girls. The house was off the beaten track. The parents never came by. The basslines boomed out across the land, audible for miles.

As he locked up his racing bike Daniel remembered his first day at intermediate school, standing in the classroom and asking Volker if the seat next to him was free, going over to Paul and Jens and asking the same, the class teacher Mrs Nanninga coming in and wanting to know why he wasn't sitting down when there were so many seats free. He knew some of them from primary school but they kept on looking at him like a stranger and bunching together as soon as he went near them. He had long since started regretting leaving grammar school. If he'd repeated the school year he'd be one of the oldest in the class now. But then he'd also have had Herlyn again, for Latin and German, and he'd have had to go through everything all over again, the metal box, the speech, the Latin texts, the German poems, twelve months of déjà vu, twelve months caught in a time loop, in a slightly shifted and yet strangely familiar world without Stefan, Onno and Rainer—and without Peter Peters. And while he was thinking about that he realized how little his actual life differed from the one he was imagining; in both versions, he was alone on his own two feet and confronted with his past whenever the opportunity arose.

Every time Daniel went to one of Jens' parties he had to pay an entrance fee. Paul and Jens and a few others from Year Ten sat at a table next to the entrance. They inspected the guests and decided who was allowed in, under which conditions.

'What do you see out there?' asked Paul, tugging at his strand of hair.

Jens looked at his watch, 'Tick tock, tick tock, tick tock.'

'Not a lot.'

'And what does that remind you of?'

'Tick tock, tick tock, tick tock.'

Daniel shrugged.

'What film?'

Daniel shrugged his shoulders again.

'Tick tock, tick tock, tick tock.'

'I'll give you a clue: John Carpenter.'

Jens imitated a siren.

'OK,' said Paul, 'that's it, we tried, didn't we?'

'Yes, siree.'

They poured a glass full of vodka for Daniel, put it down in front of him with the words 'Down in one,' waited until he'd emptied it, and laughed because they knew from experience what would soon happen to him. I'llgetthebutcher'sknifeoutandram itintoJens'chestpullitoutandramitinagainticktockticktocktick tockthebastard'sgurglingandgaspingandsmackinghislipsatevery stablistentothiseveryonetheperfectsymphonyredbubblescoming outeverywhereoutofeveryholeevenbubblingoutofhiseyesand thenhecollapsessostrangelybackwardssosurprisedyessireeand Paul'sjuststandingtherestaringasifhe'dseenaghostorwhateverand thenslaphe'sgotthebladeinhisthroatbutitwon'tgothroughitgets stuckinthemiddlethebloodybladestuckinthemiddleofhisthroat bloodshootinginmyfacebutI. One fantasy broke off and was superimposed by another. They patted him on the back, pressed cherry liqueur into his hand, corn schnapps, Kruiden, and forced him to write stuff he'd have forgotten the next day: *The Manifesto of Trash.*

Daniel cycled home an hour later. On the way he kept getting off his bike to vomit in front gardens. By the time he was finally in bed and the walls were revolving around him he felt absolutely void, without a past and without a future. The next day he kept it up for longer. He had followed Volker's advice and eaten a big meal to line his stomach beforehand. Now he was stumbling from room to room. They were standing around beneath him, and above him on the gallery they were lying in the beds and smoking a new kind of grass imported from Holland, which was so strong, as Paul and Jens never grew tired of saying, that a couple of milligrams were enough to lose your mind. Daniel had kept his distance so far. Alcohol was enough for him. But once, he'd been upstairs and tried it on with one of the girls. He didn't know her name. He'd never seen her before. She wasn't from Jericho or from Drömeln and she didn't go to the intermediate school or the grammar school either. Long brown hair, natural look, dark eyes, no necklace, no earrings, no make-up, a girl from another planet. He had sat down next to her and talked to her, but she obviously didn't feel like talking, or she didn't understand his language. She hadn't said a word all along, only watched his lips. At some point she simply fell backwards, and a boy sitting there, Ubbo Busboom from Year Ten, started kissing her and stroking her breasts. Then he pushed up her T-shirt and she let him get on with it.

Daniel stood up and leant against the bannister, a can of beer in his hand. He couldn't remember where he'd got it from, if it was new or old and he just hadn't drunk out of it yet. He took a sip and then another and another and another. Downstairs they were dancing to music he wouldn't even listen to on the radio. Jens was standing by the CD player, one hand on the headphones pushed over one ear, the other hand in the CD box, shaking his head as soon as anyone leant over and talked to him. Paul was walking through the crowd, a crate of Karlsquell beer on one shoulder. Volker was holding a bag of crisps right over his mouth so that the content landed directly in his gullet.

When he turned around Daniel saw that the beds had new occupants, except for the girl he'd been talking to and Ubbo Busboom, but they were both asleep, closely entangled as if they'd been a couple for ages. He recognized Simone in the pulsing light of the lava lamps. She was squatting on the floor-boards, her feet turned inwards, her arms clutching her knees, and her head drooped forward and flipped up again every few seconds. The orange that illuminated her made her face seem less bony, less rectangular. Her skin took on something gentle and soft, something precious, and Daniel caught himself touching it, whereupon she pressed herself against him so greedily that they both tipped over sideways. Her tongue ran over his tongue, his lips, his teeth, and her hand went between his legs. She said something he couldn't understand at first, a word that sounded like 'yes,'—'yes,' 'yes,' 'yes,' as if telling him to do the same. And he did. And she opened her eyes, pushed him away and stumbled to the staircase. Later he saw her next to the stereo, sucking on Jens' swollen, blue upper lip. Even later, outside in the field, leaning retching over a fence and surrounded by billowing fog.

The next day his brother and sister woke him for lunch, ran into his room and dragged him, still in his pyjamas, to the kitchen.

His mother clapped a hand to her mouth and took it away again. 'What do you look like? Were you drinking last night? Or were you out on your wanderings again?'

Daniel shook his head. Once, two months previously, he had got up at night and gone into the living room, and his mother had found him there the next morning, lying on the sofa with the TV on, and he couldn't explain to himself or to her how he'd got there.

'That was an either-or question.'

'Neither nor.'

'Where will it all end?' she asked as she put potatoes, peas and half a roast chicken on the table. 'There'll be trouble if your father finds out. Hard,' she called out to the corridor. 'Lunch is ready!'

'If I find out what?' asked his father, standing in the doorway.

'Well,' said his mother, 'you don't look much better either. The two of you might as well go out together next time, then you can look out for each other.'

'You must be kidding,' said his father and wiped the sweat from his forehead. 'He's as bad as you, can't take his drink.' He pulled out a chair and sat down next to Daniel. 'Did you go out on one of your walks? . . . Or did you drink too much again? . . . I don't get it . . . Why do you always drink more than you can hold? . . . It's obvious it'll only come out at the top again.'

'Hard, please.'

'What?'

'We're eating.'

'So?'

'Right,' said his mother, 'you get started.'

The twins loaded up their plates, but they didn't touch anything other than the chicken legs, dusted in a thick coating of Fondor spice powder. 'Don't you notice . . . when you've had enough? . . . Don't you know . . . your own limits? . . . Or are you . . . unhappy . . . with school . . . your work experience . . . with yourself?'

Daniel had expected his father to lose his temper when he saw him this way, but now he was just sitting there and pausing for breath after every second or third word, as if he had to gather up his strength to finish the sentence.

'Aren't you feeling well?' his mother asked his father.

'I'm fine.' He raised his fork, as if as a sign that he still had the strength to deal with Daniel. 'But let me tell you . . . sonny boy . . . next time . . . you come down . . . to lunch decent . . . not in your pyjamas . . . that's the least . . . we can expect.'

'Eat it down now,' said his mother. 'Or it'll go cold.'

'Up,' said Daniel.

'What?' said his father.

'Nothing.'

His mother said grace and they all wished one another a good appetite.

Daniel held his head in his hands and pushed the plate away. He didn't know when and how and whether he'd even got home. Once, on the way back from a party a few weeks ago, he'd got his front wheel caught in the track on the level crossing on Hoogstraat and had a fall. He'd stood in his parents' room in the middle of the night with a grazed shoulder and a bleeding hand.

'Daniel, what's the matter?'

'Got pushed off my bike.'

'What? Who was it?'

'Don't know, didn't see them.'

His mother turned the light on. 'It looks awful. I'll call Gerald.'

'Nix. It'll get better on its own. Let me have a look.' His father leant over to him. 'Ach, a bit of Bepanthen cream and it'll be closed up by the morning.'

But his mother was already by the telephone in the hall.

'Who did you get in a fight with this time?'

'No one.'

'Can't you just stay out of the way of trouble, like everyone else?'

Then his father had taken him to Doctor Ahlers.

'The boy again, Hard?' asked the country doctor, his hair on end, his coat thrown over his nightclothes, giving off a waft of 4711 cologne.

'Who else?' said his father, also in his white coat, as they entered the surgery.

'It could be the twins. Or your wife. I treat all the Kupers. All but one—right, let's have a look at you.' He took Daniel's hand. 'Fine. It definitely needs stitches. How did it happen?'

Daniel had had to repeat the story in the surgery. But his father hadn't even listened properly. 'Why on earth did you go over there, to Drömeln? That's no place for you. No wonder you got beaten up.'

He remembered that now—no matter what he said and did, the judgement had already been made.

3

Wilfried Ennen knew it was a risk to give the men another hymn so close to Easter, but they complained often enough about only ever singing the same songs. And now that the mixed choir was out of the running—Meinders had fallen out with the director, Alwin Graalmann, as he'd found out only yesterday from Meta, the organist—it was an opportunity to try out something new.

'So tell us . . . Wilfried,' said Hard, short of breath again, 'what's it supposed to mean, *ave verum corpus*?'

'Hail, true body,' said Wilfried Ennen, and to anticipate any further questions he translated the whole hymn for them. 'Born of the Virgin Mary, who truly suffered and was sacrificed on the cross for mankind, whose pierced side flowed with water and blood. Be a foretaste for us in the trial of death.'

'And why can't we just sing it in German?' asked Johann Rosing. 'No one understands all that.'

'It's another . . . Catholic one,' said Hard. 'We don't have to . . . kneel down in church . . . on Friday . . . do we?'

'No,' said Wilfried Ennen, 'you certainly don't. And you don't have to say confession either. Don't you worry.'

'That's all right then. That would have been . . . my next question.'

'I know.'

'We haven't got the time to listen to all that,' said Klaus Neemann.

'What's that supposed to mean?' Hard stood up from his chair, his fists clenched, but sat down again straight away because he was dizzy.

'Nothing,' said Klaus.

'Are you trying to say . . . I've got something to hide?' asked Hard, who still thought Klaus and Günter had kicked him out of their regular card game. 'I don't need your . . . insinuations . . . not from you . . . Superneeman,' he pointed a finger at him, 'you get your . . . accounts in order . . . before you start accusing other people.'

'That's rich, coming from you,' Klaus replied, unmoved.

And Wilfried Ennen said, 'Two, three, four, one—and!' and banged out the tune.

And everyone but Hard sang, '*Ave, ave, verum corpus, natum de Maria virgine.*' This time there were more men there than the week before, but not nearly as many as a few years ago, and there would never be so many again. The young people had other ideas nowadays, thought Wilfried Ennen, and if they were interested in music then it was the kind where vocals weren't important. And he couldn't imagine teaching one of his choir members' sons to sing, here among their fathers. 'Yes, thank you, it's a very soft beginning, *aaave*, and at *Maria* there's the symbol for *crescendo*, that's where we have the biggest opening, and at *virgine* we go back down again. Again please. All together—and!' Wilfried Ennen didn't know what had happened between Bernhard and Klaus, and no matter what it was, the choir practice he'd moved forward to Tuesday because of Holy Thursday was for singing, not for arguing. But the way Bernhard Kuper looked, so very pale, he feared he wouldn't manage either singing or arguing. 'Very good,' he said, 'that's right, and now again—and!'

'*Vere passum immolatum in cruce pro homine.*'

'Yes, thank you, the first tenor section has to hold for five at *cruce* and the second at *immolatum*, before starting again at *cruce*. Then the two come together again at *pro*.' He started playing the melody again. The motet was one of Mozart's last works, forty-six bars for choir, strings and organ, adapted for the male-voice choir by Wilfried Ennen. He always used the same method—first he wrote the first tenor part, then he added the second bass, and he finished with the other two parts. Mozart, on the other hand, had heard everything, all at once. Whenever he thought of Mozart, he thought of what he'd read about him, about his first trip to Italy—how Mozart listened to Allegri's 'Miserere' for nine voices at a Wednesday mass in Rome and then sat down and wrote it down, note for note. The Vatican kept the score under lock and key for years, and then along comes a fourteen-year-old boy and takes it away from them without ever setting eyes on it. Wilfried Ennen had never achieved that perfect level of perception and he never would, no matter how much he listened and sang and composed, and then and now Mozart seemed to him to be an android, a robot posing convincingly as a human being.

Wilfried Ennen went through the parts one after another, but only when they sang the hymn all together again, from beginning to end, did Hard join in, because he was afraid he wouldn't be able to stay on tune the way he was feeling, and he thought his failure would be less noticeable if everyone was joining in. He still gave up at *cruce*. He had his own cross to bear; he didn't have to sit there and be humiliated, and he decided to go home during the break. But Klaus got to him first, put down a beer in front of him and said, 'Here, have a little drink.'

And he did. And he felt better already.

'We'll be in church on Friday and Saturday,' said Klaus, addressing all of them. 'And Meinders asked us if we want to sing in church again in the future. Not often, maybe four or five times a year. And the next dates would be Ascension Day, Whitsun and in October, for Harvest Festival, on election day.'

'On Super Election Sunday,' said Johann Rosing.

'Aren't we singing the evening before that at the marksmen's club fair?' asked Günter, the choir's secretary, flipping through the calendar on his lap.

'Yes,' said Klaus. 'So we can stay up all night and keep our clothes on till the next morning.'

'And we can celebrate my election victory while we're at it,' said Johann Rosing.

'While we're at what?'

'That's up to you.'

'Is it with women?' asked Hard.

'What?' asked Klaus.

'The shooting champion's ball, in the evening.'

'Dancing's usually with women,' said Klaus. 'Unless you want to dance with me.'

'No thanks.'

'As long as you leave your son at home, otherwise he'll paint all over the marquee,' said Johann Rosing once the laughter had died down. 'Mind you, maybe you ought to bring him along. For later. He certainly knows how to clean up. He's got plenty of experience at that.'

Hard stood up again but before he could say anything Wilfried Ennen clapped his hands. 'Right, men. Let's get back down to business. Over again from the beginning. Two, three, four, one— and!'

Theda Wiemers, the bookkeeper, picked Daniel up at home in the morning and brought him back in the evening. He had helped himself to an old thesaurus from the Office for Beginners so that he didn't end up writing the same thing over and over in his daily reports. *Completing a payment slip. Checking cost statements. Filing small ad treatments. Sorting insertions. Measuring size. Perfecting address list. Enveloping and dispatching income statements to delivery staff. Receiving and logging complaints.* After ten days they'd run out of things for him to do.

As one of the delivery people was off sick, a woman in the distribution department suggested they could send him out to deliver newspapers. He was supposed to learn the trade from the bottom up, after all. And he could carry on as a freelancer after his work experience was over, to earn a bit of money. When Mrs Nanninga heard about that on her inspection visit she spoke to the editor-in-chief.

Hans Meinders was standing next to the entrance in his cassock and bands, shaking hands with everyone who went past him into the church. His wife Marie handed out the hymnbooks in the vestibule, not three steps away from him. He looked at her and she returned his gaze. If it weren't for her, he'd have stayed in the desert. If it weren't for her and Meta Graalmann. The bells rang out above him and he hoped they could hear them ten kilometres south, in the Catholic part of the country, despite the fog still surrounding the village. We commemorate Jesus' crucifixion here too! And all without fasting! We break his bread and drink his blood! Until his kingdom comes and his will is done! And then we'll see who's redeemed and who's judged.

The people of Jericho climbed the hill to the church two by two, past the memorial, past the construction ruin of the mortuary onto the grave mound, the cemetery, first the old and then the young, the confirmands and the other children. There were fewer of them with every year, and even those who still came didn't know that Good Friday was a holier day than Christmas Eve. For most of them, it was just one more day off work, when they could stay in bed until midday. He had seen them on his way from the parsonage to the church: the shutters down, the curtains closed, the people half asleep at the breakfast table. And he had waved at them, had invited them to come with him, but they had stayed put and he had kept walking in the hope that they'd follow him after all. Staying sober was no easy trial.

He greeted Walter Baalmann, his neighbour the engine driver with whom he talked over his sermons on their fishing trips, and Anne-Marie Kolthoff, a loyal soul who suffered because her husband had left her for a younger woman and she was shy of entering into a new relationship. Gerald and Eiske Ahlers, both in their best outfits, stopped to talk and the three of them went over those who'd died that winter. Dine Kramer stroked his arm as if to give him courage, although it was her who delivered the *Karkblattje* church newsletter around the village and got told not to fill up people's letterboxes with her rubbish. Some of the new confirmands shook his hand while others like Tobias Allen, Wiebke Rosing and Verena Mengs walked past him with their heads down. Birgit Kuper nodded at him because the twins were holding both her hands, whinging and pulling in two different directions.

'I'm sorry.'

'What for?'

'The children.'

'The kingdom of God belongs to them.'

'Well,' she said. 'If you say so.'

Then they went inside too.

From a distance, he saw Volker Mengs drop a half-smoked cigarette and extinguish it with the tip of his shoe, and when Volker reached him he exhaled the smoke he'd breathed in, upwards.

'It is even a vapour, that appeareth for a little time, and then vanisheth away,' said Hans Meinders, holding out his hand.

Volker took it and said, 'James 4:14.'

He was always astounded at how fat the boy was and how well he knew his Bible. His flesh might be weak and idle but his mind was strong and fast. Back when he'd been preparing for his confirmation he'd hardly taken part in the lessons, although he'd always been the best in their races to find Bible quotations, and now he was the only one from the group he'd blessed almost a year ago to the day who still came to church services.

And then the male-voice choir filed past him, wearing suits and ties, with folders jammed under their arms. At the head came Wilfried Ennen, the director, and Klaus Neemann, the chairman, then Günter Vehndel, the secretary, and Johann Rosing, the deputy secretary, then the tenors, the basses—and at some distance at the very end, with no visible reason for the order, Bernhard Kuper. Perhaps coming late ran in the family.

'Moin Hans,' said Hard, reaching out a hand.

And Hans Meinders took the hand in his and said, 'Welcome, my son.'

'You can save the sweet talk. Here,' he produced a packet of Mother Superior's Melissa Spirit from underneath his jacket and handed it to him.

'Not now!' Hans Meinders looked over at his wife but she was busy with the other singers, and he folded up the cardboard and put it in the offertory box.

'You didn't come in the shop yesterday.'

'Yesterday was Holy Thursday.'

Hard shrugged. 'So? We won't see each other for a while.'

'Four days.'

'I don't want the stuff lying around in the shop, and you look as though you could use it.' With that, he turned away from him to Marie. He hugged her and she gave him a kiss on the cheek, and it hurt Hans Meinders to see how familiar they were with each other. The ringing stopped, the organ started, the verger closed the door, and as Hard climbed the stairs to the gallery Hans Meinders strode along the aisle to the pulpit.

'Dearly beloved,' he said once he'd got to the top, 'Jesus died today—he died on the cross for us, for our sins. Let us pray.' He put his hands together and spoke the words of the prayer, but because they were his own words, no one joined in. Then he called upon them all to sing together with him, the hymn 'Wood on Jesu Shoulder, Curséd by the World'.

Hard knew the words, all the men around him knew them, and they felt it was their duty to intone the hymn. They rose from the pews and sang of doubts and laments and resurrection. And after the announcements—they stayed on their feet—they sang 'Holy Is the Lord'. Their voices echoed off the white walls, and the people below looked up at them. This, thought Hard, was exactly the way it should be when they performed, eye to eye with God's emissary, making the most of the acoustics of a holy space and unattainable for the listeners, the common people. He was never to feel this way again—so strong, exalted and untouchable.

Hans Meinders read the story of the crucifixion from the Book of Luke but Hard didn't listen. He sat in the front row, his hands resting on the balustrade, thinking of the four gospels, the four voices in the male-voice choir, the four horsemen of the Apocalypse, and via that diversion he began counting the women, tallying up which of them were customers and which weren't. He wanted to make sure his customers were in the majority, no matter where, no matter when, because he feared the opposite, as an infallible sign that the competition from the neighbouring villages, especially the Schlecker chain, had gained the upper hand and his time had come. Satisfied with the results of his experiment, he tried to attract the attention of Marie Meinders, Eiske Ahlers or Theda Wiemers by clicking his tongue three times. But the only woman who looked at him was his own wife, and her glare didn't bode well.

Then—Jesus was dead at last—Hans Meinders spoke the Apostles' Creed and the congregation repeated it after him. Hard stood up too, lowered his head and put his hands together. 'I believe in God the Father Almighty, maker of heaven and earth . . . ' It hadn't been much different in the army. One word had led to another. And every soldier had to go along with the rituals. Their church service was the manoeuvre, their creed the morning assembly, their Last Judgement the war. Both, the church and the army, were practising for an emergency that would never happen, presuming their missions were successful.

They all sang another hymn, 'Lord, We Think of Your Suffering', and before silence fell again Hans Meinders said, 'The prophets foretell it. Daniel tells of his appearance—one like the Son of Man came with the clouds of heaven. Isaiah tells of his end—he was numbered with the transgressors. And so it is. The Messiah is here, but the doubters do not recognize him. He identifies himself as the Son of God, but they accuse him of blasphemy. Judas betrays him, the high council delivers him, Pilate sentences him to death on the cross. At his last supper, Jesus Christ speaks of a new covenant with God, his testament. We all know a testament can only take effect once he who wrote it has died. Moses had calves and rams slaughtered and sprinkled the blood on the people to cleanse them. That sealed the first covenant, the Old Testament. Jesus, however, we learn in the Epistle to the Hebrews, is worthy of greater honour than Moses, just as the builder of the house has more honour than the house. For every house is built by someone; he who built everything is God. Jesus didn't take calves or rams; he sacrificed himself. And God let it happen. That sealed the second covenant, the New Testament.' Hans Meinders paused and leant out over the edge of the pulpit. 'And God let it happen. Is that not an abhorrent deed, failing to help His son? God the Almighty lets His son, who looks like a man, whom he created like all of us in His image, bleed to death. He watches from on high as he takes hours to die. Does He not betray His own creation? Does He not disrespect the message that He gave him? Does it not say: "Love thy neighbour as thyself"? Yet He sees a man suffering and walks by. Is this crime not greater than the betrayal by Judas Iscariot?' There was a moment of absolute silence and then some of the congregation began asking one another whether he really wanted an answer, until Meinders swept away their doubts. 'Oh no! For the Father gives His Son for the benefit of mankind. It is better if one of the people dies than if the whole of the people were to die. The sacrifice is unavoidable. Without death, no testament! Without blood spilled, no forgiveness! Yet it is not enough to be pure on the outside. Only those pure on the inside can hope for redemption. And it is to remind us of this, of Jesus' legacy, that we drink his blood and eat his body.' And with that, Hans Meinders descended from the pulpit and invited them all to come to the Communion table. The curate distributed the bread and Hans Meinders handed everyone who came to him the silver chalice. To mark the occasion, it held not grape juice but the best Israeli red wine. Twelve times a year he held Communion, more often than the other reformed churches in the area, and every time he felt it was a trial. He breathed in the scent of the wine and poured it out and was not tempted to drink it.

Volker Mengs, fat Mengs, was the first in line. From a distance it looked like he got two pieces of bread. But the curate had dropped one of them and then gave him another, immaculate one. Then Birgit and the twins came before him, then the new confirmands, Verena Mengs, Wiebke Rosing and Tobias Allen, and then Dine Kramer, Eiske and Gerald Ahlers, Anne-Marie Kolthoff and Walter Baalmann. Some of the male-voice choir came down as well, just to 'sup a bit o' wine' and 'wet the ol' whistle,' as Old Kramer announced loudly on the staircase.

'Bet it's the cheapest he could get,' said Günter Vehndel.

'He didn't get it from me,' said Klaus Neemann.

'He must know what he's doing then,' said Hard.

'I heard he's come into money,' said Wilfried Ennen. 'They say he's doing business.'

'With who?'

'With you.'

'You're kidding. Who said that?'

'Heard it around.'

'And what kind of business?'

'No idea. But he seems to be turning a profit.'

'I thought he took a vow of poverty.'

'That's why he's sharing out his riches to us, no matter how small they may be.'

And as they went back to the gallery they discussed the wine.

'Never tasted it before.'

'Must come from Israel.'

'You mean Jewish?

'*De oll Jööd,*' Old Kramer butted in, revealing that he did understand something of what people around him said, even when they didn't shout at him.

Klaus Neemann nodded. 'Kosher.'

'What does that mean, anyway,' asked Günter Vehndel, 'kosher?'

_'It's to do with meat,' said Hard. 'Beef or pork. Jews don't eat one kind of meat, I can't remember which one.'

Before they could discuss it any further they were back in the gallery and Wilfried Ennen had them move to the front, section by section. Hard had practiced the '*Ave Verum Corpus*' at home. He owned a record of the Regensburg Cathedral Choir—he had hundreds of records of choirs—and he had put it on and listened to the piece over and over, and then he had gone back to Ennen's score and sung his part, the first tenor. Not once had he felt anything other than the slight trembling that the Latin words caused in his mouth and throat, no shortage of breath, no dizziness, no tingling in his left arm. But now that he was standing next to Günter Vehndel, his song folder open, and holding the *cruce*, he noticed the pages starting to dance in front of his eyes. The notes blurred, his head filled up with fog. He couldn't feel his lips or his tongue. Then he dropped his folder and it landed with a bang on the sandstone flagstones in the aisle. Everyone turned to him and for a moment it looked as if he was about to follow his folder down to the floor; he was leaning halfway out over the balustrade and the men around him fell silent, only he went on singing, louder and higher than ever before, until Johann Rosing grabbed him and pressed him down onto the pew. Someone, he couldn't quite see who, called for Doctor Ahlers, and at that Hard sat up straight and said, 'I'm fine.'

'Must be the wine,' he heard Günter Vehndel saying.

'It is a bit early, not even half past ten.' That was Johann Rosing.

'No, no,' said Klaus Neemann, 'he can't take the altitude.'

536

Wilfried Ennen waved both arms around in front of his face and said, 'Two, three, four, one—and!' and the men beside him started over again. Hard joined in, but he'd hardly begun when they stopped again and Wilfried Ennen said, 'Bernhard, if you don't want to sing it, why did you come in the first place?'

'But I am singing.'

'Yes, but how.'

'How am I singing?'

'Out of tune.'

'Me, out of tune?'

'It's not an impossible combination.'

'Oh, yes it is.'

'Then you're doing it on purpose.'

'What?'

'Not hitting the right notes.'

'You must be crazy. You've lost your marbles.'

'We need to turn the saying around now.'

'What saying?'

'Like father, like son.'

Hard launched himself at Ennen but Johann Rosing held him back by simply placing his sturdy body in the way. 'Hard, calm down, we're in church.'

'I won't . . . let him . . . insult me.'

'No one's insulting you,' said Wilfried Ennen over Rosing's head. 'I'm just telling you how it is. And if you don't like it you're welcome to leave.'

And at that, Hard walked down the stairs and went outside. The door slammed behind him. At first he wanted to keep walking past the graves, the mortuary and the monument until he got to

Church Road, but then he stopped. He could hear them singing through the thin windows, muffled and weakened yet still absolutely clear. It was as though anger had sharpened his senses. Never had anything been as clear and pure, as distinct. The four parts, gentle and light despite all their strength, floated above him and melded into a single voice.

On the Tuesday after Easter, they put Daniel in the editorial department. He was in the post room, a small, windowless space where he was supposed to open the readers' letters and put them in a rack, the most important letters at the top. There were dozens of them, and many of them came from the same six or seven senders. The editorial assistant Mrs Dettmers, a well-built woman with scars on her lower arms, had told him to separate the positive letters from the negative ones; they wanted a balanced mix in the paper to avoid any form of biased reporting. The only problem was, there weren't any positive letters. Some of them did start with praise but that fed into even sharper criticism of the articles or the pictures. Some readers complained they'd been wrongly quoted. Others found fault with the choice of photos and accused the editors of manipulating the pictures to their disadvantage. Most of them cast slurs on neighbours, politicians and civil servants or wrote about subjects directly related to themselves, which they considered under-represented in the public eye. Many of the readers' letters ended with the formulaic threat of cancelling their subscription if they weren't printed.

Shortly before the editorial deadline, the senior duty editor Karl-Heinz Duken asked whether there were any letters they could use; they had a gap in the local news section on page twelve that even he couldn't fill. Duken was tall and slim. When he appeared in a doorway he lowered his head, and in some rooms he went all the way up to the ceiling when he stood completely straight. Everyone, even the editor-in-chief, had to look up to him. 'Duck, Duken!' was what people shouted at him so he wouldn't bump his head on doorframes or lamps; 'Duken, duck!' was what they murmured to each other when they saw him coming into the office above the dividing walls. It was not only his appearance that granted him respect, however. Even though no one could say what he did all day apart from drinking coffee and checking up on colleagues, he proved to be a reliable organizer at key moments. If a story threatened to fall away he'd find a replacement. If a writer or an interview partner dropped out he'd get someone else—and all in a matter of minutes, without the slightest trace of panic or nervousness. His desk was flanked by two filing cabinets full of addresses and telephone numbers and there were more stowed away in his head, the kind that seemed too risky to note down. He'd been working for the *Frisian News* for almost thirty years and they said he knew everything about everyone, and that was the reason why they didn't dare give him the sack. They were scared he'd spill the beans as soon as he wasn't bound to a contract. Duken had seen half a dozen editors-in-chief come and go, and most of them had come and gone because of him. You could often hear his voice all along the corridor, and it was not advisable to visit him or call him because you were guaranteed to disturb him at something more important than what you wanted from him. 'What now?' he'd say, even before you'd spoken to him. Or he'd say, 'Duken? No!' nothing more, and slam the phone down.

Daniel handed him a bundle of paper. All the letters were about Rosing, about outstanding wages, unpaid bills, irregularities in the tendering process for the cement works. Duken skimmed the printouts, faxes and handwritten notes. 'These are cases for lawyers, not the media. You just have to look at the names of the senders, Willms, Bunger, Klaaßen, and compare them with the business directory.' He pointed at the Yellow Pages next to the telephone book on Daniel's desk. 'You'll soon see these slurs all come from Rosing's competitors. They're all contractors themselves. There's no industry where the competition's as tough as the building trade. Of course they envy Rosing his success. And it's no surprise, if you look at what he's achieved. A serious newspaper mustn't go along with this petty, personally motivated squabbling, though. A serious newspaper has to behave neutrally and report objectively.'

'But it's journalists' job to follow leads and test them for truth.' Daniel felt the blood shooting to his head. 'That's what they said in the documentary they showed me at the beginning of my work experience.'

Duken nodded. 'That's absolutely right. One of our Business section team has been on the story for months. But his research showed that the accusations made here are unfounded. All wages have been paid properly, receivables transferred on time, the tendering process was run according to the rules. Rosing simply underbid all the other applicants for the construction of the cement works by means of very clever calculation. And he sources his material from companies in the region, so he not only supports the local economy but also avoids long transport routes and protects the environment. Anyone who turns that into an accusation or calls him a Nazi because of his patriotism,' he winked at Daniel, 'is only concerned with his own profit, can't get enough. These letters,' he said, holding the papers up in the air and shaking them to and fro, 'are nothing but malicious gossip, and actually we ought to pass them on for libel.' Then he interrupted himself and looked at his watch. Daniel wanted to ask him whom they ought to pass them on to but Duken got there first, as if he'd anticipated the comment. 'I haven't got time to discuss the virtues of journalism right now. Is there nothing else, nothing positive, maybe a bit of praise?'

Daniel shook his head.

Disappointed, Duken lowered his hands and some of the sheets of paper fell on the floor. 'Then we'll just have to fill the page with an ad for the paper. That's better for the layout anyway. Too much writing's bad for the eyes—that's a scientific fact. And who reads readers' letters apart from readers' letter-writers? They don't care what they write about, they just want to see their names in the paper. They put other people down to make themselves look better. There's no room in my newspaper for that kind of business.' With these words, he crossed the corridor into his office.

The new church hall was directly opposite the parsonage. Rosing had built it for the church in eyeshot of the old one, a one-storey building consisting of three office rooms plus WCs right next to the entrance, a kitchen and a large hall with tables and chairs in front of a stage that had never been used as planned for plays, Christian concerts or speeches. Originally, confirmation lessons and the church youth club meetings were to be held there, but then the church council had decided to lay out the dead in the hall—temporarily, only until the mortuary had been extended, which had never had space for more than one coffin and a dozen mourners. That state of affairs had been going on for three years now, though, because it had turned out that the ground on which the mortuary extension was to be built couldn't take the load, and it was better to put up another building on another site on the west side of the cemetery. These circumstances and considerations had led to new church council meetings, geological reports, architectural designs and cost estimates and to the realization that the church couldn't afford another new building for the time being. And although Pastor Meinders repeatedly pointed out in his sermons that the collection was only for their own purposes until they'd come up with enough funds, that hadn't led to higher donations. No Jerichoan who attended services on Sundays ever put more than a few marks in the collection bag.

When Hard went outside the shop in the morning to get the bikes out of the garage and set them up in the bike stand, he could see the new church hall at the end of the road. And every time he looked that way he rubbed his hands. He'd tried for years to convince Enno Kröger he could make pots of money with his Beach Hotel if he'd let him take his bets at the back, in the hall, rather than at the bar in the front. 'Then we can do it in totally different style, Enno, much more professional, with odds and all that, really big time.' But the landlord hadn't gone for it. And since he'd started employing Birgit, Hard couldn't do those kinds of deals in the drugstore any more. Every time she'd caught him at it she'd let him know how much she disapproved of his hobby for weeks.

'What's the matter?' He rolled back onto his side of the bed.

'When are you going to give it up?' she asked, not looking at him.

'Give up what?'

'You know what I mean.'

'Desiring you?'

'All your gambling.'

'It's not gambling.'

'Oh no, what is it then?'

'A sure-fire business model.'

'For who?'

'For us.'

Now she did turn around to him. 'We're in debt, Hard. We still haven't paid off the extension. It's been more than seven years! And now you come along with the new shop fittings on top of it all.'

'I know,' he said, and put a hand on her belly. 'But we'll be free soon.'

Sometimes he'd still stand at the counter with investors, as he called customers who only bought cameras, film or fishing rods out of embarrassment, and talk about football, casually and not mentioning the odds, but usually now he told them to come to the old church hall, where they'd gathered every evening since the new construction had begun and handed in their bets for the German leagues. There was a match played somewhere every day, and every day there was an item in the newspaper or on TV that was worth staking a bet on. They not only gambled on results, on victories or defeats, goals or points, but also on which teams were drawn to play each other, corners, goal scorers, yellow and red cards, changes of coaches, injuries and even the type of injuries. Hard himself bet with another bookmaker—one in the county town, just as unofficial as he was—against HSV, after years of disappointment, and unlike Richard Wiemers, Anton Leemhuis, Klaus Neemann and Manfred Kramer he was convinced that, with Rosing's help, Germania Jericho would turn into a top team in the not- too-distant future and make it to the fourth division, and that brought him astounding winnings as a bookmaker. And unlike in the past, when he'd put the money straight back down again and lost it, he now kept most of it for himself. His problem was that he'd bet *against* Germany in the football world cup in Italy. That was the only reason the bank still owned the storeroom, the basement and half of the shop. But before the season he'd put a lot of money on Kaiserslautern, and seeing as they'd been at the top of the league table for a week—thanks to beating Bayern Munich—he hoped his courage would pay off this time.

To begin with, Hans Meinders had rejected his suggestion and said, 'You're not making my church into a betting shop.' Then, two years ago, he'd approached him of his own accord, shortly before he shut up shop. 'Do you still need a place?' He swayed on his feet and held onto the counter.

'A place for what?'

'For gambling.'

'I can always use somewhere. What were you thinking of?'

And once they'd agreed the conditions—Hard wanted to give him twenty per cent of the profits—Hans Meinders had pressed the key onto the palm of his hand.

'You'll have to leave as soon as the mortuary's built.'

Once, when they'd run into each other in the church hall as if by coincidence, Hard asked, 'How does it go together, anyway? Isn't it a contradiction—the church and commerce?'

'If you mean this,' Hans Meinders pointed at the table covered in paper, covered in numbers and slips, 'a betting office doesn't contravene the Ten Commandments.'

'That depends on the stake.'

And another time, after he'd asked Marie a few questions, Hard asked, 'Isn't greed one of the seven deadly sins?'

'It certainly is.'

'So how can you allow all this?'

'Bernhard, what's the point of all your questions? Do you want me to throw you out? Or should I absolve you of all guilt?'

'I'm just asking.'

'And I'm answering: brazen greed devastates its victims and makes them the laughing stock of the enemy. Good greed helps those that are bowed down to reap their just desserts.'

Every evening except on Sundays, Hans Meinders came to the drugstore and every evening Hard handed him a bundle of notes, rolled up in an empty box of Mother Superior's Melissa Spirit.

He was surprised every time to see the pastor in civilian clothes, without his vestments. Hard thought everyone ought to follow his example and never go out without a costume, so as to gain permanent respect. Easter might have spelled the end of his time in the male-voice choir but it had also filled his pockets. A great deal had happened that weekend—the women had given their families two Sunday dinners in a row, the children had gone on egg hunts in the garden, and the men were in the best gambling mood after four days off work. They thought they had God on their side, seeing as the pope had blessed them on TV two days previously, so they'd doubled the stakes.

And now that the last women had left the drugstore and Birgit had gone to pick up the twins from swimming—they were doing their Seahorse beginners' certificate—Hard counted off a couple of blue hundred-mark notes and rolled them up.

Mrs Wiemers the bookkeeper pulled up outside the drugstore and turned off the engine. She'd often keep talking to Daniel, tell him stories about Hard, look longingly over at the house and ask him to say hello to his father from her. Daniel had promised to do so but hadn't kept to it. He found their conversations unpleasant and would have preferred to cycle to the *Frisian News*, even though it would take him more than an hour on his racing bike, but her offer to pick him up and drive him home again had simply been too tempting, so he let her words wash over him as he sat with his hand on the door handle. 'Looks crowded,' she said. 'He must be very busy.'

'Not really.'

'But look at all the bikes outside.'

'Oh them, they're always there. They're ours.'

'What's the point of that?'

Daniel shrugged and repeated the words with which his father had answered his own question. 'It's psychology. Doubters find it easier to come in when they assume someone else is in the shop.'

'Oh, I see,' said Mrs Wiemers. 'Psychology. Well, that never was his strong point.'

Daniel said 'Bye then,' and 'See you tomorrow,' and jumped out of the car, a red Saab 900i, 1989 model, 126 PS, 92 kW. Unlike the other times, he heard not only his door slamming but hers too, and they both went into the shop together. Daniel was surprised to find his father on his own after all; he was usually still standing at the counter with Klaus and Günter or another of his friends shortly before closing time, discussing the state of the world, the red peril, the war in Iraq, the Kurdish invasion, or if nothing else, nothing world-moving was happening, at least the results in the football leagues. Now he was standing in the middle of the room holding a box of Mother Superior's Melissa Spirit; not even the women who otherwise populated the drugstore at this time of day were there. 'So how did it go, young man?'

'Fine,' said Daniel and walked past him to the office.

'Thanks for giving him all these lifts, Theda,' he heard his father say. 'It really saves me time. If there's anything I can do for you?'

'I could use some cream. My hands have been so dry for a while and I thought maybe you could recommend something.'

'Oh yes, I can. I can always recommend something. But you're a real challenge. I really don't know how your skin could get any softer.'

Daniel overheard more. 'You haven't felt it for a long time,' and 'You're right about that,' and then he was on his way up the stairs. He stopped for a moment in the hallway. No children screaming, no clattering of pots and pans from the kitchen, no voices, familiar or otherwise. He threw his parka and his army rucksack with its *KUPER* name patch—another Christmas present from his father—on the telephone table, went into the living room and switched on the TV. He tipped the seat back, zapped through the eight channels and stopped at *Jeopardy*. Before the Easter holidays, he and his mother had watched the quiz show almost every afternoon. And every time the presenter Hans-Jürgen Bäumler entered the studio, she'd stopped ironing and said, 'He used to be a figure skater. He even won something at the Olympics, but only in pair skating, with Marika Kilius.'

Since then, of all the TV presenters with a past—'Karl Dall went to school in Leer'—'Joachim Fuchsberger used to be an actor'—'Rudi Carrell comes from Holland'—Hans-Jürgen Bäumler seemed to be the saddest. He'd never be able to pick up his old life where he'd left off, not without making a fool of himself, and he'd only achieved his greatest successes with the aid of a woman who was no longer by his side. Instead, he spent day after day alone on the brightly coloured stage set designed to look like the inside of a computer, reading aloud answers from a board, for which three contestants had to come up with the correct questions.

'Short or long one hundred: To make the profits flow, a bar-man may give you this.'

'What is a short measure?'

'Species and creatures three hundred: bluish-white baking ingredient, medicinal narcotic, Papaver somniferrum.'

'What is opium poppy?'

'Dragons and sirens four hundred: He's as fast as the wind. His sandals have wings.'

'Who is Hermes?'

Maik from Erfurt, bleached blond hair, earrings, denim shirt, was almost always the fastest. The red light on his desk lit up, five seconds ticked away, and when they'd gone by he couldn't remember what he'd wanted to say.

Sinikka from Kiel, the oldest on the show that day, large glasses, gold necklace, brightly coloured blouse, couldn't deal with the reversed questions.

'Short or long three hundred: Due to an anatomical trait, lies don't run very far.'

'Lies have short—' she said, broke off, ran her hand over her face and tried again. 'What kind of legs do lies have?'

'What are short legs?' asked Cord, the champion, winning the round as he had done all the previous weeks.

Hans-Jürgen Bäumler came out from behind his desk and strolled over to the contestants. He asked them questions to which he already knew the answers. 'Sinikka, you have an interesting name. It's Scandinavian, am I right?'

Sinikka closed her eyes, smiled and said, 'It's a very old Finnish name.'

'You have a lovely job. You make people happy, I assume.'

'I do, yes, I'm—'

'You run a dancing school!'

'Yes.'

'And who comes to you? Older people or mainly the young generation?'

'Mainly young couples,' she looked first left, then right and then straight ahead again, 'just like my fellow contestants here. They grew up in a time, the beat era, when everyone danced on their own, and now they want to get their arms around the girls again.'

Hans-Jürgen Bäumler spread out his arms, took a step to the side and pretended to embrace an invisible partner. 'I always wanted to get my arms around the girls.'

At these words Daniel was once again overwhelmed by pity, prompting him to switch off and go outside. As he left the house he thought perhaps it was true of everything that your passion was spent at some point or was no longer enough to fulfil your wishes, and then your second, less auspicious life began and you had to go along with it whether you wanted to or not, unless—and this thought made him shudder—you did what Peter Peters had done.

Theda Wiemers' car had gone and his parents' gold metallic Audi was parked outside the shop in its place. His mother, her coat still on and clung to by the twins, knocked on the shop window from inside and mimed for him to do up his zip. She too, he went on thinking as he pulled up his zip, had already entered that second life, after she'd stopped working at Knipper's and started at Kuper's, as he knew from her stories.

He walked aimlessly around the village in his parka, past the post office and the pool hall, across the sleepers, and balanced along the tracks to the old freight shed. The sun had dipped into the fog above the hammrich and shone out of it as a white dot. Daniel put coins on the tracks and waited for a train to drive over them. Some disappeared between the stones of the embankment, some melted into the rails. He went on walking, not knowing where he was going. The farmers were sowing seeds in the fields alongside the tracks. Flocks of jackdaws flew up from the trees and settled on the ground. A low-flying combat plane thundered over him. The air was warm and spring-like.

Suddenly, Wiebke was standing in front of him. 'Here you are at last,' she said, chewing gum. 'I've been waiting for you for days. You promised to come back.'

'No, I didn't.'

'Yes, you did. Where've you been?'

'Working.'

'That's no excuse.'

'What is then?'

'You know what happens if you don't keep promises.' She took a step towards him and he could smell her breath, fruity and artificial as if she'd rinsed her mouth with apple shampoo. 'Dad said it's called trespassing.'

'What is?'

'When you break in somewhere.'

'I didn't break in anywhere. The door was open.'

Wiebke stood on tiptoes, stretched up to his ear and sheltered her mouth with her hand. 'I haven't told him anyway, if that's what you're thinking.' She slid back to her original position. 'Not yet.'

'What haven't you told him?'

'About us, you know.'

A brown Mercedes 560 SE Coupé, 1987 model, 279 PS, 205 kW, pulled up next to them. The engine cut out, the window glided down and a man wearing sunglasses leant out. 'Here you are,' said Johann Rosing. 'I've been looking for you everywhere.'

4

The next day Daniel was moved on to the Sports section, without being told why. There were monitors on the desks around the room, their screens shimmering green, the walls were hung with pennants and posters, and on the shelves were cups and small silvery figures holding footballs and tennis racquets, lined up like awards for special journalistic achievements. The editors had gathered in the conference room next door. He could hear their muffled voices through the glass door. He made out isolated words, 'Kaiserslautern', 'Labbadia', 'Boom-Boom-Becker' and roars of laughter. At one point someone came in and tossed him a couple of old *Kicker* magazines. 'Here you are, you do a bit of background reading.'

At lunchtime up in the cafeteria he thought, they don't want me to be any good. And as it turned out when he asked Masurczak, the editor-in-chief, they really didn't think he was suitable for sorting readers' letters. 'Maybe you're a bit too young to judge criticism correctly.'

'I wasn't too young for it yesterday, and today I am,' said Daniel, standing opposite him in his office. 'And today I'm a day older than I was yesterday.'

Masurczak laughed. He asked Daniel to take a seat on one of two leather armchairs and offered him an espresso. Daniel sat down. He drank the espresso like vodka, tipping it down his throat in one go. For a while his tongue and throat were entirely numb, as if he'd had a local anaesthetic to have his wisdom teeth pulled. Then it started burning. Masurczak leant back, crossed his legs and folded his arms. 'I've already heard that you take everything people say very literally. So you mustn't understand the transfer as a reprimand. It's a promotion. In the Sports section you'll take part in the editorial meetings and you can go along to football matches at the weekend. That's what every boy dreams of, isn't it?' Masurczak began biting his fingernails.

'My work experience is over on Friday,' said Daniel. 'There won't be any matches before then.'

'Never mind that,' said Masurczak, then raised himself halfway out of his seat, scratched his head and dropped down again. 'There's always plenty to do there. Most sports reports run during the week. Yesterday for example, on Tuesday, there were Bundesliga matches because of Easter. And the season's nearly finished now. People want their attention held. You have to keep up the excitement. Feed fears. Nourish speculation. Destroy certainties. It's not enough to watch the game or read the results. What counts is the stories behind it all. They're what gives the numbers meaning, gives the tragedy and triumph a face. And anyway you're here to learn about journalism, and a journalist always has to be flexible, adapt to every situation, make instant switches.'

'That's the same for the editor-in-chief, though,' said Daniel. 'So if there's nothing for me to do in the Sports section, why don't you just let me write an article for another section, just as a try?'

'What section were you thinking of?'

'Politics.'

'No way.' Masurczak reached into a dish on his desk and took out a boiled sweet, offered Daniel one too and didn't withdraw his hand until Daniel had shaken his head several times. 'Right now we're full up, with Rohwedder and the Iraqi refugees, the Kurds. If it goes on this way they'll all end up coming over here. And apart from that you've already done a couple of dodgy things. We all know that. First the story with the UFO, now the graffiti. I can't possibly put you in Politics. You've got a credibility problem, plain and simple.' He made slurping sounds as he transferred the sweet from one side of his mouth to the other. 'But I do want to give you a chance. I'm not a monster and I was young too once, you know. No one knows that better than your father. Go ahead and ask him if you like. He won't tell you anything, though. At least I hope not. It wouldn't be in his best interest. Or yours, either. Just a moment,' he said, scrabbling around on his desk and extracting a notebook from a pile. 'I've heard only good things about you from Accounts.' Masurczak looked at him, picked up a ballpoint pen and clicked the cartridge up and down a few times. 'And from the Ads department too.' He winked at him. 'So if you've got ideas you're welcome to suggest something to me. For the Culture page, if you like. I'm the acting Culture editor. All the items have initials so people aren't likely to realize it's you behind an article.'

Daniel agreed.

Masurczak gave him an event to report on. That evening—it was Wednesday—he was to go to a concert by Cpt. Kirk &. at the youth club in the county town, but it started so late, after ten, that he was only allowed to stay for the beginning. His father waited outside in the car. There were dozens of cars with number plates from elsewhere parked in front of the building, a nineteenth-century villa, cars from Bremen and Hamburg. The room was full of people, packed close together up to the stage. Daniel forced his way through the crowd and took photos of the guitarist, bassist, drummer, keyboarder and singer during the sound check. From this short distance, pressed up against the stage, a long shot was impossible. He couldn't get a view of the whole picture from where he was standing. Before he pulled the door closed behind him he heard the drummer counting in the beat for the first song with his sticks. Then he was outside. His father started the engine.

The next day when he got the pictures back, he saw that they were all out of focus. He put the CD he'd bought at Negativeland the day before on the stereo in the editorial office and turned up the volume to drown out the construction noise, and then he pulled the keyboard up closer and started writing, typing directly into the editorial system where everyone could see it.

None of the editors could deal with the music or the band's name.

'Captain Kirk and—what's that supposed to mean?' asked Tammo Tammen, the trainee, across the dividing wall.

'Captain Kirk and,' Daniel said as if to himself.

'And what? And Commander Spock? And Lieutenant Uhura? There's something missing!'

When a Panorama editor seconded to Culture by Masurczak read the article, she asked him not to write any more novels in future. She cut the piece down to half its length—twenty lines—and sent him to another event.

This time he had to interview a local band, Necrosis, who had just brought out their first demo tape by the name of *Necato*—five long-haired youths in leather outfits in the basement of the dairy which had closed down in January. He knew some of them by sight from the grammar school. The floor was covered in several layers of old carpet and the walls were lined with egg cartons. Daniel sat down on an amplifier, took out a notebook and a ballpoint pen and asked them questions, what their names were, what bands had influenced them, where they came from and where they wanted to go, and all of them answered him more willingly and in more detail than he'd expected—all except one, the drummer. He sat mutely in the corner all along, drumming the ends of two sticks against his thighs.

Daniel kept glancing over at the boy, but he only looked at him properly when he spoke to him directly. His hair came down to his hips and draped his face from both sides so there wasn't much to see of it, but there was still no doubt—it was Onno, Onno Kolthoff. Daniel hadn't seen him since the race in the hammrich. His heart thudded in his throat. 'And what about you, Onno?'

'What about me?' asked Onno, jamming a strand of hair behind one ear.

'What d'you want to do after you finish school?'

'I'm not going to finish school. I'm not going to waste my youth at school. If I spend another year in these,' he waved his sticks around in mid-air, 'classrooms I'll be dead, mentally and physically jaded, brainwashed, fit for society.'

The others, sitting around him in a semi-circle, agreed in principle but wanted to be on the safe side. The singer said, 'At least we'll have qualifications if our metal career doesn't work out.'

'That's exactly the problem,' Onno told them. 'Qualifications are the end of the line and your need for safety is the reason why your metal career will never get off the ground.'

'Yours won't either, though,' said Daniel.

'What d'you mean?'

'You can hardly make it on your own as a drummer. Unless you start singing and playing the guitar and bass, and you record it all one track at a time.'

'Who says you need all that to do metal? Metal's an attitude thing, it's about determination, not instruments. And that's why I'm leaving school at sixteen. Go ahead and write that in your,' he waved his sticks again, 'report or whatever. The teachers might as well get used to the idea.'

'What idea?'

'That I won't be here much longer. Or actually, that I'll soon only be here.'

This time Daniel asked him what he meant.

Onno said he was asking way too many questions and he only had time for one more.

'All right,' said Daniel. 'What's the meaning of your album title, *Necato*?'

'Actually,' said Onno, '*necato* is Latin and means *I have killed*.'

'I may have had to repeat the year because of an E for Latin,' said Daniel, 'and then I left grammar school for intermediate school because of that E for Latin so I didn't have to repeat the year, but I can tell you for sure that *necato* doesn't mean *I have killed*. *Necato* derives from *necare*. *I have killed* would be *necavi*.'

At that, Onno said, 'Right, I've had enough of your nitpicking.'

This time the others didn't just agree in principle.

At home that evening, Daniel called his old Latin teacher. Herlyn couldn't remember him right away, but while he was thinking out loud by mumbling 'Kuper, Kuper' over and over again, it dawned on him. Daniel could tell by his voice; it got higher and louder every time.

'I've got this question for you, Mr Herlyn, maybe a stupid one, the answer is probably really simple but I can't work it out.'

'There's no such thing as stupid questions,' Herlyn corrected him. 'Only stupid pupils. What's it all about then?'

Although Daniel assumed Herlyn knew nothing about the music, he told him the genre, the name of the band and the album title.

'*Necato*, Herlyn repeated.

'That's right,' said Daniel. 'The drummer, he's a pupil of yours by the way, Onno Kolthoff, says it means I have killed. But I don't think that's correct.'

'So you did learn something after all. I'm afraid I can't take your grade back now though. Under certain circumstances, for instance in the sentence *Caesare necato Brutus eiusque amici gavisi sunt*, *necato* fulfils the function of a predicate in the abl. abs. Then it's an autonomous element of the sentence and not formally linked to any other element, so it's absolute.' Herlyn paused. 'What do we call this participal construction?

'I don't know.'

'I've just said it. And anyway we covered this over and over. You must remember! *Cursus Novus I*, Lesson 68, Ablativus absolutus: Function and tense relation. *Militibus fortiter pugnantibus Drusus Germanos superavit!* Drusus conquers Germania, *Florus*, *Epitome II*. In this case we're not dealing with an ablativus absolutus, but with the rare imperative II, future imperative, and that means *necato* means: He shall kill! Or: thou shalt kill!'

For a moment Daniel had the feeling he'd discovered something important. The devil's first commandment. It seemed to him like a prophecy. To make himself look cleverer, he wrote that the band had no command of Latin. When he opened up the paper on Friday and found his article below the press agency report that the writer Max Frisch had died, it was like with the readers' letter-writers—a clear conscience but no outside interest. Only the Necrosis singer informed him that the band didn't want to have any more to do with him. 'It's better you don't hang out at gigs for a while. Otherwise Onno and I might put our album title into practice.'

'Which one? The right one or the wrong one?'

'Both. First the wrong one, then the right one. It's all the same in the end, anyway.'

'What end is that then?'

'Yours.'

Theda Wiemers knew Hard from dancing. She was a couple of years older than him, but it had still been her he'd asked to dance at the May Ball in the Friesenhuus while his friends had launched themselves at the young girls. Back then in the mid-sixties, she and Richard and Birgit and he weren't yet married but she did feel obliged to Richard, who was ill in bed that evening, and with every step she took on the dance floor with Hard she thought of what he'd think if he saw her like this, in another man's arms. Then Hard had trodden on her foot and they'd both fallen over.

Hard had helped her up and got her a glass of sparkling wine and apologized at the bar for his clumsiness. 'It's never happened to me before. I don't know, I must have just lost all control of myself.'

'It's fine. We managed to get up again.'

'I think it's your fault.'

'My fault?' She took a sip and tried to avoid eye contact. He was looking at her all the time, but not at her eyes—at her lips.

'Yes.' He'd never seen lips like hers. 'You make me feel dizzy.'

And she'd laughed so hard that the wine came shooting out of her mouth and onto his dark suit.

'Now we're quit,' said Hard, unmoved.

'No. Oh God. Wait a minute.' She picked up a napkin from the bar and began rubbing at the fabric.

'Sparkling wine doesn't stain.'

'It does on silk.'

'I've got five of these, all from Vehndel and all at a special discount.' He stroked down his tie, touching her fingers. 'One more or less makes no difference.'

'It needs soaking.'

'Nix. There's no need. Really.'

But she'd already taken him by the hand and was leading him to the ladies', determined to remove the stain she'd made on his suit and tie. And as she undid the tie by one of the wash basins he pressed her up against him, like he had on the dance floor, and she let him, even though they weren't turning to the rhythm of the music any more but following the beat of their hearts. Then the door had opened, they had moved apart, and Eiske Ahlers, back then still Eiske Folkerts, said, 'I didn't see a thing.'

Shortly after that Theda had got engaged to Richard and Hard to Birgit, but whenever they ran into each other they looked for a way to be alone together. And then she'd undo his tie and he'd press her up against him. They'd pretend to fall to the floor by accident, as if it were all just clumsiness, something they had no control over. And every time they got dressed afterwards, he'd say, 'I didn't see a thing.' And she'd answer, 'That's good. There wasn't anything to see.' He knew it wasn't true and she did too. He'd seen something in her she didn't see herself, and neither did Richard, and she'd liked that but she didn't dare to talk to him openly about it because she was scared her life would lose its balance if she did. At some point Richard had proposed to her and she'd accepted, mainly to thank him for having the courage to make a decision that Bernhard didn't want to make, and that was the end of the episode, as she called their affair. And she was glad it had ended. Nevertheless, it had taken a long time for her to stop comparing one Hard to the other. She'd never found an excuse to come to the drugstore again, and he'd never taken her aside at a party and complimented her skin, her scent or her plump, soft lips. Instead, they chatted on the street or in the hammrich like two old friends who have a past but no present or future, politely and attentively but with no genuine interest.

'How are you?'

'Oh, fine. And you?'

'Everything's going well.'

'How are the kids doing?'

She never asked after Birgit and he never said a word about Richard.

'The twins get more alike every day. And Daniel, well, you'll have heard about the thing with the UFO.'

'Yes.'

'But he's back on track now.'

'That's good.'

'And what are your two up to?'

And then she'd tell him about her two daughters, who were older, almost grown up now, and sometimes as she stood there with him she'd think about what they'd have done if she'd got pregnant by him, despite the pill, if her children were his and his were hers. And every time, she's be overcome with such yearning that it made her look at her watch in the middle of a sentence and say goodbye. 'Oh goodness, I've got to run, sorry.'

'Nice to see you again.'

'Yes, lovely.'

Suddenly twenty years had passed, her daughters had left home, her husband was immersed in his second love—politics, the Free Democratic Party—and she was all alone with newspapers and numbers and invoices and Irma Geuken. Twenty years in which everything could have been different if she had made a decision herself back then instead of leaving it up to the men. She had the feeling she wasn't too old at fifty to take her life in hand and make up for what she'd missed. And when she heard from Harald Sievers which high-schooler would be keeping them company on his work experience programme for the next three weeks, she decided to use the opportunity to remove the stain Hard had left on her heart.

To her surprise, he had played along straight away the day before yesterday. 'This really is good.' She put the hand cream on the counter and took out her purse. 'How much is it?'

'Nix.'

'Hard, I don't want to owe you anything.' She held out a bank note.

'You don't.' He folded his arms. 'Is there anything else I can do for you, Theda?'

'Yes.'

'And that would be?'

'I need a stain remover.'

'What kind of a stain?'

'A pretty stubborn one.'

'Then I'm your man.' And then he really had gone over to the shelf with the cleaning fluids and shown her several tubes of Dr Beckmann's Stain Devils, until she'd drawn him into a corner and explained what she meant.

Now, two days later, they were lying next to each other on the loose parquet floor and a pile of money in the old church hall, naked and exhausted and wiping the sweat off their thighs with the bank notes. It was already dark outside but the fog reflected the light of the streetlamps and illuminated the room in what she thought was a ghostly way.

'Does Meinders know?'

'Of course. Nothing happens here without his blessing.'

'And this is all yours.'

'Part of it. This is just the stake, not the profit.'

'And who has the risk?'

'The investors.'

'Sounds like a good business model.'

'The banks don't do it any differently.'

'All or nothing.'

'That's the way it is.'

'Hard.' She looked at him. 'Shall we give it another try?'

'Any time.' He leant over her and pushed her legs apart with his pelvis.

But she pushed him away. 'That's not what I mean.'

'What then?'

'I mean, should we give it another try together, just you and me?'

'Theda, we're not twenty any more.'

'*We* never were twenty.'

'I was.'

'What would Birgit do if she knew about this?'

'You mean my side income?'

'No.' She propped herself up and watched his penis shrink. 'About us.'

On his last working day, Daniel wanted to suggest a story to the editor-in-chief that had been on his mind since his conversation with Simone in the school canteen and that seemed to be a better subject for the *Frisian News* than for the *Chalkeater*. He had sat in a corner during the morning conference, staring at the words in his notepad and drawing red circles around them like Robert Redford in *All the President's Men*. After that he'd sat down at his desk and read the newspaper. The telephone had rung twice and he'd got up to get a cup of coffee. Since then he'd been looking at his digital watch—quarter to one. Another fifteen minutes until lunch break. He took a couple of deep breaths, then he picked up his workbook and his notepad and set off for the second floor. He had thought it all out precisely. He hoped he could restore his credibility with a single spectacular story in the paper. He had to prove himself, best of all by uncovering a minor scandal, as a diversion to get at the major one, at Rosing.

Passing down the corridor, which ran straight through Politics, he heard someone on the telephone. 'They're all very good pitches . . . Yes, really . . . Great . . . I like your third suggestion a lot. I'll have to take it over myself, though . . . What? . . . No . . . It's just too big a story for you . . . The others? . . . They don't seem quite finished. You'd have to go back and . . . Yes . . . Right . . . But you're welcome to pitch me more stories . . . Yes . . . You too . . . You're welcome.' Then he hung up, came out into the corridor— it was Tammo Tammen, the trainee—and dashed past Daniel, chasing the story. Daniel stood still and watched him go, suddenly no longer knowing what to do. He looked up at a builder fixing a long metal box onto the ceiling, a shield for a neon strip lamp. As he screwed down one end, the other hung halfway down and bobbed about at every turn of the screwdriver.

At that moment the editor-in-chief came out of his office, one hand in his jacket pocket, the other to his face, drawing a glowing cigar away from his mouth. There was no going back now. 'All right,' said Masurczak as he blew the smoke to one side, 'what's that long face for? Just seen an alien, have you?' He laughed and coughed at the same time. Then he said, 'Just kidding. Don't take it personally. I don't bear grudges. Or have you come to complain?'

'No, I, er—'

'Well then, there's no reason to be unhappy.' Masurczak took a step towards him, removed his hand from his pocket and put it on Daniel's shoulder. 'You've made a good start. Two articles in one week. A lot of people here,' he swiped his cigar along the corridor, 'can only dream of that. You've got a bright future ahead of you. I was cycling from house to house delivering newspapers at your age. And you're a step further along already. If I don't watch out you'll be sitting on my chair in a couple of weeks.' He laughed again. 'Just kidding, son. Masurczak likes a joke. But seriously now—if you have anything else for us, go ahead. Just send it on over.'

'Well, the thing is,' said Daniel. He mustn't do anything wrong now. Above all, he mustn't let them take it off his hands, neither Tammo Tammen nor anyone else. He had to do it himself, all on his own. 'Today's my last day here, and I need to get my work-experience book signed, the daily and weekly reports.' He held up the book. 'Is Mr Sievers back yet?'

Masurczak took his hand away and stepped to one side to make way for the builder, who'd finished with one end of the shield and was moving his ladder to screw down the other end. 'Sievers? I shouldn't think so. Wait a sec.' He went over to one of the open doors that branched off the corridor every few metres, stuck his head through it and called, 'Has Sievers turned up today?' Daniel couldn't hear whether anyone answered but less than five seconds later Masurczak was back. 'I'd have been surprised if he was. He won't show his face before Monday.'

'Taken up smoking again, have you?' Duken appeared in one of the doorways with a coffee cup. 'Since when?'

'Since now,' said Masurczak, staring at his cigar as if he couldn't quite believe it himself.

'Does she know yet?'

'Who?'

'Your mother.'

'Not if you don't tell her. I certainly won't.'

'How should I do that? I'm not the one who lives with her,' said Duken, then blinked and walked towards the staircase, ignoring Masurczak's cry of 'Duck, Duken' until he bumped his head on the dangling lampshade.

'Watch where you're going!' said the builder.

Duken rubbed his forehead, glared at first the lamp shield and then the builder, said 'Watch it yourself!' and 'Idiot!' and disappeared down the stairs.

Once Duken had gone, a red-faced Masurczak, his temples thinly veiled with sweat, asked, 'Where were we?'

'Sievers,' said Daniel.

'Oh yes, right,' said Masurczak, grateful for the change of subject. 'He's been under a great deal of pressure recently. Now that the conversion here means new dismissals, the works council is practically ground down between the management and the staff.' Masurczak twisted the heels of his hands against each other and grinned, manoeuvring the cigar from one corner of his mouth to the other. 'I'm sure you've heard about the restructuring measures.

Merging the editorial departments, slimming down Distribution. It was all in the newspaper. But don't let all that stuff bother you. You're still right at the beginning, you've got your whole life ahead of you. If it's just a signature you need, that's no problem. I can do that for you.' Daniel opened up the book. Masurczak took a ballpoint pen out of his breast pocket, signed everything and repeated his encouragement to send him more stories.

'Even for Politics?' asked Daniel.

'No, but convince me I'm wrong,' he said. 'And say hello to your father from me.'

In the mornings, once the children were out of the house, Birgit came back to bed to him. She hoped to spend another half-hour lying there in the dark before she swapped her nightshirt for trousers and a blouse and a pair of shoes. She hoped that every time. But he felt the tremor, the movement transferred from her mattress to his, and that woke him up. And then he turned around to her, reached out a hand for her and whispered in a cracked voice, 'We're alone.'

He knew that what she'd once yearned for herself, an hour together for the two of them, was no longer as important to her as in the old days. She told him again and again how much she enjoyed the moments when she lay in his arms, in the bathtub, on the sofa, on the beach on holiday, those rare moments of pure tenderness. It was enough for her to kiss him, to touch him, to feel his warmth—and then to take a shower, watch TV or play in the sand with the twins. But that wasn't enough for him.

She was doing well in the shop, better than he'd expected. Her presence had opened up a whole new field of customers for him— women who didn't want to ask him for advice because they thought a man wouldn't be able to understand their needs or because they were embarrassed to talk to him about them, about their periods, their cellulite, their soft, baggy tummies. In fact, he knew the true extent of their problem zones; they were afraid they weren't attractive any more, couldn't show themselves to him and their own husbands any more, and he saw it as his job to give them back their confidence—by whatever means necessary.

Some came in and asked for Birgit right away, and if she wasn't there and wouldn't be back within the next half hour they'd walk straight out again. He tried to hold them there by assuring them there was nothing feminine that he wasn't familiar with, but they were rarely convinced. Especially the young girls, teenagers who had once bought sweets from him and now needed sanitary towels for the first time, felt uncomfortable around him. They lurked in the aisles, spending hours reading the packaging, and when he asked if he could help them they shook their heads or said, barely audibly, that they just wanted to look around, only to disappear for ever without another word. In the old days they'd have come back to him at some point, seeing as there was no alternative nearby, but now they'd go to Superneemann or to Schlecker in Achterup if it weren't for Birgit; they'd use the anonymity of the larger stores and they'd be intoxicated by the diversity of their ever-expanding stock ranges.

He had noted with some satisfaction that Birgit also profited from her not-quite-voluntary decision to work with him instead of for his two friends. Since she'd started in the shop she'd been more even-tempered, more self-determined and open. Her cooking had improved too. When she drove to the weekly market in the county town, she now brought home vegetables they'd never eaten previously, courgettes, aubergines, chard, and she'd fry minced meat—half beef, half lamb—or pork schnitzel or chicken to go with them. But it was also tiring for her to stand up in the drugstore all morning and then make the lunch. Living and working under one roof meant always being there for everyone, at all times.

If one of the kids was ill she'd stay upstairs to look after him or her, and if she heard the bell ring in the shop several times in a row she'd go down to serve the customers. And the minute she lay down next to him in bed at night or in the morning, absolutely exhausted from selling, cooking, speaking, he'd slide over to her and say, 'We're alone.'

He considered himself in the right; they had little time for themselves and he wanted to savour that time before the day began and put paid to all feeling. In the morning they were both in the shop and in the afternoon she had the twins to look after. Andreas and Julia were forever trying to persuade them they didn't have to do their homework. Or they'd come up with excuses for why they hadn't been given any that day. 'I did it at school.'—'There's no maths tomorrow.'—'Mrs Wolters is off sick.' They needed constant monitoring. Apart from that, someone had to take them to their sports clubs, their music lessons, the children's birthday parties all over the village or in the neighbouring villages. Daniel was still causing difficulties, unavoidable at his age, but Hard hoped his work-experience placement would give him a better perspective for dealing with his anger at the world. Only yesterday, Theda had told him how well he'd gone down with the editors, and that had made him confident that from now on Daniel would do something that didn't immediately make him look bad himself. And in the evenings Hard was out, either at Meinders' place or at the Beach Hotel, even though he didn't play cards there any more but watched Klaus and Günter getting fleeced by Gerald, their new third man.

As long as he didn't spend his free time at home and vie for the spot in front of the TV, Birgit wouldn't get any wrong ideas. He didn't have a guilty conscience. The way he saw it, he wasn't cheating on Birgit with other women—he was cheating on other women with Birgit. She should be grateful to him for the attention he gave her. She was allowed to claim the largest share of the blessing that ought to be due to all of them, and although he pointed out that privilege often enough, she rarely made the most of it.

His strategy of subtly referring to her prominent position every morning in bed had only worked once every few weeks, so far. He'd still stuck to it almost every day, though. So she ought to be all the more surprised when he stayed on his side of the bed this particular morning. The shutters were down, the only light piercing the gaps between the slats, she saw his cover rising and falling, he was breathing, he was alive, and she leant back, closed her eyes and thought of him, Hard the sexy stallion, *de geile Hingst*, who else would she think of, thought of him coming home late last night from a meeting with Meinders and pouncing on her in the dark, fresh from the shower and still high on unexpected winnings. He knew that she knew what he was up to, his dirty games with words and numbers, and he also knew that she didn't want to know any more than that. Both of them, they'd agreed at the beginning of their marriage, ought to be allowed to have secrets. And that still held now, almost twenty years on.

Birgit was an impatient woman. If he'd promised her to swap over an advertising sign or get a new light bulb for the bedroom, she'd remind him until he got it done; she could never wait to open her presents on her birthday; and everything that wasn't the same as always instantly aroused her suspicion. She'd lie there like that for a few seconds, her gaze fixed on the ceiling, her arms held close to her body, relieved he wasn't pressurizing her, but then she'd ask herself whether something was the matter with him, whether something was worrying him that stopped him from greeting her as usual, and she'd lean over to him to find out.

'Hard?'

'Mmh?'

'Is everything OK?'

'Mmh.'

She put her hand on his bare shoulder which protruded above the cover. 'Are you all right?'

'Mmh!'

'I think you ought to relax for once and not worry so much. You mustn't take everything so personally, like that thing with Klaus and Günter. You always say yourself, a game's a game. And maybe you should talk to Ennen again. How long were you in the male-voice choir? Twenty-five years? You can't just leave. You really weren't singing well in church on Good Friday. That happens sometimes. Even to the very best singers. Even to you.' Slowly, she stroked his torso, his nipples, his chest hair, and when she reached his navel she noticed he wasn't wearing his usual boxer shorts or pyjama bottoms. She drew her hand back spontaneously, but he held on to it and said, 'Biggi.'

'What?'

'We're alone. We're finally alone together.'

5

It was still the Easter holidays, the school and the cafeteria were still closed and there was no one there for him to ask. But Daniel knew someone, Simone had told him about someone, a boy from a more senior class, who'd worked there for a while and had then been fired from one day to the next.

'Oh, you mean Ronnie.' Her voice almost cracked.

'Yes,' said Daniel. 'Ronnie.' It was the first time he'd heard the name.

'Hold on, I'll have to look for his number. But don't tell him you got it from me.'

'Why not?'

There was a rustling sound on the other end. Then a bang. 'Shit. What did you say?'

'Why not?'

'Just don't tell him, OK?'

'OK,' said Daniel and jammed the receiver between his ear and his shoulder. 'So why not?'

'Oh God!' said Simone. 'Because I promised not to pass on his number. That's why.'

'And because you had a thing, the two of you.'

'How do you know that? Did Volker tell you?'

'Since when have you talked about that kind of thing to Volker?'

'Volker can be very discreet. Not like you.'

'You're not having a thing with him, are you?'

'With who?'

'Volker.'

'Are you crazy?'

'So you are, then.'

'To be honest I think Volker's more into guys, if anything.'

'Rubbish. Just because he's never had a girlfriend, doesn't mean he's—'

'I can think of someone else like that, by the way.'

'—into guys . . . What?'

'I can think of someone else like that.'

'Are you going to give me Ronnie's number or not?'

'No need to get offended.' She took an audible breath. 'Man, are you sensitive. There's nothing wrong with it. You'll find the right girl one day. Or the right guy.'

'Simone!'

'All right. I'll stop. Hold on. Here it is. Right. Have you got a pen?'

Hard had played with Marie Meinders when they were children. Their grandmothers, both farmers' daughters who had become farmers' wives, were cousins, she and he were three years apart and she'd taken care of him at family get-togethers as if he were the brother she'd never had. Then, when they got older, she saw more in him than that, a friend and a confidant. And at some point they'd found themselves drunk on their first beer in the hay, he in a shirt and trousers, she in a dirndl dress, and while he was stroking blades of hay out of her hair he thought it was time the two of them got to know each other even better. He kissed her, but only briefly, then his tongue followed his fingers to the very end of her décolleté. He pushed up her skirt and pulled down her knickers with one hand, as if he'd done it a hundred times before. She wanted to undo his flies but she was shaking so much she only managed the top button and he had to do the rest himself. Before he penetrated her she asked if he'd marry her and he, incapable of saying anything else, promised her he would.

From then on they met in the farmyard after school, spending hours and hours in the barn, watched the cows calve, the pigs suckle and the farmhand bludgeon the puppies to death. Until one of the grandmothers died and the other moved into a home and the house and the land were sold. He looked for new places, in the wheat, in the oats, in the high grass on the fields this side of the dyke. And she followed him, with a blanket, a tent, a bag full of bread and fruit.

But after a while she said, 'It can't go on like this.'

'What can't go on like this?' He removed his hand from her blouse.

'We can't go on doing this for ever. So casually. It wouldn't be right.'

'Who says it wouldn't?'

'God.'

'Since when have you listened to Him?'

'Since He opened my eyes.'

'I though it was me that did that.'

'Hard, I'm serious.'

'I must have missed something, though.'

'I just didn't raise the subject before because I was scared you'd finish with me if I told you.'

'You were right. Thou shalt have no other men before me.' He leapt up, bumped his head against the roof of the tent, although he was ducking, and clenched his fists. 'He's called God is he? And what's the rest of his name? Where do I find the guy?'

And then she knew it was all just a game for him.

Not long after that she married the new pastor, Hans Meinders. There was much indignation when people found out that such an old man—he was in his mid-thirties—was going to wed such a young girl—she was nineteen and under age. But anyone who saw them together in the village or the church had to take them for a happy couple. They held hands when they went out walking, they welcomed everyone with a smile before the church services, and Meinders spoke in his sermons of paradise, of lights in the heavens, of beasts and plants on the earth, of Adam and Eve, of golden rivers, of fruitful fields and sweet seeds that sprout and beguile the world with their scent and their beauty. Except his seed didn't sprout inside her. And that cast a shadow over their love.

They still walked hand-in-hand around the village and they still smiled at all the congregation before the church services, but Pastor Meinders' sermons grew harder and darker with every Sunday. Suddenly they were about murder and killings, about disasters and plagues, about first-born sons and human sacrifices—about how it was better not to have children in some circumstances.

'Be fruitful and multiply,' Meinders called from the pulpit. 'So it is written in Genesis. But where does this growth lead us? Are there not too many of us already? When will the seas be empty and the land full? And when will it be too late to end the misery sent into the world by God's very first commandment?' Many, especially the younger ones, saw him as a prophet denouncing over-population as the cause of poverty and war and exploitation, and calling attention to the limits of growth, but the older ones turned away from him and it was a great deal of work for Marie to bring them back to the fold. Yet only a few years later, he started again. This time he wasn't concerned with the big picture but with 'the mob,' as he put it, 'which is striking fear into our country.' He slammed the Bible shut and leant on the pulpit balustrade with both hands. 'The kingdom of heaven, Matthew tells us, belongs to the children. But what about those who, before they are grown up, become sinners? How do father and mother deal with that? What do the parents feel? Do they not ask themselves, have we not done everything in our power to raise them as good and just people? And what has become of them? Was it worth all the effort? Has it paid off? Or do they wish their spawn had never been born?'

And this time it was the other way around. The young ones felt betrayed by him and the old ones—Old Kramer above all—felt he'd confirmed their assessment of the young generation. But again, it was Marie who calmed the waves of his words. She organized children's Bible days, convinced confirmands to stick with it when they doubted the point of being confirmed, and as she felt useless otherwise she took charge of Religious Education lessons at the primary school, even though she had no teacher training.

The more time she spent with children, the more painful it was for her not to have any of her own. Her and his parents had long since given up asking when they were going to be grand-parents, but when she sat with her women friends and they showed off about their sons and daughters, she thought she made out an allusion to her childlessness in every sentence.

Marie's gynaecologist couldn't find anything to indicate infertility and Hans Meinders refused to see a urologist and hand over a cup full of sperm. 'If God wanted us to stay alone, then we will.'

They argued over it and didn't sleep together for months. And at some point they stopped trying entirely, and by the time they made up shortly after her fortieth birthday it didn't work any more. That was when she let Hard in on one of the village's best-kept secrets, not by telling him but by shopping at the drugstore.

'Marie,' he said when she put the tin of maca powder down on the counter. 'I know how much you long to have children. Everyone knows that. And I can help you. I can help both of you.' But when she found out how, she turned him down, left the shop without buying the universal remedy and swore never to come back.

She kept her word for exactly four weeks. Then she was back at his counter. And soon she was one of Hard's main customers for maca, which was supposed to work miracles on men, as the enclosed brochure claimed, but met resistance from Hans Meinders. She mixed it into his food, she dissolved it in his water, she even ordered maca roots directly from Peru via a Hamburg importer and served up nothing else for days, but the only visible result—if there was one at all—was that all these measures aroused his thirst, his thirst for schnapps.

She felt tied to Hans, in good times and in bad, and she'd never divorce him, even though they were too rarely 'one flesh', as he said, for his and her taste. He suffered just as much as she did; he had suggested adopting a child from Africa who would starve without them, as an act of compassion, but she'd resisted, not because of the child but for her own sake. And she was gradually running out of time, good time and bad. Even now, at her age, the gynaecologist had said, a pregnancy was a major risk.

'Every ovulation could be your last.' These words echoed within her as she left the parsonage in the afternoon and walked along Church Road and Village Road to the drugstore. In principle, she thought as she reached out a hand for the door, it wouldn't be adultery because Hard had been her first husband, even though they hadn't made their vows to God but only to each other. She would warm up an old love for a few minutes and then let it cool down for ever.

'Hello?' The voice sounded rough and brittle.

'Ronnie?'

'Daniel. Daniel Kuper. I'm a friend of Simone's and—'

'Oh Jesus. Leave her of it.'

'It's not about her.'

'What is it about then?'

'The cafeteria on the school campus. Simone said you worked there for a while.'

'That's not a good subject either.'

'Exactly, that's just why I want to talk to you.'

'I don't want to talk to you, though. Who are you anyway?'

'Daniel Kuper.'

'Yeah, you said that already.'

'My parents own the drugstore.'

'Condom Kuper! They must've forgotten to use one with you.'

'Probably,' said Daniel. 'So the thing is, I'm writing an article for the *Frisian News* about the hygiene there, and Simone said you—'

'Have you got a hearing problem? I said I don't want to talk about it. And anyway, I thought that wasn't right for you, I thought you weren't interested.'

'Who?'

'You journalists. I told my mother all about it, she works in Accounts there, and she said no one there would believe me anyway.'

'We can do a background interview,' said Daniel. He remembered the documentary about the history of the *Frisian News*, where someone had talked in an altered voice with his back to the camera in a darkened room. 'You'd be absolutely anonymous.' Then he thought of *All the President's Men*, of Deep Throat, the informer in the underground parking lot. 'Or you could just confirm what I already know.'

'What do you know?'

'Not much.'

'I can confirm that.'

'Come on, don't be like that.'

'You really must be deaf.'

'I thought you'd have an interest in getting the cafeteria closed down, after everything that happened. But if you don't want—'

'Hold on,' said Ronnie. 'I didn't mean it like that. And you can promise me my name won't show up anywhere?'

'Sure.'

'Where and when shall we meet?'

In the afternoons, when Birgit was looking after the household and the children, Hard received his regular female customers. Some of them came during the morning as well, but they were pensioners who waited for the moment he opened up the shop and asked his advice for hours on end to kill time. He'd been surprised to begin with how much patience he found for them, in his determination to break their habits. There was nothing more difficult than recommending a new product designed for their skin when they'd been rubbing Nivea cream into their faces for forty years, but he managed it. He held their hands in his, showed them what to pay attention to, and then gave them so many free samples that they couldn't resist trying them out at home. He'd been surprised because he'd never found that much patience for Birgit. Instead of convincing her with arguments he'd pay her compliments, massage the nape of her neck with special Dead Sea oil and give her flowers, and if that didn't get him what he wanted he'd stop and put his plan—whatever it was—into practice without her permission. And when she got angry with him for excluding her yet again, he'd say, 'I told you about it.'

'Yes, but I didn't want you to do it. And you did it anyway.'

'And now you can see that this investment was only to our advantage.'

'How are new shop fittings to our advantage? The old ones were still good for a few years.'

'We have to move with the times, Biggi. We have to constantly renew ourselves, otherwise others will end up renewing us.'

'Like who?'

'People more powerful than us.'

'And who's going to pay for all this?' She gestured at the new shelves.

'*Da mook di man kien Kummer um.*'

'But Hard, I *am* worried. Your money's my money too. And if you go under you'll pull me down with you. Me and the kids as well.'

'Do you know what you sound like to me?'

'No, I don't.'

'Like Günter Vehndel.'

And that was usually the end of the discussion. The idea of bearing even the slightest similarity to one of his friends—Günter or Klaus—didn't match up to Birgit's image of herself, not after both of them had rejected her applications on his instructions. And as soon as he compared her to them now she'd get so angry that she'd leave the room, because as she told him afterwards she couldn't look him in the eye without shouting.

Sometimes Marlies and Sabine came by in the afternoons, first to him and then to her, and then they'd sit in the living room with the door ajar—Birgit was on call upstairs and he didn't want to have to phone her—and have tea and cake, and he'd listen to their stories from downstairs in the office.

'Have you tried this one? Escape?'

'No,' said Sabine. 'Smells like sandalwood.'

'It is sandalwood. Among other things, anyway.'

'No, that'd be too strong for me.'

'You're just not the right type for it.'

'No, I'm a flower,' Sabine put on a funny voice, 'an acacia, hyacinth, magnolia. And flowers have petals.'

'And stamens.' Marlies started giggling and then said it again. 'And stamens.'

'Yes, Marlies, I heard you the first time. But I've got something here, better than all the stamens in the world. . . . Here . . . Wait . . . Just a moment . . . It's too soon. Wait until the heart note comes out. It'll knock you out.'

Almost everything they said, 'sandalwood', 'type', 'flower', 'petals', 'stamens', 'heart note', they had from him, and he was always amazed at how strongly his words dazzled his female customers' judgement; a few expressions they'd never heard before and he had them eating out of his hand. All he'd done was read through the descriptions in the catalogues and memorized a few features of each perfume. Still, it wasn't always the words that seduced them into buying a product, but the presentation. He didn't force anything on them if they didn't want it. He'd usually stand to one side, two or three steps away from them, and only come closer if they asked his opinion. And then there were times, like today, when he'd say something that made no apparent business sense. 'That's the most expensive thing I have in the whole shop, Mrs Kromminga. And even so, through the pungent sweetness it exudes it comes across as cheap. That might awaken desires or leave a false impression, depending on the occasion you wear it on. Don't let the big name fool you. For a woman like you, with your natural elegance, a subtle scent is absolutely sufficient to emphasize your aura, a breath of bergamot, papaya, pineapple, something fresh, like this.' He handed her a flacon. 'Try this one.' He left them the choice until the end, merely making recommendations to steer them in the direction in which he wanted to send them, but at some point he'd say, 'You're welcome to take a sample home and ask your husband.'

'My husband? He doesn't know a thing about it.'

'Now don't say that. Who's an expert on your scent if not him?'

'He doesn't care what I smell like, as long as I don't stink. No, no, I'll take this one here, with pineapple, something nice and fresh.'

And while he was cashing up and registered Marie outside the window out of the corner of his eye, he remembered that he'd talked Birgit round in a rather similar way after their evening out dancing on the island. He'd still been a soldier at the time and had only put on his white coat to make a good impression on the girls staying there on their holidays. And as he led her onto the dance floor he said, 'Your skin's like alabaster.' His father had recently taken consignment of a dozen mineral fragrance lamps for the drugstore, Hard had broken one of them as he unpacked it at the weekend, and he meant that Birgit was just as fragile because her skin was transparent and the veins showed through beneath it, but she thought he'd paid her a particularly original compliment.

'Oh, thank you. Alabaster. I've never heard of it. What is it?'

'A crystal.' He could have said 'a stone' and not been lying either. And that was when he noticed what a difference a word made, and that it took on a different meaning depending on how and where and to whom it was spoken, like Compunist Corner, like Hard, like nix. Anything was possible. Perhaps he really had wanted to pay her a compliment, with no bad intentions—other than getting her into bed. One word had changed his life. And Birgit's too. But after Daniel was born the alabaster-like quality had given way to an even, doughy pallor.

There was another party that Saturday. Daniel had wanted to go with Simone and had phoned her to suggest they cycle there together, but she'd said she didn't have time and she already had other plans, something better to do.

Paul and Jens were just putting the beer on ice when he arrived and he helped them to set everything up. He still had to drink the vodka though, more than usual because he couldn't answer the question of which horror film featured alien parasites landing on earth and all the characters had the names of famous horror film directors. At first they were the only ones there, then the rooms began to fill up around ten, and soon there was no space to move. For a long time, Daniel sat on his own at a table in the corner, a full, unopened can in his hand. No one took any notice of him until Volker sat down next to him and held out a bag of salt sticks.

'Want a game?'

Daniel shook his head.

'Come on. It's really easy. Even my sisters beat me at it.' And when Daniel showed no reaction he said, 'For one gram of this miracle stuff. It'll make you weightless.'

Daniel shook his head again, not knowing what Volker meant, but then he saw that he was playing pick-up-sticks against himself with the pretzel sticks and opening a new pack after every round, spreading the contents on the table and rewarding himself for every point.

Daniel snapped the beer can tab against the metal to the rhythm of the music, sometimes fast, sometimes slower, sensing that if he took a gulp, if he even opened it, it'd be all over for him. He wanted to stay until the end for once, see what happened, experience what the others always talked about afterwards—how things slipped out of control, how there was one girl for every boy, how fathers came for their daughters and the cops came for the amplifier. At some point he dropped the can, stood up, both hands pressing against the arm rests, and swayed downstairs. On the stairs he ran into Paul, his hair gelled into short spikes, his shirt unbuttoned. 'Alright Kuper, want to add something to your *Manifesto*? Mind you, the way you look, you'd better not.' Comeon Danielyouhavetopunchhimrightintheballsthat'sthekindofviolence youwanttoseeifnotfeelyouhavetopunchhimsohardhedoublesover goesdownonhiskneesbeforeyoubegsformercythentakearunupand kickhimfulloninthehead overandoveruntilhisearfallsoffuntilhefalls downthestairsonhisarsearseovertitandallthatsoyoucanhearhis bonessplittingandbeforehecomesroundagainjumprightonhis facerightinthemiddleofhisuglymugandthenyoutakeabanisterpole

583

andmakemincemeatofhismeatloaffacegirlsscreamingintimeto
yourblowsgirlscomeuptothebanisterstakeoffyourpantiesand
throwthematme. The light of an old fifties standard lamp shone
on Paul from below, and for a moment Daniel stood in Paul's
huge shadow and saw nothing but his dark head and the corona
surrounding his skull, like during an eclipse. Then Daniel stepped
aside. Paul walked past, pulling Simone along behind him. He
almost didn't recognize her with her hair blond. In the hallway he
collided with Iron, motorbike helmet jammed under his arm, a
sports bag thrown over his shoulder, John Lennon glasses misted
over, like fog. They were the same height now and had the same
stature, and Daniel stood firm against the jolt that Iron dealt him.

As he opened the door he heard Paul saying, 'Ah, the Shadow-
man's here. Fresh supplies at last, guys.'

And Jens: 'About time too. My brain's started working again.'

Then he was outside. On the way home he tried to keep his
balance. His view, when he looked up, didn't reach ten metres away,
and when he looked at the ground the contours overlapped in his
head. He kept scraping the pedals along the bushes, or veering
onto the grass verge next to the cycle path. As he passed one of the
bus stops on Village Road, he thought he'd seen something. A
swastika, a slogan, one of the symbols he had painted over and
wiped away, but when he cycled back and stopped there was
nothing, only concrete.

Before Eiske Ahlers entered the drugstore she took a moment to
inspect her reflection in the dark glass door, her new hairdo, her
new lipstick, the new chain of pearls around her neck. Then she
was standing in front of him. She'd put on a short dress cut low
at the front, although it was really too cold at this time of year. In
the summer the young girls threatened to outstrip her but now, in

spring, she was the only woman in Jericho who dressed in as little as possible, and no one, not even her husband, could stop her from doing so.

She came by once a month, but not always at the same time on the same day. Hard never knew when she'd turn up and sometimes he had the feeling she wanted to ambush him, waiting outside in the street, on the pavement, in the post office opposite, checking whether the coast was clear, whether Birgit was in the shop or upstairs in the house before she visited him. He'd simmered with excitement for these encounters for twenty-five years, but after the evening in the church hall with Theda Wiemers, after Marie Meinders' announcement that she did want to accept his help after all, he feared he was no longer up to Eiske Ahlers.

'What's the matter, Hard?'

'Nix.'

'You seem so nervous. There's no one here but us.'

'It's all just down to you.'

'Oh, come now. I'm more of a habit to you now.'

'How can that be, when you look different every time and every time younger and more beautiful?'

'Well, that's all down to you.'

'Speaking of which. I've got something for you, extra gentle for maximum moisture.'

'And this, this new product, it's in the stock room, I assume. And you can't get it all on your own because it's too big and long.'

'How did you guess?'

'I just sensed it.'

'Well, let's have a look and see if you sensed right.'

He went ahead and she followed him. The shelves reached from the floor to the ceiling. On one side was the entrance to the basement and on the other, beneath a small window, was a steel desk covered in a fine layer of dust. A hole gaped in the wall above it, the plaster knocked off, the brickwork exposed. And next to it were a few cardboard boxes, boxes full of cotton wool and nappies and kitchen paper rolls. And that was what they were heading for now. They didn't have much time. They never had much time. Unless Birgit took the children to visit her sisters in Bad Vilbel.

In all the years they'd been together like this, it had happened two or three times that they heard the bell ring and someone calling for him when they were in the middle of things—whenever Hard or whenever she had forgotten to turn the sign on the door around, like today.

'Excuse me a moment.' He rose from her, buttoned his coat and went back into the shop. She lay for a while in semi-darkness, adjusted her clothes and waited until they could go on. Then, when the wait got too long and the conversation next door too dull, she tried out the products stored around her and pocketed a few of them. She always took something from the drugstore, even when she was standing out front in the shop and Hard was still serving another woman—as a souvenir of her adventure. And it was always something she'd never come across before. Sometimes she told Hard and sometimes she let him catch her in the act.

The names on the packaging sounded exotic—ginseng, guarana, maca and kava kava—and made her think of faraway worlds, places she'd never been and would never go. Some of them Hard got delivered and others—like night milk crystals, colloidal silver or the hair-growth compound Procapillaris—he made himself. Many of the patients who came to her husband's surgery called Gerald the medicine man, as a joke, but for most of the women the village's true shaman was Bernhard Kuper.

'Right,' said Hard as he came back in. 'What were we up to?'

'We were more down than up.'

'Oh, yes.' He leant over her and pressed her back onto the cardboard boxes with his torso. Several tubes and packets fell on the floor and while she picked them up and put them on the shelves he said, 'You've no need for that.'

She was never sure what he meant by that, whether he was referring to her money or her health, and she never asked.

Then he said, 'Just you wait, you little minx, I've got something much more effective for you, all natural,' slapped her face several times and unbuttoned his coat.

The household remedies that Eiske regularly pocketed so that he'd punish her for her crime were an inheritance from his father. He didn't believe in all the properties attributed to them but back when he was just about to take over the shop from his parents, they'd been the only way to position drugstores against the pharmacies. To begin with he'd considered throwing all that stuff away, to show everyone there was a fresh wind blowing in Kuper's Drugstore. Then Birgit had persuaded him to keep it, because women from outside the village came to them especially for it. 'Leave it in stock. Even if the only effect is making people feel better about themselves.'

'But it's a con.'

'You don't have to put it in the display window.'

And he didn't, in fact he didn't advertise it at all, but neither did he hide the homeopathic products under the counter. Still, there were women who waited until they were alone with him before they dared to ask for them. Apart from Mrs Zuhl, Daniel's former class teacher, none of them had ever complained to him, and that had encouraged him to expand the range. The stock room had got more and more crowded and he missed the space they'd once had at their disposal.

She liked the idea of doing it with Hard in the back room, surrounded by the elixirs of the devil, as Gerald called the tubes and

587

bottles and tins she brought home after each of their assignations. She felt dirty even on the way to the drugstore, and when the dust above them came dislodged by his and her thrusts and settled on them, she felt it like a blessing of evil, which aroused her more than anything else. What she liked most about her visits, though, was the risk of getting caught. It made the short time they had together something valuable.

They hadn't always met in the stock room, however. After she'd seen Hard and Theda in the ladies' toilet at the Friesenhuus, she'd often arranged to meet him in Aurich. Gerald thought she was visiting her parents and siblings in the neighbouring village of Haxtum, and she was but she always added an extra night, booked a room in town and waited for Hard to come over from the barracks. And later, when Mrs Bluhm had worked for him and Birgit was busy with the children, more so than now, they had driven one of their cars to the hammrich, to remote spots where only farmers went to get to their crops.

'I *am* just a habit for you.'

'No.' Hard had stopped moving. 'I don't know what's the matter.' He couldn't stop thinking of Theda Wiemers, what she'd said to him, what she'd asked him. And almost simultaneously, Marie Meinders crossed his mind. Normally, his discipline helped him to keep thoughts like these at bay and concentrate entirely on old or new tasks ahead of him.

'It's never happened to you before.' Eiske stroked his back but Hard sat up, reached into one of the cardboard boxes and took out a roll of kitchen paper so that she could wipe the lipstick off him. First he gambled away his good luck, then his voice failed him and now this.

'Maybe you should have a try of maca.'

'That doesn't work.'

'That's not what you tell the women who buy it for their husbands.'

'I'm only telling them what they want to hear.'

'And that works?'

He nodded. 'Just not on me.'

'Maybe we should go for a drive like we used to.'

'You mean to the hammrich?' She'd take command out there.

'Yes,' she said, wiping his cheek with the scrunched-up piece of kitchen paper. 'We should make the most of the fog while it's still here.'

The Beach Hotel was more than a place for travelling salesmen and tourists to stay. There were the rooms upstairs, but downstairs there was a pub where men and women sat at the bar in the evenings and outdrank each other or—like his father and his friends—played card games like skat. And at the back, facing the lake, there were two function rooms, a large one and a small one, where club members met once a week to discuss rabbits, ammunition or football or sing songs, until they were hoarse or too drunk to go on. During the day, especially at weekends, the Beach Hotel was a cafe and restaurant and the only place in the village open at half past nine in the morning.

When Daniel entered the room he saw lots of old women at the tables in their best dresses, ready for church, and only one young man right by the entrance. Even if Ronnie hadn't raised his hand, Daniel would have been certain it was him. No normal person under the age of twenty went to the Beach Hotel on a Sunday morning.

'Aren't you that kid who was in the paper?' asked Ronnie once they'd made their introductions. 'The one with the swastikas?'

'I was trying to get rid of them.'

'You managed that all right.'

'But not the way I wanted.'

'Right,' said Ronnie. 'What do you want to know?'

'Why did you get the sack?'

'Because I wanted to make a complaint.'

'To who?'

'To Schulz.'

'What about?'

'About the conditions.'

'About how plastic cups are taken out of the rubbish and used again?'

'Not just that.'

'The rats!'

Ronnie gave a dismissive wave of his hand. 'You know the minced pork rolls, right?'

'Yes,' said Daniel tonelessly. He suddenly thought he could taste raw meat and onions. 'I know the ones.'

At that moment, a young woman in a black shirt and a black apron stepped up to their table. 'What can I get you?'

'A coffee,' said Daniel.

'A coffee, *please*.'

'What?'

'Oh, forget it,' said the woman and looked over at Ronnie. 'Are you going to be here long?'

'Why?'

'Because Enno's been asking after you.'

'Oh really? Has he now?'

'Yes, he has,'

'Then tell him my shift doesn't start until half an hour from now.'

'Tell him yourself,' said the woman, turning on her heel.

'I will,' Ronnie called after her. 'When I see him.'

'You work here?' asked Daniel.

'Out the back,' said Ronnie. 'In the kitchen.' He nodded over at the counter.

'Anyway,' said Daniel. 'The minced pork rolls.'

Ronnie looked both ways and leant over to him. 'If there are any left over at the end of the day, they drizzle lemon juice over them,' he held his hand above the table and rubbed three fingers together, 'put them in the fridge and mix the old ones in with the new ones the next day. In the end no one knows which ones are which. And if any of them are left over they go back in the fridge overnight. Once I had one in my hand one morning and it was already pretty far gone, half grey and half yellow, and I was just going to throw it away when the boss came in and asked what I was doing. I told her it was gone off. And do you know what she said then?'—Daniel shook his head—'It's still good for making meatballs.' Ronnie leant back again. 'And then I told her I was going to make a complaint about her. And then she said, go ahead, but then I'll tell Schulz you've been stealing money.'

'What money?'

Ronnie pointed a finger at Daniel. 'That's exactly what I said. And then she said, the money you stole from me.'

'You stole money?'

'Who did you steal from?' asked the woman from before, putting the cup of coffee down in front of Daniel. 'From Enno?'

'No one.'

'I'm going to ask Enno.'

'No you're not.' He grabbed at her hand but she dodged and took a step back.

'Scared, are you?'

'No, I'm not.'

'Well, that's all right then,' she said. 'Then you've got nothing to worry about when I ask Enno.'

'Do what you like. I don't care.'

'Really?'

'Yeah, really.'

'Right then—and when it comes to you,' she turned to Daniel, 'a thank-you never harmed no one.'

'Thank you,' said Daniel, but so quietly that he could barely hear it himself.

'Pardon?'

And Daniel said 'Thank you' again, louder this time.

'That's better,' she said and disappeared behind the counter.

'Who's *that*?' asked Daniel.

'Gesa.'

'Gesa who?'

Ronnie shrugged. 'Don't know her surname. Student in Münster. Only works here on the weekends and in the holidays.'

'Anyway,' said Daniel. 'What about the money from the cafeteria, did you steal it or didn't you?'

'Of course I didn't. The old bag just said that to make me look bad. She said money'd gone missing on my shift. Allegedly. And she said she'd meant to report it immediately, just after she'd noticed, but hadn't out of consideration for my future—I'd get chucked out of school. And then she threw me out.'

'But you didn't do anything.'

'I couldn't prove that, though. It was her word against mine. And who believes a schoolkid? I'll give you three guesses.'

'Have you seen it yet?'

'What?'

'The ad.'

'What ad?'

'This one. In the *Sunday News*. Underneath the story about the Kurds who occupied Wiemers' office. As if the FDP could help anyone over in Iraq.'

Birgit wiped her hands on her apron and looked over Hard's shoulder.

'Terrible, as if someone had died.'

'Someone is dying.'

'Yes, but people don't usually hire contract killers publicly.'

'They haven't found anyone yet.'

'Might not be long now though.'

'How come?'

'I've heard the laundry next to Vehndel's is closing down.'

'When?'

'Any day now, at the end of April. Sabine told me today. Günter can't afford to have the space vacant. They need the rent, and you know how hard it is to find anyone.'

'First Klaus with his new range and now Günter.'

'It doesn't mean they'll rent it out to *them*.' Birgit turned back to the saucepans. 'How come there's no name in the ad?'

'How should I know, but it's definitely from Schlecker, it looks exactly the same as the other ones.'

'Schlecker. What kind of a name is that anyway? Sounds more like an ice cream company.'

'They're not druggists, they're just checkout girls, they don't know a thing about pharmacy, medicine, chemistry, botany. It's a mystery to me how they're supposed to advise anyone. But people don't want advice any more, as long as it's cheap.'

'Stop moaning.'

'It's true.'

'Do you know what you sound like to me?'

'Don't tell me.'

'What happened between you and Günter anyway?'

'Nix.'

'So go and talk to him then.'

'You must be kidding. If there's anyone who ought to be talking it's him to me, not me to him.'

'I can't help you either then.'

'You don't have to. No one has to help me. I can manage on my own.'

6

At school on Monday, everyone reported back on their work-experience placements. Mrs Nanninga questioned them all, one after another. Many of them were disillusioned. Most of them said the three weeks had shown them they weren't cut out for the job they'd been interested in. They hadn't been able to square their image of it with reality. People had made it difficult for them though, they said. They'd often spent all day standing around and weren't allowed to work properly, for insurance reasons.

'Jens,' Mrs Nanninga asked. 'How did it go for you?'

He shrugged his shoulders. 'Badly.'

'Why?'

Another shrug . 'I just realized plumbing's not right for me after all.'

'Why not?'

'Cleaning up other people's shit until I retire doesn't fit in with my life plan, it's really kind of boring, you know.'

'What were you expecting?'

He shrugged a third time. 'Don't know, just something else. You do get around a lot, you work a lot with people, but I think I will do something different now.'

'Like what?'

'First I didn't want to, but now I think I will do an apprenticeship with my father.'

'At the solarium?'

'Right, yeah.' He licked his top lip. 'That seems like it'd kind of be a more promising outlook, you know.'

'What outlook would that be?' asked Paul, who sat next to him, tugging at his strand of hair.

The boys laughed and groaned. The girls accused them of being primitive and superficial. To calm them down again, Mrs Nanninga asked Paul how he'd enjoyed his work experience placement with the police force.

'It was crap.'

'Why?'

'Nothing happened. Nothing cool, anyway, no muggings or murders. We just drove around all the time, for hours at a time, it was really stupid. And most of the call-outs were just for loud music, small accidents and confused old folks, and we had to track them down like runaway pets. There was this one old woman we had to fetch down from a tree. And the worst thing was, I had to listen to their whole life stories on the back seat. How they were in the war and on the run from the Russians and all that. Or whatever was left over, it was all muddled up in their heads, totally crazy. No way do I want to end up like that.'

Simone put her hand up. She clicked her fingers three times until Mrs Nanninga called on her. 'I can't see any development,' Simone said to Paul. 'I'm always seeing you confused on the back seat.'

Paul's face turned red. The boys and girls laughed. Mrs Nanninga asked for quiet.

Volker leant over to Daniel and asked in a whisper, 'What time is it anyway? I've got lung yearnings.'

Daniel looked at his digital watch. 'Just after eight.'

Volker gave a brief sigh and stowed the cigarette packet he'd just taken out back into his jacket pocket. 'The best thing about my work experience was the smoking breaks,' he said as quietly as possible, which was never quiet enough not to be heard by everyone else too, due to his deep, scratchy voice. 'We went out to Busboom's service station for a ciggie every half hour. The stupid thing is, I've got used to the rhythm now. I have to make greater use of substitute drugs from now on,' he said, then reached into his satchel and took four aluminium-wrapped halved slices of wholemeal bread spread with liver sausage out of a plastic box. 'I've doubled the daily dose to be on the safe side, to ward off any withdrawal symptoms right away.' A low-flying combat plane thundered over the building. Mrs Nanninga made a note in the register. Before the bell rang she collected up the work-experience books.

During the second break of the day, Daniel bought one of the minced pork rolls from behind the glass counter in the cafeteria and took it out to the corridor. He wrapped it in cling film and put it in his army backpack. He walked across the foyer and the bus parking lot to the bike stand, snapped open his lock and cycled off into the ever-thickening fog, across the fields and the dykes, past the back of the rubbish tip and alongside the railway tracks, a narrow path strewn with potholes and broken glass which he only managed to dodge at the last moment. In the county town, on the other side of the river where the air was clear, he pedalled against the wind. Every road he turned into was like a wall. It seemed as if the wind kept turning in the direction from which he'd just come, as if trying to hold him back.

By the time he got to the Public Order Office, Department of Veterinary Medicine and Food Inspection, Office 23, a brick villa directly on Frisian Road, he saw that he was too late, that it wouldn't be open until the next day. He turned around and cycled against the wind, against his anger at not being able to do anything, all the way back to the village. The next day he bought another minced pork roll, wrapped it up again and cycled into town to the public order office, skipping his two last classes. His parents would have to write him a note. He'd tell them he hadn't been feeling well, he'd been sent home and had a dizzy turn on the way, sat down on the grass and lost consciousness for a while. They'd send him to Doctor Ahlers, as they so often had. And he'd examine him and not find anything. He'd give him a sick note to be on the safe side and a new appointment, or refer him to a neurologist or say circulation problems were not uncommon at his age. It might get him a week off school, a week's time.

The office was housed in a residential building that looked no different from the outside to the other houses on the street, all of them villas, but once he went inside Daniel immediately heard the clatter of electric typewriters from several rooms. On the walls were diagrams of cross-sectioned cows and sheep and horses, and in the corridor was a display case full of shiny intestinal needles, mouth wedges, tooth forceps, ear notchers, emasculators and eye hooks, illuminated by a spotlight. Doors went off the corridor on all sides, most of them not shut, and Daniel approached one of them, knocked on the door frame and took a step into the room. Two women huddled together in one corner turned around to him in synch and asked what he wanted. Daniel said he had a sample with him, holding up the roll as if to prove it. 'That's upstairs,' said one of the women, 'on the first floor, room one oh one.' Only as he left did he notice she was holding a scalpel and there was blood dripping onto the linoleum from her fingers.

Upstairs, all the doors were closed, and if there had ever been signs on them with room numbers they'd been removed and replaced with names. He knocked at one door and when no one answered, he knocked at another with the name *Theo Houtjes* on it, beneath it the words *Food Inspection*. A man called out, 'Just a moment.' Daniel held the handle down but waited minutes for permission to enter, maintaining his position for an eternity, it seemed to him, until a loud 'Come in' granted him redemption.

Daniel had expected a laboratory with bubbling test tubes, apparatus and tiled walls. Instead, he found himself in a room full of filing cabinets and bookshelves, which might just as well have been one of the newspaper editorial offices. Even the man who'd asked him in was leaning over a typewriter and clamping in a new sheet of paper. The only thing to distinguish him from an editor was that he was wearing a white coat like a doctor or a pharmacist, or a druggist.

Among the notes on the board occupying almost the entire rear wall, a photo was pinned up showing the man in a flannel shirt, army trousers and clunky shoes, clutching a huge green fish to his chest.

Daniel got straight to the point and put the minced pork roll down on the desk in front of him.

'Where did you get that?'

'From a snack bar.'

'Which one?'

'Can you still eat it?'

'You can eat almost anything.'

'Should you still eat it?'

'Why do you want to know?'

'I'm working on a story.'

'What kind of a story?'

'I'm writing an article about this snack bar, and someone told me they sell old minced pork rolls here. And it seems there's something wrong with the coffee as well, or the coffee cups, because they fish them out of the rubbish. That's what I've heard, anyway.'

'Aha, that's what you've heard.'

'Yes, I don't know myself quite yet whether the accusations will hold, so I don't want to give too much away yet. But if you inspect the place now, maybe it'll all come out and someone with more influence at the newspaper than me will get to it first. I've seen that happen before.'

'Aha,' said the inspector. 'You've seen that happen before. You've seen all sorts at your age. You're young Kuper, aren't you, the one with the graffiti. I know your father from fishing. I'm sometimes over in Jericho. And if I have enough time afterwards I drive out to one of the old sand pits or the kolk on School Road. And then I buy my bait from you, tiger nuts, the best around, by the way. But the thing with the pork roll isn't possible the way you've planned it. As long as I don't know where this,' he picked up the roll, 'comes from and what the spatial and hygienic conditions are like in this snack bar, I'm not allowed to commission an examination at the county office. And if I did it myself it'd only prove that this one roll has gone off. Nothing more than that. That's not nearly enough to issue a warning to the operator or withdraw their licence. And it wouldn't be enough for an article either. Apart from that, this looks more like minced pork and onion to me, not pure minced pork, smells like it too, a bit acidic maybe, slightly too acidic, but there could be plenty of reasons for that.' He turned around in his chair, pulled open a drawer, took out a hanging file folder and returned to his original position. 'Let me make a suggestion. I'll send in a sample if you tell me where you got it from, and as soon as the result comes in I'll do a spot-check. And even though I'm not obliged to do so, even though I'm not actually allowed to, I'll let you know. It might take a few days, though.'

Daniel agreed and cycled through the hammrich and the fog back to Jericho.

They had taken Hard's car. Eiske had her own, a Peugeot 205 CTI 1.6, 1987 model, 104 PS, 76 kW, but it was too small and too open for what they had in mind.

'I still don't understand why you didn't get yourself an estate car after Gerald's accident,' said Hard, driving along farm tracks at walking pace. 'We could have folded down the seats.'

'Gerald's got an estate.'

'Yes, but he had the accident in your car.'

'Because mine was faster than his.'

'Did it have to be another convertible after all that?'

'I never thought it would come to this again afterwards.'

'Come to what?'

'To us. I think that every time.'

'Then why have you turned up outside my door once a month for the past twenty-five years? Maybe we should celebrate our silver anniversary soon.'

'I've tried to give it up but I can't. I tell myself every time, that's enough, it's all over.'

'Maybe it is. Over, I mean.'

'That's entirely up to you.'

'I'm back in shape now.'

'I should hope so too. For your sake. And for mine. I couldn't live without it.'

'It's like an addiction.'

'Exactly right.'

'You can't resist me.'

'It's nothing to do with you.'

'Oh, isn't it?'

'No.'

'And who then?'

'It's to do with me.'

They turned onto Hoogstraat, the windscreen wipers flapping left and right on the lowest speed and the fine droplets left on the glass by the fog trickling down the sides, and still they could barely see the asphalt ahead of them. From the white walls all around them emerged fences, trees and cows' heads, then vanished again. At one point they saw two suns heading towards them, which turned out when they halted on the grass verge to be the head-lamps of a tractor. The man behind the wheel raised a hand in greeting, and Hard returned the gesture.

'That was Watermann.'

'I know.' Hard eased off the clutch.

'Did you see his eyes?'

'He always looks crazy like that.'

'They nearly fell out of his head.'

'So? We're not doing anything that's not allowed.'

'Aren't we? I thought that was the reason why we came out here. What are we doing here then?'

'An expedition to the animal kingdom.'

'Gerald says it's because of the dyke.'

'What is?'

'The fog. The dyke and the railway embankment. The hamm-rich is like a valley.'

'Could be. It's just strange that it's staying put here so long. It's normally gone after two or three days.'

'Maybe it's smog.'

'Here? In this area? Surely not. There's nix here that makes smoke apart from the custard factory. And even if it was you'd smell it. And I can't smell nix. Can you?'

Eiske shook her head.

But as they drove further into the fields a mouldy smell dispersed around the car and the glass misted over on the inside, so that Hard turned up the heater and switched on the ventilation and they both pulled the sleeves of their jackets over their hands and began to swipe them across the panes.

'We ought to open the windows.'

'That's no use.'

'Let's stop the car then.'

'This isn't our spot.'

'This spot is good enough,' said Eiske, putting a hand on his thigh and sliding it gradually upwards.

'We're in the middle of the road.'

'We're in the middle of nowhere.'

'We're not even here.'

'Precisely.' Her hand was now right where it always ought to be, in his opinion.

'We don't even exist.'

'Enough talking.' She undid his zip and Hard just managed to press the central locking mechanism before she leant over his lap. For a moment he thought it wouldn't work out that day either, but then he felt the wet heat of her mouth and it made him forget everything that had gathered in his mind over the past few days, his fears that Theda Wiemers might tell Birgit about their affair, that Marie Meinders might be pregnant by him, that he was getting to the age when it all went downhill. Deep inside him, in the remainder of his brain still being supplied with blood, he regretted having cheated on Birgit, should it really be nearly the end for him, but Eiske removed the pressure that weighed on his soul and granted him absolution.

Afterwards they sat on the back seat, next to each other, half-undressed. Eiske was asleep and Hard had nodded off for a moment too and then been woken by a sound, by the clack of the door handle. There was someone at the window. At first he saw only a hand, a minute later a face, its nose pressed to the glass, a blurred outline. Whoever it was, he went away. Hard breathed out and reached for his trousers, which had slid down to his ankles, he couldn't remember how, and just as he went to pull them up there was a knocking, five times in a row, and his heart trembled beneath the blows, he thought he couldn't draw breath and sweat broke out on his forehead.

Eiske awoke with a start and whispered, 'What's the matter?'

And almost at the same time he heard his son's voice. 'Mum, is that you?'

When Daniel walked into the drugstore his mother was behind the counter serving a customer, Simone Reents.

Simone blushed, as far as that was the right word with her permanent pallor, said, 'Hello, Daniel,' and shoved a box of o.b. tampons into her bag.

'Where have you come from so late? You've missed lunch. Did you have to stay at school longer today?' His mother looked first at Daniel, then at Simone.

'Our car's parked in the hammrich.'

'Your father wanted to get a close look at the fog.'

'And enjoy the view, or what?'

'What were you doing out in the fields?'

'Taking a diversion.'

'A three-hour diversion? You could at least have let us know.'

'I got dizzy. I lost my bearings.'

'What, again?'

'No big deal.'

'No big deal? It could be anything. Let me have a look at you.'
She came up to him and took his head in her hands.

Daniel took a step back. 'And then I had the feeling there was someone in there.'

'Where? In the fog?'

'In our car.'

'And was there someone in there?'

He shrugged. 'Don't know. Couldn't see anything.'

'I'll be going then,' said Simone and walked out past Daniel.
'Bye.'

'Bye,' said Birgit and then, turned back to Daniel, 'You ought to go to Doctor Ahlers. Get yourself checked up.'

'Maybe it was just low blood sugar.'

'No wonder, if you don't eat anything at school.'

'That rubbish?'

'Then take the sandwiches I make for you, at least.'

'I'm fifteen years old.'

'Your portion's on top of the cooker. And I'm sure you know how to turn it on.'

606

'Yes. With the remote control.'

He warmed up his lunch and sat down in the living room with the plate. On TV, one of the new *Jeopardy!* candidates was threatening to beat Cord, the champion. His name was Timo and he came from Tübingen, had long hair tied back in a ponytail and pinched his nose every few seconds. In the first round, he was not only the fastest but also knew the correct questions to all the answers. On his lectern was a bronze figure, a creature with four arms and an elephant's head.

Between rounds, Hans-Jürgen Bäumler strolled over to him and said, 'Six thousand seven hundred. Wow, Timo, you've really cleaned up.'

'I like to do my best.'

Hans-Jürgen Bäumler folded his hands together. 'You told me you've finished your degree.'

'No, not quite. I dropped out and now I'm starting again.'

'And what do you want to be when you've finished?'

'Originally a Germanist, but I went to India in the holidays and now I'm going to be a primary-school teacher.'

'I hear the job situation is getting better.'

'It's easier for men anyway. Men don't want to work in primary schools. But I've recognized my *ātman* now, so I know my true wishes.'

'And I'm sure they'll come true, seeing as you've brought your talisman along.' Bäumler pointed a finger at the bronze figure on Timo's lectern. 'Has it helped already?'

'Ganesha helps me to overcome hurdles.'

'Ganesha?'

'Ganesha stands for new beginnings, he's the preserver of good fortune.'

'Well, you've had plenty of good fortune so far—let's see if it stays that way in the second round.' Hans-Jürgen Bäumler took a step back. 'Now we're playing for double the points in new subject areas.' The music started up and the new headings appeared on the screen one after another. 'Prussian helmets. Carrot and stick. Goethe and co. Heads and tails. Galactica. Intimacies.'

But even at the first answer, Timo pinched his nose and gazed questioningly into the spotlights above him.

'Intimacies two hundred: Dungeon and asylum for a noble Frenchman for writing about violent fornication.'

The time ticked away.

'Marquis de Sade,' said Hans-Jürgen Bäumler. 'Ah well, Timo. That would have been one for you. Random round.' He clicked his fingers and one of the candidates was selected by a random generator.

'Goethe and co. four hundred,' said Katharina, who hadn't scored yet.

'Goethe's criticism is said to have prompted his suicide, not *The Broken Jug*.'

Cord's lamp lit up. 'Who was Kleist?'

'Correct.'

'Goethe and co. six hundred.'

'The loss of language plays a role even in *The German Lesson*.'

'Who was Kästner?' said Timo confidently.

'Wrong,' said Hans-Jürgen Bäumler. 'I'm starting to see why you dropped out of studying German.'

'Who is Lenz?' said Cord. 'Goethe and Co. eight hundred.'

'Döblin makes him fail, although Franz Biberkopf means well in this novel.'

The candidates were all silent.

'There's a film adaptation,' said Hans-Jürgen Bäumler. 'By Fassbinder.'

Cord's lamp lit up. 'What is *Berlin Alexanderplatz*?'

'Correct.'

'Intimacies one thousand.'

'Sancho Panza, the loyal companion, understands Don Quixote, who yearns for this beloved.'

Timo's lamp lit up. 'What are windmills?'

Hard sat opposite him at the dinner table. Daniel stared at him and he returned his gaze. No giving in. Don't show weakness. His hair was still damp from the shower and instead of his white coat, which smelled of Eiske's perfume—Obsession—and was now in the laundry basket, he wore a pale blue shirt and a fresh, new pair of trousers. He spread butter on a slice of black bread, put salami on top and divided it into two equal halves. The twins picked the raisins out of their rolls and shoved the rest into their mouths.

Birgit dropped a sugar *kluntje* into Hard's cup and poured hot tea over it until it crackled. 'How was the hammrich?'

If she knew something, if Daniel had told her anything, she gave no sign of it.

'I saw you,' said Daniel.

For a moment he felt caught out. 'Nix. I couldn't even see myself.'

'That's not possible,' said Andreas.

'Yes it is,' said Julia.

'No it's not.'

'Yes it is,' said Julia. 'In the mirror.'

'There aren't any mirrors in the hammrich.'

'I've seen some there.'

'Where?'

'In a lake. Lots of them.'

'Not true.'

'It is true.'

'Stop squabbling,' said Birgit.

And Hard said, in Daniel's direction, 'I heard you had another dizzy turn.'

Daniel looked at his mother—and with that, Hard had won. 'And you lost your bearings. I'm just wondering when.'

'What, when?'

'When you lost your bearings.'

'I don't know,' said Daniel. 'It can happen easily enough in this fog.'

'That's true,' said Hard, 'but your school's in another direction entirely.'

'Isn't that the whole thing about losing your bearings, that you suddenly wake up on the other side of the world and can't remember how you got there?'

'I think you need a check-up.'

'That's what I said,' said Birgit. 'But he won't listen to me.'

Daniel lay on the rolled-out sheet of paper like a piece of meat ready to be weighed and wrapped, and a deep, scratchy hum came out of his throat. He'd been to the cinema with Paul and Jens and Volker the night before, to see *Darkman*, and his head was still pulsing from the schnapps and beer, and his hand was burning from the cigarette Paul had extinguished on it. Doctor Ahlers took the wooden spatula out of Daniel's mouth. 'Right, right. Everything's fine so far.' He pushed himself off against the examination couch with both hands and rolled back into the middle of the room on his office chair. 'Do you often feel dizzy? Do you have headaches? Is there something troubling you?' He wrote something on a piece of paper. 'Does it happen often, this loss of orientation? Do you sometimes walk around the house in your sleep?' He dropped his pen and rolled back closer to Daniel. His thin white hair shone in the neon light. 'And where did you get this stigma?' He felt Daniel's palm. 'It looks fresh to me. Do you smoke? Smoke marijuana? Do you know what this reminds me of? That film, what's it called again, *Logan's Run* or something, it was on TV the other day, and they all have these diodes in their hands and when they extinguish, they're thirty and they get renewed or something like that. But really they kill them. You should be glad you're not thirty yet. Mind you, this seems to have extinguished as well. Have you been having any problems recently? You can talk to me about anything, Daniel. About your father as well. I know he can be quite rough sometimes.' Then he got to his feet, rubbed his hands together as if to charge them electrically, and put them around Daniel's neck from behind. 'Right, right. Well, not if you don't want to. I always say: no pressure, but anything's possible. Perhaps your skull's just a bit out of joint.' His hands closed around the back of Daniel's neck and his fingers made circling motions. 'I can feel a lot of tension on the left-hand side, everything's tensed up, absolutely stiff. That comes from you spending too long too close to the screen. The moment you came in, I noticed your typical computer game-player's posture, slightly bent, shoulders drawn in, head forward. It's no different with my children either, they spend hours staring at the screen, the most they do is lean over in one direction or another, depending on

611

where they're steering their characters or their spaceships, and then they freeze in the middle until my wife calls them to their meals. I have to put their heads right every evening. I always say, put their sense back in place, and that's exactly what I intend to do with you now. You'll see, you'll feel better in a minute. You won't feel a thing, perhaps a bit of a crack, a jab like from a needle, a mosquito bite, no more than that.' Even before he'd finished his speech there was a jolt. For a moment Daniel felt like Doctor Ahlers had broken his backbone. His vision went black, he saw stars, tiny stars sparking and going out, the rain of fire before the end of the world. 'Right, right. It doesn't always help, of course. If you get dizzy again I'll have to send you to see a colleague of mine,' said Doctor Ahlers and went over to his desk and his computer and pressed a few keys. 'I don't have the equipment for a thorough neurological examination. For now, you should take it easy, get plenty of fresh air, take a walk in the hammrich in the afternoons, well, better not in this fog, if you fall down no one would ever find you, you'd better stay in the village after all. I'll prescribe you diazepam, something to calm your nerves. And cream for your hand. My assistant will give you a prescription and a note for school. I can't do any more for you at the moment.'

Once she'd put the twins to bed Birgit had come into the living room and they'd watched the evening news together. Then Hard had got up and gone to see Meinders—it was the twenty-sixth day of play in the football league—and when he got back he took a beer out of the fridge and came into the living room. Birgit was lying prone on the reclining chair, wrapped in a blanket. She only turned her head in his direction. Her cheeks were glowing with happiness and her gaze was glassy. The footrest was folded out and underneath it, on the carpet, her shoes lay as if thrown off.

There was a bottle of red wine on the table; it has been almost full before he left. And now, illuminated by the floor lamp, he saw that there wasn't even enough in there to pour another glass. She could take a lot of drink, and apart from the shine on her skin and in her eyes, her drunkenness wasn't noticeable. She never got abusive, never talked nonsense or lost her balance. All the symptoms other people displayed in this state remained concealed within her. And that, that impenetrability, was something he valued in her and that he also credited with her success in the shop, her success with men. She treated the few men who came in there the same obliging way, even though she couldn't stand the sight of some of them, as she admitted to him afterwards. It was only for him that she sometimes let her mask slip, and what came to the forefront then was not something he liked to remember, a cold gaze full of contempt. He closed the door behind him and adjusted the seat he'd been sitting in before, moving it closer to her.

'What have you got up your sleeve?' The colour had vanished from her face from one moment to the next. And she was looking at him exactly as he'd expected.

'Excuse me, I live here.'

'It's Tuesday.'

'I know, your holy Tuesday.'

'Don't you have to go to the Beach Hotel?'

'I'm not going any more. They can sing much better without me anyway. No one stands out any more now.' The male-voice choir had been practising on Tuesdays instead of Thursdays, since Easter.

'You usually have something else more important to do than sitting around at home.'

'Not today.'

'What about Meinders?'

'Just been to seen him. Wasn't much going on today. Lots of them are at the Beach Hotel. And now I've got an evening off.'

'It's my evening off as well, an evening off from you.'

'I know. But I thought we could spend it together for a change.'

'No, we can't.'

'Why not?'

'That goes against the principle.'

'What principle?'

'The principle of my evening off. Anyway, I bet you don't want to watch *Dallas* with me. That's exactly what I'm going to do.'

'I know. Tuesday's *Dallas* day.'

'Yes, but not for long. Mind you, who knows, Bobby was dead and then he jumped out of the shower bright and breezy one morning six months later.'

'I don't understand a word.'

'This,' she gestured at the TV, even though it was still showing *Report*, a feature about the Germans' relations to foreigners and asylum-seekers, 'is the last-but-one series. It'll all be over in the autumn. And up until then I'm going to enjoy every second.' She folded the footrest back down, threw off her blanket, got up and went over to the wall unit to take a new bottle out of the bar section. 'And I'm going to get drunk while I do it.'

'You go ahead. It's your right.' He raised his beer. 'And if you don't mind, I'll join you.'

'All right then,' she said, sitting back down. 'But only if you don't take the mickey and don't comment on every scene. Here,' she handed him the bottle and the corkscrew across the table, 'make yourself useful.'

'I will.'

'What? Take the mickey?' Her tone had changed, softened, and he liked the sound of it. He'd broken her resistance, and if he didn't make a wrong move now she'd come to him later, over to his side of the bed.

'No.' Hard put his beer on the table, screwed the spiral into the cork and pulled it out with a plop. 'Definitely not. I'd never do a thing like that. So, what's happened so far?' He half-filled her glass and put the bottle next to her, within her reach.

'Bobby and April got married last week, at last,' she said with growing enthusiasm, 'and Clayton made up with McKay, much to J.R.'s annoyance because he can't stand McKay, they're too similar, both pretty nasty guys who'll stop at nothing, and—'

'No,' he interrupted, 'from the beginning, I mean.'

'You've never watched it?'

'Maybe once. Ten years ago.'

'You've missed a whole lot.'

'An entire life.'

'Dozens of lives.'

'Can't you at least try to sum it up for me in two or three sentences? Just so I know what's going on.' He reached his left hand out to her.

And she took it. 'No. And now sit down and shut up. It's starting.'

7

Daniel spent all day pacing his room. He bit his fingernails and the skin around them. When he could take no more, he went down to the shop and asked his parents whether anyone had called for him.

'Who's going to call you?' asked his father, kneeling on the floor and shelving packets of sanitary towels according to absorbency. 'Biggi,' he stood up raised his head above the Hygiene Articles sign, 'has anyone called for Daniel?'

'No. Not that I know of.' His mother returned a camera she'd just dusted to the shelf and turned around to Daniel. 'Who are you expecting a call from?'

By their faces, their wide eyes and smiles, he could tell they assumed he'd finally fallen in love. All the signs, the dizziness, the lack of appetite, the nervousness, suddenly made sense to them. His mother had already clasped her hands in front of her chest and his father had a hand on her shoulder from behind. They were both ready for happiness.

'I'm doing this project at school. We're working on health in Biology, contaminants in food, and I talked to a food inspector and—'

His father nodded. 'Houtjes.'

'What Houtjes?'

'Theo Houtjes.'

'Theo Houtjes.' His mother repeated the name several times but couldn't make a connection to anyone she knew. Then she said, 'What was his wife's name again?'

'Frieda. Frieda Voss.'

'Really? I thought he was married to Kaselautzki.'

'Martin's step-sister?'

'Which Martin?'

'Martin Masurczak. The editor of the *Frisian News*. I went to school with him. I told you about that just the other day.'

'Mamasurczak.'

'Exactly. His mother married Old Kaselautzki a couple of years ago. Then he died. Of cancer.'

'Yes, I know, yes. But I thought his daughter used to run around with a Houtjes.'

His father shook his head. 'No, you're getting him muddled up with Hoyer from the Farmers' Cooperative Bank.'

'Oh yes.'

'Not Houtjes.'

She still looked incredulous.

'Tall one with a beard. Theo Houtjes. You know the one, he always comes here for his bait.'

'Oh yes. I know, yes. And what have you got to do with him?' his mother asked, turning to Daniel.

'I want to invite him in to class.'

'But you're off sick. Can't Volker take care of it?'

'He's got another project.'

'You really ought to go back to bed now,' said his mother and turned back to his father. 'He still looks a bit pale, don't you think?'

'Nix. Where's he going to get any colour in his cheeks from if he stays in bed all day?'

On his way upstairs, Daniel passed the bathroom, opened the mirrored cabinet and pressed several tablets out of the packaging, five or six at once. He didn't look as he swallowed them and washed them down with water.

He felt bad at dinner.

'Eat it down,' said his mother. 'I made fried eggs especially for you.'

Daniel didn't correct her. Instead, he held his head and his stomach, and at the sight of the yolk streaked with white he broke out in a sweat.

'You need to get a good meal inside you,' said his father. 'That'll get your strength up. Then you'll be right as rain, believe you me.'

'You can see the boy's not feeling well,' said his mother, horrified. 'He must have the flu.'

'Nonsense, he's just unhappy with himself. Or he's been drinking too much again.'

'When would that've been? We'd have noticed. You'd smell it.'

'A lot of them take these things nowadays.'

'What things?'

'Ecstasy. Happy pills. You can't smell nix. You don't even notice anything. Not until they pass out.'

'Stop it, will you,' said his mother. 'The boy's sick, that's all.'

The twins played with their food, building towers out of the portioned pieces of bread, bread towers and bread walls, bread fortresses held by bread soldiers, which were attacked by more bread soldiers until they were eaten. His mother sent Daniel back to his room. Later, when the twins were asleep, she brought him chamomile tea and rusks. He lay in the dark and dozed from dream to dream.

The next day, Volker came round with his homework. English, Unit 5, Exercise 4a and 4b: Finish the following short conversations. Example: Jim: *I feel terrible. I'm hot and my whole body is aching.* Mrs Ward: *You'd better not go to school then. You'd better stay in bed.* Biology, structure and life of flatworms. Tapeworms and liver flukes have no sensory organs and no digestive organs. Why can they survive nonetheless? Physics, Mechanics 2, Exercise 2: A hamster runs in its wheel but doesn't appear to move from the spot. Describe the state of the hamster's motion (a) in relation to the inner surface of the wheel (b) in relation to the surface on which its cage stands. An essay in German. 'Nanninga says we don't have to do the test if we write a novella,' said Volker, one hand on Daniel's bed cover, stroking slowly from top to bottom. 'You can choose the subject yourself. You just have to stick to the form.'

Daniel's eyes kept falling closed. He tried to concentrate on what Volker was saying, he wanted to stay awake, answer him, reach out a hand to him, but he couldn't manage it. He was fighting against something that weakened and lamed him, something in his innermost self that was stronger than him. Was it the tablets? Rosing? School? His parents? Was it his unhappiness with himself? He didn't know. He felt like a tapeworm in a hamster wheel—incapable of cutting back the speed at which he was being whirled around. He saw Volker put the note with his homework on his bedside table, stand up, turn around to him and leave the room. Then he fell asleep.

After three days he felt better. He sat down at his desk and opened up his spiral pad. He took the lid off his fountain pen and inserted new cartridges as if loading a gun. Over and over, he started and broke off after the first few sentences because what he'd written didn't seem appropriate enough. He tore out the pages, crumpled them up and tossed them across the room. Suddenly, as though something inside him had snapped, it came almost automatically: *I am travelling on the orders of the Privy Council. The initiates forgot the deeper motives for my journey at the very moment they dispatched me to fulfil their will. No one knows where I am flying to and why. I deleted the files that might have informed anyone before I set out. No one knows my route; even I have lost sight of it. Officially, I am on an exploratory mission. According to the coordinates, there ought to be nothing at the place where I am now, nothing but the dark emptiness of outer space.*

On the fourth day, the inspector called. His father put the call through to him upstairs and said, 'I'm hanging up now.' There was a click on the line, but when Daniel heard Houtjes' voice he thought he could still hear someone else breathing at the other end as well.

'The results indicate a whole lot of bacteria, mainly lactobacilli and pseudomonads, which shouldn't be in there in such a high concentration. I'm going to pay a visit to the cafeteria. It was about time anyway. Is it open all morning or only during the breaks?'

'All morning,' said Daniel. 'Until one.'

'I'll call you as soon as I get the results.'

Daniel left the house after lunch. He took his racing bike across the railway tracks into the hammrich, into the fog. Shortly behind the sign for the village he stopped, looked at the construction pit, the muddy hole out of which the community's fortune was supposed to grow, and then mounted his bike again in anticipation of his triumph, the first stage of his victory. The further away he got from the village, the denser the fog became; it was no longer only resting on the fields but reaching up to the treetops and the gables of the farmhouses. The cows and the tractors had vanished and their noises and sounds came through as if from a great distance. For a moment, as Daniel cycled up the dyke, he thought he was floating above the clouds. Below him stretched a white sea from which little protruded, only the tip of the church tower, the Beach Hotel, the custard factory, the power lines and— like lighthouses warning boatmen against steering towards a cursed place—the eight navy radio masts.

The telephone's ring made Hard jump. It wasn't the usual ring, not one that came from outside, but a more muffled, less shrill one. He had dreamed of it, of this sound, but now that he'd sat up he couldn't remember the context. He looked at the clock on the wall above him, just before three, and when he got up everything went black and he held onto the table because he was scared he'd fall over if he didn't. Then he went out into the corridor to the telephone, to put a stop to the ringing.

'All right? Got up at last, have you?'

'Yes,' he said, still dazed. 'Why didn't you wake me?'

'You looked tired. I thought you could do with a sleep.'

'But not in the middle of the day.'

'You're awake now.'

'I don't feel like it though.'

'Can you come downstairs? There's someone here to see you.'

'Who is it?'

'Theda Wiemers.'

He hadn't heard from her or seen her since she'd left the old church hall with the parting words of 'Think about it.' And that

621

had been more than two weeks ago. Theda Wiemers. Had she come to tell Birgit about the two of them? To explain to her that the world, her world, was nothing but a simulation behind which real life went on? He noticed he was beginning to panic. But what would she want with that? She'd destroy two families, his and hers; she'd lose something in which she'd invested a great deal of time and love, and apart from her freedom she'd gain nothing, because—he was certain of one thing—he wouldn't do what she wanted. The game was played by his rules and not by hers. In the bathroom, he scooped water onto his face with both hands; for minutes, so it seemed to him, he held his head under the tap. The cold did him good and refreshed him, but not enough to drive out the shadow of sleep still weighing him down. Theda Wiemers. What on earth was she thinking of? Did she think you could just turn back time and start over from the beginning again? That he'd give up everything he'd built up, for her sake? He took a towel from the pile, dried himself and looked in the mirror. His wrinkles might have got deeper but he still had dark, full hair which he tamed with pomade and combed back until every strand was right where it belonged, in his opinion. He rinsed his mouth, brushed his white, even teeth and decided, after feeling his chin and cheeks, that it was too early for a second shave and that he would excise what had happened between Theda and him, then and now, from his memory. Nonetheless, he did shake a few drops of aftershave onto his palm and rub them into his cheeks and neck. Everything was absolutely fine. Nothing and no one could harm him, Hard. He buttoned up his shirt, fastened his tie, which he'd put on top of the laundry basket after lunch, and took his white coat off the hook.

'There you are at last. Where have you been so long?'

'Upstairs,' said Hard and nodded at Theda. 'Hello. How are you?'

'Fine. And yourself?'

'Great.'

'The stain's still there.'

'What stain?'

'The one from the other week.'

'Blood and that,' said Birgit and put a bottle of Dr Beckmann's Stain Devil—for blood, milk and protein—back onto the shelf.

'Oh, really?' He didn't know what he found more surprising, that his wife still didn't dare to speak the word *sperm* after twenty years of marriage, or that his lover had dared to mention it to her.

'Yes,' said Theda Wiemers, looking at Hard. 'And I even have the feeling it's got bigger.'

'That happens sometimes,' said Birgit. 'Blood spreads out in the fabric but only until it dries.'

'Yes,' said Theda Wiemers, 'but what if it gets wet again?'

'You mean the blood?'

'Well, as I said, if it gets wet again.'

She'd changed her tactics. The threatened frontal attack had not taken place; she was trying to wear down the enemy instead— Birgit or him, he wasn't quite sure which of them was her target— using guerrilla tactics. Asymmetric warfare could be successful, Algeria, Cuba, Vietnam, no one knew that better than he did. What he was intending with Schlecker was nothing different when it came down to it. But he had a plan whereas he feared that Theda didn't have one and was acting in an entirely unorganized, flexible and impulsive way. Had she revealed their dirty little secret to Birgit he'd have simply denied it and declared her insane, as he'd prepared himself to do on the stairs, on his way down to the shop. Now he had to come up with a new strategy. There was no way to predict her steps.

'You recommended a natural method,' said Theda Wiemers, addressing Hard, 'to get rid of old stains. A household remedy. Your wife didn't know what I mean. What was it called again? You can use it to thicken sauces as well.' She snapped her fingers. 'Damn. I can't remember the name.'

'You mean starch?'

'Ah yes, that's right,' she said. 'Starch can bond all sorts of things—and loosen them.'

'Yes,' said Hard.

'But not everything, unfortunately. Some things still come through again.'

'Yes,' said Birgit. 'I know. You get these ugly outlines. The stain's gone but you can see there used to be one there.'

Daniel went back to school on Monday. In Social Studies, they talked about Hitler's birthday and its effects on the present day. In Osnabrück that weekend, three skinheads had attacked a group of Kurds who were on hunger strike to draw attention to the fate of the refugees in Iraq. In Oberweser, fifteen Nazis smashed parked cars with baseball bats. In Wennigsen, unknown arsonists tried to set fire to an asylum-seekers' hostel. And there were attacks on foreigners in Verden, Wunstorf, Hanover and Holzminden. Mr Engberts reminded them of the test on Thursday and handed out preparatory material, a brochure from the Federal Agency for Civic Education and a few hectographed sheets for them to look at for the next time. No sooner had he let go of them than he wanted to collect them up again. Not only did the boys spend minutes sniffing the sheets before they glanced at the content but one of the handouts, presenting the reasons why asylum-seekers fled their countries, also showed a naked woman, her hands tied, her eyes blindfolded and her legs spread. Next to the picture were the words: *Using a fire hose, water is sprayed at high pressure at the women's genital areas. They are very shocked.* Paul and Jens weren't shocked but aroused. They kept pointing at the picture.

Simone put her hand up. She clicked her fingers three times before Mr Engberts called on her. 'This is misogynistic.'

'Yes,' said Engberts. 'It is.'

'That's not what I mean.'

'What *do* you mean?'

'That you chose this example, that's misogynistic.'

'No, Simone,' said Paul, who hadn't put his hand up. 'It's hot.'

Simone's face turned red and she called him a sexist. Paul and Jens threw balls of paper at her from behind, over the others' heads. Mr Engberts asked for quiet. Daniel stared at the picture. The thought of spraying anything on a naked woman, even only water, churned him up. Volker couldn't tear himself away either. He wolfed down his liver-sausage sandwiches as if he hadn't eaten for days. A low-flying combat plane thundered over the building. Mr Engberts made a note in the register. Then the bell rang.

During the first break, everyone in the schoolyard talked about the woman and the fire hose, until Paul and Jens started in on the *Manifesto of Trash* on the way to the gym, calling it the one true revelation. No one knew what the *Manifesto of Trash* was, and no one asked—some out of lack of interest, the others out of fear of Paul and Jens punishing them for their ignorance.

In the changing room, Mr Schulz, the headmaster and sports teacher, said to Daniel: 'You still look a bit pale. Are you really feeling fit enough to join in again? We're not going to be taking it easy today.'

Daniel nodded.

'We're practising over on the cinder track for the Federal Youth Games. Long throw, long jump, high jump, hundred-metre- and eight-hundred-metre run.'

Daniel threw and jumped and ran.

He achieved average scores in all disciplines.

If he'd been slightly more attentive Hard might have interpreted the signs correctly, but there was a lot, too much, occupying him at the moment. Klaus Neemann and Günter Vehndel had stabbed him in the back, one with his new stock range and the other with their card games, Wilfried Ennen had thrown him out of the male-voice choir more or less outright, Theda Wiemers was stalking him—who could blame her in view of his outstanding qualities—and the Schlecker chain was threatening to ruin his business. And all that had happened in less than four weeks; the only thing that wasn't a problem any more was his son, since he'd found the meaning of life in writing.

On Sunday, Birgit had come home from church and said over lunch—snirtje pork with red cabbage and potatoes—'It was pretty tough today.'

'The meat? I think it's just right, actually.' Hard put the last bite in his mouth.

'No, I mean the church service. Meinders seemed totally different, like he used to be when he was really emphatic, you know, really passionate, only more positive, but what he said then—'

'Sounds good to me. A bit more spice at church at last, not always his dull, out-of-touch sermons that no one understands apart from him. Maybe Berger at most.'

'Berger?'

'The pool player. The crazy guy from Petersen's Pool Hall. Always used to buy baby powder. For his cue.'

'Oh yes. Haven't seen him for ages.'

'Me neither.'

'Is he still alive?'

'Definitely. People like that don't die. Unless they do it themselves. They all lose it at some point, right when they realize their picture of the world doesn't match up to reality, they've been worshipping the wrong gods all along. Holy cows that turn out to be perfectly normal beef cattle, or,' he cast a glance over at Birgit and Daniel, 'people with no navels who have all the other parts you'd expect. Or doppelgängers. Not like you two,' he looked at Andreas and Julia, 'identical twins who grew up in two different places.'

'He reeled off Jesus' entire family tree. You know—Abraham begat Isaac. Isaac begat—'

'Andreas, sit up straight and take your elbows off the table, that's bad manners. And you, young miss,' he pointed his fork at Julia, 'eat down your plate.'

'—Jacob. Jacob begat Judah and his brothers and so on and so on. And then he started in on the whole story of Jesus' birth, even though Christmas is ages away still. But it was like on Christmas Eve, like if the saviour—'

'What are you talking about, Birgit?'

'Meinders. I told you. He was so different to usual, so strange, so happy and relaxed. And it was quite nice really to see him like that. But still long and tough to follow.'

'Oh right, yes.'

'And in the end he threw his hands in the air and shouted Hallelujah, and then we all had to sing Hallelujah, over and over, three times in a row.'

Hard jumped up, threw up his hands and sang, 'Ha-llelujah, hallelujah, hallelujah! Ha-llelujah, hallelujah, hallelujah!'

And the twins joined in. 'Ha-llelujah, hallelujah, hallelujah! Ha-llelujah, hallelujah, hallelujah!' Only Daniel and Birgit stayed in their seats and looked at each other as if the whole family apart from them had fallen prey to a blissful disease.

'Ha-llelujah, hallelujah, hallelujah! Ha-llelujah, hallelujah, hallelujah!'

And then, three days later, Marie Meinders had been in the shop, while Hard was out in the county town, officially, to buy film cartridges from the competition, a photography shop, because he'd forgotten to order new stock and the customer, Manfred Kramer, Old Kramer, refused to wait any longer. And when he and Birgit went over the day after dinner, after the evening news on TV—him holding the receipts and asking who had bought what—she interrupted him at some point and said, 'Marie Meinders.'

'When did she come in?'

'This morning. You'd just left. She said to say hello.'

'And she bought all this?' He read out every single item. 'Plasters, cleaning vinegar, magnesium tablets, shampoo, iron capsules, conditioner, folic acid, toilet paper, vitamin C, dishwasher salt, skin oil, tonic—'

'Yes.'

'What tonic was it?'

'Double Heart.'

'The strength of two hearts.'

'Yes, that's the one.'

'This is a really long list. What's up with her?'

'No idea.'

'She usually makes sure she never buys too much at once.'

'Yes,' said Birgit. 'So she can come back as soon as possible.'

'Biggi, we're related.'

'As if that ever stopped you.'

'What do you think of me?'

'Only the worst.'

'Oh really? I didn't notice that the other night.'

'What night?'

'Last Tuesday.'

'Can't remember it.'

'I'll take your word for that. You were pretty far gone.'

'Look who's talking.'

'I can remember it all though.'

'Oh yes? All what?'

'All this.' And he stood up and walked towards her, his hands stretched out, and she screamed 'No,' and 'Go away,' in a high, girlish voice that showed him she meant the exact opposite of what she was saying, so he leant over her and pressed her against the seat with all his weight.

'Hard,' she said once he'd taken his tongue out of her mouth, 'what if the kids come bursting in?'

'Then they'll learn something useful.'

'Let's go to the bedroom.' She tried to free herself from his grip and he let her go, propped up half on the armrests and half on the floor. Then she slid through beneath him and went to the door, unbuttoning her blouse. And as he didn't care where and how they did it—every couple of weeks—he followed her to the next room.

On Thursday, Daniel sat next to Simone, with his backpack and her bag on the desk between them. Daniel wrote: *The most important differentiation for understanding fascist youths is that between protest behaviour and targeted political actions. The latter are embedded in a strategy with the intent of removing the democratic system. Protest behaviour can be derived from an alienation situation which can range from specific rejection by a teacher to general lack of perspectives in society.* As he wrote, he had the feeling he knew everything. Before Engberts collected up the tests, Daniel read through what he'd written. Suddenly the sentences seemed hollow, like a poem he'd learned by rote and never understood.

Over lunch his mother said Houtjes had called that morning and would try again later. Daniel couldn't wait; he got up and ran to the telephone in the hallway.

'They're civil servants,' his father called after him. 'They're all on their lunch break.'

Daniel refused to admit his father was right. He tried over and over again. He didn't get through until three.

'Yes,' said Houtjes. 'There's plenty to criticize in that place, especially when it comes to good manners. But I can't find any evidence for a gross violation of the hygiene regulations.'

'But what about the minced pork rolls you examined, and what about the employee I talked to? Everyone at the school knows there's something up.'

'Your suspicion wasn't quite unfounded, the meat had been treated with nitrite pickling salt, it was onion mince, not pure raw pork, the labelling's not correct, but apart from the sample you provided, the entire stock was fine. Absolutely tip top.'

'Couldn't you do another check in a couple of days?'

'There's no need to. The original suspicion wasn't confirmed.'

Daniel tried to rescue his story. They talked to and fro. By the time he hung up he felt like when he cycled against the wind—inferior but determined not to give up.

The name was still above the entrance but the steam that had always surrounded the laundry had vanished away. There was not much to be seen of the sign next to the door; only the words *mangling service* and *closet-ready* stood out clearly from the weathered and paled symbols. Through the windows, which had previously been covered in a milky adhesive foil, Hard could now see into the space—pale tiles, on which the tables and machines had left a number of marks. If Schlecker really did move in here they wouldn't even have to renew the floor. Everything was flawless and ready to rent immediately. The dying was beginning, first the laundry, then Kuper, then Vehndel, Superneemann, Kramer's Furniture Paradise and all the other shops until the whole village was dead, and Günter of all people was helping to dig their grave. Perhaps he only wanted to see his own prophecy come true and was accelerating an unavoidable development, seeing as he couldn't stop it.

He ran his fingers along the edges of the door—plastic, easy to prise open. A few years ago he'd broken into his own house; Birgit and he had locked themselves out and he wanted to save the money for the locksmith. Afterwards the panorama window had to be replaced after all, because it wouldn't close properly any more and his attempts to undo what he'd done had ruined the fittings once and for all. He took a step back and looked over at Vehndel's and the tailor shop next door. The textile triptych, as Birgit had once called the three houses in a row, had been destroyed without Hard even lifting a finger. Now it was time to prevent a further destruction, his own, through destruction. The doctor's surgery. The pharmacy. The drugstore. His business was the weakest link in the medical-care chain. It would hit him first and he had to defend himself. But breaking in? Into a vacant building where there was obviously nothing left to steal? To do what? Set fire to the bare tiles? If only the dirty laundry had been left behind, a pile of old rags, cleaning cloths, anything that was more than nothing. It had to look much more hasty, more chaotic, like a randomly chosen target that had fallen prey to vandals, youths. The windows smashed, the walls graffitied. Bottles filled with methylated spirits flying through the night, a burning rag in their necks, the sky illuminated by their comet's tails.

In the week after that, Mrs Nanninga gave back the assignments. Under Daniel's she had written, 'Point of the story neither stringent nor surprising. Too many mistakes in expression, no complete sentences. A complete sentence has three elements: subject, object, verb.' Simone got a B. Jens got a C. Volker got a D. She told Paul to come to the front of the classroom, held out his book and asked him what the point was, whether it was a bad joke to hand in a story by Hebbel, 'Paul's Most Remarkable Night', one of the best-known novellas, copied down immaculately. 'You didn't change anything. Apart from the writer's name. You could at least have changed something. I have to assume you think I'm absolutely stupid. It's an unprecedented cheek.'

'An unprecedented event,' said Paul.

At that, she threw him out of the classroom, threatened him with a black mark on his file and shouted through the closed door, 'There'll be consequences.' No one said anything, all staring down at their exercise books. They'd never seen Mrs Nanninga like this, so unravelled and wiped out. Once she'd calmed down she said, 'I have graded your assignments, but in some cases I'm not sure whether you really wrote the texts on your own. Especially in your case, Daniel, I get the impression that you copied from somewhere, at least in part. This,' she held up his exercise book, 'is nothing more than a story glued together out of fragments.' She lowered it again, stood up and went over to the window, unsure of what to do now. She'd never been so humiliated, even during her training placement in Hamlyn. The more freedom she granted the pupils, the meaner and less considerate they got. They filled in gaps with words that altered the meaning of the text. They used silent working periods to send each other letters. If they watched a film adaptation they messed around in the darkness and parroted the lines. They were like slaves whose chains had been loosened after years of imprisonment—incapable of making anything out of their possibilities. She turned around to them. 'That means I can't give a grade for the assignment as a whole. I'll set a date and think up a question for you to answer in writing here in the classroom under my supervision. I won't let you get away with this again.'

When the bell rang she asked Daniel to stay behind. She waited until everyone had left, closed the door herself, came up to him, pulled up a chair and sat down opposite him. 'I'm not speaking as your German teacher or your class teacher now. As you know, I'm also a guidance teacher. You can tell me anything. It doesn't matter who you copied from and whether you knew about Paul's attempt to cheat or not. I'm thinking of something else now, something more fundamental.'

The bright voices of the kids outside came in through the windows. Daniel looked past her into the schoolyard, at the groups standing close together, at the benches and trees and concrete plant pots. Volker disappeared behind the gymnasium. Paul and Jens followed at a distance, their hands in their pockets, strolling, their sports bags thrown over their shoulders as if they were really on their way to the sports hall.

'Hello, Daniel, wake up!' Mrs Nanninga waved her hand in front of his face and a scent, a perfume, rose up to him but he couldn't think of its name.

'I've been talking to a few colleagues about you, about your behaviour. Some of them are of the opinion that you've changed since the Easter holidays, that you haven't been on the ball since then. I've noticed it too. You're too easily distracted by other things, like now. Something is occupying your mind, I can tell, and the essay you handed in confirms my suspicion—that you're obsessing over something and can't find your way out on your own, that you've lost the way. You're like someone in a labyrinth, who knows all the paths and turnings and yet still follows the markings he's made himself. They're all pointing in the wrong direction, but you follow them as if you were taking that path for the first time. That's why you're not making any progress. You're turning in circles at high speed. Inside, you're running at a hundred and eighty kilometres an hour. Are you still thinking about the thing with the UFO or the one with the symbols, the ones you washed away? Your father had hoped your work experience at the newspaper would take your mind off that, and I did too. Johann Rosing is a controversial figure for lots of people, for good reason. Because he stands for a position that hardly anyone dares to speak out loud in Germany. Because he touches on taboo subjects and looks at difficult issues from a different perspective. I know what you think, Daniel. But he's not the man you think he is. He's not a Nazi. I taught his son for years, God knows he's not easy, and still I never heard a bad word from him about Michael. Not a one single time. He helped him with his homework, helped organize school trips to Austria and Poland, and he was always in the front row at all the performances here in the school hall. If Michael was absent without an excuse a one single time, then Johann came to see me to apologize in person for his son's behaviour. And unlike many other fathers and mothers, he always came to parents' evenings, on time down to the minute. And all that even though he has a company to run and no one to take anything off his hands. As you may know, his wife passed away a few years ago. And after her death he devoted himself entirely to bringing up the children. Family always comes first for him. He works himself into the ground for his family.'

Simone broke away from the other girls, rummaged in her bag, walked along the side of the gymnasium, looked around, turned the corner and disappeared. Mrs Nanninga waved her arms in front of his face again. This time he recognized the perfume, the light, mild note that she fanned towards him. Daniel couldn't help thinking of the slogan, the poster hanging above the cosmetics shelf: *With Tosca came tenderness.*

'Were you even listening to me? Did you even understand what I'm trying to say to you? You see enemies everywhere and feel surrounded by them. I remember it well from my own school days, that powerlessness that presses you down and keeps you on the ground. You want to get up and you can't. You defend yourself and take blows. You fight and you lose. I'm sure it wasn't easy for you at the beginning, when you transferred from the grammar school. Anyone who transfers from grammar school has a hard time at intermediate school. Not because of the school work—because of the other pupils. That's absolutely normal. A perfectly natural procedure. At the beginning you just have to a make a few adjustments if you don't want to be an outsider. And you did, then. At the beginning you deliberately got bad marks, to show the others you're no better than them, that you're not above them in terms of school achievements. Do you think I didn't notice? By now I assume you've realized where that strategy will get you—to lower-secondary school. And you don't want to end up there. But you're not at risk of dropping down a level any more now. You've finally found some friends, as I've heard from some of your fellow pupils. At the parties at least, they say you're a firm feature.'

The two teachers on yard duty, the smoker-hunters Mr Mengs and Mr Kamps, popped up in front of the gymnasium and pointed first left, then right. One of them, Mr Mengs, took the path that Volker, Paul, Jens and Simone had taken, turning the corner and disappearing into the bushes just as they had. Mr Kamps went the other way around.

'But still, and I fail to understand why, you keep running up against brick walls. But let me assure you one thing—it's not the wall that will break that way, Daniel, it's you.'

As soon as Hard saw the sign that he was entering Achterup, less than ten kilometres away from Jericho, he always thought of Hamann, Alfred Hamann. His greatest competition for a long time. Fifteen years his senior, in his early sixties, but not yet old enough to retire. Yet that was exactly what he'd done after a branch of Schlecker had opened up five doors down, across the road from him. In the old days Hard used to drive over to him if he didn't have a product in stock and it would take too long to order a new delivery. Then he'd put up with Hamann's comments. 'You don't even have any Ladies' Gold Tonic in stock? What kind of a shop is it, your Kuper's Drugstore? Jericho's pride and joy. That never would have happened to your old man. He always had everything in reserve. It was more likely to be the other way round in those days. I was the one who came grovelling to him.' This time, though, Hard was going to see him for another reason.

'What do you want here?' Hamann had opened the door a crack. A dog barked.

'I want to talk to you.'

'What for? To gloat over my downfall?'

'To prevent mine.'

'That's enough now, Hero. Stop it!' The dog fell silent. 'You must be doing marvellously, now that I'm not in your way.'

'Do you think they'll be satisfied with that? They won't stop until there's none of us left.'

'Who do you mean by us? You and me?'

'Is your wife in?'

'One woman's not enough for you now, eh?'

'One never has been enough for me. With one I'd have been dead long ago, financially.' Hard didn't want anything from her; he just didn't want any witnesses to what he was planning.

'As dead as me?'

'Is she in or not?'

'No, but she'll be right back.'

'Let me in then.'

And he did. The dog, a beagle, sniffed at him and jumped up on his leg, but after Hard had stroked him he lost interest and vanished into one of the rooms. Hard knew Alfred's wife; he'd run into her a few times in the shop. The walls in the hallway were hung with black and white photos of her—a short blonde in a white coat, behind the counter, outside the shop, with her children and his dog, Hero's predecessor. But in the living room, it looked like Hamann had been on his own for more than a few hours. The sofa and chairs were piled high with gear—animal skins, shot cartridges, a khaki gilet, a leather bag—and the table was covered in empty beer bottles. Hamann cleared a few of them away and took them past him. 'Had a bit of a celebration last night.'

'A big catch?'

'My freedom. My daily freedom.'

'Doesn't seem to have done you much good.'

Lost in thought, Hard looked at the antlers on the wall, the tin soldiers in the display case, lined up in front of a few books— *The Night of the Generals*, *South of the Main Offensive*, *Foxes of the Desert*, *The Prisoners*, *Scorched Earth*—ran a finger along a bayonet and flicked at its tip. His gaze drifted over to a photo of Hamann in uniform, a child in uniform, and he realized he must have been in the war. He had been through the steeling process. He'd been baptized. The ideal partner. The dog squatted down in front of him, following his every move.

Hamann called from the kitchen, 'Do you want one?'

'What?'

But instead of answering he came back clutching two opened beer bottles and put one down on one side of the table and one on the other. Then he sat down, picked up his bottle and held it in front of his face. 'Cheers.'

Hard took off his jacket. It was hot and close; he felt sweat running down the back of his neck. He dropped down into the seat opposite Hamann. 'Cheers.'

'To the past.'

'To the future.'

'Come with me,' said Hamann, before drinking a sip, and stood up. 'I'll show you the future.' The dog barked again and wagged its tail. 'Stop it, Hero. That's enough now.'

Hard picked up his beer bottle and followed Hamann and the dog next door. And then they were standing in his shop. The neon tubes above them went on with a flicker. There were curtains in front of the windows now, and the shelves were empty and coated with dust, but otherwise everything looked exactly as he remembered it—a bright, white room with a counter and a cash desk and old advertising signs on the walls, not unlike his own drugstore, only smaller, much smaller, because it didn't have a photo studio or a dark room and Hamann had never refurbished or extended his store. It looked like a museum with no exhibits, as if it had been looted and vandalized and then cleaned up again, so as to take in the removed exhibits in case one of the thieves showed unexpected regret and brought them back. The only thing left was a few blue canisters with orange stickers covered in black crosses and flames and skulls, in one corner of the room. 'Looks more like the past to me.'

'Call it what you like. Makes no difference.'

'Maybe not for you.' Hard drank a gulp of beer and walked across the dust-dulled linoleum to the windows, pushed the net curtain aside and looked out.

'That's the present,' said Hamann behind him.

'Are you still in the volunteer fire brigade?' asked Hard, not turning around.

'Right now the only flames I'm putting out are my own.'

'I've got a job for you, you see.'

'Where's the fire?'

One evening, Rosing held a speech in the village hall. Outside on the street, local antifascist activists demonstrated, ten or fifteen young people with whistles and banners—*Resist to Exist, Nazis Out, Germany Never Again*. Inside, in the large room entirely panelled with wood, there was nothing to be seen or heard of them. The windows were closed and the curtains drawn. Across the whole length and breadth of the auditorium were four hundred stacking chairs, their legs interlocked. Only in the middle and at one side, on the way to the toilets and the bar, had they left two narrow aisles which, however, gradually filled up with people once all the seats were taken. Soon there was no getting through, neither in one direction nor the other.

Almost everyone was there, almost the entire village, Mrs Wolters, Daniel's former primary-school teacher, the Kamps and families, the Pfeiffers and the Reicherts, all present and correct, the Szkiolkas, Michalaks and Zywczgks and a few other men and women who had moved into Compunists' Corner from Poland and the Soviet Union only a few months ago, Schulz the blacksmith, the mayor, with his sons Philipp and Jörg, one almost twice the age of the other, the footballers Heiner Oltmanns, Marco Klüver and Guido Groenewold along with Coach Sandersfeld, Wessels the baker with his three employees the Hibben sisters, their hair still dusted with flour, Wilfried Ennen, who was wearing a sash and a chain over his suit as he was Jericho's current champion marksman, Hilliger the dentist, Heiko Hessenius and Gerrit Klopp, the two long-distance truck drivers usually unemployed due to drunkenness, Theda and Richard Wiemers, Irmgard Geuken and Ronnie, the chef from the Beach Hotel, Onken the lawyer, Klaus Neemann and Günter Vehndel—Hard's old friends— Jens Hanken and Paul Tinnemeyer—Daniel's new friends—the village policemen Frank Tebbens, Joachim Schepers and Kurt Rhauderwiek in uniform next to the entrance, Nella Allen in a white, floor-length tulle dress, Tammo Tammen, the trainee at the *Frisian News*, Harald Sievers, the work-experience supervisor with his health restored, Karl-Heinz Duken, towering over everyone even seated, Martin Masurczak and Inge Kaselautzki, the operator of the school cafeteria, Postman Schmidt, Ewald and Edith Reents, who didn't understand what their daughter was protesting against outside and talked about it in loud voices, Dirk and Meidine Mettjes and Lüpke and Elfriede Haak with their daughters, Messers Willms and Bunger and Klaaßen, the dairy chairman Anton Leemhuis, the director of the farmers' cooperative bank Albert Hoyer with his wife, Freerk-Ulf Dänekas from the savings bank and Gesa, the waitress from the Beach Hotel, Volker, who was sharing a tin of peanuts with his father, Eino Oltmanns with his son Klaas, the bicycle salesman, Captain Fechner, the milk-truck drivers Schoon and Korporal, who had to take their loads all the way to Oldenburg now that the dairy had closed down, Kromminga the driving instructor, Enno and Gerda Kröger, who owned the Beach Hotel over on the dyke, Fishmonger Krause, as always in a thick navy sweater with a Prince Heinrich cap pulled low over his eyes, Freese from the custard factory, Hayo Hayenga from Club 69, the farmers Appeldorn, Veenhuis, Lüpkes, Wübbena and Gosseling in a row, Brechtezende, Tönjes, Harders and Watermann in the row behind, Magda van Deest and Mrs Bluhm,

Hard's former employee, Stumpe the drinks salesman with his four rosy-cheeked sons, the food inspector Theo Houtjes and the engine driver Walter Baalmann, embroiled in conversation about carp, Anne-Marie Kolthoff, the master tradesmen with their journeymen: Electrics Plenter, Paints Benzen and Abbo and Ubbo Busboom, who must have come straight from the workshop to judge by their appearance, smeared with oil and dusted with paint, Eiske Ahlers, her neck and ears hung about with pearls, Mrs Spieker, Uli Dettmers the hairdresser, his hair combed over his bald head as usual, the organist Meta Graalmann and—close behind her, some thought too close—Hans Meinders, the pastor, and next to him Marie, his wife, and at the front, in the first row, Mrs Nanninga, Iron and Wiebke while on the very right, at the far edge, sat Old Kramer, both hands jammed behind his ears although Johann Rosing hadn't said a word yet. He was standing in the shade on the stage, behind a lectern decorated with flowers, sipping at his water glass and arranging his prompt cards, densely covered in figures and words.

Daniel leant against the back wall next to his father. Hard had undone the top button of his white coat and was wiping the sweat from his forehead with one sleeve. Everyone was gasping for air but those sitting by the windows didn't dare to open them, fearing that the chants and whistles from outside might suffocate the words inside. Instead, they left open the doors that led to the corridor and the toilets. Then the lights went out in the hall. Someone shrieked. A child began to cry. Another joined in. A man advised that someone should press the switch. And as if in response to this advice, the stage lit up and everyone looked up and fell silent.

Rosing was wearing a dark suit, a white shirt and a burgundy tie; his hair, parted in the middle, glinted in the spotlight. He tapped the microphone several times. Then he leant forward. 'Good evening, ladies and gentlemen. The election battle has now begun.' He propped himself up with both hands on the lectern and looked at the audience, but couldn't recognize anyone because of the dazzling lights. 'I've been looking forward to this day for months, to finally getting started, to presenting myself and my election platform. I know,' he raised his hand, 'many of you are thinking, what's the point, we already know him. And in actual fact,' he lowered his hand again, 'many of you have known me for years, some of you right from the cradle. But that means nothing at all. The very people we think we know best of all, we know the least. No one can see inside another person. Our thoughts they are free, who can bring them to light, they fly and they flee, like shadows by night, as the song goes that we occasionally sing in the male-voice choir, the thoughts they are free, and that's a good thing too. Everyone should be allowed to think their own thoughts and keep them to themselves. But as a politician, I'm expected to reveal my thoughts, so that you understand what's going on inside me and what opinions I represent. And I know too that there are many doubters among you, voters who don't agree with what I say. But what do I say? And what don't they agree with? What is their image of me made up of? Out of what people say about me in Jericho? Out of the articles in the press? The radio and TV programmes? The media campaign against me? I've talked to hundreds of people and I'll talk to hundreds more. I'm going to go from door to door. For five months, I'll march around the village and introduce myself personally in every one of the,' he looked at one of his cards, 'two thousand, one hundred and fifty-one households. I want to get to know every one of you, and I want every one of you to get to know me. Anyone who leads a community has to understand its members and incorporate their wishes into his decisions. In return, you express your trust in him. Of course I can hold speeches like the other candidates, speeches like this, but not a one single one of them will have the same strength and effect as a face-to-face conversation.'

'*A* single one,' said Daniel, so quietly that only his father could understand him.

'But nevertheless, I want to take the opportunity here and now to present my platform, the platform I stand for in my election campaign. This platform is inextricably linked with my life. If you vote for it, you vote for me. For twenty-three years now I've been running Rosing Construction, the company my father founded after the war was lost, the company he transferred to me. For twenty-three years I've been building houses and halls, streets and squares, just like my father before me, and all the streets and squares, all the houses and halls he built are still standing like on the very first day. Not a one single one of them has yet collapsed or ever will collapse.'

'*A* single one,' said Daniel.

His father gave him an annoyed look.

'In every project, I've incorporated local companies in the planning process and proved, against what some managers say, that it is possible to work for a good price and at high quality,' he pointed at the window, 'without falling back on components made in Eastern Europe or the Far East or employing workers from abroad.'

Nobody clapped but someone in the hall shouted, 'Exactly.'

And someone else, 'Nonsense.'

'I've built up a network for regional cooperation, to make our homeland what it was up to Reunification—a priceless value. The system of the social-market economy has proved itself in the past forty years, so why should we give it up now? Just so the rich have it better and the poor even worse? This country doesn't need Europe, but Europe needs this country! And exactly the same is true of the economy. It has to serve the people and not the other way around.'

There was applause for the first time, and Rosing used the pause to take a sip of water. Then he continued, beating down the applause with words.

'In everything I do, my father taught me to pay attention to the three Fs.' He raised his right hand and counted on his fingers. 'Hard work for the Firm, the Family, and Friendship. I grew up with these three, and I stand by these three today, because they're the foundation on which,' he counted off on his fingers again, 'happiness, security and wealth are built. I went into training under my father at the age of fifteen. And from that day on I worked for him and for myself, sometimes ten or twelve hours a day, depending on our orders book. And alongside that I got my school-leaving certificate at evening classes and studied civil engineering in Hanover. Not for my career, but because I have an objective that's larger than I am—to lead a region to the top of the world. I've never known what it means to be unemployed and I wouldn't wish it on anyone, but I'm convinced that anyone who wants to work will find work. And anyone in this hall who's willing to work,' he waved his hand around the darkness like Pastor Meinders bestowing a blessing in church, 'I promise to create a job for you appropriate to your skills, in or through the concrete works. Because these works will bring other works and other industries in their wake and bring about a general upswing. And that means everyone will profit from their success, and not a one single one of you will be left behind.'

'*A* single one,' said Daniel, and his father said, 'That's enough of that now.'

'I've never lined my own pockets,' said Rosing, putting his hands in his trouser pockets and pulling the fabric out as if to prove it, a barely visible gesture as he was still behind the lectern, and then stuffing it back in. 'I've always given my employees a share of the company's profits. That not only increases productivity but also the motivation to keep going day-to-day and shape the future together. I give pregnant women early leave, and I give mothers their jobs back after they've had their children. I pay higher wages to young fathers, voluntarily, all voluntarily. Because it pays off in the long run. I often end up training the very same children in my company. And then, thanks to their parents, they already have a level of knowledge that others of their age don't yet have and may never have. That's how I understand a family company. And in the best case, the village community is nothing other than that.'

More applause.

'As everyone knows,' said Rosing, raising his hands, 'every large family has its arguments. But like in every large family, in a family company you can always rely on each other when it comes down to it. Another part of a family company is that you budget carefully and don't waste the takings, but use them sensibly and moderately,' he looked at one of his cards, 'for new kindergartens, schools and old-people's homes, improved transport, building homes to favour families and the environment, rebuilding the station, strengthening the police force, researching, developing and supporting alternative energies, conserving the hedges, supporting agriculture, expanding the industrial estate to attract more and larger companies.'

Different listeners clapped at every bullet point. It was a circular canon of clapping that surged around the hall, like when the pope reads his *Urbi et Orbi* from St Peter's in more than sixty languages on Easter Sunday. Rosing arranged his cards, took a glug of water and raised his right arm aloft again.

'Firm, family, friendship—these three, as I said, are my maxims. But it wasn't always that way. To begin with I thought the firm and the family were all I needed. From Monday to Friday I took care of my company and on the weekend I took care of my wife and children. Both areas grew and developed superbly. That filled all my time and I didn't feel I was lacking anything—quite the opposite. Sometimes I thought, this must be what happiness feels like, a state between exhaustion and confidence in the future. There were times, tough times, when Monika and I spent every evening poring over the books, the numbers in the red, and fell asleep wondering whether it was worth going on. And at some point Michael would come bursting in with one of his little problems, a lost toy or a scraped knee, or Wiebke would cry in her cot. And that picked us back up again. That gave us the courage to fight against all odds. Until,' his voice trembled, broke off, threatened to fail, began again and talked over the uncertainty, 'until Monika had, until she,' he swallowed, 'had the accident, not long before Christmas, on the 21st of December, twelve years ago. I was at the building site over at the sports field when Kurt Rhauderwiek came along, his hat in his hand, and said that Monika's car had veered off the B70 and turned over in a field, and that the baby, our daughter, had been hurled out of it and only mildly injured, as if by a miracle. And when I drove to the hospital with Kurt and saw Monika lying there, covered in blood and unconscious, I thought, it's all over now. Nothing will ever be the way it used to be. I asked Kurt how it had happened but he couldn't give me an answer. There weren't any witnesses, no car or pedestrian she could have swerved to avoid, no animal she'd rammed into. The road was clean and dry and there were no brake marks on the road surface. Monika was in hospital for another three weeks. I can hardly remember those days, Christmas and New Year in Intensive Care while the doctors tried all they could to bring her back.'

Daniel couldn't believe Rosing was spinning his personal grief into his campaign, but most people were sitting there, leaning forward, staring ahead as if hypnotized, as if they really were at church and were saying a mute prayer without moving their lips.

'It was only after her death,' Rosing said into the silence, 'that I noticed how important and valuable, how essential friends are. Of course they couldn't possibly take away my pain at that time. But since the accident they've always been there for us, looked after Wiebke, listened, helped out. And that's what I wish for in the village, a high level of understanding, responsibility and solidarity. Of course, that requires us to understand one another, to have a command of the German language and to have learned to be considerate of one another.'

There was more applause, and again Rosing used the pause to take a drink of water.

'Because of this opinion,' he continued, 'I've often been accused of being xenophobic. And yet there's no doubt that integration is only possible if we can talk to one another. Anyone who goes on summer holiday to Spain, Italy or Greece knows how important it is to have a common cultural basis. Integration is adaptation, and I expect that from everyone who comes here. Germany is unthinkable without foreigners. Anyone who dreams of a Fourth Reich is living in another time, another world. Foreigners are a significant economic factor. Foreigners are prepared to work more for less money than Germans. Foreigners take on jobs no one else wants to do. Their annual consumption demand has a supportive effect on the economy, and their savings with German banks are considerable. And victims of political persecution, so-called asylum-seekers—let me add this explicitly—are also welcome at any time. Including the Kurds from Iraq and Turkey. However, we have to give them a possibility to find work without taking a job away from a German.'

Some people whistled, and others, his supporters, drowned them out with clapping.

'In view of more than two and a half million unemployed in this country, reason dictates we must limit immigration, select foreigners by their skills. That's consensus across the political parties. A company doesn't employ anyone without checking them first, without a written application followed by an interview, not a one single person.'

'*A* single person,' said Daniel.

And Hard said, 'That's enough.'

'Not everyone talks as openly about this as I do,' said Rosing. 'But not everyone is standing for a political office. I don't want to give anyone promises I can't keep later, least of all myself. But I don't want to skirt around difficult issues either, out of fear of failing. For far too long now, problems have been put off on the federal level or fobbed off on the states and local authorities. And now it's time to clean up, and thoroughly. Your vote decides whether everything stays the same as it's always been or changes for the better.'

Rosing rearranged his cards. He put some of them aside and patted the rest into order. The audience had fallen silent. He shielded his eyes from the spotlight with one hand but he could still hardly recognize anybody, only glasses, necklaces, brooches, things that reflected the light, and his daughter's eyes. Now came the difficult part of his speech, the ending.

'The modern age deliberately attempts to dissuade the individual of the significance of the term *homeland*. This is necessary to make the people ripe for deeds of political insanity. For the more one uproots them, the more one pushes them to the big cities' machines and offices, the more one drives them into a frenzy of advertising, cinema, of industry, speed, traffic, all the more does one alienate them from their soil until no one has any notion of where their daily bread actually comes from. The victims of this development are not the millionaires but the farmers, the small businessmen, the wage earners. And so the catastrophe begins. International capital cannot make use of a nation of people still rooted in their soil. And so they dismantle tariffs, so they tear down borders, and so the rural people migrate to the towns and cities. There, the masses conglomerate, and the call resounds for ever-cheaper food and ever-cheaper clothing. The consequence—increasing destruction of agriculture, of retail, of family companies, increasing unproductivity, once again migration to the towns and cities. An atrocious cycle that will destroy the land, the village, Jericho.'

An upsurge of applause.

'The worst, however, is the destruction of trust in our nation, in our people, the elimination of all hopes and all confidence in the future. How can we evade this fate? The basic idea of high finance consists in there being only one fate—the mortal world. This fate depends on the opportunity for a livelihood that the individual obtains in terms of material goods. You all know the saying: Every man forges his own fate. True good fate depends, however, on the earth and the soil, on Mother Nature, and on the people, on the quality of the people. Every nation can only seal good fortune for itself if it leads its own life, if it obtains the goods it is capable of producing itself. Just as the individual only finds satisfaction through his own work. One can only be proud of what one has achieved oneself, with one's own strength and effort. No lottery ball brings true good fortune.'

Rosing was talking on and on. Daniel looked over at his father, who nodded after every sentence. That silent agreement. Daniel felt paralysed. The words stabbed at his flesh like needles but he felt no pain, only dull rage.

Rosing said, 'The state is charged first with providing the opportunity for a livelihood and way of life for the citizens. Whoever has no citizenship is to be able to live in Germany only as a guest, and must be under the authority of legislation for foreigners.' Boos came from somewhere and someone whistled on two fingers. 'The first obligation of every citizen must be to work both spiritually and physically,' said Rosing, unmoved. 'The activity of individuals is not to counteract the interests of the universality but must have its result within the framework of the whole for the benefit of all. Consequently, I demand the abolition of unemployment benefit.' He looked at his cards again. 'A division of profits of all heavy industries. An expansion on a large scale of old-age welfare. The conservation of a healthy middle class. Immediate communalization of the great warehouses and their being leased at low cost to small firms. To whoever asks me what my vision is,' he said and looked up at the light, 'I will answer, to create a new platform onto which every German can step who is willing to act in favour of his nation. That is my goal, and every road that leads there is right. Resistance is there to be broken. If the community comes to awareness and organizes its strength logically, if every one of you here in this hall takes up his position and fulfils his function, then an inseparable, an invincible community of fate will come about, a real family.' He looked up from his cards, stretched out his right arm and pointed his forefinger at the audience. 'And I believe in that family, I will fight for that family, and if necessary, I'm prepared to die for that family.' In the front rows, several listeners rose from their seats and clapped their hands wildly, animating others behind them, who had held back so far, to stand up as well and applaud Rosing. The movement swept from front to back through the hall like a wave.

'So, how was it?' asked Birgit when father and son returned shortly after nine and came in to join her in the living room one after another, dropping into their seats. The TV was showing *A Palace on Lake Wörther*. She switched off the sound.

'Pretty crowded,' said Hard. 'We had to stand all the way through. Half the village was there. But he didn't convince me.

What he said about communalizing the warehouses is all well and good, but practically it means expropriation. It's bordering on socialism. The economy has to stay free.'

'At least the German economy,' said Daniel.

'Everywhere. They've even realized that over there now,' he waved out of the window.

'But that's not what he said. He only talked about Germany. And that *is* socialism—National Socialism, if you ask me.'

'No one did ask you. And anyway, how do you know? You weren't even listening properly.' Hard looked at Birgit. 'He kept making stupid comments.'

'Who?' she asked. 'Rosing?'

'Daniel. He gave a good speech, though, you've got to give him that, he can certainly talk.'

'Daniel?'

'No, Rosing. What he said about the family and Monika, about her death and how you have to stick together, no matter what happens.'

'Did you two know his wife, actually?' asked Daniel.

'Monika? Oh yes, she was a good customer.' Birgit looked at Hard. 'You had more to do with her, didn't you? I wasn't in the shop in those days.'

'Is that supposed to be an accusation?'

'No.'

'You could have started part time whenever you wanted. But you didn't want to. You wanted to keep your independence.'

'Just like you.'

'So what about Monika then?'

'She came in almost every day. Pretty as a picture, very graceful and always dressed tastefully, well read, educated, witty.'

'That's more compliments than you've ever paid me.'

'She was very good fun, especially, really enjoyed life.'

'Just because she laughed at your jokes.'

'Bought a lot of perfume. A different note for every occasion.'

'She just knew how to wind men around her little finger without anyone noticing.'

'That's all just rumours.'

'Marlies saw her.'

'Who with? With Klaus?'

'She used to flirt with everyone, with you too, and you went for it.'

'Excuse me, Biggi, that's the basis of our business.'

'What? Adultery?'

'Love.'

Birgit almost fell off her chair laughing, but Hard was serious.

'Love of our own and foreign bodies. The lust of the flesh.'

'The curse of the flesh, more like.' Birgit had calmed down again. 'Its excretions, its imperfections, its decay.'

Daniel asked, 'So how did it actually happen?'

'What?'

'The accident. I mean, how did she die?'

'If you'd been listening you'd know. Rosing said it. In the hospital.'

'I mean the car. Rosing just said she veered off the road.'

'How should I know? Maybe she was driving too fast. Or the steering wheel jammed. Used to happen often with that model, at that time.'

'What model was it?'

'Didn't she have a Scirocco?'

'You know that better than I do,' said Birgit. 'I never drove it.'

'Me neither.'

'But you sat in it.'

'Once. She gave me a lift into town once because we'd run out of nappies and you were out in our car. I can't believe you keep dredging it up. I'll have to listen to that story until the day I die.'

'You might be right there.'

'Where were you that day, anyway?'

'I had to go to hospital. Remember? Your son had something wrong with his eyes. He had to have an operation.'

'Oh yes.'

'What was wrong with my eyes?'

'They were always all sticky. You always had this clouded look.'

'You couldn't cry.'

'Your tear ducts were blocked.'

'What are we watching here, anyway? *Dallas*?'

'It's Friday.'

'Doesn't look like *Dallas*, no.'

'A cheap copy.'

'Turn it off then.'

And she did.

9

Birgit had dropped a roll-on deodorant earlier and it had shattered on the floor, the last one from bac, and now she was sweeping up the shards and wiping up the spilled fluid with a floor cloth. And Hard was just about to look in the stockroom for the only customer in the shop, Marlies Neemann, to see if they did have another one in there, when Hans Meinders came in. Hard was amazed to see him. He usually came half an hour after closing time to make sure they were alone. 'You seem to be a man in need today,' said Hard, and he removed a box filled with a fifth of the previous day's betting takings from the shelf behind him.

'Leave it,' said Hans Meinders, raising both hands and nodding at Birgit and Marlies.

'What? No Mother Superior's today?' asked Hard. 'How will you manage without it, Hans?'

'It's over, Bernhard.'

'What's over?'

'I don't need it any more,' said Hans Meinders, pointing at the box. 'I'm doing much better now. No restlessness any more, no tense muscles.'

'You ought to take it a while longer, just to be on the safe side. The symptoms can come back at any time, as long as the cause isn't put right.'

'That's the thing. I think I'm healed.'

'Nix.'

'Yes I am, Bernhard, and do you know what's even better? Mind you, perhaps it's related.'

'What?'

'The mortuary's being built.'

'When?'

'This summer. Rosing said it wouldn't be as expensive as we originally thought. We sat down after his speech yesterday and talked it all through. After all the toing and froing I wasn't sure what to think of him any more, whether I ought to vote for him in October or not. As you know, my vote carries a certain weight. We went through the other estimates in the church council and talked about a new call for tenders. And just think—he gave me a new estimate.' He looked at the women. 'And in the past few weeks, thanks to several generous donations, we've had so much in the collection bag that we can afford it now.'

'That must be a real relief, I assume,' said Marlies Neemann.

And Birgit said, 'A relief for who, that's the question.'

On the weekend Daniel wrote everything down, his conversation with Ronnie at the Beach Hotel, Simone's observations in the schoolyard, the results of the microbiological examination. He spent hours bent over the white Olympia typewriter, typing letter by letter onto the paper—with such vehemence that the symbols pressed into the platen. Now and then he heard a train approaching from the distance and speeding past the house, and he raised his head and looked out of the window, at the road, the level crossing and the broad, white land behind it. Only when his parents called him for meals did he leave his room for a few minutes, silently wolfing down his food at the kitchen table and pondering over the right words while his father talked insistently at him.

Early on Monday morning he cycled to school and dashed straight across the yard to the cafeteria to confront the woman who ran it. The room was already brightly lit and the floor shone as if it had just been washed. The coffee machine, a wide monster that occupied half the counter, snarled and steamed, and the scent that rose from it filled the air around it with a sharp, spicy aroma. From the kitchen, he heard an abruptly expelled laugh, and he made out a shadow through the gap in the swinging door. As he walked towards it Mrs Kaselautzki came out backwards, lifted a tray of minced pork rolls onto the glass counter top and wiped her buttery hands on her apron.

'How old are they?' Daniel asked.

Her smile froze. 'Just made. All fresh.'

'That's not what I've heard.'

'Oh really?' she said, folding her arms in front of her chest. 'And what is it you heard?'

'That they're from yesterday.'

'Yesterday was Sunday.'

'From Friday, then.'

'Who told you that?'

'So you admit it.'

'Ronnie Geuken!' She lowered her arms. 'I should have known. I knew it was a mistake not to go to the police. What other lies has he told you? The one about the coffee cups?'

'So you admit that too.'

'It was *you two* who set that inspector onto me! Of course! It all makes sense now. You just wait a minute,' she frowned and then pointed a finger at him, 'I know you from somewhere.' Daniel took a step back. 'I've seen your face before somewhere.' He was almost in the corridor leading to the classrooms when he heard her saying, 'Aren't you the one, doesn't your father have the—' He didn't catch the rest.

While the others went to the cafeteria during the breaks, Daniel sat outside on one of the concrete benches and added Mrs Kaselautzki's double confession to his article, in handwriting. At the end of the last lesson, in Biology, he read through what he'd written. He had everything he needed, two independent sources and written proof, even though the food inspector hadn't sent it to him yet. Mr Mengs was absorbed in the chapter he'd given his pupils to read for homework, 'Human Sexuality'. Inspired by its content, Paul and Jens sketched out roughly how they imagined reproduction with Simone and passed the folded pieces of paper to her at the front. Even Volker, already completely occupied by the approach of lunchtime, didn't ask him what time it was. A low-flying combat plane thundered over the building. Mr Mengs made a note in the register. Then the bell rang.

Hamann had picked up Hard in his car, a white VW Passat, 1987 model, 90 PS, 66 kW, which he had used to deliver orders in the countryside—that had been his advantage over the other druggists—to the old widows in remote villages. And now they were sitting in the car at the far end of Village Road, each of them with a beer in his gloved hand, looking over at the former laundry. The streetlamps were already switched off and there were no lights on in any windows; only the red S above the savings bank and the red A for *Apotheke* above the pharmacy shone out into the night. They had abandoned their original plan of attacking the building while driving past. The risk of missing it had seemed too great to Hard and Hamann wanted to avoid Vehndel linking his car to the attack.

'What's in there anyway?' Hard held up one of the bottles, distinguished from the one in his right hand only by its stopper, and eyed its contents, although little more than outlines were visible in the darkness.

'Petrol and sulphuric acid.'

'And what's this here? On this rag?'

'Potassium chlorate.'

'And it definitely works?'

'Why did you come to me in the first place, Hard? Here in your Compunists' Corner there's plenty of people who know better. They studied it at their universities—street-fighting, Molotov cocktails, armed resistance.'

'I thought you were the chemist around here, the man for dangerous materials.'

'They're all things you can get at drugstores.'

'Maybe in your day.'

'The Finns beat the Russians with these in the war. Bottles against tanks. Satellite against superpower. We ought to do fine with them too.'

'You should know.'

'I was only in the flak. Hitler's last resort.'

'Better than nothing. And apart from that,' Hard returned to Hamann's question, placing the bottle back in the crate as carefully as possible as he was scared it might go off in his hand, 'you hate them as much as I do. Even more.' Since the card-game evening at the Beach Hotel, since he'd dashed out of the church, he wanted nothing more than new friends, a new connection, and he hoped that Hamann, similarly to Klaus and Günter before him, was someone he could confide in who'd support his plans when push came to shove. A tiny matter had shifted in the cosmos—a shop owner had changed tenants—and now everything was different. Until now they'd been on enemy sides, and suddenly, in the face of their death, they were fighting evil side by side. What was it Hans Meinders had said? Without blood spilled, no forgiveness.

His kingdom come.

His will be done.

On earth as it is in heaven.

Hamann said, 'I'm just wondering whether our message will get across. There's nothing written on the house. Are you sure they're moving in?'

'Dead sure. There's nothing else free in Jericho.'

'But this here is just an attack on a vacant house. It could have been a couple of youngsters.'

'That's exactly why.'

'I know that. But the reason why we're both sitting here together is Schlecker.'

'Right.'

'And what we want to read in the paper is *Schlecker Attacked*. And not *Laundry in Flames*.'

'The laundry's not even in there any more.'

'Maybe it'd be better to burn down the Achterup branch. To emphasize our cause.'

'That would fall back straight on you.'

'That's why you ought to do it. Me here. You there.'

'Nix. That's a whole different league.' Hard drank a gulp of beer. All of a sudden he felt every muscle, every nerve in his body, and then he said, 'OK. I'll do it. This is so insane, so absolutely paradoxical, it deserves something in return. A druggist who destroys a drugstore, and a fireman who starts a fire.'

'That's nothing new. *Fahrenheit 451.*'

'You're speaking in riddles, old man.'

'Science fiction.'

'A book?'

'I've only seen the film. Long time ago. They set fire to books.'

'That's not new either.'

'All books.'

'Even the Bible?'

'That first of all. I can't remember the rest. Not a trace.'

'Gone with the wind.'

Hamann tapped his head. 'Absolutely empty.'

'Like my beer.'

'Let's go then.'

'Let's douse that house!'

After school, Daniel cycled to the newspaper. He knocked on the doorframe of Masurczak's outer office. The secretary had the telephone receiver jammed between her ear and her shoulder, raised her hand, said, 'Yes, yes, I'll tell him . . . yes . . . yes, absolutely . . . bye,' and hung up. 'Daniel, what's up?'

'Erm, I'd like to talk to Mr Masurczak.'

'On what business?'

'On my business.'

'Mr Masurczak's in a meeting. You're welcome to wait for him here.' She gestured at a leather chair opposite her.

Daniel didn't want to wait any longer though. He had waited long enough, at least that was how it felt; his time had come. At the same moment as he turned to the door, the secretary leapt out from behind her desk.

'I . . . er,' she stuttered as they both found themselves in Masurczak's smoke-filled room. 'He just barged through.'

'It's all right,' said Masurczak, who was standing by the window with Duken, a half-smoked cigar in his hand, staring from one fog to the other. 'No problem. Come on in, Daniel. Take a seat.' He waved him over and pushed a chair towards him. 'We were just talking about you.' Daniel removed his army backpack and sat down. 'What would you like to drink? Espresso?' Daniel nodded. Masurczak looked over his head. 'Mrs Houtjes?'

'Right away.' Not much later, the secretary put a cup on the desk in front of Daniel and asked, turned to the two men, 'For you too?'

'No, thank you,' said Masurczak, now perched on the other side of the desk, one leg dangling above the floor.

Duken shook his head, 'I've still got a coffee,' and held up his cup.

The secretary shut the door soundlessly behind her.

Once again, Daniel drank the espresso like vodka, and once again his tongue burnt afterwards as if he'd rinsed his mouth with fire.

Masurczak took one last puff and then put out the cigar stump in the ashtray. 'I'm glad you're here, Daniel. I was just saying to Mr Duken, that young Kuper, he's got potential. He's got an eye for subjects and situations and he's confident, he talks to people, asks the right questions. He's not like other boys, the ones who come in here all the time and want to make something of themselves and then never open their mouths. Isn't that right?'

'Yes,' said Duken. 'That's right.'

'He takes after his father,' said Masurczak. 'Bernhard Kuper! He was the same at that age. Do you know what he used to call himself at school?'

'No,' said Duken without a trace of enthusiasm. 'What?'

'Hard. I'm Hard! Call me Hard! Always had a big mouth. Always making some stupid comment. Not always right and especially not at the right moment and usually to the wrong people, but still.' He raised both hands. 'He got what he wanted back then. He didn't take it the wrong way from me and I didn't take it the wrong way from him. Your youth, I always say, is one thing and the time after it's a different matter. You can't hold people to blame their whole lives for what they did wrong as children. I think everyone ought to get a second chance, everyone ought to be able to prove themselves. But I'd never have thought,' he shook his head, 'that he'd have sent me such a Trojan horse. You live and learn.'

'Never have thought it,' said Duken, still unmoved.

Daniel looked from one man to the other. He had no idea what they were talking about.

Masurczak sighed, ran a hand through his hair and stood up. 'Right, what can we do for you?'

Daniel took the pages held together with two staples out of his backpack and handed them to him. Once Masurczak had read the whole thing he passed them over to Duken.

'Well, that's quite something,' said Masurczak. 'Don't you think so, Mr Duken?'

'Yes,' said Duken, his eyes glued to the paper. 'Very brave. Really amazing.'

'I've heard you've been researching this story,' said Masurczak and cleared his throat. 'Do you know who the cafeteria belongs to, by the way?'

'Yes,' said Daniel. 'To the school.'

'No, I mean, who runs it, who this woman is who you keep mentioning here.'

'Yes,' said Daniel. 'It says her name.' He pointed at the sheets of paper in Duken's hands. 'Mrs Kaselautzki. Inge Kaselautzki.'

'Are you taking the piss?' Masurczak grabbed both armrests and pulled Daniel towards him, his face red with rage. 'Have you made a bet with your father or what? Is this about crossing some kind of line? As in, see how far you can go with him before he notices what you're playing at?'

'I don't know what you mean,' said Daniel.

'What's the stake? How much did he offer you? Five hundred? A thousand?'

'For what?'

'For what? For what? For your father, for you to mess with my mind, you in his place because he doesn't dare, that coward, he's always been a coward, a big mouth and nothing to back it up with.'

'My father's got nothing to do with all this.'

'Nothing to do with it!' Masurczak whirled around. 'Look at him, Mr Duken, look at him sitting there like butter wouldn't melt.'

'I just wanted,' Daniel started, broke off and began again, 'I just wanted to write a good story.'

'A good story! Now you listen to me, my boy. Either you're as stupid as you're acting, or—'

'Maybe he really doesn't know,' said Duken.

'—it's just another . . . What?'

'Maybe he really doesn't know.'

'Impossible. No one could be that stupid. Apart from the fact that these accusations here,' he gestured at the pages, 'are plucked out of thin air, I can't believe the name of the woman from the cafeteria didn't make you wonder. Kaselautzki! Masurczak! No one round here has names like that! No one. Nobody else has names like those, refugee names like that! Your father must have told you that Inge Kaselautzki's my mother. He certainly told everyone at school. And that she married again later on. At her age! At fifty! Old Kaselautzki, who had cancer even then. And why?' He was shouting now.

'For the money?' asked Duken.

Masurczak stared at him, stiff with anger.

'Out of pity?' asked Daniel.

Masurczak jerked around to him, his fists clenched. He was dizzy. It had been a rhetorical question; he hadn't expected either of them to answer it, and now he wondered which of them to grab first. 'Oh no,' said Masurczak once he had himself back under control. 'My mother was never interested in money. And she's not one for pity. She did it because she was homesick. Homesick!'

Duken handed the text back to Masurczak.

'I find it very difficult not to take this personally.' He waved the pages around in front of Daniel's face. 'Didn't I treat you well during your work experience? Didn't I do everything for you? How am I supposed to take this? Is your father trying to get revenge on me this roundabout way, via my mother? Is that what it is?'

Daniel had collapsed into a bundle on the chair.

Masurczak went back to the window and said, not looking at him again, 'Under these circumstances I can't employ you here any longer, of course.'

The words drove Daniel out of the room.

After the phone call, Hard had put up a sign on the front door—
Please use business entrance—and explained to Birgit up in the
kitchen that the doorframe had warped out of shape once and for
all. 'We'll probably have to replace the whole thing.'

'About time too. It hasn't closed properly for ages.'

'And now it won't open any more.'

Then he'd gone downstairs again to wait for Daniel. There
hadn't been much business all day, just a few women and Old
Kramer, who asked when he could pick up the latest set of pictures of his son. He brought in a black-and-white film for development every few months. Whenever his son came to visit from
studying in Berlin—most recently at Easter—he would take photos of him, to 'document his drift into the underground,' as he put
it. He was convinced he'd joined the terrorist Red Army Faction,
and he thought he could prove it by the wanted poster on display
in the post office opposite.

'Should be ready tomorrow,' Hard shouted.

'What?'

'Ready tomorrow!'

'Ready to murder?' Old Kramer shouted back, 'Oh yes,
they're good at that, that's true. Buback, Schleyer and now that
Rohwedder. But not for much longer,' he brandished his stick in
front of Hard's face, 'we'll get them soon, we'll get them all, and
then we'll hang them. Where are my pictures?'

Hard had made a couple of attempts to explain and then given
up, written a random date on a piece of paper and held up the
numbers to him.

'That long? It only takes three days at Schlecker.'

'Why don't you go there then?'

'What did you say?' yelled Kramer, but he'd already turned
to leave. 'I'll be back next week. You can count on that. And woe

betide you if they're not ready by then.' He gave another threatening shake of his stick.

Hard's anger subsided after that; the shouting had done him good. But he knew it would come back as soon as he saw Daniel. And that's exactly what happened.

'What's the matter with the door?'

'Broken. Someone slammed it too hard too often.'

'Well, it wasn't me.'

'No. You're never responsible for anything.'

Daniel shrugged. 'Not for that anyway.'

'Do you know who just called me?'

'Nope.'

'Martin Masurczak.' Hard came out from behind the counter.

At the same moment, Daniel backed off, took a step into the shop, and as Hard launched himself at him he dropped his backpack and ran, along the perfume shelves, past the hygiene articles towards the back wall and from there back to the counter. And Hard ran after him. Hard kept stopping for breath, the payback for hardly sleeping the night before, and that gave Daniel a break as well. Then Hard got moving again and Daniel did too. Birgit, surprised by all the trampling, came down the stairs and shouted across the counter, 'What's going on here? Have you lost your minds?'

The door opened, the bell rang, and two policemen entered the drugstore, Kurt Rhauderwiek and Frank Tebbens, their legs wide, their thumbs hooked behind their belts. Hard and Daniel stopped at the same latitude, at a safe distance to each other, separated by a row of shelves.

'Sorry to bother you,' said Kurt Rhauderwiek. 'You can go on playing in a minute. There's been a fire at Vehndel's.' He held his cap in his hand and fiddled with the visor.

'Sabine told me this morning,' said Birgit. 'The laundry.'

'Word's got out already,' said Hard, still out of breath. 'Nothing stays a secret in Jericho.'

'If that was true we'd have nothing to do. But it's not that simple, Hard, I'm afraid. And you can't usually tell if people are crazy, pyromaniacs, kleptomaniacs and whatever else there is, you can't even sense it. Some people see that differently, mind you. But maybe they have a gift we don't possess.'

Hard remembered now. He was with that *crazy woman*, the one from the cinema, Nella Allen. She disapproved of all perfumes but she still shopped at the drugstore, mainly for the things he made himself and the few creams and lotions that were absolutely pH-neutral, *absolutely pure, free from toxins.*

'There was another fire in Achterup,' said Kurt Rhauderwiek. 'At Schlecker.'

'And we've got a witness there,' said Frank Tebbens, taking a step forward, standing on tiptoe and peering over the shelves.

'You don't say. Who?'

'A man. Lives across the road. Went out to walk his dog at night.' Frank Tebbens slid back to his original position.

'And he saw who did it?'

'Exactly right.' Frank Tebbens took out a notepad and opened it in the middle. 'Black hat, black jacket, black trousers. Height: one metre seventy to one metre eighty. Build: athletic, slim.'

'The fire brigade think it must be someone who has access to chemicals and knows about them,' added Kurt Rhauderwiek, looking around the shop.

'And that narrows down the suspects a lot, of course.' Frank Tebbens snapped the pad shut. 'There's not many left.'

'We're actually fairly sure who's behind it.'

'So why don't you arrest him?'

'That's what we're doing. That's why we're here.' Kurt Rhauderwiek grinned and Frank Tebbens planted his legs even further apart then they already were.

What did they know that he didn't know? For a moment, Hard was confused. He'd expected them to come by after Hamann's description. After all the unusual things that had happened in Jericho over the past few years, this new story, the arson attack, must have had its origins at Kuper's Drugstore as well. But what if they weren't going after his son, but him? What if Hamann had betrayed him? Or, even worse, what if their witness wasn't his witness? Then the whole plan was redundant.

'And as I see,' this time Kurt Rhauderwiek stood on tiptoe, 'he's here as well. You can come out, Daniel Kuper, we saw you before from outside when you were running around in here. I'm afraid you won't have the pleasure of a well-earned beating. I bet you were looking forward to it.'

'You'll be safe with us.'

'It wasn't me.' Daniel emerged from behind the shelves.

Kurt Rhauderwiek asked, 'Where were you last night?'

'Here. At home. In bed.'

Birgit nodded. 'I said good night to him.'

'That didn't stop him from going out again last time.'

'I was in my room.'

'When?'

'The whole time.'

'Between three and four in the morning?'

'Daniel, have you got anything to do with this?' asked Birgit.

'No.'

'Don't lie to me.'

'Really.'

'When did it happen?' asked Hard.

'What?'

'The fire.'

'Which one?'

'Both.'

'One at three, the other at four. We're assuming they were both the same person.'

'Why?'

'Let's just say there are some conspicuous similarities.'

'Such as?'

'That's something only the arsonist can know.'

'I don't understand. You know it too, don't you? And you're not the arsonist, or are you, Kurt?'

'You won't hear any more from me.'

'Weren't we both in the kitchen at three?' Hard said over the top of the shelves.

'What?'

'You had a hot milk because you couldn't sleep, you'd had a nightmare. Remember? When was that?'

Daniel shrugged.

'Must have been around three,' said Hard. 'Yes, we had the radio on, the news. It's terrible what's happened in Bangladesh. Two hundred thousand dead, seven million homeless, you can't imagine it. And then we sat there for a while and talked about it, about life, how fast it goes past and how you ought to enjoy every moment, even when you think you can't go on.'

'Yes,' said Daniel. 'You talked about the army. About the barracks. Staff Sergeant Freese. Standing to attention for hours and getting shouted at. For nothing.'

The two policemen exchanged glances.

'When I heard about the fire this morning,' said Hard, 'I thought the same—who here would be capable of that apart from my son? But he was here, Kurt. And the boy can hardly be in two places at once, can he?'

'Some people say it's happened before,' said Frank Tebbens. 'It's theoretically possible.'

'Maybe you'd be better off going over to Old Kramer. His son lives in Berlin but who knows. I've got a couple of nice photos of him here, and if you ask me he looks pretty damn similar to one of those terrorists,' he pointed out of the window at the post office opposite. 'And maybe he wasn't at the Mayday riots in Kreuzberg last week, but here in our village.'

Kurt Rhauderwiek put his cap back on and tapped his forefinger against the visor. 'Have a nice day.'

10

Daniel couldn't sleep and didn't want to wake anyone, so he tip-toed along the hall past the twins' rooms and up to the attic. He'd been lying in bed and thinking for hours, about his father who had suddenly been on his side, about Masurczak and Kaselautzki—and about Rosing, about what he'd said in front of all the people in the village hall. He couldn't get the words *deeds of political insanity, daily bread, rooted to the soil, lottery ball, legislation for foreigners* and *community of fate* out of his head; he thought he'd read them somewhere, and then, just as he threatened to fall asleep, it occurred to him where, in which article, in which book.

Now he was standing upstairs on the landing outside the door to the attic. He felt in the darkness for the key, which his father kept on top of the doorframe, and once he'd found it he felt for the lock. He inserted the key, turned it, pressed down the handle and pushed the door open, which he managed once he'd put his weight against it. Just as quietly but without any resistance, he closed it behind him and flicked on the light. It was only then he became aware of the hurdles he had to overcome to reach his goal. The whole space was filled with cardboard boxes full of toys, rubbish sacks stuffed with clothes and bedding and curtains—things no one in the family needed any more, which his mother still considered too good to throw away. Three decades' worth of furniture, a television cabinet, a record-player console, a kidney-shaped side table. He hadn't been up here for months. He stepped carefully on the floorboards; his parents' bedroom was directly below him. As he forged a path through the junk he felt as though he were treading through his own life, from the present, which began directly behind the door, back to his birth. First he pushed aside the cardboard boxes containing his old school books, *Texts for Secondary Level 8* and *7*, *Language Practice 8* and *7*, *English 4B* and *3A*, *Music around Us*, *Cursus Novus I* with the grammar booklet, exercise books full of his handwriting, with his name written on them more and more clearly the older they got, and a few ragged copies of the *Blackboard Jungle*. He heard a car approaching from the dyke, the engine and the music getting louder and louder and then quieter and quieter again across the level crossing and along Village Road. He rolled aside a round, artificial leather footstool and put the cuddly ET toy on top of it that his father had won for him at the village-fair shooting contest. Rubbish sacks towered ahead of him. He opened one out of curiosity—it emitted a strong scent of lavender—and rummaged around in it. T-shirts, checked carrot jeans, batwing sweaters, clothes for which he was too big and the twins were too small. When he moved the sacks, cardboard sheets drawn on on both sides and held together with parcel string fell over next to him. The top one depicted a two-dimensional jet plane dropping bombs on two-dimensional people—a subject that had fascinated him for a long time and given rise to hundreds of variations. He loosened the knot and looked at several pictures of tattered bodies, but the light wasn't bright enough to make out every detail of his early ball-point-pen drawings. So he tied them all up again, got to his feet—the floorboard beneath him creaked—leant the bundle against the record player console and came across shoe boxes full of autograph cards from *Bravo* magazine and stickers of actors and singers and bands. In-between there were lots of things that didn't belong to him—fishing rods of all lengths and types, a tackle box, a net, empty suitcases, boxes of Christmas baubles and Easter decorations, a bag of rattles, babygros and bibs, a song folder printed with *MVC*, instruction manuals for the Opel Rekord E2 2.0 S, the Miele G540 dishwasher, the Grundig studio 2000 hi-fi and the Nordmende Spectra Color which they had long since replaced with a Galaxy, several years' issues of *Kicker* magazine and the *Karkblattje*—the church newsletter that old Mrs Kramer put in their letterbox after every church service, no matter whether one of them had been to church and taken one home or not—advertising flyers for Kuper's Drugstore: *Attention all housewives: Spring is on its way!*; *Summer, sea and sunshine! Practise your backstroke with sun cream!*; *Autumn—time to get cosy! Special offer on all baby items!*; *Heat up the winter! With vitamin capsules, herbal teas and condoms!*, which Daniel had had to deliver around the village for his father every year, blushing with shame, tin cups, crystal glasses and porcelain dogs, presents from his aunts in Bad Vilbel, an old egg timer that started ticking when he brushed against it but then fell silent again before he'd taken two steps, a chest full of old clothes, a pile of magazines with a yellowed copy of the *UFO News* on top, a dozen semi-transparent scented lights made of stone, half of them broken, and scattered over all of it skat playing cards from many different decks, the suits mixed and mingled.

Underneath the attic window was a chair with its backrest broken off, the loose spindles interwoven with cobwebs. Daniel put one foot on the seat and looked out, but he couldn't make out much other than his reflection. Only the logo *Jericho Cooperative Dairy*, advertising something that no longer existed, stood out from the night and made everything around it appear even darker, never-ending. Somewhere out there was the flat roof onto which Volker had wanted to climb when they'd played hide and seek. Had he managed it, Daniel's life would have taken another course.

He wouldn't have escaped to fantasy worlds; the thing in the snow would never have happened; he would have gone to intermediate school with Volker from the very beginning, would never have got to know Stefan, Onno and Rainer properly and driven Peter Peters onto the railway tracks; he wouldn't have had a problem with Pastor Meinders; he wouldn't have cared about the signs on the walls; he'd have done his work experience with a plumber, a car mechanic or the police force, like the other boys; no one would suspect him of smashing windows or burning down houses. A parallel universe. Diffuse, blurry, hard to imagine—unless he attained a higher level of illumination or travelled into the past like Michael J. Fox in a De Lorean DMC 12, 1982 model, 132 PS, 97 kW, equipped with a Chevrolet V8 engine, nuclear reactor and flux compensator, and then from the past back to the future. The gates at the level crossing closed, the lights of a train engine lit up the sky, and Daniel stayed on the chair as long as the freight cars sped past the house. Beneath him, he heard his parents, his mother moaning, the bed squeaking. Imagining them doing it together churned him up. He paused, thought briefly about turning back because he found it so repulsive to be so close to them, and then continued after all, hoping he could devote himself entirely to the task at hand as long as they were occupied.

Once he'd removed a wall of advertising signs he discovered new old objects: Fisherman's Friend tins now containing coins squashed flat by trains, screws and nails and staples, a Panini sticker book from the football world cup in Italy, which he still hadn't managed to fill completely despite his father's mass purchase of sticker packs, a C64 with a floppy disk drive, joystick and diskettes, inactive since the twins had spilled juice over it, a pair of leaky boots, a Kelly Family record that he was so ashamed of that he didn't keep it with the other records in his room, a pair of old Chucks entirely coated in mud, a Zippo lighter that Onno

Kolthoff had given him and never demanded back, which he now reclaimed in a moment of grim determination, several dozen rolled-up posters for the Kill Mister concert in the school auditorium and a yellow Reclam booklet of *Poems and Interpretations 2, Enlightenment and Sturm and Drang*. On a pillar, the chimney, hung the nylon thread with the glass droplet and his confirmation certificate with the aphorism: *And before the throne there was a sea of glass like unto crystal: and in the midst of the throne, and round about the throne, were four beasts full of eyes before and behind*. Below it was his old satchel, still holding school books as if he'd just shrugged it off, *Texts for Secondary Level 6* and *5*, *Language Practice 6* and *5*, *WES—World and Environmental Studies, English G*, books *2* and *1*, the pencil case with his spaceships and galaxies and alien life forms, and behind that was a high pile of his Perry Rhodan collection, one thousand, three hundred and six pulp paperbacks and twenty-five silver editions. Only a step further were the adventure novels, *Gulliver's Travels, Robinson Crusoe, Treasure Island, The Deerslayer, Huckleberry Finn, The Sea Wolf*, on top of them a recorder and a book of notes for it. A dusty display cabinet held rows of model kits he'd never finished making, and some that had collapsed again due to the temperature variations in the uninsulated attic because the glue had dissolved, a Phantom, a Cobra, a Gazelle, a Lux, a Marten, a Fox, a Beaver, a Leopard. He had chained his bike, a BMX 2000, the reward for his first school report, to one of the roof beams to protect it from being claimed by the twins, and had hidden the key so well that he'd never find it again. And there, right at the end, below a slanting beam, under a shabby waxed tablecloth, it was—the wooden box with his name on it, his grandmother's legacy. Between his mother's moans and the squeaking bed he heard another car coming from the dyke. He knelt down—the floorboard beneath him creaked—and lifted the lid. Photo albums full of black-and-white pictures appeared, atlases of anatomy, the *Pschyrembel Clinical Dictionary*, journals like

The German Christian and *The German Druggist*, slim volumes entitled *Sexual Developmental Disorders* and *Thou Shalt Lead a Chaste and
Virtuous Life*, their covers stained with mould, a guide to identifying
flowers, the *ABC of Good Manners*, *Be Beautiful—Stay Beautiful*, *My
Path to God, My Son*, and at the very bottom the thing he'd been
looking for all along: *Mein Kampf*, the anniversary edition for the
Führer's fiftieth birthday, bound in blue leather with gilt edging
and a golden sword. As he picked up the book he thought that the
sword looked like an inverted cross. And he opened up the anti-
Bible, the work of the devil, and a newspaper cutting about a
speech Hitler had given in Jever fell out. Then he went back to the
door—the floorboard creaked again—and began reading as he
walked. His mother had fallen silent below. No moaning, no
squeaking. With every line, with every step his heart grew lighter.

On that first warm night of the year, Hard lay awake for a long time
as well, the window open at the top, the net curtains billowing in
light gusts of wind, and listened to the sounds of the cars coming
from the dyke with thudding basslines, approaching from the
hammrich, changing down a gear before the level crossing and
accelerating after it the moment they arrived in the village, so hard
that the engines howled. Their lights jerked through the gaps in
the shutters, illuminated the room for two or three seconds, cast
long, bizarre shadows and then disappeared, never to be seen
again.

In his mind he went through the stocktaking again, which he'd
worked out hours previously in the office, his own personal stocktaking of the month that had just ended. He kept account of every
event, and every event could be listed under assets or liabilities,
depending on how he interpreted it. The crisis, prompted by
him leaving the card-game circle and the male-voice choir, was

overcome—an asset. Pastor Meinders' revelation had made less of an impression on him that he'd have thought possible; he'd reckoned with a sudden end ever since they'd made their agreement, and although it meant a drop in turnover he was sure he'd soon find a new, better place for his betting office—another asset. The danger of being supplanted by Schlecker had been averted for the time being, and until the Achterup branch reopened, which nobody expected until June, his catchment area would be expanded by three thousand potential customers, at least half of whom he hoped to keep by means of personal advice and free gifts—also on the positive side. He heard a creak above him and waited for it to repeat itself, but when it didn't he went back to his internal accounting. The only major blow to his accounts was Daniel's failure at the newspaper—a definite liability. The boy was developing into a problem that couldn't be dealt with through corporal punishment alone. And he felt he couldn't devote himself to him with the same dedication as usual because he needed him, because he was his alibi, his insurance against a much larger problem, the downfall of the house of Kuper. Daniel's failure at the newspaper had certainly stung him, but that was at a time when he thought he was invulnerable. Hard had never felt as alive as that spring, as alive and as close to death. It was just how he imagined war—new frontlines opening up at every turn. The borderlines blurring between friend and foe. Bullets pierce his flesh and yet, driven by an unbounded will for victory, he makes a big haul. Nothing and no one can resist his weapon, his own fast shots, he has them all at his feet, just as alive or dead as he is. And the only thing he has to pay attention to is not catching anything he can't get rid of later, when it's all over. Two women he thought he'd lost for ever had come back to him and he had given them what they asked for—assets. He considered it only natural that one of them was demanding more than she was entitled to, now that she had savoured his prime cuts after years of voluntary renouncement of good quality. And April had been extremely successful in his marriage, compared to the year's first quarter; Birgit and he had slept together three times, less often than he had with other women but more often than usual—an asset. She may only have given in to his early-morning wooing on one occasion, but the new investments, sympathy, interest and alcohol, had paid off immediately. Apart from that he had heeded her promise that she would give herself to him if he let her come. The more space and time he gave her, the more love she was prepared to give him. The further he moved from her, the stronger her urge for him. And it was the same this time—under cover of darkness she opened up to him, he felt her hands stroking his chest hair, his belly, his hips and thighs, slipping through the slit in his pyjama bottoms and gripping his penis as if they had to tame a wild thing, with a strength and determination he'd missed in Birgit for a long time.

'Pretty hard,' she said in a low, almost masculine voice.

And he said, 'Hard by name, gentle by nature,' almost without expression, surprised at her tone, at the force with which she commanded him.

And as she sat atop him, completely naked unlike him, and he reached greedily for her breasts, he thought once and for all that a being from an alien world had taken possession of her, so willingly did she accommodate his wish to touch her. Everything else, however, she fended off. When he grabbed her and wanted to turn her over she slapped his hands away, and when he wanted to say something she kissed him so long and hard that he tasted blood, hers or his of both of theirs, impossible to distinguish, for at last they'd become one again, one flesh and one blood. She pressed him against the mattress with all her body's weight. Her legs latched around his and her fingernails, long and pointed, dug into his shoulders. She set the rhythm and he, grateful for the experience, succumbed to it. He stopped taking stock, stopped moving, thinking of others, thinking at all. He had entered a state of supreme bliss. All the assets and liabilities had dissolved into thin air, all sounds were muffled; he perceived the train speeding past outside and even Birgit's moans as if from a great distance. All he heard was his heart beating, so loud and hard that he feared it would burst and rip him to shreds from inside. But he was willing to take the risk. Better to die in bed or on the battlefield than in hospital, pumped full of medication, under a doctor's scalpel. And yet he had to hold himself back if he wanted to extend the few seconds that sex usually lasted between them, and he did want to—at least until they were both exhausted, too exhausted to get up in the next few hours and go about their old, sedate lives again. Birgit had turned back into the woman he'd married, proud, mature, insatiable; he didn't know how and why it had happened, and he swore not to ask her, but to savour every moment of her lust in silence. All he knew was that she'd used to mount him like this before, after days of grief and contempt—so she could lie in his arms afterwards. They each had a different understanding of closeness, and perhaps that was still the case, perhaps she hadn't changed at all, perhaps they were merely exchanging their interpretations, and perhaps they'd both gain in their own way, gain confidence to close the gap between them beyond just that night. Sweat ran from all the pores in his body and he felt like he did in the sauna, the purpose of his existence fulfilled—up to now it had merely been hot, but now his innermost self opened up, swelled, glowed, pulsed, stopped beating—and started again.

Once again a car boomed closer and strips of light fell onto her body, her long, sweat-soaked hair, her shiny, bobbing breasts. 'Yes, Biggi, yes!' With ever faster thrusts she drove him and herself towards their climax, but then, just as she had introduced her hand to assist things, just as they were both ready to come, she above him, he inside her, she paused and signalled to him, her finger pressed to her lips, emitting a quiet hiss, to be quiet. She looked up at the ceiling.

Then the car was past and the spell was broken. 'What's the matter? Why are you stopping?'

'I heard something. A creak.'

'That was us.'

'It came from up there. There's something up above us.'

'Nix.'

'Yes there is, I'm certain.'

'Right now you're above me. That's all that counts. And now carry on.'

But she got off him and flopped onto her side of the bed.

'You can't stop now.'

'Do it yourself. I can't any more.'

And he followed her advice before the pictures she'd conjured up in his head faded away. But he'd barely started to redeem himself when he heard it too, a creak directly above him, and he removed his hand, buttoned his trousers and got up to see who or what had robbed him so cruelly of his blessing.

Despite the fact that Daniel had experienced the most unpleasant thing children could experience, in his opinion—been a witness to his parents having sex—he could hardly wait to show them his discovery. He had taken the book to school but hadn't dared to take a look at it during class or in the breaks, fearing he'd be caught by the teachers or his fellow pupils. The former would have drawn the wrong conclusions and felt confirmed in their opinion that he, the UFO boy, was responsible for the symbols. And the latter would have ridiculed him as a swot for reading something they didn't have to read, and perhaps told their parents what he, the crazy kid, had found out. Both fears proved unfounded; they wouldn't have paid any attention to him anyway. All anyone talked about was that there had been arson attacks in Jericho and Achterup and the fog in the hammrich had disappeared overnight. The teachers and his fellow pupils speculated over who might have set the fires, not coming to any conclusion. And unlike the snow five years previously, the fog only seemed to warrant major attention at the moment of its disappearance. In Geography, Mr Kamps didn't talk about earthquakes but about meteorology, weather phenomena on a global scale with apocalyptic force and effect. Mrs Nanninga had brought along texts on the subject—poems by Eduard Mörike ('September Morning'), Theodor Storm ('October Song') and Christian Morgenstern ('November Day'). And in Physics they were supposed to use steam to simulate fog, which was not possible, however, because the other Physics class was using the Bunsen burners at the same time for the same reason. Volker suggested using smoke and offered to fill the room with it himself, but his father didn't take up his suggestion. Daniel knew he could trust Volker. He was sincere enough to keep everything to himself if you asked him to, as Simone had recently confirmed on the telephone, but Daniel also knew that Volker's affinity was no use to him; he didn't have enough power. No one would believe Simone and her antifascist friends if she made the accusations public. Whatever they said or did, every flyer, every demonstration, every gesture was nothing but propaganda, no matter how obvious the proof might be. He couldn't go to the *Frisian News* any more. And he didn't want to let Rosing's political adversaries in on his secret, Bernd Wübbena, Didi Schulz, Richard Wiemers or Jürgen Engberts, because they were certain to misuse the information for their election campaigns without giving him credit as the true originator. Then Rosing would be out of the picture but he, Daniel, wouldn't be rehabilitated. He had thought about the problem all morning, about how best to share the news, and at the very end, on his way home—he was just cycling towards the drugstore—he'd realized there was only one person who could advise him on how to proceed. He hoped his father now saw him, his prodigal son, in a new, better light and the new bond between them was strong enough to bring Rosing to his knees. But when he was sitting opposite him at the kitchen table over lunch he was suddenly not sure whether his parents were open enough to support him in what he intended. The twins had smeared the tomato sauce in which their pasta was drenched across one side of the table, his mother was impaling slices of courgette on her fork but not putting them in her mouth, and his father was sitting behind his plate, cutting his potatoes into ever-smaller pieces and staring at him with a tired, tense look on his face. 'Where were you last night?'

Daniel rolled his eyes. 'Not that again.'

'I asked you where you were.'

'In my room.'

'When?'

'The whole time.'

'And you didn't hear nix?'

'What was there to hear?' He looked at his father and his mother.

'Nix.'

'Nix is what I heard.' And to avoid giving his father a reason to reach across the table, although he didn't look as if he was in any state to do so, as pale as he was, he added, 'I was asleep. Until you came in.'

'Ah, so you noticed that.'

'It was hard not to. You turned the light on.'

'To see if you were there.'

'I was. The whole time. I'm always here at night.'

'That's all right then.'

'Yes,' said Daniel. 'It is.' He took the book out of his backpack, deciding the right moment had arrived. 'It's all in here.'

'What's in where?'

'What Rosing said. In his speech in the village hall. *Deeds of political insanity, daily bread, rooted in the soil, lottery ball, legislation for foreigners, community of fate.* It's all in here and in this article here.' He held the book out to his father, and he took it in his hand, opened it at the very beginning, at the page with the author's photo, and slammed it shut again.

'Where did you get this from?'

'From the box.'

'What box?'

'The one from Grandma.'

'The one in the attic?'

Daniel nodded.

'So you were up there after all.' His father stood up, one hand resting on the back of his chair, but sat straight back down again.

'I've had that,' Daniel pointed at *Mein Kampf*, 'for a long time. I've had it all my life. But I only remembered yesterday that there's a link between what Rosing said and what it says in here.'

'This here ought not to exist at all any more.'

'I know.'

'You don't know nix. Your grandma ought to have left it buried in the ground, with the flag and the medals.'

'What flag? And what medals?'

'Everyone here in Jericho,' his father gestured around the room, 'had a swastika flag outside their house. Everyone. And

684

before the Poles came everyone with an ounce of sanity burnt them or buried them in the garden. Along with this book here. Only your grandma didn't. The Poles burnt down every house with a swastika flag, you see. Every one. Out of revenge. And once the Poles were gone your grandma dug everything up again. Everything except for the flag and the medals.'

His mother looked up from her plate. 'She always said you should never burn books, and you shouldn't throw them away either, books are there to be read.' Her eyes were red and swollen.

'Well, obviously no one here read this book, otherwise none of it would have happened.'

'What wouldn't have happened?' asked his father.

'Auschwitz.'

'Does it say anything about Auschwitz in here?'

'Not directly.'

'There you are then.'

'But they could have known where things were heading.'

'How do you know that? You weren't even there.'

'You don't have to have been there to know what it was like.'

'Oh yes you do, otherwise you can't judge properly. Back then,' said his father, who hadn't been there either, 'you had to decide what side you were on, for or against Hitler. We only found out about Auschwitz after the war. And that's why we couldn't decide for or against it. That's the thing your green and commie teachers didn't tell you during their brainwashing sessions. And they've read much too many books.'

At first Daniel wanted to say, 'Better than nix,' but then he'd have taken his father's bait, and he couldn't open himself up for attack or the conversation would take a totally different turn to the one he'd intended. 'In any case that proves I'm right. Rosing's read it, *Mein Kampf*, he quoted from it.'

'Nix. Words like that crop up in every book and the news-papers are full of them.' He unfolded the report about Hitler's speech in Jever. '*Lottery ball*. I read that every day. Don't know anyone who's ever won more than a few marks.'

'I do,' said his mother, 'Gerald . . . Doctor Ahlers won a car. That Porsche. The one he had the accident in.'

'Eiske won the car. And anyway it wasn't in the lottery.'

'Where did she win it then?'

'How do I know? Am I the one who's constantly running over there or you?'

His mother looked out of the window. 'At least the fog's cleared up at last. Otherwise there'd have been *another* accident.'

'I know I've made a mess of things, I admit that,' Daniel said quickly before they changed the subject. 'The thing with the news-paper was stupid. And I'm sorry. But now, this here, this is absolutely clear. And I think we ought to tell them.'

'Tell who what?'

'Tell people. That Rosing's a Nazi.'

'You still don't get it, do you? We're all in the same boat here. And you'd better not tell anyone anything any more, if you don't want them to string you up. Because that's what they're planning.'

'Hard,' his mother said. 'What are you talking about? Who's planning what?'

'What do you think,' said his father, ignoring what she'd said, 'I've had to hear because of you over the past few years?'

'That's why I thought,' Daniel said, 'that *you* could tell them.'

'Nix.' His father picked up the book as if testing its weight and then lowered it again. 'And even if it's true, it's all a long time ago. No one can remember it. We ought to leave the past in peace. What's done is done.'

'History repeats itself.'

'History lessons maybe.'

'And people trust you.'

'They used to. The name Kuper has suffered a lot recently.'

'I thought we were supposed to leave the past in peace.'

'That's what we're doing.'

'And what happened to Grandpa's medals? Are they still buried in the garden?'

And at that, Daniel did get a slap around the ear, not very painful but resounding, for immediately breaking their agreement.

Hard couldn't remember when he'd last been so alone, so perfectly at one with himself and the world. No women asking his expert opinion, no men wanting to talk about their public or secret passions—photography or fishing or betting—no teenagers ashamed of their blossoming bodies—no customers at all. It was just before four; he was behind the counter in the shop, the children were out of the house, Birgit had taken the twins to their swimming lessons in the county town again and Daniel was hanging around outside somewhere, on the streets of Jericho. He was presumably looking for another way to prevent Rosing's election after all, but Hard wondered how Daniel would manage that now that he'd taken the book away from him. There must be other copies in the village, carefully hidden and locked away so that none of the children got their hands on them and asked questions no one wanted to answer. Mind you, with the Compunists he wasn't sure they didn't have it lying around in plain sight, as a display object and constant reminder. But Daniel didn't go there any more. And the Reichert boy and the other two long-haired louts Daniel had hung out with at grammar school hadn't shown their faces in the drugstore since Daniel had switched to the intermediate school. Although they'd avoided the drugstore before that as well, he remembered now, after he'd recommended in all seriousness that they try using conditioner on their hair. And he assumed the Reents with their anorexic, politically over-motivated daughter didn't have *Mein Kampf* on the living-room shelves, or Volker's parents either—at least he hoped not. Arne Mengs was capable of anything. He shuddered as he thought of the barbecue Birgit and he had held for the *Utlanners*, the New Jerichoans, on their terrace, and of Mengs' absolutely bizarre statement *that you should let children do anything they liked, that they'd come up against their boundaries of their own accord at some point, that life would punish them.* Anyone could see by Daniel's example how incapable children were of learning from their own mistakes—despite the strictest upbringing. He was glad he'd rendered him harmless. He had defused the bomb and at some point Daniel would come to terms with the fact that it was sometimes better not to want to change the world, for him and for the world as well. For a while now, though, since his last encounter with Theda Wiemers, he'd been thinking about giving his vote to Johann Rosing after all. If her husband made it to mayor, she might not just put him under private pressure but cause trouble on the business side too. And maybe then she'd even pull strings to get Schlecker to Jericho, if need be under police protection, just to ruin him. He thought he knew her strategy precisely—if she couldn't have him for herself, she wanted at least to see him suffer for his decision to stay with Birgit. Dictators acted much the same way in the face of their own defeat. The country, the nation they'd exploited was not to fall into enemy hands, at least not undamaged, not in its full magnificence and size.

He looked around the shop. The boxes were unpacked, their contents shelved, the rows were full of products and the floor was shiny clean. The PVC squares reflected the green of the maple leaves outside the house. Spring at last. At last the fog had dispersed, the fog out in the hammrich and inside him. Everything was perfectly fine and he thought everything ought to stay just the way it was. He picked up a camera, a white Dynax 8000i Prestige, the latest Minolta model, inserted a colour film and took a few shots, like he only otherwise did when customers came to him after their holidays or family get-togethers and pressed their cameras into his hands with the request to fill up the film, wind it back and develop it, so they could finally enjoy their blurry pictures of the beach and the mountains or weddings and birthdays. He photographed the counter display, the empty aisles, the advertising signs up on the walls, and himself in front of and behind the counter. And when he'd finished, removed the film and put it in an envelope, he turned the sign on the door to *Closed*, which he never did during business hours unless Eiske was there and dropped a flacon of some expensive perfume into her handbag in front of him. He went into the office, took *Mein Kampf* out of the desk drawer and went upstairs with it into Daniel's room to hide it there, behind the collected volumes of Goethe and Schiller, assuming Daniel would never suspect it was in his own room. And he looked forward to seeing the stupid face he made when he found it, which he didn't expect to happen until the end of the year, until Daniel next tidied his room at Christmas, and he hoped he'd be there then to savour every moment of his victory over his son.

At dinner they were all sitting around the table together again. Hard and Birgit, Daniel and Julia and Andreas, the whole Kuper family.

'Could you pass the butter please,' Daniel said, and Hard passed it to him.

None of them mentioned a word about what had happened over lunch. The twins went to bed without resistance. Daniel cleared the table, did his homework in the kitchen and then disappeared to his room. And at night, as they lay alongside each other, Birgit turned to Hard again to relieve her conscience, as she admitted to him, because she hadn't managed to make him happy the night before.

11

During the night before Ascension Day his father came into his bedroom and told him he had to get up; something had happened. Daniel got dressed and followed him downstairs. He asked him why he'd woken him, what had happened, but his father didn't answer, merely opening the front door and pointing outside. The sky was covered by low clouds. The streets were dark, the lamps switched off hours ago. There were no lights in the windows of the houses. And yet—aside from the *S* of the savings bank and the *A* for *Apotheke* on the pharmacy—there was a weak glimmer as if someone had lit fires in different places at the same time, so as to set the whole village alight, inextinguishably.

Then Daniel saw the people. They were standing in semi-circles in front of the walls. Some were wearing nightclothes, others had put jackets over them. None of them turned around to him or his father. The two of them walked together past the empty houses, the concrete pillars of the bridges, and everywhere there were people standing and staring at the symbols that Daniel had washed away weeks ago with cellulose thinner, which were now glimmering like glow-stars stuck to the ceilings of children's bedrooms.

His father grabbed him by the arm, dragged him forward and pointed at one of the swastikas. 'Was that you?'

Daniel shook his head.

'How did you make the stuff come through again?'

Daniel shook his head again.

'Stop it! Stop it right now!' His father raised his hand to hit him.

Daniel felt them all crowding around them, coming towards them from every direction and forming a circle from which there was no escape.

The next day the symbols had all vanished, but as soon as it was dark they appeared again and there were more of them with every night that passed. To begin with they were only on the shops along Village Road, Schröder's Shoes, Dettmers' Hairdressing, Wessels' Bakery, Krause Fishmongers, Vehndel Fashions and the Flower Barn; then the ones on Station Road, Kramer's Furniture, Benzen's Paints, Hanken Solar, Tinnemeyer Upholstery, Plenter Electrical, Busboom Autos, Oltmanns' Cycles and Kromminga Driving School; then, a week later, they were also on the houses in the new estates, the farmhouses in the hammrich, the old dairy, the Beach Hotel, the custard factory, even the church, everywhere there were swastikas, *NPD, foreigners out, Germany for the Germans*. Only next to the drugstore window did it say *I love you*. That was why the angry villagers gathered outside the Kupers' door, rang the bell, hammered their fists against the shutters and yelled up at the brightly lit windows. Hard was afraid something might get broken and he called the police.

Kurt Rhauderwiek and Frank Tebbens, waiting outside the house with the engine running, beat a path through the crowd, escorted Daniel to their car to roars of applause and took him to the police station in the county town. The officer who had questioned him the first time, Uwe Saathoff, questioned him again now, in the same white, windowless room.

692

'So you can't remember anything?'

'I wasn't there.'

'It says here,' he leant over a sheet of paper, 'you're a sleep-walker.'

'I'm not.'

'How long have you been sleepwalking?'

'It was only once.'

'Once is enough.'

'For what?'

'Henning does it too sometimes, gets up at night, sits down in the living room, watches TV with his eyes shut, even though there's nothing on at that time of night, just the blank screen and white noise, and then goes back to bed.'

'Poltergeist.

'What?'

'A horror film.'

'Have you seen it?'

'No.'

'Do you often watch films like that?'

'No.'

'Do you know Kenneth Parks?'

'No.'

'Not surprised. Interesting case. 1987. A small town in Canada. Kenneth Parks is twenty-three. He works as a project manager for an electronics company, has a wife, a five-month-old daughter and a problem—he's lost a lot of bets, on the horses, and he's run up huge debts. To pay them off, he steals a lot of money from his boss and then gets the sack. Still, everyone in the family stands by him, especially his in-laws. One night, the 23rd of May, he gets in his car and drives twenty-three kilometres to their house.

He breaks open the door with a crowbar, injures his father-in-law, stabs his mother-in-law to death and then drives to the police station because his hands are covered in blood and he can't work out why. And all that—'

'With the crowbar?'

'—in his sleep. He couldn't . . . What?'

'Did he stab his mother-in-law with the crowbar?'

'The police didn't believe him either to begin with. Interrogated him for hours, different officers on different days—no inconsistencies. Lie detector—no abnormalities. Always the same story. And then the defence applies for him to be examined by sleep specialists, neurologists, and they find out there's something wrong with his brain activities and he really was sleepwalking at the time of the crime.'

'Yeah, right,' said Daniel. 'Your whole life's a dream, and then you wake up and you're dead.'

'Could be. Wouldn't rule it out. In his case, the jury found him guilty anyway. Supposed to be a retrial next year. Wouldn't surprise me if the supreme court classifies sleepwalking as a new mental illness and he's acquitted this time.'

'Who?'

'Kenneth Parks. Were you even listening to me?'

'Not all the time.'

The next day, Daniel was arraigned before a magistrate and immediately released because, as he was told, the witness had contradicted himself and they had no evidence against him. The *Frisian News* blamed a gang of youths for the new graffiti. At school, Paul and Jens bragged that they'd done it. They were picked up from home as well, questioned, arraigned and released. Homeowners stood guard outside their properties. Amateur marksmen and hunters positioned themselves on driveways with loaded guns. The police patrolled the streets. It was no use. No one climbed over the fences under cover of darkness and painted on people's walls. And yet it happened. No house was left unmarked.

In the evening, as soon as the sun set, they wiped over the paint from top to bottom. Superneemann and Kuper soon sold out of sponges and cloths and placed orders for special gloves, and the Raiffeisen farmers' cooperative shop was running out of canisters of cellulose thinner. Some tried tougher methods. Those who could afford it commissioned cleaning firms from outside the village. Others used sandblasters. A chemical corporation offered breathable graffiti protection and delivered several vanloads at a special price. During the day the village shone like a new pin. But at night all the symbols were back again.

On Saturday evening the news made it onto the local TV show *Reports of the Day*. On Sunday, reporters and camera crews descended on the 'ghost village', the 'Nazi village', like flies upon the cows' heads behind the slaughterhouse. Like in the old days when the news of the corn circle spread around the world, outside broadcast vans with satellite dishes and light masts lined the streets. Tourists arrived from all over the country, by buses and trains, most of them in their own cars, neo-Nazis especially, who pitched their tents at the campsite by the lake and by the dyke. Those who wore shoes and suits rather than boots and braces and had hair longer than scalp-length could rent a room at the Beach Hotel or a holiday apartment. At night they paraded around the village, some clutching lit torches, others beer cans, video cameras, photo cameras. They filmed and photographed the symbols and their comrades in front of them. Some saluted with their right arms, some didn't. They got the pictures developed at Kuper's but all of them turned out badly. It was too bright with a flash and too dark without. Hard took his own photos using a long exposure and offered them for sale under the counter. But shortly after one of them was reproduced in *stern* magazine, Kurt Rhauderwiek turned up in the shop and said, 'Get rid of that stuff, Hard. People have started talking.'

'Have they, now?' said Hard. 'And what are they saying?'

'They don't think it's right for you to make a profit out of it and all.'

'Out of what?'

'Out of all this here. The thing your son did.'

'Daniel's got nothing to do with it. The magistrate said so.'

'That's not how people see it. They think Daniel started it, so he's responsible for it, no matter who's doing all this,' Kurt Rhauderwiek pointed out of the window, 'this time around. And you shouldn't be making money out of it.'

'Oh, and it's fine for the others, is it? The Krögers have got their whole hotel booked up. Hayo Hayenga had to get new girls from the East for his club because the lads are beating his doors down. Fokken, Neemann, they're queuing up everywhere. And Vehndel's even selling bomber jackets now. But I'm not allowed to make money out of it.'

'Hard, it's for your own good. Take my advice. Otherwise I can't guarantee anything.'

'What can't you guarantee?'

'Your family's safety.'

'What do you get paid for, if it's not that?'

'People are angry, Hard, you have to understand that.'

'And you think I'm not?'

Later, at dinner, he still hadn't calmed down. 'You get a few sales and along comes the state and spoils it all.'

Birgit put her hand on his. 'You mustn't get so upset all the time. Rosing will put an end to this nonsense. Marlies told me he's got this stuff that he uses on his building sites, to polish up old bricks, and—'

'Rosing! Rosing! He's not going to do anything!' Hard wanted to say something else but then they heard the sound, footsteps, hundreds and thousands of footsteps coming closer, and a hubbub of voices rising up to them from below, from the street outside. 'Resist to exist.' 'Nazis out.' 'Germany never again.' They got up, looked out of the window and saw demonstrators marching past with banners, circled by police officers, neighbours and neo-Nazis blocking the crossroads and greeting them with raised fists, sticks and stones flying through the air, police vans and water cannons driving up and separating the groups. 'That rabble,' said Hard, and closed the net curtain. 'That's the end of our peace now.'

On the Sat1 show *Us in Lower Saxony*, Daniel saw the drugstore, his father raising the shutters outside the windows, his mother taking the twins to school, himself walking past the angry crowd, fetching his racing bike out of the garage and setting off for school, pursued by journalists. RTL plus offered him money for an exclusive interview, lots of money. His parents pressured him to take the offer, to make a statement, present his view of things, to think of his future and theirs, to wash the family name clean.

The candidates for the mayor's job used the attention for their election campaigns. Bernd Wübbena, standing for the Christian Democrats, said that anyone developing in the wrong direction ought to feel the full force of the law. The Social Democrat Didi Schulz was against that. Richard Wiemers pointed out the right to freedom of expression but added, 'Damage to property is a crime.' Jürgen Engberts hoped the paint could be removed without harming the environment. Johann Rosing objected to the phrase 'Nazi village'. 'A whole village is being held unjustly responsible. It's one isolated criminal. No, it's not me. Everyone knows his name.' Paul and Jens reported on the parties, how Daniel couldn't take his drink and always lost control of himself. 'How he got hold of alcohol I don't know,' Paul said with a shrug.

'Maybe he hid the bottles somewhere along the way, to get a head start. For Dutch courage.'—'He doesn't have any experience with girls yet,' said Jens, completing Paul's thought, 'or not any good experiences.' Volker said, 'It's because of his diet. Daniel often has low blood sugar. He's never eaten enough, especially meat.' Frank Tebbens flicked through a folder and read aloud, not looking at the camera, 'Daniel came to our attention at an early age. Fishing on private property at seven, breaking the church hall windows at nine, ruining a field of maize at ten, insulting the pastor at fourteen, and so on.' Nella Allen brushed her hair out of her face and said, 'I told him, *Namu amu Myōhō Renge Kyō*, but he didn't listen.' Mrs Nanninga had no explanation for his behaviour. 'There was no sign of aggression on the outside.' Martin Masurczak said, 'Daniel has a disturbed relationship to reality. He's in a state of war. The battle line divides his brain into two halves at all times— him against the others.' He said the same thing, only in more detail, in a commentary published in the *Frisian News* the next day. Doctor Ahlers called for a general ban on computer games. Pastor Meinders called, his arms outstretched to heaven, 'And the blood shall be to you for a token upon the houses where ye are: and when I see the blood, I will pass over you, and the plague shall not be upon you to destroy you.' A scientist said the paint was highly likely to contain zinc sulphide, copper and salt, which explained the glowing. Wiebke asked one of the reporters whether he'd rather see her sluice gates or her sluice chamber, and added that Daniel had always got to see both, had been crazy to see them. His father said nothing. His mother said, 'Well, yes, Daniel has changed a lot recently. But that might be his age. Boys often have it difficult at his age.' She rejected accusations that she hadn't taken good enough care of him, had neglected him for the sake of his younger siblings. A psychologist said it was due to the lack of creative opportunities in the village, the perpetrator hadn't found any form of legitimate recognition in the village or at school and was looking for a way out. 'In my view he was left alone by his parents, carers and teachers, and that's why he escaped into a parallel world. The symbols are nothing but an expression of emotional desperation. How else can we explain the words *I love you* on his own wall? Xenophobia and narcissism are often close to one another. At advanced stages of this personality disorder, however, the thought processes are often reversed. Then xenophobia turns into altruism, narcissism into self-hate.'

Hard was beside himself. Someone had smashed the shop window and looted the display, even though he'd let the shutters down like every evening. They'd been pushed up and fastened with lengths of wood at the sides to give the stones free rein. He feared it wouldn't stop at stones and he'd end up with the same fate as the Schlecker shop in Achterup. So he called in Old Kramer to barricade the whole shop with chipboard against new attacks, once the police and the insurance people had registered the damage—with a certain satisfaction, it seemed to him.

'There's no point,' yelled Manfred Kramer, Old Kramer, when he came along with his carpenter to measure the windows. 'You should get the problem out from under your roof instead of locking yourself in.'

'And where am I supposed to send it, the problem?' Hard yelled back. 'To Berlin perhaps? To the capital city of problems?'

'The politicians might stay in Bonn.'

'Leave me in peace with your Bonn.'

'Better than here. Then you'd be rid of it at least.'

'You mean,' shouted Hard, his strength waning, 'like you did with yours?'

'New York?' Old Kramer bellowed. 'What would he want there?'

Hard waved a hand in despair and went back inside. The shop was just as empty as a week ago, but now the silence was threatening. He thought he could sense the calm before the storm.

Although all the objects in the room were still in the same places, right where he'd put them, they seemed to have suddenly taken on a different meaning. He asked himself whether you'd be able to tell in the pictures if he took some now, see the difference, see that the light came in directly rather than falling through pristine panes of glass. But he didn't feel like taking photos. What he really felt like was sweeping everything off the shelves and hacking all the new shop fittings to pieces. He wasn't a religious man but if he were, if there were a religion that elevated his shop to a deity, then he'd see its desecration as the greatest sin. And that's why he picked the stones out of the display and swept up the shards and threw the rubbish in the container behind the garage. Then he put on a clean overall and experienced a feeling that had previously been totally unfamiliar: waiting for customers. No one came to buy anything all morning, a few women expressed their sympathy when they saw the mess and a few men hinted that he'd been lucky and everything could have been much worse, but none of them took anything away with them, as if the bad reputation that Kuper's Drugstore now had in their eyes extended to its goods. In the afternoon two workers, the carpenter and his assistant, mounted the chipboard. One of them got a splinter, and when he took it out a drop of blood spilled out too, and he smeared it on the wood from the outside.

'D'you need a plaster?' asked Hard.

'It's fine,' said the man. 'It'll be over in a minute.'

Under normal circumstances Hard would have shared that view but he didn't want blood on his shop, no matter what Pastor Meinders said in church about blood as a sign of righteousness, and he went inside to get the man a plaster. First he tried to find his way in the dark, and then he did switch the light on after all, and when the telephone started ringing as if in reaction to the movement he jumped with shock and stopped motionless by the door. People had been calling since dawn, not to order anything or ask his advice because they couldn't work their new camera

700

properly, but to hurl abuse at him. To begin with he'd answered the phone with 'Kuper, Jericho,' and listened to the tirades that rained down on him—he didn't want to lose any customers and he thought he might change the callers' minds if he showed understanding, but they didn't let him get a word in edgeways, they'd only called to dump their hate on him. He saw that someone had picked up the phone upstairs, a small green dot lit up above the dial, and when he came into the kitchen later on—the children were in their bedrooms by that time—completely exhausted by the feeling of permanently having to defend himself against everything and everyone, Birgit said, suppressing a sob: 'Margret rang, she saw us on TV.'

'Your sister. No wonder. I could've bet on that.'

'The only question is who you'd bet against.'

'Against you.'

'She and Jochen offered to come and collect Daniel. They'd come up in the car tomorrow. She said he can stay in Bad Vilbel until the whole thing's blown over. And Gerhild offered her help too. Maybe we should all go down there for a few days.'

'No way. They're the last thing I need.'

'But when he's gone and all the nonsense goes on, people will realize it can't have been him.'

'That's not the point any more, Birgit. Daniel put the idea into the world and other people are putting it into practice now, bigger and better than him.'

'What if he talks to them?'

'Who? Daniel?'

'Yes, what if he tells them to stop?'

'He doesn't even know who's doing it.' He gestured out of the window.

'Maybe he does.'

'Believe me,' said Hard, putting his arm down, 'if he knew he'd have told me.'

'Maybe that's the reason.' Now she did start sobbing.

'What are you trying to say? That it's all my fault when it comes down to it? Who started it all off? Him or me?'

Birgit shrugged.

'Him or me?' Not noticing, he started talking in the same tone as to Old Kramer, as if she were hard of hearing or stupid, or both.

'Him,' she said and turned away from him.

Just after Whit Sunday there were parties in the Hankens' barn during the week as well as on weekends.

'What is *The Thing*?' asked Paul, pushing a glass of vodka towards Daniel.

Jens looked at his watch, 'Tick-tock, tick-tock, tick-tock.'

'A film,' said Daniel.

'OK, let me put that more clearly,' said Paul and lit a joint. 'What is the thing in John Carpenter's film *The Thing*?'

'A human being,' said Daniel, though he hadn't seen the film.

Paul and Jens exchanged glances.

'Not quite right,' said Paul, 'but not quite wrong,' and he handed Daniel his joint as a reward.

And Daniel took it—to his own surprise.

They were all still in bed when the police came to search the house in the early morning. Kurt Rhauderwiek and Frank Tebbens started down in the cellar and then worked their way from room to room up to Daniel's bedroom.

'Why don't you just move in with us?' asked Hard once he'd got dressed. The policemen were taking boxes off the shelves in the shop storeroom, opening one after another and scattering the contents over the floor. 'Then you won't have to keep coming round specially. That'd save us all time and money.'

'You're in the way, Hard,' said Kurt Rhauderwiek. 'Or are you trying to obstruct us on the job?'

'I'm just wondering what you're looking for down here. Why don't you start at the top? Then we'd get it over with. I thought you were here because of Daniel.'

'Have you got something to hide?'

'No, nothing.'

'Then just let us do our job and don't worry about anything.'

Birgit followed them with a bucket and cloth, wiping down the now empty shelves and starting to put back every book, every folder, every box of her own belongings they'd picked up, but the twins cried when the men started rummaging through their toys and there was no consoling them. She phoned the school, bundled the two of them into the car and drove them off to the seaside.

When they finally examined his room, Daniel stood mutely alongside.

'Don't you want to tell us where you've hidden the stuff, Daniel?' asked Frank Tebbens, one hand on his holster. 'Speed the whole thing up a bit.'

'What stuff?'

'Forget it, we'll find it anyway. New information. Someone saw you. Yesterday and the day before too.'

'Who?'

'Your behaviour's making it worse for you. I don't know how you do it, night after night. But I do know one thing: Sooner or later you'll blow your cover, sooner or later we'll get evidence, like back then with the UFO thing. Everyone leaves traces. You can't wipe them away. That would be a trace of its own. That's the way it is.' He pointed out of the sloping window down at the street, down at the people gathered there calling Daniel's name. 'How much further do you want to go? Have you no sense of decency?'

Those words reminded Daniel of Pastor Meinders. Of the clip round the ear in the old church hall, of the necklace with the glass droplet and the motto he'd given him when he was confirmed in church, which was now framed in gold and hanging from a beam in the loft. He wondered whether it would help, whether faith was a way out. But then he told himself he hadn't done anything. And he was reminded of Volker, of what he'd said about the first-born. That they didn't stand a chance, no matter how hard they tried. He shook his head as if to bring himself round again. Everything was spinning, everything was moving around him. He closed his eyes and opened them again. He tried to concentrate, to fix his gaze on one point, holding himself firm by it like everyone else did. It didn't work. He kept thinking the same thoughts, about Iron and the corn circle, about Peter Peters and *you too*, about the symbols, about Rosing, his parents and the twins, about Wiebke and her sluice, about the parties over at the Hankens' place, about Simone, about Paul and Jens, about Volker with his liver-sausage sandwiches and his lung yearnings, about the newspaper and the cafeteria, about Pastor Meinders and the policemen, about school, his classes and his teachers, whose answers didn't match up with his questions. It was like on TV, like on *Jeopardy*!

Daniel props himself up on a game-show lectern. In front of him on the display board, his Christian name is noted in handwriting. He looks at the video wall and chooses a category. The host Hans-Jürgen Bäumler reads the text from the screen, even though it's clearly visible for both Daniel and the audience. Before he finishes the sentence Daniel presses the button. The red lamp lights up. He knows everything beforehand. He's still not going to win.

Moving-coil meters for alternating voltages and alternating currents contain a built-in rectifier. They are built to display the respective effective value.

What can be used to measure happiness?

This category is used to identify something prospective.

Will Germany be unbeatable for years to come?

The Reichsbank printed more and more money so that the public could pay the spiralling prices.

Do we only stay true to ourselves if we change?

A total of thirty-five hens and rabbits are contained in one cage. They have ninety-four legs altogether.

How many opportunities can you give away without losing hope of ever taking one?

When a pseudopod comes across nutrient particles, the latter are engulfed. This results in a bubble-like vacuole.

What is life?

Double Jeopardy!

FEELINGS 200

Its cathode consists of a tungsten wire with a high melting point, which can be brought to white heat by a heating current of approximately 40 A.

What is rage?

When mixed they produce white light.

Is there really nothing to see here?

CLICHÉS 600

This is a simplified version of reality.

What is literature?

PUBERTY 800

On a hiking map (scale 1:25000) the distance between the churches in two villages is 8 cm.

How far removed am I from myself?

PLANT PORN 1000

The sperm are transferred to female mosses by falling water droplets. They penetrate the archegonia and fertilize the egg cells.

How did it come to this?

Final round! Hans-Jürgen Bäumler says Daniel now has to type in the sum he's willing to risk. Daniel bets nothing. That's all he has. Although he's alone and there's no one he could copy from, Bäumler tells him to put one of the concentration helmets on, like headphones with blinkers on the side. Bäumler tells him to take the writing tablet and the writing pen, prepare himself to write, get ready to write for his task in the category

DISPROVEN HYPOTHESES

1848, 1918, 1989.

Daniel writes: *Is resistance pointless?*

The answers to the questions and the resulting new questions flashed past in a second, as if someone had blown a hole in his head to flood it with information, to churn up his memory and swirl it up into a vortex that swallowed up everything. Suddenly there was silence. The sounds had fallen mute, the movements frozen. He felt like behind glass, casketed in a glassy sea. Frank Tebbens was holding something out. He had four eyes and four arms, and in his four hands he was holding four books, two identical copies each of Goethe's *Theory of Colours* and Hitler's *Mein Kampf*.

12

When Daniel came to, it was bright and white. A white room. At first he thought he was in the interrogation room but then he saw a window, roofs of houses, tops of trees, birds in the sky, clouds. He was lying in a bed and being taken care of by a woman in a white coat. She hung up a new bag above him, from which a transparent liquid dripped into a tube and into his arm. The woman turned around, said, 'I think he's waking up,' and disappeared from his view.

His mother leant over him. She was crying, her tears falling onto his face. She hugged him and pressed him to her and said something into his ear, something he couldn't understand because her mouth was pressing up against his cheek. She stepped back, took out a handkerchief and blew her nose. Daniel sat up, pushing himself against the pillow with all his strength. His father was standing by the window, his hands behind his back, and staring out.

Daniel said, *I want.*

His mother paused mid-cry. 'Hard, come here, he said something.'

'What did he say?' His father approached him.

'I couldn't understand it.'

Daniel said it again. *I want.*

They approached him from either side, leant over him, shook their heads.

'I'll go and get a doctor,' said his father and left the room.

'You have to save your strength,' said his mother, gently stroking his hand. 'You've been through a lot. But they checked you inside and out here and didn't find anything.'

A doctor came in, his father behind him, both in white coats. The doctor looked into his eyes, dazzled him with a flashlight and asked, 'Can you understand me?'

Daniel nodded.

'Good.' He took away the flashlight and put it back in his pocket. 'How many fingers am I holding up?' He held up three fingers.

Daniel said, *Three*.

'Oh God,' said his mother and burst into tears again.

'That's perfectly normal,' said the doctor. 'It'll come back.' He turned to Daniel and told him to put his right forefinger on the tip of his nose, to follow the pen he was moving to and fro with his eyes, to hold up the same number of fingers as he was holding up. Then he pulled back the covers, tapped a rubber hammer against Daniel's arms and legs, ran the end of the handle from bottom to top along the soles of his feet, asked him to sit up, stand up, on two legs, on one. 'You can lie down again now.' The doctor looked at his parents. 'Have you told him?'

'Told him what?' asked his father.

'What happened to him.'

'What did happen to him?'

Daniel pulled up the covers and leant back.

'You lost consciousness and banged your head. Three days is unusually long. We thought that was it.' The doctor turned around to his parents. 'Looks like it was just an episode after all. But we'll keep him here to make sure, for observation.' He stood up, shook hands with Daniel's mother and father, pressed the handle of a soap dispenser next to the door and rubbed disinfectant into his hands.

'What happens now?' asked his father. 'What are you going to do with him?'

'Lumbar puncture, cranial CT, EEG. We'll take another good look at everything, especially how he reacts now that he's conscious again.'

'EEG?'

'We'll measure his brainwaves, check the neural pathways, and if we don't find anything you can take him home again for the weekend.'

'And then?'

'What, and then?'

'What if he keels over again?'

'We can never totally rule that out.'

'But he reacted badly to the medicine,' said his mother.

'What medicine?'

His father said, 'Diazepam.'

'I'd recommend Tegretol, it has fewer side effects and makes the nerve cells less excitable and blocks the excitation propagation in the brain. That helps the nerve cells to keep their membrane potential stable.'

When they were alone again, Daniel said again what he'd been meaning to say all along. 'I want to be alone.' He said it very gently and quietly with a rough, scratched voice. His mother still started crying.

'Come on, Biggi,' said his father, helping her up. 'The boy doesn't know what he's saying. He's not all there again yet.'

His father led his mother out of the room. They left the door open and a nurse came in, folded down the bedside table and put a tray of lunch down on it—veal in gravy, peas and carrots and a potato patty—and before the hospital noise swallowed up their voices, he heard a few sentences. 'Doctor Ahlers says he has it too.'

'What?'

'Epilepsy.'

'Just because he fell over once, that doesn't mean he's sick.'

'First the Peters boy and now Daniel.'

'Peters?'

'The farmers. From Drömeln. You know the one, the boy who got run over by a train.'

'Oh yes. But that was an accident.'

'I know.'

'He was in the wrong place at the wrong time.'

'Do you think it's catching?'

'I think we should get a second opinion.'

Hard drove the car to the county town to pick him up. Despite the situation—business was bad and Birgit was a bundle of nerves—he had the feeling he had everything back under control. Daniel was sitting on the edge of the bed in a tracksuit, his stuffed sports bag already in his hand, and when Hard went to take it off him he stood up and swayed to the door. Hard grabbed him just in time before he fell over again. Supporting each other, they walked along the corridor to the exit.

'Where's Mum?'

'At home. She's in a bad way. She won't leave the house. They're laying siege to us, Daniel.'

'Journalists?'

Hard nodded. 'They're like a plague.'

'They came here too. Pretended to be patients. One of them even came in my room. But not for long. They threw him out right away.'

'They're still there.'

'Where?'

'Outside the front door.'

'Round the back as well?'

'Not when I left.'

But when they got outside there was a camera crew around the car and a woman—mid-thirties, long dark hair, low-cut dress; under normal circumstances Hard would have flirted with her— held out a microphone and asked, 'How are you feeling, Daniel? What do you say to the news that swastikas have appeared in other villages? Do you think that proves your innocence? Do you think that absolves you?'

Hard shoved her aside, opened the passenger door and made Daniel get in. The moment he was in the car himself he locked all the doors at the touch of a button. The woman knocked on the window as the cameraman squatted down. Hard turned the key in the ignition.

On the B70 once they'd reached the rubbish dump, there were still corpses on the lane, squashed flat and shredded, dried pieces of skin and bones and fur. Hard was reminded of the day when he'd driven Daniel to the newspaper, the rain and the hare, and he drove over the dead animals like over fallen leaves in autumn. Then he said, 'These two guys from the child-welfare office came yesterday, wanted to make sure you live in an orderly household.'

'And?'

'They made sure.'

'That's all right then.'

'Yes, everything's going great. Apart from the fact that they've filed charges against us, you for criminal damage to property and vandalism and me for negligence of parental duty.'

'Who? The men from the child-welfare office?'

'Practically everyone in the village.'

'They must be crazy.'

Hard shrugged. 'Onken says they won't have a case, there just isn't enough evidence against you, but a whole load of people swear they saw you.'

'While I was in a coma?'

'It's a mystery to me too how you're supposed to have done it, lying in bed totally out of it and under constant observation, and at the same time running around the village and spraying on houses. I thought about it for a long time, how you manage to disappear unnoticed and come back before all the action starts again in the hospital the next morning. You must have either an accomplice or a doppelgänger.'

'I haven't got either.'

'Or you're doing it yourself. Maybe you give other boys orders, using the power of your thoughts, boys who look just like you.'

'Yeah, right.'

'Then you'd better stop it right now.'

'Why?'

'It's doing you in. That attack, it was a signal, an alarm signal. That'd get all my alarm bells ringing, something like that would. Your body's putting up resistance to your mind. Happens a lot at your age.'

'What does?'

'That phenomenon.'

'Funny, I've never heard of it.'

'I have. It's medically proved.'

'Where did you get that crap from?'

'Ahlers.'

'I thought you couldn't stand him?'

'I can't. I didn't get it directly from him. But he's right—if you go on like this you'll finish yourself off, you and the family along with you. Your mother hasn't slept for days, not since you sent us away. She keeps asking herself what she's done wrong, and I'm wondering the same thing, I have been for a long time. Haven't you always had it good with us? Haven't you had every freedom? We gave you everything you ever wanted. First that BMX bike, then that computer you insisted on having, the best jeans, the most expensive shoes, always the very best. Every day people pester me on the street about you, every day. I practically can't go anywhere without people talking about you, and every day I defend you. My son? What's supposed to be the matter with him? He's fine. There's nothing wrong with him. And do you know what they say then? Nothing a good beating wouldn't put right.'

Daniel stared at the countryside. Cows were grazing in the meadows between the hedges, the wheat was blossoming in the fields, the maize was at half-height. An even landscape swishing past them, green and yellow and back and white, above it the sky, white and grey and blue. Then Hard turned off the B70 and they passed the village sign for Jericho. There were posters on the street-lamps, for Wübbena, Schulz, Wiemers, Engberts and Rosing. *A clear line at all times. Uncomfortable. Independent. Nonpartisan. Down to earth. Competent. In touch. Confident. One for all. One of us. A man*

738

from here. A man who can do the job. Actions not words. Change not stagnation. Work not poverty. For a new Germany.

'What's all this?'

'The election.'

'They all look the same.'

'Actually,' Hard said, to finish his previous train of thought, 'human beings are nothing but televisions. Sometimes you have to give them a good bash to get them working properly again.'

'Must not have worked on me.'

'Maybe I haven't found the right spot yet.'

'You can rule out the back of my head then.'

'You think I should try the front again?'

'Definitely,' said Daniel, holding out his left cheek, 'here,' and then his right one, 'and here as well. And a bit harder this time, please.'

'I'll have a think about it.'

'But don't take too long. Otherwise someone else will beat you to it.'

'Maybe him?' Hard pointed out of the window.

'Maybe.'

'He'd have good reason, anyway, more than one reason.'

'I wouldn't be surprised at him. Him or Iron.'

'Iron?'

'His son.'

Johann Rosing was walking towards them along the pavement, on his way from door to door, and Hard greeted him by raising his fingers from the steering wheel, by nodding and saying 'Moin,' even though Rosing couldn't hear him. 'He hasn't come to see us yet but he's been almost everywhere else, Utstürven,

Verlaten, Swaarmodig, Achterup, Uphangen, Drömeln and Drömelnermoor. He's gone through three pairs of shoes. It won't be long before he comes to see us.'

'Won't that be fun?'

'The question is, for who. He didn't convince me with his speech, and he won't manage it over tea and cake either. I've been having a good long think about who to vote for.'

'I thought you were an FDP supporter?'

'I am, but I ended up in serious doubts, about myself and my decision. I asked myself, is it right to hold onto something your whole life, even when times are changing? Don't you have to give something up sometimes, let go of people and opinions if they only ever disappoint you?'

'And now you can see clearly again?'

'Yes. Now I say, yes to Wiemers. And yes to the FDP. It's my party, and you stay true to your party like you stay true to your religion and your profession and your family.'

Daniel went back to school on Monday. In History they talked about National Socialism, the final solution, but many of them already knew the subject and showed how superfluous they considered having to talk about it again. The teacher, Mr Engberts, interpreted the text with them that the class had read during Daniel's absence, the *Wannsee Protocol*. Everyone except Daniel and Simone stared at their desks, bent forward, writing something in their exercise books that had nothing to do with the lesson or drawing the cross and the star depicted in their history book. And when Mr Engberts asked Jens what the formulation 'treat accordingly' might mean, Daniel guessed that whatever Jens said would revolve in circles.

'Anything, really.'

'Like what, for example?'

And because Jens shrugged his shoulders, Mr Engberts said, 'Paul, what do you think?'

'It depends on the context.'

'On what context?'

'The context it was said in.'

'And in this case that is?—Yes,' he looked around the room, 'anyone else?'

Simone put her hand up, clicking her fingers three times before Mr Engberts called on her. 'Treat accordingly means kill.' An hour beforehand, in German, literary criticism I, interpreting song lyrics, she had pointed out that Udo Jürgens' protest song 'Dear Fatherland' was not only about Germany, but perhaps also, perhaps only about Austria, as Jürgens came from Klagenfurt. So now Paul said, 'Treat accordingly can also mean expatriate, lock up, re-educate,' and to provoke Simone and Mr Engberts he added, 'if you talk about the Jewish question in Germany, you have to talk about the nigger question in America.' Simone's face turned red and she called him a relativist. Paul and Jens threw balls of paper at her from the back, over the others' heads. Mr Engberts asked for quiet.

Volker asked in a whisper, 'Hey, what time is it? I'm having lung yearnings.'

Daniel looked at his digital watch. 'Quarter to nine.'

This time Volker didn't groan, though, only sighing as if he'd accepted that time was always against him, and stowed the cigarette packet he'd just taken out back into his jacket pocket. He took six aluminium-wrapped halved slices of wholemeal bread spread with liver sausage out of the plastic box and explained that he'd increased his daily ration for the end of the school year, because of his fear of examinations. 'I had to decide. Either more cigarettes or more liver-sausage sandwiches. I spent whole nights weighing up the pros and cons and then decided on the middle way—more cigarettes *and* more liver-sausage sandwiches, but both in moderation.'

Mr Engberts cleared his throat and said, 'Volker, we'd all like to find out what you have to say about it.'

'About what?' asked Volker with his mouth full.

'About the Holocaust.'

He shook his head so that he didn't have to speak with his mouth full again.

'And stop eating in class, that's what the breaks are for.'

'They're much,' Volker swallowed, 'they're much too short for that.'

'Maybe for you,' said Paul, but no one except Jens laughed.

'And what about you?' asked Mr Engberts, turning to Daniel, 'this is your subject, you know all about it.'

Daniel did want to say something; he knew exactly what he wanted to say.

But then Mr Engberts said, 'You've always had something to say about it otherwise.'

It sounded like an accusation, as if he wanted to coax something out of him that he could use against him later, a confession, an admission. So he didn't say anything; he looked outside at the low-flying combat planes breaking through the clouds and shooting over the school in split seconds. Mr Engberts made a note in the register. Then the bell rang, and while everyone got up and packed their bags and left the room, Mr Engberts came over to his desk. 'Listen, I don't want you to have to repeat the year because of this, because of your illness. You've got a doctor's note. It's all signed. But you do have to catch up. You're not getting special treatment here.'

Daniel nodded distractedly. He looked past Mr Engberts out of the window into the yard, saw Volker, Paul and Jens and—at a distance—Simone disappearing behind the gym.

'There's still a week to go before the exams start.'

When Daniel got outside, determined to follow his friends, Mr Kamps and Mr Mengs, the smoker-hunters on duty during break, came up to him from either side.

'Hello there,' said Mr Kamps, 'where are you off to?'

'To the gym.'

'You haven't got Sport now.'

Daniel thought about what to say. They knew he had no choice; either he spoke or he didn't, either way he looked guilty. So he said, 'So what?'

'Have you seen Volker?' asked Mr Mengs.

'He went to the cafeteria. He was hungry.'

'He had a whole pile of sandwiches with him this morning.'

'Can't have been enough for him.'

Mr Mengs walked off towards the cafeteria and Mr Kamps followed him, and before they realized they'd been sent on a wild-goose chase Daniel ran to the gym to warn the others.

On the way home Simone offered him her help to say thank you and handed him a list of the most important things they'd done in the classes he'd missed. Maths, inverse of quadratic functions, root functions. 5(a) First, sketch the graph of the given function $f = [x \rightarrow (x-1)^2 - 4; x \in \mathbb{R}]$. Then restrict the domain so that the new function f_1 has an inverse function $f_1{}^*$. Define the domain and range of $f_1{}^*$. (b) Repeat the procedure for the remaining function f_2. (c) Check your result by reflecting the graph of f about the main angle bisector. (d) Then repeat for: (1) [x → 1/2 (x − 2)²; x ∈ IR] (2) [x → − ((x + 2)² − 4); x ∈ IR]. (6) Justify: A function is invertible if the graph of the function only increases or only decreases. Physics, optics, light diffusion, (a) Show that the equation A = B/G = b/g also applies to silhouettes, when measuring g and b respectively from the point light source. (b) A light source has a diameter of 3 cm. A body with a diameter of 2 cm is at a distance of 4 cm to the light source. Construct the umbra and penumbra of the body on a screen at a distance of 6 cm from the light source. Show that no umbra appears when the screen is more than 12 cm distant. (c) Explain why a solar eclipse can be observed only in some areas on the day side of the earth, whereas a lunar eclipse can be seen in all areas on the night side. Biology, forest habitats, heterogenesis in common haircap moss. As soon as the calyptra is shed from a mature capsule, the peristome becomes visible, a crown of sharp teeth on the edge of the capsule inclined over the opening. The lamellae consist of thick-walled cells; they are erect when dry and adopt their original position when moist. Examine the peristome using a strong magnifying glass. What is the importance of the movement of the peristome lamellae? English, Unit 6, Exercise 5:

> *Here's a question for you to think about:*
> *The more we learn, the more we know.*
> *The more we know, the more we forget.*
> *The more we forget, the less we know.*
> *The less we know, the less we forget.*
> *The less we forget, the more we know.*
> *So why learn?*

At home, he opened up the textbooks and exercise books. He couldn't shake the question *so why learn*? He kept coming back to it—why was he learning? What for? For himself? For his parents?

For life? He didn't know. He wanted to answer the question; he started, broke off, and the pages flew around the room, half-filled with his handwriting. He couldn't get beyond these new questions. He stood up and paced up and down, up and down, for minutes. Then he went over to the stereo and put on a record. He turned up the volume and closed his eyes. He didn't want to hear anything, see anything, all he wanted was to jump, hurl himself against the wardrobe, the wall, anything. For a moment he felt like in *Awakenings*, and at the same time he felt that his awakening had not yet come. Exhausted, he lay down on his bed. The moment he lay there he thought he'd never get up; it was like he was fastened in place. Simone wanted to help him, Simone of all people, the girl who'd rejected him at the party in the Hankens' barn, the girl for whom everything went smoothly, who was always the best at everything and knew exactly how to get through life without harming herself. What could she give him apart from the right answers, that which was expected of him? But what was right? And what was wrong? Who decided that? Who checked?

His mother came in. 'What's the matter? Didn't you say you have to revise for your exams?'

'I'm just having a little rest.'

'How can you rest with this racket on?' She turned off the stereo and put a hand on his forehead. 'Aren't you feeling well? You look very pale.' She took her hand away.

'I always do.'

'Have you taken your tablets?' She picked up the pack of Tegretol from the table and unfolded the information leaflet. 'Side effects: double vision, involuntary eye movement, headaches, weight loss, apathy, disturbed consciousness, coordination defects, memory defects, mental defects, speech defects, diarrhoea, digestion complaints, disturbed perception, loss of appetite, tiredness, gaze palsy, nausea, vomiting, convulsions, dizziness, trembling, fatigue, increased excitability.' She shook her head. 'Increased excitability—what a lot of nonsense. It doesn't make sense to take something that causes exactly what it's supposed to prevent.'

The instant he was alone again he went on thinking about why he learned. His hands folded over his stomach, he looked up as if the solution was on the ceiling, and he saw himself mirrored in the skylight window. He wasn't a graph or a function, he didn't only increase, he didn't only decrease, he wasn't invertible, he was a white penumbra on the night side of the earth.

Then he examined his peristome.

'I saw Johann this morning.'

'Johann?'

'Rosing. He was in the Vehndels' shop.'

'We saw him the other day too. Walking down Village Road.'

'He's been to see the Neemanns as well. Marlies says he manages ten to fifteen visits a day.'

'He must have had a lot of walking to do out in the hammrich, visiting the farms.'

'He took the car for them.'

'You seem to know all about it.'

'I'm just interested.'

'In politics or Johann Rosing?'

'Both.'

'I thought he was going to walk all the way. I thought it was like a missionary trip. Behold, I'm castigating myself for your sins. Vote for me and heaven will be yours.'

'He only drank one cup of tea and ate one piece of cake at the Neemanns' place.'

'And that's what he does—drink tea and eat cake?'

'No, he presented his manifesto, but only quickly. He left after a quarter of an hour.'

'I've heard different.'

'What then?'

'A customer told me he spent all afternoon at her place and ate half a Frankfurt crown cake.'

'What customer was that?'

'Eiske Ahlers.'

'She lies as soon as she opens her mouth, she does. No one can stand to spend long at her house.'

'Why do you say that?'

'Because I've been there.'

'When?'

'She invited us round a few months ago—Marlies, Sabine and me. I told you, remember? She wanted to get to know us—after twenty years as neighbours.'

'Did she?'

'Don't you think it's odd—a woman with no female friends?'

'No stranger than a man with no male friends.'

'You mean like you?'

'I mean in general.'

'I almost got stuck in her heavy, low armchairs. The tea was really bitter. And her Black Forest gateaux was out of a catalogue, she got it from Bofrost.'

'Did she tell you that?'

'No, I could tell by the taste. We've had it as well once.'

'But you froze a cake for him as well.'

'Only for an emergency though. He doesn't give you any notice that he's coming. And anyway, I baked it myself.'

'So that's why you're always baking cakes these days—for him.'

'And for us. Are you complaining? Don't you get enough from me?'

'Enough cake, anyway. But you could make something other than rose-swirl cake.'

'I just want to be prepared.'

'But why that rose-swirl cake, for goodness' sake? You've never made it before.'

'Because of the name.'

The twins chanted, 'Swirl cake, swirl cake, swirl cake,' hammered their forks and fists on the table and refused to go on eating beans with bacon and pears and potatoes.

'You eat that down now,' said Hard. 'The swirl cake's for dessert.'

'Swirl cake, swirl cake, swirl cake.'

'If you say swirl cake one more time you're going to your rooms. And then you can forget the lake this afternoon. In this weather . . . ' and he looked outside at the clear blue sky.

'Swirl cake, swirl cake, swirl cake.'

'Right, that's enough.' Hard crumpled up his napkin and slammed his hand on the table so hard that the plates jittered.

'Oh, let them. I've got more than enough. As long as they eat something.'

'They're supposed to eat something healthy.'

'My rose-swirl cake's healthy enough. And there's bound to be a slice left for you.' Birgit went in the other room and fetched the cake plate. She cut two slices for the children and one each for Hard and Daniel and herself as well. And when they were all finished they wanted another slice and another. 'We have to leave one slice though.'

'I want another one,' said Hard in the same whiny tone as the twins beforehand, having suddenly realized how he could shorten Rosing's visit.

'This one's for Johann.'

'Who's more important to you?' asked Hard, serious again. 'Him or me?'

'You,' she said, and Hard speared the slice on his fork and shoved half of it into his mouth.

'Now I don't know what to offer him if he comes round today.'

'The frozen one.'

'That was the frozen one,' she pointed at the crumbs. 'I took it out of the freezer this morning, especially.'

Daniel, who'd been sitting between them in silence all along, his head in his hands, his elbows on the table, said, 'Then make him a nice German apple strudel.'

'That takes far too long. It'd take me all afternoon. And I haven't got any apples left. And I have to do the washing and the ironing.'

Hard folded up his napkin and stood up. 'Well, you'd better get started then.'

An hour later, Johann Rosing rang the doorbell. As it was Saturday, Hard hadn't taken a nap but started on the accounts right away, and Birgit was still busy in the kitchen when she heard the bell.

In white coat and apron, the two of them ran out of their respective rooms into the hall and down the stairs.

Rosing was wearing a suit and tie despite the heat. His hair, dark and sticky, drooped over his face. He hugged Birgit and kissed her on the cheek, shaking hands with Hard. 'Having a spring clean for June, I see. New shop window and a new door. Good choice.' He was hoarse; his voice threatened to fail at every word.

'They're from you, after all,' said Birgit and went up the stairs ahead of them.

'All I did was recommend them.'

'As long as the glass holds up to strong tremors.' Hard raised his forefinger and whispered, 'He's upstairs.'

'And the twins?'

'At the lake. Working off a bit of energy.' Hard led him into the living room, the reception room, where Birgit was already busy laying the table.

'Nothing's changed in here.' Rosing paced once across the room for which he'd laid the bricks years ago, stroked the walls and the window frames and gazed absent-mindedly out of the panorama window, his hands in his pockets, onto the terracotta terrace, the level crossing, the old dairy and the hammrich fields.

'It's good German craftsmanship.' Hard stepped up to him from behind, and as they were standing next to each other he registered an unusual scent. 'What's that?'

'Sweat.'

'No, the other smell, underneath it.'

'You mean my perfume? I got it from you.'

'I should hope so too.'

'You'll never guess.'

'Want a bet?'

Birgit rolled her eyes and went into the kitchen.

'How much?' Rosing held out his hand.

And Hard took it. 'A hundred. Tosca.'

'Davidoff. Am I a woman?'

'Who knows? Smells more like Tosca.' Hard gestured for him to sit at the head of the table, taking a seat opposite him on the recliner. 'You could have picked it up—from a woman.'

'You're the expert.'

'Johann, what's that all about? How long ago is that now? Fourteen years? And it was only once. I know we haven't always been the best of friends, but you can't hold grudges for ever. We've both made mistakes and we've both paid for them.'

'That's true.'

'We should drink to that. Biggi,' he turned to the door, raising his voice, 'have we got any cold schnapps?'

'I'll get it,' she called back at the same volume, filtered through two rooms.

And while Birgit went next door to get a bottle out of the freezer, Hard positioned two glasses on the table. Birgit poured them drinks and the men toasted their new friendship.

They'd barely put their glasses down when Rosing said, 'Don't you want to come back to the choir?'

'What, to listen to more comments?'

'If you can't take the heat, stay out of the kitchen.'

Birgit, anxious not to let the mood slip, put a hand on Rosing's shoulder. 'I've got nothing here for you now.'

'What haven't you got here for me?'

'Cake.'

'All the better. I'm full to the brim with cake. I'm sure I could make room for a cup of tea, though.'

'I'll get you one,' said Birgit and darted to the kitchen.

'And what about me?' called Hard, but Birgit didn't hear him. And when Daniel came in and sat down on the sofa without shaking hands with Rosing, Hard leapt up and said, 'You,' and launched himself at him, but Rosing held him back.

'Leave him be. I don't want a fight.'

'I do,' said Daniel.

'I suppose you still think I'm a Nazi.'

'More than ever.'

'Perhaps I can convince you of the opposite today.'

'If you say the opposite of what you said at the village hall, then you can.'

'I was just sketching out my manifesto, I just wanted to make it clear what—'

'Before you start your speech, Johann,' Hard interrupted, 'I want to say right away that I won't be voting for you, no matter what you say. It's got nothing to do with your political convictions or with you. Some of your views are sensible enough, in themselves. And I'm right behind you on one or two topics, although I don't agree at all when it comes to the influence of the state on the business world. It's just that I've always voted FDP, all my life.'

'I know,' said Rosing. 'But the mayor's elected directly. I have to get an absolute majority or there'll be a second ballot. And if your Richard Wiemers, who we all love and respect, isn't among the chosen ones, maybe you'll make use of your right to vote a second time and decide in my favour.'

'Maybe. Maybe not.'

'Maybe your vote will make all the difference.'

'Everything has its price.'

'And no one knows that better than you.'

'That's a fact.'

'But what really surprises me is that you're still standing by a party that's been undermining you for years. The free market is breaking us. Not just economically, culturally too. Just look at what happened to the dairy,' he waved out of the window, 'or to Vehndel.'

'Why Vehndel?'

'The laundry. The minute something's vacant the vandals come along.' Rosing cast a meaningful glance at Daniel.

'Or the big corporations,' said Hard, 'which is the same thing in the end.'

'Now we're on the same wavelength. I don't want to persuade you of something you reject outright. I'm not a Jehovah's Witness,' he took out a leaflet, 'going from door to door with the *Watchtower* to convert people. This just details my aims and objectives, what I want to take as my yardstick when I'm in office. And maybe you'll have time to have a quick look before the election.'

Rosing handed Hard the leaflet and Hard took it, although Daniel had reached his hand out for it as well. 'Oh, you'd like that, wouldn't you?' said Hard. 'To see if you're right.'

'About what?' asked Rosing.

'Daniel thinks you copied passages for your speech.'

'Copied? Where from?'

'From *Mein Kampf*,' said Daniel.

'But that's banned.'

'Yes,' said Hard. 'If only you had a copy so you could prove it.'

'And?' asked Rosing, still facing Daniel. 'Have you got a copy?'

Daniel looked at Hard. 'Not any more.'

'The police have got his,' said Hard, scanning the leaflet reluctantly. 'That's where it belongs.'

'The question is, of course, why did you even have a copy in your room?'

Birgit came in with a pot of tea. She had changed her clothes, put on a flower-patterned dress and red court shoes, and dabbed on perfume of her own, 4711 eau de cologne.

'You're all dolled up,' said Hard.

'It's a special occasion.'

'You never get dressed up like that for me.'

'You're here every day, aren't you?'

'Do you want me to leave?' Hard stood up halfway from his chair, but sat down immediately when no one reacted to what he'd said. 'Is that it? Do you want me to get out of your way? You just have to say the word and I'll be gone.'

Birgit rolled her eyes and poured the tea for all of them. The rock sugar crackled and the cream formed clouds on the surface.

'These are big *kluntjes*,' said Rosing. 'They hardly fit in the cup.'

'From Knipper's.'

'Oh yes, you used to work there, didn't you?'

'Long time ago,' said Hard.

'Before your time.'

'I keep wondering how you manage it,' said Hard.

'Manage what?'

'Politics and business.'

'I've taken a few weeks' leave.'

'We can't take leave, Johann. Business doesn't have holidays.'

'I've handed the management over to my son.'

'Iron?' asked Daniel.

'Michael.'

Hard cast a punishing glare at his son. He'd never been able to envisage handing Kuper's Drugstore over to him, and now, after all the trouble he'd caused, he certainly couldn't. But he had to admit that it pained him to see how natural it was for other businessmen to pass on the baton to their offspring. 'How old is he now?'

'Nineteen, so he's legally competent.' Rosing cleared his throat. 'I want to train him on the job—he should be taking over the branch in Jerichow.'

'You mean the other one, the one in the East?'

Rosing nodded. 'The W makes the difference.'

'W for witty,' said Daniel, at which Hard glared at him again.

'No,' said Rosing. 'W for West and East reunited.'

'As if the two villages ever belonged together.'

'That's what we call PR. You could use some too. For your image. It's taken a few knocks recently.' He cleared his throat again. 'We went to look for a new location over there, Michael and me. Drove around, Schwerin, Parchim, Wittenberge, Stendal, and then we came through Jerichow for a bit of a joke, and he says, why not here? We'd have bought something anyway, there or somewhere else. And it's not bad at all. Berlin's nearby, and the A2's not far either. The claims will all be staked soon. Nothing ventured, nothing gained.'

'Life punishes those who delay.'

'Whoever has no house now will build no more—that's my motto.'

'That's stolen too,' said Daniel.

'Isn't everything really run down over there?' asked Birgit. 'There was something on TV about it the other day. Honestly, it looked awful.'

Rosing nodded. 'In a desolate state. Absolutely falling apart.'

'They still have cobbled roads. And the houses.' Birgit shook her head.

'About time someone builds it up again.'

'Someone like you,' said Hard.

'Just like I said, we're on the same wavelength.' Rosing sipped his tea. 'It might surprise you, but I'm not here to talk about business or politics.'

'I am surprised,' said Hard. 'I thought that was why you'd started preachifying.'

Birgit asked, 'What did you come to talk about?'

'About your son.' Rosing looked at Daniel, and Hard and Birgit followed his example. 'I'm very worried about him, you see.'

'You're not the only one,' said Hard.

'I can imagine. Daniel's made a lot of mistakes, and his biggest one was perhaps turning all of Jericho against him. His behaviour must be having a negative effect on your turnover.'

'Oh yes,' said Hard.

Rosing leant forward and said, now facing back to Daniel, 'Don't you ever think of your parents? They've got it hard enough already. Not only do they have to stand up against the big corporations, now they're losing their regular customers as well, because of you.'

Hard looked at Rosing and suddenly wondered again if he ought to vote for him instead of Wiemers.

'They might have to close the shop down soon. And then? What happens then? What are they going to live on then? And you? What will become of you? Have you ever thought about that? Even a one single time?'

'*A* single time,' said Daniel.

'What?' asked Hard, dropping the leaflet and rising from his seat again.

'Nix.'

Hard sat down again, picked up the leaflet and wiped the back of his hand across his forehead.

'Are you not feeling well?' asked Birgit.

'I'm fine,' said Hard. 'Everything's all right. I just sometimes feel like your son's squatting on top of me and ripping my heart out because he's a bit peckish.' He grabbed his chest to show her the place he meant.

'He's your son just as much as mine.'

'I'm not so sure about that any more.'

'What's that supposed to mean?'

'As a man,' Hard said, looking over at Rosing as if he hoped for his support on the matter, 'you can never be sure whose child it is that comes out of your wife.'

'Are you trying to say I had someone else?' asked Birgit, her voice distant and trembling.

'I'm not trying to say nix.'

'So why did you say it then? We decided against a caesarean, despite the complications, and now we just have to both stand by him.'

'What complications?' asked Daniel.

'You were the wrong way round all along,' said Birgit as briefly as possible, not wanting to mention all the details in front of Rosing.

'You decided against it,' said Hard. 'It was all your decision in the end. Even Ahlers advised you against it, and so did I—I was scared to lose you during the birth.'

'It all turned out all right though,' said Birgit, crying now, her head lowered and looking around for a tissue. 'With me and with him as well.'

'All right? Is that,' he pointed at Daniel, 'is that what you call all right? They had to pierce his tear ducts for him. It's not normal, a child that never screams and cries and just stares at you instead with big round eyes.' He pushed up his eyelids with two fingers.

'I'm not talking on my own behalf here,' said Rosing. 'The whole thing's not actually on my agenda. But it's been put on my agenda by the election. And the person who put it there was you. This painting business has to stop. You have to tell us how you did it, what you used. It's starting to wear the village down.'

'Oh yes,' said Hard, and as he'd had enough of only ever saying 'Oh yes,' and confirming Rosing on everything and anything, he added, 'You can see Birgit and I are worn right out. We're at the end of our tether.'

'I mean it's wearing down the houses,' said Rosing. 'The walls are starting to disintegrate from all the cleaning fluids.'

13

A few days later it was almost like before. The symbols were still there but they left the streetlamps and garden lanterns on at night and the glimmer was hardly visible. Many Jerichoans had planted ivy or vines in front of their houses and put up screens or advertising panels. And Rosing had built new walls and re-plastered old ones. The reporters and camera crews no longer waited outside the drugstore, no longer accompanied Daniel to school, had moved on to the next arena. Isolated demonstrators and a few neo-Nazis still marched through the village, but since they were no longer being filmed, since they were only filming themselves, they no longer carried flaming torches. The homeowners no longer stood guard outside their properties, and the amateur marksmen and hunters no longer guarded the crossroads and driveways with loaded guns. Only the police were still there, outside the bank, the village hall and the drugstore, for safety's sake— in case something did happen after all.

Daniel rode his racing bike along the roads as if through a tunnel. It was dark on either side, the only light came from in front and behind, but no matter how hard he pedalled or which direction he turned, he couldn't find his way out. Slides flashed up on the walls, thousands of slides in magnificent colours, the same picture wherever he looked: the flowerbeds have been weeded, the lawns have been mown, the flowers are blossoming in the front gardens, the cars gleaming in the sunlight. In the mornings they get up and go to work—if they have work—and in the evenings they sit in front of the TV, sedated by series, chat shows and quiz shows, the news of all the world. On Saturdays they clean up or drive to the county town and walk up and down the pedestrian zone, examine the cheapest and the most expensive wares, buy new outfits until they're tired and happy enough to go back to their boxes made of ticky-tacky. On Sundays they go to church or to the cinema and watch a film with their children, or they go on a trip to the seaside, to some restaurant with a sea view, perhaps they go to the Hansa Park or the Heide Park for the rides or take a walk in the moor or the forest. Some have birthdays, others get married or have children; there's always some reason to celebrate. When the sun shines they can have a barbecue, if not there's always football or tennis or the bar at the Beach Hotel, the disco, the UFO in the industrial estate. Men go hunting or sit by the kolk at night, or at one of the sand pits, rods in one hand, beer and cigarettes in the other, waiting for something to bite. Women take evening classes in silk painting, ikebana or sewing for beginners and re-learners. Children learn to swim, ride, play tennis, football, handball, volleyball, chess, guitar, accordion or recorder, and when they're older they sing in the school choir, join the volunteer fire brigade or the scouts. Once a year they all fly south or east or west, to a foreign country where you can't see the poverty at first glance from the hotel, to an island or a peninsula, with or without palm trees, that's not that important, what's important is being somewhere else, leaving everyday routine behind, at least for a few days, before they go on with what they call their lives. At some point they take retirement or get made redundant because they're too old and no one needs them any more, or they simply stop because they've had enough of their own accord, they keep going for a few more years, dragging it out, supporting their children, their grandchildren, and then they get cancer, Parkinson's disease, Alzheimer's or, if they're lucky, they have a heart attack or a stroke and fall down dead. Daniel couldn't talk to anyone about it, no one would understand him, he didn't understand where it came from all of a sudden, his fear of complying with necessity, of resigning himself to everything being the way it was. But how was it? Was it like this? Or was it different? Who could tell? Who knew? All he knew was that they wouldn't serve him at Supernee-mann any more, that when he went shopping for his parents and stood at the cash register in the supermarket they took his shopping off the conveyor belt like something that had to go back on the shelves because he didn't have enough money to pay for it all, that they didn't say hello to him any more and turned away when he came towards them, that they put the phone down when he picked up the receiver, that his aunts in Bad Vilbel were advising his mother on the phone to send him away, to boarding school, to a home, best of all abroad. Only at the parties did they let him in without his compulsory drink as an entry fee. The tablets he had to take to help his nerve cells *to keep their membrane potential stable,* as the doctor had said at the hospital, and the joints he now smoked, replaced the effect of the vodka.

Once he woke up in his bed on a Sunday morning and everything was littered across the floor, as though a sprite had whirled around the room. Someone had pulled all the records off the shelves and broken them, scattered the books around the room, swiped everything off the desk and the console for the stereo. Daniel got up and got dressed. He checked whether anything was missing but all the valuable objects he possessed were spread out in front of him. Some things, like the typewriter and the radio alarm clock, were unharmed, but most of it had been smashed to pieces. The posters were hanging off the walls in tatters. The books were missing their dust jackets, the records their covers. What remained of the bible, countless scraps of paper, black and white confetti, was sprinkled over everything like snow. The letters and numbers formed new combinations, the spirit of truth,

if the whole body were an eye

people

19

99

four horsemen

prophets

a day of clouds and thick darkness

firmament

God

Gog and Magog

22

because I live, ye shall live also

cities are destroyed

turn thou

madness

wizards

Go to the ant, thou sluggard; consider her ways, and be wise

Nebuchadnezzar

seal

kingdom of God

23

covenant

primitive times

wisdom

lights of the world

that they shall walk like blind men

shield

transformed

33

salvation

pour out my spirit

loot

but be ye doers of the word

a great white throne

source

26

and the sea gave up the dead which were in it, words and numbers that flashed up in his consciousness and extinguished again. Then he unlocked the door, a gust of wind crossed the room and the scraps danced in the air like snowflakes, and he went downstairs to the kitchen and asked his parents and the twins who'd trashed his room during the night.

'No one,' said his mother.

'You did,' his father.

They followed him up to his room, the twins at the rear. His father could hardly get up the stairs. He wheezed at every step.

'My God,' said his mother when she saw the chaos. 'What's happened here?' The twins tried to push past her but she held them back. 'You two stay here. This is none of your business.' Then she began gathering up the shards, returning the books to the shelves, folding the clothes.

'It wasn't me,' said Daniel. 'Someone came in my room while I was asleep.'

'And who might that have been? The Plutonians?' She gave a short, shrill laugh and shook her head, as if she couldn't believe she'd said that.

'Very funny.'

His mother took a step up to him, the smile wiped off her face. 'You're still totally out of it.'

'One beer, two at the most.'

'I didn't say anything about alcohol.'

His father was leaning against the wall. 'Locked from the inside, you said. Very strange.' Once he'd got his strength back he ran his hand over the lock and the doorframe. 'Doesn't look like anyone's broken in. Maybe he came through the wall. Or out of one of the power sockets.' He leant over to the next best one and poked a finger in it. 'Or,' getting up again and twitching around as if watching a fly, 'he's still in here, just that we can't see him.'

'A ghost,' said the twins in perfect synch and ran into the hall towards their rooms, screaming loudly.

'Hard, stop scaring the children.'

'We can't see him because he's right in our midst.' He looked at Daniel and Daniel took an instinctive step back, almost stumbling over his desk chair which lay prone behind him, its rollers in mid-air. But his father went no further than the look. He spread his arms and said, 'Now you can see where it takes you, what happens to you at those moments.'

'What moments?'

'You forget yourself and then it comes out, then it shows its face.'

'What shows its face?'

'Your true self.'

The sun was high in the sky and Hard was walking, dressed only in a shirt and trousers and shoes, along the train tracks into the hammrich. Cows were grazing in the meadows, sheep on the dykes. Children's clear laughter sounded out from the lake. He hoped a long Sunday walk would drive away his worries—that Daniel wouldn't get a grip on his drug problem, that Theda Wiemers would put more pressure on him and Birgit, that the customers would stay away and he'd never make the most of the winnings due to Kaiserslautern coming out top in the championship, now that everyone who had bet on Bayern Munich had left and taken their stakes with them, now that Meinders had taken the church hall away from him.

Along the way, lots of cyclists and walkers came in the other direction, often compelling him to stop and talk. Some of them, those who had their dogs with them, asked him about dog food and flea collars, whether the ones with dimpylate had arrived yet, others asked what he thought about the Bundesliga outcome, whether he'd expected Kaiserslautern to beat Cologne so easily on the last day of the season, but most of them wanted to know what measures he was planning to take against his son or whether he was still behind him all the way, which they assumed he wasn't.

Soon he turned off onto a smaller path, fearing he wouldn't get enough exercise if he stayed on the Hoogstraat. He ascribed the sweat on his forehead, under his arms and on his back to the heat which had descended over the land for the first time of the year. He put his shortness of breath and the pressure on his chest down to the fact that he'd hardly left the house for weeks because of the journalists and tourists, at most taking the car to go shopping, take the twins somewhere or visit Daniel in hospital.

The air was full of butterflies and birds and flies, cats dozed on top of silage heaps beneath their white tarpaulins and black tyres, and dandelions and marigolds had shot up around him.

Paper boats were floating on the Wallschloot, forming jams at the weir. The longer he walked, the lighter his thoughts grew. It couldn't get any worse, he thought, than it was now. Daniel was going through a difficult stage, like all boys his age, and one day, he was convinced, he'd be able to laugh at what he'd done, like he himself sometimes laughed about his own young days, about the school-boy tricks, the races, his shyness about talking to girls and asking them to dance. He'd got over all that, and Daniel would get over his anger too and find another task for himself other than revealing the secret of life through writing. He'd fall in love and stop drinking and smoking and he'd finish school and learn a trade and start a family. And he, Hard, would set a good example and swear off all women to whom he wasn't married, pay off his debts by honest means, forgive Klaus and Günter, join the male-voice choir again, drink less and spend more time with the kids.

Sometimes he looked around but apart from the dairy chimney, getting smaller and smaller, there was not much to see of the village behind the blossoming hedges of Jericho. He walked all the way to the dyke. Sheep paused in their chewing, stared at him and then went on chewing. He climbed up on one side and down on the other, waded through the reeds with his hands aloft, clambered onto the wobbly rocks of a breakwater, stood for minutes by the river as it flowed dull and sluggish, and watched the freight ships floating downstream.

Then he set off homewards. Birgit had warned him to be back home in time for lunch; she was making a special meal for the end of the asparagus season—plaice with shrimp and boiled potatoes and asparagus and salad—and he had promised her to keep an eye on the time. He climbed up the dyke and down again and walked along the path he'd taken before. Not far from him, on the one-track railway embankment leading to Holland, a train passed. A few of the passengers waved at him from the open windows, with handkerchiefs or bare hands, and he waved back.

Clouds chased above him, changing shape every few seconds. For a minute, an hour, he stood still and saw a dog, a whale, a tank, a woman's face, her breasts, bombs, all floating above the earth. The wind picked up. He heard the leaves rustling in the trees and the stalks on the fields colliding. He felt a tickle on his head as though something had got blown into his hair and got stuck, a twig, a leaf, an insect, but when he reached for it he couldn't find anything. White lights danced in the air ahead of him, fireflies in the middle of the day. A wasp buzzed around him, attached itself to his shirt at heart level, and he felt the vibrations of its wings passing over to him and making him shudder gently.

Suddenly it was silent. He was lying on his back on the grass between the path and the Wallschloot. He stretched his arms and legs, wanted to get going again; it was time. Every muscle strived to walk on, every thought, and he did walk on, with large strides, heavier and slower than before but still fast enough to have reached the farmyards kilometres away, the Hoogstraat shimmering in the summer fug. Then he opened his eyes and saw he was asleep.

His mother stood over his bed, her hair messed up, her eyes red from crying. Over and over, Daniel drifted off again, falling back into the dream from which she'd wrenched him. She said something, 'Get up,' and 'Hammrich,' and 'Half dead.' The words made no sense. She wouldn't stop shaking him. It took a while until his mind was clear enough to get up. He followed her along the hallway, past the twins' rooms where the two of them were squatting on the floor, still in their pyjamas, surrounded by dolls and plastic figures, entirely submerged in their games.

Downstairs, his father was in the double bed, his face shiny with sweat, his shirt unbuttoned down to his navel. Doctor Ahlers listened to his chest and arm, pumped up a cuff, looked at his watch. 'Right, right. You should have come to me earlier, Hard. I can't do anything for you now.' He removed the stethoscope and put it into his case. 'You have to go to hospital. There's no other option.'

His mother ran to the telephone in the hall to call an ambulance. 'What's the matter with him?' she asked after she'd hung up.

'Heart attack.'

'Will he make it?'

'I can't say, Biggi. We'll have to see over the next few hours.'

While she accompanied Doctor Ahlers to the front door, Daniel went back into his parents' bedroom. His father waved him over and told him in a weak voice what had happened. He paused after every sentence. Daniel handed him a glass of water. His father drank it in one go.

'I'm taking Julie and Andy over to Marlies' place,' said his mother from the doorway, 'and you,' she nodded at Daniel, 'put something else on and wait for the ambulance.'

'I can look after the twins.' There was nothing he wanted less than to see a hospital from the inside again. 'Really, I don't mind.' He was even prepared to spend time alone with the twins instead.

'I don't want them to notice anything.'

When the paramedics finally arrived, after what seemed like hours, they put his father on a stretcher, carried him downstairs to the ambulance and slammed the doors behind him. They drove off to town with flashing blue lights.

Shortly after that, his mother was beeping the car horn in the driveway. Daniel ran out of the house and the door fell closed behind him with a bang.

'Well, haven't you done well?' she said when he was sitting in the passenger seat.

'What?'

'You know what.' Then she put the car in reverse, moved back without checking the mirror, switched to first gear, accelerated, went into second, third, fourth, fifth gear, and they shot along Village Road far too fast for Jericho. Above them, they heard the bells ringing; the roads were empty, only a few pedestrians on their Sunday pilgrimage to church crossed their path. Daniel spotted Volker on the pavement, a walking balloon, his bulky body squeezed into a suit far too small for him. Daniel raised his hand to greet him, and Volker greeted him back, paddling his arms, his head stretched well forward as if it had to pull his weight.

On the B70, his mother overtook a tractor at a hundred and twenty kilometres an hour, in the county town she sped across a junction on a yellow light, and near the hospital, in a thirty-kilometres-per-hour zone full of one-way streets, she ignored all the traffic signs. Daniel had never seen her driving that way, so recklessly, against every rule. Brakes screeching, they stopped on a disabled parking space right outside the entrance.

'Emergency,' was all she said about it as she headed for the casualty department. She went straight to the reception desk and asked after his father.

'Bernhard Kuper?' said the nurse.

'He's just come in.'

'Diagnosis?'

'Heart attack.'

'Then he'll be in Intensive Care. Just through there,' the nurse pointed at a glass door at the end of the corridor. 'Wait, I'll take you.'

'Doesn't everyone here,' his mother looked around the room, 'end up in Intensive Care?'

'No, most of them don't end up anywhere,' the nurse gestured at some of the patients sitting on benches either side of them, holding their heads or bellies and groaning and crying and cursing. 'We send them straight back home again.'

Daniel thought they'd be going straight to his father but instead they spent hours in a waiting room with cheap prints and scribbly children's drawings on the walls. The cold light of the neon tubes reflected off the linoleum. Daniel got his mother a coffee out of the vending machine and a Coke for himself. A doctor came and said, 'Mrs Kuper? You can go in now.'

'How is he?'

'Not doing well. Took a pretty hard knock.'

'Will he, I mean, is he going to die?'

'We're all going to. Sooner or later.'

'And him?'

'Do I look like God to you?'

The room he led them into was darkened. Daniel's father was in a bed, electrodes stuck to his chest, five on the left and one on the right, and there were tubes coming out of his arm and nose, connected up to flashing, humming machines. His father said something to his mother. From where Daniel was standing, in the small room outside the door, he couldn't understand what. His mother wiped tears out of her eyes and waved him over. His father's hand was resting on the sheet, his fingers barely moving, more of a tremble but still he managed to reach out for Daniel. His father whispered, 'You look after the twins. And don't give your mother any more worries, you hear? You're the man of the house now.'

The desks had been pushed apart and distributed around the room. Daniel was sitting next to Simone again. This time the class was divided into two groups, all with different worksheets so they couldn't copy from each other—his had an *A* at the top, hers had a *B*, his questions and answers weren't the same as hers. Daniel calculated and wrote; he had no idea what. He couldn't stop thinking about his father. There were three tests that week, and the next week as well, plus three more the week after that, History, Music, German, Physics, Social Studies, English, Religion, Chemistry, Maths. What links Beethoven's nine symphonies with the Nuremberg Rally? Karl Kraus' 'Hour of the Night' with radioactive decay? The social-market economy with population development in Africa? The past participle with the antitheses of the Sermon on the Mount? Acids and alkalis with the normal parabola? During his revision he'd tried to work out a connection; he'd thought there must be a system, an objective towards which everything was headed, like with two parallel lines that intersect at infinity, except that here there were dozens, hundreds of parallel lines striving away from him, into darkness, into the universe, dozens, hundreds of paths and possibilities he had to take, over and over until they touched and caught fire through the power of that touch and exploded and unleashed an energy in his head more powerful than a thousand atomic bombs.

He looked at the clock every few minutes, not getting anywhere. Simone put her pen down and rubbed her eyes but didn't hand in her paper. Instead, she put a new sheet of paper on her desk and started over from the beginning. As she packed up her things, cleared everything but that sheet off her desk and went up to the front, he wanted to jump up and tell her she'd forgotten something at first but he stayed in his seat, said nothing, passed the tests.

He didn't know why she'd done it, what she wanted from him or where it came from, this sudden interest. Because he hadn't told the teacher on her in the schoolyard the other day? He kept thinking about it but he didn't come to any conclusion. He didn't dare to ask her either though, accepting it like a gift. He told himself, she doesn't want me to repeat the year or change schools so I don't have to repeat the year, doesn't want me to lose all grip now that my father's in hospital. She wants me to stay, for whatever reason.

They visited his father every day. The twins weren't allowed to go with them. Daniel stood by the bed as if alongside a coffin. Sometimes he felt as though his father were already dead. Daniel wanted to say something, he did say something, he started talking about school, saying he'd get through and pass the year, but he broke off again straight away because his father didn't react, just lay there, his face pale and collapsed in on itself, his body limp, not even the blankets moving when he breathed. The consultant asked them into his office, showed them images of his heart, white lines and white shadows, and explained what had happened. 'Your husband had a posterior myocardial infarction.'

'What does that mean?'

'The heart is supplied by its own vessels. There are two main vessels, here and here. The posterior wall gets its blood supply from the *arteria coronaria dextra* and by the *ramus interventicularis posterior*. Theoretically, you can also stent that in a posterior infarction. During the coronary catheterization, however, we established that the affected vessel is too stiff and can't be expanded. A bypass is too risky at the moment; he's still too critical. So we have to use conservative treatment. And that means—it may take weeks, or months, until he's back to health. What he needs now is absolute rest.' They didn't say a word on the drive back home. It was only when they got into the garage with the engine idling that his mother said he had his father on his conscience.

'Pretty shit, the thing with your old man,' said Paul, leaning against the gym wall in full view of the teachers.

'Yeah,' said Jens and ran his tongue over his teeth. 'You gave him a pretty tough time of it.'

They were conducting a dialogue in which Daniel and Volker were nothing more than an audience for them. The fact that they even tolerated their presence was solely because they were in the same class and they'd need established allies as soon the Year Ten kids were gone, to cement their new power.

'I don't understand it. Everyone wants to get on TV, they do all sorts of crap to get there, and as soon as they're on it, they topple over, some out of enthusiasm and the others, well, because there's bad news.'

'It's just too much of a shock.'

'What's a shock?'

'Seeing yourself.'

'Doesn't seem to bother our friend here.' He thudded Daniel on the shoulder. 'The opposite, really, look at him. He's really blossoming with all the attention.'

'Have you finished now?'

Jens said, 'Oho, he can speak.'

Paul put his arm around Daniel, reaching far enough to put him in a headlock if he wanted. 'The Year Tens are having a party.'

'Their leaving party.'

'So you know about it then.'

'Everyone does.'

'What you don't know is that they've got the keys from Schulz.'

'What keys?'

'The keys to our beautiful school here.' He stretched out his other arm and gestured along the two dual-storey blocks. 'They're allowed in the night before, access to the foyer, the school hall, all the corridors. Free entry all night long.'

'And we've offered them our help,' said Jens. 'So they can get everything ready.'

'Get what ready?'

'He really doesn't get it,' Jens said to Paul.

'He's too young to understand. Let me put it like this—this is the perfect opportunity to really show the eco-freaks what's what, to do something against all their bloody understanding and saving the world crap.'

'Like what?' asked Daniel, his voice scratchy with suspense.

Paul loosened his grip slightly and said, 'You're a regular and welcome guest at our parties. We have a lot of fun together. But a party takes a lot of hard work. You can't always imagine it from the outside. Getting hold of drinks, getting something to smoke, choosing the music, getting hold of girls.'

'That must be a lot of work.'

'Yes siree,' said Jens. 'And all the mess afterwards.'

'Don't forget that. There's a lot of rubbish left over. All fun has its price. And there was no overlooking that you've had fun. You've drunk a lot, sometimes a bit too much at once maybe and mixed your drinks too much, especially. You've smoked, the best stuff on the market right now. You've danced and laughed and cried, or at least that's what it looked like, maybe it was just snot. You had a go with girls, not always successfully—but who apart from me can say he's always a success with girls? You've done a hell of a lot, Daniel Kuper, things other people will never do, not in a hundred years. You've seen heaven. And now, we think, it's time for you to pay for it.'

'You mean you want me to pay a proper entrance fee? Money?'

'No, man, I mean you owe us, something you can't make up with money—you owe us to be there. Volker got it right away that you have to pay something back, and he sold us his soul. And now we want yours. And that's why Jens and I've decided to take you with us.'

'Where to?'

'The leaving party. We want you to take part in the preparations.'

'What an honour.'

Paul jammed his arm around Daniel's head until he paddled with his arms. LetgoofmeyouarseholewhenIgetoutofhereI'llmess youupI'llbeatyoutoapulpwe'llseewho'sthebigkingroundherebut notanymoreonlytheoreticallynotanymoreyou'retheonlyonewho thinksyoucandowhatyoulikewithmeyouthinkIwon'tfightbackI wouldnotdarenotDanielthatsoftiethatweaklingthatmentalcaselet goofmeyoustupidarseIcan'tbreatheI'llsplityourcheekswithawrench andpulloutyourtongueI'llburnyouruglyclothesandyouruglyhair I'llstickpinsineveryporeofyourbodyI'lluseahotirontostampfuck youfuckyoufuckyouintoyourskintillthere'snoroomlefttostamp fuckyouintoyouyouwankerI'llpourpetroloveryouifyou. Then Paul let him go and slapped him on the cheek. 'You have to make your mind up, Kuper, decide which side you're on. Either you're here, with us, and then you have to show yourself, for everyone to see, and take the blame if something goes wrong. Or you're out. It's as simple as that.'

Hard kept drifting off; lying down made him sleepier than all his medication. Doctors came, inspected his stats, spoke to other doctors about his condition and left again without having talked to him. He didn't know whether no one visited him because Birgit didn't want them to, so that he didn't get upset, or because everyone was scared to see him this way, so weak. It was fine by him though; he was alone and had more time for the nurses.

When he was doing better he was moved to Cardiology, to a two-bed room. The man already in there—porous skin, yellow fingernails, thinning hair and ten years older than him—was no competition. Nevertheless, he was annoyed at having to share all the attention from then on. Birgit came by after closing time in the evening, put clean clothes in his locker, filled the glass on his bedside table with mineral water and sat on the edge of the bed for a moment before finding a reason to get up again—the flowers had wilted, the window was open too wide, the blinds too far up.

'Biggi, just sit down, will you, you're making me nervous.'

She didn't sit though; she leant against the wall, her hands together behind her back.

'Are you managing?'

'Managing what?'

'The business.'

'I've got everything under control apart from the books. And that can wait until you're back.'

'Won't be long before you take over the shop.'

'That'd suit you, wouldn't it? I do all the hard work and you enjoy the autumn of your life.'

'That's the way it works already.'

'Oh, Hard,' she stepped close to him and brushed a hair from his forehead. 'You're in your mid-forties, you'll be bored if you stop working now.'

'No. I'll enjoy it.'

'Who with?'

'With you.' He pulled her to him but when he noticed she felt uncomfortable being kissed in a stranger's presence he let go again. 'Could you go out for a moment?' he said to the man next to him. 'I've got something to discuss with my wife, something personal.'

'Very funny.' A smoker's voice. A smoker's cough.

'He snores.'

'So does he.'

When the other man went back to staring at the screen above him, Hard explained, 'His operation's tomorrow. Bypass.'

'Why aren't you getting a bypass?'

'Too complex.'

'What is?'

Hard thumped his right fist against his chest. 'My heart.'

Sometimes she brought the twins with her now and sometimes she didn't. Daniel had been to see him three or four times, had sat on the chair next to the bed and given monosyllabic responses to his questions, because Birgit had insisted to both of them that they weren't to provoke each other. 'How are you?'

'Fine.'

'How's school going?'

'Fine.'

'And the village?'

'Fine.'

Then Hard had decided he wasn't strong enough to listen to any more of his lies, and asked Daniel to stay at home until he was fully recovered. The consultant was optimistic he'd soon be discharged but recommended he didn't go back to work immediately but check in to a rehabilitation centre. 'For as long as possible. At least two months.' And to his own astonishment, Hard consented. The prospect of finally getting out of Jericho prompted such a rush of euphoria that his stats went haywire for a day. He couldn't remember the last time he'd had a holiday, least of all on his own. And the thought of the possibilities that freedom offered, after years of family life, made him feverish with anticipation.

After two weeks he was sufficiently recovered that he thought he'd survive any news that Birgit told him. But when it rained down on him in one go it was as if he'd been struck by lightning.

'Guess who came in the shop today?'

'Theda Wiemers.'

'Almost—Richard.'

'What did *he* want? Was he out canvassing for votes?'

'He doesn't need to with you. He bought perfume. Obsession.'

'For Theda?'

'No.' Birgit raised her eyebrows. 'For his girlfriend.'

'He told you that?'

'He didn't, Marlies did. And she got it from Klaus.'

'That puts paid to his election chances then.'

'Looks like it.'

'And who is it? I mean, who's his girlfriend?'

'Eiske Ahlers. Apparently they've been having a thing for a while now.'

'I can't imagine that.'

'I can. I told you, she's only got eyes for men. And she goes out so often. Her own husband hardly set eyes on her. He started getting bored.'

'How do you know?'

She blushed and looked away. 'That's what I heard.'

'And what else have you heard?'

'Marie Meinders is pregnant. I thought as much—she's been in such a good mood recently, she hasn't stopped smiling. And you can see it now, a bit. And Hans is like a new man on Sundays. Probably because they've started on the new mortuary now too. It couldn't have gone on, the way it was.'

Hard felt his heart stumbling.

For a second he thought it had stopped beating.

Then it started up again.

'Oh, and just think, they know who set the fire now.'

'What fire?'

'The one in Achterup and at the laundry next to Vehndel's.'

'Who?'

'Hamann. Rhauderwiek came round today, with that boy, what's his name?' She looked at him again and clicked her fingers. 'Tebbens. They found all sorts of chemicals in his house.'

'And that's why they came to see you, to tell you that? Haven't they got anything better to do?'

'No, they wanted to check your alibi again because Hamann said it was you.'

'What?'

'The thing with the fire.'

'But it wasn't me.'

'That's what Daniel said too.'

'That's all right then.'

'Yes, especially because Sabine and Günter will be getting some money out of it soon. They had a tough time finding a tenant, what with it all being so shabby with the broken windows and the soot stains.'

'Don't tell me Schlecker's opening up in there.'

'No, a betting shop.'

'By who?'

'What d'you mean, by who?'

'Who's running it?'

'Günter himself, I think. All official. With a licence and everything.'

Hard sat up in bed. 'He doesn't know the first thing about it.'

'Don't go getting excited. The doctor said you have to avoid stress.'

'How can I, when you tell me things like that? Günter Vehndel. Good God.'

'He doesn't have to make his own bets.'

'I'll say.'

'Not like you.'

Hard ignored her snide remark. 'And all that happened today, on one day?'

'More or less. I wanted to wait until you were feeling better.'

'I am.'

'I can see that.'

'I'm totally out of touch in here. Apart from with what's on TV.'

'Plenty happening there.'

'Yes, but nothing I can influence.'

'That's how it's supposed to be.'

'Absolutely out of the loop.'

'It would have been the death of you otherwise.'

'And nobody asked after me?'

'Everyone's always asking after you, whether you're still alive.'

'And? Am I?'

'Looks like it.'

14

It was a Wednesday, after midnight, and his mother and the twins had gone to bed hours ago. He'd been in bed too, fully dressed. His mother had come into his room one last time to check up on him. As soon as all the sounds in the house had died down, he pulled on his parka and crept on stockinged feet, his shoes in one hand, down the stairs to the basement. He took a few newspapers and magazines out of the wastepaper basket and the sacks of cans and plastic tubs. It wasn't much—the rubbish was collected on Mondays. Only the empty cardboard boxes were piled up to the ceiling against one wall, because Daniel hadn't got around to breaking them up during his work experience and taking them to the dump with his father. He fastened the big rubbish sacks to his handlebars, put a few of the small ones in his jacket pockets and stuffed newspapers and magazines in his backpack.

He took a detour through Compunists' Corner, past the fields, straight across the hammrich. He heard the cows at their water troughs, their scraping and stamping and snorting. As he passed a farmyard a dog started barking, making others do likewise. Then it was silent and stayed silent, for minutes. The sky was clear and starry. Above him in the distance, the red flashing lights on the navy radio masts, ahead of him the outlines of Clay Road, where Doctor Ahlers had come off the road and the Kelly Family's double-decker bus had broken down. Then, at the level crossing, he turned onto Hoogstraat, where Rainer and Marcel Pfeiffer had held a race. Hundreds of times he'd cycled along here, as a child with his father on Sunday mornings and later on his own to the UFO on Saturday evenings. He could have cycled blind without bumping into anything, and now he did cycle blind.

Once, a few months before, the police had stopped him on his bike. Every weekend they parked on the side of the road opposite the bus stop and checked the alcohol level of the car drivers coming from the disco. He had almost passed them when the driver wound the window down, stuck his head out and called, 'Hey you, lights on!'

As he cycled, Daniel tapped his foot against the dynamo to press it against the tyre, and he noticed that it wasn't working, that it turned and turned and nothing happened. But instead of dismounting and walking the rest of the way, he had picked up speed. He heard the engine roaring behind him, saw the blue lights flashing through the night and hoped he'd make it to Compunists' Corner with its barriers and bollards and speed bumps. But they overtook him, parked diagonally on the street and leapt out of the car with their guns cocked.

'Stop where you are,' said one of them—Kurt Rhauderwiek—and Daniel stopped.

And the other one—Joachim Schepers—said, 'That's gonna cost you.'

They noted down his details in the light of their headlamps. He had to show his ID although they both knew him. 'He's got it on his person, Jo,' one called to the other over the roof of the car.

'Exemplary behaviour.'

'Mitigating circumstances?'

'Zero tolerance.'

'That'll be twenty marks then.'

Daniel showed his wallet. 'I've only got ten.'

'We'll take that.'

'We'll take anything.'

'Can't I do a bank transfer?'

'He wants to do a bank transfer, Jo.'

'That costs extra, of course.'

'Otherwise I'll have to go home again and get the money.'

'Where are you going at this time of night—after twelve?'

'To the UFO.'

'UFO? Did you say UFO, boy?' Joachim Schepers came around the car.

'So you saw it too?' They made that joke with everyone.

'He must have done, you couldn't miss it, there was this light, really short and really bright.'

'Like lightning.'

'A shooting star.'

'A meteorite.'

'Excellent camouflage.' Joachim Schepers handed back his ID and put a hand on his shoulder. 'You've fulfilled your mission and now they've come to get you, right? You'll get in the stone and fly off with them. And then they'll destroy the earth, their creation.'

'Take us with you.' Kurt Rhauderwiek went down on his knees before him. 'Please. We'll submit to you. Here,' he took his gun out again, 'we'll put our weapons in your hands. Command us. Do what you want with us. We're at your service, master of the universe.'

Daniel said, 'I mean the disco.'

'We know.' Kurt Rhauderwiek put his gun back in its holster, stood up and patted down his trousers.

'You're not allowed in there at this time of night.'

'Bedtime.'

And then they sent him home, following him all the way to the drugstore at walking pace.

If they caught him now, with no lights and loaded down with plastic bags, it would be all over. They wouldn't let him get away with it, not for all the money in the world. They'd take him to the station and interrogate him, and he'd admit everything, even if he couldn't explain his crime of cycling around with a load of rubbish in the middle of the night. 'Bring rubbish and wrappers,' Paul has said. 'You know—wrappers.'

Daniel pushed his racing bike into the cycle stand, snapped the lock shut and walked past the staff room over to the main entrance. He shielded his eyes and pressed his nose against the window; everything was dark inside. When he knocked on the glass Paul appeared out of nowhere and let him in. In the foyer he saw Jens and Volker and a few older kids he knew from school and the parties. They were kicking at something he couldn't make out. 'Are you crazy? Keep that away from me.'

'I think I've trodden on something.'

'Time for a round then.'

'It wasn't the cat. Felt more like one of your rotten oranges.'

'Did you have to bring the thing along?'

'Paul said we needed an animal.'

'Not a dead one. A live animal, he said.'

'Put your hand in it, then you'll know. Oranges don't have fur.'

'Your ones were pretty furry though.'

'Gimme the flashlight, will you?'

'Not now. We'll have the cops here otherwise.'

'I thought they knew about it.'

'They do but the neighbours don't. And if they call the police they have to come. It goes via police headquarters.'

'Good job I'm wearing rubber boots.'

The floor was soft and feathery. Whatever it was that Daniel's sneakers were sinking into, it stank like it was half-digested. Paul and Jens took the bags and the army backpack off him and tipped out the contents.

'Just plastic,' said Paul.

And Jens said, 'And paper.'

'Oh great. Haven't you brought any compost? This is no use to us.'

'I told you to leave the kids out of it.'

'Volker thought of it himself.'

'Volker's a sly fox, isn't he?'

'You can still eat some of it.'

'Maybe *you* can. You eat anything, you do.'

Daniel was already regretting having come but then Paul gave him a beer, as if to numb his doubts, and they all raised their cans. 'Welcome to the club.'

'What club?'

'Your club.'

Give him one of those papers. Here.' Paul handed Daniel a flyer and switched on the flashlight.

'And now it's OK to turn the light on, or what?' someone said.

'Read it out.'

It took Daniel a while to decipher the handwriting, his own handwriting.

'No one can read this.'

'You are no one.'

'What is it?'

'Read it out, I said.'

'The teachers . . . imagine . . . the world in which they . . . rule as the best world.' He struggled from one word to the next, like he used to in German or Latin lessons. 'Everything that . . . contradicts their . . . ideals is worthless. That's why they are only . . . concerned with . . . defusing our . . . energies. The daily . . . lessons, the constant . . . examining and . . . evaluating, serve only one . . . purpose, to . . . break our will, to . . . free our thoughts from all . . . emotions . . . and distract us with . . . knowledge that we'll never . . . use. We are the . . . disorder, the . . . unpredictable, the . . . revolutionary, the element . . . that annihilates . . . school. May the . . . trash be with us!'

And then the others threw a handful of copies of it up in the air.

'I didn't write that.'

'Who else was it? It's got your signature on it, or hasn't it?'

'Could be.'

Paul switched off the flashlight. 'Do you know another Daniel Kuper with such messy handwriting? Let's get out of here. We've got a lot to do.'

In the yard, they tipped over the rubbish bins and went on to the caretaker's tool shed. One of them had a crowbar with him, another a pipe wrench. They used them to break the lock. Paul mowed the sunflowers around the biotope with a scythe. Jens dug up earth with a spade and chucked it in the goldfish pond. Volker pulled the flowers out of their beds with his bare hands.

Ubbo Busboom from Year Ten asked Daniel why he'd spared the school.

'Spared it?'

'You know, with the swastikas everywhere else.'

'I've got nothing to do with that.'

'Yeah, right,' he pointed at a tree without branches, 'and you've got nothing to do with this either.'

'Maybe he didn't,' said Volker.

'What?'

'Maybe you just can't see anything because the cladding on the ground floor is white, because the symbols don't stand out against it.'

'Not such a stupid thought,' said Paul.

'I'm telling you, he's a sly fox, even though you can't even tell he's got a dick.' Jens raised the saw to the branches again.

'So why didn't he use a different colour paint then? That's dumb, that is, white on white.'

'As camouflage. White eagle against a white background.'

'What d'you mean?'

'What I just said. White eagle against a white background. East Frisian war flag.'

'Are you taking the piss, fatso? You might have a lot of padding, but at some point these here,' Ubbo Busboom held both fists up to Volker, 'will get through to you anyway.'

Then they heard an engine, a stripe of light flashed across the buildings, and a moment later a motorbike cruised onto the forecourt, a blue-black Yamaha FZR 600, 1991 model, 91 PS, 67 kW, water-cooled four-stroke engine with a top-mounted double camshaft. The driver took off his helmet. When they saw who it was, Paul and Jens and the Year Ten boys went up to him from all sides. Only Daniel and Volker took a step in the other direction, thought about whether to get out of there, decided against it and stayed back in the shade of the school.

Iron said, 'Not bad.'

'Thanks,' said Paul.

'To start with.'

'We haven't finished yet.'

'And I see you've got Arthur Dent with you. Not out travelling the galaxy today? But what are you doing *here*? I thought Earth had been demolished to make way for a hyperspace express route.' Daniel took a step forward, now that he'd been spotted, and Volker did the same. 'Oh boy. And Fat, Fatter, Fatty Mengs is here and all.' Iron turned back to Paul and Jens. 'What a great team. What else are you planning?'

'Vietnam.'

'Huh?'

'We're going to defoliate the schoolyard.'

'And that's it?'

'Hey, you should see the foyer.'

'And the school hall.'

'Rubbish everywhere.'

'Vietnam, you say?'

'Yeah.'

'Jeez, are you as stupid as you look or are you just pretending?'

'Why?'

'Because Vietnam won't work. You're not America, you can't just walk in and smash everything up and then walk away.'

Paul and Jens exchanged glances.

'You've got to turn up in the morning, and then they'll just make you clear everything up. Before eight, I'd say. They'll make sure of that. The whole point is for classes to be cancelled—because it's impossible to use the building. We did it with butyric acid in my year—we had the keys to the chemistry lab and that was that.'

'Right, so now what?'

'I've got an idea. I only thought of it after I left, though, otherwise I'd have done it myself.'

'What is it?' asked Jens.

'Might get you in a lot of trouble.'

'We're in trouble already. More or less trouble doesn't make any difference.'

'It's out of your league. And I don't want you to piss your pants over it.'

'Come on, just tell us.'

'Stick pins in the locks and then break off the heads.'

'And what's the point of that?'

'Then they won't be able to get in tomorrow morning, you idiot,' said Paul, slapping Jens round the back of the head. 'They'll have to get the locks changed.'

'And that could take hours.'

'But we haven't got any pins.'

'I could drive over to the office and get some, there's loads of them lying around there. We use them to flag up our customers. The radius of our power. And I could bring along some extra troops while I'm at it.' He looked up at the school. 'There's a lot of doors in there. And we haven't got all night. We want to get some drinking time in as well. Have you got anything?'

'Sure,' said Paul. 'Always.'

'You guys wait here till I get back.'

'We're not going anywhere.'

Once Iron was gone they went back to pruning the bushes and trees, but they had no beer and cigarettes left so they dropped their tools and crossed School Road to the kolk, a small lake lined by poplars, lindens, birches and a two-metre-high wire fence.

'We'll go right back again though,' said Paul after they'd all slipped through the hole in the fence.

'Yes, siree,' said Jens.

A trampled path led from the road past a transformer station to a green turnstile with fish motifs and the initials JAC. None of them was a member but Paul and Jens claimed they'd been angling there years ago, with bamboo rods and nylon lines, with bread and worms, until the cops had come and called their attention to the signs staked into the ground around the lake: *Private Property!—No entry!—All fish theft will be reported to the police!—Parents are liable for their children!*

'We got some really big 'uns,' said Jens, his hands outstretched as far as possible. 'Twenty-kilo carps.'

'With bread and worms? They must've been pretty desperate.'

'Almost starving.'

'I never knew bamboo could take that much weight.'

'And nylon. Did you use thread or tights?'

Then they'd reached the tents. One of them lit a campfire, one handed out cans of beer, one tore open a bag of crisps and passed it around. The sound of chirping crickets filled the night. They had only brought along the tents and sleeping bags in case the girls they'd invited turned up after all. No one expected that to happen but they wanted to be equipped for all eventualities.

'No beer, no crisps, no compost.' said Paul. 'Did you at least bring along some wrappers, Kuper?'

'Of course,' said Daniel, took a couple of condoms out of his parka, held them up so that everyone could see them and then threw them on the fire.

'What are you doing, are you crazy? We might need them.'

'What for?'

'For fucking.'

'Who were you planning to fuck?'

And the fact that no one answered that, not even with a joke, made each of them painfully aware of how far removed they were from sleeping with a girl, with or without a condom. They really didn't know how to go on; they had no plan other than staying up all night and drinking and smoking until dawn, until the bell rang and enough pupils and teachers were there to admire their contribution to the leaving party.

Paul crushed his beer can. 'We ought to be heading back now.'

'In a minute,' said Jens. 'One more beer. Iron will take at least half an hour, and that,' he looked at his watch, 'isn't up yet.'

'And apart from that I've got this here,' now Ubbo Busboom held up two wrappers, but they were something different to what Daniel had sacrificed to the flames, transparent, shimmering green in the reflection of the fire, 'excellent stuff.' A murmur instantly passed through the group and some of them, those who wanted to be the first to try it, slid closer to him on the tree trunks. Soon Iron was forgotten and they drank and smoked and told tales like the angling story. Daniel squatted silently between the others, taking an occasional puff, and then stared at the embers. They drew his gaze like a magnet draws metal—he couldn't tear himself away. He drank and drank and tried to extinguish the fire in his head but the more he drank, the hotter it got. And still he went on drinking, unable to think of any other means, until he noticed that the others, stripped naked, were jumping into the water next to him.

For a while he watched them as they dunked one another, hanging on to one another like children, shouting and splashing. Then he undressed as well and jumped in after them, scared they'd pull him in as he was, in his parka and sweater and trousers and shoes. The moment he hit the water he gasped for air; feet, hands, branches whipped him in the face. He got his head above water, beat his arms, looked for something by which he could pull himself out but found nothing but a hand that pushed him under. Later, long after they'd left him alone, he panted back to the bank and up the slope.

He suddenly had the sense that a storm was coming. He looked at the trees and the fire but the leaves and the flames weren't moving; only his skin flickered like from an electric current. He gathered up his things; they were damp and covered in sand and lay scattered in front of the tents. He couldn't remember throwing them there. His parka was missing. He went from one boy to the next. They all turned their backs on him. He wanted to ask them where his jacket was, but then he saw it—Paul was carrying it triumphantly above his head, stretched between both hands like a sail. Jens had thrown it over his shoulders, the sleeves dangling down at the sides as if his arms were missing. Volker had shreds of fabric hanging out of his mouth and shoved more in after them as he chewed. The Year Ten boys had rubbed themselves down with it and put it in the embers to warm up. They had doubled it, multiplied it, he didn't know how; only for him was there no jacket left. No matter who he went to, everyone shook their heads, grinning broadly; they shoved him from one to another and back, him keeping his balance with some effort; until he stumbled over one of the ropes with which the tents were tightened. He wanted to lie down but when he unzipped the mosquito nets they were both occupied, three boys in each, snuggled up close, snoring as though they'd been sleeping for hours. He too fell asleep and when he woke it was raining and the fire was out and it was absolutely silent. He looked around, didn't know where he was. The tents, the lake, the white cans on the black water, the folding knife, the blood in his hand, it all seemed alien, as if from another world.

At the school, an engine roared and lights swiped across the horizon. He looked for his parka again on the path. When a car, a brown Mercedes 560 SE Coupé, 1987 model, 279 PS, 205 kW, stopped outside the turnstile, he crouched down between some bushes because he thought he'd seen the parka over there, behind the transformer station. Two boys got out, bent back the fence and slipped in to him through the hole. Daniel didn't recognize them at first until one of them picked something up off the ground and the other stopped right next to him, undid his flies and pissed against a tree trunk. 'Are you sure they're here?'

'I saw their tents earlier.'

'Maybe just hooting's enough. Maybe they'll come out then.'

'No, Frank. We've waited long enough, much too long for those cowards. They promised to wait for us. And then they didn't. Now they're going to have to pay penance.'

'And what are you going to do with that jacket?' Frank— Frank Tebbens—zipped his flies and turned to Iron. 'Hey, I know that parka. It belongs to that crazy kid.'

'I'm putting it on.'

'A perfect fit.'

'Just right.' Iron pulled the hood over his head.

'What are you going to do?'

'You'll see.'

Daniel cycled along Broadway, past the school and the maize fields. In the morning twilight he saw only outlines, the cobs, the tips of the stalks, the beginning and end of the sowing. He considered whether to stop and go in, like back on that summer day when snow fell over Jericho out of the blue, but then he told himself it was too cold to survive the night outdoors, in wet clothes with no jacket.

And so he cycled on and on all the way home, accompanied by birdsong that sounded just as agitated as he felt.

He leant the racing bike against the wall beneath the almost entirely faded *I love you*. The shutters in front of the new display windows were down and upstairs too, on the other floors, there was nothing to see but the firmly closed white slats. His mother and the twins were still asleep. He patted his trouser pockets for his keys, in vain. He must have lost them at the kolk. Or they had been in his jacket pocket. He couldn't remember. Perhaps it had been that way, or perhaps it was different. Anything was possible. He looked across the extension, the garage. Up there on the flat roof was where Volker had meant to hide from him, and later they'd both smoked their first cigarettes there, drunk their first beer, ducked out of mowing the lawn, shopping and homework, up there they'd laid on their backs, stared silently at the sky for hours or simply sat there, their legs dangling over the abyss, and watched people living their lives. The flat roof was a hiding place that only worked in summer and only when it wasn't raining or stormy, a hiding place that offered protection for a few hours, not for days or weeks, and which was out of Daniel's reach now, because even if he managed to lever open one of the windows to the garden he'd have to go through the house from downstairs and would be caught up there if they did find him—unless he jumped down.

It was shortly after dawn. No light fell yet through the gaps between the boards and it was perfectly silent. Only once, when a train passed, was there first a rustle, then a roar and a rumble, and the walls trembled for seconds like in an earthquake. He had taken off his damp clothes and laid them over the glass wool bales to dry. He had wrapped himself in a dusty blanket and tried to find a position in which he could sleep. He drew up his knees, doubled up but didn't sleep, only dozing from dream to dream.

In one, he was lying outside on the train tracks. They—he didn't know who—had just been kicking him with their boots, and now they were jamming his arms beneath the rails. He felt the buzzing leaving the rails and crossing over to him, the shrill, rising tone, something came towards him, something large and heavy, something he had to let pass over him no matter how hard he tried to get away. In another there was a fire; the door to the freight shed was pushed open, the gust of wind fanned the fire, commands were yelled into the room, dogs barked, sirens howled, above him and around him the lights went on, blindingly bright and so penetrating that looking into them singed his retinas. The blindness wasn't black, as he'd thought it would be, but white, never-ending white.

Daniel dreamt of the future, and for the first time he was as if nailed to the spot. His father stood over him. He lifted him up and cradled him in his arms, like a child that can't find rest. He spoke to him without moving his lips. The time to sacrifice the first-born son had come. The ceremony could begin. His mother cut him open. The twins put their fingers in his wound. Paul and Jens threw stones at him from behind. Volker offered him one of his human-liver-sausage sandwiches and then bit into it himself. Simone recited the Lord's Prayer, her arms behind her back, her dyed-black hair plaited, in her best dress as if she was standing around the Christmas tree with her family, full of impatience and anticipation, until she couldn't wait any longer and tore open his skin like the wrapping of a present—using both hands at once.

'Hey, this is mine. This is my place.'

Daniel opened his eyes and turned on his back, the blanket slipping off his shoulders.

'Oh. I didn't know that was why you came. Have you been waiting for me all night? If I'd known I'd have come sooner, before breakfast, I'd have brought cushions and candles and beer and something to smoke. Micha lets me have a puff sometimes but I know exactly where he hides the stuff, in the cellar behind the work bench, sometimes I go down there just to have a smell of it. Do you know what it smells like? Like boys' hair when they come out of the lake in summer and lie down next to me on the grass and stroke all the way up my legs, all the way up—up to my sluice. Do you want to have a look?'

Daniel propped himself up on his elbows and watched Wiebke, as she went on talking, pulling her dress up to her hips to reveal her underpants, white with embroidered flowers.

'He'd have noticed straight away if I'd stolen any, he's not stupid, not like me, but it'd be worth it.' She raised her dress a little higher. 'I'd even let myself get caught on purpose, for you, doing whatever.' And before she could pull her dress over her head Daniel was standing beside her and holding her still. At first she stretched out her arms but then, realizing he didn't want to help her undress, she dropped them again and looked down, following his hands. 'That's the wrong direction.' She looked up at him. 'That's the . . . Hey, will you look at that? It's huge. I knew right away we were made for each other.' Automatically, she reached out a hand for him and he took a step back to evade her grip, stumbled over the blanket scrunched up on the floor and hit his head.

When he woke she was lying next to him, one arm flung around him, and whispering more words, her mouth directly by his ear ' . . . imagined it differently, longer especially, but I'm not complaining, for the first time it wasn't . . . Hey there—finally woken from the dead?'

'What?' asked Daniel, still groggy. 'What happened?'

'A whole lot—in your life, anyway.'

'I can't remember anything.' He ran his hand over the back of his head.

'You don't have to.' Wiebke cast off the blanket and put her underpants and dress back on. 'There'll be plenty of times you will remember. You know my sluice like the back of your hand now, but you don't know this yet.' She pushed one of the bales of glass wool aside and lifted a tarpaulin. 'I don't show this to everyone, you know.'

'I know cardboard boxes like the back of my hand.'

Wiebke unfolded the topmost flap and tossed a few books and pieces of clothing at him. 'From my mum. Dad didn't want it in the house any more but he couldn't bring himself to get rid of it. It's all mine. And one day,' she turned in a circle, 'I'll put it all on and take it off again, just for you. I'll dance in it and sleep in it and get married and die in it, and all along you'll be reading to me out of these books.'

Daniel said, 'You ought to burn it all.'

'No! Why should I?'

'It stinks.'

'Yes, I know. A box of perfume got knocked over back there somewhere. She used to collect that too.' Wiebke lowered the tarpaulin. 'And now I'll get us something to eat and drink. And clean clothes for you. These,' she picked up his things, 'will take ages to dry. And we haven't got that much time. Mind you, I wouldn't mind seeing you like this for ever.' And as she passed him he grabbed her and pulled her down to him. 'Stop it, let go, you're hurting me.'

'You mustn't tell anyone I'm here.'

'I'm not going to.'

He loosened his grip.

'You're a spy on the run.'

'You don't even know what that is.'

'Yes, I do. A man with no shadow. And I know what they do to spies when they do step into the light.'

'Oh yeah? What?'

'They do their worst.'

'It's true what the others say about you—you really are crazy.'

'So are you.'

The minute she left he fell asleep again. He didn't dream any more, though, or at least he couldn't remember anything when he woke up. A train weighed down with iron ore thundered past the freight shed, trucks stopped at the loading bay and left after unloading their charge, someone pushed the door open and closed it again. A helicopter circled over the village, sirens howled, people passed by outside, bellowing incomprehensibly. Later—in the evening, it was dark already—Wiebke came back to him. She had two bags with her, one small and full of salami, bread, chocolate, bananas, apples, beer and water.

Daniel wolfed down everything as though he hadn't eaten or drunk for days. Except for the can of beer, which Wiebke grabbed out of his hand after he'd taken his first gulp, and emptied in one go. 'Tomorrow,' she said and wiped her hand across her mouth, breathless, suppressing a belch, 'tomorrow I'll bring more. I can't take too much at once or they'll notice.'

'And what's in there?' Daniel pointed at the other, slightly larger bag.

'Clothes.' Wiebke pulled out a leather jacket, a T-shirt, a yellow sweater, a faded pair of jeans with threadbare knees, a pair of socks and underpants. 'They're Micha's. They ought to fit you.'

'I'm not wearing them.'

'OK. Don't then.' She stuffed the things back into the bag, put her head on his shoulder and stroked his chest. 'I like you better like this anyway.'

'Hmm,' said Daniel and got up. There was still a cloud of smoke in his head but thanks to the food his mind was clear enough now to realize that he wouldn't get far as he was, dressed only in a blanket. 'Well, I can try them on.' Two minutes later, he looked like the world's biggest arsehole. At last what most Jerichoans imagined as an arsehole now matched up to what he imagined too. Though the clothes were freshly washed, at least— apart from the leather jacket, which gave off a sour, spicy smell.

It took Wiebke a while to stop laughing. Then she said, 'You ought to see yourself in a mirror—it's a riot.'

'Better not.'

'Here,' Wiebke removed a pair of wire-framed glasses with thick lenses from the bag's side pocket, 'put these on. They look funny.'

'Won't he miss all this?'

'No, the bag was right by the old clothes collection sack.'

'But the jacket looks pretty new to me.'

'Dad says they're gonna get you this time. But you're safe here with me.'

'The question is, how long. I have to get out of here at some point. Out of Jericho.'

'Where do you want to go?'

'I don't know. Just out of here to start with.'

'You were on TV.'

Daniel shrugged. 'So what?'

'So everyone knows your face.'

'Not in Holland they don't.'

'They can watch German channels there too.'

'Yeah, but they're not interested. Germany's Germany and Holland is Holland, and it's only thirty kilometres to the border.' The thought of walking so far made him dizzy. He was glad he could even stand upright. And so he sat back down next to her, but a metre away so she didn't launch herself at him again.

'You won't get far.'

'Why not?'

'There's police everywhere. On every street corner. At every bridge. Dad says you're in big trouble this time.'

'What have I done?'

'You tipped all that rubbish out at school and broke the doors. And then the thing with the tents.'

'The tents?'

'Micha says there were some kids camping by the kolk and you pulled out the things, the pegs, and you kicked the kids inside them, in the tents, and stabbed at them. Micha saw you, and he called the police, and they found your knife and your parka with loads of pins in the pockets.'

'That's not right.' He knew he'd regret putting on Iron's clothes. But he hadn't thought that moment would come so soon.

'What's not right?'

'All of it. The whole world. You, me—it's all wrong.'

'But some of it feels right, don't you think?'

Wiebke slid closer to him, tweaking at the hem of her dress, and lowered her voice. 'I like bad boys, did you know that?'

'I thought as much.'

'And do you know why?'

'I bet you're going to tell me.'

'Yes,' she called out, forgetting their situation, and she took his hand and put it between her legs, 'because I'm a bad girl.'

'Shit, Jesus, you're just a child.' Daniel leapt up, lost his balance and fell onto one of the glass wool bales, then sank to the ground.

'I'm thirteen.'

'That's what I mean.'

'It didn't bother you earlier.' Now she came towards him on all fours, her dress hanging so low at the front that the deep neckline gave an insight into her physical development. He couldn't help looking directly into it. And her eyes followed his, and she only raised her head again when she was directly above him. 'Not now either.'

He didn't know if it was a crime to get mixed up with her. All he knew was that if he did it—if he hadn't done it already—he'd be in even more trouble. And as her hand slid down him, something inside his new jeans reacted to Wiebke like a divining rod to an underground stream and something else in his head ordered him to start drilling right then and there.

'Not at all.'

Then they heard the door rolling to one side.

'Why's the light on in here?'

'Don't know.'

'That was me,' called Wiebke, stood up, patted the dust off her dress and disappeared between two bales.

'I told you not to come in here so late.'

'All right, Dad.'

'What if that boy's hiding in here?'

'What boy? The one Micha told me about today?'

'That's the one.'

'He's not. Why would he?'

'That one's capable of anything.'

'I've brought us something.' She held up a small, transparent wrapper.

'Where did you get that from?'

'From Micha.'

'Are you crazy?'

'Hey, don't panic. The bag fell out of his jacket.'

'Put it back in then.'

'Coward.'

'It's no use to us anyway.'

'Why not?'

'I haven't got any tobacco.'

'I have.' She reached into her shoulder bag again and brought out a pouch. 'And a lighter.' She lined everything up in front of him like hunting trophies and then admitted she couldn't roll a joint.

'There you are then,' he said, 'that's the end of that.'

'You can't either.'

'I don't want to. Not now.'

'All right, we can do it afterwards.'

'After what?'

And she was clinging to him again.

If only he hadn't asked. She was worse than his father. Every word she said was bait. *His father*. Daniel wondered how he was and whether he'd have another heart attack when he heard what Daniel had done this time.

He had to get out of this shed. He couldn't go home and he wouldn't get far on foot. He assumed they'd be patrolling the streets until midnight and guarding the most important roads, and by dawn he'd be somewhere in Rheiderland, where the fields were so open and wide that you could see in the morning who'd be visiting you in the evening. The best thing would be for someone to put him in the boot of their car and drive him out. Volker didn't have a driving licence but he knew how to drive. To get to Compunists' Corner, though, he'd have to walk halfway across the village, and even if he managed to get there unnoticed, with all the police about they wouldn't even get to the end of the driveway. Apart from that Volker had changed sides and there was no ruling out that he thought Daniel had kicked and stabbed at him through the tent to get his revenge on him and the others. The only person who could help him now was Simone. She lived the closest. And perhaps he could send her a letter via Wiebke, perhaps she could persuade her mother to take a trip to Groningen tomorrow—with him in the back. And then, when they'd sat down at a table somewhere and placed their orders, Simone would say, 'Oh, I left my sunglasses in the car, can you give me the key for a minute?' But there were gaps in the plan. What if her mother said, 'I'll lend you mine,' or 'Just sit in the shade,' or offered to go with her. And even if everything did run smoothly, what then? He had no money, no ID, no destination. He didn't even have his own clothes on.

'What are you thinking about?'

'Nix.'

'Takes you a long time to think about nix.'

'It takes up a large part of my life, if not the majority, and it totally fulfils me.' As he said that he stood up and folded back the tarpaulin over her mother's belongings.

'What are you doing?'

'I just had an idea.' He stuck his hand in one of the boxes and pulled out a book.

'Do you want to read to me?'

'Have you got something to write with?'

'There's a pen in there somewhere.'

Daniel dug down through fabric and paper until he felt a ball-point pen at the very bottom. At first he thought the cartridge had dried out, but then it worked.

'What are you writing?'

He tore out the first, mainly blank page of *The Spy Who Loved Me*, the one with the title printed on it, folded it up and handed it to Wiebke.

'A love letter? For me?' She unfolded the piece of paper and cast a glance at it. Then she threw her arms around him.

'What does it say?'

'That you love me and want to be with me for ever.'

'And what else?'

'That you don't dare to tell me personally.'

'So it's right then?'

'What's right? You and me?'

'You can't read.'

'Yes I can.' She blushed, let go of him and lowered the piece of paper.

'It's for Simone.'

'Which Simone?'

'Simone Reents. Lives on Station Road. The house—'

'I know the one.'

'—with the green . . . How come?'

'Everyone knows her.'

'I want you to give it to her. Please. This evening, before you go home.'

'What do you want from her?'

'I want to ask her a favour.'

'I knew you had someone else. That's why you're like that.'

'Like what?'

'Cold.'

'I haven't got anyone. And if I had anyone, it'd be you.'

'So why don't you let me do it?'

'Can you drive a car?'

'No.'

'You see.'

'But she can, or what?'

'I thought you wanted to help me?'

'You want to get away from here.'

'Don't you?'

'Away from me.'

'Wiebke, your father just showed up. How long do you think it will take him to find out?'

'Find out what?'

'That I'm here. They're constantly putting things in here and taking them out.'

'This stuff's been here for ages.'

'Will you do it or not?'

'And what's in it for me?'

'Me.' And when she put her hands on him again he said, 'Tomorrow night.'

'Only if you take me with you.'

'OK.'

'Promise?'

'Yes, I promise.'

By then he'd be long gone.

'Daniel!'

It took a while for the voice in the dark to separate from the dream into which he'd slipped.

'Daniel? Are you here?'

Simone. The floorboards creaked beneath her feet. She really had come.

'Hello?'

Daniel threw back the blanket, stood up and stuck his head between the bales. A weak ray of light wandered across the floor.

'I'm here.'

She shone the light in his face. Then she was standing before him, reaching her free hand out to him, and he pulled her in.

'Can you please take that out of my eyes?'

'Sorry.' The beam of the flashlight migrated down him and hovered over the tobacco pouch and the wrapper.

'Thanks.'

'What do you look like?'

'What do you mean?'

'Aren't they Micha's clothes?'

'Some of them,' said Daniel, not wanting her to think he was wearing Iron's underpants.

'Where did you get them from? From Wiebke? If anyone in this village was abducted by aliens, then it's her.'

'At least she was clever enough not to go running to her father or her brother with my message.'

'I was pretty amazed when she brought it. She didn't say a word. And then she scooted right off again.'

'How far have you got?'

'Everything's ready. We're leaving tomorrow morning, around nine. My mother was totally surprised. She said,' her voice went up an octave, 'What? You want to go shopping with me? With *me*? In Groningen? What did I do to deserve it?' and down again, 'She's always wanted to. Probably more in Oldenburg or Bremen or Hamburg though. I hate shopping, it's totally dull, totally, at least the shops she wants to go to, all these posh boutiques, do they even have them in Groningen? Never mind, it's the only way to get her to drive there with me. She couldn't believe her luck.'

Daniel began gathering up his own, clammy clothes and stuffing them in the travel bag Wiebke had left for him.

'What's all this?'

'I'm packing.'

'I told you we're leaving in the morning.'

'I thought we'd set off while it's still dark.'

'Do you want to spend all night in the car boot? Do you know how cramped it is? You might be dead by the morning if I shut you in there now.'

Daniel pressed the top button on his digital watch. Two thirty. 'What are you doing here so early. I wrote *at four*.'

'I've just got back from the UFO, it was totally dull, totally, and I thought I'd come straight to you, because if I have a kip first I'll never wake up, not even if I set three alarm clocks.'

'What now?'

'We'll stay up all night.'

'We haven't got that much time left. It gets light at five.'

'Then let's make the most of the time we do have.'

'And do what?'

'Well, we could have a smoke, for instance. Seeing as you've got some gear here.'

'It's pretty strong stuff.'

'What's up with you?' And she put down the army backpack she had over her shoulder, squatted cross-legged on the floor, jammed the light between her legs, rolled out papers and tobacco, sprinkled some of the dried blossoms on top—rather a lot, Daniel thought—and licked along the edge.

'Need a roach?'

'It's fine without. Have you got a light?'

Daniel took out the lighter he'd put in his pocket. The flame was turned up so high it almost singed her red-and-black-streaked fringe.

'Careful!'

'Sorry.'

The smoke rose from her nostrils, making her look as though she were burning from the inside. 'Want a go? It's pretty strong.'

'I'd better not. Otherwise I'll be totally wasted tomorrow.'

'That doesn't matter now.'

And seeing as she was right about that, he made no reply and sat down next to her and took a draw, and for a moment he thought he couldn't breathe. And then he felt this thoughts relaxing, growing soft and supple, pliable. Simone Reents. The prettiest and cleverest and most popular girl in the village—and him, the most hated boy in Jericho. Her thigh on his, her shoulder on his. And he thought of the party at the Hankens' place, when they'd kissed, too briefly for his taste, and he wondered if he ought to try it again, seeing as it meant nothing to her anyway, as she never tired of saying.

'Hey,' she said just as he was about to lean over to her, 'leave some for me.' And then, her lamp weaker now, 'Oh, right.' And he inhaled what she'd inhaled, their lungs exchanged chemical information, their hands wandered from their cheeks to their calves and back, their fingers slid along their thighs, felt along the seams of their jeans, and then, as they were both almost there, they tipped over and so did Simone's backpack, out of which several cans rolled across the floor.

'What's this?' asked Daniel, picking up two of them. 'Phosphor spray. They're empty. Where did you get this from?'

'It was over there by the door, I almost tripped over it,' said Simone and pressed out the joint, burnt down almost to her fingertips. 'I thought it was yours.'

Then the lights went on above them and the glass wool bales were pushed aside as fast as backdrops on a TV show.

'I thought we'd never see each other again.'

'I thought so too.' His voice sounded nasal.

'What did you say? You're not speaking clearly.'

'I thought so too.'

'What did you think too?'

'That we'd never see each other again.'

'I think that every time. And it's almost always not the case. Maybe I should change my expectations.'

'Maybe.'

Daniel was sitting in a windowless room. He pulled down the bandage, and when he looked around he realized he'd been here twice before. There was a table in the middle with an intercom and around it were two chairs, three including his, and there was another chair in the corner. Everything was white apart from the hands and the numbers on the clock above the door. But it could have been a different room every time, he thought now, two or more rooms that are absolutely identical.

Saathoff opened up the file. 'Fractured skull, concussion, cerebral laceration, fractured nasal bone. Orbital fractures. What about your teeth? Says something here about front teeth trauma.'

'They're gone.'

'Where?'

'Here.' Daniel opened his mouth and showed him the gap.

'Falling from a platform onto tracks like that can have bad repercussions. Even though it's not high. It's easy to underestimate. How high's the platform at the Jericho freight shed, a metre, one fifty? Depends what you hit when you land, of course. You were lucky. There's people who've broken their necks that way.'

'I didn't fall.'

'What did happen then?' When no answer came, he asked, 'What's the last thing you can remember?'

'The last thing before what?'

'I've got a boy your age. Henning.'

'I know.'

'I know you know, but I'm going to tell you again. Can't be said often enough. I told him once, when he was little, Henning, you watch what you get up to. No matter what, it always comes back to you like a boomerang. And to me as well. The good and the bad things. I've never had problems with him since then. And do you know why? He knows his boundaries. He knows perfectly well what he's allowed to do and what not. He's no angel, mind you, God knows. He's come home drunk in his time, just the other day he puked all over his bed, but—and this is the difference— he's not funny in the head. He only makes mistakes once. He learns from them. And he only takes things the body can get rid of. Sooner or later. Out of one orifice or another. What was all that stuff by the way?'

'What stuff?'

'The stuff you smoked beforehand.'

'I don't take drugs.'

'I can't confirm that.' He flicked through the file. 'Your urine was full of it, Tetra-hydro-cannabinol. Sound familiar? How long have you been dealing now?'

'What's this all about?'

'You know what I think? I think you didn't injure yourself in the maize as a kid, and it wasn't aliens either, it was Michael Rosing, and since then you've had a bone to pick with him. That's why you did the graffitis, that's what's behind all this fanaticism. I've got a whole load of statements here from people who saw you selling gear at parties in his clothes—White Shadow.'

'Rubbish.'

'And then there's the tablets.' Saathoff held up a bag containing several blister packs and lowered it again. 'Some of them aren't even legal in Germany. Where did you get them from? From school? Or from home?'

Daniel looked to one side.

Saathoff leant over the file again. 'Mainly diazepam. Side effects: rage attacks, hallucinations, suicidal tendencies, derealization experiences, emotional coldness and weakness for criticism. Could count in your favour. At least partly.'

Daniel looked at the clock above the door. Quarter past seven. He didn't know whether it was morning or evening. Everything felt like far too early in the morning. 'Where's my lawyer?'

'Do you want to play games with me?'

'I want to talk to Onken.'

'Fine, we'll play games. He's on his way. Be here any moment.'

'I'll wait, then.' Daniel folded his arms and leant back.

'What a shame. I thought we'd just warm up and go over what you did again. A confession would be better for you, you know.'

'I haven't done nix.'

'So why do you keep finding yourself here?'

'That's what I'd like to know.'

'No UFOs, no swastikas, no broken tent, no broken bones, no stab wounds. No criminal damage, no actual bodily harm. It all dissolves into thin air. On closer inspection. Nobody did it in the end. In the end none of it ever happened. Nix is, nix was, nix will be.'

'Something like that.'

'So you weren't at the kolk?' He opened the file to a different page. 'On the night of 3 July?'

'I was, but—'

'And you didn't hide for three days in the freight shed, in Rosing's storehouse by the railway?'

'I did, but—'

'And what about the Rosing girl? You had nix to do with her either?'

'I never touched her, at any rate.'

'That's not what she looks like. It's not what she says either.'

'But she's got a screw loose.'

'And you haven't?'

'She's lying.'

'And the doctor's lying. And her father. Her brother. All liars.'

'Yes.'

'All except you. And what about the other girl you had at your mercy? Simone Reents? You didn't touch her either, I assume?'

'No.'

'And this,' he put the army backpack with the spray cans on the table, 'isn't yours either.'

'Right.'

'Of course not. It doesn't have your fingerprints on it either. And the name here,' he pointed at a patch bearing the word *KUPER*, 'is nothing to do with you. You're absolutely innocent, a blank sheet of paper.'

'In that sense, yes.'

'In what sense are you not? Sexually?'

'That's none of your business.'

'Everything here's my business, everything about you. I'm your shadow, you see.'

'I haven't got one.'

'The Rosing girl told you that.'

'How do you know?'

'I know a whole lot about you, Daniel Kuper. More than you think.'

'Oh yeah?'

'Oh yes.'

'What, for example?'

'Peter Peters. Oh yes, that surprised you, didn't it? That's not in here.' He tapped at the file. 'The true stories are never in here. What really drives kids like you. What they don't ever want to talk about. Or do you want to tell me you had nothing to do with it, with his death? That he stood on the tracks of his own accord to see what it's like to be ripped to shreds by a train. Shall I call him in?'

'Who?'

'Peter Peters.'

'Peter Peters is dead.'

'You will be too when you get out of here. *If* you get out of here. You're looking at detention.' And when Daniel looked at him questioningly, he said, 'Youth detention centre. You can imagine what they do with someone like you there.'

'No, I can't.'

'It's better if you talk. They'll rip you to pieces in there.'

'Wild beasts.'

'Without blood spilt, no forgiveness.' Saathoff pressed the button on the intercom. 'Mrs Freese? We're ready now. You can send him in.'

'No, wait,' said Daniel and leant forward. 'I'll tell you what happened.'

Marksmen's Club Fair

Green-White Jericho

05–06 October 1991
Programme

Saturday	4 p.m.	Bird shooting by the ladies' company
	6 p.m	Great Tattoo and flag consecration
	8 p.m.	King's Ball with the male-voice choir and the Sunnyboys dance band
	9 p.m.	Proclamation of the King
		Tombola
Sunday	7 a.m.	Reveille with the Drömeln marching band
	2 p.m.	Memorial ceremony at the war memorial
	3 p.m.	Reception of non-village associations and parade
	4 p.m.	Children's entertainment

Village square. Free entrance to the festival tent on all days. IDs will be checked at the entrance. Residents are requested to flag their homes.

I Have Overcome the World

I have a hundred and forty-one friends on Facebook. Most of them are people I studied with or shared houses with in Göttingen, whom God has scattered across the world, a few travel acquaintances from Israel and Italy, men I met on forums, lovers, eternal searchers, car freaks like me, confirmands who grew dear to my heart during my church internship in Verden, congregation members to whom I still feel obliged despite the distance, my sisters Verena and Venja, but also half a dozen people I went to school with, to whom I'd lost contact over the years and who now inform me in more or less coded form of what's on their mind every day.

Jens Hanken *omg. on a sunbed. not alone* :)

Paul Tinnemeyer *at the office. nix doing here. what's going down?*

Simone Rosing *aaaaaaarrghh! be glad you don't have kids.*

Every few weeks they inform me of events, birthdays, concerts, class reunions, and although I never turn up to any of these occasions they still persist in trying to win me as a guest the next time. They've uploaded photos showing us at a time when we thought we had control over our lives, photos in which it's not age that determines our hairstyles but our youthful intellectual standpoints, and we, high on various drugs, are laughing although we felt like crying only seconds before. The comments beneath them (*wow, we were so young; those were some cool parties; we had so much fun,* etc.) suggest to me that they've forgotten or supressed everything important and only remember experiences that never happened.

Apart from my profile photo there are no pictures on my page (*invidia, tamquam ignis, summam petit*). I invite them to every church service via my wall. I've put a few short texts on the net, weekly selected pericopes from the Revised Common Lectionary and extracts from my sermons, beneath which they (what else can they do?) click *Like*. In the mornings, when I boot up my computer and log in after my asanas, I see the faces of my life lined up simultaneously before me, illuminated by their own screens, with children or pets on their laps, in bed, at the table, on the beach, on holiday, in cars, in planes, in free fall, as though they had been there in this way from the very beginning, linked to one another through me. But before I post the week's Bible verse as my status, all these faces make me aware that one is missing and always will be missing, as long as I never find it embodied in another.

I send my message out into the world, *Be not overcome of evil, but overcome evil with good,* close my laptop, roll up the anti-abrasion, skin-friendly foam mat and drink a mouthful of carrot juice. Then I take my jacket off the hook and go outside to buy the *Weser Courier* opposite, at the Grubes' newsagents (my predecessor cancelled the subscription). On a morbid impulse, I take a diversion across the graveyard. There are unfamiliar names on the stones and beneath them rot unfamiliar stories. I'm new here and all the living look at me as though I'd floated directly down to them from heaven after years of darkness. *Mundus senescit.* Old women look up from the graves, plucking at weeds, old men walk towards me with firm steps and extend their wrinkled, age-spotted hands. I greet them all with the greatest possible friendliness of which I am capable at eight in the morning and walk past them, pulling my jacket closed to ward off the autumn weather.

In the churchyard I run into the sexton, Mr Kerkhoff, a short, grey-haired man sweeping up leaves despite the wind, rake in hand, and his activity prompts me to begin a conversation about the weather and the tall, hundred-year-old trees. 'In my village back home they felled them all and replaced them with Japanese maples.'

'Good idea. It's all protected here though. Every derelict house, every rotten tree. They won't let anything decay.'

'Paradise for Buddhists.'

He gives me an uncomprehending look. Then he goes on, 'But they just make a mess and block out the light. Is that your car?' He nods over at my grass-green Beetle convertible, 1951 model, 24.5 PS, 18 kW.

'One of them.'

'I used to have one of those once. My first. Always went like a dream. Did long journeys in it, across the Alps, to Lake Garda, Florence, to the Adriatic and from there—'

'You presumably had a closed VW Beetle. This one's a convertible from Karmann.'

'What difference does that make?'

The black artificial leather roof, the Petri steering wheel with the Golden Lady horn button, hinges with grease nipples, ivory-coloured Schenk ashtray on the gearstick, to name but a few; too many small details that would take too long to list. Every man who has ever owned a treasure (without being aware of it at the time) feels under pressure, in the face of my treasures, to compare his experiences with mine—a method that very rarely leads to us coming closer. And every man whom I refuse this exchange of secret male knowledge comes up with some different way of taking revenge on me for what he misinterprets as arrogance.

'When's your wife arriving, did you say?'

'I said I didn't have one.'

'Oh, yes.' He takes the rake in both hands again and scrapes its steel prongs across my soul.

Every day the devil leads me into temptation. I walk down the thirty steps of my brick Jacob's ladder, let a horse and carriage full of tourists pass, cross Findorff Road and enter into my own private hell. Revolving racks of newspapers, magazines and books, birthday, wedding and condolence cards, a lottery-ticket sales point, and in the display pipes, lighters, matchboxes—many ways of experiencing good and bad fortune, but none of them as effective and subtle as what penetrates in parallel through every pore of my sinewy, yoga-steeled body.

I've barely closed the door behind me when the scent of finest tobacco takes my breath away, fresh tobacco that hasn't yet dissolved into the air, spicy and moist. And as I search my pockets for change at the counter, hallucinating on the memories and visions released by these smells in my lungs, my eyes alight on the shelf at the back, where my venial sins are neatly ordered: Marlboro, L&M, Davidoff, Pall Mall, R1, R6, Stuyvesant, Reval, Lord, HB, Gauloises, Gitanes, Lucky Strike, Camel, John Player Special, Chesterfield, American Spirit, Schwarzer Krauser, Samson, Van Nelle, Drum, Javaanse Jongens. I've had you all and I savoured every single one of you, albeit without warnings such as *Smoking can kill*, *Smoking can lead to circulatory problems and causes impotence* or *Smoking causes considerable damage to you and the people around you*, which shine in a particularly glaring light now, in view of why I gave up smoking back then. My fingers trembling, I place the money, one euro ten cents, on the indulgence tray next to the till and disappear with the *Weser Courier*, not getting embroiled in the conversation that Mrs Grube (the herald of my damnation) attempts to begin.

Back at the house I make a cup of herbal tea, cut three slices of wholemeal bread while the water is boiling and scan the headlines, leaning against the table. *Thorny Issues Raised on Turkey Visit, Geißler against 'Take It or Leave It Policy'*, *New Accusations against Facebook*. I start one of the articles, the one about Christian Wulff, and from the third paragraph on I notice myself waiting for the first opportunity to stop reading because I still can't imagine Wulff as German president. Driven by my own impatience, I flick through the pages, simultaneously grateful and disappointed not to have to read any more about myself. I redeemed all the hopes congregation members had expressed of their new pastor in the newspaper in only three Sundays—and squandered them again on a single one. I spoke to them, not from the pulpit, shielded by God's radiant tetragrammaton, but on an equal level. I talked not about the past, but about the future. I let the children come forward and I blessed them. I joined the ranks of the choir and sang every hymn from the gallery in my angelic castrato. I celebrated Holy Communion with them, and all of them, their hands folded, their mouths wide, were ready to take the body and the blood of Christ into them and believe in a new beginning, when, in the midst of this blessed atmosphere, my mobile phone began to ring. I reached under my cassock into my pocket and hung up on the caller (my father). I apologized, red with shame, to the congregation, yet the moment was destroyed. Some stood up from their pews and left the church without receiving the sacrament. Others, however, joined me in singing 'In the Name of God I Shall Begin What Is My Due', as a sign of reconciliation. And when I said goodbye to those who had stayed, outside the church door, they assured me it could happen to anyone (in other words, that I too was not infallible).

I pour the water in my teacup and start a nerve-jangling search for the accursed mobile phone, sullying my morning purity—that state of absolutely no wishes or desires. I pull my trousers out of the washing machine and go through the pockets, I throw back blankets and bedspreads, push aside magazines—*Auto Motor Sport*, *Beetle Review*, *Vintage Cars*—and in the end call myself from the landline. I walk all around the house with the cordless telephone and listen out for the ring tone (the first bars of Beethoven's Fifth Symphony). In the bedroom—nothing, in the living room—nothing, in the bathroom—nothing. I go over to the parsonage without a jacket and initiate the same procedure in the office, with the same result. And where do I find it? In the church on the altar, switched to *Meeting*, my meeting with God.

After breakfast I go through the week's schedule. Prepare confirmation lessons for Tuesday and Thursday afternoon—What were Luther's theses directed against and what significance did they have for church history? A boy has been coming to kindergarten absolutely filthy for days—Tuesday evening, gain insight into family situation. Write sermon for service—Philippians 1, Verses 3–11, *Thanks and intercession to the congregation*. There are two baptisms lined up for next Sunday—Wednesday evening, visit children to be baptized and their parents. No senior parishioners' birthdays. No deaths, no funerals. No pastoral emergencies—not yet. Instead, the deacon turns up, Malte Snores, sorry, Schnaars. We'd vaguely arranged to meet although he'd claimed only yesterday that the pastor's Sunday, as he calls my Monday, was sacred to him and he didn't want to disturb me with his matters. But his matters are my matters too. The deaconry is looking for new qualified staff for its home care services, and he asked me to look through the applications with him. He's just as new as I am and doesn't want to put a foot wrong, seeing as he's had little practical experience so far. He seems to have great respect for me because he calls me Pastor and prefaces every question with 'I wanted to ask you,' which tempts me to put my hand on his thigh to calm him down. But I'm sitting too far away to do that (the desk is between us). Two hours later—we decided, on my advice, to invite three men for interviews—he leans over to me and says, 'I wanted to ask you where you come from, Pastor.' He's from Ritterhude and studied Social Education in Bremen. There, he apparently developed not only a burning interest in other people's personal lives but also a poor memory, because he's asked me the same question before.

'Jericho.'

'Not *the* Jericho?' he asks with a wink (*nihil novi sub sole*).

'No,' I say with a straight face, 'the one in East Frisia,' although that's not strictly true, but it's closest to the place I mean—a place that doesn't exist and perhaps never existed, except in my imagination. The real Jericho looks different. When I visit my parents, which is a rare occurrence nowadays, thank God, I arrive in a village that seems to consist entirely of Compunists' Corner. As soon as I turn off the B70 a sign instructs me not to drive more than thirty kilometres per hour. I've barely cut my speed before I'm bumping over the first of twenty-three speed bumps. Twenty-three speed bumps on the way, twenty-three speed bumps on the way back. Every one of them deals a blow to my crew cab, so that I feel a second's weightlessness, the joy of floating on air, before I hit my head on the roof and fall back onto my seat.

Where cows grazed twenty years ago there are now houses. Children bounce on netted-in trampolines as if trying to imitate me in my car, men trim lawns and hedges with noisy machines so as to encourage the neighbours to do the same, and women plant seeds and bulbs, their arms inserted into plastic gloves up to their elbows. One garden borders on the next, one traffic-calmed road branches into the next, Poets' Corner into Actors' Corner, the Bird Estate into the Tree Estate, the Tribe Colony into the Island Colony. Like a cancer, they grow from all directions towards the old village and cut off its air. The Reformed Church still towers above it all, but the sound of the bells now competes with the banging and scraping of the concrete works out in the hammrich. Of the farmhouses in which Jericho's founders and their descendants lived, three generations under one roof, not a single one has been left standing since the marksmen's club fair, after the devastating fire that year. The Friesenhuus—demolished, Schulz's forge—demolished, the dairy—demolished, Schröder's Shoes, Tinnemeyer Upholstery, Oltmanns' Cycles—demolished, demolished, demolished. In their place there are uniform purpose-built structures housing ALDI, LIDL, KIK and EDEKA (including a post-office counter). Klaus Neemann sold his last supermarket, the headquarters, to a company called BEVPET—Beverages & Pets. Günter Vehndel expanded his betting business and replaced the clothes shop with a slot-machine hall. And even Bernhard Kuper abandoned his fight against the world and rented the drugstore out to Schlecker. You see them again now, the Necessary Three, slamming cards on the table in the Beach Hotel and debating football, their faces glowing with beer and schnapps.

Malte Schnaars has meanwhile got up to admire my library, which ranges from Aristotle to Zwingli, three thousand books that occupy almost the entire back wall of the room on their shelves. At the very bottom are ring binders (*in alphabetical order*) with material on Stephanie Beckmann, Onno Kolthoff, Bernhard, Birgit and Daniel Kuper, Rainer Pfeiffer, Simone Reents, Stefan Reichert and Johann, Michael and Wiebke Rosing.

I look at my mobile phone—almost ten. 'Is there anything else we need to talk about?' And before he can ask me another question, for example whether I've read all the books and what the names on the binders refer to, I get up, put my hand on his back and accompany him to the door.

Next I drive over to Farmer Kück. My treasures are stored in his thatched timber-framed barn behind the old mill, treasures that I intend to take to my grave, should that time ever come (build me a seven-door pyramid-shaped garage and put me in a car boot, sheathed in asbestos against purgatorial fire and brimstone)—a white Mercedes 280 SE W 116, 1979 model, 185 PS, 136 kW, with double-wishbone front-wheel suspension, mechanical fuel-injection system, solid wood panelling, chrome-plated metal applications, central locking, air-conditioning; a red Opel Commodore GS/E, 1970 model, 150 PS, 110 kW, electronic fuel injection, dual exhaust, halogen high-beam lamps, vinyl roof; a grey Borgward P 100, 1960 model, 100 PS, 75 kW, ponton bodywork, air suspension, straight-6 engine, crossbar between sills and transmission tunnel, independent suspension on trapezoid wishbones; a yellow Porsche 911 2.4 S, 1971 model, 190 PS, 140 kW, five-speed manual transmission, six-cylinder boxer engine with dry-sump lubrication; an orange Ford Capri RS 2600, 1969 model, 150 PS, 110 kW, bucket seats with wide wale-cord covers, key steering wheel, Weslake V6 engine, central camshaft with spur gears, magnesium Minilite wheels; a marine blue and cream flatbed pickup with a double cab (hence the crew cab), VW T1, 1962 model, 39 PS, 31 kW, divided windscreen, leather seats, two-spoke steering wheel, load bed folds down on three sides; and the remains of a VW T2 fire engine, 1975 model, 68 PS, 50 kW, which I bought ten days ago on Ebay for one thousand, five hundred and thirty-four euros and twenty-five cents and collected from Ibbenbüren. Contrary to the description, the bodywork and engine weren't in working order, which I only noticed on the A1 motorway when there was a bang near the Holdorf junction and the con rods came out through their casing. Now I'm in the process of taking it apart bit by bit and putting it back together.

Old Kück comes out of his house to give me a hand as soon as I drive into the yard. Since he gave up livestock and agriculture and started renting out his stables and barns (to people like me), he's been offering his services to anyone and everyone. He knows a bit about cars, more than most people who claim to know a bit about cars. He doesn't know the fine details, the specific features of every single model, but he does know what to do if I tell him, and he can deal with anything as long as he needs no more than a screwdriver, a 13 mm spanner and a pair of pliers to repair it.

After the two of us have filed off the welding seams with an axle grinder and smoothed them over with filler, we sit on two dismounted driver's seats and drink water and beer. He offered me a Beck's too but I turned it down with the true excuse that I had to drive, although it's the first time in years that I haven't felt like drinking. I only bought the red nag so I can leave my best horses in the stable over winter, and now I have to wait until it has new shoes, which, as I've asked an expert friend (one of the hundred and forty-one) from Verden to do the smithing, may take until mid-December.

Kück spits on the floor as if he had to cleanse his mouth before making an admission. 'You're the first pastor I'd go back to church for.'

'You shouldn't go to church for my sake,' I say, 'only for your own.'

'I didn't say I was going to do it, not for me, not for you and not for God's sake either.'

Next Sunday, I'm sure of it, he'll be sitting in the back pew.

In the afternoon I go for a walk in Devil's Moor. The wind has dropped off and the clouds have cleared. On my arrival four weeks ago, I'd anticipated dense, dark woods and black, moist earth and not kilometres of flat, open land as I was familiar with from the hammrich (even that no longer exists in Jericho; another industrial estate has grown up around the concrete works, with fields and hedges making way for warehouses and roads). Long paths lined by ditches, a sluggishly flowing river, few, already almost entirely defoliated trees, rustling reeds. Ants crawl over stones and feet, geese flap chattering through the sky, cows graze in the meadows, horses stand neighing at gates, farmers spray slurry on the fields. On a side path, I lie on my back on the grass and close my eyes. I hear cyclists and walkers passing me, hear them whispering to one another, that's the new pastor lying there like a dead man, like a man struck down, only to continue on their way, strengthened by that realization. A dog sniffs at my hair; I feel its tongue licking my pate, bald not for religious reasons, and then he too has gone, enticed by new, more interesting smells, and thus, crawled upon, chattered over, licked across, I fall asleep. When I wake and look around I'm alone. Not a soul far and wide. Only me and nature (καὶ εἶδον οὐρανὸν καινὸν καὶ γῆν καινήν). The sight reminds me of how I began to doubt in Christianity during my final year at school, prompted by reading *Siddhartha*, and turned to Buddhism and Hinduism, read Lao-tze and the Upanishads and saw all plants as thinking, suffering beings equal to the peak of creation (which further radicalized my already radical diet), until I came across Alanus ab Insulis at university, whose theory that a divine force inhabits everything and reflects back onto ourselves reconciled me with my faith (*Who never ate his bread with tears*). Shortly before my first theological exam I hit another stumbling block when I spent two semesters working through Giordano Bruno's universal substance, the foundation of all forms, the untransformable—and the infinity of the universe. Perhaps I'd still be stumbling if he had written more and the Catholic Church hadn't burnt him and his work.

Instead of warming myself on this memory, I feel the cold drawing in beneath me. I pat blades of grass from my trousers and complete my circle by passing my car and calling in at Café New-Helgoland. On the terrace on the north-western side of the building, all the tables are occupied. The guests, most of them elderly, greet me with friendly waves. One of them whistles the first bars of Beethoven's Fifth Symphony. A young man with long hair and paint splashes is sitting at one table, flicking through a catalogue with his legs crossed and raising a cigarette and a Moor Beer to his lips by turn. There's a box of JPS on the table with a lighter on top. I ask whether the seat next to him is taken and he gestures to me to take my place by his side, not saying a word. I order a cup of East Frisian tea (*Draußen nur Kännchen*). For a while we gaze silently at the midges dancing in the sun's glare. Then he puts his catalogue aside and says, 'So you're the pastor.'

And I answer, 'So you're the artist,' as though there were only one in this village. After that our conversation instantly becomes halting again, prompting me to add the not-terribly-original question, for lack of alternative ideas, of what brings him here (but sometimes the dumbest questions lead to the most interesting conversations).

'Coincidence.'

'What coincidence?'

'One day before the deadline, I ran into an old friend from Aachen in Hamburg, who had a residency here once, so I sent my portfolio and they chose me. And now I'm here, in the back of beyond. And you, Pastor?'

'A pastorate. I even converted for it, from Reformed Church to Lutheranism.'

'That's a bigger sacrifice than mine.'

'Not if you knew what I gave up for it. If I was allowed to, I'd preach my own faith.'

'And that is?'

'A proto-Christian faith, despite all the contradictions resulting from the strict interpretation of the Bible, one that includes all later forms of the faith, a difficult undertaking when they're based on such a complex, ambiguous text and the resulting entanglements. Interestingly enough, by the way, the two most opposing Christian confessions, Catholicism and Calvinism, are united on one point— in denying coincidence, what you say brought you here, and in understanding everything that happens as divine providence. And although I don't feel a hundred per cent in accordance with either of them, I do agree with them both on that matter.'

'Can I tell you a story?'

'You won't convince me of the opposite.'

'Do you know Cees Nooteboom?'

'*All Souls' Day.*'

'My father was an odd fellow, a man who hugged trees in the woods and that kind of thing. The girls loved it in those days, in the late fifties. After he finished school he travelled alone to Turkey and Afghanistan and taught German at the royal court in Kabul, and he drove trucks all across India. An adventurer, a day-dreamer—with a talent for languages. He wanted to be a writer but then he studied German Literature in Berlin and moved in the same circles as Hans Magnus Enzensberger and Uwe Johnson— probably he just went to a couple of their readings or drank with them in bars and scratched his red beard, what do I know. It all happened before Fritz Teufel and Co. declared their flats were communes; by that time he was already a teacher in Lemgo. In any case, he translated Cees Nooteboom's first novel *Philip en de anderen* into German, not for a publisher, just for uni. It was a cult book back then, had a lot to do with freedom and travel, with girls, loneliness and being different. That's where I get the second part of my name from. The first part is from my great grandfather Jan Wachowiak—he was a policeman on duty at Celle Castle and was stabbed to death one day on his way home from work. My parents have old newspaper clippings about it, pictures of the trial. The murderer was executed on Hangman's Hill in Hanover. My father often told me about my roots but by the time I got to the age when you read books about the meaning of life, Nooteboom's first novel was out of print, and at home we had the Dutch original but my father couldn't find his translation. Then a friend and I went inter-railing halfway around Europe, and to Paris to see the Louvre, and on the way there I saw Nooteboom's *Philip and the Others* at Bielefeld Station and realized it was the book my father had told me about, and then I read it and the Philip in the book goes to Paris as well. He hitchhikes and I was on a train, but it was still pretty odd to be sitting on a train and reading the book that's responsible for my name. And then we got to Paris and I sat down at the top of the Île de la Cité and took the book out and read there, at the exact place where Philip is sitting at the top of the Île de la Cité as well. That was my literary epiphany. You can't get much more amazing for a mixture of reality and fiction.'

'Divine providence.'

'Wait, there's more, it gets better. When I got back home I wanted to tell my father right away, but as soon as I'd started, as soon as I mentioned Nooteboom, he told me he'd been hiking in the north of Norway while I was in Paris, and he's sitting on a hill and sees another person on the next hill, and they both wave at each other, and when they go down their hills and meet in the middle, my father recognized the person he was waving at.'

'Cees Nooteboom.'

'The two of them built a fire, talked and shared their last whisky. And a few years later my mother gave me a book, a collection of Nooteboom's travel writing, and in one piece he describes this meeting with a red-bearded Westphalian hiker.'

'There are hundreds of stories like that, that owe their fascination solely to the fact that the backstories are cut out, all the apparent chaos that surrounds us, the endless information that floods over us, the banality, the irrationality, the infinity of the universe—Αρμονίη αφανής φανερής κρείττων. Nooteboom and you necessarily belong together, we all do, we're all part of the whole, and sometimes the paths that lead us to one another are longer and sometimes they're shorter, and some are so short you can hardly believe it. A poet could never write such a thing without being criticized, but as soon as he says it really happened, it takes on a metaphysical dimension.'

'This really did happen.'

'That may well be, but you're concentrating your story on that outcome, and that's the only reason why what happened seems to you like a miracle. Had your father not read Nooteboom he wouldn't have recognized him, but they'd still have met. And had your father not translated Nooteboom it would have been simply a meeting of two old men. They'd have sat down and drunk together and then gone their separate ways without all the surprise. What about all the other everyday encounters? Aren't they just as significant, more significant even? What about us, for example? Why are we sitting here? And what results from it?'

But he doesn't pick up on that. Instead, he stares into the setting sun, puts out his cigarette and says he wasn't listening and was thinking about something else all along, 'If the Messiah was among us now, we wouldn't recognize him either, not even by his deeds.'

'We don't have to,' I say, swallowing my disappointment. 'Jesus is the Messiah and he died for us, for our sins, and since then he's been within us.'

'Then why do we have to keep eating his body?'

'To remind us of him, of his legacy.'

'I though Jesus was coming back before the world ends, to awaken the dead and take along the living to the kingdom of heaven?'

'Parousia. The date and the time is known to no one, though, not the angels in heaven, not the son, only the father.'

'And you believe that?'

'Don't you?'

'I believe I'm hungry.'

'Me too.'

'We can talk at the station.'

'The station?'

'Yes, in the restaurant.'

It's getting dark but there's still enough light to appreciate my car sufficiently. Now that he's standing upright next to me and surmounting me in height and width, he comes across like a long-haired Buddha, and he radiates that calm and composure, that inner smile that I'd ascribe to a reincarnation of Siddhartha Gautama, had I not returned to the Christian path. In the car, Jan-Philip runs his hands over every detail, and I let him.

When I walk into the old station behind him, blind through my misted-over glasses, the restaurant owner decides to treat us to green cabbage and sausages. He seats us at a large table where several other guests are waiting for their evening meal, and hands everyone a drink on the house (I take apple juice and exchange green cabbage and sausages for a tiny slice of vegetarian quiche).

Jan-Philip is sitting at one end of the table and I'm at the other, between us men and women who could be our parents if they'd had children young. They introduce themselves one after another, Georg and Antje, Helmut and Magda, and when I start to tell them who I am they wave it off and inform me they recognized me when I walked in the door and know perfectly well who I am; that gets around quickly in a village like this even if you don't go to church every Sunday. Each of them has a story to tell about me, things they've heard from congregation members or read in the newspaper. My reputation, Georg says, precedes me, and Helmut assures me he's only heard good things about me, and they talk about me, heap me with praise, as if I were the Messiah and not (which is more likely) a gay double-murderer.

After we've eaten, Antje asks the artist what he's working on.

'An installation for an exhibition in Syke. I've sawed letters out of fibreboard, painted them and added LEDs and these fairground caps.'

'What letters?'

'Mycobacterium vaccae.'

'What's that?'

'It's a bacteria found in cow dung. It was discovered a long time ago, but now scientists have injected mice with deadened mycobacteria and found out that it stimulated serotonin release in their brains.'

'Makes you happy,' says Magda, revealing herself to be a pharmacist.

'Anti-anxiety,' says Antje, not revealing how she knows that.

'Hey,' says Helmut, rising halfway off his chair, 'let's eat shit. We've got more than enough of it round here.'

'Exactly,' says Jan-Philip. 'We even breathe it in when the farmers fertilize their fields.'

'Oh, so that's why I'm so happy here,' I say after a long period of not commenting. 'And I thought it was down to the people.'

'And what do these . . . boards look like now?' asks Antje.

'Come and have a look,' says Jan-Philip. 'I'll show you.'

Once they've admired my car and described their most wonderful VW Beetle experiences at epic length, they march ahead of me in the dark, from the station to his studio in the artists' houses by the horse paddocks. My headlamps light up the way for them. Jan-Philip opens the door and invites us in. Several rooms lead off the hallway, a bedroom, a kitchen, a bathroom, but he takes us into a large, bare space containing a workbench, a black leather sofa, a bookshelf and, leaning against the wall, the negatives of the letters he told us about.

'And where are they now?' asks Magda, pointing at the holes in the wood.

'Out there,' says Jan-Philip and indicates out of the window.

We turn to our reflections, and at that moment a light above us switches off and another one in front of us goes on. Red, yellow and green flashing light, floating far above the field, illuminates the night, and we press our faces up against the glass like children, and I'm suddenly a child, filled with bliss by this anagogical, meditative-ecstatic view of letters lit up in series *my ca co ca bac acc ter va ium vaccae coba ca va myco ae bact cc erium va my acterium m baba reibt y curie vibrato cemiratromb bart maiba umc beute ett beirut america rumtriebi verbot myria mumaborte erotic v microtumor eamiet barcabaretc vorbau beac victor came raabe ta arbeitet abuembry o beirat beauty beatrice vorbeit rauma trieb roycet rabieiterbertae acca vmiret rabbit cabcymatari- obaca braum eat my bra rabiat mumie taube amateur ebortereimtamber orb it bravo auto bete armut autor ramboy come ertor eier aorta turbocter*

comicum vaamouribm votum merci reto boetore eurotreu actarammaorira
be a bromo rt mao city may a atom mama art yeti cae creme cobra boterio
army bavaria amoeb e meteor reite trabe aroma car a m ba va cobacteri
mycoba um vaccae.

'Is it always the same order?' asks Antje.

'No, it works through a random number generator—it's coincidence.' Jan-Philip pauses as if expecting an objection from me, that God is at play here too, and steps closer to me. 'I have no influence over it.'

What a day—first I meet a real artist in this artists' village, then the spiritual takes shape through him and transfigures itself into the coloured light of a superhuman, supernatural creative power, which shows itself not only in the purity of the sky, in the shimmer of the sun, but also in the mud of the earth, in the faeces of cows. *Deus in minimis maximus.* Oh, sweet theophany! I feel rejuvenated by years, sense Philip next to me, his breath, his warmth, his hand on my shoulder—and a vibration in my trousers.

I take out my phone in the hallway. My father's name on the display. The first thing that flashes into my mind is d e a t h, because whenever he makes repeated attempts to call me he has news of a death to impart, of Didi Schulz and Uli Dettmers, Enno and Gerda Kröger or, just recently, of Hans Meinders, my mentor. I answer and he hands the receiver to my mother after pointing out how hard I am to get hold of.

'Arne and I,' she says, 'have decided to move to War's-inxed-fun after all.' That's a joke. The place is called Warsingsfehn, twenty kilometres away from Jericho, and Arne, my father, has been head of the local high school for a few years. 'We've bought a house there, smaller than this one, two bedrooms.' She pauses to let the size sink in. 'And you're all independent now. You hardly ever come to visit anyway and we don't need as much space just for the two of us.'

'What are you trying to say, Petra?'

'That you'll have to clear out your room.'

'By when?'

'By Sunday.'

'This Sunday?'

'We have to move out on Monday.'

'And why are you only telling me this now?'

'We kept trying to call you but you always hung up on us.'

Once I've hung up on her again, albeit not without saying goodbye first, I say goodbye to the others because tomorrow's the only day this week when I can go to Jericho without postponing any appointments. Instead of leaving with me, which would have allowed me to find an excuse to go back to Jan-Philip, the others try to persuade me to stay by telling me the night is young, etc. But I haven't got time to wait until they've all gone. I have to go over to Kück's farm and swap the Beetle for the pickup so I'll have enough space for furniture and boxes, and leave early tomorrow morning so that I'm back in the afternoon in time for communion class.

At home, I go online again. I have three Facebook friend requests from my new friends, Jan-Philip Scheibe, Helmut Meyer and Antje Brinkmann, all of which I confirm, and Simone Rosing has updated her status, *poo, joris just did a poo*. Carried away by the moment, I click *Like*.

Jericho. I speed through the thirty-kilometres-per-hour zone, my head and behind polished by twenty-three speed bumps, accelerate to eighty over the last few metres, brake abruptly and come to a standstill with smoking tyres at nine in the morning on Mozart

Road, eyed by the neighbours ('And he's supposed to be a pastor?' etc.). The drive is blocked by a skip, into which Arne is just heaving his worn office chair. I take the laptop off the passenger seat. With an elegant twist, I swing myself out of the car, slam the door so loudly that the net curtains behind the closed windows all around start twitching, and greet my father with a handshake, as befits a son with an unorthodox but polite upbringing. The two of us go inside the house. The hallway has been cleared already, the living room is piled up with boxes and a bumping noise comes from upstairs.

'Most of it's gone already,' says Arne. 'Petra and Venja are just taking a load to the dump but they'll be back any minute. We waited for you to have breakfast. The kitchen and bathroom are the only rooms still usable—and your room, of course.'

'Did it have to be now?'

'Well, you know,' he says, inserting his thumbs behind the straps of his dungarees, 'it suddenly went very quickly, the house, the contract, all the loose ends tied up, we hadn't thought it would come through at all, but then it suddenly couldn't go fast enough for Kolthoff—he's got three children with that Mettjes girl now. Didn't she go to school with you?'

'I thought he was with Susanne Haak.'

'That was ages ago, they split up years ago now. Anyway, we wanted to use the autumn half-term holidays for the move because otherwise we'd have had to wait until Christmas. And you know how it is between Christmas and New Year. Try finding a removal company then. And that would have been much too much stress for you too, with all the religious holidays.'

'Does that still work?' I ask, pointing at the cables and boxes on the floor where the telephone table used to be.

'Of course. Everything still works here.'

'Good, I have to go on the net.'

'Who've you got down there?' I hear Verena calling from downstairs.

'Your brother,' says Arne.

And as soon as she hears that she's on the stairs, down in the hallway, in my arms. Her pearl earring tickles my cheek. We haven't seen each other for months. She sends me an email every couple of weeks or calls me, crying, at the end of her tether, looking for consolation when things aren't going the way she imagined in her relationship or at the office (what she wants never matches up with reality; everything always has to be perfect and bigger and better, etc.). I hardly get a word in edgewise and when I do say something she feels I've misunderstood her. 'What's that supposed to mean? I don't give a shit about God.'

'I wasn't talking explicitly about God, I just think you should talk to someone neutral.'

She accuses her sister of being our parents' favourite as a child, and me of having begrudged her everything. Officially, she's training as a German and History teacher in Munich, but apart from our parents everyone in the family knows she hasn't set foot in the university for years (she's not even registered as a student there) and ekes out a living with short, not very lucrative PR jobs in the music industry; she has a husband (Lothar, forty-seven, a lawyer and member of the Bavarian conservative party), two step-daughters, lost a lot of money on shares and holds various dubious views, which she tries to suppress when she comes home to avoid arguments, although that rarely works because she feels provoked by Arne's mere presence. 'They practically gave away the house,' she whispers to me, loudly enough for Arne to hear it, and releases herself from our hug.

'We're glad to be rid of it at last.'

'A hundred thousand! Lothar says you could easily have asked twice that. You have to think of your future, you're no spring chickens now, and a house like this is practically your pension plan.'

'You mean your pension plan.'

'I don't need your money.'

'Well, if that's the case I can cancel that direct debit.'

'You're still giving her money?' I ask.

'Until she graduates—like all of you.'

Verena gives me the evil eye to remind me of our deal not to give away our secrets in front of our parents, and that if I don't stick to it she won't hesitate to reveal mine to them (she only knows one of them).

'How old are you now?' I ask her, 'thirty-two?'

'Thirty-one.'

'And when are your final exams again?'

'Just so you know, I'm entitled to the money.'

'Why?'

'As compensation.'

'What for?'

'For Venja and you.'

'You've got a real competition problem, Verena!'

(Αἱ γυναῖκες υμῶν εν ταὶς εκκλησίαις σιγάτωσαν–curses and execrations I consider it inappropriate to utter as a man of God.) Once she's calmed down again she makes an obvious effort to enter my cosmos and make herself understood, saying that it's easy for me to talk, the first-born and the last-born are always sufficiently appreciated in the Bible, whereas the ones in between 'play practically no role at all,' at most getting punished and dying

843

early deaths, etc. pp. I repeat my diagnosis and she renews her curses and threats, until Petra and Venja come in the front door.

'Oh boy,' says Petra, 'what's going on here?' and launches herself at me. 'How lovely to see you.'

Although I evade her puckered lips through a skilful turn of my head (thanks to my muscular neck), she manages to plant '*een Ballerduutje*', as she calls it, on my cheek. Since moving to Jericho twenty-seven years ago, she's tried to veil her existence as a non–East Frisian through an exaggeratedly complete adoption of Low German dialect. Venja, on the other hand, I hug long and sincerely. Her dreadlocks smell like hay and when I stroke her back I notice she's got fatter since we last met (three months ago for Petra's sixtieth birthday) and still isn't wearing a bra. She's the shortest and youngest and fastest of us all. She completed her degree (Social Management) in Emden in six semesters and has worked in a project supporting adults with learning disabilities ever since. Money and faith aren't important to her but she doesn't get much fun out of her job any more, too many clients and too few staff to support them, and she split up from her boyfriend this summer when she caught him in bed with her best friend (she aborted his baby, that's her secret). So she wants to make the most of her newfound freedom and use her talents in another area (environmental protection). With Arne and Petra and some eco-activists from ReSist who she met on the Internet, she's going to go to Gorleben in November and chain herself to the railway lines to block the nuclear waste transport, and in December she wants to fly to Cancún with another group, Plant for the Planet, to plant a hundred and forty-nine ceiba saplings outside the conference hotel, one for every state taking part in the UN climate conference. Arne and Petra welcome their daughter's determination, although they're sceptical about the flight to Mexico (too dangerous and too far away). Verena didn't even try to talk her out of the plan, being convinced that everyone has to go through things of their own accord and it's therefore pointless to give anyone advice (I don't ask her why she keeps calling me, if that's that case). I haven't actually signed any of the petitions to which Venja has called my attention in multi-recipient emails over the past years, but I do support her in her fight for a better world, especially because she's the only one of the three of us who's declared herself willing to bring as many children as possible into said world, once she finds the right man—despite all her traumatic experiences and apocalyptic rhetoric.

'My room's empty,' she says. 'Verena's taken the valuable stuff to sell off on Ebay.'

'The autographed Michael Jackson CD,' says Verena, 'is worth at least three hundred euros.'

'You should know.'

'He should have died twenty years earlier, then we'd have made more money out of his death than out of his life.'

'Who's we?'

'Sony and me.'

'But there are still a couple of books that might interest you,' says Venja.

'You can have them, they're not first editions.'

'I can take a look at them.'

'But not until after breakfast,' says Petra and walks past us into the kitchen. 'I need a coffee and something to eat. I'm starving to death.' We follow her and sit down at the laid table, each of us in his or her place, the last time before the positions are rearranged in the new kitchen. As usual, we all talk at the same time, about the house, money, the climate, and as usual we end up arguing. At some point, in a moment of calm, Arne stands up, takes a piece of paper from the dresser and hands it to me. 'Look, I found this today.'

'What is it?'

'A betting slip.'

I take the crumpled piece of paper, transparent with grease stains, and unfold the following prophecy:

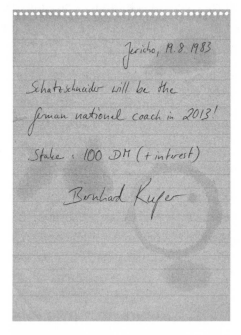

'And yesterday,' says Arne, 'I took it over and showed it to him. And do you know what he said? The thirty years aren't up yet.'

After breakfast I go upstairs, my laptop and two folded removal boxes jammed under my arms, to my room, to the museum of my childhood, and face into an abyss (figuratively speaking). It's been gathering dust on the shelves for years—Viking models ordered by their real-life manufacturers, most of them HO scale, a complete replica of the cars of Jericho between 1983 and 1991, the books of my youth (for example, Hermann Hesse's complete works), several volumes from the Protestant Book Mission (including *All We Want Is Your Soul—Rock Scene and Occultism: Data, Facts, zackground*), historical encyclopedias, school textbooks, ring binders full of notes, photo albums—all of it producing an absolutely false image of my past. On the desk is a diary from 1995, the year I finally moved out of the parental home. Above the bed, stuck to the sloping ceiling, are posters of local bands that have long since split up (Deichwart, Kill Mister, Paranoia Park). The other half of the room is occupied by a wardrobe full of trousers, sweaters and T-shirts now far too big for me. I've arrived but I haven't yet reached my goal. I don't know where to start (αϱχὴ ἥμισυ παντός), and as so often when I want to begin something disagreeable, I go online again first. Jan-Philip informs me (and all his other friends) via Facebook that he's uploaded a video of his work to YouTube: http://www. youtube.com/watch?v=5SlNy5cAzo0. The sight sends a rush of blood to my head. I suddenly feel his hand on my shoulder again and his hot breath on the back of my neck. I'm tempted to send him a message, to pour my heart out to him, but I close my laptop before I'm overcome by this sentimental daze.

I unfold the two cardboard boxes, set them up side by side and begin to separate the important from the unimportant. I sit down on the bed and open the top drawer of the bedside table—pencil drawings of people and animals, rock-hard modelling clay figures, ink-stained school books, sticky pages covered in sticky poems (the lyrical you was always D.)—all artefacts of my submerged ego—a packet of condoms (very possibly from Kuper's), cigarettes so dry they crumble in my hand, a Swatch with a dead battery, love letters never sent and, at the very bottom, a photo of a boy with a bare chest, my desire, my demise: Daniel Kuper.

From the very first moment I saw him I knew we belonged together. The way he sat there in front of me, alone at a desk, his legs tucked behind the legs of his chair, his head propped on his hands, with that expression of absolute boredom and composure. Mrs Wolters introduced me to the class but no one listened, not even I did. While she reeled off my not-yet-very-complex biography in as much detail as possible, I couldn't take my eyes off him. My entire thinking concentrated on the empty seat next to him. I hoped she'd put me there and that's what she did, although there were several other free places on the margins of my perception.

I wasn't left-handed from birth; I became left-handed for my own sake. Whenever he wrote something in his book, on the pre-ruled lines, a stroke, a curve, a dot, I tried to be as close as possible to his arm, and the only way to do so without raising suspicion was to lean halfway over the desk, curve my hand around my fountain pen and push the tip across the page while his right elbow was claiming the space occupied by my left elbow. From his point of view, naturally, I was always getting in his way, and less than three hours later he suggested we change places, which I, just as naturally, rejected with the remark 'I can't sit by the window, there's a draught.' We came to an arrangement. I curbed my desire, he his rage.

The only time I could watch him undisturbed was when he prayed before class, which everyone did apart from me. I hadn't yet been baptized and Mrs Wolters had left it up to me to take part in the morning ritual or not. And so, for a minute at the beginning of every school day, I looked at him from the side, in profile, watched him moving his lips, his eyelids twitching at every word he breathed, his hands containing one another, and I joined in the prayer with open eyes and asked God to make sure that his hands might one day contain mine like that.

At break times I stayed out of the way. He was surrounded by boys, normal boys, and I felt there was no place in their midst for me, at most when they needed someone to punch, because they looked over at me every few minutes and then broke out in peals of laughter. I'd hear my name in conjunction with a not-terribly-original metaphor from the field of mathematical measurements—sack, barrel, ton—and other, more ribald references to my weight—flab-face, fatty, greedy pig. But nothing they said ever hurt me. And even those incidents revealed the quality that later distinguished Daniel—he didn't join in.

Sports lessons were a problem. The teacher demanded physical contact in team games (unlike in other lessons, where we weren't even supposed to put our heads together). He told everyone, even the girls, to go more into tackles, and if necessary to put our whole bodies into them and bring our opponent to the ground. Some of my fellow pupils, particularly those whose only evidence of brain activity in all other lessons was stupid comments, soon became astoundingly ambitious in this regard (*beati pauperes spiritu*). And I too discovered the advantages of my size and knew how to use it. No one storming towards the goal ever got past me. I stood in their way and let them bounce off me like a rubber ball against a wall. The only one I received with open arms was Daniel.

How I'd have liked to shower with him afterwards, just the two of us. But how was I to hide my affection for him there, even under more positive, intimate conditions, in the thrill of our nakedness? My body was in my way, in all respects. I had no control over its needs. It acted without my involvement. Looking at Daniel, touching him, was a reflex. At that time I didn't know what it was that drew me to him. All I knew, out of instinct, was that he didn't feel what I felt, and I had to learn to keep my distance so that he didn't move away from me. Yet no matter how hard I tried to be invisible and soundless, that was exactly what he did. If I didn't move towards him he wouldn't move towards me. If I said nothing he said nothing. And so I abandoned my plan, three days after I'd come up with it, dialled his number in desperation or circled the drugstore on my bike like a moth around a light, in the hope of at least catching a glimpse of his face at the window. He never called me back when I wanted to meet up with him after school and his father or mother picked up the phone, and he got them to say he wasn't home when I paid spontaneous visits. But that didn't scare me off. And I was almost grateful to him when I knelt before him in his garden sand pit, spade in hand, and he hit me on the head with a hammer. At last there was a connection between us.

It was he who sparked my passion for cars. The plastic tank, the Leopard that his parents made him give me on my sickbed, in the ridiculous assumption that it might undo what had happened, is now the dearest item in my collection. Like it once was in his room, it is on the very top of my shelves, above all the other exhibits of my life. Though its market value may not be particularly high, for me it's irreplaceable. It's the only tangible thing left of him for me.

We played together like children, positioned figures in front of shoe-box forts and castles and acted out simple conflicts through them, whereby our proxies were immortal, falling down and getting up again as soon as we needed them. Sometimes I'd let him win just to see how happy it made him to have beaten me, and sometimes he'd let me win, to salve his conscience with regard to the plaster on my forehead. That hammer hurt him more than me. The more time we spent together, the braver I got. As if by coincidence, I'd stroke his hand as he repositioned his troops and I happened to be hiding mine behind the same rebel-basis bedpost at the very same time; as if thoughtlessly, my soldiers would move towards his from the most remote post, armed only with their bare fists, and only admitted defeat once he'd sufficiently tickled them with a bayonet in close combat; and as if pointlessly, they'd say with their dying breath that they couldn't get enough of it. I'd provoke him until there was nothing he could do but launch himself at me and silence me, his knees on my arms, my head jammed between his thighs; and once, on that hot summer day when his father first beat him, I came to him dressed only in a pair of red towelling underpants so as to encourage him to cycle to the lake or the sea with me, equally scantily clad, so that I could drag him into a meadow along the way where we'd be undisturbed. My heart quaked, my skin shone (the treacherous poison of transpiration), I had dabbed talcum powder under my arms. The plan almost succeeded, albeit differently than expected, but the excitement at the thought of being discovered by him on the flat roof, the best hiding place in all of Jericho, had made my blood surge so fiercely that the window slipped out of my sweat-lubricated fingers and shattered. When his father appeared in the doorway with a wooden clothes hanger to chastise Daniel, I was willing to sacrifice myself for him. There I stood, bent over, my backside outstretched, my hand on my pants, but his father wouldn't allow it. And so a new wound sealed our friendship.

Then came the snow and with it the cold. I visited him in hospital, shook his hand to say hello, felt the tubes in his arm and sat down, as though it were the most natural thing in the world, on his bed. Gravity drew him towards me. He was too weak to resist and too confused to say anything other than what he kept repeating— *iron, lock, sign, bike, field, clearing, maize*. None of it made sense, he was severely traumatized—by whatever had happened—with far-too-low blood sugar, and he ate too little meat as well, and I had resolved to take better care of him than his mother. I picked up my bag from the floor, tipped it upside down, unzipped it and let dozens of chocolate bars and mini salamis rain down on the sheet. His Eve had looted the tree of knowledge and there was no snake in sight (it was twitching in its den). What troubled our paradise was the self-proclaimed gods who watched over us—his parents—chiding me for my therapy and insisting I put it all away again and take it with me. As compensation, I stuffed a Mars bar in my mouth in the corridor.

From then on Daniel was the crazy kid. Everyone claimed he claimed to have been abducted by aliens and set down again in the maize field. In fact he was incapable of speaking about what had actually happened. Even a faith healer like Bernd Reichert couldn't change that, in his long, expensive sessions. Daniel repeatedly asserted that it hadn't been the way they presented it in the newspaper, but how it had been he couldn't say. I was the only one who believed him without the slightest doubt. But if I thought my trust would be an advantage to me, I'd thought wrong. I don't know whether he secretly reproached me for not coming with him that day (who would have turned down the offer of being driven in his father's car through the wind and snow?). All I know is that whenever the subject came up, at school, on the way home, at the cinema, he'd look at me with his dark, sad eyes—as though I were from another planet and simply unaware of being different.

It took me weeks to get back in his good books. I tutored him (officially, not in love, but in English and Biology, World and Environmental Studies, German and Mathematics—we repeated what he'd missed in his absence). His mother was grateful that her son had some company, his father that he didn't have to pay a penny for the extra teaching, Daniel not to fall behind at school, and I was grateful for the time spent with him. Everyone was happy. Once I brought along a biology textbook I'd stolen from my parents' shelves, and explained that Mr Kamps had hinted he'd ask questions from it in his next test, although it was material for Year Seven or Eight.

'What kind of questions?'

'On human anatomy.'

Daniel stared at me uncomprehendingly.

'Where which bodily organs are and what function they have.' Once he'd read the chapter I said, 'If you've got any questions, go ahead and ask.'

'I haven't, though.'

'Mr Kamps said he might bring the dummy.' The dummy was a model of a human with removable body parts to allow us to look inside.

'What for?'

'So we can show him the organs—from the outside. He said we have to be able to feel them through the skin, in case, well, in case one of us has another accident and someone else has to perform first aid on them. Kiss of life, heart massage and all that.'

'Why another accident? Who's had an accident?'

'You. In the maize field.'

'It wasn't an accident.'

'I know.'

'And he said that?'

I nodded like a boy insane, full of joyful anticipation at putting my lips on his, breathing into him, massaging his heart and running my hands from there over his lungs, liver, stomach, intestines and down and down. 'We did it in class. On each other.'

'Who did you—'

'Simone.' I rolled my eyes.

Daniel pulled a face.

'Yeah, it was pretty pointless. You can see all her organs through her skin.'

'You can't see yours.'

'I'm a real challenge, that's what I am.'

'OK,' he said, 'let's get it over with.'

He was cautious enough to close his bedroom door—a thought that would never have occurred to me. 'I don't want those annoying twins coming in. You never know what idea they might get.'

'Like what?'

'The wrong idea.' We took off our sweaters and vests but when he saw me peeling my jeans down my thighs he paused. 'Them too?'

I nodded again but he looked at me unwaveringly as if still expecting an answer, and then I remembered that my nodding was often not recognizable as such due to my lack of neck, looking more like a tremble as though I had Parkinson's disease. 'We have to.'

'There aren't any vital organs down there.'

'You have no idea.'

His jeans slipped to the floor. 'And now?'

Now we were naked down to our underpants. I was wearing red ones again, but a larger size than on the roof three years previously, made of thinner fabric, the finest satin, which played about my thighs and which, although it was tight at the front, I barely felt at the back. His, in contrast, were cotton, printed with fire engines (nothing seemed more appropriate, seeing as he was to extinguish my fire).

'Lie down.'

Daniel did as he was told, leaning back obediently, even closing his eyes for a moment, although—and this marred my joy—he kept his hands folded in his lap like a football player in the wall, as if he sensed what I was aiming for. The sun fell on his milky-white, vein-marbled boyish body, displaying him in all his magnificence. Slim and small-boned and immaculate and well proportioned. His skin had no fluff, no spots, no bruises (at least not at the front), only freckles as if dabbed on by the creator (*similis simili gaudet*). I rubbed off the excited moisture from my hands on the bedcover and set about my task.

He opened his eyes with a start.

'Here,' I stroked his chest, 'is the heart,' my hand moved on, 'and here's the left lung, and here,' my other hand came to my aid, 'is the right one,' I circled his nipples with both thumbs as if that was part of the exercise, slid lower and lower, 'liver, stomach, spleen,' I no longer had the patience to deal with each organ separately, 'here,' I had reached his hips and pinched at his flesh, gasping and struggling for air, dizzy on the frenzy of my desire, 'are the kidneys,' I almost lowered myself onto him, so far had I embraced his delicate body shivering beneath my grip, 'and here, last but not least,' I raised myself up to look at him at the point when the touch of my fingers set his fire engines in motion. But it didn't come to that. As I lifted the edge of his underpants he rolled off the bed and jumped to his feet before I could finish my lesson.

'Your turn,' he said, absolutely tonelessly.

Submissively, I stretched myself out for him but his touches were without passion, more a tap with his fingertips, interrupted by constant sidelong glances at the textbook to reassure himself that he'd definitely found the right place (he hadn't). I wanted to teach him, take his hands and guide them, and I grabbed them, conducted them in a zigzag over the hill of my chest and down into the valley of my lust—

'Daniel?' Knocking, banging, giggling. 'What are you two doing in there? MA-MA,' a piercing, ear-splitting screech in stereo, 'they've locked themselves in.'

855

—and as he got dressed I sank back onto the pillows, exhausted by my unsuccessful arousal.

At the moment when our childish games promised to turn into more, I succumbed to a religious fervour due to that very rush of hormones. I strived for higher things, wanted suddenly to merge not with worldly matters but with the heavenly, and for lack of spiritual alternatives began to read the Bible, at first selectively, *The Creation*, *The Flood*, *The Ten Commandments*, *Daniel in the Lion's Den*, *Jonas and the Whale*, *Jesus' Nativity* and *Crucifixion* and *Resurrection*—stories I'd heard before, then the Old and the New Testament from front to back. I went to church every Sunday (not to the children's service, to the advanced one), I got baptized, joined the church youth club, sang in a Christian band and spent the summer holidays on group trips to the North Sea or the Baltic coast, where they swore us novices to chastity, sedentarism, poverty, daily repentance and obedience. The food was strictly rationed and didn't invite anyone to ask for second helpings. The days consisted of Bible lessons, talks and hikes—silent marches that served to clear our minds. During this time, I even took part in morning exercises and lost, in combination with my only remaining scourge, ten kilos in three weeks every time (which I'd put back on only ten days later). I was convinced it was my calling to lead a virtuous life and become a preacher, and that God demanded a sign from me so that he'd see how serious I was. I renounced our afternoons together on the flat roof, when we drank our first beer and smoked our first cigarettes huddled close together, and decided on intermediate school although we'd both been recommended for grammar school. My asceticism was supposed to cleanse me and sharpen my senses. It did the opposite, however. My fantasies grew dirtier and more pressing. Barely a day went by when I could concentrate on the teachings of the prophets, evangelists and apostles without reading Daniel into all their words.

A bruised reed shall Daniel not break.

Now there was leaning on Daniel's bosom one of his disciples, whom Daniel loved.

For many deceivers are entered into the world, who confess not that Daniel is come in the flesh.

A bruised reed!

Leaning on his bosom!

Come in the flesh!

I was going through my first severe crisis and the only way to find joy was to eat more than ever.

Daniel, meanwhile, was amusing himself with his new friends, Stefan, Onno and Rainer. My parents' house is strategically positioned on Mozart Road, in the middle of Compunists' Corner between Lortzing, Verdi and Bach. And my room back then was already a ten square-metre cell of tongue-and-groove wood panels, which looked even smaller due to the shelves along the wall for my model cars. But it had one key advantage over my sisters' rooms (which were at the back of the house)—from my desk, I would see Daniel several times a week, cycling or walking in all weathers, coming from one friend and heading for another, rushing past beneath my window. Then he'd look up at me briefly but couldn't see me through the net curtains (I had checked) as long as there was no light on, then lower his head and continue on his way, seemingly relieved. If he was—relieved—I certainly was. Only knowing that he was nearby made my self-imposed loneliness bearable. I knew all I had to do to speak to him was go outside, and sometimes I did that, always assuring it seemed as natural as possible. In the summer I'd mow the lawn; in autumn I'd sweep up leaves; in winter I'd shovel snow (thus convincing

Petra and Arne that anti-authoritarian parenting really did make children into better people). In spring of all times, the hardest season for me—everything stirring, budding, blossoming—I couldn't think of anything rational to do in the front garden, on the pavement or in the road without appearing to be lying in wait for him, and so confirmation lessons came at precisely the right moment. They brought together my two passions, although the long breaks between the spiritual exercises meant they didn't raise me to the same level of ecstasy and epiphany as playing doctors and nurses with Daniel or group trips to the sea. The communal prayer, the interpretation of the Holy Scripture, the smoking breaks outside the church were both consolation and pain. With every word he said, every gesture he made, I felt the vicinity and the distance between us. Those two years with Pastor Meinders were our examination, and we both passed it. He recognized that a defeat could also be a victory and that one person's triumph brought another person's sorrow in its wake, and I that there was rapture in renunciation and virtue in vice. By splitting apart, we released new forces. Despite that, I have to admit that I felt satisfaction when I—once again from my desk—watched Rainer, Onno and Stefan separate from him. At the beginning of their friendship they had all flowed in one direction and hadn't parted ways until late in the evening. By the end they ferried Daniel from one house to another in the afternoon because they didn't want to be alone with him, and as soon as they'd passed on responsibility to the next person they took to their heels.

I can see it all in absolute clarity now—each of them had a gift that Daniel found lacking in himself, but none of them was strong enough to bring it to fruition. At the time I didn't understand what he thought was so great about them. And it drove me crazy to listen to them and watch Daniel hanging on their every word when we met outside our house, coincidentally or deliberately. Stefan would be talking about serial interfaces as he passed, specialist software and the 'SE with its GPIB or CPU cards and the internal SCSI port'; Onno would show off his knowledge of music, 'S.O.D. were a thousand times better than M.O.D., Nuclear Assault and Anthrax put together, they really wasted their potential'; and Rainer would rave about an enchanted Vespa, '133 ccm Polini dual spark cylinder, 24 mm Dell'Orto carburettor, air filter and flow-optimized ETS long stroke flowed crankshaft for suction motors,' with which he would one day overtake his brother, so dramatically that the latter, the first-born, would never again match up to the former, the younger. They greeted me with guarded nods, never interrupting their monologues, as if they despised me, the teachers' kid, for having to perform lowly tasks such as gardening in that weather and at my size. My greatest objection to them, however, concerned their appearance. Their hair looked either dull or greasy, no matter whether they'd washed it or not; their skin was by turns pimply and bloody and scabbed from scratching; and their clothes consisted entirely of sneakers, jeans and black band T-shirts, which their mothers weren't allowed to wash under pain of hellish torment, because they didn't want the prints on them—skulls, zombies, gravestones, musclemen—to fade (which they all did nevertheless). Daniel possessed none of all that, and in their presence his extraordinary beauty and wise reticence were all the more obvious. That was the only recognizable advantage to this four-man gang, provided you had an eye for that kind of thing—and I do.

How often did I wish I could knock one after another of them out of the way and have him all to myself again. But when it did happen, when we were back at the same school together, I thought I had to prove to him that I could do without him. We did go to the cinema together as often as possible—dark hours in which my entire attention was focused on his hand on the armrest—but I spent most of the time with Paul and Jens. I'd introduced them to him as 'my new friends' on the very first day. And after only a few weeks I had fallen so prey to this illusion that I genuinely believed I was obliged to them. From then on I went along with everything. I watched their films. I went to their parties. I drank their beer. I smoked their joints. I listened to their music. I scattered their rubbish. I slept in their tents. I spoke their language. I exalted their idols. I demeaned their victims.

That's the one thing for which I can't forgive myself, and that, along with the other thing, is what made me the person I am now, a fanatical Catholic in the garbs of Martin Luther, a servant of God who swings the incense only for his own Mass—I confess to myself, and I forgive myself my sins, so that I may instantly commit them again.

The other thing is this (and this is also the end of the story).

(At least for the time being.)

At the King's Ball at the Green-White Jericho Marksmen's Club Fair, there was a rumour going around that Daniel was back home. A lot of people said he'd come to prevent Rosing's election as mayor, which was expected for the next day. In floods of tears, Wiebke had gone to the police and retracted her statement that he'd raped her (at my urging; I had appealed to her conscience and looked her deep in the eye). And although there were other charges pending against him (including for criminal damage, actual bodily harm and trespassing), he had been released from remand prison in Vechta. I had written him several very long letters explaining my failure in various ways and asking his forgiveness, but they'd all ended up ripped to shreds in my waste-paper basket rather than in one piece in the post box. At some point I decided it would be easier to tell him what I felt in person. And I wasn't the only one with that opinion.

'Let him come,' said Paul—like all of us, marked by slowly healing stab wounds—as he aimed a rifle at a white square behind the shooting stall. 'He can paint a red dot on his forehead like an Indian and get straight into my iron sights.' Then he pulled the trigger, lowered the rifle, reloaded and leant forward again. 'Best of all with his back to me.' His second shot countersank the hole cut by the first one in the exact centre of the paper square. 'Like this target.' And the third steel bullet hit the spot too. The woman gave us back the target, which she had stuck to the wall the wrong way round on Paul's instructions—'to make it more difficult'— and offered him the main prize, a big-eyed, big-eared cuddly toy. 'If that thing could really turn into a gremlin I'd take it,' Paul looked at me. 'I like the idea that creatures, especially such cute ones, turn into monsters when they eat after midnight. But,' he turned back to the woman, 'Gizmo's for pussies.' His new favourite phrase. The endless row of tin bunnies passing him, the plaster stars hung on nails, the plastic flowers in white tubes— they were all for pussies.

'You can give it to your girlfriend.'

What girlfriend, I was tempted to say, but I held my tongue, knowing full well how vulnerable the tender connection between us was.

'You take it then.'

'I'm not your girlfriend.'

'Not yet.'

'Never.'

'You don't know what you're missing.'

'Oh yeah? What am I missing?'

'As you can see, I'm a pretty good aim.'

'Come back when you've grown up.'

'Twenty-eight,' said Paul as he turned around, the target in his hand, and because I'd got even fewer points than Jens (five, to be precise), I had to get us a round of Kruiden, the fourth in a row. Paul had never been a member of the marksmen's club but had apparently spent his entire childhood at shooting galleries and even hit nine or ten if he'd had nine or ten shots of Kruiden, or so he said. And Jens didn't seem to be concerned he might have to pay for a drink of his choice at any time soon, either. So I decided to take a break for the moment, after we'd entered the ballroom—a magnificently decorated marquee with a wooden floor—and waited for our order at the bar. The old and new king of the marksmen, Wilfried Ennen, was sitting on a stage with his retinue and assuring his fellow marksmen and markswomen drank as much and as quickly as possible. They were all wearing uniforms, draped with cordons and medals, and some of their sleeves were decorated with patches declaring them to be a *sharp shooter*. No one from Compunists' Corner was here, not even the sports riflemen Achim and Onno Kolthoff, and I'd only come because I hoped Daniel would turn up as well. The male-voice choir had already absolved its performance but most of the listeners hadn't yet quite recovered from the divine voices. They had requested several encores and now they were sitting behind their glasses, their heads propped on their hands, exhausted from the cumulative power and strength sounding out from three dozen men's throats. The Sunnyboys, a two-man band with a beat machine, had taken to the other stage and played the opening bars of the Jürgen Drews song 'A Bed in a Corn Field', which a number of those present understood as a reference to Daniel's UFO experience. They rose from their seats and flooded the dance floor, bellowing his name. An old woman came towards us, her back bent, her face furrowed, a walking memento mori. She held a bucket under our noses and asked if we wanted to buy a raffle ticket (we didn't); there were lots of prizes and a trip to Berlin to be won. To get rid of her, I took out three of the tiny scrolls of paper, threw in a five-mark note and told her she could retain the difference. As she looked at me big-eyed and big-eared instead of displaying gratitude, I concluded that she wasn't familiar with the phrase 'retain the difference' and replaced it, in a second attempt to make myself understood, with 'keep the change.'

Our Kruiden came and we tipped them down our throats in one go.

'Right,' said Paul, rubbing his hands and looking at me, 'time for a new game.'

'Yeah,' said Jens and cleared his throat, 'I've got a really dry mouth.'

I responded—making some effort to use their jargon so as to avoid further misunderstandings—that I had to 'take a piss' before I could shoot again, and they thereupon patted me on the back, wished me a 'good shot' and released me into the night. Outside, I leant on one of the flagpoles confining the festival ground and lit a cigarette under the flutters of white and green. The festival ground was in the middle of the village, on the site of the demolished station, between the freight sheds, Rosing's bungalow and Kramer's Furniture Paradise on the other side of the road. Petersen's Pool Hall was closed and there were planks of wood over the entrance, the stairs leading down to the cellar, so that drunk festival-goers didn't fall down the dark hole or relieve themselves down there—of whatever they needed to get rid of. A few boys I knew from school were dressed up as firemen and watching every spark, as if they feared they'd be taken to account personally for a possible conflagration. Kurt Rhauderwiek and Frank Tebbens were squatting on the bonnet of their police car and keeping a lookout for potential criminals, their eyes fixed on me. Daniel was nowhere in sight.

I flicked my cigarette end away and walked along the cordon of snack, raffle and shooting stalls past the toilet truck towards the railway lines. On the far side of the freight shed, I considered myself undisturbed. It wasn't that I couldn't urinate in other people's presence, but the comments they expressed above the urinals ('Can you even see it over that belly?' etc.) had always had an inhibitive effect on me. I climbed onto the platform and watched by the weak light of a distant streetlamp as my jet hit the shimmering wood with its many layers of oil, cellulose thinner and anti-graffiti paint.

When I returned, relieved and a nuance more sober than two minutes previously, I still thought I could resist the foodstuffs on display. Krause Fishmongers' truck made no impression on me. Nor did the scents emanating from Fokken's mobile grill cast their spell on me. Seconds later, however, I was standing as if hypnotized before Wessel's Travelling Confectionary. Doughnuts filled with strawberry, fruits of the forest and rum pot jam, burnt almonds, toffee apples, deep-fried quark balls, cherry turnovers, gingerbread hearts inscribed *Little Kitten*, *Little Frog*, *Little Sparrow*, *My Hero*, *My Sweetie*, *My Honey Bee*, *I Miss You*, *I Love You*, which I've never seen anyone eating (apart from in the mirror) and all of which I'd have given to Daniel if he'd been there and I hadn't had to fear that I'd be shot for it, chocolate-coated bananas, popcorn, American-style frosted cookies, French-style cinnamon rolls, macaroons, spritz cookies, custard tarts, waffles, butter cake, honey cake, almond cake, coconut snowballs, coconut ice, marzipan horns, plain marshmallows, pink-and-white marshmallows between wafers, dipped in chocolate-flavoured coating at both ends, candyfloss, candy canes, liquorice sticks, liquorice whirls, lollies of all sizes and colours and flavours, sherbet dippers, sherbet plain, sherbet straws for biting open, sherbet flying saucers, candy necklaces, candy bracelets, blackberry and raspberry drops, aniseed balls, cola cubes, cola hearts, cola bottles, butterscotch, foam strawberries, pineapple cubes, sour apple rings, sour pickles, sour French fries, chocolate coins, peppermint creams, peppermint mice (I digress), and entered the marquee wiping sugar, flour, jam and gelatine off my face with both hands. The Sunnyboys were playing Wencke Myhre's hit 'One Mark for Charlie' and there was such a crush at the bar that there was no getting through, because they were handing out Charlies for one mark as long as the song lasted. The crowd dissolved the moment the music stopped. And lo and behold—Paul and Jens were still standing in the very same spot where I'd left them standing.

'You're a lucky boy,' said Paul.

'Why?'

'Because of us, your friends.'

'We got a couple of Charlies in for you,' Jens shoved three glasses of this emetic and narcotic combination of cola and brandy in my direction.

I took a tiny sip and put the glass down.

'Down in one,' said Paul.

And Jens said, 'We did too.'

Their dull eyes made me suspect they were telling the truth. I hesitated nonetheless, positioned myself between them, switching my weight from one leg to another, and thought of Daniel, of how they'd always filled him up at the parties in the Hankens' barn. I was suddenly overcome by such great desire that I was all but ready to leave Paul and Jens standing a second time and walk over to the drugstore to make my peace with him. But then the door opened and the as-yet-uncrowned king of the village, Johann Rosing, entered the marquee with his retinue—our class teacher Mrs Nanninga, his retarded daughter Wiebke, her no more mentally developed brother Iron and behind the latter but holding his hand, a classmate known all too well to the three of us, for differing reasons. There was a surge of applause, the Sunnyboys switched in the middle of their song to 'For He's a Jolly Good Fellow', which they'd already performed for Wilfried Ennen at the beginning of the evening, only to segue subtly into Freddy Quinn's 'Tomorrow the World Begins'.

'Oh, fuck it,' I said, put one of the glasses to my lips even though I knew it would herald my end despite my full stomach, and tipped back my head.

'Hey, isn't that Simone?' asked Jens.

'It sure is,' I said and chased the first Charlie with the second.

'Woah, what does she look like?' asked Jens, which seemed a not-unjustified question in view of her Sinead O'Connor–style shaved head, high heels and conspicuously short sequinned dress, but Paul said, 'The question is, what's she doing with him?'

I knocked back the third Charlie and put my arms around their shoulders. 'Come, friends, let's go shooting again. I get the feeling I'm going to hit the spot tonight.'

'I'm starting to like you,' said Paul.

And when Jens said, 'Watch out you don't fall in love with him,' and Paul, 'At least he's got a bit of meat on his bones—more than enough,' I thought I'd blown my cover, and I let go of them again to find out how far they'd go if they really meant it. 'You wish.'

But neither of them dared to touch me. It was only when I took a step towards the door that Paul grabbed me from behind and said, 'You've forgotten something.'

'What?'

He nodded over at Enno Kröger behind the bar. 'There's a bill to be paid.'

On the way to the shooting stall we returned to the subject—albeit briefly—of Simone. 'I never knew they were together,' said Jens, and Paul said, 'Maybe they aren't. You never know with her, one day one way, the next day the other.' And that was the end of the matter, and we turned back to what we'd begun hours previously—controlled self-destruction.

'Got a fag?' asked Jens.

And I said, 'Yes, siree.'

'I told you not to come back until you're grown up,' said the shooting stall woman.

I flicked my cigarette end away, put three marks on the counter and picked up the rifle. 'We are now.'

'That was quick.'

'It's not a question of time, it's a matter of experience,' I said, full of alcohol-induced bravado, and once she'd pinned the target onto the wall like before I shot a triangle into it.

Jens' bullet holes were closer together this time but not close enough to topple Paul from his throne. Once again, the woman offered him the cuddly Gizmo toy, and once again he rejected Gizmo. 'Hmm,' he said, turned to me, 'looks like it's time for a new round.'

'Unless,' said Jens and looked up, 'he guesses what's wrong with this picture.'

'What do you mean?' asked Paul, following his gaze.

I too looked around but even after what felt like five hours I couldn't spot anything conspicuous.

'Look at the flagpole,' said Jens, pointing at the nearest one, and added, as we still didn't say anything, 'so, what's hanging up there?'

'No one yet,' said Paul. 'But if Daniel turns up I can't guarantee for nix.'

'The flag,' said Jens.

I stared at the white-and-green flag and noticed how difficult I found it to focus on anything with both eyes.

'OK,' said Jens, 'forget it,' and he slapped me on the shoulder. 'Let's go and get a drink.'

As I walked ahead of Paul and Jens to the marquee I noticed there was hardly anyone left outside apart from the fire brigade boys, and when I opened the door I realized why. The evening was approaching its climax, the raffle, and everyone who'd bought a ticket wanted to be there when the winning numbers were called out. Seven, twelve and forty were not among them. The Sunnyboys were leaning against the bar while the woman who'd been round with the bucket was now standing on the stage and handing the winners their winnings: a mock turtle dinner at the Beach Hotel, a Club 69 voucher to the value of a hundred marks (which would have prompted Paul and Jens and any number of other boys around me to buy up the whole bucket of tickets if they'd been informed of the prize in advance), a twelve-piece Biedermeier-style silver-plated stainless-steel cutlery set from Superneemann, an imitation-suede winter jacket and a ladies' handbag with the label *VL* from Vehndel Fashions, free hair extensions from Uli Dettmers, a stuffed fox, a herd of wooden elephants with plastic tusks, CDs by Boney M., Milli Vanilli and Michael Bolton and a dozen further useless items. The trip to Berlin went to Old Kramer, who had initially understood 'Dublin', as he bellowed into the microphone, and then, once informed of the real destination, announced at the same volume that he would never go there, to Germany's future capital city, 'not even in a wooden box.'

Before they all blocked the bar again, which was a predictable outcome because, as I now found out, Rosing had announced the prospect of free beer after midnight, I ordered another round of Kruiden. The Sunnyboys returned to the stage and played the opening bars of Wolfgang Petry's 'Madness'. When they reached the chorus, mass hysteria broke out in the hall. Men and women who seemed not to have moved their bodies for years (at least I didn't dance back then) were hopping up and down not two metres away from me, ramming their fists into each other's torsos for sheer joie de vivre. I wished I had the rifle back. Instead, Paul planted a Kruiden in my hand and we drank to our own hell, hell, hell.

'Right,' said Paul, rubbing his hands and looking at me, 'time for a new game.'

'Yeah,' said Jens and cleared his throat, 'I've got a really dry mouth.'

Once again I objected that I had to empty my bladder before I could go on, this time varying the theme by referring not to 'taking a piss' but to 'milking the snake', whereupon they, as if I'd hit precisely the right tone, declared themselves willing to accompany me. I let them go on ahead, the three of us climbing the steps to the toilet truck together, and when they occupied both urinals at the top, I beat a hasty retreat.

The scent of juicy grilled meat gave me brief pause before I turned off, my hand already on my flies, into the now absolutely pitch-black ravine between trailers and freight shed. The shed door was pushed open but there was no light burning inside, that much I could still make out, and then the darkness had swallowed me up.

Once I was done I lit a cigarette, and in the briefly flickering reflection of the flame I saw him, Daniel Kuper, my honey bee, my sweetie, my hero, his hair ruffled, his skin pale and drawn, a lighter in his hand, just released from remand prison, just run away from home; everyone said afterwards that he'd returned to the freight shed to take a new stand, make a new mark, daub a new symbol and take revenge on the man who'd put him behind bars, but that's not true.

'Daniel,' I reached my hand out for him, wanting to feel him, stroke him, console him and myself, and grabbed at thin air. 'What are you doing here?'

'I want to be here when Jericho perishes,' I heard him say—his voice, too, aged by years. 'Before I disappear for ever.'

'I thought that won't be happening until tomorrow after the election. And if you want to live to see that you'd better leave now.'

Silent, we stood facing each other. The tip of my cigarette glowed at each of my deep breaths but that light was not enough to illuminate more than my fingers. For a moment I thought he'd followed my instructions and got out. From the festival grounds, music and a polyphonic 'Hossa, hossa, hossa, hossa' wafted over to us. From the inside of the freight shed came a scratching sound, as if from an animal.

I said, into that black nothingness (and that was the only way I could say it), 'There's something I have to admit.'

'What?'

'I wrote it.'

'You wrote what?'

'*I love you*,' and then, before he could say anything else, I took a step towards him, to where I guessed he was, and kissed him unerringly on his bitter-sweet lips (the longer the waiting, the sweeter the kiss).

He pushed me away. 'Are you crazy?'

'No,' I said, straining towards him.

'You're totally bent,' he said, shrinking back from me.

'I always have been.'

'Bent as in drunk.'

'I know exactly what I want.'

'So do I.'

'You.'

'But I don't want you.'

Amor gignit nullum amorem. I flicked my cigarette end away, just as carelessly as before, and turned around on the spot. Ever since I'd known him I'd anticipated rejection, but we'd never revealed our feelings to each other and now the words stood between us, as insurmountable as a wall. As I turned the corner the noises of the marksmen's club fair grew louder again, the voices and the music from the marquee and the shots from the shooting gallery. They showed me the way out of the darkness, which I wouldn't have found using my eyes alone. Halfway back, somewhere between the confectioner's and the fishmonger—I saw only what was directly ahead of me—Mrs Nanninga stopped me. 'Have you seen Wiebke?'

'Not Wiebke,' I said, but whom I had seen didn't seem to interest her because she moved on before I could tell her, calling the girl's name. Suddenly I felt the Charlies rising up inside me. I held onto one of the flagpoles for support and vomited, and when I looked up, towards the white-and-green flag, and drew in the smoky scent of the night sky, I understood what Jens had meant was wrong with the picture, and I wanted to tell him and buy myself free from everything, and then I'd forgotten it again, and then I was standing before Paul and Jens, before the shooting gallery where they'd waited for me, and instead of that I said I'd seen Daniel by the freight shed, and the news spread like wildfire across the whole festival grounds, and at the same moment I saw the flames of my betrayal licking up the wooden walls of the freight shed, and the sirens sounded, and the fire brigade unfurled their hoses, and we all ran over there and watched as a light shone out inside and a shadow walked towards it. And then he stepped into what surrounds this entire